D. J. Taylor was born in Norwich in 1960. He is the author of six novels, including *English Settlement*, which won a Grinzane Cavour Prize, and *Kept: A Victorian Mystery*. His *Orwell: The Life* won the 2003 Whitbread Prize for Biography. He is also a well-known critic and reviewer, and is author of the hugely influential *After the War: The Novel and England since 1945*. His new book, *Bright Young People: The Rise and Fall of a Generation, 1918–1940*, will be published in late 2007. He lives in Norwich with his wife and their three children.

Praise for *Real Life*:
'This is a very funny novel; it is also a serious novel and a very good one'
T. J. Binyon, *Sunday Times*

'*Real Life* is masterly. It exudes sadness and unease, like an accomplished film noir'
Shena Mackay, *Times Literary Supplement*

'Taylor has a sharp ear for speech nuances. *Real Life* is a provocative and thoughtful piece of mischief'
David Hughes, *Mail on Sunday*

'His prose has a taut unmannered elegance, with deft touches on every page'
Max Davidson, *Daily Telegraph*

'D. J. Taylor makes you laugh out loud with his mordant cynicism'
Amanda Craig, *Literary Review*

Praise for *Trespass*:
'This is a haunting, funny and altogether remarkable book'
Jane Shilling, *Sunday Telegraph*

'This is an assured and sophisticated novel . . . repaying attention and rereading: depth-charged with humour, and acutely aware of the shifts and eddies of the social currents of the past fifty years. Turning its sad and accomplished pages, one thinks of the England that Carlyle described, stuffed with wealth but dying of inanition'
Hilary Mantel, *Sunday Times*

'. . . an absorbing book, written with an intelligence and wit that compliments and rewards the reader'
John Keenan, *Guardian*

Praise for *T*
'Taylor's fic uieting . . . the many, varied and r ylor's novel its special distinction'
Independent on Sunday

'D. J. Taylor's artful re-creations of different times and ways of living never sink into nostalgia. Instead, they convey a sense of a whole world changing, of something lost, and only partly retrieved in the act of remembrance'

David Horspool, *Times Literary Supplement*

'He's wonderfully good at places . . . but even better at people. Taylor does people like the admirer of Victorian and Edwardian fiction that he is renowned for being. Ted King . . . is a real triumph of character-drawing, his story one of the most intimate growing-up narrations around, and as good as anything Taylor has managed so far'

Valentine Cunningham, *Independent*

'It reads so easily that it is only when one puts it down, with a purr of satisfaction, that one realises how much ground it has covered. From post-war Yarmouth to modern Plumstead, via the Soho of the Sixties and Seventies, Taylor has animated very different worlds with equal panache'

David Robson, *Sunday Telegraph*

'. . . quietly unsettling, even devastating . . . the narrative has a slow-burning charm and power . . . You probably had to be there. You probably ought to read it'

Robert Hanks, *Daily Telegraph*

'. . . a masterly reconstruction of a vanished age . . . it probably throws more light on what it is like to be a comedian than any work of fiction or non-fiction published in living memory'

Andrew Barrow, *Spectator*

'Taylor has written a quirky, affectionate, often very funny, very English novel; bitter-sweet, flirting with sentimentality but shying away at the last minute. There's a touch of Orwell in his attitude to England, critical but loving. He is a nicely evocative writer, with an acute awareness of the passing of time . . . Taylor . . . has found his own unmistakable voice'

Allan Massie, *Scotsman*

'. . . abrasively intelligent . . . Taylor sketches the tat and tinsel of small-time showbiz with a loving touch . . . Ravishing in its historical sweep, restrained in its attention to the tedium of everyday life, the book is too grimly real to be an uplifting read . . . But as a state of the nation novel, it is state of the art'

Christopher Bray, *Mail on Sunday*

RETURNING

Three Novels

D. J. Taylor

Real Life
First published in Great Britain by Chatto & Windus Ltd 1992

Trespass
First published in Great Britain by Gerald Duckworth & Co. Ltd 1998

The Comedy Man
First published in Great Britain by Duckworth Literary Entertainments, Ltd 2001

Returning
This edition first published in Great Britain in 2007
Timewell Press Limited
10 Porchester Terrace, London W2 3TL

A catalogue record for this title is available from the
British Library.

ISBN–10: 1 85725 221 7
ISBN–13: 978 1 85725 221 7

Typeset by TW Typesetting, Plymouth, Devon
Printed and bound in Great Britain by William Clowes Ltd, Beccles, Suffolk

With many thanks to the original sponsors: Carmen Callil, Robin Baird-Smith
and Sarah Such

Contents

REAL LIFE

So this is real life
you're telling me
and everything
is where it ought to be

Howard Devoto, *Definitive Gaze*

In real life, things are much worse than as represented in books. In books, you love somebody and want them, win them or lose them. In real life, so often, you love them and don't want them, or want them and don't love them.

Anthony Powell, *The Kindly Ones*

... the still eternal light through which we see the infinite unchanging vistas we make, from the height of one year old, out of suburban gardens or municipal parks in summer, endless grassy horizons and alleys which we always hope to revisit, inhabit in real life, whatever that is.

A. S. Byatt, *The Virgin in the Garden*

Part I

Early one afternoon in the late January of 1974 a young woman set out to walk the short distance from Piccadilly Circus underground station to the National Gallery in Trafalgar Square. Although her journey was in a certain sense premeditated she moved slowly and hesitantly, sauntering diagonally along Coventry Street and waiting for nearly a minute under the Swiss Centre clock on the outlying flank of Leicester Square. Later she could be seen drifting in the same strangely reluctant way along the square's western approach, pausing to stare at the cinema advertisements and the gaping tourist boutiques.

The young woman's name, for the purposes of this particular fiction, was Caroline. She was perhaps twenty-two or twenty-three, with square, regular features and shoulder-length blonde hair. In the fashion of the time she wore a short, belted coat and shiny, high-heeled boots, the latter impeding her progress even further and causing her to waver timorously on the icy pavements. At regular intervals she would stop and kick the toe of each boot rigorously against the kerbside to dislodge the particles of snow that had collected beneath.

Early afternoon in Leicester Square. Snow, fallen two days previously, lies banked up in off-white drifts. An opaque sky gives promise of more. A whirl of distant voices, given sudden coherence as from the south end of the square a procession of young men, shaven-headed and dressed in billowing robes, their vanguard chanting and banging small drums, comes clanking into view. Walking towards them the girl briefly disappears, caught up in the flow of shuffling movement and outstretched arms, re-emerges and turns hard right into a side alley.

In Panton Street, past a newsvendor's table and a cinema showing pornographic films, the girl's pace increases. The pavement is more crowded here – a traffic warden, a file of schoolchildren lofting satchels at one another – but she presses forward, stumbling occasionally when her feet catch on the impediments of kerb or paving stone. Two workmen's braziers, glowing against the grey frontage of shops and the muted light, give her passage into Whitcomb Street a faintly numinous quality: the hurrying figure at first dissolving into a haze of shaky air, then seen striding purposefully on past pale, empty windows towards the distant traffic.

The man stands waiting on the gallery steps. Women with heavily laden baskets, foreign students with clipboard files clamped under their arms, surge about him. Miraculously, as she approaches they clear and there is only the single dark figure, the shoulders hunched higher in the overcoat, the eyes nervous and intent. The man is in his early forties. He has sparse, receding hair which has been slicked back over his scalp with oil or grease. The girl divines that he has shaved recently – there are rough, red patches on his neck – but imperfectly, so that a small coin-sized blob of bristles sits on the point of his chin. As he sees her he flicks down a cigarette and grinds it with his heel. The eyes stray, down across the crowded pavement, upwards into the dense air, back to the girl. He says, 'I didn't think you'd come.'

'You thought wrong.' The tone is – artless? Obedient? Its precise nuance fails to register with the man. He goes on, 'It's not far. We could take a cab.'

'If you like.' The girl pauses, a look of intense concentration passing over her face. 'What sort of place is it?'

'Just fine,' the man says. 'For what you and me've got in mind, just fine.'

In the taxi – a dark, lurching vehicle allowing occasional close-ups of the passing street – the man says urgently, 'When we get back to my place I'm going to fuck your brains out.'

The girl leans back in her seat, legs splayed. She sticks out her tongue and lets it rest on her lower lip. 'I know,' she says, 'I know all about that.' She pauses again. 'Let's hope you're as good as you say you are.'

Charing Cross Road. Cambridge Circus. Past overbright shop-fronts. A brief glimpse of the lowering sky. Shaftesbury Avenue. The man, eyes staring blindly in front of him, takes the girl's hand and places it in his lap.

The flat is small, sparsely furnished. A bed. A chair. Pictures cut out of magazines taped randomly to the walls. The electric fire glows. Standing in front of it the man casts long, angular shadows. From the window behind there are views of huddled rooftops. In the distance the Post Office Tower. 'Let's talk business,' he says. 'How much is this going to cost me?'

The girl leans negligently against the door, arms folded across her chest. 'Twenty. Thirty. It depends what you want.'

'Whatever you've got. That's what I want.'

Naked, their clothes flung in serpentine coils around the room, they examine one another. It is an unfortunate contrast: the man's scrawny torso, grey haunches, white, tapering legs; the girl's plump, rosy contours, fresh dappled skin. Her right flank, edging nearer to the fire, is scarlet from the heat. Together they might form part of some medieval figurative painting: Spring and Autumn, say, or Maidenhood Sold into Bondage. The girl raises her hands above her stomach and begins to massage herself. By this stage, as the man lopes hungrily towards her, their conversation is barely intelligible, a series of muttered, raunchy monologues, spoken over each other's shoulders.

... *You London bitches just fuckin' ask for it. Think you're so flash* ...

... *I want a man who can give me a good time. Are you going to give me a good time? Are you?*

... *So fuckin' flash. I could hurt you if you wanted me to. I could hurt you so bad that I* ...

... *A good time. A good time. A wonderful time.*

... *Fuck your brains out.*

Once in the course of these poorly choreographed preliminaries, as the man lies prone on the cheerless bed, the girl sprawled across him, something unlooked for happens, something unplanned. 'Look at it,' the girl says, sinking back momentarily on her haunches. 'Look out of the window.' The man stares intently, his eyes registering both panic and bewilderment, until he sees the first restless flurry of snowflakes. 'Snow,' he says woodenly. 'Sure,' the girl says. 'It's starting to snow. Look at it.' They pause for a moment as the flakes drift down over the huddled Soho rooftops, pink and luminous in the glare of the lamp. The man smiles. 'I'm going to fuck your brains out,' he says with a touch of sadness.

Finally the act is completed, there on the narrow bed, a bizarre, self-conscious spectacle in which limbs are weirdly deployed across the white sheets, where there are strange tensings and pauses, inexplicable confusions and variations to the routine of push and shove, the warp and weft. Such is the intent synchronisation of gesture, the stylised breaking apart and coming together, that one might almost think there was a third presence in the room, staring out over the writhing bed towards the dark wall of glass. Beyond, the snow continues to fall.

Capital Pick-up, Leisurevision's first major feature, was filmed on location in central London and at the loft in Dean Street. The principal actors – two hard-up and unmemorable associates of Morty's named Jake Gordon and Irma La Douche – were paid fifty pounds apiece. I did the lighting: a row of raw bulbs placed a yard or two above the protagonists' heads. Morty directed. An afternoon's work, the editing completed two or three hours after Jake and Irma's departure, sweating and glassy-eyed, from the premises, the product transferred to an eight-reel later that night. Sound: Crazy Rodney. Camera: another of Morty's stringers. Executive producer: Terry Chimes.

Inevitably for a first feature shot on a shoestring there were problems. Chief among these was Irma La Douche's inability to learn her lines. The intent look, the grimaces of urgent concentration on which so many subsequent observers remarked, were the product not of mild over-acting but simple amnesia. Later when we had dialogue coaches, printed scripts – all the careful paraphernalia that came to characterise Morty's operations – such deficiencies were grandly overcome. As it was, the game amateurism of these early forays was thought to suggest a certain ready verisimilitude, an authenticity which later productions with their practised starlets and easy dialogue were presumed to lack. Then there was Jake's inability to respond to any word or gesture not in the script. The exchange about the snow, for example, was entirely spontaneous, a consequence of Irma raising her head from Jake's puny torso at the exact moment when the first flakes began to fall, in sheer over-excitement with scene: a random, fleeting quirk which was to invest *Capital Pick-up* with its single moment of charm.

Inexplicably, several of Morty's early films were to possess this odd, elegiac quality, a characteristic which set them apart from other more clinical ventures, undertaken by other Mortys in other, similar studios peopled by other Jake Gordons and Irma La Douches, attended by other tensions and anxieties. There is the moment in *Doctors' Wives* in which Sheri La Grange, stepping out of the pile of hastily divested clothing, ignores the beckoning figure on the couch to turn and smile briefly at the onlooker, a mysterious Delphic smile, having no relation to any event taking place on screen or off. There is, again, the scene in *Possession*, with its country-house vistas of blazing log fires and coy maidservants, in which the camera moves falteringly beyond the savage coupling on the rug to record the spatter of rain on glass, a glimpse of dense, untended foliage. In his way Morty had some claims to being an artist. A vulgarian would have given these episodes an unmistakable ironic force, had Sheri La Grange deliver only a mournful pout, timed the slap of water on glass to coincide with another more obvious conjunction. With Morty there was a sense in which these minor detours in the forward march of the plot existed wholly in isolation, played no part in the wider development of theme or content. I recall in particular *Latchkey Kid*, another Leisurevision effort from about this time, filmed once more in the loft in Dean Street, the familiar outlines disguised with heavy curtains and hired furniture. Its plot again was rudimentary. A lissom schoolgirl (gym-slip, hockey stick, straw hat – Morty liked this sort of *haute* stylisation) is presented by her mother with a door key on the understanding that the mother will be delayed that evening. The daughter subsequently returns to the house accompanied by a brawny youth in a leather jacket. An inevitable sequence of events then follows, broken only – both parties by this stage maximally aroused – by the early arrival of the mother. Seen a decade later *Latchkey Kid* has little to recommend it, apart from a curious moment when the camera, ignoring the sight of Candy Barr sleekly unrolling fishnet stockings, swivels to take in the framed photograph which rests on a side table next to the sofa. It shows a wedding couple from a period perhaps thirty or forty years before, arm-in-arm, smiling fixed, snaggle-toothed smiles, ducking instinctively as a whirl of confetti descends upon their heads. The camera lingers, trawls slowly over the archaic hairstyles and the dilated eyes, and for a moment Candy Barr and her consort are forgotten, a blur of limbs dimly descried in the distance, a swish of abandoned clothing on the crackling soundtrack: a fugitive moment, suffused with poignancy.

More moments from these early days: Morty auditioning a pool-side scene in front of a line of thatch-haired girls in swim-suits; scripting *Doctors' Wives* in a rented Harley Street consulting room half an hour before filming ('Make it tasteful,' Morty said, 'and cut the crap'); the Dean Street loft awash in coruscating artificial light. Twitches on the thread. Rushes from the endless tape. Watching the rough cut of *Possession* at the preview cinema in Wardour Street with Terry Chimes asleep in his chair. Fiery dawns, intent and red-eyed on the cutting-room floor. And the girls: Sheri La Grange, Irma La Douche and Lila St Claire, Terri da Motta, Berkeley Lush and Corona d'Amour. Impossible complexions, improbable names. They came in waves. When we started they were all Sixties cast-offs, ageing waifs who'd had walk-ons in films about Swinging London called Keki or Boo or Jade. A little later they began to be named after hotels: Tiffany, Berkeley, Ritzy. A bit later still they had men's names: Sam and Joe and Jake. Only towards the end when everybody – producers, directors, actors – were casting envious glances towards America did they assume that three-pronged, EEC-diluted uniformity: Martina La Chasse, Gaby du Pont, Cornelia del Hacienda. As the names changed so did the attitudes. At the start the girls were naïve, generous and trusting ('Listen love,' I can remember Morty instructing some pouting ingénue, 'this is a *pornographic* movie, right? You take *all* your clothes off and get on the bed'), gamely tolerant of the indignities visited upon them. Subsequently amateur warmth gave way to wary professionalism: girls with agents, contracts, artistic integrity, scruples, percentages; girls who emerged frostily from bed, shower, embrace or pose to examine small print, call for a telephone, an understudy, a renegotiation. The scenes move sharply into focus now, lose the ethereal gloss imposed by distance. Filming *Plasma Party* in bare, angular chambers streaked with artificial gore. The prodigies of costume design demanded by *Nazi Death Camp*. That grim procession of sex, money and lies, lies, money and sex. Studio lights pulse through the fog of cigarette smoke. Morty smiles his mad, off-centre smile. The cameraman grins. The figures recede and fade away. At these times Irma and her rhapsodies over the snow remain only as a faint memory, a fading tint of romanticism in a picture since given over to harsh, brutal colours.

Nearly dark up here in the study. Outside the window and its vista of identikit terraced houses the streetlamps have begun to go on in that mellow, autumnal way they have. In the remoter distance over towards Heigham Park, a frail pinkish glow. A second, keener light shines up from under the door. From below there are odd, fractured sounds as Suzi roams noisily around the kitchen. Gusts of air blow in through the half-open window.

Sometimes I listen to the sounds people make as they walk by outside. You get to know them all: the fugitive clatter of high heels – they still wear high heels round here – the slurp of trainers as some lurching oaf shuffles past on his way to the pub, the whisper of the sandals the old women wear. The noises are rarely confined to footwear. Children slither by in the gloaming, a salvo of chatter that vanishes instantly on the wind; teenagers slink past to rustle the leaves of the hedge with their shoulders; burly women loiter for a moment on the pavement by T. Coulthard's grocery shop, leaving behind a snatch of gnomic repartee. I looked out once at two a.m. on an airy summer's night, alerted by vigorous rustlings borne on the breeze, and found Fat Eric from two doors down practically giving his girlfriend one in the front garden.

Such bucolic licence is long past now. From below there is another random crash of crockery. The radio rasps on, then off. Outside the cars purr by in the murk: sleek roadsters with wound-down sun roofs, nippy Minis driven at speed. Astonishing vehicles. Fat Eric from two doors down has a squat, hump-backed conveyance which, fleeting memory assures me, is a 1966 Hillman

Husky. I listen to another gutsy squeal of rubber on tarmac, peer outside. There are lights going on all along the street now; the myriad flicker of the television sets. I light a cigarette and stand at the window considering the wide portholes into narrow, bookless rooms, the restless, screen-tethered heads. Downstairs the noises from beyond the kitchen door have quietened down to the staccato clink of Suzi chopping vegetables and Suzi singing disagreeably along to the radio. In the gloom of the hallway the telephone message pad gleams palely. Elaine rang yesterday. The message is still there, written in Suzi's Marion Richardson copperplate. 'A woman rang. Said she'd ring back.' Elaine, without a doubt. After all, what other woman would ring me up unbidden? Emma? Wouldn't have the number. One of Morty's actresses? Disappeared, disappeared into the random clutter of time. No, it had to be Elaine.

Amid the passage of a crowded life, you forget things . . . It must be two years since I last set eyes on Elaine. Not much less, for that matter, since I last set eyes on all of them, on Morty, Terry Chimes, Crazy Rodney or whoever. Two years of silent, self-imposed sequestration, broken only now by this ominous twitch on the thread. If it *is* her, that is . . . Wondering uneasily about this I pull a coat over my shoulders, step out into the cheerless streets.

Fine spray mists over the glass of the streetlamps. A bicycle weaves past. The muffled thud of flesh on metal discloses that Fat Eric from two doors down is out there doing his car. Fat Eric does this quite a lot, usually at the most unpromising hours of the day or night. Dawn on a vicious December morning finds him, an otiose scarf wrapped over his tee-shirt, full-length on the pavement guiding his freezing hands towards the chassis. Noon on an eighty-degree August scorcher reveals him splayed over the bonnet, glistening in his sawn-off jeans, morosely polishing the windscreen. As I lope by, gratefully feeling the cigarette smoke crackling in my lungs, he straightens up from his engrossed rear-wheel crouch and nods.

'Hi.'

Clad in a sweatshirt and a wantonly tight pair of tracksuit bottoms, Fat Eric is a tremendous spectacle: unbeautiful hands, face a wedge of reddening flesh. He has one of those awesome professional footballer's haircuts that resemble a bunch of grapes laid lengthways across the scalp.

'How's it going, Fat Eric?'

Fat Eric and I talk about football. I read about it in the *Eastern Evening News* and tell him whether I think Darryl McKenzie will make the city team next week and what the news is on Kevin Flack's groin strain. The result of this elementary exercise in news-gathering is that Fat Eric imagines me to be absurdly knowledge-able on the soccer scene. One of these days, he grandly intimates, we might even go and see a game together. Now he merely looks thoughtful, sets off immediately on one of his random monologues.

'You see the highlights the other night? I thought it was fucking diabolical. That ref . . . I mean,' says Fat Eric, 'I saw him when we played the Arsenal last year. Two penalties in the first half, right? And then, when Flacky gets one in the head right on the edge of the six-yard box, what does he do? Gives a fucking goal kick.'

'But Fat Eric,' I chip in earnestly, 'they reckoned he wasn't fit, you know.'

Kevin Flack is Norwich City's latest discovery: a tiny, rock-headed Scot who fled over the border at the end of last season with a couple of paternity suits and an alcohol problem that they didn't find out about until after the transfer forms had been signed. Local opinion is divided about Kevin Flack. The *Eastern Evening News*, having hailed him initially as a 'soccer sensation', devotes pointed headlines to his failure to score in the last eleven matches. But Fat Eric has other, mutinous ideas.

'Fit? Wouldn't matter if the kid was fit, would it? Papers have got it in for him, haven't they?'

'I suppose they have. Well, see you around.'

'See you around.'

I leave Fat Eric back by the rear wheel, where he looks suddenly immutable, a vast, unhappy mammoth anchored eternally by folds of permafrost. And so: on. Past the dogleg alley that leads you back into a maze of side streets and lock-up garages where tethered Alsatians whine balefully at the sky. Past the hole in the road with its arc of winking lights. Past the City Gates on the corner, where the door swings open for an instant and there is a sudden confused impression of smoke, light shining off glass, mute, aquarium faces.

The western side of Norwich was built on hills. The wide arterial roads that snake out to the suburbs – Newmarket, Unthank, Jessop, Earlham – run through valleys. Between them the side streets rise, undulate and fall: College Road. Recreation Road. Christchurch Road. Teeming terraces, away from the thunder of the traffic and the taxi roar, a discombobulated world. You can tarmac over the hills, you can turn a wilderness into an asphalt floor, but you cannot tame what lies beneath. Under the West Norwich streets there are old chalk workings, refuse pits full of vanished Saxon dung. They open up occasionally and a bus disappears, lists comfortably into a funnel of cascading earth, a tree totters inexorably to one side, a house is scythed neatly in two by the shifting void below. The past refuses to lie down here. It will not go away. Sometimes, prompted by chance malfunctions of gas and electricity, they dig up the grey streets and find Nazi bombs, or parched skeletons grown white and friable beneath the sandstone grit. The bombs come from a Baedeker raid in 1942 when Goering tried to erase Norwich Cathedral; the bones are from centuries back, from Danish burial grounds, from Angevin plague pits: a cavalcade of grim history sealed up in the wet earth, ripped open by prying fingers of iron and steel.

Up College Road. Left along the dense outline of the park. The spectral hand of a more personal heritage looms up here, the twitch upon the thread grows insistent. Each stroll through the back streets of Norwich has become a tightrope walk over a frothing cauldron of reminiscence. The house on the corner? That was where you attempted to put your arm round a girl called Alexandra Dodd fifteen years ago. The wide concrete lead-in to the park gates? Where your friend flipped lazily off his scooter and snapped a wrist. You can hear the bone crack now, screaming back across time.

I halt on the corner of The Avenues and Christchurch Road and light another cigarette, watch as two spiky-tops, a boy and a girl in the standard leather and bondage gear, saunter by. In my absence, inexplicably, Norwich has become a place of violence. Fat Eric tells me about it sometimes, waxing philosophical over his can of Strongbow: 'Fucking diabolical it is too. This old woman, friend of me mum's, comes home and finds her door's been kicked in. And then when she looks in the kitchen . . .' Fat Eric is a walking, recitative case book of the lore of local horror. 'So then they tied the kid to a tree and . . . Beat up his mother and then . . . Waited until he'd unlocked the back door and . . .' The gangs, the lads you see looking sullen and anxious outside the park gates, have designer names these days: the Steins, the Dawn Patrol, the North Park Avengers. The Steins got hold of a police Alsatian out on Eaton Park last week. According to Fat Eric's admiring testimony, it came back in fillets.

This is what they've done to my city, where I sowed my youthful dreams . . . Back outside the house there is an odd, untenanted darkness detectable in the front room. Suzi has disappeared. I admit myself cautiously, careful not to rattle the key in the lock, inch silently across the musty carpet. Here Suzi has printed a note on top of the message pad. 'Elaine rang. Will call back.'

What do you know? It was her. Unbidden, half-remembered images crackle in my head: Elaine decked out in a wedding dress, hair *à l'impératrice* for the preliminary scenes of *Virgin Bride*; Elaine romping through thigh-high bracken, stalked by three slavering, Amazonian pursuers, in a spoof Morty once made called *Daughters of Giant Hulk*; I halt on the stairs for a moment, seeing her face with its queer, intense look emerging out of a backdrop of unknown physiognomies and random paraphernalia, clamber upstairs into the raging darkness.

Later I ask Suzi, 'The girl who rang, Elaine. What did she sound like?'

'Which girl?'

'The girl who rang called Elaine. The girl who rang and you took the message. What did she sound like?'

Suzi turns from the television set where she is adjusting the video to record a snooker final. There are files of unmarked examination scripts strewn over the carpet.

'I don't know. I wasn't listening.'

'Did she sound cheerful? Angry? Preoccupied?'

'I don't remember.'

'Did she have an Irish accent?'

There is a tinge of scarlet seeping into Suzi's flabby and generally marmoreal cheeks. She says, 'You just don't have any tact at all, do you? Some ex-girlfriend of yours you've never told me about rings up and I have to answer the telephone, and all you can do is ask me, "What does she sound like?" and "Does she have an Irish accent?"'

'Did she?'

'I don't remember,' Suzi says. She slams the tape viciously into its slot. 'I just don't remember. And if she rings again do you know what I'm going to do?'

'No.'

'I'm going to slam the phone down,' Suzi says. 'I'm just going to slam the phone down.'

There is a brief, puzzling moment before I gather her up in a neutral, compensatory embrace. She cries quietly for a moment. 'You should have told me about her,' she says.

The room falls quiet again. In the distance, towards Unthank Road, the traffic hums.

I still have the photographs. They fell out of a drawer the other day and came tumbling down over the carpet: parti-coloured leaves on the dead forest floor, glistening evidence. Scuffed now, stained and split by half-a-dozen hurried removals and uneasy resting places, they have their own patterns. Contrived, formal portraits: Morty, Terry Chimes and I pictured behind desks, posed with flustered starlets at industry launches, lined up outside the office door at Dean Street; stills from the major Leisurevision productions, full of bobbing breasts and wanton undress; odd, miscellaneous shots taken in the studio, in pubs, in the Grunt Records foyer. Elaine stares intently out of a frame of cameras and lighting equipment; Morty, frozen in mid-gesture, hovers in the centre of an arc of bright, inexplicable light; a joke portrait of Terry Chimes asleep on a sofa, eyes keeled crazily to one side. There is a flawless, perfect photograph taken by David Bailey which appeared at the height of our fame: we sit stonily, side by side, behind a glossy oak table strewn with discarded film reels. Somebody – not myself – has captioned it '*Sunday Times*, November 1977'.

Other pictures. Morty and Terry Chimes shot in the Bethnal Green Road, around 1975. Crazy Rodney stands a pace or two behind them, eyes lowered, hands stuffed into his East End frightener's overcoat. Terry Chimes pictured with some of the

Grunt Records roster: with the Glasgow Express, a panorama of tartan flares, macaw haircuts, bony, Scottish faces; with Bobby Dazz, the latter encased in a white tuxedo. Countless portraits of Elaine: Elaine in black fishnets and satin camisole lying on a bed of white roses (the promotional shot for *Virgin Bride*, I recall), Elaine in a girl-guide uniform standing before a full-length mirror, shot in shadow so that her pale face stares up out of the murk. What strikes me most in retrospect is the consistency of the expressions. Morty looks nervous, uncertain, head turned half to one side, eyes permanently distracted by something beyond the camera. Terry Chimes, in contrast, is the epitome of self-possession, grinning, ironic, contemptuous. Elaine seems remote, preoccupied. There is a single photograph of the four of us taken on a boat on the Thames which neatly encapsulates these attitudes. Morty's face is averted, gathered up in shadow, the rest of his body slung to one side. Terry Chimes stares straight ahead, one hand clasped round a pint glass, hair streaming in the wind. I have my arms folded high up my chest, an odd, knowing look. Elaine is disagreeably amused. 'I am here too,' her expression seems to say. 'I am part of this, but I wouldn't want you to think that I was in any way enjoying myself.' Behind us the choppy water stretches away to a backdrop of rotting wharves and tumbledown warehouses.

Suzi's attitude to this portrait gallery is revealing. I watch her sometimes as she turns the pictures over, critically, but with cautious interest. Her comments are careful, designed in however small a way to connect her to the pantomime of face and gesture rather than to establish distance. 'I knew a woman who looked like that,' she says, examining a print of some forgotten starlet, or 'There was a girl at school who did her hair that way.' Seeing the picture of Elaine and the roses she said once, 'Wasn't that a poster? I'm sure I saw it in a magazine somebody had at school.' Her comments on my own appearance are, I suspect, purposefully mundane. 'You look ill there,' she says. 'Ill. And you haven't shaved.' The wider implications, of livelihood and past association, are set prudently to one side.

There is a faint wistfulness about these excavations. On one occasion she said, 'I was on TV once.'

'When was that?'

'At school. Every year in the week before Christmas, Anglia TV used to choose someone from one of the local schools to read from the nativity story and one year it was me.'

'Did you enjoy it?'

'They said I had very expressive diction,' Suzi says primly, 'and that I responded well to the camera.'

Later on, several stills photographs of this performance were brought out and arranged before me. They showed a small, plump schoolgirl, abundant hair falling over green blazer, reading from a heavy prayerbook. There were glimpses of festive scenery: snow-covered logs, a lavish crib, a henge of beribboned parcels, a file of choristers processing across the stage, ersatz snow pouring down above them. They seemed as remote and unreal as anything Morty and I had ever contrived.

'I was quite famous for a bit,' Suzi said. 'People used to stop me in the street and say they'd seen me.'

Only one of the photographs causes me anxiety, and that not on account of cast or circumstance. Taken in Venice, where Morty and I had gone on business, at the height of *Carnivale*, it supplies an immense, fantastic panorama. Pierrot, Harlequin, other figures out of the *commedia dell'arte*, stylised Venetian noblemen, are performing an intricate and expressive dance, their faces, white-painted, hidden behind black eyemasks, wholly absorbed. Morty and I, tourists bidden to the ball by one of Morty's associates, stand in the centre of this assembly, uncertain and somehow ill at ease. Many of the dancers wear animal masks: bear, eagle, panther, zebra. There is something mildly sinister, certainly, in the precision of their grouping around me, but the disquiet is that of association. Looking at them you think, inevitably, of fog over the Piazza San Marco, water lapping across the grey flagstones, light shining from high, desolate windows. The picture, with its hints of entrapment, the suspicion of evil disguised within a cloak of frivolity, has always unnerved me, but I have never been able to throw it away.

Suzi approved the photograph. 'Nice costumes,' she has said on more than one occasion. 'You must have enjoyed yourselves.'

Early in the morning, two days after Elaine's call, Suzi advances on me bearing something small and flimsy between her fingers. 'I found this stuck down the side of the radiator in the dining room. I thought you might want to see it.'

A photograph, yellowing at the edges and blurred by years of heat. I twitch it out of her hands, flip it face upwards on to the desk and my father stares up at me, a single figure posed beneath a tree, shading his eyes against the sun. I turn it over. There is a date pencilled on to the hard, shiny paper: 'June 1957'.

Suzi hovers expectantly. 'Do you know who it is?'

'Just my dad,' I tell her noncommittally. 'Just my dad when he used to live here.'

This seems to satisfy her. When I look up from the desk a moment later she has disappeared. In the distance I can hear her feet moving rapidly down the narrow staircase.

Although my father invariably referred to himself as a 'native' and had been known in his more elevated moments to talk about 'ancestry', his arrival in Norfolk had been of recent date: it was not until the beginning of the 1960s, with various professional commitments fulfilled and personal obligations decisively severed, that he had finally settled himself at the house in Norwich. Once installed he had lost little time in erasing those traces of his previous life which might have been thought to compromise newer affiliations. There had been a flat Midlands accent once and occasional half-affectionate references to 'Brum'. Neither of these survived the transit east. Subsequently he gave the impression of a man unreasonably absorbed in milieu, the possessor of a fund of specialised information which could be used to eke out conversations with more knowledgeable acquaintances. Precarious at first, this thin coating of local lore soon hardened into an impenetrable carapace. Though he might show mild uncertainty in dealing with more obscure areas of Norfolk life – National Hunt racing courses, say, or the history of Norwich City Football Club – he rarely allowed himself to be caught out.

This abrupt transformation – from vagrant to habitué – was typical of my father's character. Set down in an unfamiliar environment, shunted off into fresh spheres of influence and intrigue, he set to work immediately to reinvent himself, to take on some inconspicuous but recognisable shape that would be acceptable to the people around him. The new job, the chance encounter, the unfamiliar face seen across the garden fence: no introduction of this sort could proceed very far before my father had first emerged to reconnoitre, sniff the air and establish what was required of him and his ability to supply it. At the time I assumed, uncharitably, that this caution arose out of sheer deference, social uncertainty, simple fear, that the bewildering shifts of opinion which it demanded reflected nothing so much as an engrained lack of resolve. Only later was it possible to establish that they grew out of a profound desire for assimilation. My father wanted people to like him, wanted it very much, and to this end was prepared to conciliate almost any foible in the people he ran up against. While this characteristic implied deep-rooted insecurity, there was also in it the suggestion of the actor, someone happy to exchange the blander aspects of his own personality for a feigned but potentially more engrossing role. In this sloughing-off of one temporary skin and its replacement with another there lurked, not infrequently, an appreciation of comic possibilities.

My father's relationship with Morty Goldstein was invested with something of this air. They had come across each other in the early 1960s in the course of some long-forgotten business transaction: a relationship kept up on my father's side by a willingness to please and considerable amusement. In this respect, at least, the connection did my father credit. An intransigent conservative of a kind rarely found even at that time, he might have been expected thoroughly to disapprove of Morty, his race, his trade and his morality. My father's opinion of the Jews was wholly untenable. 'Look at the Middle East,' he would say. 'A perfectly decent set of people, all going about their business and perfectly amenable to British influence. And then suddenly the Jews decided to come interfering and ruin everything for forty years.' Curiously this blanket condemnation did not extend to Morty Goldstein. 'No doubt Mr Goldstein makes his money in ways which moralists would find obnoxious,' he would say. 'That is beside the point. He has never, so far as I know, committed a crime. Consequently he is entitled to any professional service I am able to provide him with that he cares to pay for. You will only find me complaining of him at such times as my bank refuses to honour his cheques, and that occasion, I am pleased to say, has not yet occurred.'

My father was a chartered accountant, specifically an insolvency practitioner concerned with the winding-up of small businesses and the reclamation of debt. It was the only subject on which he spoke with any bitterness. 'When I was a young man I had a number of talents. At school I won prizes for composition. I had a passable tenor voice. I was not unaccomplished. But they made a chartered accountant out of me. Consequently I have spent my life evaluating the contents of sweetshops and arguing with creditors over ten-pound notes.' Some hint of these early attachments still lingered: he approached the *Insolvency Practitioner's Gazette* with the air of a man determined to find fault, not so much with its professional lore as with its defective grammar; he sang in the chorus of the Norwich Philharmonic Society for twenty years. At the same time, there was something mildly defiant in the way he pulled on his dinner jacket, or lamented a faulty subjunctive: an impudent and derisive gesture to an unseen audience.

As a parent he was unapproachable. To have waylaid him on one of his journeys to or from the house, to have interrupted him in conversation, to have proposed alterations to his routine – each would have been unforgivable. It was my father who sought me out, who discussed or directed. At these times, and with affected reluctance, he would talk about his clients: 'I went to see a man today who sells vacuum cleaners in Heigham Street. Five thousand pounds owing and dropping stumer cheques all over the place. I told him,' my father would say, pausing for emphasis, 'that he was *properly in queer street* and no mistake.' The out-of-date commercial slang was characteristic. My father brought to any discussion of business an unmistakable aura of the past, the suggestion that he moved amid a world of silk-hatted clerks at their stools, financiers in Astrakhan coats and Threadneedle Street fogs. In this, as in so much else, he seemed a deliberately archaic figure.

But perhaps in this brief account I have wholly misjudged my father. Perhaps, in retrospect, there were times when the mask dropped, when the carapace of suavity and self-possession fell away and a more recognisable human face emerged. If so I do not remember them. Purposeful, intent, absorbed, he gave the impression of existing inside some remote, high-walled palisade, the key thrown away, the door indistinguishable amid the yards of fencing, the process of forcing an entry requiring a greater resolve than I possessed. Or perhaps this too is simply an illusion of hindsight and there were great tracts of my father's character that I failed to investigate, great open-cast mines simply requiring the coal to be lifted from their surface. Perhaps too the incidental remarks with which my father strewed his conversation – the hints about his ancestry, the half-revelations about his early life – were simply lures designed to draw me into a web of shared knowledge and easy familiarity. If so, the bait remained untasted. I liked my father and I think he liked me, but the gap between us was as bare and arid as any desert.

Though all this might suggest that my father neglected his duties as a parent, that he abdicated the many responsibilities conventionally assumed under this role, this was not the case. He was, for example, unreasonably exercised by my choice of career, linking it to other similar decisions of which he had some knowledge, using it as an excuse to impart a great deal of lapidary advice. Curiously, the degree of personal interference which he brought to most aspects of my life was here wholly set aside, buttressed by alleged powerlessness. 'It is a *great mistake* to expect children to imitate their parents,' he would say. 'Take Parsons' – Parsons was a crony from the Philharmonic – 'a surgeon at the West Norwich Hospital and wants his boy to go into medicine. The boy's a cretin, of course, but Parsons will fix it. You'll see. He'll write to his old friends and get the boy into medical school. Where he'll come a cropper, I shouldn't wonder,' said my father innocuously. 'Now, if I wanted to get you articled as a chartered accountant, it *simply couldn't be done*.' The glint in his eye suggested that it was my capacity rather than his own which lay in doubt.

But he approved my choice of journalism. 'It is an honourable calling. In fact where would we be without newspapers? I have often thought that the degree of coordination required to produce a single issue of the *Daily Telegraph* must be quite remarkable. No doubt at some future point you will be able to tell me how it is done.'

Later he said, 'Your cousin James had some ambitions in that direction. I believe he aspired to be the sports editor of a newspaper in Sunderland. But it came to nothing, alas. It came to nothing.'

It was here in these preparations for a new life that would be lived out far away from Norfolk, beyond immediate surveillance and recall, that my father's detachment from reality became complete. He was put out to discover that the course took place in London. 'But my dear boy, where do you intend to lay your head? I should be very sorry to think' – a rustle of the newspaper – 'that you should be reduced to the position of one of those unfortunate young people' – another rustle of the newspaper – 'who are, I believe, forced to sleep on the Embankment.' It was useless to explain about government grants, about halls of residence and accommodation agencies; ideas of this sort, once fixed in my father's head, were not readily dislodged. He cheered up, however, in a discussion of my likely colleagues. 'There is, I gather, a category of journalist known as the hard-nosed investigative reporter, who occupies his time drinking gin and peering at unsuspecting politicians through the windows of what I believe are known as love-nests. I trust that you, at any rate, will aim slightly higher.'

Time passed. I went away to London, rarely to return. My father gave up his insolvency practice and sank into retirement. The housekeeper who had looked after me and attended to his own limited wants was dismissed. Curiously, absence wrought a change in our relationship, in my father's conception of himself and the duty he might be thought to owe to his dependant. He wrote regularly in a thin, clerkly hand and there was about these letters a tinge not so much of affability – my father was always affable – but of revelation. He spoke mostly of his acquaintances, the cronies of the Philharmonic or the masonic lodge, but seldom to the exclusion of his own personal concerns. 'Parsons is having great trouble with his son. The boy has been expelled from medical school and wants to go on the stage. I was able to assure him that I had no worries in that direction.' I was touched by the compliment, if compliment it was, the more so in that it seemed to elevate me into a new frame of reference. Compared to Parsons's delinquent son I had taken my place among the various mechanisms with which my father regulated his life.

In retirement my father was not without resource. He had certain little antiquarian hobbies which he continued to work up: the antiquities of Norfolk, the route and dimensions of the old City Wall. There is a photograph of him taken at about this time, reprinted from the *Eastern Evening News*, standing beneath the walls of Norwich Castle, his eye fixed rigidly on the distant battlements. It was at this stage in his life, too, that he began to cultivate the society of his neighbours. This was an unexpected departure. Dislike of neighbouring families, of their children, personal habits and social status, was one of my father's most marked characteristics. He had an exaggerated notion of respectability, of appropriateness to milieu, vague attributes subsumed under the convenient shorthand of 'class'. It was rare for any newcomer to the neighbourhood to match up to these exacting standards. Predictably the neighbour whom my father selected for his overtures of friendship was of a more acceptable type. 'Perkins is a decent little man,' he informed me. 'Sat upon by his wife, of course, but we can't mind that at his age.' The reference to age was consciously fantastic. Perkins was a retired insurance clerk a year or two younger than himself, but it amused my father to pretend that he was a much older man, to suggest, in fact, that Perkins's continued existence was a matter for wonder and congratulation. 'It is a marvel how much Perkins gets about,' he would say. Or, 'Perkins astonishes me with his vigour.' It was a deliberate fantasy, which lent colour to an otherwise prosaic relationship, but my father kept it up. He took an obtrusive interest in Perkins's hobbies and immediate family. 'I spent an agreeable afternoon looking at Perkins's collection of cigarette cards,' he wrote at about this time. 'Apparently he shows them at exhibitions and is offered large sums of money for them by American collectors.' What Perkins made of this gentle patronage was anyone's guess. I saw them together only once, in the mid-1970s, setting out to attend a cricket match at the county ground at Lakenham, and he had the puzzled look of the man who feels, amid much ancillary politeness, that he is being made a fool of. Shortly afterwards came another letter. 'You have made a fine impression on Perkins,' my father wrote. 'He enquires after you constantly.'

And then something went wrong between them. Whether it was that Perkins grew finally to resent my father's patronage, that my father became bored with his creation, or that some other agency intervened, I never discovered. But there were no more references to cricket, to cigarette cards, or life insurance. To my father such severances were quite irrevocable. Once thrown down, the frail pontoon bridges that joined him to the rest of humanity could not be restored.

I saw my father for the last time in the summer of 1976. He had lost none of his old vigour. Oblivious to the heat he led me into the back garden, where a hosepipe lay leaking water on to the parched grass, and criticised the drought regulations. 'A ridiculous intrusion. I have had a man here from the council actually insisting that I cease to water my lawn,' he said, giving the hose a little kick with his foot. 'Naturally I told him that it was his duty to supply me with water and that I should view any interruption with extreme gravity.' I had not seen my father so gleeful since a rival for masonic high office had fallen down drunk at the festive board in front of the Senior Provincial Grand Warden. Later, as we sat drinking tea beneath the cloudless sky, he revealed a new and consuming interest.

'What do you think of that tree?'

There was an old lime tree which grew a yard inside the neighbouring garden. Long unpruned, its yellow foliage fell low over my father's rose bushes; sweetish scent hung in the dead air.

'It does seem rather overgrown.'

'*Exactly*. That is exactly what I said to the man from the council when he came to inspect it. Overgrown. Neglected. A health hazard too, I shouldn't wonder. Naturally, I am taking legal action.'

The neighbouring property was owned by a bedridden spinster. 'Couldn't you ask her to prune it?'

'I should have thought that you at least might have supported me in this,' said my father mildly.

Clearly in the matter of the tree my father had become rejuvenated. At dinner that night he was more animated than I had seen him for years. We ate in the kitchen, as the shadows fell over the gloomy garden and the smoke from his cigar rolled against the windows and lay curled there like grey cotton wool. In this final encounter his conversation was a simulacrum of the prejudice of the last twenty years. Later when, searching for memories of my father, I came to reflect on the scene, it seemed to me that there was a suspicious fluency about these remarks, that they existed, albeit unconsciously, as a kind of apologia, patiently rehearsed over many years and only now thought suitable for display. In their triumphalism – the triumph of one who had survived, endured, maintained rigid principles in an age of dissolution – there was an unmistakable note of elegy, tempered by complete isolation from the ordinary processes of life. 'Do you know,' my father said, 'those people I see at the club, Parsons and that sort. All they ever talk about is the past. You know, the women they had thirty years ago and how happy they were. I never heard anything so deplorably sentimental. I have lived for seventy years, followed a more or less respectable calling and, I trust, behaved adequately to my fellow men, and do you know I never stopped to consider whether I was happy. In fact,' said my father, '*happiness never came into it*.'

I had a sudden glimpse then of bright, flawless machinery put to some ugly purpose, of a rare and subtle mechanism grinding inexorably on out of trim.

Later, we walked out once again into the garden and the tree wrought a final, magical effect. 'Do you know,' said my father, 'I shouldn't wonder if it was a very long dispute.'

It was his final victory. By a curious stroke of fate the solicitor's letter informing my father of his neighbour's capitulation arrived on the day of his death. It was returned to me amongst a pile of unopened post: masonic communications, requests for unpaid subscriptions, the paraphernalia of comfortable old age. He was found collapsed in his bedroom, having failed to keep a lunch appointment in the city. 'I should like to die in my chair,' he had often said, 'like an old Viking. Not in hospital being chaffed by a lot of silly nurses.' In this as in other areas of his life my father was narrowly triumphant.

In the week after his death I received two letters which shed some light on my father's character. The first was from the elderly lady who lived next door. Its tone was conciliatory. She explained that while she had not spoken to my father for some years, she was 'inexpressibly pained' by the news of his death, which might be construed as 'a warning to us all'. As a mark of respect she had given instructions that the tree should immediately be cut down.

The second letter was from Mr Perkins.

It was a diffuse, rambling document, clearly written under some constraint, concluding with a request that I should call at the Perkinses' house to receive various 'items' – the word was underscored – lent to Mr Perkins by my father and never returned. I called at the Perkinses' by appointment some days later to be handed, without explanation, a large brown-paper parcel. It contained several hardback books with titles such as *The Jewish Conspiracy: and what can be done about it.* I remembered a remark of my father's early on in their relationship. 'Perkins is very strong on the Jews,' he had said. 'It is one of his many agreeable features.'

My father had left a thousand pounds; a handful of trifling debts. The whole realised a sum in three figures. I was his sole legatee. There remained the question of the house. At an early stage I had felt confident in disposing of my father's estate. The property would be sold, I thought. Children would come and run over its musty staircases and despoil the regularity of its well-kept lawn. The estate agent, a jaunty young man whose brother I remembered from school, had another suggestion.

'You want to rent it,' he advised. 'People coming into the city these days, they're schoolteachers, students. They can't afford to buy property – letting's what they want. A bedsitter or a flat. You could make a hundred a month from this place if you went about it in the right way.'

I took him at his word. A contracting firm gutted the downstairs rooms, stuck Fablon on the kitchen walls and painted over the cracked ceiling. I spent a day in the city buying cheap, serviceable furniture for the three bedsitting rooms. A second contracting firm came to instal coin-operated gas and electricity meters, and finally the business was done. I left the letting arrangements in the hands of the solicitor, who promised to acquire 'a good class of tenant'. I can remember thinking, as I signed the necessary documents, that my father would have approved the sentiment.

All this took place in the long summer of 1976. At first Morty had grown nervous at the prospect of my long absence and for a time I received sharp, admonitory reminders of the world I had left behind me. 'The least you can do while you're down there is to read a few scripts,' he remarked a day or so after my departure.

* * *

One day in early September, having collected a set of keys from the solicitor, I paid a final visit to the house. Six weeks had elapsed since my father's death and already all trace of him seemed to have been expelled from the bright, nondescript rooms. There was a television set occupying the far end of the lounge – something he would have abominated – and a long angular sofa had replaced the narrow chintzes. Only in the dining room, with its cluster of mahogany chairs and the framed sporting prints out of Surtees, was there any hint of his departing spoor. Curiously it was here in this meagre, ill-furnished space, motes of dust dancing in the flood of sunlight, that the memory of my father, long kept at bay, rose up finally to disturb me. For a moment it seemed to me that in refurbishing his house along these bland, anonymous lines I had destroyed him far more effectively than any stroke. Subsequently, such was my distress, I went rapidly from room to room in a search for other tangible reminders of his presence. Little had survived the enthusiasm of the contractor's men. A cupboard on the landing disclosed a dusty edition of the works of Sir Walter Scott, each volume firmly inscribed on the flyleaf with my father's initials; there were patent medicine bottles collected in the bathroom cabinet. Back numbers of *Accountancy* still lay piled up in the spare bedroom. But these were insubstantial ghosts. I went downstairs and stepped into the garden.

Here everything was much as I remembered it. In my absence the solicitor had sent round a jobbing gardener and the square lawn and the gravelly walks retained their original character. There had in any case been little for him to do. The drought had lingered on into September and the grass was white and friable. At its fringe a few plantains grew to knee height. Beyond, the summer's rose heads lay mouldering. I had never liked the garden, which from an early stage in his occupancy my father had appropriated entirely for his own use. It was here that he had sat on summer evenings reading newspapers or listening to classical concerts on the radio, here that he had stood gossiping with his odd, anonymous acquaintance. To have played football on it or skirmished through its borders would have been an act of despoliation. There was something neat and pedantic in its arrangement – a whiff of the fussy, authoritarian side of my father's nature which required the

symmetrical draping of tablecloths, the measure
dried crockery. I would have preferred a wildern
garden in its later incarnation had always re
girlfriend from the early days with Morty, a
spectacular beauty that its maintenance seemed
form of intimacy, flawless yet inhuman.

Moving on over the dusty grass it was possible to detect the first hint of autumn. Dry leaves crackled underfoot. A faint breeze blew in from across the park, bringing with it the scent of smoke. It would rain soon, I thought, that relentless Norfolk rain which sweeps in from Jutland to saturate the landscape and provide the characteristic smell of wet compost and extinguished bonfires. Older memories crowded in now, of an attempt to dine outside cut short by thunder, of the scurry to convey food, tables and chairs hurriedly inside, of my father's panama hat left alone and unclaimed amid the downpour. Dead, I thought. Gone. Rising up before me with its high, lonely windows, brickwork dark in the faltering light, the house seemed as remote and tenantless as any desert island. I went indoors.

I saw my father twice after his death. On the first occasion he walked into the cutting room at Dean Street late one evening as I sat talking to Morty and stood just inside the doorway, his shoulder pressed against the wall. I have no idea how long he remained there: in the half-light, the neon gleaming above us, it took some time for me to establish that the accretion of lines and shadows was a human form, still longer to establish that the form was my father's. In the brief instant before he disappeared I had time to register only an impression of mild bewilderment, as if he had strayed into a long-remembered room whose furniture had now been changed out of all recognition. Indeed, such was the speed with which the sensation passed that I was not completely sure that it was my father. Tired, preoccupied, I would have dismissed it as a trick of the light had it not been for the smell: that odd compound of tobacco, tweeds and chalk, as distinctive as musk.

The second occasion was on an underground train at the end of the Metropolitan line near Uxbridge, late one winter's afternoon when the fog lay over Watford and the distant spread of Metroland.

n recognition came late. It was not until the short figure in the ackintosh had stepped off the train and stood uncertainly in the frame of the closing doors that I realised who it was. He was gone in an instant, leaving me half out of my seat staring at the empty platform.

Morty took a great interest in these visitations. He said, 'You saw your old man? Here in the studio and then again on the tube? That's really unusual. Once I can understand, but twice, that's really spooky.'

'It was disagreeable, I'll give you that.'

This was intended to stop the conversation, but Morty went on, 'What did he look like? Would you say he looked unhappy?'

'Not unhappy. Preoccupied, perhaps.'

'Uh huh. Usually they look unhappy. Did I ever tell you about the time I saw a ghost? Girl called Angela who used to work here, but then she died. Drugs or something. It was before your time. I saw her in Leicester Square and she looked *deathless.*'

Later he said, 'You see him again, I want to hear about it. And this time look into his eyes. That's a sure sign.'

It was an unnecessary injunction. I knew I would never see him again.

Once, out of curiosity, late one night at the loft in Dean Street, I asked Morty, 'Tell me about my father.'

Morty looked surprised. 'Your old dad?'

'My old dad. Tell me about him.'

For a while Morty thumbed dejectedly through the clumps of shiny models' portfolios that lay strewn over his desk. Then he said, 'I dunno, Martin . . . What do you want to know?'

'Well, where did you meet him for a start?'

'Where did I meet him? Jesus, Martin, it was a long time ago. 'Sixty-two, 'sixty-three maybe. Time some nudie magazine wholesaler went bust: he had to liquidate the stock. Which was a laugh, when you think about it, getting someone to liquidate eight tons of fanny mags. But he did me a favour, your old dad did. Let me take a whole run of *Cleavage* out of the warehouse and no questions asked. You remember *Cleavage*?'

'Before my time, Morty.'

'I suppose it was . . . Well in those days the only way you could get away with nude shots was to call it art. You know, you have a row of strippers waltzing round in bits of gauze, but you have a caption that says, "East Sussex Ladies' Greek Dancing Championships", that sort of thing . . .'

'But what about my old dad?'

'Your old dad? Your old dad did me a favour once in a while. Any time a wholesaler called in the receiver I'd give him a call.'

'Just that? Nothing else?'

'Like I said, Martin,' Morty said vaguely. 'It was a long time ago.'

The first time that I saw Elaine she was lying face down beneath the male lead of a pornographic film called, if memory serves me, *Girlschool Janitor* during a shooting session at the upstairs loft of the studio in Dean Street. Bright days, gems amid the confusing clutter of the years, not beyond recall. Morty Goldstein's studio . . . I can see it now. Ten a.m. on a basting July morning with the windows open to admit the scents of the clotted streets below. Morty's film crew, intent veterans of *Manhunter* and *Innocence*, loitering around a tray of sandwiches, plastic bags of ice which were applied every five minutes or so to the nipples of the female lead, the piles of scabrous paraphernalia: there was a school uniform hanging on the wall in its neat dry-cleaner's sachet. I was moving determinedly on towards the office when Morty grasped my arm.

'No, Martin, you have to see this. One of Frank's best. And the chick.'

They still called them chicks in those days. I glanced over at the set where a gaunt, unhappy-looking actor named Frank Fellatio was positioning himself meticulously between the legs of a tall, busty girl with abundant dark hair. In these early days the physique of pornographic film actors still seemed worthy of remark. Even the American ones, the surging hunks with names like Pete The Prong and agents and six-figure salaries, sported beer bellies and toupees. Frank Fellatio was a terrible specimen of humanity: lank, receding hair, badly chewed nails, a few feeble hairs rising from the marbled drum of his chest.

'Are you sure he won't drop dead from exhaustion?'

'He's a good boy, Frank is,' Morty said without much conviction. 'One of the best. Okay he may not look much, but the punters like that. Say you were going to a dirty movie, right? Who would you want to see up there on the screen giving it to Talia Silk or Nancy Slick? Ask yourself, Martin. Someone who looked like Mr Universe or someone who looked like you? Viewer identification, that's what I'm after.'

'What about the girl?'

'Opposite rule applies. Obviously the girl's got to be the best that money can buy.'

'I meant this girl.'

'Elaine or Eileen or something. Another one who wants to do fucking *Hamlet* at the RSC. The agency sent her along. Look, just watch, will you. It's quite a turn-on.'

It was, as Morty maintained, quite a turn-on. Back on the set Frank Fellatio and Elaine or Eileen or something were in the middle of an athletic routine which involved Elaine or Eileen splaying her muscular legs on either side of Frank's puny torso while Frank attempted to burrow gamely into her midriff. I caught a glimpse of the girl's face as Frank flipped her over on to her front and skated airily over her buttocks. Not a happy face: resentful and remote. But – and this is the remarkable thing – the film crew were raptly attentive, bug-eyed faces bent low over the zoom lens. Now, adult movie film crews are a silent, indifferent breed. I was in a studio once when an actor named Hank Mohair led Lynsey Laguna through a devious food-and-drink routine, ending up by munching *pâté de foie gras* out of her navel, without so much as a raised eyebrow. Not here. When Frank got to the part where he had to roll his eyes and carol with fictitious lust there were whoops of encouragement and handclapping. Red-faced and perspiring, the bodies rolled apart.

'It's a wrap,' Morty Goldstein said. 'Give it ten minutes, will you, and then try the scene where Frank finds the gym mistress in the shower.' He draped his arm over my shoulder in a gesture that was meant to convey brotherly affection. '*Hey*. Come into the office, will you?'

I followed him warily over the set, nearly colliding with a burly scene shifter carrying a lacrosse stick. This was the mid-1970s. Now at that time in pornographic films, or in the sort of pornographic films that Morty Goldstein shot, or in the sort of pornographic films that Morty Goldstein shot in London, the characters did not have sex. Soft-core. It was only in the early Eighties that the studios became full of straining members and gynaecological close-ups. Still, Morty was doing his best to nudge forward the frontiers of his art. A chain of adult cinemas on the south coast had even sent back a recent Leisurevision production – a thirty-minute tape called *Thrash* – on the grounds that it offended public *decency*. These were proud scars.

Morty's office: a lurid booth decked out in red plush. On the wall hung a framed photograph of Morty's son being bar mitzvah'd. Morty waved me into a chair, a grim, eager chipmunk searching amid the detritus of his desk for a cigarette lighter.

'Fuck, am I glad to see you. I've got problems like you wouldn't believe.'

'The agency again?'

'Uh huh. You wouldn't believe the sort of thing they're sending me, you wouldn't.' For a moment Morty looked as if he could cry. 'Thirty-five-year-olds with outsize tits. Fourteen-year-olds with no tits at all. Plus *Milkmaids* got taken out of Smiths again.'

'No?'

Milkmaids was one of Morty's milder men's magazines, of the sort that more or less got sold legally. It got taken out of Smiths every three or four weeks. 'We're going to have to redesign the cover,' Morty said cheerlessly, 'and take out a whole four-page spread.'

'That's too bad, Morty.'

A telephone rasped from the desk. 'Yeah,' Morty said wearily into it. 'No. The fuck? Tell me about it.' I watched him interestedly as he hunched himself back into his chair and cradled the receiver around his neck. Occasionally when a Sunday newspaper runs a vice exposé you get to see pictures of pornographers captured in all their meretricious glory: greying grandfather types with bouffant hairdos and roguish glints in their eyes. Morty did not correspond to this stereotype. Morty, it is fair to say, looked like a chartered accountant. In fact, Morty *was* a chartered accountant: at any rate there was a framed certificate on the wall made out to 'Mortimer Goldstein FCA'. Morty found these letters magically efficacious in his occasional dealings with the Inland Revenue.

Morty's history. The *News of the World*, when they did the series, maintained that he had been to Harrow. In this particular, though not in others, the *News of the World* was wrong. Morty attended Rotherhithe Council School, which he left at sixteen with an open scholarship in Mathematics to Magdalen College, Oxford. Which he left at seventeen after a slight misunderstanding. Apprenticeship served as clapperboy in his uncle's back garden in Poplar making shorts with a hand-held Rolleiflex. At eighteen he was art director on *Cutie*. The rest is history. Scary history. It was a fact, for instance, that Morty knew the Krays.

'Ron and Reggie? Reggie was a gentleman. Very polite. You know, always used to hold the door open if you were walking into a pub or anywhere.'

'What about Ron?'

'Ron? Well now, Ron . . .'

Scary history. Once when he was drunk Morty told me about a famous fight in which the Krays had neutralised a Maltese pornographer who had tried to muscle in on the youthful Morty's patch in Dalston ('And then Ron got this cutlass . . .'). You didn't want to listen. Back at the desk Morty had finished his telephone call and was staring morosely into space again. Out of the tail of my eye I could see the tall girl being togged up in a plastic mackintosh.

'That was Baff Thackeray' – nearly all Morty's friends in the adult cinema trade had names like Baff or Griff – 'owns the Regal in Brighton. Said ever since we sent the tape of *Thrash* the council have been sending inspectors round to see the reels. Says he can't do *Girlschool Janitor*. Says it's too much of a risk.'

'What's so bad about *Girlschool*?'

Morty sighed. 'Nothing. We've done worse than that, *much* worse. I did a count on the scenes. Twelve straight hits. Some messing about with shaving cream. And the bit in the changing rooms where the lacrosse team finds the vibrator. Christ, you don't even get to see Frank full-frontal. But Baff reckons the Festival of Light are really big down there. One sniff of *Girlschool Janitor* and there'd be a demo outside the cinema, that sort of thing.'

'I've done the rewrites on *Prime Time* plus I called Starfinder, and they think they can get us Minty Greenbaum.'

'Great.' Morty slapped his fist down on the cluttered table. His eyes glinted with pleasure. 'Now, would you mind excusing me? I have to make a phone call.'

I nodded. Whenever Morty made a particularly chanceless killing, it was his innocent habit to telephone his wife – a refined little woman who lived in Ongar with Morty's three children – and tell her about it. I remembered other such calls. 'Honey, I got the UK rights to *Sweet Body of Bianca* . . . Baby, you'll never guess, I just managed to sign up Lynsey Laguna.' I left him crookbacked and intent over the receiver and wandered outside into the airless studio.

They were still filming. Bright, merciless lights. Cigarette smoke rising in dense, vertical lines to the leprous ceiling. Occasionally a bulb popped with an edgy, fragmenting noise like an egg being smashed. Elaine was standing mid-set, wearing a plastic mackintosh, beneath a shower arrangement of serpentine hoses and see-through curtains. As I approached, Morty's director, a cerise-shirted homunculus with tattooed forearms, was saying sternly to the sound man, 'Look, if we drop the fucking mackintosh we don't have anything for her to take off, right?'

'You ever know a chick who went into a shower with a mackintosh on?'

'I fucking do as well, if it comes to that.'

A few threatening gestures later and a reminder from the sound man that Morty would be along in a minute or two to see how things were progressing and they get the cameras rolling. Elaine whisks the curtain back to its fullest extent and begins languorously to finger a bar of soap, inching the raincoat off her shoulders as she does so. I smoke a cigarette and look nonchalant, as if I've seen it all (I have, I've seen it *all*). Meanwhile furtive Frank, clad in mechanic's overalls, stalks leerily round the back of the shower. Elaine arches the raincoat over her midriff. Frank lays a furry paw tentatively on her shoulder. And then, 'There isn't any water.'

The director and the sound man exchange weary, incredulous glances.

'Sure there's no water. This is a film. That's a set. You're supposed to pretend.'

Elaine shoots out one of those intransigent looks I will come to know so well. 'Look, how am I supposed to do a shower scene without water?'

There are some goblin chuckles at this. Morty's crew can do without the Gielgud dramatic verisimilitude bit. Who needs accessories? I once heard a director called Andy Scrod maintain that you could shoot *War and Peace* using a bed and a couple of shotguns. Elaine starts to button up the mackintosh.

'Forget it. I quit.'

The onlookers stare. A whinnying intervention from the director is brushed aside. I pause to take in the scene: the sound man is wheezing over a cigarette; Frank Fellatio emerges trouserless from behind the shower curtain and starts to examine a vivid red weal on his thigh. Another bulb pops.

And then, imperceptibly, I knew that this was the start of something, that some queer, ineluctable mechanism had cranked noisily into gear, seizing me up and bearing me away into unfathomable distance. As in some crowded Elizabethan drama, the incidental characters – cooks, scullions and gentlemen attendants – had faded away, moved back into the surrounding tableau, allowing hero and heroine to step forward and transact their business.

I stood up as Elaine swooped purposefully towards the doorway where Morty and I loitered,. her charcoal hair sweeping in the breeze of the fans.

'Now you listen to me, Mr fucking *Goldstein*, or whatever your name is. This was supposed to be a proper *film*, that's what you said. None of this, "I'm sorry, darling, we're economising, so the set for the next scene is this bed here," none of these fucking actors who have to get finished by four so they can get back to their fucking *milk-rounds* . . .'

'But baby . . .' Morty began brokenly.

'. . . Who're practically *bald*. "Oh baby, you have to work in this new feature I'm planning"' – the mimicry of Morty's nasal East End drawl was surprisingly accurate – '"with all these *major stars* and this *big-time director*"'

'Listen, Eileen . . .'

'It's Elaine, actually. Elaine. But I don't suppose you noticed that, did you, when you were staring at my tits in the audition, Mr

Big-time Producer?' She turned to me for the first time. 'Have you ever been to one of his auditions? You say a couple of lines and then he goes, "Perfect baby, just perfect. Now go ahead and take your clothes off." '

'Listen, Elaine, we can work this one out, okay? We can just . . .'

And then, quite unexpectedly, she burst into tears. Morty shrugged, hunched his shoulders into his jacket and backed away. I said, 'You mustn't mind him.'

'What do you know about it? Who the fuck are you, anyway?'

'Oh, I just work here. But you mustn't mind Morty.'

'No?'

'No. Why don't you put some clothes on and we can talk about it?'

She looked up suspiciously. There was an ancient director's deckchair a few feet away with a dressing gown hanging over the back. With this wrapped around her gleaming shoulders, shielded from the gaze of prurient onlookers by my cautious arm, with Morty staring resentfully from the doorway, Elaine allowed herself to be led away.

'He's not really called Frank Fellatio,' Elaine said later.

'He isn't?'

'He's called Frank Bence-Jones. He's got a wife and two children and he lives in Walthamstow.'

'He does?'

We were having dinner in a restaurant on the Bow Road, a favourite resort of Leisurevision staff after filming sessions in Docklands, urinous studios down by the river in Millwall and Cubitt Town where guard dogs prowled restlessly over the asphalt floor. For Morty, now vanished on some mysterious errand up west, this was a venue of impressive personal significance. It was here, according to legend, that a sixteen-year-old Morty had run messages for gangsters, sold stolen number plates and burnished counterfeit jewellery.

'How do you know he's called Frank Bence-Jones?'

'He told me. In the coffee break. He told me some other things. Like he owes Morty five thousand pounds. And Morty has the deeds to his house.'

'That as well?'

'He's only got one lung,' Elaine said reprovingly. 'And he has to do the next two films for free to pay back the money Morty lent him for the operation.'

I was used to hearing these stories. Whereas about Morty's actresses there hung a faint, intangible glamour, over Morty's actors there rose only the fetid stink of desperation. They came from places like Forest Gate and Chingford. They moonlighted from day jobs as taxi drivers, fruit-stall barkers, ambulance men. Ambition, alone, marked them out as components of Morty's improbable, ramshackle cortège. Late one night in Dean Street, while Morty frowned over a defective storyboard, I once questioned a harassed, balding father of three who appeared under the stage name of Johnny The Wad over his motives. 'I want to be a *star*,' he said simply.

'And you,' Elaine said, 'what do you do?'

'I'm the writer.'

'The *writer*?' I stole a look as she applied herself busily to the contents of her plate: charcoal hair emerging out of her scalp like a giant furzebush, wide, sloping chin, tilted nose, an air of massive, deep-rooted intransigence only narrowly appeased. Beyond, Terry Chimes appeared in the doorway, dressed in a mauve suit, stared pruriently towards us and then departed noisily in search of a table.

'Who's that?'

'He's called Terry Chimes. He works with Morty.' It seemed a prudent description.

'That figures. He was there at the audition.'

'What made you choose Morty?'

'The agency. They said it would be good experience.'

'Good experience for what?'

'*For being an actress*.'

You got a lot of this. Burly twenty-year-olds with appendix scars who'd failed for RADA anxious to 'broaden their perspective', game veterans of provincial rep naïvely bewildered by the sight of a cine camera. Elaine seemed a novel addition to their ranks.

There was a loud interruption from an adjacent table as Terry Chimes, now grown innocently boisterous, flipped a wine glass on to the floor. 'Listen,' Elaine said. 'I'll tell you about it if you like.'

And so, as the dusk began to fade over the striped plastic tablecloths and the lights of the Bow Road flashed up furiously behind us, disturbed only by the blare of the police sirens and the raucous interventions of Terry Chimes, Elaine explained. It was a considerable monologue, taking in her parents' removal from Cork twenty years before, grey North London Irish childhood, the linoleumed floors of the convent school, a philosophy degree at Birkbeck, the general effect oddly unrevealing. When we emerged at length into the dense streets of the East End it was as if I somehow knew less about her, that the result of this rambling autobiography was to conceal rather than to disclose.

Time telescopes now, emerges from the scrambler in random, piecemeal fragments. Elaine turning up at the flat in Hammersmith a month later with a suitcase; her mother's rich Kerry brogue echoing down the wire; waking up once in the small hours and finding her sitting crosslegged in the front room, white face staring through the gloom, expressionless as a sphinx; effortful, energetic sex. What do I remember about her? The usual things, I suppose. *Anger. Irishness. Unpredictability* (not turning up when expected, turning up when not expected). Seeing her at work once in Morty's studio and thinking fitfully of the unreality of it all, as if we were merely children at play, and that our real lives were being lived out somewhere else, far away from the tapering snout of the zoom lens, in echoing space and silence.

Pornography. These days, of course, I can no longer rely on the magazines and the impedimenta of the film studio. These days, I have to make my own.

'Tell me about those boyfriends of yours.'

'I already told you.'

'Tell me again.'

'If you want. First time when I was fourteen. It was after a party. I didn't know what I was doing. I thought it was going to be just kissing and so on. Then there was Adrian, about the time I was doing my O-levels. I was serious about him: I'd have married him if he'd asked me, given up school and everything.'

'Then there was Keith, and the one who worked in the bank?'

'Steve?' Suzi's face assumes a look of dreamy reminiscence. This, after all, is her past being unfurled. When she considers the bleak expanse of her life to date, these are the meteors which spring up to irradiate it with their phantom light. Adrian, Keith and Steve. 'He was sweet. He used to take me to school on his motorbike.'

'And after that?'

Slowly Suzi ticks off the names on her fingers. 'Mike. Robert. Anthony. He was the one who got upset when I went to college. He said it was going to break his heart.'

Mike, Robert and Anthony work for the Norwich Union now, or at the big garden centre up the Daniels Road, or in the jewellery shops along Gentleman's Walk. Suzi sees them with their families sometimes when she goes shopping at Sainsbury's and they stare gamely at her.

'Then when I went to college there was Ashok. I was really serious about him.'

Ashok was the son of a Nigerian chieftain, sent out on a Commonwealth scholarship, who on the first occasion they went to bed together presented Suzi with a dozen fifty-pound notes. The relationship foundered when she discovered the existence of three other wives back in Lagos.

'. . . Bob, Marcus, Justin . . .'

Suzi, of course, would greatly resent the suggestion that she is promiscuous. She is a modern girl, taking her pleasure as modern girls do, but each of her relationships is invested with a patina of moral seriousness. She has been engaged three times – short, tense engagements foundering on ill-will and uncertainty – nearly engaged another four times. Moreover the whole progress, this modern Wife of Bath's tale without the marriage, has been framed from the outset within strictly defined limits. When she was sixteen, Suzi told me, she set down a catalogue of the men who existed beyond this pale: men who were married, men who were more than five years older or five years younger, men of whom her parents might be expected to disapprove. This last category I found touching.

I look at Suzi for a moment as she reaches the end of the story of her last engagement ('Everybody there at the party and we were in separate rooms not speaking to each other'). It broke down a month before the wedding and the engagement presents lie gathering dust in her parents' loft. There is about her a fundamental self-possession, a hard inner coating, a disconcerting refusal to be drawn. Mike, Robert and Anthony and the dusty file of fellow-conspirators had been no match for this pitiless intelligence, I thought.

'Seventeen. That's quite a lot.'

'I was *serious*,' says Suzi firmly. Nothing infuriates her more than the imputation of light-mindedness. 'I've always been serious.'

The faint hint of ulterior motive drifts over the conversation, loiters for a moment, goes away.

Some memories of Elaine:

Unpunctuality

In the early days of our relationship Elaine elevated unpunctuality, formerly a traditional female wile accepted with a good-natured shrug of the shoulders, into a rare and devastating weapon in the sex war. Invited to dine at eight, she compromised on nine-thirty. Asked to be at a theatre half an hour before the performance, she might saunter in mid-way through the second act. Her record was one of Morty's supper parties, convened in honour of a beetle-browed American hard-core director named Scazz Fogelburg, when – the company bidden to assemble in Ongar at 7.30 – Elaine arrived at a quarter to eleven. Insouciance, cultivated negligence, might have made these failings narrowly tolerable, but in fairness Elaine always volunteered perfectly plausible explanations for her tardiness. For example, the excuse for arriving late at Morty's party involved two defective underground trains, an epileptic mini-cab driver and a bomb scare closing the A12.

Indifference

Related, I suppose, to the foregoing. Once, exasperated beyond measure by some chance delinquency, I asked, 'Why do you behave like this?'

'Behave like what?'

'Who do you turn up late to places? If I tell you the table's booked for eight, why do you always get there at nine?'

She thinks about this for a bit. Then she says, 'Listen Martin, why don't you find someone who'll do what you want?'

'What do you mean, "What I want"?'

'Someone who'll turn up at places by the time you want them to. Someone who'll go to bed with you at the time you want them to. In the way you want them to. Why don't you find someone like that?'

Elaine specialised in unanswerable questions of this sort. Eventually I said, 'Will you have dinner with me tonight?'

'A girl's got to eat.'

'Will you make a special effort and turn up at eight?'

'All right.'

I cheated, of course: I booked the restaurant for nine. It was a futile gesture. Elaine arrived at thirteen minutes past ten.

The Rose of Tralee

Have you ever heard of a magazine called *Ireland's Own*? They sell it at London mainline stations and you can occasionally see fuddled Irish labourers poring over it in pubs. The subtitle – *A Little Piece of Ireland* – is printed in outsize capitals on the cover, generally beneath a black-and-white drawing of Parnell or O'Connell, and the inside is devoted to potted biographies of nuns, viscidly sentimental short stories and pictures of gap-toothed children captioned 'A fine young man from Leinster'. Well, Elaine's family subscribed to *Ireland's Own*: 'Every year when I was a kid Dad used to take a picture of me in my party dress and sent it in. You used to have to say how old you were, where you went to school and what your favourite article in the magazine was. There was a series about an old lady who was a private eye – "Ireland's twinkliest detective" – so I always chose that. Every year Dad used to send it in and we'd get the paper and see if they'd printed it, but they never did. In the end, when I was about fifteen, Dad was going to give up – he thought it was a fix, you see, and they just printed pictures of people they knew or who'd sent them money – but then he thought he'd give it one last try. Only this time he made me write down that I came from Tralee, because they liked captioning girls' photographs "The Rose of Tralee", and sure enough they printed it: "Elaine Keenan, the Rose of Tralee". I got people writing to me after that, terribly polite letters from boys at Irish private schools who wanted a penfriend from England. And a dirty letter – from a priest it was as well – who said I was a pure vision of Irish loveliness, and a lot of other things too. Dad took that one to Father Michael, who said it was very shocking and he had a good mind to write to the other priest's bishop . . .'

I saw the 'Rose of Tralee' shot once. A face of sharp, extraordinary beauty, like a cross between a Kate Greenaway girl and something out of Alma-Tadema, and, in its intimations of future obduracy, quite terrifying.

Her manifold suitors

The distinguishing mark of Elaine's allure was the number of people who wanted to marry her. Not to sleep with her, more or less obligatory in circles where not wanting to sleep with a woman was near proof of inversion, but to marry her. The serious thing. Morty asked her. Terry Chimes asked her. Even Crazy Rodney, late one night in an otherwise deserted studio, shuffled across with unignorable evidence of his regard. This last request fascinated me above all.

'What did he say?'

'He was very formal. He said he wanted me to know that he'd always liked and respected me.'

'Anything else?'

'He said his old mother in Romford would die happy if I said yes.'

'What happened when you said no? You did say no?'

'I thought he was going to get nasty. But in the end he just looked sort of sad and backed away.'

There were other, equally unlikely, aspirants to Elaine's hand. Frank Fellatio. Bobby Dazz. Two members of the Glasgow Express. Her manifold suitors included a Conservative MP, an American porn tycoon and the merchant banker who inhabited the flat downstairs from us in Bishop's Park.

'What do you tell them?' I asked once, a lunch date with the proprietor of a West End model agency having ended in the inevitable declaration.

'I just say I'm sorry but it's impossible, and in any case there's someone else.'

'And what do they say?'

'They just look upset. Sometimes they start crying. Hugo' – Hugo was the Conservative MP – 'said he was going to kill himself.'

Late one night in a taxi coming back from Morty's place in Ongar, drink and intimacy having wrought a conducive atmosphere, I asked her. Elaine shook herself slowly awake out of the nest of furs.

'You want me to do *what*?'

One eye fixed nervously on the black conveyor belt of the road, I repeated the request.

'You want me to *what*? Well I'll tell you what you can do for a start, Martin, you can get the fuck out of this car. Right now. Go on, just get the fuck out.'

What do you do in such circumstances, with the fog rising up over the Mile End Road and the taxi driver chortling over the intercom? I smiled. I got the fuck out.

And where are they now?

In Dean Street Morty works on into the darkness. It is past midnight and the tribe of PAs and art directors has disappeared, gone away to the Zoom Club or Tokyo Joe's, but Morty labours on. It will be two or three before he drives back through the dead streets, off through the East End and along the A12 towards the Essex rabbit-run. It is quiet in the studio, quiet but not inert. There are three video screens running simultaneously and Morty watches them all, head bent low down over the desk, framed in the beam of the anglepoise. Sometimes he flicks a switch and the screens stop while he examines the frozen images with their improbable conjunctions of human flesh. Morty is busy censoring hard-core movies for an American cable network, wiping out the appalling close-ups and the jittery climaxes – two seconds here, ten seconds there – running the resulting gaps and sound-breaks effortlessly into one another until all that remains is a seamless web of anodyne soft-core. The task is to his taste. It is, after all, the pornographer's abiding challenge – establishing what you can get away with. Beside him on the desk there is a checklist sent by the American cable network marking out forbidden areas, but Morty rarely consults it: his intuition is an infinitely superior guide. Onscreen a burly, tumescent actor breaks out of a clinch and turns briefly towards the camera. Morty flicks another switch and winds the reel forward, ponders for a moment, winds the reel back again and scrubs the offending exposure. Later the trained eye will detect a tiny hiatus in the action, a momentary wavering of tangled limbs, but how many trained eyes watch American cable networks late at night? Morty lets the blemish pass. Somewhere in the outer office a telephone rings; Morty ignores it. He works on amid the flickering light.

In Suffolk Terry Chimes wanders back from the fish farm with a brace of rainbow trout swinging fatly on his arm. The farmhouse yard is empty, as well it might be, for this is not a proper farmhouse yard but a show country gentleman's estate and there is a suspicious regularity to the piles of baled straw and the row of shiny agricultural implements. In the kitchen a great deal of gleaming pine, a counterfeit kitchen range and a blonde woman in her thirties drying dishes. Terry Chimes says disconsolately, 'I got these. The rest of the fuckers are dying. I fished a dozen out of the overflow pipe just now. Covered in gunge and stuff.' He sits down heavily on a pine armchair, hoists one Wellington over his knee and lights a cigar.

'I told you those fish were a mistake,' the woman says neutrally. She has a peculiar, stylised hairdo, like a parrot's, the fringe teased up in spikes over her forehead, the rest curling down over the nape of her neck.

'Not my fault,' Terry Chimes says listlessly. 'Fucking nitrate in the water, isn't it? Fucking farmers pumping it into the river.' He brightens. 'Why don't we get the car a bit later and go into town? Go to a club or something?' The woman nods. They stare at each other, two people massively out of place and out of time, achingly bemused by their unfamiliar milieu, the sensation oddly disagreeable.

In the flat in Romford Crazy Rodney says, 'Turn over.' Outside a watery November sun shines over the roofs of council houses disappearing up the hill. On the bedside chair a radio rasps football results.

'What do you want me to turn over for?' the girl asks. She has pale, dirty features and there are odd purple bruises on the skin of her inner arm.

'That's a bloody stupid question,' Crazy Rodney tells her tolerantly. 'So I can stick it in you from behind, of course.'

At least that is how I imagine it.

But of course the chief ornament in this ghostly picture gallery eludes me. Morty and Terry Chimes are at the end of telephones somewhere. Even Crazy Rodney I could track down if I had the time and the interest. But Elaine. I don't know. I ceased knowing two or three years ago. And now that I want to talk to her again, now that I have this urge to find out what she wants, the trail is cold. Curious, isn't it? After the crash, when Morty panicked and Terry Chimes stopped answering the phone and barricaded himself into his office, I didn't hear from her in a long while. Just rumours, vague, absurdist rumours pulled out of thin air. In Paris with money. In London without money. In New York with a recording contract and a duplex. Rumours of that sort. Then, when Morty and I nervously re-established contact a year or so later, her name began to flit warily again across the wires, a sharp parenthesis in the bland recitation of sleaze and sensuality.

'So how was the launch, Morty?'

'It was a scene. Scazz Fogelburg had these chicks flown in on a Lear jet . . . Yeah, and that Elaine was there.'

'She was?'

'Sure, with some record producer I never heard of. She said to say hi.'

A few months later the postcards began to arrive, undated, unsigned, the only clue to provenance contained in the postmarks and the vivid pictures on the front. Postcards from New York, from Venice, from Reykjavik. Postcards from exotic or strange locations: from Tunis, bless you, from Tromso, from Consett, County Durham once with a picture of a derelict steelworks. And always from these furtive, cosmopolitan outposts the same laconic messages: 'Here for a couple of days . . . a couple of weeks . . . a couple of months . . . weather good . . . weather bad . . . weather mixed', the same familiar handwriting.

The postcards continued to come. One a week on average, corresponding to no known geographical trajectory or series of flightpaths. From Rome, then Delhi, then Tokyo. From Albuquerque, then Rio, then Fiji. Eventually after two dozen or so of these

I made a brief, resipiscent effort to track Elaine down. I spent a day over it. I telephoned people I hadn't spoken to in three years, people who slammed down the telephone as soon as they heard my name, people who babbled threateningly about forgotten debts and ancient scores until I too slammed down the telephone, people who couldn't or wouldn't remember me, people whom I couldn't remember. I phoned Morty. I phoned Terry Chimes. I phoned booking agents all over Europe. I phoned record company A&R men. I phoned Elaine's parents in Wembley Park. At one point I even acquired an Irish telephone directory and phoned some people with Elaine's surname in County Cork. It was all to no avail. The frail alliances of the past lay endlessly exposed. Morty thought that he might have seen her at a party in San Francisco a year since. Terry Chimes thought she might have got a part in a film called *Lick My Decals Off, Baby*. One or two of the A&R men recollected fuddled encounters in the grim days after the crash. Elaine's parents accused me of corrupting their innocent child. It was a relief, in these circumstances, to turn to the Keenans of County Cork and their voluble relish of unknown callers.

So where did she go? I like to think of a life of low-key exile; a deracinated Becky Sharp yawning sadly over the cocktail glasses and the ashtrays while Rod or Mack or whoever it was attended screen tests or record studios, a ghostly revenant to the great cities of Europe. I like to imagine that her first flight wasn't far, to Paris perhaps, or Frankfurt, where she could read the English newspapers and meet queer half-acquaintances in the record company offices. And I can see her smiling over the defeat of it all, the defeat of watching Rod or Mack or whoever making his third-rate films or records, of Sunday mornings in hotel bedrooms far away – but I don't think she can have liked it. I don't think she can have liked Rod or Mack or whoever, I don't think she can have liked the hotel bedrooms, or the queer company. Every city in Europe has its contingent of English exiles – the foreign correspondents who no longer correspond, the demure chanteuses who had a hit in 1972 and have just emerged from ten years' litigation, the bit-part actors who appear in films that even Morty Goldstein wouldn't care to know about. A reckless, rackety life, this attendance at studios in

Munich or Hamburg or Amsterdam for previews or press launches or parties, but I don't think she can have taken to it.

She did not quite disappear, of course. People never do. Later I discovered that Elaine had left her own unreasoning footprints through several of the capitals of Europe. A promoter claimed to have seen her backstage at a concert in Lille. Somebody said that they saw her in a preview cinema at the 1982 Berlin film festival. But then the trail went dead. A number I had in Hamburg said she had left six months previously. A letter I sent to an address in Cologne came back unopened. And so Elaine slipped away, a faint, negligible scent, leading off into rocky, unpromising terrain, kept alive only by memory and rumour.

There's something else, though, that has to be dealt with first. The photographs come in a sagging brown envelope, bunched in half and squeezed within a coil of Sellotape. Name and address handwritten in frail, spinsterish scrawl. A half-inch pile of Polaroids, the work of someone with scant chance of a future in this line of business. However, on this occasion the form interests me rather less than the content. There are twenty-four pictures, consecutive. In frame one the hero and heroine sit on a sofa in some cluttered, featureless room, he in a suit, she in one of the joke tart get-ups in which people attend fancy-dress parties. Identifiable items amongst the debris at their feet include a Marlboro cigarette packet, the *Daily Mail* and a copy of Keith Thomas's *Religion and the Decline of Magic.* Frame two is broadly identical, except that a packet of Polos has appeared mysteriously in the region of the *Daily Mail.* And then, as in all decently constituted narratives, sequentially and with consecutive revelations, things start to happen. By frame four there is a definite loosening of clothing. Yet this is not your standard hot-action stuff. Increasingly, as frame succeeds frame, it becomes clear that whoever perpetrated this horror is something of an artist in his or her way: frame seven, for example, consists simply of the suit, hung cursorily over the back of the sofa, while frame eleven involves sundry manoeuvrings with lofted limbs and mirrors. Later on things become quite strenuously athletic, but there's some droll, off-camera symbolism, frame eighteen ignoring the on-sofa frenzy altogether to linger over a phallic, table-bound cactus.

Except that there are two reasons why this isn't funny. First, towards the end, things turn nasty. In frame twenty the man in the suit – who isn't wearing the suit by now – has just smacked a hefty backhander into his accomplice's face. Frame twenty-three is a nightmarish thrash of frozen, jerking limbs. I steal a single glance at the last shot and then tear it shamefacedly in two.

There is another reason why it isn't funny. The man in the suit is me.

As the hours pass, the photographs become a pivot on which the day turns. Left on a desk-end, lodged two feet down in a choked cardboard box, hidden under a carpet, they are a magnet drawing me back, through the dense, headachy air. *I didn't do this*, I say to myself at intervals during the mesmerised contemplation of these shiny, perfidious rectangles, *I wasn't there.* There is a faint – a very faint – comfort in the knowledge that I have nothing to do with this *at all.* And yet in minor, muted ways this sort of thing has happened before. I remember . . . I remember five years back, one autumn, strolling out of the Grunt Records vestibule towards the murk of Oxford Street and walking into an actor called Jim Woodward. You will not, perhaps, have heard of Jim Woodward. He played bit-parts in films ten years ago that perhaps you didn't see: the stolid chauffeur in *Driven to Lust*, the leery headmaster in *Spank Academy*. The encounter took approximately half a minute. A second or two for Jim to wheel into view, a further five for me to detect a vengeful glint of recognition in his vague but unpromising eyes. The rest consisted of Jim's fist flapping weakly against my chest once or twice, a little badly staged grappling, and me giving him a double-fister in the throat that made him burst into tears. I left him sitting cheerlessly on the pavement and thought no more of the episode – after all, actors are violent people, they frequently accost you in the street without warning. Two days later at one of Morty's parties in the loft at Dean Street something equally queer and inexplicable happened. Picture the scene: Morty and I in our shiny leather jackets exchanging confidences, an ellipse of attendant women, a rough cut of *Man-eater* showing on the wide screen in the viewing room, when suddenly one of the women craned forward and attempted to jab a champagne glass in my face. Have you ever had a champagne glass pushed into your face? The trick is to deflect, thus, meanwhile doing as much damage as possible to your opponent. I remembered this and did quite a lot of damage. While they were cleaning her up I had a word with Morty.

'Who's the girl?'

'Who's the girl? You tell me who's the girl. I thought she came with you.'

'I thought she came with Vanessa and Scazz and that lot.'

'Vanessa and Scazz thought she was with *Adult Video World*.'

Morty made enquiries: Jim Woodward's girlfriend. But this, it transpired, was a mild preliminary. Two days later someone hurled a postcard reading 'Martin Benson must die' through the window of the flat in Bishop's Park, attached to a brick. Twenty-four hours after that I took delivery from a messenger boy of a registered letter containing a dozen razor blades. 'Maybe you upset him or something,' Morty suggested, when pressed for explanations, 'how the fuck should I know anyway?' Jim Woodward turned up frequently over the next few days: on the far side of street corners feigning an interest in window displays, a lurking troglodyte presence on the edge of parties, late at night on the end of telephones. I couldn't establish what it was that I was supposed to have done to him, or what it was that I was supposed to do in recompense. On the day after two undertakers had rung, unbidden, to offer sympathy and discuss my funeral arrangements, I decided on the magniloquent gesture and sent a thousand pounds in ten-pound notes on a bike to Jim Woodward's flat in Leytonstone. They came back the next morning in fragments. After that Morty sent Crazy Rodney round in a mini-cab. I don't think he hurt him much.

Amid the passage of a cluttered and eventful life you forget things.

Later on, in the soft, misty twilight, I make a closer inspection of the photographs. I deal the pack out card by card on the kitchen table and search anxiously for the inevitable clues of time, location and identity. The room? The room is the sort of room in which these sort of pictures get taken: minimally accoutred, devoid of those revelatory knick-knacks. Frame nine gives a hint of French windows somewhere in the background. Frame thirteen, shot at floor-level, discloses a vista of white, rolling carpet. It could be anywhere. Time? A magnifying glass applied to the copy of the *Daily Mail* reveals a date sometime in March 1978. What was I doing in March 1978? I don't recall. It might have been the time we did *Girls on Top* with Talia Silk, but it might not have been. The girl? Five nine. Maximally endowed. Morty had a file of them half a foot thick. This one didn't work for a month or two afterwards though, that's for sure.

Unless, unless . . . In pornographic cinema, as in more rarefied art-forms, artifice is all. Towards the end of the 1970s Morty got into making splatter movies: *Slash*, *Mad Surgeons*, *Plasma Party*. Given the low budgets and the prognathous actors Morty was forced to employ, they were narrowly realistic. Thus in *Cannibal Island* a man and a woman arrive in tropical paradise, frolic for a while in Bounty hunter fashion, only to be caught, molested and eaten by the randy, starving inhabitants. It was, for a late-period Leisurevision film, brilliantly executed. Morty shot it at low tide on Sheringham beach, the cannibals were all extras blacked up with boot polish, and the horrific finale – in which everyone chews daintily on splayed human limbs – involved some dextrous sleight-of-hand with cocktail sausages. And yet *Cannibal Island* was nervously declined by four German hard-core importers on the grounds of taste.

Dissimulation. Illusion. You can do anything with pornography. You can prune away puny genitalia and paste in hulking substitutes. You can graft on bogus torsos, turn that rictus of rheumy disgust into a calm, gratified smile. Wise to these tricks I ran the magnifying glass over that taut, pitiless body looking for signs: the tiny blemishes a shade or so darker than flesh which show that someone has been tampering, the faint blur of retouching at neck level. It was to no avail. There was one particular shot of me in close-up, the girl clasped disinterestedly over my lap. Quite flawless. You can even see a grainy, pointillist swirl of dust on the girl's shoulder. You can't fake a shot like that. Even Morty, I reason, couldn't fake a shot like that.

After that I scoop up the photographs and put them back in the box.

Back in early '82 when I finally came back here, it was the snow that I remembered, just as I had remembered other snows falling in other cities long ago: in Paris late one night in the parks by the *École Militaire*, in Venice where it descended softly and fruitlessly out over the windy lagoon, more mundanely over thronged Midland rooftops in a silent dawn, snow falling gracefully through the thin air. Now as the train rattled eastward over low, flat countryside it brought back other memories, some recent – a white carpet stretched over Kensington Gardens stained by a single trail of footprints – others more remote, connected indelibly with childhood. Oddly these recollections were linked with landscape rather than emotion. Taken as a child to the high expanse of Mousehold and invited to look out over the wintry city, its spires and office buildings rising up out of the pale dusk, one remembered only detail: the square outlines of Norwich Castle, light neatly constrained to reveal the glowing banks of the city hall. Whatever profounder sensations might have been stirred now lay dormant.

The train out of Liverpool Street was crowded. Generally at such times – Thursday, late in the afternoon – one counted on a degree of uniformity: business people, City men in dark suits with copies of the London evening paper going back to commuter stations down the line, a rare seagoing tourist bound via Harwich for the Hook. Now something had weakened this homogeneity. Students, ticketless and self-absorbed, sat on their bolster-shaped rucksacks ready to scurry off at the guard's approach. Elderly chattering ladies with mysterious parcels. A rugby team back from the

Continent, their luggage stacked in doorways and under seats, skirmished fitfully in the bar. Later as the train passed Colchester they would divide and dwindle, leaving only a handful of long-distance commuters, but for the moment their effect was to impose a spirit of willed raucousness upon the teeming carriages, a capacity for collective action. Alone in their seats, bent over coffee cups, books or crosswords, the passengers none the less displayed a definite unity: an announcement crackling over the Tannoy causing them to stir like troubled dreamers, a rugby ball sailing overhead producing shy, fugitive smiles.

Colchester. Manningtree. Ipswich. Stowmarket. Diss. The familiar names ran in my head. Recalling ancient, deep-rooted associations, suggestive of other, more innocent days, they combined with current doubts and anxieties to produce a context in which the past took precedence over the present, in which latent uncertainties were replaced by a hardening of resolve. This was unusual. Previously I had found myself resisting any deliberate step, gaining comfort from the dense hinterland which exists between thought and action, fascinated simply by my own inanition. Now I found that I no longer cared what Morty Goldstein might say or what Terry Chimes might do, what the consequences of this escape (for that is what it amounted to) might be, no longer cared about future reckonings or contingencies. As the train rattled on through the damp Norfolk landscape, past the shrouded churches and the dark, endless fields, as the remaining passengers – the old lady with her circle of cases, the sallow schoolgirl – slept noiselessly on, I found myself gripped not by doubt but by a queer exhilaration. As the outlines of Norwich station slid into view, awash suddenly in blinding light, a glimpse of distant, scurrying figures, I registered neither fear nor anxiety, only the satisfaction of a successful retreat.

I left London in winter; returning to Norwich I found spring. There were crocuses out in the briny fields on either side of the Wensum; beyond them small river craft lay at anchor, motionless beneath clear grey sky. Next morning the sun was shining and I walked through damp, airy streets to the Cathedral Close.

In the past six years I had had little contact with the solicitors. They wrote occasionally giving details of new and departing tenants and forwarding rent cheques. In recent years these had declined to the point where the house barely covered its expenses: the result, successive letters had explained, of a glut in the local rental market. At the same time the number of tenants had markedly fallen off. At first the property had attracted a steady stream of lodgers: students from the local university had lived for years at a time in the small bedsitting rooms, hung Indian broadcloths across the doorframes and decorated the landing with Athena posters: unmarried schoolmistresses had arrived to fill the lounge with bowls of potpourri and hold housewarming parties in the draughty kitchen, but over the years they had fallen away. Now only a single tenant remained: a woman in her late twenties who, six months before, had been allowed to take over the entire house. It was this arrangement that I wished to disturb.

The solicitors' premises lay in the oldest part of the Close, their frontage directly opposite the west door of the cathedral. Episcopal coats of arms rose over the brass plate of its entrance: and within there was a short, tiled passage with a glass roof where ferns grew in buckets and queer clumps of foliage curled up towards the light. The reception area, unlit, containing quantities of musty furniture, preserved this air of grave, clerical gloom.

It was the same solicitor whom I had dealt with six years before. He greeted me effusively. 'Hullo. How are you? I was wondering when you'd look in. Have a seat, won't you?'

'I take it you received my letter?'

'I did. About the property in Unthank Road?'

'Glebe Road.'

'The property in Glebe Road. And you want planning permission, that's right?'

'On the contrary. I want to live in it.'

He was older now, in his early thirties, and there were family portraits clustered at one end of his desk. Beneath the bonhomie I detected deep, unconquerable reservoirs of disquiet. Eventually he produced from his desk a statement of account covering the previous three months: the amount owing was inconsiderable.

The solicitor watched nervously as I read.

'You'll see there have been one or two extras in the past few months. Repairs to the property and so on.'

I ran my eye over the closely typed columns. 'Item: replacement of roof tile; item: renewal of doorframe; item: replacement of panes in greenhouse.'

'Who authorised all this?'

'Well, the tenant – a Miss Richards – gave the actual instructions. Naturally the bills were settled by us.'

The solicitor hesitated. Clearly I had touched some tender nerve of reminiscence. 'Between you and me we find this Miss Richards a bit of a trial. Always on the telephone asking for this and that to be done. Writes letters too. You see, there is a clause in the tenancy agreement about maintaining the fabric.'

I felt a momentary stab of irritation at this fussy, sensible spinster and at the complicity which abetted her.

'You might have spared me the greenhouse.'

The solicitor laughed. For a second I caught a glimpse of that bright, hard sheen of professional detachment. It was the client, I thought, having the client's little joke. But there were other, more pressing, matters at hand.

'When can I expect to move in?'

'Let's see. It's the end of February, isn't it? We do six-month tenancy agreements. The current one expires March thirty-first. I think you might expect a month.'

Later I walked out into the Cathedral Close. It was midday now and small files of schoolboys were passing on their way to the Norwich School refectory at the back of the old bishop's palace. Beyond them towards the Ethelbert gateway besuited figures from accountants' offices proceeded to lunch. On impulse I turned into the cathedral and jostled for a moment with the early tourists collected before Bishop de Losinga's tomb and the Lady Chapel, but it was to no purpose. A shadow had fallen over the day and I had no place here among the grey stones and the demure memorials to a thousand-year, ecclesiastical past. I went back to the small hotel on the west of the city near Chapel Field and slept until dusk.

The days passed swiftly. I set out to explore the city of my childhood. I wandered over Mousehold Heath. I ate lunch under the high Georgian chandeliers of the Assembly House and browsed in the secondhand bookshops of St Benedict's. Norwich was much as I remembered it. Here and there new buildings had risen above the ancient thoroughfares and passageways, there was builders' rubble piled up over the cattle market, but the bones of the old city shone through, a bright, gleaming skeleton impervious to this modern camouflage.

At an early stage I returned to the office in the Close. In the interval the solicitor's enthusiasm – his name, I remembered, was Robey – had waned.

'There seems to have been some mistake. Apparently the tenacy agreement runs annually from New Year's Day.'

'The tenant knows about this?'

Mr Robey handed me a typewritten letter. Its purport was unambiguous. It contained, additionally, a request that the solicitors should instal a cat-flap 'as a matter of urgency'.

'Have I any legal rights at all?'

'Not really,' said Mr Robey cheerfully. 'You could try offering her money, of course, but it would look very bad if the case ever came to court. In any case you'll be in by Christmas.'

It wanted a few days to the end of March.

'Let me get this clear. I am expected to spend nine months living in a hotel as a result of some legal oversight?'

For the first time in our dealings, Mr Robey looked pained. 'I wouldn't put it like that.' He seemed for the first time a less solid figure. 'Of course I can write to Miss Richards and explain the situation in any way you think suitable.'

I said, 'At any rate you can tell Miss Richards that there is not the slightest chance that I will consent to pay for her cat-flap.'

I resolved to take matters into my own hands. I wrote to Miss Richards the same afternoon, informing her of my intention to inspect the property. Then, two evenings later, as the light faded in little crimson streaks over the western edge of the city, I left the hotel and walked purposefully through the narrow streets towards Glebe Road. The route lay southwards, past the Chapel Fields and the Roman Catholic cathedral. Here, at last, I found evidence of the changes of the past six years. There were hotels now in Unthank Road, crowding out the private houses with their wild little gardens, turbulent roadhouses ablaze with light. Traffic thundered past in the direction of Cringleford and the Ipswich

Road. I had an exact notion of what I might find. Miss Richards's letters with their careful language and their intimations of cats and greenhouses told a familiar story. I imagined a middle-aged woman with a choice vocabulary and distinct political opinions, her evenings devoted to frugal suppers and conscientious housework. There would be ironing going on, I thought, the room draped with white, austere garments which would be hurriedly removed from my sight. But there was no way of proving this hypothesis. Though lights shone at the house in Glebe Road and noise resounded from within, no one answered the doorbell. I stood waiting for several minutes and then went disconsolately away.

In despair I returned to Mr Robey.

'I simply do not believe that she has a right to deny me access to the property. Surely as her landlord I am allowed to carry out an inspection?'

'That depends on your motive. She could argue, you see, that your intent is a hostile one and not in the spirit of the agreement.'

'And is that what she does argue?'

'I've had a letter,' Mr Robey said indifferently, 'which accuses you of harassment. If I might say so, you really are putting yourself in an unfortunate legal position.'

I saw how it was. Mr Robey had grown bored with my predicament. He saw me as an annoyance, motivated only by an unreasonable, personal anxiety, dug into a pit of my own making.

'Is there any other solicitor in your firm who could help me with this situation?'

It was a fatal remark. 'The law is the law, Mr Benson,' Mr Robey said stiffly. It was as if I had begun to cross-examine him on some delicate aspect of his private life. There was nothing more to be said. I walked out into the Close, leaving him amid the damask draperies and the mouldering ferns.

On the next morning I wrote to Miss Richards offering her five hundred pounds for immediate repossession. She replied by return of post, enclosing a copy of the tenancy agreement with the crucial clause underlined in red. I wrote again, doubling the amount. This time there was no response.

And then, curiously, fate lent a hand. Quite by chance, having tea one afternoon in the Assembly House, I met an old friend of my father named Mrs Stephens. My father had possessed few female friends, tending to regard even the wives of his acquaintances as exercising a wholly doubtful influence, but he had made an exception of Mrs Stephens, who taught French and had been expelled from the local Conservative Association for undemocratic views. We had a long, reminiscent conversation about the circumstances of my father's death.

'I thought it such a shame,' Mrs Stephens remarked, 'that even when he was ill he should be harassed by the business of that tree. In fact, after the funeral I wrote to that dreadful old woman and told her so.'

Here, plainly, the flame of remembrance still burned. But there was another surprise. When I mentioned the problem of the house, Mrs Stephens grew thoughtful.

'Dear me. I have a feeling I know this person. I believe she teaches in our junior department.'

'It's a common enough name.'

'No, this one lives in Glebe Road, I feel certain. *Such* a pretty girl and so delightful with the children.'

For the first time, obscurely, I had an ally. Mrs Stephens promised to make enquiries and, if necessary, to intercede. 'Your father was a very dear friend of mine,' she explained as we said goodbye beneath the city hall clock.

With the vision of the punctilious spinster fading rapidly I wrote again to Miss Richards proposing a compromise. I had no wish to disturb her arrangements. It would be sufficient, I suggested, if we could merely occupy the house together. Two days later another letter arrived. It said simply: 'I don't mind, Suzi.' I sent Mrs Stephens a bunch of flowers. It seemed the least I could do.

Mr Robey provided me with the keys to my father's house. Now that a compromise had been found he seemed strangely animated, as if, I thought, he had played some subtle role in the negotiations of which I had previously been unaware. He insisted on standing me what he called a 'celebratory drink', so I allowed him to take me to a small pub near the cathedral gates and buy two glasses of bitter sherry. Once installed in the meagre barroom he grew confidential.

'Of course, I remember you from school. You were in Nelson, weren't you?'

'Parker.'

'Parker, was it? Odd how your memory can play tricks on you. I still keep up with some of the old gang, you know. You ought to come along and say hello to us one evening.'

'I should like that *very much*.'

Presently he was joined by a couple of lawyer cronies; I slipped away and took a taxi to the house. In daylight it seemed a frail and insubstantial edifice. There were sprigged lace curtains that had not been there before. Within, the hallway disclosed a number of unfamiliar furnishings. Letters lay on the mat – Miss S. Richards, Susan Richards, Miss Suzi Richards. Obeying some proprietorial instinct I picked them up and arranged them on a small occasional table. Here, in addition to the telephone, was a pile of neatly snipped-out soap-powder coupons. The house no longer retained its own smell, an odd, musty compound of pipe smoke, chalk and tea. In its place was an artificial, feminine odour of air-freshener and the hint of perfume.

For a while I roamed around the downstairs rooms, matching the contents against their imagined former state. There was little I remembered. Cheap, unfamiliar pictures hung on the walls. The kitchen had been repainted, badly, so that feathery brush strokes strayed downwards on to the wainscoting. The place had that generalised, impermanent look that I knew from my own days as a student – neutral, unloved, a receptacle – but here and there were signs that a single personality had attempted to impose order: jars of herbs, neatly labelled, stacked up in the kitchen, a file of glass animals – cats, mice – that ran crazily across the mantelpiece in the lounge. Two or three invitation cards rested against the back of this carnival procession: an old girls' reunion, a tennis club supper, a parent–teachers'-association ceilidh. They seemed grim entertainments.

In the ramshackle porch that separated the kitchen from the back door there were tennis rackets, discarded tracksuits, a smell of sweat. I opened the door and stepped out into the garden. Whatever memories I might have preserved of it received no answering call: there was a mound of bare earth where the lime tree had been; the rose bushes were wild and unkempt.

Later, as the light began to fade and footsteps resounded on the pavement outside, I wandered through the upstairs rooms. Here the trail was firmer. There were Monet posters on the landing, chiaroscuros of blue hills beneath mounting shade; the second of the two smaller bedrooms had been converted into a makeshift study with a desk, a chair and a typewriter. The door of the third room, my father's bedroom, now appropriated, was slightly ajar. I found nothing I recognised. A single bed, its pink coverlet folded back, took up the far side. There were flowers in the ancient fireplace. A line of toy animals – bears, hippopotami, raccoons in day-glo yellow – marched along the dressing table. It was a schoolgirl's room, I thought, wanting only the pony club rosettes, the posters cut from *Jackie* and *Just Seventeen* to produce a final, authenticating touch.

A female voice said sharply from the doorway: 'Do you always snoop around in people's bedrooms?'

Turning back I saw a small, plump, sulky-looking girl regarding me balefully. In her late twenties, perhaps, dressed in a bulky tracksuit, her face pink from recent exercise, the effect was not prepossessing. She gave the impression of some small but rapacious creature of the field, cornered in its lair and liable to turn nasty.

'Suzi,' she said, advancing briskly into the room. 'Suzi Richards.'

'I didn't mean to take you by surprise.'

'It's all right. The solicitor told me you were coming.' She gave me a cross look. 'I just didn't expect you till later.'

There was a large basket-chair in the corner of the room. She sat in this, still frowning, and began to unlace her tennis shoes. 'Look. I know you're the landlord and there're all sorts of questions you probably want to ask me, but I have to get changed and go out. Tuesdays are one of my busy nights. So perhaps you'd be kind enough to just go away and let me get myself together.'

I had come badly out of that. From the doorway I looked back, but she was already seated in front of the dressing table, head lowered intently over the mirror.

I spent the evening contriving a bed in the second spare room, occasionally returning downstairs to search for blankets or pillow-cases. Once the telephone buzzed; I let it ring on unanswered. Later I sat in front of the television and drank gin out of a bottle I found in the kitchen; at eleven I went to bed. She came back, noisily, at midnight. Lying in the darkness I heard her moving about in the bathroom. There was the occasional slamming of a door. At eight I awoke to find the house empty.

It was the first of many similar evenings. Miss Richards kept odd hours, I discovered. Often I would return to the house late in the afternoon to find that she had been and gone, that the remains of a frugal supper already lay on the kitchen table. She rarely came back before eleven. At weekends, the time at which the denizens of lodging houses traditionally emerge to sniff the air, she became still more elusive, often disappearing altogether to return late on Sunday night, flustered but unforthcoming. From an early stage I was intrigued by these absences. Did she visit her parents or relatives? Did she have some boyfriend many miles distant? There was a pile of Duke of Edinburgh Award Scheme literature on the coffee table in the lounge. From it I devised an elaborate fantasy in which she led groups of romping schoolgirls along mountain paths or pitched tents amid lakeland scenery. There would be mugs of cocoa around the camp fire, I thought, and prurient discussion of sex. Such visions had no grounding in reality and were soon abandoned. Miss Richards remained as an intermittent, vagrant presence, reluctant to be drawn into wider orbits of conversation or complicity, like some child on the edge of a crowded playground, happily intent on a game of its own invention.

Slowly and imperceptibly fractures emerged in the ice.

'I should hate to think that you were avoiding me,' I said one evening, meeting her on the stairs.

'I'm not avoiding you. I just happen to be very busy at the moment.'

'Too busy to set foot in the lounge?'

'Much too busy.'

Later that evening she appeared in the front room with a basketful of washing and an ironing board.

'Will I be disturbing you? By doing this, I mean?'

'No.'

She ironed studiously for an hour and then went away. The clothes lay in a pile on the sofa. They were utilitarian garments: pairs of plain white briefs, Aertex shirts woven in the spongy, punctured cloth that I remembered from my childhood, a dirndl skirt or two. I had a working knowledge of women's clothing – the rucks of discarded underthings which the models left in the changing room at Dean Street, the fanciful camisoles that Elaine wore around the flat – but these struck an unfamiliar note. They combined with the glass animals and the girlish bed to suggest a recognisably older world – homely, economic and inviolate.

I set about subjecting Miss Richards to deliberate study. As a palaeontologist takes a fragment of bone or a scrap of fossilised vegetation and extrapolates from it some cumbersome beast roaming in a primeval swamp, so I assembled a gesture, a look, an intonation, and construed a personality. Tiny accretions of detail – an overheard conversation, a chance remark – each played some part in this grand but notional design, like a vase reconstituted out of shards so tiny that only the glue gives it pattern and coherence. The archaeological metaphor was, I found, appropriate to a process of re-creation demanding the weighing-up of evidence, the dismissal of untenable early theories. In particular, I thought, I had been mistaken about her appearance. She was a short, well-built girl – no more than five feet high, perhaps – but there was a definition about her features which set her apart from the plump Glebe Road housewives. Her most original feature was her hair – copious and corn-coloured – which when treated with the appropriate lotions and mousses fell in rippling cascades on to her shoulders. I suspected artifice, but its shade never varied and there was upstairs no trace of incriminating bottles. She was vain of this adornment, settled it occasionally against her neck with a complacent gesture and spent long periods combing it out in front of the mirror. It had particularly impressed the Nigerian prince, she told me.

There were other reassessments, other readjustments to this frail early prognosis. She was erudite in a small way, the possessor of a stock of specialist lore that enabled her to name an obscure foreign capital or a chemical symbol. It was a false erudition, I thought, born of the general knowledge required to excel in after-dinner games and television quizzes: it was, I suspected, from the files of MasterBrain cards that most of her information was derived.

What she did at the school I never wholly determined. Cars, presumably driven by colleagues, occasionally called for her early in the morning or returned her late in the afternoon; their owners remained unseen. There were stray references – it was a small independent school, precariously financed – to the headmaster and matron. She taught for the most part small boys, nine- and ten-year-olds, and was oddly well informed about their personal circumstances – which had parents who were divorced, for instance, or were being pressed to fulfil vicarious parental ambitions. Beyond this tightly coralled arena the landscape of her private life stretched out into shadow. She had no women friends, I concluded. Her interests, such as they were, were entirely masculine. She watched sport on the television in an absorbed, critical way. There was a snooker player named John Marshall whose progress she followed around the professional tournaments and whose performances I was occasionally asked to video. Her social life seemed mapped out by the invitation cards on the mantelpiece, but there were hints of wider affiliations beyond the tennis club dances and the old girls' reunions. In the fortnight after my arrival a man named Christopher telephoned repeatedly. It became a kind of ritual between us. 'Christopher rang,' I would say as we met on the stair. 'Did he? Thank you.' 'Who is this Christopher?' I asked once. 'He seems very anxious to speak to you.' She shrugged. 'Oh, just someone I know.' It was, in its way, a rebuke. The small barrier that we had imposed on our dealings had been breached and she resented it.

Once, passing outside her room late at night, I heard the unmistakable sounds of sexual activity. The noises went on for a long time: strange heavings and ululations, pantings and grunts, a man's voice raised in recrimination. To one who had presided over so many simulated expressions of ecstasy, wheeled microphones close in to get what Morty called a 'killer soundtrack', it seemed vaguely indecent, a sharp gust of realism blowing over Morty's bland, tidy dreamscape. I listened for a while and then, ashamed of my own voyeurism, went away.

It was another tiny dent in the barrier. Next morning Suzi said, 'Do you know, I sometimes think that the worst thing about men is that they make assumptions about women that they'd never dream of making about a car or an electric drill.'

I had heard this sort of remark before. It had not seemed to bear repetition. 'Not quite as mistaken as the assumptions women make about men.'

'I hadn't thought of it that way.'

'Women never do.'

Looking back I can detect a sense of shared confidence that almost certainly did not exist. Hindsight imparts complicity. At the time, I am sure, we saw ourselves as nothing more than two ill-assorted people whom chance had thrown together in circumstances beyond our control, uneasily determined to make the best of things. Meanwhile there was news from other quarters, flickers of continuity burning beneath this slow, disjointed progress. Postcards came from London, Rome, Los Angeles, postcards from Morty, Terry Chimes, Crazy Rodney, messages from other queer denizens of the world I had left behind. I took them into the kitchen and read them looking out over the bleak garden – bleak even in spring – with unmitigated wonder. They had no place, I thought, in the placid low-key landscape I was fashioning for myself, were no more than dispatches out of a battlefield from which I had long since retreated. Afterwards, out trawling the wet Norwich streets with their quotas of dull Norfolk faces, they lost even their zestful, energetic quality and became only memorabilia, regimental buttons wrested from decaying cloth, spent cartridges pulled out of the mud. Eventually I lost interest in these mementoes, leaving Suzi to collect them from the mat and arrange them without comment on the mantelpiece.

Summer came. The wind blowing in from the sea lost its sharpness and there were ice-cream vans in the streets. Suzi believed in the restorative powers of sunshine. On Sunday afternoons she put on odd, formalised bathing costumes – relics, I correctly diagnosed, of her schooldays – and reclined decorously on a garden chair, her face raised towards the heat. There was a painful innocuousness about these performances: no artifice attended the arrangement of limbs or the choice of pose. It was, I saw, a routine, something that one did in Norwich at certain times of the year when the temperature had reached a certain point, regardless of personal consequence, like my father's compulsion to eat outdoors at any date after May Day. Suzi burned in the sun. An hour in the garden chair left her skin red and angry, her face contorted in a mass of fat scarlet flesh, her fine hair bleached out of recognition, but she persevered gamely. Watching her from the kitchen window through the glaze of reflected sunshine, one was aware only of an intent, silent figure, motionless amid the heat.

Once around this time she said, 'I could cook you supper tonight if you like.'

'I should like it very much.'

'It wouldn't be anything very special.'

'I should still like it.'

So she cooked me supper: a substantial meal as it turned out, eaten formally around my father's dining table with place mats produced from the kitchen cabinet and previously unseen china. She ate copiously. In the intervals between courses she told me about Christopher. 'It was just one of those things that you do,' she explained, 'just one of those people that you meet. But I could see it wasn't working out.' Later she said, 'He was very demanding. He always expected me to be there, round at his house, going over to see his mum and dad, and he used to get angry when I had to do marking or go to something at school, so in the end I finished it.' The vague, talismanic phrases were familiar. It was how people talked, I remembered, about cast-off lovers, bogus affiliations finally given the lie. '*Just one of those things . . . could see that it wasn't working out . . . so in the end I finished it.*' So Morty, abandoning one of his improbable mistresses, would talk of 'knocking it on the head'. I had a glimpse of a brief, arid courtship, cut short by cynicism and good sense. It was a new phase in our association.

Our relationship prospered. We ate long, scrappy meals together on summer evenings, emerging from the wreckage of plates and tattered cellophane to wander through the streets to pubs on the edge of the city, in sight of the wheat fields and the water meadows. Suzi was knowledgeable about pubs. She knew which served Adnams Ale, the treacly local beer, at which of them you were likely to find a Norwich City footballer smoking furtively at the bar. Such knowledge was oddly agreeable, a proof that one had deciphered the abstruse codes by which the city was governed, that one was somehow as representative of milieu as the white-flannelled bowls players with their tankards, or the crop-haired students from the Norwich School of Art. Later we ventured further afield to Mulbarton, Hempnall and Brooke, tiny villages in the southern half of the county, each with their symbols of neat, regimented rural life: church spire, war memorial, green, occasionally a cricket pitch. No wild country existed now in Norfolk. There was a hint of display in these excursions. Suzi was not in any strict sense a local girl – her parents lived in Bungay on the Suffolk border – but she had been to school in Norwich and taught there since her graduation. In her unveiling of out-of-the-way beauty spots and rare lych gates I detected the authoritative note of the tourist guide.

Suzi did not talk much about her parents, whom she referred to as 'Mother and Father'. There was a photograph of them on her bedside table: the man's face weatherbeaten, canny, obstinate; the woman's bland, emollient, grey hair cut on roundhead principles. She said once, 'Mother and Father didn't hold with university. They wanted me to work in a shop and get married.' There was no trace of bitterness in this, rather one of pride. It suggested that she admired her parents, respected even the more questionable among their beliefs, and yet admired most of all herself for her ability to flout the conventions they had imposed upon her.

At the beginning of August Suzi took a fortnight's holiday. In the interval beforehand I found myself speculating on her choice of venue. It would be Corfu, I thought, or Mykonos, French provincial church architecture or Rhine castles: that was where these single, independent-minded schoolmistresses went of a summer vacation. I had not reckoned on a streak of insularity. It was the Lake District. She went with a schoolfriend named Lucy, a girl who had hitherto existed simply as a voice on the telephone, but who was, I gathered, frequently brought out and put to service in this way. There was the additional fact that Lucy required consolation. 'Lucy's been badly let down by a man,' Suzi explained. She wrote postcards from the guest-house on Lake Windermere in a crisp, girlish hand. It had rained. It had not rained. Lucy had been ill. Lucy had recovered. They were brief, characterless messages, giving no hint of the sharp, self-contained intelligence which had indited them.

In her absence I grew restless. Solitude, long anticipated, swiftly became irksome. At night I prowled through the empty house, or sat watching the blaring television. Once, in desperation, I sought out Mr Robey and spent an evening with him and his friends in the Maid's Head Hotel. They were professional men, assistant solicitors, junior partners in accountancy firms: heavy-set thirty-year-olds who laughed boisterously at their own jokes. Several of them had vague memories of me from adolescence. They said, 'Weren't you in old so-and-so's house? Didn't you play in the fifteen?' A dozen years on, the school still exercised an unreasonable hold over their personal lives. They wore its old boys' ties and looked forward eagerly to its reunion dinners. But amid this opulent nostalgia I detected a faint air of unease. 'Of course it isn't the same,' they said, 'not any more. They've closed down the boarding house and they say the new head's keen on soccer.' I listened to them with amusement. I was detached from their world, I thought, I could leave it at will. Their ties were physical: they had jobs, wives, children. Mine were abstract, I thought complacently, the ties of memory, instinct, association; they could be lived out wherever I chose. The ten thousand pounds I had brought from London lay gathering interest in the building society.

Mid-August came and Suzi returned. I saw immediately that absence had wrought a decisive shift in the way that she regarded me. The holiday had not gone well. 'Lucy got cystitis and had to stay inside a lot,' she explained. 'I spent most of my time bringing her cups of tea.' 'What else did you do?' 'I went for walks,' she said, '*lots* of walks. Or I listened to Lucy telling me about what she does in bed.' I saw how it was. Intimacy to her meant roguishness, innuendo, the exchange of slightly lurid confidences. She had brought me back a comic postcard, bought on a daytrip to Barrow-in-Furness. It showed a tiny, pallid cleric escorted, or rather propelled by a voluptuous woman in a tight skirt. Two crones looked on. 'Does that vicar have any children?' 'No. They say his stipend's too small.' There were other signs of our changed relationship. She came down to breakfast in a dressing gown, or walked around the house in her nightdress searching for a handbag, a mislaid newspaper. Once I surprised her sunbathing topless in the garden: she was unabashed. This newfound role did not suit her, I thought. Flooziedom, with its range of gesture and response, its comedy of titillation, seemed alien and inappropriate. The short, plump girl turning on the garden mat, the white breast, the sloping grin: none was in the least erotic.

As a signal, however, it was unmistakable. Later that evening she appeared in the lounge, clad in her nightdress, and grasped my hand. 'I want it done,' she said, 'I want it done now.' I followed her upstairs along the lightless passage. In bed she was brisk and commanding. 'Wait,' she said at one point. 'Now . . . and then wait again.' There was calculation, I thought, in the practised arrangement of her limbs. Afterwards she gave a short, commendatory sigh, like a small child who has completed a not very enjoyable task to the best of its abilities.

'How do I match up to Christopher?'

'Pretty good. Christopher was always very concerned about Christopher.'

I let the matter lie. There would be other revelations, I knew, other disclosures from the dark catalogue of past intimacies that would come my way. Lying there on the narrow bed, the ridged sheet stiff and uncomfortable, the air heavy with musk and sweat, I thought inexplicably and yet with infinite longing of Elaine.

'The thing to do if you're drinking pints, is not to hang about.'

'Too right it is.'

'After three then. One, two . . .'

'One, two . . .'

It's Saturday night and I stand in the front bar of the City Gates with Fat Eric from two doors down. Several other of Fat Eric's *convives* are posed negligently about the place – a character called Woody, who I think sells Fat Eric misappropriated car spares, and an exophthalmic teenager called Mad Trevor, and through the shifting, smoky air I can make out the figure of Kay, Fat Eric's girlfriend, buying another round of crisps at the bar.

'Bloody hell.' Fat Eric slaps down the glass, a fragile goblet in the dense wrapping of his fist. 'Your round.'

'Adnams?'

'Adnams it is.'

I saunter off to the bar and purchase another four pints of the local beer, while Fat Eric renews a menacing conversation with Woody about a flat car battery. I like it here. I feel at home here with Fat Eric in the bar of the City Gates, drinking pints of Adnams and watching people who resemble Fat Eric's younger brother playing snooker. A little later, if I feel so disposed, I may have a game of darts, or join Kay over by the jukebox and see what they have in the Sixties and nostalgia section. These are simple pleasures. I relish them.

Back at the table – anxious onlookers deferentially making way as I wander past – Fat Eric hoists a pint glass expertly off the tray.

'After three then. One, two . . .'

'One, two . . .'

We have been in here half an hour and Fat Eric is on to his fifth pint of Adnams. Me, I've had three and I'm already noticing that the cigarettes are becoming harder to light and that I've joined in a raucous singalong to 'Hi Ho, Silver Lining' on the jukebox. Now, Fat Eric can *drink*. I'd put him into the Terry Chimes class, without question. I once saw him and Mad Trevor stage a drinking contest in here one evening after a horse named Dandruff, the repository of much local goodwill, had splayed itself nonchalantly over the final fence in the National, twenty lengths clear of a receding field. They began by drinking six pints of Adnams each, Fat Eric helping his down with sundry handfuls of pickled gherkins, cheesy snacks and whatnot. They then had a couple of gins apiece, Fat Eric in the meantime sending out to the takeaway for a brace of cheeseburgers. After this they went on to snappers, a high-octane cocktail composed of lager and brandy, exclusive to the locality. They stopped after seven of these, when Mad Trevor passed out, whereupon Fat Eric went off for a curry and an informed discussion of whether Kevin Flack could shoot with his left foot.

Saturday night in the City Gates. Occasionally Fat Eric takes me to other places – to the Romany Rye up by Bunnett Square or the Farmhouse in Colman Road, but predominantly we come here. Fat Eric likes a quiet pub. The City Gates is a quiet pub: full of silent, slimmed-down versions of Fat Eric and their mournful, hilarious women. Fat Eric is a species of god here, a molten monarch. People get out of his way when he lumbers up to the bar: the tough boys with the lacquered hair queue up to buy him drinks.

Fat Eric and Woody have now left the subject of the flat car battery in favour of Norwich City's craven performance a few hours previously against some bunch of northern cloggers. I shift gallantly to one side as Kay, Fat Eric's girlfriend, steams back from the bar with her cargo of crisp packets. Kay. About fifteen years ago in this part of the world I used to know girls like Kay. Kay is perhaps twenty-one or twenty-two, but looks older, much older. As it happens, Kay isn't from round here. They come in from the country, people like Kay, from godforsaken hamlets like Holt and Fakenham, tiny towns on the bare Norfolk plains where the wind sweeps in from the sea and you spend your teens in the market square smoking cigarettes and waiting for something to happen. At seventeen or eighteen you leave that job in the wool shop or the chicken-packing factory, say goodbye to your parents' bungalow on the squeaky clean estate where the air always smells of salt and the gulls hover endlessly, and head towards the grey bedsitterland of the city. Norwich is full of people who come from somewhere else, from Lynn or Thetford or one of the dead towns on the coast. Kay comes from Framlingham, twenty miles over the Suffolk border, and you can tell it in the way she speaks, clipping the vowels to say 'hey' instead of 'have', 'rud' instead of 'road'. Fat Eric, alternatively, is stage Norvicensian. If he admires something it's 'reely nice'. He doesn't ask me what I think of something, he says, 'What you reckon?'

It grows pleasantly comfortable here, pleasantly blurred, as Kay jams her pit-prop calves against mine beneath the table, steals a look at her mutinous complexion in a hand-mirror, monitors Fat Eric who is flexing his wrists in preparation for an arm-wrestling bout with Mad Trevor. Fat Eric nods benignly and tells me that City have an evening match on Wednesday and do I fancy coming. I nod back as Kay and I start one of our regular conversations about music. Ever since she found out about my former career, Kay has treated me with beguiling deference. I could tell her anything. Tonight, flapping stubby, carmined fingers over the Babycham, she wants to know, of all people, about Bobby Dazz.

'And did he really . . . do what they said in the papers? Found a deer sanctuary and give all that money to charity?'

'We all liked Bobby.'

'And Barbie. I read an interview where he said that even after twenty years the first thing he did every night when he came off stage was to phone her.'

'She's a great girl, Barbie.'

'And do they, you know, *keep in touch*?'

'I get a Christmas card. A telephone call every now and then.'

Bobby Dazz. I could tell Kay one or two things about Bobby Dazz. Imprimis, the deer sanctuary was actually a venison farm. Even when I knew him, which was in the mid-Seventies, he hadn't spoken to Barbie (real name, Edna) for five years. The one thing you could say in Bobby Dazz's favour was that he had a good PR man. Whenever he cracked up it was always in the papers as 'overwork', and even when a tabloid newspaper grew fractious once about the drink Barbie weighed in with a felicitous mastectomy.

'I joined his fan club when I was a kid,' Kay says moistly. 'He sent me a signed photograph once.'

No he didn't. I happen to know that all the photos were signed by Bobby's agent, but this is not the time to despoil childish illusions. Instead I call over to Fat Eric, who has just finished grinding his opponent's fingers into the table top.

'So who are we playing on Wednesday, Fat Eric?'

'Fucking *Newcastle*. Beat us in the Cup last year.'

'Any good?'

'Fucking soft cunts,' says Fat Eric. 'No trouble.'

Another thing about Kay: Fat Eric hits her. I once heard him do it, round at Fat Eric's house, two doors down, where we had retired for coffee and a browse through Fat Eric's video collection (there was a tape of *Girlschool Janitor*, which levied a faint, Proustian smile). I was in the lounge when it happened, staring at the record rack and darkly conscious that the raised voices in the kitchen were some way beyond the customary lickerish banter. They were arguing about . . . I forget what they were arguing about. Arguing with Kay, along with Norwich City FC and drinking, constitutes Fat Eric's principal hobby. It is his habit to argue with her about things she doesn't actually know about: about how you revived a defunct car battery, whether Manchester United had won the FA Cup in 1971, that sort of thing. On this occasion, however, they were arguing about something on which Kay did have some, admittedly tenuous, view: Kay's mother.

'I suppose you want the old girl to live here?'

Kay made some muffled rejoinder. I recollected that her mother lay bedbound in a council bungalow outside Saxlingham. The volume of noise increased.

'I suppose you want the old girl living here and telling me off about *drinking* and *smoking*, then?'

Silence. I could imagine Kay's dull realisation that, yes, he wasn't joking and, no, there wasn't anything she could do and, yes, there wasn't any point in appealing to me and, no, there was no obvious course to pursue except to wait for something to happen, that something which would hurt but take the fear away.

'I suppose you want the old girl ringing me up every day and telling me to get a *proper fucking job*?'

More silence. Meanwhile the air had grown tense and headachy. I remember taking a purposeful interest in a framed photograph that hung askew on the wall, finally recognising the Norwich team from four years back. The blow, when it came, was nothing: no explosion of sound, no clamour of voices, merely a soft twinge of bone on flesh, followed, a little later, by an encore of furtive scuffling. Two minutes later Fat Eric came and lowered a cup of tea nonchalantly into my lap.

'Girl's a bit upset,' he said. 'Gone upstairs for a bit.'

That nonchalance. I remember Terry Chimes once coming to blows in a pub in Shaftesbury Avenue with some failed rock dinosaur he had recently erased from the Grunt Records roster. It took precisely half a minute. Half a minute later while they were sweeping up the broken glass and retrieving the two halves of the pool cue which had been smashed over his opponent's head, Terry Chimes was back in his chair nursing a large brandy.

Such disagreements are in abeyance this evening, however, here in the City Gates where the air grows thicker and the women ever more tired. Each female face conceals, narrowly, its own quiet resentment, its own desire for solitude, the absence of the raucous, convivial partner. Each would rather be with its children, asleep, in front of the television, anywhere. There is a faint, ominous pressure on my shoulder as Kay begins her slow, somnambulistic slide. Seeing this Fat Eric lurches across and slaps her jovially.

'Carm on, girl. Can't have you falling asleep. Not in here. Not in front of everybody and that.'

For a moment Kay's head rolls, glassy-eyed, until she remembers where she is and that the prospect of sleep is at least three hours distant.

'Sorry,' she giggles weakly. 'Must be the gin.'

Or the Pernod. Or the Bacardi. Kay drinks enormous amounts in a wry, disinterested way. 'A real *alki*,' Fat Eric will say proudly, 'a real *boozer*,' when this fact is drawn to his attention. He plods away again to conduct some vague superintendence of a pool game in which Woody and Mad Trevor are now engaged. There is a brief exchange of chatter. He saunters back. 'Why not come back to my place?' he suggests. 'Come and have a talk?'

On these occasions Fat Eric is very keen that I should come back to his place, come back and have a talk. The reasons for this are almost exclusively financial. Fat Eric thinks I have money. Further, Fat Eric thinks I have money which could be harnessed to the lurching tumbril of his own commercial ambition. For oddly enough, despite the hours tethered to the bar-stool, Fat Eric is a businessman at heart, part owner of a mini-cab and a stall on Norwich market, hitherto trammelled only by want of capital. At an early stage in our relationship he began to hint outrageously that I might make up this deficiency. He did this, subtly enough, by means of newspaper headlines. The libel award, the out-of-court settlement to the discarded girlfriend, the damages paid to the Joan Collins lookalike with the champagne-bottle shoulders – Fat Eric uses them all for the purposes of invidious comparison. 'Course,' he says. 'Wouldn't mean anything, would it, to a man in your position?' There are more of these genteel clichés: 'Someone of your standing', 'A man with your resources', more phrases from the soaps and the tabloid court reports. Once I came clean. 'Look, Fat Eric,' I told him. 'I've got no money at all. Just forty quid a week I get out of the building society and what Suzi pays me in rent. What about that? Will that do?' Unfortunately, or perhaps fortunately, Fat Eric treated this as an enormous joke.

'Why not come back to my place?' he suggests again. 'Come and have a talk?' He stands over me, a brooding, solicitous giant. There is no alternative but to acquiesce. Kay, prodded, poked and propelled by Fat Eric's saveloy fingers, shambles before us to the door. Fat Eric turns, modestly adjusts his jeans, waves – there are nods of recognition from the boys at the snooker table, a smile from mine host – and we move out into the night air.

Outside the street is damp: a gust of fine rain. An infant whirls by on a skateboard ('Watch where you're *fucking going*!' Fat Eric yells good-humouredly after him.) Passing the house I wonder if I can hear a telephone ringing. Nothing. A week has passed now since Elaine rang. Wedged in his doorway Fat Eric is suddenly stricken by atavistic proletarian formality, ushers me in, sweeps a strew of cans from the sofa, plumps cushions, instals me by the glowing gas fire, plods to the kitchen. Kay disappears up the narrow staircase. I watch the dispirited droop of her shoulders. Doors slam. Taps go on. In the distance, through the adjoining wall, the buzz of television.

The decor of Fat Eric's house is oddly familiar. I remember ten years back watching *Coronation Street* and marvelling at the flight of ducks which adorned Hilda Ogden's wall. Fat Eric has an identical set, a dart pinioning the head of the leading bird. There are splayed record covers: *Now That's What I Call Music Vol. 23*, Bobby Dazz's greatest hits. Alone, in an alcove, four books: *The Rothmans' Football Yearbook*, *On the Ball City*, *Norwich City: The Divison One Story*, *Flying High with the Canaries.* Inspection reveals that the latter has been autographed by the entire Norwich team. A square foot of cigarette packets stacked neatly like bricks against the far wall recalls the two thousand Benson & Hedges that were Fat Eric's price for silence after one of Woody's recent escapades. Fat Eric trips back into the room with a tray to disturb their symmetry, fingering the corner packet and searing the cellophane with his thumbnail. I draw his attention to *Flying High with the Canaries.*

'All eleven of them, Fat Eric. Plus the substitutes. How did you do it?'

Fat Eric looks modestly around him. 'End of last season. They came down the Gates. Some charity do or something. So I said, if you want me to give a fiver for crippled kids, you got to sign this. They *signed*,' says Fat Eric truculently, 'they *signed*.'

Smoke rises. Fat Eric flicks the television on, coaxes Bobby Dazz's greatest hits out of their sleeve and puts them on the turntable. From above, the sound of footsteps. Fat Eric moves his head upwards with unfeigned disgust.

'Listen,' he says. 'Let's talk *business*.' Without encouragement Fat Eric talks business for the next fifteen minutes to the accompaniment of a police serial and Bobby Dazz intoning a series of ballads of glutinous sentimentality. The gist of it appears to be that Fat

Eric's plans for his market stall are being sorely frustrated by his timid partner. At present they don't possess a van, which means that the produce, which comes in every morning from New Covent Garden, has to be purchased at extortionate rates from a local supplier. Fat Eric wants to cut out the middleman and have his own truck sweeping up and down the A12 six days a week. Then there is the tame farmer in Lincolnshire from whom Fat Eric maintains he can extract a concession for beetroot and curly kale. Then there are the exotics. At present, he claims, Norwich market furnishes a subsistence diet of fruit and root vegetables: swedes, turnips, parsnips – the queer ethnic fodder of Norfolk. Fat Eric wants to bring in yams, mangoes, passion fruit, nectarines. There is poetry in the way he talks about them.

Naturally, all this will cost money. How much money? I fear that Fat Eric doesn't know. There are contemptuous references to someone called Ron, presumably Fat Eric's partner, and to the City Hall, which won't let them put up a neon sign. Our avid colloquy is cut short by the re-emergence of Kay wearing a pastel-pink dressing gown and drying her hair with a portable dryer. Without her make-up, seen in the haggard late-night glare, Kay looks pale and white, very pale and white. A dropsical calf peeps momentarily through the folds of her gown. Fat Eric regards her with distaste, examines his watch and mutters something about wanting to see Woody before the pub closes. I watch him prowl off, the cigarette a tiny, glowing stub in his mottled fist.

Kay says, 'You don't want to listen to what he tells you about that market stall.'

'I don't?'

'Him and that Ron. Couple of crooks they are.'

'Yes, well . . .'

'No. Couple of crooks they are. I been out with them on Sunday afternoons. Out in the country. Out near Wroxham. Digging up cabbages and that out of people's fields.'

Kay pauses, as if to let this entirely predictable piece of intelligence sink in. Flopped down on the sofa she looks sad, tired, exasperated. These East Anglian girls lose their looks very quickly. Twenty-one, twenty-two, and the subcutaneous fat rises up to fill in their cheekbones, puff out the skin around torpid eyes. Wet, torpid eyes.

'Kay . . . Don't . . . Please, don't *cry*.'

'I'm sorry.' She snuffles for a while, face averted. 'Listen,' she says. 'Would you . . . Would you tell me some more about those people you know. About, well, Bobby Dazz and the others.'

'Sure, Kay. Anything you want. Who would you like to hear about?'

Kay lights a cigarette, the tears already a fleeting memory. 'Did you ever know Lulu Sinde?'

As it happens I did know Lulu Sinde. I came across her in the mid-1970s, when we were on the way up. Lulu Sinde, predictably, was on the way down. 'These old women,' Morty remarked, having briefly considered her for a part in *Indiscreet*, 'incredible the way they keep going. Just incredible.' I sense Kay's questioning stare.

'Sure. I knew Lulu. A real trouper.'

'That's what my dad used to say. In those *Carry On* films.'

'That's right. She's a great girl, Lulu.'

We look at one another in that helpless, inarticulate way. 'Oh Martin,' Kay begins and I tense myself for some epic revelation about Fat Eric, about how he wants it eight times a night and threatened her mother with a chainsaw. It never happens. Instead a moment of confidence is shattered by the crash of the front door and the return of Fat Eric, monstrous and triumphant, clutching a bottle of whisky.

'Later,' I say, patting Kay's dormant hand. 'Tell me later.'

An hour later everyone is drunk. I am drunk. Kay is drunk. Fat Eric is drunk. Here, however, the resemblance between us ends, for while I am drunk and exhausted, Kay is drunk and sad and Fat Eric is drunk and boisterous. In this condition we have watched a video Fat Eric has recently acquired of a badger-baiting excursion, sung along to Side One of Bobby Dazz's greatest hits, and discussed Norwich City's abject mid-week performance against Sunderland in the Littlewoods Cup. To the accompaniment of raucous laughter – his own – Fat Eric has ferreted gamely inside his beloved's dressing gown and Kay has fainted gracelessly on to the sofa, only to be revived by a jug of water poured over her face. At midnight, as I stumble through the doorway I can hear Fat Eric bawling with a complete absence of self-consciousness into the dead air:

On the ball, City.
Never mind the danger.
Steady on, now's your chance . . .
Hurrah, we've scored a goal!

Outside the street is moist and silent. The lights flash and boomerang around my head as I move on into the pressing darkness.

Back at the house, chaos threatens: in the front room a sprawl of billowed sofa cushions; in the kitchen a stack of ancient, unwashed crockery. I loiter in the kitchen, which has somehow taken on vast, Brobdingnagian proportions; nervously I totter past huge foot-stools, stretch yearning hands up at remote, unreachable cup-boards, negotiate the monstrous obstacle course of chairs and tables. It scares me, this giant's clutter. Knives and forks, stacked on the draining board, are obscure implements of war, the saucepans gaping cauldrons. Grappling with a remorseless, un-wieldy blanket – a tea-towel probably – I come upon the morning's post, concealed there by Suzi. Two items. A postcard and a large, squarish parcel. The card is post-marked 'St Tropez'. On its cover two bare-breasted beauties sit at the poolside drinking from frosted glasses. On the back are the words, 'Unfortunately Brigitte and Dolores already have agents.' The writing, that pinched, doubtful hand, is unmistakably Elaine's.

The kitchen continues to enlarge: each fork a barbed infantry-man's pike, each plate a gleaming spacecraft. The parcel, bound with string, with thongs, with electric cables, with tentacles, contains . . . an obelisk? A mattress? A block of concrete? Eventually, undone and placed on the kitchen table, it discloses a small plastic container. I stare at it for a moment and then at the piles of leftovers, the festering coffee cups, trying to find some explanation for the rank, heavy odour. I prise open the gaping maw of the oven: empty. Realisation dawning, I look half-heartedly at the soles of my shoes. Nothing. Despairingly I move closer and, three feet distant, take a sniff at the container. After this I don't bother to open it. Gingerly I convey box and wrappings to the dustbin and loft them inside. On the way back I find a black-bordered card which must have fluttered to the floor during my transit. It says, 'To Martin Benson, from an admirer.' I cry silently now, face down on the kitchen table, as the Queen of Brobdingnag cackles airily above my head.

In the autumn of 1969 I went to London to train to be a journalist.

My father came of a generation which emphasised the significance of partings, seeing them as a finite, concrete barrier beyond which lay only uncertainty, and the excuse for a great deal of lapidary advice. 'I daresay,' he said, as we assembled my baggage on the platform, 'that you'll find London much as I found it. A lot of queer people living an ever queerer lot of lives.' It was a prophetic remark. As the tide of passengers began to move purposefully towards the waiting train another thought seemed to strike him. 'You must write to me,' he said. 'You must write to me *often*. Don't do what Craddock's boy did. He didn't write to his father for over a year and finally when they decided to investigate they found him in a squat in Camden Town with a lot of Buddhists.' As the train pulled out through grey, desolate sidings and on into the wet Norfolk countryside the image of him, intent and waving from the platform, persisted, until at last, at Diss or Stowmarket, it faded away and there were only the fields, the distant church spires and the angry skies. Later on, in the ensuing months, fragments of this homily would occasionally settle in my head. 'There is a class of undergraduate known, I believe, as professional agitators. Stay out of their clutches.' Their influence was negligible. To me they seemed as remote and insubstantial as cracker mottoes.

I remember London, this early innocent London, as a series of textures, a city given definition by colour: the dark earth thrown up by the road diggers near Waterloo – they were building the office blocks above Lambeth then – overbright buses trawling the streets near Oxford Circus, the russet expanse of treetops seen from Hampstead Heath. Textures, colour and names.

I had enrolled myself at Goldsmiths' College, a choice deplored by my father on geographical grounds. 'South of the river,' he had observed. 'You'll end up spending all your money on taxi fares, I shouldn't wonder, and find yourself having to leave concerts before the end to catch the last bus.' But he would have approved of the college and its unassuming premises in Lewisham. Barely a year had passed since the turmoil of 1968, its influence still traceable in the whitewashed graffiti on the concrete walkways and bellicose articles in the student newspapers, but little sign remained of the bruising encounters of the previous autumn. On my second day, I recall, we were addressed by a bearded postgraduate in a Lenin jacket who informed us that further education was an instrument of social control and that examinations were socially divisive. We paid him no heed. 'That sort of thing,' as Roger Garfitt remarked with prescience, 'had rather had its day.' In contrast we were a studious group, already much exercised by the thought of sub-editorships and outplacement schemes. Two or three students who had already served a year on provincial newspapers were regarded with awe. We wrote passable imitations of *The Times* leaders, read *The Economist*, then regarded as the acme of journalistic style, from cover to cover and on two evenings a week were instructed by our professor, a courteous middle-aged man who had once been literary editor of the *New Statesman*, on the importance of the point of view.

The time passed quickly: an intense, hermetic life lived out largely beyond the college borders. Of all the people with whom I came into contact in these early years, it was Roger Garfitt who exercised the most profound influence. He was a tall, ambitious boy from a Yorkshire grammar school and, at nineteen, a figure of enviable sophistication. With him I roamed around south-east London. We lived in Brixton, Brockwell Park, Hither Green, queer suburbs known only from the street maps, rented furnished flats in decayed mansion blocks in Streatham Hill and Penge. We ate in Chinese restaurants in Half Moon Lane and Denmark Hill with occasional forays further afield to Nunhead and Peckham Rye. On Sunday afternoons we took buses to Richmond and Hampton Court Park, or loitered by the river at Mortlake. It was not, I am happy to admit, a relationship of equals. It was to Roger, for example, that I owe my first experience of women. His own attitude to the girls we met at Goldsmiths' or encountered in the course of our travels was unfathomable. He liked women, he was happy to be seen with them, to take them out and spend money on them, but he shrank from any deeper involvement; an involvement that most of them were anxious to prosecute. The result was that at any given time there existed a gaggle of admirers simultaneously attracted by Roger's inscrutability, marked down in the phrase of the time as 'lack of introspection', but puzzled by his indifference. Though they could occasionally be detached from this grouping – 'Roger's harem', not entirely a joke – and offered consolation, the original impetus still lingered. 'Doesn't he *like* women?' a girl called Alice once asked me late at night in Streatham. 'I mean, he knows I'd take my clothes off now, right here on the spot, if he wanted me to.' I had no answer.

But in any case our paths had begun to diverge. There was nothing obvious about this, no violent disagreement or deliberate treachery, simply a slow, spreading fracture that grew a little wider on each occasion that we met. He had changed, I thought, in some subtle, ineluctable way; his ambitions now social rather than academic. The Alices and the Julias gave way to the Camillas and the Jennifers, braying upper-class girls from secretarial colleges or the Lucie Clayton, who smoothed their skirts carefully over the battered sofa of the Streatham Hill flat and declined the pungent cups of tea. There was an eager, wholly unselfconscious pride in the way Roger showed off these acquisitions, as if they were exotic, brightly plumaged birds brought down by skill and cunning. What game he was playing, what snare he had laid down to entrap Camilla and her kind, what great prize he hoped to emerge with, I did not discover until later. Shortly afterwards, at the beginning of our third year, Roger moved out of the flat. I did not regret his passing. There was something unreasoning about him, I decided, a self-possession unwarranted by the facts. Like a nervous small boy on a games field he had assumed a superiority over his peers which did not exist; the next scrum, the next tangle of arms and boots, I thought, would see him exposed and derided. In his absence Streatham Hill became a place of ghosts.

Though our professional lives took separate paths, Roger and I kept up in a small way. We met infrequently in the corridors of newspaper offices, in pubs near the old *Daily Mail* building in Carmelite Square. It was a relationship founded on telephone calls, sightings across crowded rooms and imperfect memory. 'Martin is one of my oldest friends,' Roger would say if any third person happened to intrude into one of those brief reunions. If that person happened to be a woman he would go on to say, 'Martin knows secrets about me. You see, at one point he was my father confessor.' This canvassing of past intimacy in a way designed to leave the listener at once bemused and intrigued never failed to annoy me. I supposed it a consequence of his job, in which these small revelations and greater mysteries seemed to cohabit in a rather uncomfortable way. Roger was a gossip-columnist on a London evening newspaper – a considerable position for someone of his age and background; it seemed reasonable to suppose that this talent for public mischief-making should infect his private life. He spoke knowledgeably about 'Paddy' Lichfield and 'George' Weidenfeld. The photograph of him which appeared above the column – black-tied, hair swept back and looking rather like Ronald Firbank – seemed to confirm his elevation into rarefied circles where I could not hope to penetrate. There was something about Roger in these days, something hard, shiny and engrossed, which had not been there before. Like the carnival reveller who places a white, sculpted mask over his face as a prelude to saturnalia, he had whirled off, disguised and ungovernable, into a landscape of private fantasy.

Meanwhile I set to work, laboriously, at the job of becoming a freelance journalist, a task not without its satisfactions. I wrote feature articles for trade journals – *The Retailer*, *Haberdashers' World* – sober chronicles with large circulations. I wrote book reviews for the *New Statesman* in the brief, rancorous period under Crossman's editorship. For a bizarre six-month period I acted as resident sub-editor on a magazine devoted to the construction of plastic aeroplanes. Later, during the years with Morty, souvenirs of this time would surface to embarrass me.

A year or so passed. Looking back I can already discern the first faint outlines of the world that would rise up to claim me. I went out for a time with a girl who worked as a glamour model and was occasionally photographed for the Sunday newspapers. Later, under the auspices of a satirical weekly, I was sent to interview the publisher of a range of what were then known as 'male interest' magazines. Each of these encounters impressed me less by their exoticism than by the sense of ordinary people making do in the face of unpromising circumstance. The glamour model with her lavish bathroom rituals and her sturdy self-possession, the pornographer, found in his office eating sandwiches amid bundles of page proofs, neither seemed to me more than casual vagrants picked randomly from a debris of similar flotsam, uncertain of motivation or destiny.

One day late in 1973 when I was at work on an article called 'Why stay-at-home housewives may soon be a thing of the past' the telephone rang. It was Roger. He said, rather wearily, 'I *insist* you come to dinner next Friday.'

I knew from the tone of his voice what had happened. A string of other acquaintances had let him down.

'Anyone interesting coming?'

'Lots. Caroline Mallender.'

'Who's she?'

'Writes children's books. Rather good children's books.' Roger's attitude to his dinner guests was that of a loyal flat-racing trainer, anxious to defend his stable against imagined slights. 'And Keith Harrison.'

Keith Harrison was a recently retired first division footballer whose memoirs Roger was supposed to have had a hand in ghosting.

'I nearly forgot,' Roger went on. 'It's rather exciting. There's a pornographer coming. Morty Goldstein.'

Roger found all his dinner guests, these minor novelists and strident television producers, 'exciting'. For a moment I wondered what Morty Goldstein had done to commend himself to this all-seeing intelligence. Then I remembered a newspaper report about the prosecution of a newsagent under the Obscene Publications Act. A magazine Morty produced had been mentioned in court.

Roger interpreted the silence as indecision. 'Come on,' he said heavily, 'do me a favour. Say you'll come.'

'All right,' I said, with equal heaviness. 'I'll come.'

In the week before Roger's dinner party, events of wider significance intervened. It was the time of Mr Heath's confrontation with the mineworkers, of the national overtime ban and the three-day week. Looking back it is hard to assimilate the passions that were roused in that silent English winter of 1973–74, a time when phrases like 'collapse of government' and 'breakdown of law and order' were bandied about and the scent of anarchy hung in the air. It was the time, too, when my father finally achieved a certain immortality on the occasion when he wrote and had published in the *Daily Telegraph* a letter beginning with the words, 'Dear Sir, Writing by candlelight . . .'. The phrase, appropriated by a socialist historian and used as the title of a famous essay, resonated through the later 1970s as a byword for bourgeois hysteria in the face of minor inconvenience.

I began the evening of Roger's dinner at a publisher's launch party in Bedford Square. Here the atmosphere was grimly festive. Arc lights and a generator had been procured in case of power failure. People – publicists, book trade habitués, literary agents – stood in twos and threes discussing the prospects for a settlement of the dispute. 'It can't last,' they said gloomily. 'Heath will have to settle.' 'It can't last,' they said later, after the room was suddenly plunged into darkness. 'Gormley's a reasonable man. They'll have to settle.' I exchanged a few words with the author in whose honour the party was being held, a small, shy American academic. 'I didn't realise things were so bad as all this,' he said. 'I suppose it must have been this way in the Blitz. Now they tell me there's a real prospect of the government being overthrown.' Later the lights came on again. Optimism, like some long-neglected plant suddenly allowed to luxuriate in sunshine, was briefly renewed.

'They'll have to settle. They say the money's leaving the country and at this rate it might not come back . . .'

'I know a man who knows Heath, and he said . . .'

'I know a man who knows Wilson, and he said . . .'

'Back where I come from we have recognised procedures for dealing with this sort of thing: declare a state of emergency and call out the National Guard.'

'It was a mistake ever to expect the miners to be reasonable . . .'

'It was a mistake ever to nationalise the mines in the first place . . .

Later I walked out into the Tottenham Court Road and took a bus through the empty streets to Kentish Town. Here both electricity and gas had failed at a crucial stage in the preparation of Roger's elaborate menu. We ate out of tins in Roger's cramped kitchen, at a table lit by strategically hung torches.

It was not a successful meal. In later years those people who dined out in the winter of 1973–74 were eager to devise tales of straitened conviviality and unexpected pleasures. The reality was less appealing. Miss Mallender and the professional footballer arrived late and regarded each other with barely concealed distaste. Roger, depressed by culinary disaster, scarcely spoke. Morty, alone amongst the row of minor celebrities, seemed to be able to take events in his stride. He ate a large meal of beans on toast. When in Roger's sitting room, fortified by brandy and cocoa, some sort of conversation began it was his voice which rose decisively above Miss Mallender's remarks about her Carnegie Award and Keith Harrison's homely interjections, an intent monologue whose substance I can remember even now.

The provocation was Miss Mallender's account of *Last Tango in Paris* – now a rather elderly scandal – to which she had been accompanied by her literary agent.

'I suppose it was his way of making a proposition,' she said, 'sitting there for two hours in a darkened cinema – and do you know it really was *very* dark – watching people crawl all over each other and catching his breath, poor man, when anything particularly objectionable happened.'

'It sounds horrid,' said an epicene young man who worked on Roger's newspaper.

'Cut to ribbons,' Morty said suddenly. It was the first time I remembered hearing him speak. 'Guy I know works for the editing company told me about it. Forests of pubic hair all over the cutting-room floor, Brando's cock, everything. Just popcorn. You could take your grandmother to see it.'

'Well, I don't know that I'd want to take my grandmother to see it,' said Miss Mallender skittishly. 'In fact I don't think I could ever look a knob of butter in the face again.'

Morty made a small growling noise, suggesting a sedate yet rackety motor vehicle brought rapidly into gear.

'Let's talk,' he said, 'about pornography. Now, you mightn't think that pornography concerns you. Forget it. Pornography concerns every one of us, every one of us down throughout time. You've seen those Roman frescos, the stuff you get in the Pompeii exhibition? Pornography, every inch of it. Go back a couple of thousand years and ask the man in the street what turns him on and he'll tell you: pictures of people fucking. Or rather, not people fucking, but people looking as if they're about to fuck. Because pornography,' Morty said, 'is about delayed gratification. A girl who's taking her clothes off is more exciting than a girl who's taken her clothes off, right? A naked girl sitting there on a chair showing you her tits is *beautiful*, okay? A girl who's just taking her top off and doesn't know if she'll let you see what's underneath is *erotic* . . .'

Miss Mallender muttered something about titillation. Morty ignored her. 'Let's talk,' he continued, 'about the varieties of pornography. There's the pictures you see in the newspapers, the page three girls. That's not pornography, that's just a picture. Let's consider pornography as a social force. All those guys sitting there in their bedsitters beating off over *Penthouse* and *Men Only*. Power. Unusual power. Bring it together and it would terrify you . . .

'I'm not a sexual libertarian, I'm a businessman. And an artist. I'm not telling people to have sex. Jesus, fourteen-year-old girls coming home and telling their mothers they've just fucked for the first time and what's going to happen! Disgusting, just disgusting. I'm telling people to look at sex. Safety valve, social control, whatever you like to call it. People would be fucking in the streets if it wasn't for me . . . Books, music, pictures hanging up in fucking stately homes. You can forget about all that. Well let's just say pornography, *pornography is the new art form* . . .'

It was an impressive performance. Even now, ten years later, I can see Morty hunched in his chair, the pale light gleaming on his bald head, declaiming his text with the fervour of some medieval hedge-priest. But it had an ironic fervour, a series of complex codes given unity and design by sheer force of delivery. Like the amateur debater who proposes fascism or compulsory euthanasia as a way of exercising his rhetorical skills, his was a triumph of simple oratory.

The party broke up early: Miss Mallender and Keith Harrison in search of taxis, Morty and I to walk the few hundred yards or so to the tube station. As we lingered on the empty staircase he said, 'You're a writer, aren't you? Always looking for writers. Come and see me tomorrow. Come and see me and we'll have a talk.'

Our trains arrived simultaneously, his to go northward, mine to go south. Through the opening that divided the two platforms I watched him for a moment, face pushed down into his collar, jammed between the tall, leather-jacketed youths and the Irish navvies with their knapsacks: he was wholly absorbed. Then there was a grinding of gears, a slow, painful rattle of far-off machinery and the train bore him away.

I went and saw Morty: we had our talk. The studio at Dean Street was at this time half-built: decorators moved carefully around the piles of sawdust and exposed woodwork, studiously avoiding the three or four girls who had assembled for what Morty described as 'a screen test'. Seen in this environment, blinking in the haggard morning light, he seemed a diminished figure, anxious over minor alterations to schedule, tiny setbacks. 'That cameraman's on double time,' he said more than once, 'so where the fuck is he?' It was only then that the splendid battlements of the previous night swung aside to reveal a frailer edifice. We went into Morty's office where there were glistening ozalids lying over the desk and a pile of empty cigarette packets.

'A lot of people in this business can't write a script,' Morty said. 'They think it has to be like a sitcom, like something on the BBC. And lots of nudge-nudge dialogue. This is an outline.' He threw me a plastic wallet containing two sheets of paper stapled together. 'I want to make a twenty-minute film. Take it away and see what you can do.'

I spent a week on *Hookers in Hampstead*, a short feature which in the event never progressed beyond the big storyboard in Morty's office. The plot was of slight dimensions: a young man picks up a prostitute outside Hampstead tube station. They go to a house in the High Street. There in mid-coitus the man remembers a vital appointment. The remainder of the story concerns his frenzied efforts to extricate himself both from the girl and a bevy of playmates who inhabit the floor below. I gave it minor strokes of irony – the man nearsighted, unable to move without his glasses, the prostitute given the same name as his wife, their dalliance continually interrupted by the ringing of the telephone. I imagined the dialogue to be hard-boiled but with occasional touches of comedy, although in fact, it achieved neither of these aims. Oddly Morty approved.

'Not bad,' he said. 'Not bad for a first go. But what the punter wants is action. Or at any rate he wants to think there's going to be action, and that it's going to happen soon. And don't take the piss out of sex too much. Last thing a guy who pays money to see a pornographic film wants to think is that you're taking the piss out of sex.'

I persevered. For a month I declined all other commissions and sat in my room devising scripts from the storylines Morty supplied. I wrote another twenty-minute feature called *Stately Lust* in which a group of elderly libertines, each dying of some unspecified complaint, arrive at a country house for a last, epochal orgy, and a longer piece, a costume drama centring on a Victorian cleric's futile attempt to reform a woman of the night. Oddly the task was to my taste. I became adept at refining dialogue, at allowing the plot to advance by means of gesture or intonation, at inserting punchlines, at conferring rhythm and pattern on to the chatter about sex. As the power cuts grew longer in duration, as Mr Wilson succeeded Mr Heath – the only image I remember, curiously, that of Mr Heath's piano being removed from Downing Street – I persevered. At the time there seemed no more enviable destiny than to sit in a room in a city, alone and unregarded, and to write.

At the beginning of March Roger telephoned. I had not spoken to him since the evening of the dinner party. He said in a subdued way, 'Are you going to Morty Goldstein's party tonight?'

The invitation, florid and embossed on manila paper, had lain on my mantelpiece for a fortnight. I had planned to spend a hard evening working on a script called *Mandy Does Mayfair* which had arrived that morning, but somehow I did not feel like telling Roger this. 'I don't think so.'

'I'm going. There may be a story in it for the paper and I need someone to show me round. Say you'll come.'

The subterfuge, I realised, was wasted. Roger knew all about my association with Morty.

'All right. I'll come.'

And so we went to Morty's party, held on the very evening when Harold Wilson accepted Her Majesty's request to form his third administration. At the loft in Dean Street the atmosphere was chaotic, the heavy press of people made indiscriminate by music and flashing lights. I knew a few of the guests by sight. None was known to Roger. At first this detachment seemed not to trouble him and he roamed happily enough around the curtained rooms, peering into doorways and examining the garish decor. Later, when the volume of the music lessened and various exotic dancers began to perform on a raised dais at the rear, he grew restive.

'Do you think it would be a good idea to call the police?'

'Why should you want to do that?'

By this time Roger was very drunk. 'This is practically an orgy. And it would make a good story, don't you think?'

Roger went outside to a telephone box and called the police. They came almost immediately, a harassed-looking sergeant and a brace of constables from West End Central. The music stopped, the lights came on and there was general consternation. The policemen knew Morty of old. 'Sorry to trouble you, Mr Goldstein,' they said. 'Complaint received from a member of the public and we had to investigate.' They made a cursory inspection of the premises, after which the party resumed. I caught sight of Roger smiling inanely. At least, I thought, he had got his story.

A little later Roger said, 'Do you suppose those policemen are corrupt?'

'I shouldn't wonder.'

'That's a pity. The editor doesn't like attacks on the police. I suppose I shall have to keep that side out of it.'

A few days later a short item about the party did surface in Roger's column. It bore no relation to any event that either of us had witnessed. But a week after this his portrait ceased to appear above the page devoted to society goings-on and metropolitan gossip. Morty, as Roger discovered to his cost, had powerful friends. He hung on for a year or so – he wrote for one of the London listings magazines, a genre then in its infancy, I heard his voice once or twice early in the morning on a commercial radio station – but it was to no avail. From time to time, loitering in the Fleet Street pubs and drinking dens, I came across his old colleagues and acquaintances; their silence was an eloquent testimony to what had happened. Roger continued to telephone me sporadically, the gaps increasingly drawn out, so that, hearing his voice, I would have to concentrate for a moment before I remembered who he was. When he rang for the last time, early in 1975, I failed to recognise him. Shortly afterwards he left London to work on a provincial newspaper and our relationship, such as it was, came to an end. Later, when some odd juxtaposition of memory and circumstance brought him back to mind – walking past Goldsmiths' College, an afternoon in the late Seventies spent with Elaine at Hampton Court – it was hard to believe that Roger had ever existed. He seemed to belong to an older, less concrete world whose boundaries and prohibitions I had long since left behind. Occasionally when some rare acquaintance who had known us both, some woman met years later at a party, asked, 'Do you remember Roger Garfitt?' I would have to pause a moment before answering: a cruel memorial, perhaps, but one which I was not inclined to alter or dispute.

Early evening, two days after Fat Eric's *soirée* and the Tupperware box full of shit. Waking up this morning, late, in bright sunshine, with Suzi already departed to school, I had one of those glorious daybreak amnesia sessions. I came down the stairs whistling, I scanned the post with guiltless interest and I was halfway through breakfast before my eye fell inexorably on a shred of wrapping paper lying in the wastepaper basket. Instantly, like iron filings obeying the call of a magnet, everything fell back into place again – the pictures, the stinking parcel, Elaine – and, no, it wasn't something I could just write off, wasn't something I could file cheerily under Life's Little Ironies. *I have to find out who's doing this to me.* And I have to find Elaine, because I want to know about this sudden interest in my whereabouts and why it stops short of actual contact, and whether she knows anything about the photos and the parcel. Which, knowing Elaine, she will.

I lock into a round of phone calls. Suzi is at the parent–teachers' association. The odd car shudders past outside. First I try Morty. I try Morty a number of times. I try him at his house in Ongar and get an answer phone telling me that Mortimer Goldstein is not presently available. I try the studio at Dean Street and get nothing at all. I try the timeshare cottage in Devon and get a piece of posh trash who claims never to have heard of him. Then I remember the flat in Greek Street. The phone rings for quite a long time before Morty picks it up.

'Martin. Good to hear from you. How are things?'

'Fine, Morty. Just fine. What about you?'

'I can't complain. *Jungle Lovers* went in the adult video ratings at number two.'

'That's great, Morty . . . You ever hear of Jim Woodward these days, Morty?'

'Jim Woodward? Sorry, Martin.'

'Jim Woodward, the actor.'

'The one who was in *Spank Academy*? Haven't seen him in two years, not since he married the bimbo who threw the glass at you that time . . . Something worrying you, Martin?'

I tell Morty a bit about the photographs. Morty whistles through his teeth down the line.

'And you're sure it's you? That's bad, Martin.' There is a swirl of random gusty movement somewhere. Morty's voice edges back into focus. 'Sorry about that, Mart. I have someone here right now . . . Listen, you have anyone you owe money to?'

That's a laugh. The bastards all owe me money. Morty. Terry Chimes. Elaine . . . 'No.'

'Not Eddie Lyle? Frank Rosati?' – Morty mentions a brace of time-honoured Soho frighteners. 'No one like that?'

'No.'

'No bimbo after a pension?'

'Not that I can think of.'

There is a silence, followed by a faint scuffling noise in the remoter distance.

'Are you there, Morty?'

'Sure, Martin. It's just that I have someone with me right now. Look, if I hear anything off the wall I'll let you know. Okay?'

I cradle the phone handset for a while against my shoulder, hoist it reluctantly back on to the table. The silence echoes.

Eight a.m., two days later. Mist coming close up to the window. The garden is half obscured by queer, vaporous trails. Suzi, cross, whey-faced, hair tied back with a sliver of ribbon, bustles noisily around the kitchen in her dressing gown. At one point she says, 'I'll be late back tonight.'

'How late?'

'Eleven. Twelve. I don't know. It's the school concert.'

Later I watch her reversing the car out of its parking space in that neat, fussy way she has, each precaution, each cautious manoeuvre and glance in the mirror wholly exaggerated. Suzi is immensely proud of her driving. The car moves off and Fat Eric lounges past, head nuzzled into his collar against the cold. He does not look up.

Yesterday another batch of photographs arrived, neatly done up in cellophane and packed tightly into a padded bag. I didn't bother to take them out and look at them. There is a drain twenty yards down the street opposite T. Coulthard's grocery shop. I waited until the pavement was empty and T. Coulthard, seen through the plate-glass window, had disappeared into his storeroom before posting them eagerly through the grating.

Shortly after this I have an idea. A good way of finding out if Elaine is still around, is still in the business, say, would be to phone one of the Soho model agencies Morty used to deal with. There were numbers of these sad, dead-eyed procurers sitting in endless repose in flyblown offices at the top of staircases in Wardour Street or Golden Square: Starfinder, Movie Girl, Screen Talent. In the guise of a Social Security *fonctionnaire* I do the rounds of telephoning. Movie Girl and Screen Talent have never heard of her, but at Starfinder I get a bored-sounding American who preserves some faint recollection of Elaine's accomplishments.

'Elaine Keenan? Yeah, I remember her. Irish chick who frowned all the time. Used to be in *Driven to Lust*, *Spank Academy*, all that early Leisurevision stuff Morty Goldstein used to put out.'

I murmur something about being more interested in Miss Keenan's whereabouts than in a résumé of her career.

'Okay. I get the picture. Haven't seen her for a while, but she's probably still on the books. You want me to go take a look?'

He returns with a phone number. Unfamiliar. I make a great show of thanking the American for his assistance.

'Glad to help,' he says. 'Who'd you say you were calling from?'

'Department of Health and Social Security.'

'Uh huh. Nothing to do with the IRS?'

'Nothing at all.'

'Glad to hear it. I hate those fuckers.'

Later on I ring the phone number. A man's voice, incomprehensible amid a blare of noise. I try again until, halfway through the second attempt, realisation dawns. West End Central Police Station. You have to hand it to those Americans.

A bit later the implications of the West End Central joke begin to dawn on me. The phone number is a plant. Question: who planted it there? The American or someone else? Having brooded about this for an hour or so, I ring Starfinder again. The same bored-sounding voice.

'Hi, man.'

'This is the Department of Health and Social Security. I believe we spoke before.'

'Sure. The guy who said he wasn't from the IRS, I remember. What can I do for you?'

'Well, the thing is that we're having a slight problem contacting this Miss Keenan on the number you gave us and I, that is my colleagues and I, were wondering if you could give us any further information.'

'What sort of information?'

'Have you spoken to Miss Keenan recently?'

'I got forty girls on the books here. I don't make a ledger note every time one of them rings up to tell me she's putting on weight. Wait a moment, though. I got a feeling she rang in last month, to tell me she was on a new number.'

'Elaine . . . Miss Keenan telephoned you?'

'Could have been her. Could have been some guy. Sometimes they get their boyfriends or their managers to phone in. I don't remember.'

'Last month?'

'Last month. Two months ago. Who knows? Hey, I've got plenty of other girls here. Sure you don't want one of them instead?'

'I don't think that will be necessary, Mr . . .'

'Zappa,' intones the voice. 'Francis Vincent Zappa.' As I said, you have to hand it to those Americans.

More artefacts from the Goldstein years. A stack of Grunt Records press releases advertising Terry Chimes's progeny to the world: the Glasgow Express on tour; Bobby Dazz coaxed out of retirement. A

Leisurevision illustrated calendar from 1978, of the sort which Morty sent out to the trade, featuring Miss Lila St Claire and 'Legs' Alice La Faye. A photograph of Morty lugubriously eating *paella* in a Spanish restaurant in Maddox Street. A frail, crumbling copy of *Pages*, Mr Tovacs's literary magazine, with contributions from García Márquez and Kundera. Press cuttings from the *People*, *Daily Mirror*, *News of the World*. A shot of Terry, Morty and me at the poolside, relaxed, quizzical, the prone bikinied body behind us probably Elaine's, difficult to tell. Pictures of Morty with various East End frighteners, with Charlie Kray, the Major, Mad Jimmy Parsons. One of Morty's election bills. Elaine in an SS officer's greatcoat at the head of a file of stormtroopers. Dead things, out of a dead world. It has never occurred to me to throw them away.

The stormtroopers I can date with some precision. Towards the close of Morty's late-Seventies period, the period of *Plasma Party* and *Body Snatchers*, there was a mild vogue at the smart end of the hard-core market for war and sex films. They bore titles such as *SS Experiment Camp* and *Unmarked Grave* (there was even a gay one, I seem to recall, full of thrashing young members of the Hitler Youth movement, called *Nazi Lust*). The high street cinemas were chary, naturally enough, but the bleary video shops were interested, and one or two of the continental distributors. Emboldened, Morty hired two dozen Nazi uniforms from a theatrical outfitter's, acquired a number of dummy stenguns and persuaded a friend to lend him a remote island off the Hebridean coast for a week's shooting.

The film was called *Blitzkrieg Bondage*. The treatment, which I devised during the course of the rail-trip to Stranraer, was unexpectedly imaginative. A crack SS unit arrives stealthily on the Isle of Muck late in 1942, cleverly forestalling the efforts of a handful of bewildered crofters to raise the alarm. The local laird, a monocled fifth columnist, gleefully makes over his ancestral house as headquarters. Holed up in Castle McIntosh and amusing themselves with the local womenfolk, the SS men unveil the purpose of their mission: a bacterial rocket loaded with a deadly virus trained on Glasgow. All would be lost, were not busty Flora McKillop able to persuade the treacherous laird of the error of his ways . . .

It was a disaster. Late November, a pale, watery sun scuttling across the crags and blasted cliff tops. It rained continuously for seven days. Hunter Stagg, the American hard-core star imported at vast expense to play the part of the SS *Gruppenführer*, came down with pneumonia. Half the cast were nearly drowned attempting to film the landing scene. Eventually, frustrated by the crepuscular light and the onset of darkness shortly after lunch, Morty decided to film most of it inside the castle. An all-action scene in which Flora McKillop, played by Elaine, abseils to safety from a top-floor window was aborted when a sound man fell to his death from the slippery ramparts. In the end Morty decided to cut his losses and had me rewrite the script to accommodate a rugby team arriving by mistake for an evening at a Scots health farm.

Morty and I had a serious ethical chat about *Blitzkrieg Bondage*. Our first.

'Doesn't all this bother you?' I asked, early one morning as we stood on the battlements staring unhappily at the rain.

'No.' Morty peered down to the spot where half-a-dozen of the extras were rehearsing their initial molestation of Flora McKillop. 'It doesn't bother me.'

'But what about the Jews, Morty?'

'What about the Jews? Martin, you don't want to worry yourself about the Jews. Listen, I'll tell you a joke. It was my father told it to me. They're herding this pile of Jews into a gas chamber, right, and because it's the camp commandant's birthday every prisoner is allowed one last request. For some it's a cigarette, for others it's an extra five minutes alive. But one little guy wants a piano, that's right, a piano, and the sheet music to Beethoven's Fifth. So they set the piano up in the corner of the gas chamber, close the door, switch on the taps, and that's that. Quarter of an hour later they open up again. Everybody's dead except the little guy who's playing away like there's no tomorrow. "So what's all this?" asks the commandant. "How did you do it?" "Well," explains the little guy, "I guess tunes help you breathe more easily." '

As I said, a serious ethical chat.

Some more history: Morty's fledgling career as an entrepreneur during the early 1960s had been blessed with certain advantages. Not least among these was the location of the Goldstein senior dwelling at 174 Valiance Road, E2, two doors down from homely Mrs Kray. Then there was the *éclat* of the Goldsteins themselves. This derived not so much from Councillor Goldstein's political affiliations, substantial though they were, as from sheer weight of numbers. There were a lot of Goldsteins, variously at large in the thoroughfares of local commerce. They kept pubs, sold radios, worked as kosher butchers and used-car dealers. Collectively their numbers were sufficient to populate Morty's adolescence with a series of lurid exemplars, a pageant of weird uncles, mad aunts and desiccated cousins. Periodically in the early Seventies they re-emerged, surfaced like bloated, long-forgotten fish above the waters of some stagnant pond, and then were gone. Oddly bejewelled women waving to Morty across Oxford Street, gnarled elderly men nodding from shop doorways; nervous at first of these tangible reminders of his past, Morty swiftly anaesthetised such wraiths by means of anecdote, each revelation firmly checked by the barrier of family solidarity. 'My Uncle Hymie,' Morty would begin reminiscently, 'now take it from me, Martin, it just wasn't true about the . . .' About the used-car racket, the leant-on shopkeepers and all the rest.

Crazy Rodney enlightened me about the Goldsteins once. There were a lot of Goldsteins, a few too many for comfort. They beat people up, intimidated their children and – a traditional East End expedient – threw paraffin heaters through the windows of rival shopkeepers. According to Crazy Rodney's appreciative testimony any threat of competition – a new used-car lot, shutters taken down from some long moribund grocery – sparked a paranoid campaign of clan activity, meticulously planned, extending across three or four generations.

In the early 1960s a small shopkeeper was unwise enough to set up a modest emporium across the street from Uncle Hymie's extravagantly decorated Food Mart in the Bethnal Green Road. He lasted a fortnight. On the opening day Uncle Hymie established two of his nephews, armed with air rifles, in an upstairs window of a house across the road. Undeterred, a few customers dodged past the spray of pellets to negotiate the fragmenting doorway. When the shopkeeper replaced his windows with heavy-duty shatterproof plate glass Uncle Hymie sent gangs of juvenile Goldsteins in to pilfer from the bags of stacked confectionery and mouldering fruit.

Denied access by sternly worded signs they gave way to intent Goldstein pensioners who roamed noiselessly through the silent corridors, blundered innocently into the neat, geometric stacks of tins and left vast orders which they then declined to collect. Midway through the second week, none of these expedients having proved immediately effective, Uncle Hymie persuaded Morty's father to exert some influence on the council works department. Subsequently two workmen with pneumatic drills and a heavily bribed road-digger operative spent two days and nights breaking up the adjoining pavement. Miraculously the shop struggled on. A lesser man might at this stage have permitted his opponents some modest respite, but Uncle Hymie, animated at first by this new diversion, had now grown bored. Late at night two days later he stole an elderly Landrover, drove it at speed in the direction of the shop's frontage and jumped out seconds before impact.

It was an impressive heritage. These were proud exemplars.

A characteristic sight in late-Sixties Norwich was the fat girl skipping. Threading your way through the dead Sunday-morning council estates, a trail of scuffed verges and burly middle-aged men washing their cars, you could be confident of seeing them: at the edge of the roadside, in somebody's driveway wedged between a juddering pram and a wrecked Mini. There would generally be three of them: two to hoist the rope, one, the fat girl, heaving herself over it in that shambling, splay-footed way they have. The fat girl. Twelve or thirteen. Torso, stomach quite undifferentiated, the whole like a large flat bolster crammed into the print dress, the too-small frock. The red face. The helmet of dun hair bouncing from side to side. The *intentness.* Always the fat girl: the two spindly rope-turners simply stooges, accessories to the fact. Sometimes there would be two or three to a street, the only movement beside the loafing car-washers, the only sound except the faint rasp of a radio somewhere beyond the yellowed hedge. And always the fat girl, pausing a moment perhaps outside the rope's arc to regain her rhythm, engrossed in her hop-skip-and-jump routine, immobilised on tiptoe by some ill-judged twist.

Those fat girls. I fear they don't exist now, that they get put on diets at birth. I went looking for them once. I loitered around outside school playgrounds. I spent an afternoon trawling Eaton Park, I even followed the old Sunday-morning paper-round route through the West Earlham estate, past the ragged grass and the glittering cars. There was no sign of them. I looked in vain for those anaconda legs labouring grimly over the zebra crossing, the drowsy, lymphatic smiles, the neutral, filled-in features, looked in vain for those brooding puffball families – fat, youngish mother, butterball four-year-old, pudgy baby. Those fat girls.

Suzi is a fat girl. Sometimes, watching her arrive from the upstairs window, noting the cautious decanting from the car, I speculate about Suzi's early life, wonder about that lost, alien girlhood. They have tough childhoods, those fat girls: the snickering cronies in the changing room, the chalked outrages on the bike-shed wall. Later, in the tense huddles of adolescence, the fat girl is fair game. An unwritten law of courtship. Everyone knows you can do what you like with a fat girl, pull her hair, chew on her breasts, lose your fingers in the folds of her rump. They have to tolerate it. Later they marry thin, sullen men who hit them.

I watch Suzi now as she extricates herself from the worrying harness of the car, pauses uncertainly before the gatepost, contemplates the troublesome two-yard dash to the door. Suzi is one of those fat girls to whom life is a strenuous denial of unshakeable evidence. Like the murderer found carrying the blood-stained bundle she coaxes a whole style out of her phantom blamelessness. And she's *not* fat, because the scales said nine stone three this morning and considering her height and . . . Suzi is five feet tall, and edging towards stoutness. The flaming cheeks. The heavyset tread. The thick high heels. Various aspects of the traditional fat girl routine are starting to descend upon her. As she bustles towards the door I look at the car, the cluttered Renault with its hapless paraphernalia of tennis rackets, badminton gear and bunched swimsuits (sport, that useless fat girl panacea) and smile.

For one with such a precise appreciation of the public taste, or of the avenues down which the public taste might be induced to wander, Morty was surprisingly slow to investigate the potential of what were at the end of the Seventies coyly known as 'special interest publications'. Such diffidence was all the more curious in that Leisurevision prided itself on attention to market research, customer relations, consumer attitudes – all the wool-pulling, hoodwinking phrases that Morty gleaned from his occasional trawlings through shiny American management magazines. At the time, subtlety having come late to the backward UK pornography market, such an attitude smacked of novelty. Deep into the mid-Seventies there lurked the conviction that pornography was *easy*, that all one needed was a woman taking her clothes off in suitable surroundings and a minimally proficient cameraman. The girl, the bed, the slow divestiture – anything more, any variant on this elementary narrative theory, and the purchaser rebelled, switched his allegiance back to staider certainties. Morty didn't think this. Morty thought pornography was *difficult*, that it needed to be worked out, that there were complex laws by which it functioned and flourished. A characteristic sight at this time was the spectacle of Morty leafing respectfully through some Scandinavian import, some bristling display of Technicolor pudenda, and adducing sophistication from the artful conjunction of limbs and the tricksy plotlines. It was about this time, too, that he began to consult books with titles like *Strategies of Eroticism* and conduct deep, theoretical discussions with baffled art directors.

'. . . You see, Martin, there's what they call "a *trajectory of desire*" in all this . . . I mean, I don't want to get heavy, but okay, the chick comes into the room, right, and looks at you. When's the time you start fancying her?'

'That depends, Morty. It depends on what she looks like.'

'Okay. She's a looker, we'll take that for granted . . . But tell me the point at which you actually *desire* her?'

'That depends as well. It depends on what she does.'

'Look . . . I realise this isn't an easy concept to handle, but . . . What I mean is, there's a sort of what they call *erotic grammar* working here, right? Say you're in a pub watching a stripper. Now the turn-on, the real turn-on is not when the chick's taken her top off, it's the split-second before she's taken it off. It's the *suggestion* of what she's got underneath.'

'You're saying that we ought to print pictures of girls just before they take their clothes off?'

'No. All I'm saying, Martin, is that we're underestimating the punters. There's ten, fifteen other fanny mags out there in the paper shops and we ought . . . we ought to be *educating* them.'

The upshot of this was a surfeit of reader questionnaires in *Bouncers, Upfront* and the rest of the Leisurevision stable, a file of returnable coupons, a mounting two-way traffic of editorial canvassing and reader response. Reader response. As occasional editor of the correspondence sections I was familiar with the unquantifiable varieties of reader response. 'Dear Sir,' writes N.G. of Huddersfield, 'I was fascinated to examine your picture spread of Miss Lila St Claire in the recent issue. Does Miss St Claire ever have cause to visit the West Lancashire region? I can assure her of a hearty welcome at 17 Acacia Avenue should she ever chance to pass this way.' That was in the mid-Seventies, the old, polite days of genteel locution and elegant italic script. The 'bountiful charms' of Miss Aimée Ortez, the 'girlish sensuality' of Corona d'Amour, the 'pouting insouciance' of Martika: all were hymned, not unmovingly, in such terms by C.J. of Ewell, Surrey, M.B. of Highgate N6 and 'Your faithful reader' of Skegness. Only later did the tone turn nasty, the intimations become less veiled. 'Tell Terri da Motta if she wants a fucking good time to ring Lowestoft 57002 and ask for Rod.'

The worst transformation took place in the 'Readers' Wives' section, where the coy photographs of plump housewives – middle-aged women waving from bathtubs, spreadeagled on pastel eiderdowns, emerging from grubby kimonos – gave way to nightmares, to scarred waifs bent over sex toys, to frightened, gaping teenagers. I remember one picture from these earlier times. A lurid, overlit room, in the background a rumpled, unmade bed. The woman – well into her forties, feigning a game smile – stood sideways on to the camera, one haunch jutting forward. Balancing on her hip, tethered by means of a flowery garter belt, was a rosette with the number '1' stencilled on to it. A feeling of infinite sadness enveloped the moment in which hubby put down his lager and his cigarette to brood over the tapering zoom lens.

The questionnaires were printed, returned, examined and collated. Hitherto the readers of the Leisurevision stable had subsisted on a steady diet of blondes, brunettes and redheads, tall, small, fat and thin. Invited to state their preferences, to select some garish exemplar, they chose redheads, brunettes and blondes. They wanted them small, tall, meagre and plump. They wanted homely scenes and exotic scenes, they wanted girls on hearthrugs and desert islands, in the backs of cars and on the backs of motorbikes, singly and severally. Confronted by such a roster of heterodox opinion, Morty was frankly perturbed. Casting his eye over the neatly tabulated statistics ('large breasts, twenty-seven per cent') he could find no clue as to his customers' salient desires, no hint – in a phrase suggested by his business magazines – of a reader profile. At the conference staged to discuss the findings such confusion plainly disturbed him.

'Okay, Martin. We print fifty thousand copies of *Bouncers* every month. We send them out and the newsagents sell them. Who reads them?'

'Christ, Morty . . . people like you. People like me.' The fixed gaze instructed me to elaborate. '. . . Schoolkids. Men on building sites. High Court judges.'

'Uh huh. I'll run with that. But what distinguishes them? What sets them apart from other people?'

'They're men, Morty. That's what sets them apart from other people.'

In conversation, Morty and irony existed in remote, watertight compartments. He went on, 'It might surprise you to know, Martin, that I took a pretty good look at that last bunch of readers' letters, a pretty good look. I think I have an idea of the sort of person who reads the stuff we put out.'

'You do?'

'Sure. If you asked me to describe our typical reader I'd say this: I'd say he was a married man, in his thirties maybe, with a couple of kids. I'd say he was successful, attractive to women. An educated man – some of those letters were well-written – but dissatisfied, wanting more. And that's why he comes to us.'

If you had asked me to describe our typical reader I would have said that he was an unmarried man, in his twenties or his teens, unsuccessful and unattractive to women, and thick as a plank. Just an ordinarily furtive masturbator, in fact.

Morty continued, 'But what excites them? What is it they want?'

'Blondes, brunettes, redheads . . .'

'These are sophisticated men, Martin. Men of the world. Not kids with their tongues hanging out because they've just seen a stripper in a pub. What sort of trajectory of desire is that . . .? Did you look at that stuff Terry brought back from Sweden last week?'

'We couldn't sell it here, Morty. It's not legal. Not in England.'

'I know, Martin. I know that. But did you look at it?'

As a matter of fact I had leafed cursorily through the copies of *Scandi-Sex* and *Erotomania.* They depicted fresh-faced Swedish women staring at bananas or daintily urinating into glass jugs. 'Pervert corner, Martin,' Terry Chimes had said. 'Just pervert fucking corner.'

'It's a bit . . . specialised, Morty.'

'A hundred thousand copies a month, Martin. That's how specialised it is.'

'You mean we ought to sell pictures of girls with bananas?'

'No, Martin, I'm just saying that there are other things, that there are other types of woman. Look, they did a survey at the National Gallery the other month – I read about it in the paper – and do you know who was the favourite painter of male visitors under the age of forty-five?'

'Rembrandt?'

'Try again.'

'Cézanne?'

'And again.'

'Rubens?'

'Correct,' said Morty. 'Absolutely correct.'

The upshot of this was an addition to the Leisurevision stables, the first of Morty's special interest magazines. Slight initial conflict over the title having been resolved – base Terry Chimes wanted to call it *Wobblers* or *Double Helping* – Morty eventually compromised on *Outsize.* Fat girls, thirty-two pages of them. Girls with vast, distended breasts gazing up out of cascading bath foam, girls with wanton, dewlap haunches crawling distractedly on all fours, engaged in nude mud-wrestling sessions or frenzied netball games. Even here in a medium encouraging the blatant and the overblown Morty's sense of artistry did not wholly desert him. His favourite trick was juxtaposition, the establishment of a context which was then mocked and deflated, a reality undercut by crass yet unsuspected illusion. Thus two monstrous female twins, clad in the regulation schoolgirl gear, are pictured side by side in the act of undressing. It is, to the fascinated observer, an identical divestiture: the same otiose skirts removed to uncover bolster thighs, the same blouses unpeeled to disclose identical pudgy forearms. Only in the final frame does the joke emerge, as the second girl tugs free of her undergarments to reveal a pair of inflated balloons. Another of Morty's variations on the stream of adipose female tissue was the introduction of a male element, a male element at once cowed, puny and ambiguous. Flushed out effortlessly from places of concealment, tiny, insignificant men with meagre torsos and harassed expressions were driven hither and thither by these bulging Amazons, were balanced across stalwart knees and callously thrashed, pinned down beneath the rolling flesh and endlessly humiliated. Sad, pitiable dwarfs in boxer shorts were confronted by mountainous dames bearing hockey sticks, wistful homunculi with washboard ribcages craned over by eldritch rolypolies. In a small, insidious way *Outsize* impinged on the public consciousness. Its pages were robbed to supply calendar illustrations, or the frontispieces of novelty greetings cards. You will remember the picture, so many times reproduced now that it must be famous, in which – the environment a bedroom and a gaping hearth – a wizened Father Christmas is shown pinned to the ground by his tormentor. Morty's memorials were many. Trailed over the dense, unpromising terrain of the 1970s, his footprints strayed over several minor pathways and marginal defiles before returning to broader routes and sturdier destinies.

More memorabilia from the early years with Morty: some rejected designs for the Grunt Records logo; a frayed, stretched tartan scarf; a picture of Terry Chimes standing next to a Radio One disc jockey; a *Music Week* singles chart from late 1975. Having left them scattered on the kitchen table I return to find Suzi turning them over. She seems oddly animated.

'Isn't that the Glasgow Express?'

Four cowed-looking Scottish teenagers, unhappily marshalled in their suits, staring at a framed replica of a silver disc.

'Don't tell me you were a fan of the Express?'

'My sister was. She even joined the fan club and bought a pair of tartan jeans. Father used to try and stop her wearing them.'

The picture stays on the table for a day or two before I take it away again.

Grunt Records, formed by Terry Chimes late in 1974, maintained a heterodox roster of artistes. There were all-girl groups with names like Candyfloss and Pussycat, ageing male vocalists encountered by Terry Chimes in his old Sixties Tin Pan Alley days, bands of plausible-looking boys next door put into suits and given arresting soubriquets such as Kenny or Biff. 'Music,' Terry Chimes used to say at around this time, 'music is about *gimmicks*.' The Express's gimmick was tartan and sawn-off jeans, together with stylised North-of-the-Border names like Rory and Kelvin. They were huge, no question. When they arrived at Selfridges once for a guest appearance a thousand adolescent girls rioted in the street outside. When Wee Jimmie the midget drummer appeared on a television chat show to announce his engagement the studio got burned down and there was an actual suicide. They sold two million copies of a record called *Pillow Talk*. Yet the Express's ascent to stardom was not without its problems. For a start they couldn't play their instruments, they really couldn't, and the bass player was a mental defective, but it was nothing that Terry couldn't fix, nothing that couldn't be glozed over by his tender ministrations. Session men were imported to make the records, the band went nowhere where somebody might casually ask them to sing or pick up a guitar and Kelvin the bass player stayed safely locked in his hotel room. All went well – sales, acclaim, television – until the day on which their manager sidled shamefacedly in to see Terry Chimes and confided that the boys had been thinking very seriously about their careers, very seriously indeed, and the upshot of this deliberation was that they wanted to play live. In fact they wanted to play live so badly that they had, on their own initiative, booked themselves into a week at the Apollo Theatre, Glasgow, and the ticket details had already gone out. Terry Chimes tried to talk them out of it, of course. He told them that it would be bad for their careers, he assured them (less plausibly) that no one would come. Their manager was offered a quarter of a million pounds to stop being their manager (he declined). But the music papers were already running 'EXPRESS TO TOUR' headlines, the tickets sold out in a day, and then there was nothing for it but to go ahead.

It was, naturally enough, a disaster. Grade A. Amid conditions of lavish security Terry had employed a session band to play behind curtains at the back of the stage and spent a week giving the boys intensive mime coaching. What could go wrong? In the event Tam the lead singer tripped over a microphone wire halfway through the opening number, flopped off the stage into the orchestra pit and sprained his ankle. As the band craned anxiously out into darkness the music blared on, almost drowned, fortuitously enough, by the noise of the screaming girls. Eventually, when they had dragged Tam out of the orchestra pit, given him emergency first aid and sent him back on stage, things got worse. Unbeknown to the backstage minders Wee Jimmie had packed his drum kit with flash powder. It went off three bars into *Lassie I Love You*, sending Wee Jimmie head first in the air, deafening the first six rows and blowing a small hole in the roof. As the band reeled dazedly around the vibrating stage, Kelvin the bass player began to have an epileptic fit. Finally the curtain fell away at the back of the theatre and the session men were revealed in all their embarrassed glory.

A day or so later Suzi says, 'What happened to the Glasgow Express?'

Broke up. Re-formed. Broke up again. I can remember asking the same question of Terry Chimes, six months after the concert. 'So how are you doing with the Express, Terry?'

'Bloody bad. I thought I'd fixed Wee Jimmie up to do a series on Scottish TV. You know, *Edinburgh Rock*, something like that. It turns out the cunt can't read the autocue.'

'What about Tam?'

'Haven't seen Tam for a month or so, now you mention it.'

'And Kelvin?'

'Kelvin's dead . . . At least I *think* Kelvin's dead.'

What happened to the Glasgow Express? Died, disappeared, went the way of all flesh. Vanished into that lost, boreal world of betting shops, dole queues and remembered, evanescent glory.

What happened to all of us, for that matter? Morty goes on making his films in a muted, low-key way. Terry Chimes, that monstrous epitome of twentieth-century urban man, retired to the country. Crazy Rodney? Lost in the random clutter of our times. Elaine, alone amongst these shadowy wraiths, these gaunt reminders of another world, continues to haunt me.

Another thing about Elaine: I hit her once. Quite hard, in fact, my only excuse extreme provocation. It was at a dinner party given by some friends of hers whose names might have been Jason and Amanda, who might have lived in Holland Park. Elaine's friends occupied no recognisable social category and performed no obvious function in her life. Stray, incidental baggage, picked up in the course of foreign holidays or retained from her university days, they appeared to have been chosen on an entirely random basis or to fulfil obscure criteria of which they themselves could hardly have been aware. Jason and Amanda were wholly representative of this tendency, happy to entertain us, but conspicuously baffled by the way Elaine spoke to them and her complete inability to distinguish them from other similar friends met in other and apparently indistinguishable circumstances.

I hit her quite early on in the proceedings, just as the prawn cocktail had given way to the veal escalope ('They're vegetarians, by the way,' Elaine had said in the cab), when she turned to me and said, 'One of the troubles with you, Martin, is that you're such a wimp.'

'Oh, I am, am I?'

'Yes' (meditatively), 'a real wimp. Has anyone ever told you that before, Martin?'

'As a matter of fact, no.'

At this point Jason made some cautious deposition about the food getting cold. I gave him one of my God-isn't-she-a-scream looks. 'Listen,' I said, still keeping it joky, 'if I'm such a wimp, how come I could render you immobile in five seconds flat if I tried to?'

'Go on then. Try.'

It took, as I had suggested, approximately five seconds. Pulling the chair carefully to one side I yanked her to her feet, twisted both arms behind her back and applied a double Nelson.

'Point taken?'

'Point taken.'

Pausing only to note Jason and Amanda's smiles of relief, I relaxed my grip. Next minute I was bent double and retching on the carpet, marvelling simultaneously at the pain and the fact that I'd managed to miss such a carefully signalled express-train knee in the groin.

I hit her after that. Just a single backhander across the face. Nothing you could erect a court case around. We left soon afterwards.

One a.m. Three days after the round of phone calls to the model agencies. Suzi comes slowly awake, eyes blinking furiously in the relentless light. The side of her face is creased from the sheet. I watch her as she shakes her head bewilderedly from side to side, slides over on to her hands and knees and rambles clumsily over the pillows. Naked, there is a squatness about her that I try not to notice.

'Why's the light on?'

'I don't like the dark. Don't like it at all.'

Later, somewhere in the early dawn when there is pale sky lurking outside the window, the phone rings in the hall.

'Martin? Sorry to get you so late.'

'Morty. It's four a.m.'

'Is that so? Well, I'm sorry. Only I had these Americans here and they only just left. They said to say hi.'

Morty's Americans. I remember Morty's Americans from the distant days. I suppose it's good that they still remember me. The line crackles: I hear a siren go by a hundred and twenty miles away.

'. . . Anyway, I asked around like you said. For a start, you can forget about Jim Woodward.'

'I can?'

'You can forget about Jim Woodward because I talked to him last week. He's retired; hasn't made a movie in years. He didn't even remember you.'

I slide a fingernail down that mental check list of suspects.

'What about Frank Rosati?'

'Hey, where've you been? Frank went down to Brighton a year ago with his wife and kid. Last thing I heard he was opening an antique shop.'

'Anyone else?'

'Act your age, Martin. Act it. You know the business. People move on. People pull out. People die. It's all over now. Nobody remembers. Nobody cares.'

For some reason I start crying at this. I don't know why. Perhaps it's something to do with the thought of the look on Elaine's face when I hit her, or the memory of Suzi's coltish smile, that tensed anticipation. I cry silently, staring out into the haggard dawn, the street with its rows of bunched cars, unyielding curtains. After a moment or two I say, 'So who is it, Morty? Nobody remembers. Nobody cares. So who's sending me this stuff? Who's doing this to me?'

A pause. Suddenly I wish I were a hundred miles away, sitting in Morty's office, as in the old days when we returned from a jag and couldn't be bothered to go to bed, talking on into the morning or heading for an early breakfast in the all-night café in Dean Street. Or . . . forget it. Dead. Gone. I look down at the street again and see, of all people, Fat Eric loafing round a gatepost, bent on some mysterious matutinal errand.

'I don't know,' Morty says coldly, 'I just don't know.'

Where have I been? I've been sitting on my backside here in Norfolk for the past two years, that's where I've been. You lose touch. You forget things. At first I tried to maintain some neat, peripheral vantage point on all this. I subscribed to *Adult Video World*. I worked up a few tired scripts. I even had Morty send me copies of his showreels. And from afar I watched the spectacle of Morty picking up and disentangling the cats-cradled threads of his career.

People moved on, pulled out, died. Lila St Claire became a straight actress. Johnny The Wad ended up as a prison warder. Frank Fellatio became a traffic warden. I know because he once tried to give me a parking ticket in Wigmore Street. Parched, resentful faces. I grew used to seeing them in unpropitious circumstances, in underwear catalogues, in furtive pubs south of the river, in another world.

I once asked Morty about his retirement. He became prodigiously animated. 'Retire? Listen, Martin, if there's one thing I can tell you about my retirement it's that it's going to be perfect.'

'Tell me about it. Describe a typical day to me.'

Morty's face creased over. 'You aren't kidding me? Okay, I wake up and I'm in bed with Cindy Lu Win. Or better still, Cindy Lu Win and her daughter. We fool around for an hour or so and then it's breakfast. Fruit juice. Bacon. Eggs . . .'

'*Bacon?*'

'Sure. I'll have dropped all that Orthodox stuff by then. After breakfast I have another session with Cindy Lu Win, only this time she goes on top. Then I get the car to take me to whatever race meeting happens to be on that afternoon. I'll stay to the end of the card. I'll always win.'

'How come?'

Morty was shouting now. 'Because I'll back every horse . . . Back to London – I'll have Cindy Lu Win with me in the car, of course – and tea at my club. White's. The Athenaeum. I'm not fussy. Maybe then a little roulette, or Cindy Lu Win. Depends on how I feel.'

'Won't you ever get bored? Doing all that, I mean.'

'No.' Morty shook his head emphatically. 'I won't get bored. Ever.'

Pornography has its own codes, its own subterfuges, its own way of doing things, its own paradoxes. It is not a matter of revelation but concealment, not of gratification but denial. Morty, in particular, was obsessed by the suggestive nature of his art. 'Tease them,' he would say. 'Tease them right up to the end.' Each of his films followed the path suggested by this maxim: a slow progress of tiny advances and smaller retreats, the construction of vast exotic panoramas which were subtly defused and undermined, the whole easily reinterpreted as a complex ironic device. Students of the Leisurevision *oeuvre* grew used to characteristic tricks, the thumbprints he appended to standard scenarios of window-cleaner, pick-up and virgin bride. A favourite Goldstein stratagem was moving scenery, the incidental effect at first glimpsed from afar, but later usurping the dramatics of the centre stage. A young woman stands undressing before the saloon-bar doors of an opulent shower-room. The doors, animated by some spectral breeze, blow back and forth as she completes her preparations. She is seen, in a split-second collision of frames, first, clad in a towel outside the door, second, naked but partly concealed, from within. On another occasion, at the high point of a film called *Al Fresco Lust*, shot in the New Forest, Morty hired a road digger to traverse slowly across the set as the film's climax was played out. It is an impressive yet confusing finale. In a woodland glade ten yards distant a young couple remove each other's clothes: an alluring spectacle this, the occasional glimpse of breast and buttock, the frequent exhalation of breath, but all the while the viewer is conscious of the momentous distraction moving into vision on the edge of the screen. At first it is simply a matter of noise: the hissing of steam, a grinding of gears, mechanical screeching, but even this, curiously, is enough to distract attention from the mounting frenzy beyond. By the time the digger appears the onlooker is completely absorbed, indifferent to anything but the inch-by-inch progress of this lumbering juggernaut across the clearing. Perhaps three minutes elapse before its hindmost part disappears. The couple lie decorously in each other's arms, spent and exhausted.

Censorship accounted for much of this evasion, but there was a sense in which Morty relished the prohibition of the classification boards and the ukases of the industry watchdogs. They gave him scope, he said, they furnished a framework for the particular conceits he wished to nurture. I asked him once to describe an ideal screenplay. He thought for a moment and said, 'A guy's wandering about at night in this old castle in the woods, through these passageways lit with flaring torches. All the rooms are like cells, barred up, but with spy-holes so you can see what's going on inside. He looks into one of them and sees this girl taking her clothes off, very slowly, button by button. He shouts at her, but she doesn't hear, just goes on taking her clothes off. So he starts breaking down the door. By the time he makes it inside the girl's disappeared. So he walks off down the corridor, looks through another spy-hole and there's the girl again doing the same thing. The door's even more barred up with locks and bolts, but he goes and gets a power drill and busts his way in. No sign of the girl again. And so it goes on: six or seven different rooms. And each time it's more difficult to get in, and each time the girl's coming on stronger, waving her fanny at him and feeling herself. One time she's even got another guy in there with her. And so finally he makes it in there for the last time and what does he find? I'll tell you. He finds an inflatable doll shrivelled up on the floor and hissing away as the air falls out of it.'

The Kafkaesque imagery, the predicament of the hero – baffled, confused, unappeased – were typical. So was the setting, the vistas of stone and firelight, the Rackham-like interior. Morty disliked 'realistic' pornography on aesthetic grounds. I remember in the early Seventies watching with him a hard-core German tape, the first either of us had seen for that matter, bought by Terry Chimes in one of the Beate Uhse shops and smuggled home on the cross-channel ferry. It went on for thirty minutes and consisted simply of a man and a woman in a room on a bed having sex. Morty was scandalised. 'It was just so . . . so fucking boring. I mean, nothing happened, nothing at all. You mean to tell me, Martin, that in Germany there are poor, cabbage-eating, Teutonic fuckers paying money for this?' Morty wanted costume, he wanted spectacle, dark forests, vagrant, scurrying humanity. There was a baroque air to his productions in later days, a deliberate cultivation of artifice. At one point he did indeed make a film very like the imagined screenplay. It was a costume drama called *Codpiece* (ironist though he was, Morty never scrimped on the titles) set in fifteenth-century Sweden and almost obstinate in its refusal to let the hero approach the heroine. Its high point came midway through the second half when, in a tunnel beneath the mountain fortress, two lovers standing five feet apart appraise each other's naked bodies. Moving forward, the hero's foot activates a hidden switch, whereupon a massive iron gate crashes down between them. *Codpiece* did badly at the box office.

And of course it isn't funny. In its broader implications it isn't funny at all. I once saw a film, or perhaps I should say part of a film, in which a woman was beaten with baseball bats. I watched it at the screening room at Dean Street along with Morty and the obscure, wretched acquaintance of Terry Chimes who thought that

Morty might be able to help him distribute it. He was a small, badly shaven man with red eyes and a flat Northern accent. As we watched he apologised nervously for the poor quality of the print – it was in black and white with scratches on the surface, for the absence of a soundtrack. 'Easy dub one on later,' I remember him saying, 'if you like it, that is.' Transfixed by the slow arc that the bats made as they descended, neither of us paid him any attention. It seemed realistic, which is to say, there were bruises where previously there had been only pale unblemished skin, and the choreography was amateurish, with the people who were doing the beating knocking into one another or occasionally stumbling over furniture. There was a terrible moment when the girl, naked now and dragging one leg awkwardly behind her, got as far as the door only to find it locked, a sudden lurch of camera angles suggesting sharp, intrusive movement behind her. We watched for about ten minutes, until Morty said very quietly, 'No. Yeah, turn it off.' The small seedy man stared uncertainly as I flicked the cassette out of the machine and handed it back to him. Morty said, 'Look, there's no market for this stuff, this S&M freakshow stuff. You might sell it abroad. Amsterdam. Berlin. You might sell it there. But not here.' The small man shrugged, unabashed, gathered up his case of tapes – he even had a business card, I remember, which he pressed upon us – and went out.

Later Morty said, 'You think all that happened?'

'What do you think?'

'I don't know . . . Jesus, you can do anything these days with films. I've been on sets in the States where they cut chicks' heads off and ran them over with motorbikes, and then seen them come up smiling in the hospitality lounge half an hour later.'

I remembered the look on the girl's face as she clutched for the door handle. 'You'd have to be a pretty good actress to pretend all that was happening.'

'I don't know, Martin, I just don't know. There's some queer cunts Terry knows, some real filth. *Real* filth. All right, I'd slap a chick around once in a while – who wouldn't? – but I wouldn't have somebody standing behind me with an eight-reel for ten minutes while I was doing it.'

'Neither would I.'

Morty gave me that indulgent, Jewish paterfamilias grin. 'No, you wouldn't, would you? No, of course, you couldn't, could you?'

Here in Norfolk people have their own nomenclatures, their own ways of doing things, their own subterfuges. Fat Eric has names for cars, names dependent on the circumstances, on the value, on the ownership, names finely judged and capable of endless shifts and tergiversations. Waggons. Machines. Grids. Jalopies. Each carries its hint of disparagement or approbation, each, more to the point, depends for its effect on the intonation Fat Eric chooses to give it. 'Like the motor,' he will say with genuine admiration as some turbo-charged Metro passes us on the ring road. Set against this was the occasion when Woody from the City Gates acquired a fifth-hand purple Ford Capri with stripes and a spoiler. 'Like the *motor*,' Fat Eric told him with thinly veiled contempt. With particularly exalted or desperate vehicles his names leave the realm of actual description – registering something in terms of its characteristics and resemblances – and become purely emblematic. A super-charged Bentley to Fat Eric is 'class' ('class coming up on the outside lane . . . class reckons he can overtake us'). Minis and baby Fiats, for some reason, are 'bastards' ('cut up a couple of *bastards* coming down Newmarket Road tonight').

When I came back here I assumed, wrongly, that the Norfolk people had no irony. They would have descriptions for things, I thought, that actually described; they would have words for objects, people, words even for states of mind, that saw these artefacts or conditions for what they were. Above all, I assumed, they would see things without artifice: their reactions would not be filtered through any stream of over-conditioned self-consciousness, but simply emerge out of an authentic perception. It would be the difference, I assumed, between actuality and metaphor. And yet I was wholly in error. To Fat Eric language is a finely honed instrument, a subtle code of communication, awash in barely uncoverable nuance. He has a way, for example, when asked if he is going to do something, or if he has done something, of replying, 'Reckon I will,' or 'Reckon I did.' This is ironic, but it is not simply ironic; it has its own twists and ambiguities, it is not merely the opposite of what is implied. It does not mean, 'I will not do what you have suggested.' It does not even go one stage further and indicate the inadequacy of the question; it does not mean, 'You must be very stupid if you assume I will do what you have suggested.' It admits a relationship. What 'Reckon I will' means, approximately, is, 'Our intimacy is such that you know already that I will not do what you have suggested. Therefore, by suggesting it, you have given me the opportunity of making a joke at my expense – as it discloses my own incapacity – but also at your expense, because it indicates the futility of your asking me to do anything which I do not want to do.' At the same time it is more even than this. It is evidence of a power struggle in which Fat Eric, from the outset, has the upper hand. For asking Fat Eric to do something which you know he will not do, and even, as Kay does and I do, asking it simply in furtherance of an ironic ritual, is to acknowledge your own inferiority in the relationship. It is the relationship which exists between the stand-up comic and his feed: a series of dialogues, fair enough on the surface, which will always end in effortless victory.

Suzi has this characteristic. From time to time in our relationship, people – colleagues from work, wistful men – would telephone her and suggest that she accompany them to cinemas, football matches or restaurants. 'I might do,' Suzi would say, 'I might do.' 'I might do' in this context did not mean 'I might not'. It meant 'I am in charge here.' It meant 'By making this request you have placed yourself in a position of extreme vulnerability. I may choose to do what you request, on my terms and in accordance with my stipulations, in which case you will have allowed yourself to become a victim of my condescension, or I may choose not to do it, in which case my indifference will render you foolish and resentful.' A less subtle thraldom, perhaps, than that practised by Fat Eric, but no less powerful.

When I came back here I assumed, again wrongly, that I would find directness, a way of life that was unfeigned, a manner of doing things that was in some way authentic. Instead I found Suzi and Fat Eric, with their evasions and their unwritten charters of superiority. I found the Norwich shop assistants who, if you miscount the money you hand to them, say, 'Whatever are you like?' which means, paradoxically, 'I know exactly what you are like.' I came looking for what I conceived of as real life, for some definitive gaze on these shifting landscapes, and found only subterfuge, illusion, a persistent refusal to be drawn. Like some soldier, the veteran of months of jungle warfare, who moves on gratefully to open country, I had discovered only the same camouflage, the same bunkers concealed beneath fronds of ersatz foliage, the same howitzers grouped menacingly together behind unbending, painted trees.

If there was one cinematic technique which Morty distrusted above all others it was realism. The commodity in which he dealt was, as I have indicated, in his eyes the least straightforward of functions. To have reduced it to an elemental basis – the man, the woman, the bed – would have been to him a betrayal of the imaginative faculty. This assumption – that one needed trappings, incidentals, continual embroidery – had deep roots. He was, for example, one of the few people I have met who found the sexual act, or at any rate its depiction on film, uninteresting. Sex to Morty figured as a slightly unappetising and somewhat frugal meal, requiring endless titivation and decoration to render it palatable. To film it he needed above all room for manoeuvre, ideally some greater knowledge that he could spring on an unsuspecting cast. A typical Goldstein trick was to impose some extra dimension on to the filming of a screenplay, some unthought-of contingency to which the actors themselves had not been made party. In the late Seventies, for example, I was present at the filming of *Mayfair Orgy*, a project which represented the high point of this approach. The plot was straightforward – suspiciously so for anyone acquainted with Morty's techniques – involving no more than the convening of a group of libertines at a mews house in Berkeley Square (specially rented for the purpose). Halfway through the proceedings the sound of sirens could be heard in the street outside, to be followed a few moments later by the breaking down of the door and a full-scale police raid, its conclusion the herding of the cast, most of them half-clad or draped in blankets, into waiting vans. Only I, Morty and the cameraman knew that the dozen or so policemen were in fact extras, hired from a theatrical agency which specialised in such deceptions. It was perhaps Morty's finest hour. To the sound of police whistles, amid rapid, obtrusive movement, as terrified actors fled hastily to places of concealment, he continued to film. The result is an impressive piece of verisimilitude: moments of genuine antagonism, the camera occasionally dislodged to provide unexpected angles, a final shot of abject terror on the face of Cindy Lu Win as she is led away protesting. Several of the actors refused to work for Morty again, yet he remained triumphant. He had created something novel, he thought, something splendid and coherent from the unpromising chaos around him. When I protested that his creation was realistic – actual surprise, authentic terror – he disagreed. To Morty one level of unreality had been strengthened by a second. The emotion might have been genuine, but the circumstance trailed gossamer threads of fancy and that, for him, was enough.

For a brief period Morty caught the spirit of the times. The pornography of the late Seventies cultivated an attachment to fantasy. It was the time of the *Emmanuelle* films, of which Morty made several low-budget spin-offs, the time of *Mitteleuropa* costume dramas, of erotic parodies of the famous and innocuous. Leisurevision's adult versions of *The Sound of Music*, featuring a nymphomaniac Julie Andrews lookalike, and *Chitty Chitty Bang Bang* date from around this time. He shot desert epics, sex dramas acted out on Swiss ski-slopes, spoof Westerns: lavish productions with extensive casts. Later on, when the chill, elemental winds blew in from the Continent, he was dismayed. You could buy German sex videos on the underground market by the late Seventies, Swedish sex soap-operas, gory works of realism in which grim Scandinavian businessmen could be seen paying energetic court to their secretaries before proceeding homeward to perform the same efficient service for their wives. It should be said, in his defence, that Morty's distress was genuine. He was appalled not by the crudity, by the tendon-grinding close-ups, but by the underlying assumption, the thought that the pattern of everyday life, however highly charged the sexual atmosphere, should be considered a fit subject for cinema. 'Real life,' he used to say around 1980, 1981, whenever some foreign salesman caught him unawares, 'real life is for people with no imagination.'

* * *

The fat girl was generic. There were other figures that I remembered from the Norwich past, specific figures, framed in their own peculiar landscapes. There was, for example, the man with the dog. At a remove of twenty years I cannot recall precisely when it was that the man with the dog first strayed into my consciousness, but it must have been sometime in the mid-1960s. Certainly by 1967 or 1968 he was as fixed and immovable a part of the local terrain as the Carrow ironworks or the lofty tessellations of the City Hall. As a fixture on the Norwich streets the man with the dog was not unique. There were others like him, other faces with whom one became familiar – flustered women in mackintoshes, broods of noisy children – but somehow they lacked the man with the dog's staying power, his regularity, his range, fell away until they became vague attendants in a tableau where the central part had already been cast: it was the man with the dog who rose above them, who, by means of his continual presence, confirmed the narrower patterns of their lives. At the time I was scarcely conscious of the fascination which he exercised. It was only later, when I left Norwich, that I realised how central he had become to any re-creation of these fading landscapes, how consistently he emerged to inhabit the memories of familiar streets and parklands. This role was all the more puzzling in that I could remember nothing concrete about him – what he wore, what, specifically, he looked like – only the fact of his presence. It was, I supposed, simply that he was always there, marginal but unshakeable from the corners of this mental picture, down there on the edge of things, inviolable.

The man with the dog had the advantage of longevity. But there were other characters, less prominent perhaps, but capable of exercising an equally potent spell. Chief among these was the man with the shoes. The man with the shoes first appeared in the Christchurch Road area of Norwich in perhaps early 1968. Whereas I recall nothing about the man with the dog other than the fact that he was there, I remember the man with the shoes precisely. He was young, a year or two into his twenties, with tousled hair and a put-upon expression, and with a fat woman whom we supposed to be his wife, and with his shoes he began to walk past our house on perhaps three or four afternoons a week. I often speculated about those shoes: stack-heeled boots in vivid colours, a pair of scarlet sports bootees with grandiloquent, guttering laces. Where did he buy them, I wondered? What shop or salesman had been prepared to sell them to him? The highlight of his wardrobe, a sight so incongruous that it would bring my father hurrying joyfully to the window, was a pair of curving, canary-yellow moccasins. The effect was as if the man with the shoes had acquired two outsize bananas, hollowed out a portion of the pulp and simply placed his feet in the gaps.

The man with the dog. The man with the shoes. Even when I left the city in 1969 I had managed in a small way to keep up with them, to maintain some hold on their remorseless trajectories. My father referred to them in his letters. Then, on my visits home, I would assure myself of a sighting or two: the man with the dog seen late on a winter's afternoon crossing the westernmost corner of Eaton Park, the man with the shoes prancing once again at breakneck speed past the house. Each survived deep into the 1970s. I saw the man with the dog as late as 1975 on the corner where Christchurch Road meets The Avenues, and as the car taking me to my father's funeral moved away from the house the first person whom we met was the man with the shoes. Each, I thought, was immortal. And yet coming back to Norwich in the early 1980s I discovered that neither had survived my departure. They had gone, disappeared, and I had returned to a city devoid of human landmarks.

Of the two it was the man with the dog whose absence I most regretted, so much so that in time I began to haunt parts of Norwich where I thought I might encounter him: by the river near Earlham, out in the Cringleford marshes, nearer at hand down the long sweep of the Newmarket Road. It was no use. I never found him. But even then the suspicion lingered in my mind that he was still there, that his absence was merely a puzzle deliberately imposed upon me, wanting only my own ingenuity to solve it. For this reason, even until quite late on, when all reasonable hope had passed, I walked the Norwich streets with the hope, the very faint hope, that here in the dogleg leading across from Meadow Rise to Colman Road, there at the point where Earlham Park meets the university, I might find him, that this vital piece of the jigsaw might be restored.

And then, nearly a year after I returned, I did find something: something only marginally connected to the man with the dog, but enough to convince me of the folly of my search. In the centre of Norwich, a good mile or so out of his natural orbit, I met the man with the shoes. It was early in the morning, raw and damp, and he stood in the doorway of a supermarket with the collar of his jacket hunched up to his chin. Though I had not seen him for six or seven years it was unquestionably the same man: the same tousled hair, the same half-nervous, half-insouciant look. He even gave me a faint quarter-glance of recognition, the scintilla of a nod, as if he remembered me, but could not quite locate me in his own mental landscape. And yet, staring at his feet, at the white baseball boots, mildly outlandish, certainly, but in no way as bizarre as the stacked heels or the platform soles of long ago, I realised that he was no longer the man with the shoes, but simply an ordinary middle-aged man glimpsed in a shop doorway. Like the man with the dog he had lost his glamour, the one through absence, the other through removal of that single defining quality. Like the Gaumont Cinema or the old thoroughfares of London Street, each had either disappeared or been changed out of recognition by the intervening years, and I had sought refuge in a past that no longer existed.

In the late Seventies Morty got ambitious. It was a gradual process, so gradual that medium-term associates like myself and Terry Chimes scarcely noticed, a process made manifest in tiny changes to routine and procedure. Crazy Rodney, who had once had the unhappy privilege of delivering Morty to his meetings in a superannuated post-office van, was given a chauffeur's uniform and a Lagonda. Morty's accountant, who had worked first above and latterly in a pub in Maddox Street, was dismissed in favour of a Big Eight firm in the City. Stray touches, minor adjustments to the smooth trajectory of Morty's career. There was one lawyer who vetted the magazines and films Morty put out on the legal market and another lawyer who advised him unofficially what he could get away with in the illegal trade. The primitive distribution system – Crazy Rodney and the van – was replaced by a svelte firm in Twickenham. A little later I began to wear suits to meetings and was referred to as 'our creative director'.

Cautious, watchful, but ambitious. By 1975 Morty had a stockbroker. A year later he had finessed an entrée into one of the City livery companies – it might have been the Worshipful Company of Dyers – and was parcelling the money together for an American distribution deal. Slowly, subtly, imperceptibly there emerged a new resplendence to Morty's operations, an annual sheaf of pointers to these shifting horizons and beckoning goals. It was at about this time that he began to place what were for Morty crazily unprecedented sums of money on horses with fanciful Jewish names that were brought out for weekly humiliation at minor race-courses in the north of England. It became an engrossing daily ritual: the flustered exit from a shoot in one of the warehouses down by the river at Bow or Poplar, the scurry through the mist, the late-afternoon phone call to the on-course correspondent at Doncaster, Towcester, York, the unfailing intelligence that Solomon's Fancy or Star of David had fallen at the third or thrown its rider at the seventh, emerging with Morty into the pale autumn light of the East End to hunt for a pub. Matters came to a head when a horse named Samson's Delight, on which Morty had staked a thousand pounds at 13–1, failed to emerge from its stall in the Cesarewitch and was summarily disqualified. 'It dies, Martin,' Morty told me subsequently. 'For that it just fucking dies.' I hadn't realised that he'd owned it. Neither, it transpired, had anyone else.

The secrecy was characteristic. Not overtly clandestine, it proceeded out of Morty's conviction that you kept the various parts of your life in individual compartments. Only later when the journalists got to work did anyone realise just what Morty was up to in the 1970s, how truly circumspect he was, the types of people he hung around with. The people Morty hung around with had names like Bald Ernie and Terry the Blade, had pale, mad eyes and wore suits that were twenty years out of date. Morty knew them from way back, back from the old Bethnal days. I was once clambering up the stairs to the loft at Dean Street when an unassuming man in a brown suit, the sort of man you see sitting on his own in the corner of a pub nursing a half-pint glass, ambled by.

'That was Charlie,' Morty said, shuffling the papers on his desk intently. 'Haven't seen him for a while.'

'Charlie?'

'Charlie Scaduto.'

Charlie Scaduto. Mad Jimmy Parsons. The Major. Morty knew them all. Morty's ambition? It was, it is fair to say, colossal. It was unrelenting. It hovered high above the slot-machine arcades and the bookshops that he bought his way into in '76, '77, the desolate frontages in Greek Street and Brewer; underpinned the criminally favourable deals he did with the Maltese club owners and the nervous two-man printing outfits in Commercial Road. It embraced plans for floating Leisurevision on the unlisted securities market. More narrowly it brooked no opposition. By the late 1970s you didn't mess about with Morty Goldstein, you just didn't. A series of less than trustworthy associates limped off into penurious retirement. A bookshop proprietor in Frith Street sustained a fractured skull. Did Morty do that? I don't know. I know only that he bought the lease when it came up for sale a fortnight later.

Trammelled by law, weakened perhaps by the disadvantages of background and profession, Morty's ambition was capable of fitting into more conventional patterns. Respectability, held at bay by the bread-and-butter necessities, by the films, the magazines and the escort service in Nottingham Place, was never far distant from his more grandiose schemes. Morty's business cards, updated every year, now in embossed black type, then with *Mortimer J. Goldstein* engraved in trellises of gold leaf, underpinned this sense of continuous refinement. In the mid-Seventies the inscription ran simply 'MORTY: MAGAZINES AND FILMS' and the telephone number belonged to Morty's solicitor. A year later it was '*Mortimer J. Goldstein FCA & Associates Printing Consultants*'. By 1978 it was 'Leisurevision', an actual company with paid-up share capital and a tame peer who owed Morty money sitting on the board, and one of its subsidiaries made up the plates for the *Radio Times*. That was how far Morty had progressed by the late 1970s. There was, to be sure, the comic paraphernalia – the grim vans full of pallets of *Bouncers* and *Upfront*, the swivel-eyed gentlemen on the pavement in Meard Street ready to inveigle you down the tapering steps – but the accountants were Messrs Saffery Champness of Gutter Lane and the fixed assets included two drinking clubs and a wholly legitimate warehousing business in Deal.

And what about Morty? Morty didn't change. Morty sat tight. Morty burrowed on relentlessly through these dense, populous years, an intense, guttering light, never wholly extinguished, always capable of flaring dramatically upward. Often towards the end of the Seventies he was abroad: in America with Terry Chimes, in Europe where he had connections with one of the big German porn houses. Returned to London he grew restless, dissatisfied, a sullen figure decanted from a taxi to complain about airport delays or roadside litter. 'What this country needs, Martin, is a good shaking up,' he said once or twice on these occasions, an ominous remark, forgotten at the time, but remembered in the light of what came later. Abroad had a galvanising effect on Morty: most of his foreign excursions were followed by some unrelated business coup, some gross extension of his sphere of influence. Early in 1979, recalled from Hamburg to an England of piled snowdrifts and industrial unrest, he unveiled his most ambitious scheme to date.

Morty's office in Dean Street. Outside thin rain was falling over the grey rooftops. In the aftermath of a power cut the lights had fused: from the studio beyond the doorway electricians murmured softly to one another. Morty said, 'I didn't think things were this bad. You should have rung me up and told me.'

'We didn't know where you were.'

There were galley proofs lying on the desk in untidy coils, the first fruits of a plan to produce an intimate-contact magazine. Morty flicked through them unhappily for a moment and then held one up a foot or so in front of his face.

'Adult male, 42, well-built, seeks afternoon playmates . . . Do you think this stuff is going to sell?'

'Circulation thinks it will. There's a big order from the Midlands.'

Above Morty's head a lightbulb fizzed for a moment and then went dead. He frowned at the greying sheets again and went on, 'It's all right, Martin, I'm not getting at you. It's just . . . Do you realise this morning the power went halfway through a shoot? There're three actresses sitting down there wrapped in blankets freezing themselves to death. Scazz left in a taxi half an hour ago. He says he won't come back unless I can lay on heating. What am I supposed to do about that?'

Dressed in a fur coat, thinning hair brushed low over the front of his head, Morty looked more than usually depressed. He said, 'You know, Martin, would it surprise you to know that I was thinking of going into politics?'

I had grown used to these bizarre revelations. There was a fantastic side to Morty's make-up composed entirely of ungovernable whims. Periodically there emerged the idea that he should start a national newspaper, or buy a football club. Nothing ever came of them. I shook my head.

'What sort of politics?'

Outside the tempo of the rain had increased. Morty picked up a copy of a model directory that was lying on the corner of the desk and began to leaf through it. He said evasively, 'These girls ought to be more truthful. It says here that Candy Ingrams is twenty-four and has starred in several full-length feature films. Now, I know for a fact that she's thirty-one.'

'Do you want me to go and see how the actresses are?'

'She was in those black and white shorts that Frank Rosati used to make and that was ten years ago. No,' Morty said decisively. 'I want you to stay and listen to me. Seriously, Martin, I'm thinking of going into politics. Proper politics. Not pissing around on some town council with a lot of old women in twin-sets. The real thing.'

'The real thing?'

'Sure. All right, Martin, I admit that I may not give the impression of being a serious person. I can see that. But I've been doing a lot of thinking about the way this country gets run. A lot of serious thinking. On the plane coming back from Hamburg I . . . Jesus, Martin, that fucking Labour Party. I mean, do you know there are people dying out there because the ambulances won't take them to hospital? And when some ambulance-man stops playing cards long enough to take them to casualty, ten to one a goon turns up with a placard and tells him to go away again.'

'It's a disgrace, certainly.'

'*Exactly*. A disgrace is exactly what it is. And you know, Martin, it breaks my heart to say this because, well, I don't know if I've told you this before but my father used to be big in the local Labour Party. In fact, you know the Goldstein Daycentre off Bethnal Green Road? Well, it was my father that raised the money. They had Aneurin Bevan down for the opening ceremony. And, well, it breaks my heart to see the fucking *Labour* Party responsible for all this.'

In fact I knew about Morty's dad from Crazy Rodney, whose own father was an embittered veteran of the Bethnal Green Labour Party. A colourful grocer with premises off the Bow Road, Councillor Goldstein had gone down before one of the great town hall corruption scandals of the late 1950s, when he was found to be supplying all eight local old people's homes under a complex system of aliases. A little later his chairmanship of the local schools board had coincided with all six Goldstein progeny passing the 11-Plus. I knew all about Councillor Goldstein.

'. . . Anyway,' Morty went on, 'I've been talking to one or two business contacts – you know, Charlie Scaduto and Bald Ernie – and they've convinced me that I ought to stand.'

Unbelievably he was serious. He was, I later discovered, so serious that all previous undertakings became invested with the retrospective taint of lightmindedness. In fact, investigation revealed that the plan to become a Conservative MP was already well in hand, attended with all Morty's characteristic foresight and attention to detail. At the time Trotskyist entryism into the Labour Party was a subject much in vogue for newspaper exposés. Morty's takeover of his chosen constituency would have done credit to the wiliest revolutionary cadre. The moribund Conservative association in the carefully selected East End seat – Labour majority 14,000 – stood scant chance. Within a month of Morty's decision to take over the seat – this was late 1978 – membership mysteriously doubled. Within three months Morty had Charlie Scaduto, a horrifying figure who sold secondhand TV sets somewhere in Forest Gate, installed as party chairman. Crazy Rodney, voted in as constituency secretary at an extraordinary general meeting attended by nineteen of Charlie Scaduto's drinking companions and eleven appalled members of the local bourgeoisie, helped by throwing the filing cabinet containing the membership lists into the Thames.

Inevitably there were problems. Chief among these was the prior existence of a prospective parliamentary candidate, a motherly woman who sat on Newham Council. Charlie Scaduto cultivated her assiduously in the bar of the constituency association headquarters after meetings. I record an early dialogue.

'The problem about the Labour Party, right, is that they're a *load of fuckers.*'

'Well, I . . .'

'A load of fuckers. Take my business, right? Two years I've been trying to extend down the street, put in a showroom with a couple of neon signs, something tasteful. Can I get planning permission? No. And all because the fucking Paki in the sweetshop over the road keeps complaining.'

'It does seem a little unfair . . .'

'*Unfair?* One of these days I'm going to get hold of Mr fucking

Aroni, Mr fucking Aroni with his fucking *turban*, and jam one of his sticks of fucking London rock right up his . . .'

The prospective parliamentary candidate's resignation, for reasons which she would sooner not disclose, having arrived fortuitously at Conservative Central Office on the day before the fall of the Callaghan government, the field was clear. Morty won the hastily convened selection conference at a canter.

There were some other problems. Most obviously there was the question of what Morty did for a living. At first he featured in the local press as 'businessman Mortimer Goldstein'. A little later he was being referred to as 'businessman Mortimer Goldstein with his interests in the adult entertainment market'. Two weeks into the campaign the *Daily Mirror* ran a story headed 'PORN KING'S BID FOR PARLIAMENT'. Then there was Charlie Scaduto and what he did for a living. Charlie Scaduto specialised in long-firm companies, an auspicious piece of fraudulence popularised by the Krays. The theory is time-honoured. You buy up some likely-looking high-street site, stock it with a shelf-full of pricey electrical goods (all legitimately acquired from suppliers) and put in a manager to run it. The manager signs the cheques and deals with the suppliers, and nobody knows you exist. For the first six months you administer the shop like an ordinary business. Every week or so you place an order with the suppliers (you deal with lots of different suppliers) and you pay them on the nail. The manager ingratiates himself with the local bank, talks plausibly about expansion and cashflow, and negotiates a loan. Finally you send in a large order to all your suppliers, take delivery of piles of stock and preside over a grand sale at knockdown prices. The manager disappears to Switzerland with a percentage and the suppliers, when they come to investigate, find only a boarded-up shopfront concealing a pile of mildewed invoices. This is the theory. Charlie Scaduto's practice of it, characterised by meanness and the tendency of his stooges to relocate in places like Upminster, ran sadly adrift. Barely had Morty got his libel writ in at the *Mirror* than Charlie Scaduto appeared on the front page of the *Star* under the caption 'TORY CHIEF IN ELECTRICS SWINDLE'.

In the teeth of these difficulties Morty fought a lively campaign, finely attuned to the locale and its traditions. He had himself photographed eating whelks in the Bow Road. He went to his public meetings in a brewer's dray attended by Pearly Kings. When the local Labour Party headquarters got firebombed – the publicity happily obscuring the simultaneous arrest of Charlie Scaduto – he sent a widely quoted message of sympathy. Bright, tense days; in commotion. Once or twice I went canvassing with him down in the dark tenements of the East End. At night, trawling the gloomy corridors of the towerblocks in Rotherhithe, negotiating the urinous staircases, monitoring the thump of hectic jungle jive, Morty became an uncertain, deracinated figure, someone out of his milieu, out of his time, out of his mind. We took Crazy Rodney with us on these occasions, Crazy Rodney with a baseball bat stuffed inside his jacket: Morty had no illusions about canvassing in the East End. The mission accomplished, the fruitless hammering on the doors of silent, terrified pensioners, the confrontations with sullen black youths having duly taken place, back in the Lagonda cruising through the dead streets, he grew reflective.

'You know something, Martin? You know something? We've failed these people. All of us. You. Me. All of us. We've failed them.'

'We have?'

'Sure. People have dreams. They want things. They have a *right* to want things. And what happens? People let them down. Society lets them down.'

'It does.'

'I won't let them down, Martin. I promise you that. I won't let them down.'

He lost by 10,000 votes. Back at the loft in Dean Street, as the faces thronged around a television blaring election results, Morty got drunk on the champagne purchased in anticipation of his victory. Rocking unsteadily on splayed feet, plump, knuckleless hands clamped round the endlessly fisted glasses, he looked alone, vulnerable, purposeless. It was then, perhaps, that I realised Morty's chronic unsuitability to his environment, his apparent inability to perform the exacting role in which he had cast himself. Whereas other actors in this noisy drama played their parts with conviction – Terry Chimes with his pantomime leer, Crazy Rodney's guard-dog eyes – the impresario, the actor-manager for whose delight the play had been convened, seemed sadly ill at ease.

It was a salient defeat. Years later I came across the election result in an old Whitaker's Almanack, but the twinge of recognition was unconvincing. Reinvented, unpicked and restitched in stronger, brighter colours, the fabric of Morty's past could not accommodate these frail outlines.

A week now from the last chat with Morty. Early in the evening there is a mild diversion when Kev Jackson telephones. Kev Jackson: quite a well-known name these days, at any rate in the rarefied circles in which I once moved. Thirty-one or thirty-two, but a ten-year veteran of the industry, the first staff reporter on *Adult Video World* and in this capacity escorted by a deferential Morty Goldstein around many a crowded Leisurevision set and through many a thronged Dean Street cutting room. At this time Kev's interviewing style was that of the respectful ingénue.

'Basically, Kev,' Morty would say, propelling him into the armchair and proffering the half litre of brandy, 'I see *Plasma Party* as the first attempt to bring American hard-core slash to British screens in a form acceptable to the British censor.' 'Basically,' Kev's report would begin a week later, 'top UK director Morty Goldstein sees *Plasma Party* as the first attempt to bring American hard-core slash to British screens in a form acceptable to the British censor.' Such reliability was comforting to Morty in a world characterised by fickle friendships and savaged reputations. 'That Kev Jackson,' he would say, 'that Kev Jackson, he's *all right*.' Later when he moved to Los Angeles as *Adult Video World*'s resident stringer, returning subsequently to work as a showbiz reporter on one of the London dailies, the connection was sustained. I haven't seen him in three years.

'Martin. Kev Jackson. How are you?'

'I'm fine, Kev. What can I do for you?'

In fact I know exactly what it is that I can do for Kev Jackson, Kev having told me copiously on each of the two previous occasions on which he telephoned. However, as old comrades-in-arms we eschew this sort of directness.

'I saw Terry Chimes the other day, Martin. He said to say hi.'

'Terry Chimes,' I say. 'What about that? Say hi from me as well next time you see him.'

'Sure ... Look, I'll get to the point, Martin. I need to know if you'll help me with the project.'

'The project ... Look just run that one in front of me again, would you, Kev?'

Kev Jackson's project. The news that Kev Jackson, hitherto considered barely able to hold a pen and to subsist merely by transcribing the press releases sent to him by eager publicists, was writing a book had sent a steely dart winging into the carapace of the adult film world. Even Morty had condescended to telephone me late one night and tell me about it.

'That Kev Jackson,' he had explained. 'Yes, well the word is he's pulling some exposé stunt. "My life in the skin trade", that sort of thing. Some Sunday supplement did a piece on him last week. I wouldn't worry about it, but I thought you ought to know.'

'Who's talking to him?'

'Beats me. *I'm* not talking to him. Terry isn't talking to him. Nobody's talking to him. Somebody told me he flew over to see Scazz Fogelburg though.'

'What did Scazz say?'

'Scazz drove him back to the airport – you know those fancy cars Scazz has – and told him if he ever saw him again he'd kill him.'

'That won't look very good in the book.'

'Aw, Scazz was only joking. You know Scazz. Anyway, like I said, I shouldn't worry about it, but I thought you ought to know.'

Now I listen again as Kev Jackson goes through his list of valiant objectives. 'Basically, Martin, what I have in mind is a serious study – I should say that the *Observer* have already expressed an interest in the serial rights – something that will set the industry in context, reopen the censorship debate, examine, you know, the human consequences of it all.'

'That sounds good, Kev. Could I ask who you're talking to?'

An ominous question. There is a pause down the line. I can imagine Kev Jackson, hunched over the phone in his cramped writer's flat somewhere in London, wondering how much to tell me, wondering in fact if this is a suitable enterprise for Kev Jackson to have involved himself in in the first place.

'You'd be surprised, Martin. For instance, I've recorded interviews with Sheri La Grange and Corona d'Amour.'

Starlets, both of them. Worse, ageing starlets. Sheri La Grange, the younger of the two, hadn't worked since 1976 to the best of my recollection. Corona d'Amour might have appeared in three photomontages in as many years. Collectively useless.

'On the business side I've talked to Ernie Mackay and Rufus Stokes.'

Dim, know-nothing wholesalers in the north of England. No trouble there.

Another pause down the line. I am visited by the sudden, pleasing sensation that Kev Jackson, haughty Kev Jackson with his leather jacket and his sideboards, is waiting for me to respond.

'Well, with that sort of help, Kev, I can't see you needing any assistance from me.'

'Listen, Martin,' Kev Jackson sounds mildly distraught now. 'I'll be frank with you. I got a ten-thousand-pound advance for this – I don't know how much you know about publishing, but take it from me that's a lot of money. That was six months ago. Since then I've got a dozen sides of notes and taped three interviews with people Morty Goldstein might have slept with in 1970. No one's talking. Morty won't talk. Terry Chimes won't. That psycho who used to drive the van . . .'

'Crazy Rodney.'

'Crazy Rodney. He won't talk. I spent a thousand pounds going out to see Scazz Fogelburg.'

'What did Scazz say?'

'He said if he ever saw me again he'd kill me.'

'He was only joking. You know Scazz.'

'Listen, Martin. You have to give me a break. Talk to me, please. No names, no dates if you like, just talk to me. I won't mention you as a source and I won't tell anyone else you spoke to me. I promise.'

'Why me, Kev?'

'Christ, Martin. You spent eight, nine years working with Morty Goldstein. That's longer than Terry Chimes, longer than anyone. Right from the start. *Capital Pick-up*, *On Heat*. Right the way through you're down on the credits. Writer. Sound man. Executive producer. If I'm going to finish this, you have to give me a break.'

It strikes me that I need to think about this. I need time to balance the manifest disadvantages (Morty finding out) with the definite benefits such an association with Kev Jackson would confer. Outside there are raised voices in the street, the squeal of car brakes. Lights flick on and off.

'Look, Kev,' I say, 'it's seven o'clock. Ring me back in a couple of hours when I've had time to think about it and we'll see.'

'Tomorrow if you like.'

'No, nine o'clock and we'll see.'

'Okay, okay.' He is chirpy now, chirpy and deferential. 'Hey. You remember the last time we met? Back in Suffolk, early '81?'

'No,' I tell him, making sure it's the last thing I say before I put down the phone. 'I don't remember.'

Subsequently a more major diversion, its outlines emerging rapidly from the closing moments of the conversation with Kev Jackson, rises up to claim my attention, as outside the window, enacted in a queer slow-motion manner reminiscent of primordial cinema, a genuine domestic drama is noisily and patiently unravelled.

Drenched as it is in bar-table bonhomie, roadside conversation and late-evening confidence, the neighbourhood harbours several continuing domestic dramas, each of them exposed, discussed and monitored by a circle of avid observers. This is live soap-opera, its allure markedly more concrete than the nightly stake-out around the television set, in which my chief informant is Fat Eric. It is Fat Eric who keeps me up to the minute on these single-parent tragedies, these child-batterings, these chronicles of intrigue and violence, whose conclusions appear so tardily in the columns of the *Eastern Evening News*. 'Those two kids at Number 16 got put on remand,' he will say as he loiters into the City Gates of an evening, or 'Little Angie at Number 27's up the spout again, so her dad told me.' Divorces, pilfered virginities, minor rumbles – these are the street's stock-in-trade, a bush telegraph transmitting widely and effectually at the smallest provocation.

Lately our attention – my attention, Fat Eric's, the attention, in fact, of people residing several streets away – has been largely focused on the Ferguson family seven doors down on the other side of the road. In a world of stylised humanity, the fat fathers with their six-packs, the tired housewives proceeding in Indian file to Friday-night bingo at the Norwich Mecca Rooms, the Fergusons are giant, comic-book caricatures: Mrs, occasionally encountered in the grocer's, a mass of stunning and unsatisfied female flesh; Mr, a harassed, sat-upon taxi driver; each astounded and embarrassed by a brood of delinquent children. Mrs Ferguson's paramours were legion, so numerous for it to be safely assumed that Mr Ferguson no longer cared, no longer troubled himself about the file of hulking labourers, the besuited salesmen, the easy despoilers of his marital bed. Certainly it must be owned that Mrs Ferguson sometimes looked a little strained, a little more *distraite* in her afternoon saunter from shop to bus-stop to compromised hearth, that Mr Ferguson's pained self-absorption knew no bounds, that his cheerfulness, when encountered in pub or by roadside, became almost tragic, that he grew nearly desperate in his chatter about football, or the vagaries of the city council hackney-carriage licensing department, but bless you, these were queer people, queer people indeed, and Mr Ferguson's return home at this unexpected hour in these unexpected circumstances was the queerest thing of all.

Objects. Movement. Sound. Black taxi-cab slewing to a halt at right-angles across the street. Slam of car doors. Mr Ferguson, a grim, remorseless figure, seen in hurried transit from driver's seat to front door. A loud hammering. Lights flicked on, then off. A sash opening at an upstairs window, a head staring out and then withdrawn. More hammering. A silence which Mr Ferguson abets by stumbling back from the door and then extinguishes by seizing a flower pot from an adjacent hedge and hurling it through the glass of his own vestibule. Then a sudden issue of figures out of the gaping doorway: Mrs Ferguson, hair tumbling down her back, arms upraised in supplication; a pale, middle-aged man, shoeless, in shirt sleeves and carrying, incongruously, a briefcase, who trips over the raised step and sprawls for a moment on the concrete with his limbs beating in several directions. Shouting: Mr Ferguson, Mrs Ferguson, the middle-aged man. Then a complicated game of hide-and-seek: the middle-aged man crawling to a refuge beneath the meagre hedge while Mr and Mrs Ferguson bicker, being found and chivvied out again by Mr Ferguson into the doorway; Mrs Ferguson skipping nimbly out into the street, where she flutters anxiously beside the taxi before being dragged back by the hair.

More shouting: the middle-aged man, Mrs Ferguson, Mr Ferguson. A grey cat, which has sat until now on the gatepost of a neighbouring house observing the proceedings, streaking fearfully off into distant gardens and alleyways. A sudden flight of all three parties back through the open door, a vicious slamming of the door behind them, a certain amount of interior scuffling, and then silence. The black taxi lies drunkenly across the pavement. A few people come and stare over the hedge, where all that remains is the briefcase discarded by the middle-aged man and a fragment torn from Mrs Ferguson's dressing gown. The grey cat prowls carefully back and resumes its position atop the gatepost. Within, the house is dead and quiet, the light still shining from an upstairs room.

Later, as the dusk extends over the slate rooftops, as the groups of children assembled on the pavement fragment and melt away into the dark, as the streetlamps go on and curtains slither into place, I go out to the front gate and smoke a cigarette. Fat Eric lumbers by in a tracksuit and scuffed trainers, pauses, catches the second cigarette in his giant paw, lights up.

'Out jogging, Fat Eric?'

'Doing it for my health, aren't I? That keep-fit lark, isn't it?' says Fat Eric contemptuously. He hunkers down on his knees for a moment, chest heaving, hawks into the gutter. 'You hear about them Fergusons, then?'

'There was a lot of noise. Earlier on.'

'That's right. A lot of noise. Never heard anything like it. *Fuck* of a lot of noise. Kay reckoned I ought to go and do something about it. Didn't reckon on that though.'

'Why not?'

'Domestic disputes,' says Fat Eric grandly. 'Not a good idea, sticking your nose into domestic disputes. Bad news they are. Know what happened? Someone tipped old man Ferguson the nod that he might learn something to his advantage if he comes home early. What's he find? Old woman in bed with that little bloke the council send round to see people about home improvements.'

'What did he do?'

'Ferguson? Kicked him around a bit. I mean, who wouldn't? A week in hospital, I mean he's fucking lucky really, isn't he? Old Ferguson being soft the way he is. After all,' says Fat Eric with surprising seriousness, 'it's something you can't ignore, isn't it? I mean, a couple of months ago we was in this pub over West Earlham way and this bloke starts giving Kay the eye, offering her drinks and that. Some cunt in a suit. Some rich cunt.'

'What did you do?'

'Punched him in the throat,' says Fat Eric. 'Told him it was lucky for him I wasn't a violent man. But you can't, you can't ignore something like that, can you?'

'You're right, Fat Eric,' I tell him. 'You're right. It's just something you can't ignore.'

Back inside the phone rings. I let it ring seven or eight times, then pick it up.

'Martin. Kev Jackson. Did you have a chance to think things over?'

'Maybe, Kev. Maybe.'

'Come on, Martin. Don't play games with me. A couple of conversations, that's all it would take. I'll even come down and see you if you want . . .'

Obscurely there is fear in this, the hint of a threat.

'Kev. You remember a girl called Elaine?'

'Elaine? Was she the one in *Shameless*? The one who gets out of the pool and . . .'

'That was Elaine Le Brun. Elaine Keenan. You must remember her.'

'Got it. Tall girl with dark hair. With Frank Fellatio in *Girlschool Janitor*. Supporting roles in *Obsession*, *Heartburn* . . . You think she could tell me anything about Morty Goldstein? You think I ought to talk to her?'

'I think you ought to find her.'

Encouraged by Kev Jackson's eager silence, I explain the plan. He finds me Elaine, where she is, what she does, who she's with. I tell him whatever he wants to know about Morty Goldstein, Terry Chimes, about Leisurevision, about the millions of feet of shiny celluloid, about the glossy secrets of the cutting-room floor. Anything he wants.

'Okay, I'll buy it,' he says. 'Elaine. Elaine Keenan. I've got some numbers I can call. Give you a progress report in a week. Now . . . you mind if I ask you some questions straight away? Tell me about Morty and those Americans.'

'Anything in particular?'

'Where they got the money for a start.'

I tell him a bit about Morty and Scazz and the little men in suits. Faint noises of static crackle down the line. 'They did *that*?' Kev asks at one point.

'If you think I'm lying, Kev, we can stop right here.'

'No,' Kev Jackson says with gratifying humility, 'I don't think you're lying, but . . .' I talk some more. He listens.

The late Seventies: my tornado years. An interview Elaine and I granted to *Adult Video World* circa 1978 gauges the febrile tenor of the times. Beneath the caption 'THE ADULT FILM WORLD'S HOTTEST COUPLE' the two of us are pictured seated in the front room of the Queensway flat, the shot taken from the doorway to give an impression of endless rolling carpet. Elaine – languid, wearing a see-through, peach-coloured camisole – confides that she is negotiating for a 'major' Hollywood project; I announce sternly that I am poised to enter a collaboration with 'Harry' Pinter. It was the sort of thing you said to *Adult Video World* in those days, back when Morty really was having discussions with Ken Russell and Roger Vadim about a script of mine with the working title of *God: The Movie.* I forget who was to play the starring role, but John Belushi had certainly been marked down for a cameo appearance as the Pope.

The money, of course, came from abroad. The English market lay dead, snuffed out by censorship and timid investors, Soho was in retreat as the council cracked down on the film theatres and the bookshops and the rents flew up. Morty made a few low-budget features for the home market around this time under the general title of *Adventures* (*Adventures of a Teenage Girl*, *Adventures of a Travelling Salesman*): in their decorous flashes of breast and thigh lurked only a scintilla of lubricity. But if England slumbered, the Continent was waking up. By 1977 Franco had been dead for two years and you could smuggle film canisters in through the border run to Spain, where six months later they were shown in Madrid art cinemas while armies of mantilla-clad matriarchs protested noisily in the foyer. *Academia Spanko!* was showing in Torremolinos when Elaine and I spent a week there in 1980. The French, of course, took everything they could buy. Where Morty nosed radically ahead of his time was in forging connections with the Eastern bloc. He had a Hungarian distributor as early as 1976 and there was even an implausible exchange scheme, fixed up through the Russian embassy, whereby Morty, masquerading as a fellow-travelling educational publisher, supplied sealed parcels of 'text-books' in exchange for propaganda histories of the Second World War and enormous subsidies.

I came across the *Adult Video World* interview only the other day. It seems so obviously fraudulent, so self-evidently self-deluding, that one can only marvel at the lame, pitiable intelligence that shepherded it into print. Nevertheless, it is an authentic document.

'So, Martin, tell us how you went about scripting *Imbroglio*?'

'How does a script get written? Some words. Some tinkering. Some more words. Some more tinkering. How long is a piece of string?'

'And now the word on the street is there's a chance of an American deal?'

'Well, we're not counting any chickens, but let's just say that it's next stop Sunset Strip.'

Subsequently the adult film world's hottest couple were photographed holding hands, staring out of the window at the wilds of Kensington Gardens, examining a framed copy of the screen-writing award presented to me by *Adult Video World* for my work on *Manhunter*. My chief memory, though, is of Elaine picking a quarrel with the interviewer, an inoffensive, toupee'd thirty-year-old named Harold Dakin.

'If you don't mind, Martin, I'd like to ask you a few – uh – personal questions which our readers are keen to know the answers to. Now, your lady Elaine . . . I take it this is a very special relationship in your life?'

At this juncture Elaine slid off the sofa on to the floor and enquired, 'Do you want me to get my tits out?'

'I don't quite . . .'

'No, for the interview, I mean. I mean, why don't I get my tits out and you could take some pictures? There's him as well. He could get out his cock.'

'I'm not . . .'

'I mean, we could do it right here on the rug if it would help the interview.'

They loved it, of course. Elaine was described in the piece as 'smouldering' and 'temperamental'. After Dakin had gone, I said, 'He was only asking questions.'

'Yes, well there are questions and questions. I can just about take stuff about sex scenes and *exposing your baddy*, but special relationships? Forget it, I quit.'

'You needn't take it personally.'

'I needn't? How the fuck else am I supposed to take it? Oh baby, Harold Dakin with that bloody wig falling over his ear and having to write everything down in capitals and that drooling photographer. It could all be an enormous joke, only then it isn't a joke at all.'

For some reason this exchange sticks in my memory.

We move on now: history comes tumbling randomly out of the opened locker. I sell the place in Queensway, dull now and cheerless, buy another one in West Kensington. I sell the other place in Newbury – I never went there anyway – and buy another in Salisbury. I sell the Aston Martin and buy a Lagonda. I lose heavily on all these transactions, but it doesn't seem to matter. 'The money's all there, Martin,' Morty breathes whenever that vulgar subject is mentioned, 'the money's all there.' And the money *is* all there, all of it. Morty and Terry Chimes, by this stage, are grandly opulent beings, weekend in the Seychelles, think about buying Scottish castles, Irish salmon farms, Welsh mountains. The first Mrs Goldstein gives way to the second, the second Mrs Goldstein to the third. There are accountants, lawyers, estate agents, stockbrokers, telling us to spend money, to maximise assets, to upgrade our investments. Not to be outdone, I give Elaine a cheque book and a Peter Jones expense account, come home one day to find the flat strewn with gift-wrapped parcels: stereo systems, cookers, fridges, clothes, and Elaine sitting amid them like a child in a toyshop. 'What did you buy all this for?' I ask, not unkindly. 'I don't know,' she says, 'I just wanted to. Do you mind?' 'Of course not,' I tell her. Later I haul the collection up to the loft, inventory it and calculate the bill. It comes to £11,000. It sits there for a year until I instruct Crazy Rodney to take it away and sell it.

I do other things. I bring home travel-agents' brochures and instruct Elaine in the catechism of the high-powered international tourist.

'Mykonos?' 'No.' 'Madagascar?' '*No.*' 'Java?' 'If you like.' I do like, I like very much. Overcoming this initial reluctance, we go on long, aimless, sun-drenched excursions. We traverse Samarkand, we sidle beneath avenues of lamp-post-high rhododendrons in the foothills of the Himalayas, take pot-shots at wildebeest from the back of a jeep scuttling through the veldt. It is all very expensive, all very odd. Back home I razor pictures out of the *National Geographic* with a Stanley knife, plot new forays, establish fresh locations. Sometimes in these vagrant trawls through distant continents I explore the business angle. I go to Hamburg and check out the porn *kinos* and the latest sex hardware in the Beate Uhse shops. I traipse through the stacked warehouses of Amsterdam, piled high with technicolor pudenda. I attend lavish promo launches in Munich preview cinemas, nod my head sadly over the on-screen thrash and regret that it won't do for the British market. They all know Morty, these serious German pornographers with their designer suits, these fresh-faced Dutch sex traders with their university degrees and their MBAs. 'Herr Goldstein,' one tells me at a trade convention in West Berlin, '*ist ein grosse* libertarian.' I listen to the chatter about the latest victory in the censorship war, the latest feminist assault, shake my head, collect my plane ticket, fly back to an older, prohibitive world.

I do more things, different things. I give parties, grand parties, expensive parties. At the place in Fulham, sometimes, or at Tramp's, Xenon, Stringfellows, whatever the latest fashionable hotspot is. Everybody comes. Morty comes, Terry Chimes comes, and their impossible women. The industry is there, of course (it's called an industry now: it has trade papers in which Morty, Terry and I are occasionally profiled), the grizzled veterans from Fifties Soho, the starlets, the moneymen up for the night from their Essex hideaways, but also other people. Pop people. Morty's East End frighteners. The odd footballer, page three girl, darts player, snooker ace. And still, mysteriously, it is affordable, still it is there. It is at this point in my life that, for the first time, I am unable to comprehend how much money I am earning. This fact is visited on me one Sunday morning in 1977 when I attempt to open the top drawer of the bedside table, in which I am accustomed to store loose change, credit-card counterfoils and the like. The drawer is wedged shut with fifty-pound notes. Taken out and counted – a surprisingly laborious task – it realises £1700. 'What do I do with this?' I demand of Elaine, marching into the bathroom where she sits amid ski-runs of lather examining her toenails, and depositing a fan of notes on the mat. 'Take it round to the bank.' 'No, you have it.' 'No, I don't want it. You have it.' We compromise by spending half of it. On lunch. In Paris.

Raging, restless years. *Intimate Strangers* and *Love in a Void. Thrash, Splash* and *Confessions of a Sex Maniac.* Years of change, both in Dean Street and Tin Pan Alley. Punk rock arrives and suddenly Terry Chimes and I are spending three nights a week in clamorous holes in the ground off Oxford Street listening to the Clash, the Jam, the Damned, Buzzcocks. Bobby Dazz and the Sugarlumps are jettisoned from the Grunt Records roster in favour of the Crabs, the Cut-throat Razors and the Bicycles from Space. Briefly we are punk prophets, New Wave impresarios. Morty thinks about making *The Great Rock 'n' Roll Swindle* with Malcolm McLaren, turns the idea down; the Sex Pistols do, however, get to play a couple of tracks on *Oh Bondage Up Yours*, a short that Morty made around this time, and Sid, always hard up for a bob or two, had a cameo in *Leather Rat.*

Raging, restless years. I sell the place in West Kensington, dull now and cheerless; buy another one in Bishop's Park. I sell the place in Salisbury – I never went there anyway – and buy another in Winterbourne. I sell the Lagonda and buy a Ferrari. Morty and Terry Chimes, by this stage, are even more grandly opulent beings, weekend on Martha's Vineyard, think about buying French chateaux, Greek islands. Where is the money coming from? Sometimes, during the course of modest, day-long lunches and drinking sessions, Terry Chimes and I ask ourselves this question. There seems no ready solution. We make *Blood Feud, Slash, Trash* and *Organ-grinder.* And in the intervals of this restless, rackety existence there is Elaine.

I do mad things with Elaine. I recall a conversation from around this time. Early summer. Late morning. The day gapes before us.

'So what do you want to do? Sex?'

'No.'

'Food?'

'No.'

'There's five hundred quid in the drawer. We could go and blow it at the races.'

'No.'

Try again, more circumspectly.

'There's a new outfit in Paris Morty got a letter from, asking about the export situation. We could fly over there, check them out, stay the night and come back in the morning.'

'No.'

'Terry Chimes is making a video with some new band he's found, halfway up a mountain in Scotland. We could fly up *there*, check *that* out, stay the night and come back in the morning.'

'No.'

'We could get Crazy Rodney to take us to Hackney dog track . . .'

'No, for fuck's sake.'

Try again, more cravenly.

'So, tell me what you'd like to do. Tell me what you'd like to do and we'll do it. Anything. Anywhere. Think about it.'

She thinks. I wait. Rio de Janeiro? Some new, unprocurable drug? Nothing? Eventually she says, 'I'd like to get in the car and go to Oxford for the day. I'd like to have afternoon tea somewhere in the country. With scones and jam. And I'd like to go in a punt. You can take me.'

Incredibly, we pursue this unprecedented course. We take the Ferrari and proceed at a gentle pace down the A40. Unflustered, I negotiate the complex local traffic system. We examine the cool greenery of college lawns, silent in the afternoon shade, nimbly evade the skidding cyclists in the Broad, peer into the windows of Blackwell's bookshop, mingle with loud, confident undergraduates on the riverbank. Later, as we cruise back along the Westway to help Morty entertain a couple of East End moneymen the expedition takes on otherworldly shapes and proportions, becomes wreathed in mystical trappings, an Alice in Wonderland trip deep into some wholly fantastic bolt hole. The incident is never referred to again.

* * *

Sometimes, early in the morning when the haggard light spilled out over the eaves of Dean Street, Morty grew serious.

'I mean, what do you think about all this, Martin?'

'All this?'

'The books. The films. The mail-order shots. The chicks who'll sit there at the other end of a phone and tell you they'll eat you for five quid an hour.'

'It's a living.'

'Sure, it's a living. Did I ever tell you about my mother, Martin? Lives in a retirement home now at Ponders End. I go see her on Saturday afternoons. She thinks I'm a chartered accountant. Well, I *am* a chartered accountant, but that's not the point. You remember my kid? I brought him to Terry's barbecue that time. He thinks I run a toy company. He's fourteen. I found a copy of *Bouncers* in his room the other day. How do you think I felt about that?'

'I imagine you felt pleased and proud, Morty. I hope you did.'

'Did I *fuck*? I tore it up and threw it away. Plus I stopped his allowance for a month . . . What I'm trying to say, I suppose, is . . . What I mean is, do you believe in God, Martin?'

The question arose periodically in our line of business. Terry Chimes had once asked it of me immediately prior to his departure inside a massage parlour in Wardour Street. Cindy Lu Win had once asked it between takes on a film called *Jungle Frenzy*.

'It's best not to think about it.'

'Uh huh. I think about it *all the time*. I do. When we're on a shoot. When we're tying up a deal. Night times. That time last week when we were trying to get Katy, er Julie . . . that time we were trying to get Julie to go down on the guy who was . . . I was thinking about it all the while, thinking, what does God think about this? What will God do to me because of this?'

'God's tolerant, Morty.'

'Jesus, don't give me that, Martin, don't give me that liberal crap. Ever. You ever read the Bible, Martin? *Our* Bible. Have you any idea what God does to people who don't shape up? Even to people who're just minding their own business. You ever read about Job?'

'He was the man who scratched himself with a piece of pot?'

'Sure, Job. Job was just sitting there one day looking out over his vineyard and suddenly God comes along and really fucks him up.

I mean really screws him. And he wasn't even doing anything. "The unmerited suffering of the good man". That's what the books call it. Now if God can do that to Job, what can he do to me?'

'Perhaps Job had done things the Bible never revealed. Perhaps it was simply reparation?'

'Listen, Martin, you don't get my point. Job was just an ordinary guy. Okay, maybe he fooled around a little, maybe he coveted his neighbour's ox – we don't even know if he had a neighbour. We're none of us perfect. Job's sins must have been, well, *marginal.* But that doesn't save him. God just comes along and walks all over him.'

'It was a long time ago.'

'Jesus, Martin, don't you understand about religion? As far as God's concerned it was last week, yesterday. The rules don't change. Nobody ever renegotiated the commandments. Now, take a look at me. I make dirty films. I print dirty magazines. I got a barracks full of flats down in the East End – shit-heaps, most of the tenants are pensioners – and I never do any repairs and I raise the rent three times a year. I have half-a-dozen, a dozen people owe me money and if the interest doesn't come in on the first of the month I send Crazy Rodney round with a sledgehammer. I had a guy's arm busted last week. Do you think that's bad?'

'Pretty bad.'

'I'm unfaithful to my wife and I'm ashamed to tell my kids what I do for a living. I'm telling you, Martin, sometimes I lie awake at night just imagining what it's going to be like up there, just wondering what it is that God's going to do to me.'

Morty's guilt. At the time Morty's guilt seemed merely fanciful, a half-humorous gloss, the buccaneer's momentary regret at the pall of smoke rising over the burned-out port, the ravished doxy and the jemmied casket, as the Jolly Roger flaps in the breeze and the pirate galleon sweeps on into the sunset. But what about my guilt? The guilt of the accessory, I suppose, the bosun's diminutive mate who creeps up to the strongbox after everyone else has taken their share and is last in the line for the ravishing. Guilt nevertheless, and just as fit for retribution. Sometimes I lie awake too, just imagining what it's going to be like up there, just wondering what it is that God's going to do to me.

* * *

The thing of horror sits four feet away on top of the video. It came first thing this morning. So far I've played it through three times, with breaks for coffee, cigarettes and restless, edgy stares out of the window. Provenance London, typewritten name and address, postmark scuffed into anonymity. At first I thought it was one of Morty's showreels, a negligent secretary using an old mailing list, but it wasn't, *Christ* no, it wasn't at all.

Shot in colour, with good lighting and deft camerawork, which is to say that the close-ups don't waver and there is accurate panning to and from the action. Unlike the photographs, somebody subscribed for a lavish set: acres of bedroom, fluffy carpets. A brief trawl past an open window discloses neat, rolling gardens. The film is a standard surprised-by-a-stranger short. It begins with a few establishing shots: the room, landscaped from the doorway, the bed with its casually ruffled sheets, dressing table. After perhaps ten seconds spent straining to hear the soundtrack I realise that there isn't one. This is one of those jokey, money-saving ones they made in the mid-Seventies using captions. Sure enough, just as the saucy, fur-coated blonde steps in through the door the first of them slots into focus. HOME EARLY FOR A CHANGE. The girl smirks into the camera, jinks the fun-fur inch by inch off her shoulders and drops it on to the carpet to reveal – a touch improbably – a scarlet camisole and stockings. Removing the camisole takes a good two minutes (TIME TO RELAX) and there is an interesting diversion with a hairbrush. I take a good look at the girl's face as she does this: the standard minor actress's grin, off-centre, stultified, masking layers of unconquerable resentment. Naked, finally, monster breasts cradled in pudgy dairymaid's hands, she plumps herself down on a chair by the dressing table.

There the camera leaves her, angling off to the window where, sure enough, a burly oaf in white overalls is leering away through the rungs of a stepladder (NOT ALONE!). After this I could write the shooting script myself: the anguished gesticulations, the feigned surprise, the scrabbling at the glass (I HAVE TO TALK TO YOU), the meticulous coupling. Whoever shot it was a stylist in his or possibly her way, a subtle user of props (the bedside candlestick over which the camera lingers, the light bulb which detonates at a crucial moment). The conclusion, in which the couple lie spent and exhausted on the bed while the camera tracks over discarded rose petals on the white carpet, released an odd, elegiac note.

You will have anticipated the conclusion. The window-cleaner was me. Worse, I remember nothing. For a moment I cast around in my memory for an odd fragment or two, those tiny pieces of rubble which might somehow be fashioned to authenticate this vast, appalling edifice, but there is only bare, level terrain. Tearfully I wind back the last minute or so of the tape and watch it again, see myself roaming effortlessly and with Herculean attack through this past which I never knew existed, this unimagined secret life. Afterwards I curl up on the sofa in a tight, foetal ball. Outside the rain falls endlessly.

Part II

Extraordinary things continue to happen.

This lunchtime in the City Gates Fat Eric, after various achingly polite preliminaries, asked me to lend him three hundred pounds. I declined. This afternoon as I sat anxiously rewinding the window-cleaner tape for the umpteenth time I discovered a second and yet more indirect request, specifically a copy of *Brides* magazine wedged down the side of the sofa. I took this away and hid it. Later on Suzi says, 'Have you seen a magazine I left in the lounge?'

'What sort of magazine?'

'It's called *Brides*,' Suzi says without apparent self-consciousness. 'Have you seen it?'

'No. I haven't seen it.'

Later on, looking up from her marking, Suzi says, 'Do you know how old I am, Martin?'

'Thirty. Thirty-one.'

'Thirty-two. Do you know what that means?'

'Tell me.'

'It means I have to start deciding about things. It means I have to start deciding about my *career*, whether I ought to carry on what I'm doing, whether I ought to do something else.'

Such utterances are readily decoded.

Suzi goes on, 'About my career. About *babies*. Do you know what it's like to be thirty-two and not be married? I saw a girl I used to be at school with today in the city. Three children and the eldest is twelve. Do you know how I felt about that?'

'Tell me.'

'No,' says Suzi, 'you tell me. You're the one who's so bloody clever. What do you think I've spent the last two years doing? Why do you think I've stayed here?'

Oddly there is no rancour in this. Suzi says reminiscently, 'Do you know why I went into teaching? Because I liked children. I mean, *liked* children. Not just didn't mind having them around, or wanted to form their characters. That's what a lot of teachers want to do: they want to form kids' characters. I don't. I just *like* children. Do you know when I was sixteen, when I was going out with Adrian, all I could think about was getting married and having children. Live in a house like this and see Adrian off to the Norwich Union every morning and have children. There'd be three of them . . .'

'Suzi . . .'

'Three of them,' Suzi says firmly, 'two girls and a boy. And I'd call them Tom and Ceridwen and Natasha . . .'

'Suzi, will you just . . .'

'Tom because of that children's book *Tom's Midnight Garden* . . . Did you ever read that when you were a kid? Ceridwen because Mother came from Wales and that was her grandmother's name. And they'd all be terribly clever and do well at school and I'd be terribly proud of them. And you, you just . . .'

'Suzi,' I say, 'Suzi. You don't even like me.'

'No,' she says, 'I don't, do I? I've been living here for two years and I must have been to bed with you two hundred times and I don't even like you.'

'What about the others? What about Bob and Marcus and Justin? Did you like them?'

'I don't know. I haven't a clue. You don't know what it's like, do you? Being a girl. Having tits and blonde hair. Suddenly there are all these men wanting to go to bed with you, and you . . . well, it's just something you do. You have a boyfriend and he takes you places. Do you understand?'

'I understand.'

'No, you don't,' Suzi says patiently. 'You don't understand at all. I'm thirty-two and I want to have a baby and I've been wasting my time here for two years and you don't understand at all.'

Later, after she has gone out, the telephone rings on endlessly in the hall. I stand there in the darkness for a moment cradling my hand over the receiver, think better of it, turn away.

'Do you want to stay for the second half?'

'I ought to make that phone call.'

'It would be a pity to miss the violin piece.'

'I suppose it would.'

'In any case I just went and looked at the telephone kiosk and there's a queue.'

'Yes.'

Somewhere in the recesses of panelling above our heads a bell rang shrilly. Nearer at hand two men in evening suits who had been speaking to each other with disagreeable emphasis raised their heads and then lowered them abruptly. The smell of cigar smoke hung heavily on stagnant air. Elaine stood examining me with the air of a child convinced that some treat, long unreasonably denied, might still be won through sheer persistence. 'Make sure you're still here when I get back,' she said finally.

Returning to the Wigmore Hall after a ten-year absence brought back older memories, of a kind not usually associated with such places. Happily, they were not those of familiarity – the decor changed now and anonymous, the framed portraits scarcely remembered – but of past association, the whole conveying an air of threatened gentility, liable to sink at any moment beneath an encroaching, vulgar tide, but until that time still capable of keeping its head narrowly above water. Dark panelling, the raised dais strewn with chairs, the glimpse here and there of piled programmes and fussing officialdom – all these suggested a school prize-giving, hedged about with all manner of pleasurable anticipation and incidental spectacle. But there were older memories too, accumulated in childhood, prompted now by the discarded instruments propped up against chairs, sheet music flapping against its wire supports, harsh concert-hall light: memories of my father commenting with his usual asperity on an amateur performance in St Andrew's Hall, or seen himself on the edge of a remote and crowded chorus. Rehearsed and brought out again in this way, these associations had the effect of undermining present reality.

The hall with its cavernous ceiling, the Wigmore habitués in Dickensian subfusc, the conductor with his white tie – all this was an insubstantial pageant wheeled out to impress case-hardened tourists. It was my father in his shabby dinner jacket, showing his teeth as he sang, who was real.

Standing at the entrance to the foyer, the crowd first thickening and then falling away into a succession of tightly ordered queues, one could establish a perspective on the apparent chaos. Seen at this remove the throng of concert-goers was no longer random, but instead took on recognisable shapes and divisions, was transformed into tightly knit centres of conversation, each grimly maintained against knots of turbulence, or single figures, armed with cigarettes and wine glasses, staking out a patch of personal territory. Beyond, a darkened corridor hung with photographs led to the street. Here, deaf to the clamour, a commissionaire sat drinking tea out of a mug.

Elaine came back carrying two glasses of wine. She said, 'I was the only person in the ladies who wasn't speaking Polish.'

'Did you try them in Russian?'

'That's not even funny.'

Leaflets, scattered here and there over the seating area, piled up in foot-high bundles at the door, bore out this remark. Their tone was unambiguously menacing, the images they evoked – workers massing behind shipyard gates, tanks crawling over the white country – uncomfortably out of place amid the genteel furnishings, as if I had discovered one of Morty's magazines in a nursery. On this dark November evening the concert preliminaries had been solemn. Two Poles, uncomfortable in hand-me-down English clothes, spoke hastily of the situation in Gdansk. An academic from the University of London discussed possible government responses. The dull English faces watched impassively. Afterwards Elaine had heard a woman say, 'It's all very sad, but I don't see that there's anything we can do.'

Convened at short notice, for the Polish crisis had risen suddenly to claim the attention of the public, the night's audience was appropriately polyglot. Shabby expatriates, their arms queerly folded high up their chests, lingered in ones and twos near their seats. A few Polish aristocratic ladies of elderly vintage sat in state on cane chairs near the foyer, attended by a woman who claimed to be secretary to the government in exile. It was to this group and its paraphernalia that the eye returned: a vista of raised, beaky faces, silent gravity, the lorgnettes archaic even for the Wigmore Hall, the effect at once alien and historical, a Cracow drawing room of the last century mysteriously transported into the present day. An elderly man, previously half obscured as he disposed of a coffee cup, shuffled hesitantly forward, his eyes straining in recognition.

Elaine said, 'It's Mr Tovacs.'

I had not at this point met Mr Tovacs, or even seen his picture, yet there was about him a disconcerting air of familiarity, as if one knew all that it was convenient to know and that a common ground conducive to dialogue already existed. Mr Tovacs was at this stage in his long career quite a well-known man. He conducted intermittently a small, cosmopolitan literary magazine, seldom seen on bookstalls, but mentioned favourably in newspaper arts pages, but he was better known as an obituarist, the chronicler of hectic artistic lives lived out in pre-war Central Europe. There was about these memorials a tangible glamour, deriving not so much from the choice of subject – mostly minor surrealist or expressionist painters – as from the strong scent of Mr Tovacs's own personality. Without being stated in so many words, his past affiliations were sharply apparent. You could not read a page of his billowing, un-English prose without deducing that its author had known Firbank, watched Brancusi at work, or devilled for Picasso. Obscurely, these hints had the effect of diminishing the importance of his subjects: it was Mr Tovacs who had survived, you felt, rather than the acquaintances of his youth.

Seen at close range he seemed a curiously generalised figure: the shock of white hair, stained yellow at the fringes with nicotine, rising so stiffly that it might have been suspended by invisible wires, brooding features, an oddly pained expression suggesting much inner disquiet. Dressed almost wholly in black, a pinkish cravat providing a single bizarre ornament, he looked every inch an émigré, uncomfortable, absorbed, the thirty years or so spent in a foreign country clearly of no account when set against the sharper outlines of the past. Examining him, you thought, inevitably, of fictionalised portrayals of an English exile, of seedy legations in the

Bayswater Road, World Service broadcasts and carefully nurtured, impotent resentment. There was something quaint, too, about his demeanour, something trammelled, the apparent vitality of his gestures – his first action was to kiss Elaine soundly on both cheeks – rebuffed by small, shuffling movements, the sense of innate feebleness.

He said, 'This is a memorable evening, a memorable evening. I was dining with Professor Sikorski – he is connected with the London University – and he told me about it, so of course I came straight away. A memorable evening. Perhaps, who knows, I shall write something about it if I am allowed, if I am permitted? Of course, a great many people are interested in my poor country, a great many, and that is to be applauded. But there is also great ignorance. There is also that English habit of making a judgement not necessarily connected with the facts.'

Deconstructed, its key fragments detached from more superfluous materials, this speech, as I was later to discover, provided several clues to Mr Tovacs's character. It conveyed the assumption of his own centrality while hinting at his connection with people of more formal influence and importance (Professor Sikorski was a well-known Polish expert). It advertised his literary credentials while canvassing the possibility of exclusion and even censorship, an intrigue that neither of his listeners could be expected to fathom. Above all it placed his own position beyond doubt: that of a guest, caught up in a family crisis, who knows what ought to be done, but is uncertain of the ability of his hosts – well-meaning but ignorant people – to take the necessary steps.

Mr Tovacs went on, 'This Walesa, this trade-unionist. You will not think it possible, perhaps, but I knew his father. This was before the war, of course. Everything in Poland is before the war. The man was a shoemaker, a village shoemaker. I offered to go to the BBC, to go on television and tell this story, but no, they were not interested. They did not think it *newsworthy*.'

Elaine said, 'I remembered the pianist who played in the first half. Isn't he your protégé?'

'The young man who performed the Schumann study? He is a friend, nothing more. My wife has given him some lessons at her studio. Possibly it was there that you met him.'

A faint shiftiness came over Mr Tovacs as he made these observations, as if he feared that in revealing the existence of a wife, a studio and his connection with Elaine he had somehow given himself away, disclosed some part of his personality that were better concealed.

Elaine said, 'Is Jerry here?'

Mr Tovacs said with an effort, 'She is here. That is, I am expecting her to be here.'

It was not a tactful question. Mr Tovacs made one or two more shuffling motions with his feet and then relapsed into silence. I reflected on the information which the previous few moments had yielded up. I was not at all surprised to find that Elaine knew Mr Tovacs. Elaine knew a great many people from the social category in which Mr Tovacs and his kind reposed, the category of minor poets, impresarios, failed street actors. Invited to parties at the loft, where they stood awkwardly in groups maintaining a morose, silent solidarity, they annoyed Morty beyond measure. 'Fucking *artists*,' he would say. 'Just a load of read-my-poems, pay-my-bills, fucking *artists*.'

The bell rang a second time, now with greater effect. A musician or two began to wander intently across the dais. Away behind us beyond the foyer a door slammed and there was a sudden blare of traffic. I thought of Morty's pinched, eager face, the light spilling out over the desk-tops in Dean Street, of restless days and telephone calls. A tall girl in a scarlet mackintosh came into the foyer and began to pick her way slowly through the crowd towards us.

Elaine said, 'Jerry's here.'

The girl said brusquely, but with an air of having rehearsed the words, 'I had to take a fucking taxi all the way from Finsbury Park. Six pounds and twenty pee. You could have told me where the place was and not had me screeching round like some fucking tourist.'

Mr Tovacs did not seem put out by this assault. He said, 'That was very extravagant. You could have taken a bus. I am always telling you to take a bus. You cannot expect me to give you the money, you know that.' He turned to us. 'Jerry is an American. You will have noticed how Americans always pretend that they do not know where places are in London.'

There was an unmistakable air of authority in this, the hint of some contract unfulfilled. Jerry shrugged. 'You could have told me anyway. You knew I was going to be there all afternoon.' Nearer at hand she seemed older than when moving towards us: creased in concentration, her face lost its youthful lines and grew indeterminate, caught somewhere between girlhood and middle age. She said, 'Anyway, it all worked out. You could at least give me the money for the fucking cab.'

By now there were only a few people moving back from the foyer; seated heads stretched before us back to the stage. Mr Tovacs said sharply, 'I shall do no such thing. And I will not permit you to talk in this way.' He gave Elaine a stiff little bow. 'I must apologise for this. It has spoiled a most interesting conversation.'

'Interesting, asshole,' Jerry said, by now thoroughly ill-humoured. Mr Tovacs ignored her. 'We shall meet again,' he said, 'and in more agreeable circumstances.' As he moved off towards his seat, not looking behind him, the girl following unwillingly in the rear, I caught the first brief hint of exclusion that was to dog my dealings with Mr Tovacs, the thought that I had intruded into an atmosphere, at once tense yet containing its own rules and ordinances, in which it was better not to linger. There was something unusual about the way in which he dealt with the American girl, although at this stage I knew nothing of their relationship, a deep-rooted irritation untempered by conventional courtesies, something which rose now through the cigar smoke and the declining hum of conversation and suggested deeper antagonisms. Obscurely it established Mr Tovacs in my mind as somehow a figure of power, buttressed by inner resources which it was impossible to fathom, bland and emollient, but ready to turn nasty if provoked.

I said to Elaine, 'Let's get out of here.'

'I thought you wanted to stay.'

'Just do it,' I said. There was a sudden burst of random, unfocused applause from beneath the stage. 'Just do it.'

Outside the streets were dark and empty. Light blazed out of the silent shopfronts. In the odd hour before the pubs closed and the theatre crowds departed the city lay dead, a few buses chugging in mid-lane, taxis shunted up at the roadside, sleeping traffic. Often at these times, late at night in the loft at Dean Street, cruising with Morty through the grim dawns, I played tricks on this silent, inanimate world, took the houses in the grey squares back a century and a half and populated them with East India nabobs and John Company merchants, put powdered footmen at the door, rearranged the road beyond. Altering them in this way, clearing the weeds out of rank, jungly gardens and sending nursemaids and gentlemanly children scurrying around them, somehow gave character to these buildings, a sense of proper function. The thought that where Arab banks and carpet showrooms now fought for space, infants had skirmished and Regency bucks hobnobbed brought comfort of a sort.

Lolling in the taxi, resentment yielding now to an easier exhaustion, Elaine fitted snugly into this reinvented landscape, took her own place in the charade. Given flowing skirt, bonnet, parasol, she resembled the subject of a painting by Fragonard, displayed a naïveté that was already compromised, an experienced eye that, amid the innocent trappings of swings and summer lawns, knew very well what it was about.

I said, 'Where did you come across him?'

'Tovacs? Oh, he knows everyone.' She pronounced it in the Irish way, 'uvryone'. 'He knows Morty. He probably came to a party at the loft. I don't remember.'

This in itself was not surprising. Plenty of queer people came to Morty's parties: advertising men, soap-opera queens, disc jockeys. I had once seen a minor member of the Royal Family peering uncertainly through the throng. Mr Tovacs, the translator of Cocteau, Joyce's amanuensis if the accounts were true, must have been the queerest fish to swim into that dense and populous pool.

'What about the girl?'

'Jerry? Oh, just someone of Tovacs's. One of Tovacs's women. There's a bunch of them. They put his magazine together for him so they can go round saying they slept with a man who slept with Colette.'

'He sounds quite a guy.'

'You don't want to believe all that stuff,' Elaine said.

Later I was to hear similar estimates of Mr Tovacs, the hint that these widely advertised affiliations were largely bogus, that his motives as an editor in a publication given over to famous names were no more than those of the autograph hunter. For the moment he seemed a person of infinite resource, an impresario who had wandered on to some meagre, poorly lit stage to invest it suddenly with a cascade of light and sound. And, though there were other more urgent questions to be resolved, questions about my dealings with Morty, my relationship with Elaine, it was the image of Mr Tovacs which persisted as the taxi sped westward towards Kensington and Fulham and Elaine slept, an image at once precise and oddly suggestive. The conjuror had arrived, I realised, taken out his magic box and released a flight of exotic wildlife; older memories, taking in my father, self-absorbed and aloof among the distant chorus, moving nearer at hand to include Morty's face beneath the flaring light, resting evenly on an earlier life, long forgotten but now sharply in focus, in a landscape to which, after long exile, I had returned.

More photographs. I found them quite by chance in a steel tin, wedged shut with elastic bands, in the shed at the bottom of the garden. Not vivid genitalia, but family photographs, old sepia shots from the Twenties and Thirties, muddy greys and browns, placed there I suppose by my father at some remote point in time and then forgotten. Stylised, formal attitudes. My father in his early teens, hair scraped back and parted in the middle, standing self-consciously with his hand resting on a chair back. A middle-aged woman in a cloche hat holding a baby. A holiday party arranged awkwardly in a charabanc: none of the figures is recognisable.

With the photographs came other memorabilia: a folded sheet of newspaper, unfurled to reveal the front page of the *Daily Herald* of 6 June 1944; a caricature of a small, eager mannikin perched athwart a stack of boxes the better to wield a snooker cue and captioned 'Jack Benson plays a cunning shot', a joke on my father's comparative slightness; a programme from a football match between a Celebrity XI and RAF Fighter Command Europe, printed along the edge in my father's handwriting the words 'Lawton did not play'; a closely written sheet headed 'Films seen in 1941'. I looked at them for a while. They revealed a side to my father's life of which he had rarely spoken and of which, as a consequence, I was altogether ignorant. Marrying in middle age, uprooting himself from early environments, cutting himself adrift from the ties of family, he had managed without obvious effort to detach himself entirely from this former existence, had grown up, moved on, ignored whatever memories of these early days might have risen to disturb him. Rather than bringing him closer to view the effect, oddly enough, was to distance him yet further. There was a sense of exclusion about this carefully hidden treasure trove, the air of secrets, however innocent, kept purposely out of sight, aspects of my father's life which he wished quite deliberately to conceal. There was no place for me, I realised, here among these shabby mementoes, these evocations of a life lived out in my absence. The way was barred; the door shut firmly across the path that led back to my father's early life could not be reopened.

Later I show Suzi the photographs. She looks at them with faint interest, as usual making comments that draw herself, however narrowly, into the subject at hand.

'Father used to wear his hair like that.'

'When did he stop?'

'He didn't. He says he's the last man in England who still has his hair parted in the middle.'

There is a faint, suspicious brightness about Suzi. She says eventually, 'Christopher rang today.'

'Christopher?'

'Christopher I used to go out with. You remember.'

'What did he want?'

'Just to have a chat. You know, catch up on old times. He's at the Norwich Union now. He's a *manager*.'

'Is that good?'

'He's got a *secretary*,' Suzi says.

Christopher telephones several times over the next three days, Christopher with his manager's job and his secretary. Hearing his voice I experience a faint twinge of phoney terror, like ghostly knocking heard a long way off.

A wet October here in Norfolk. Grey clouds drift in westward from the sea to hang low over the city, alternate with fierce, unexpected sunshine. Even here, twenty miles distant from the coast, the air harbours a faint tang of salt. With the clouds come the gulls: razorbills and sandpipers blown south from Jutland to perch on telephone wires and scavenge outside the fish-and-chip shops. Characteristic tokens of the Norwich autumn: overbright buses trawling the rainy streets, the scent of burning leaves, knots of blue-uniformed schoolboys. From nearer at hand come more specific signs of a changing season, an irrevocable shift in the pivot of the year: Suzi engrossed in her marking; Fat Eric and Kay back from an autumn holiday in Majorca, Torremolinos, Ithaca, wherever, the former plumper, sun-drenched, content, instigator and victor of a memorable wine-bar upset, the latter thinner, paler, more terrified. Norwich play a smattering of early-season games, canter over a set of newly promoted mediocrities, go down heavily at home to Liverpool, and the papers buzz with rumours that Kevin Flack is unhappy, won't sign a new contract and wants a transfer. Intrigued by Fat Eric's restless ventilation of these issues I agree to accompany him to the big pre-Christmas game against Manchester United. In Heigham Park the bowls and the tennis are over now, the old gentlemen and the bouncing housewives gone elsewhere and the gates locked at six. The streetlamps go on earlier. Early in the morning along The Avenues there are conkers all over the road, blown down from the big horse-chestnut trees during the night. I walk down there sometimes and pick them up, carry them back home and store them in jam-jars above the sink, get an odd, indulgent smile from Suzi.

Kev Jackson telephones once or twice: stray fragments of intelligence creeping down the wires. He says the publishers are paying for the calls. He thinks he might have known someone who might have known Elaine in the six months or so after the crash, thinks he might be able to find a phone number for one of her ex-flatmates. In return I convey scraps of speculation about Morty's private life, I advance a theory of Terry Chimes's bisexuality, I suggest that Crazy Rodney was 'misunderstood'. The hint, the pregnant deflection, the eventual compromise, 'integrity' lurking shyly in the background. He believes it all, a limitless, effortless gullibility.

In the afternoons I amble out into the countryside, through Trowse, Keswick, Intwood, Caistor-by-Norwich, along narrow roads hazily recalled from childhood where the hedgerows rear up on either side and ploughed fields stretch away as far as the eye can see, where there are quaintly overgrown pathways leading to forgotten churches smelling of damp and mildew, where the touch of a hand on the door sends woodpigeons panicking from their roosts above the stained-glass windows. Stoke Holy Cross, Hempnall, Brooke – small straggling villages, their origins proudly displayed in Pevsner and Ekwall, their forefathers asleep in the mouldering churchyards, full of reedy meres and rotting elm trees, sluggish tributaries veering off from the Wensum over the South Norfolk flat. Neatly tended village greens, blowsy shopfronts and decomposing thatch. Across country, out towards Brooke, the landscape turns bare and motionless, the silence broken only by a solitary tractor, a train heard a long way off, space peopled suddenly by an ancient on a bicycle, a loitering farmworker. Like a Thomas Hardy poem. Back along the Ipswich Road in the fading light the illusion is debunked: stretched traffic, the first neon signs of hotels and guest-houses. Not like a Thomas Hardy poem. Autumn moves rapidly on now. The beech leaves lie piled up in Jessopp Road. Norwich beat Chelsea, lose to Southampton. Kevin Flack, dropped for the Southampton game, tells the *Eastern Evening News* that he is 'thinking seriously' about his career. I have long conversations with Fat Eric about money and opportunity (my money, his opportunity). I have longer conversations with Kay about violence and resignation (Fat Eric's violence, her resignation). I make long, unsatisfactory phone calls to Morty, most of which consist of me listening into a dead receiver while the wind whistles down the wire and Morty, prised eventually from some high-octane business roundtable, arrives to offer consolation. I watch Suzi, a fleeting, marginal presence now, down there on the edge of consciousness, arrive and then depart, depart and then arrive. It all feels very stretched, very thinly spread, this dim, low-key season, somehow exhausted and furtive. I lie awake at nights on my back, Suzi a slumbering, stertorous hump beside me, trying to bite the head off the twisting darkness. Fear, like a flashing blue light, its reflection ricocheting off the walls, rises effortlessly up to join me.

* * *

Snow fell overnight. Waking in the small hours I watched it floating gently down over the shrubberies and tiny gardens beyond the mansion block. By morning a level off-white blanket lay over the grass and the paths of asphalt.

At breakfast Elaine was fractious. She sat in the kitchen, hunched in a dressing gown, her hair untended, and drank tea resignedly. At length she said, 'Are you going in this morning?'

'Not unless Morty wants me.'

'He won't want you. He told me. You know how Morty is when he's after a deal, when he's after money.' She gave the word an unusual emphasis. 'Besides, he thinks you're losing interest.'

'Why should Morty think I was losing interest?'

Nearly four years had passed since Elaine and I had met in the studios at Dean Street. In that time I had grown used to her bewildering variety of moods. At first I had assumed that these proceeded out of an extreme sensitivity to circumstance: an ambiguous remark, a momentary diversion from some standard pattern of behaviour would be enough to infuriate her for hours or days. But there was something else, I saw, a part of her character which I had never been able to appease. Elated or downcast, confidential or remote, she still displayed an inner intransigence – varying in degree from ironic sympathy to outright contempt – which was beyond the power of conciliation. Morty, curiously, possessed original views on this topic. 'Seen a lot of chicks like that one,' he said once, amid much crapulous bonhomie. 'Think about it, Mart. You spend the first fifteen years of your life growing up in some refuse heap and being shat on by your mum and dad. And then suddenly, wham, you look like a million dollars, you're five feet ten with torpedo tits and guys are literally begging you to sleep with them. So what happens? You're pretty pleased with yourself – after all, you might not like all the guys, but at least you can pick and choose – but not *that* pleased. Ten to one says you spend the next fifteen years in a permanent sulk because you're not omnipotent.'

'And then what happens?'

'After you're thirty? That's when it gets really bad. Your tits cave in, your bum splays out, all the guys are just fucking you for old times' sake and you hate yourself for not having all the things you hated having when you had them.'

Pertinent though Morty's observations were, they had no practical bearing on my feelings towards Elaine. These had long ago been frozen into sharp relief. I was, I assured myself, obsessed with her, while finding her – now more than ever before – intolerable.

Not looking up from the table she went on, 'He thinks you're lacking in *commitment*. He thinks the scripts you put in are too bloody boring for words. He thinks you laugh at him.'

It was not a new accusation. 'Morty knows where I stand.'

'Flat on your back. That's what Terry Chimes says.'

And so we bickered on, as the pale early sunlight diffusing over the snow gave it an egg-yolk sheen, as the central heating switched itself off and the room grew cold: a long, intimate disagreement at whose core lay not malice, but a gross unfamiliarity with temperament. Four years spent living hugger-mugger in West London flats, four years spent in Dean Street, or on location in odd parts of England and Europe had imposed, I thought, a false, effortless solidarity, disguising all manner of failed connections.

'Anyway,' Elaine said finally, 'at least I still seem to be working for my living.'

In these later days Elaine worked for a promotions agency in Newman Street. The job was not onerous, requiring her only to don exotic costumes and decorate merchandising stands, but she resented it inordinately. Like Faulkner in Hollywood, or Eliot in his bank, she was determined to give value for money while admitting the mundane nature of the task.

'What is it today?'

'God knows. Last week it was some new type of mineral water and I had to wear a headdress with a sort of lemon attachment. This week it's probably sanitary towels.'

She left shortly afterwards, gathering up her things in sharp, angry rushes, throwing on coat, scarf and hat without ceremony. After she had gone I wandered absently around the flat, examining the havoc of her departure: in the bedroom a tussock of spent tissues and a heap of underclothes, in the hallway half-empty coffee cups and a clutter of video cassettes. There were other discoveries. On the top shelf of the bookcase in the study I found one of Mr Tovacs's novels – *Incandescence*, an early one – and put it aside for future study. Then, as the pale winter morning wore on, I went into the front room and stood looking out over the empty tennis courts and the file of trees in the street below.

Alone in the flat, without occupation or interest, I had one infallible resource. It amused me to think of the other places I had inhabited in London, to subject them to an endless process of comparison in which there were no finite answers, but merely shifting points of view, an elaborate decor now surfacing to dislodge the memory of an inconvenient location, a leaky top-flat roof safely anaesthetising, in terms of awfulness, the remembrance of a musty basement. At thirty I was a veteran of London flatland. I had lived all over the western city, at first in Ealing, Acton Town, in queer maisonettes hunched in the shadow of the Westway, over takeaway restaurants in Hanger Lane. Later, as Leisurevision's activities had expanded, I had embarked on a remorseless process of betterment: moving steadily eastward, taking in Gunnersbury, Shepherds Bush and Hammersmith, before settling on Fulham, later more fashionable still, now designated simply an up-and-coming area. At present we lived in a side street off the Fulham Palace Road, Bishop's Park not far away, the river dimly discernible through distant treetops. I was immune to such places, the raw feeling of impermanence never quite dislodged by redecoration or long tenancy, always liable to be knocked back to the surface by a phone call for a bygone resident, the stack of unidentifiable post in the hall. Even here in a Fulham mansion block, where the flats changed hands at relatively long intervals, we still received three or four phone calls a week for people of whom we had no knowledge. Joe. Anne. Samantha. A Mr Perrick who had lived here in the 1960s. Someone called Karas. I used to wonder about this file of former tenants. Were their lives so chaotic, their homes so impermanent, I thought, that their friends had simply lost track of them, moved in a slow, vain pursuit forever two or three addresses behind? I imagined long, serpentine trails spread out all over London, a vast, spreading plant of fractured alliances and vain enquiry, letters piling up in abandoned hallways, telephones ringing on in silence. A few callers rang repeatedly, unconvinced by explanation or denial. Sometimes late at night a call came from overseas, crackling away on a fading international line. The request, conveyed by a halting African voice, was always the same:

a Mr Solomon with whom the caller needed urgently to speak. We knew of no Mr Solomon, but the calls continued, sometimes pacific, resigned, at other times voluble and excited. Elaine had an uncanny ability to predict them. 'For Mr Solomon,' she would say sometimes if the phone rang around midnight. She was rarely wrong.

At about half-past ten Morty rang. He seemed subdued.

'How are you getting on with that script?'

'Which one? The one set in the girls' school? It's not above half finished.'

'Yeah, well, don't bother finishing it. Terry's backer's gone back to the States. And between you and me the only people he's likely to be paying money to in the next few months are lawyers.'

'I see.'

'We ought to talk,' Morty went on. 'There's things happening, things you ought to know about. You want to come and have lunch?'

'I should like to have lunch,' I said.

'Great. Well, be at my club about quarter to one.'

'Which club would that be?'

Morty named an address north of Oxford Street. 'It's a proper club,' he went on. 'Waiters and all that. Make sure you wear a tie.'

Morty seemed unabashed by these instructions. After he had rung off I went back into the lounge and sat leafing regretfully through a folder which contained the fragments of *Girls' School Party*: it seemed a pity to waste it. Later I put on a tie and set off through the heavy slush of Bishop's Park to the underground station.

Morty had not prospered since his bid for parliament a year and a half before. In the months after the General Election a Sunday newspaper had run a four-part exposé of his career to date, police had called at the studio in Dean Street, and there had been talk of an Inland Revenue investigation. These were minor problems, nimbly evaded, but they were the symptoms of a deeper malaise. Whether it was that older associates had run scared of this newfound notoriety, that unlooked-for commercial pressures had come to disrupt Leisurevision's easy ascent, or that in his search for fresh spheres of influence he had simply overreached himself, the

Morty who emerged from this hectic, indiscriminate period in his life was a reduced and chastened figure. Two years before there had been a string of blonde receptionists at the loft, a party a month and a procession of transatlantic visitors. Now there was only Crazy Rodney to man the row of telephones and placate the printers' representatives, and the American businessman who called at Dean Street was a rare migrant, like some bizarre, brightly plumaged bird blown off course by high winds and disappointed by this small, arid garden. Morty did little overseas business now. There were still familiar callers. The northern cinema owners and the tape salesmen who had supported him in his early days continued to arrive, but there was about them a hesitancy, an unwillingness to commit themselves to long-term agreements and future projects. They thought Morty a risk, that, in the business jargon of the day, he sailed too close to the wind. Meanwhile the reels of unused celluloid tape lay piled up in the storeroom. There had not been a film made at Dean Street for a month and a half.

Morty's club reflected something of these reduced circumstances. It lay in a tiny mews off Portman Square. Its membership, drawn from the ranks of minor actors and obscure journalists, was undistinguished. Gloomy portals gave way to a glass cage where a porter sat smoking a cigarette, and a small, windowless cell lined with shabby armchairs. Here I found Morty conducting some transaction with a bald, elderly man.

'Paying my sub,' he explained, 'they like you to be regular here.'

We ate in a narrow first-floor dining room, looking out over the traffic. There were half-a-dozen other diners, wary middle-aged men occupied with newspapers or each other, a single resentful waitress. Morty, however, was unreasonably absorbed in his surroundings. 'You meet some pretty interesting people here,' he said at one point. 'You see that bloke over there? Used to read the news if I'm not mistaken.' Later he said, 'There's an MP comes sometimes. If he turns up today I'll introduce you to him.'

After lunch we went upstairs to a cramped, deserted smoking room filled with camera portraits of thirty or forty years previously. Morty's face brightened. 'Former members,' he said, tapping one of the glass frames. 'Know any of them, do you?' I looked for a while down the lines of heavy, dissatisfied faces. None was recognisable. Eventually, high up on the right-hand side, I discovered the face of a minor novelist of the 1930s.

There was a small silver bell on the occasional table. Morty shook it confidently. Nothing happened. This seemed to depress him and he sank down heavily into an armchair. I looked at him for a moment. In his leather jacket and canvas trousers he seemed out of place amid the solidity of this faded world.

'How are things?'

Morty shook his head. 'Things are bad. Look, I know I haven't called you for a week or two, Martin, but it's because . . . I got a letter from the bank this morning. That's okay, I can handle that. But what about the next letter and the one after that? But it's not that, it's the . . .' Some weightier grievance floated before his eye for a moment and I watched him grasp at it. 'I went down the video mart this morning, you know, the one in Shaftesbury Avenue. Used to do a lot of business there. They used to take *Thrash* and stuff like that in Fifties in the old days. Now it's all foreign stuff. Color Climax stuff that somebody's been through and wiped all the hard-ons off. In German and *not even any subtitles*! And you know those import videos used to be expensive. Ten, fifteen quid. Well, they're selling them at six now.'

'What does Terry say?'

'Terry?' Morty waved his hand ambiguously in front of his face. 'Terry's . . . Look, Grunt are strapped for cash right now. That comeback album they did with the Express last month. Well, it was a complete turkey. They paid twenty grand to have it plugged on every radio station in the UK and it sold two thousand copies. That tartan gimmick just doesn't cut it any more. Plus Bobby Dazz wants to buy Lucille or whoever some more cosmetic surgery and he's suing them for five years' unpaid royalties. So you can forget about Terry for the moment.'

Outside the window grey clouds were moving in from the west. The sky was dull and opaque. It was barely three o'clock, but already the streetlamps were going on.

'So what happens? What is it that's happening that I ought to know about?'

'Yeah, well, I'll tell you about that. Terry says that, well, never mind about Terry. You know Terry's got the clap again?'

'I didn't.'

'Straight up. Reckons it's that girl he brought to the party, the one who . . . Anyway, the thing is, you remember *Resurrection*?'

I nodded. A florid, elaborate screenplay, conceived two years previously at the height of our prosperity, it had seemed extravagant even then. The plot I remembered intimately: I had devised it myself. A notorious Victorian roué takes a young wife to satisfy his ever-more-libidinous urges. Inexplicably they fall in love. He is then struck by acute paralysis and dies. His wife, at first consoling herself with a succession of young men, mourns him earnestly. He then returns to earth as a ghost to confront her. They discuss the nice theological point as to whether one can have sex with a ghost. 'Only your love,' the spectre of wicked Sir George finally informs his bride, 'can make me rise again.'

'What about it?'

'Got a backer,' Morty said unexpectedly. 'At least I think I have. Or at least if he can't find all the money, then he knows people who can.' He shook his head doubtfully. 'How much do you reckon it would take to make *Resurrection*, Martin?'

I thought. In its original form *Resurrection* had been lavishly framed: a cast of twenty, multiple locations (including an implausible scene in which Sir George and his wife attend a *levée* at Windsor), myriad period costumes. At the very least, a fortnight's shooting time.

'Half a million.'

'I told him three-quarters. To be on the safe side,' Morty explained. 'But we'd have to trim it. Take out some of the fancy stuff.'

'The scene in the hot-air balloon?'

'And that other bit, the bit at the court ball. We could trim that if it came to it . . .'

And so for twenty minutes we plotted happily. We made Sir George a country squire rather than a minor peer, we reduced the number of his wife's lovers from six to three, shifted the scene of their reconciliation from a felucca on the Nile to a punt on the Cam. We made the grand ball at which he had his fatal stroke a select dinner party, altered Sir George's passion for stag-hunting to a mania for stamp-collecting. It was easy work and we relished it. When we had finished, Morty said, 'I like that. The client'll buy it.

Sex. History. Cutaways while the heroine takes off her crinoline, I like that. Maybe bring in some big names. Gladstone. Disraeli. That sort of thing. Find some place in the country to film it.' He looked at his watch. 'Jesus, Martin, I've got to go. Promised Terry I'd meet him at four. You feel like coming along?'

I shook my head.

'Uh huh. Right then, I'll catch you later.'

We wandered back along the narrow, linoleumed corridors, down the rickety staircase to the hall. Here in the glass cage the same porter still sat, still smoking a cigarette. A spirit of mild curiosity, which had lain dormant during the truncations and realignments of the previous half-hour, flared briefly into life once more.

'Who's the backer, Morty? Who's giving us the three-quarters of a million?'

Morty shrugged. 'Oh, some guy of Terry's. Some guy Terry picked up somewhere. An old guy, edits some magazine nobody's ever heard of. Foreign name. Tomas. Tovacs. Something like that. You ever heard of him?'

Once more the ratchet clicked slowly into place. 'Yes,' I said, 'I've heard of him.'

And for some reason I secreted this information inside me, not yet wanting to impart it to Elaine, and added it to my old worry about Morty and my new worry about Elaine, added it to the inklings of subterfuge and dissimulation which I had already detected and carried within me for a long time, seeing in these unexceptionable signs the certainty of some future reckoning, like faint trails of smoke seen across the horizon, a tiny crackle of distant thunder.

I came back to the flat to find that Elaine had preceded me. A dazzling metal-blue cape hung over a chair back. From along the hall came the sound of rushing water. Elaine lay in the bath reading a copy of the *Evening Standard*.

'What was it today? More mineral water?'

'Worse. Condoms. I had to wear this blue costume and be Captain Condom and stand in the middle of a room full of schoolkids telling them that sex was a healthy and meaningful experience.'

'Did they look as if they believed you?'

'They just looked spotty. Embarrassed and spotty. One of them tried to ask me out.'

'What did you say?'

'I was very naughty. I told him I liked it rough. I told him sex was about pain, not healthy and meaningful experiences. And then I gave him the supervisor's home number and told him that if he still wanted to go through with it he should ring in the evening and ask for Madame Domina.'

'Then what happened?'

'Oh, he just started apologising, you know how they do. But he was very sweet. He called me "Miss".'

I wandered back into the hall and to the telephone, where a series of messages had accumulated on the answer machine: messages from out-of-work actors who thought I could put in a word, casting agencies who wanted to ask me to lunch. Clearly the news of Morty's backer was out. As I bent down over the receiver it rang again.

'Martin? Morty. Something else I wanted to talk to you about.'

A great blare of noise washed over Morty's voice and faded away again.

'Where are you calling from?'

'Jesus, someplace Terry took me. The Bazooka Club. But listen . . . The thing about *Resurrection* is that we've got to move fast on this one, right? Development costs, site hire. It's going to need money up front. So basically I'm doing a debt recall. Everything that's gone out in the last two years has got to come back in. All of it.'

It was the ancient language of Dean Street. In times of plenty, distribute your surpluses in the hope that in times of hardship you might be able to call them back.

'Where do I come in, Morty?'

'It's . . .' There was another remote, clangorous eruption, as if somebody had dropped a tray a long way off. 'The thing is I want you to take tomorrow off and go and see Frank Fellatio.'

'I didn't know Frank still worked for you.'

'He doesn't. Not since *The Sword Swallower* back in '78. But he owes me two grand. I want you to take tomorrow off and go and get it.'

'Look, Morty . . .'

'Jesus, Martin. You know what I expect at a time like this? I expect a little loyalty. That's right, a little loyalty. Nobody's asking you to smuggle drugs, or beat up some old lady. Just go and see Frank and collect the two grand. Crazy Rodney'll come with you. A child of six could do it.'

'Look, Morty, I have things to do . . .'

'You know something, Martin? You disappoint me. You disappoint me a lot. Do I make myself clear?'

'You do, Morty. You make yourself perfectly clear.'

The voice blared on like some great implacable dog straining at the end of the leash. Eventually I put the phone down.

Elaine provided no comfort. Throughout her time at Leisurevision she had maintained an air of grim nonchalance about Morty's activities which allowed little compromise.

'You know what Morty's like? If somebody owes him two thousand pounds, do you expect him to put an invoice in the post? You knew what Morty was like when you got into this. Do you really expect him to turn round and act like Mr Nice Guy?'

'But why me?'

'Jesus Christ, Martin. Sometimes you make me so angry. You do. You don't realise it, but you do. I mean, what do you think these people are? I've watched you with Morty. You treat him as if he was some sort of loveable East End rogue with a heart of gold. Something off the television.'

'That's not true.'

'It fucking *is.* I've watched you. I know. You practically snigger every time he speaks to you. Him and Terry Chimes. He's a *pornographer*. He makes money out of sex. What sort of person does that? Those contact magazines he publishes, the ones where blokes send in pictures of their wives turning their vaginas inside out, what sort of a man do you think does that? A philanthropist? And where does that leave you with those bloody clever scripts you write about schoolgirls entertaining the rugby team in the shower?'

'You wouldn't understand.'

'You poor baby,' Elaine said pityingly. 'You never had a chance, did you?'

Later, when Elaine had gone to bed, I sat by the gas fire and read Mr Tovacs's novel. I had done so once before, but could remember nothing of it. It was a small, slim volume which, while printed in English, had been published on the Continent in the late 1940s. There were recommendations on the jacket from Connolly, Spender and Eliot. As I read, phrases from some ghostly unwritten review ran through my head: 'The spirit of Norman Douglas and the politics of Joseph Roth'; 'a Bohemian Sitwell'; 'Firbank in *Mitteleuropa*'. It was a queer, recondite work of a kind unfashionable even then: florid, overwritten, decked out with classical quotation, the atmosphere that of a hothouse, the prose orchidaceous. Its plot was picaresque: a young man's wanderings in an unfallen, pre-war Europe, his dalliance with the women he meets in hotels along the way, a long bravura passage retailing his impressions of a cornfield in summer. And everywhere the hint of approaching doom: aeroplanes hanging in the autumn sky, lines of marching men, crowded railway stations; a potent symbolism, honed by a key scene in which the hero, making love to his mistress in the open air, raises his head to greet a swirl of descending propaganda leaflets, each marked with a swastika.

When I had finished I turned back to the title page. Here there was a dedication: *À mon ami Jean Cocteau.* I put the book back on the shelf in the study and went to bed.

It snowed again that night and I stood for a long time at the window watching the pale, even flakes falling over last summer's rose bushes, turning the outstation of dustbins and refuse bags into angular hummocks like ancient burial chambers. Snow coming in from the west and falling over the suburbs of outer London, over Ealing, Hammersmith and the Fulham Road. As ever I thought of other snow, falling long ago, on Eaton Park where I had gone as a child with my father, of snow falling over the level East Anglian plain, over remote landscapes that existed only in the imagination. Elaine slept on, her face turned slightly to one side, and I watched her too, until other faces, other memories, emerged to fill this dense, penumbral frame: my father, other girls to whom in this silent, half-waking state I could no longer put names, a virgin field of snow seen once in the countryside outside Norwich which I had not dared to despoil. Random images, suggesting both extinction and renewal, concealment, the transformation of old, familiar things into shapes that were new and unrecognisable, the whole coalescing into unreality, dominated by colour, by whites, greys, blue-black shadow, dead, submarine faces.

In the small hours the phone rang once more. I listened into the crackling receiver for a while, silent, but appreciative of the spirit which ordained this fruitless quest, this search across thousands of miles for this person of whom nobody knew and of whom there was now no trace. The voice, for once uninterrupted, seemed appeased, content to ramble slowly on, digressive, uneasy, always returning to its unanswerable question, its puzzled disbelief, a litany given shape by recurring phrases and quirks of diction. At dawn, the snow gone now to fall over other gardens, cerise streaks of sunlight moving into the western sky, I went to bed.

I woke late to find that Elaine had already disappeared. A sheet of notepaper lay propped up against a milk bottle on the kitchen table. It read, 'Back later, just do it.' There was post on the mat: bank statements, a rent cheque from the Norwich solicitors, an early Christmas card with a scrawled, anonymous signature. I took the letters into the living room and read them staring out over the tennis courts, where two elderly men were stepping warily over the frozen surface, patting the ball dextrously back and forth. Pictures of Elaine hung everywhere: Elaine, wide-eyed and obdurate in a promo shot Morty had had taken around the time of *Girlschool Janitor*, Elaine in loincloth and warpaint for the Leisurevision remake of *Tarzan*, Elaine among a group of partygoers, an ellipse of bland, disinterested faces that included Mike and Bernie Winters and Barbara Windsor. It was then, curiously, that I became aware of what had happened. Something had gone wrong, I realised. The machine had broken down, some vital part of its mechanism had become impaired, torn adrift in a grinding of gears and blunt edges, the whole lying useless and irreparable.

There had been similar moments before in my life: moments with women, with my father, with ambitions, long tended and stoked up, whose promise had finally ebbed away. Such situations, I knew, required a decisive gesture, an uncancellable tug at solid but untenable moorings. Once in my early twenties during the time with Roger Garfitt I had seized on the first half of a novel I had written, a manuscript on which I had expended two years' patient labour, and burned it page by page. It would never be published and that realisation, at that age and at that time, was enough. The present, I realised, demanded an identical course, a slewing away from the slaughterer's embrace back to familiar certainties. And so I stood for a moment amid the pictures of Elaine, as the old men continued to play tennis and the green tennis balls rose every so often into view, wondering what I might do with myself and in whose hands the solution lay.

Time dragged.

The negotiations for the funding of *Resurrection* proved more irksome than Morty had imagined. Two years before he might have found a distribution chain, or even a bank to underwrite Mr Tovacs's promised thousands, to provide down payments for equipment and venues. Now such days were over. Influential connections, made in the boom years of the Seventies, patiently maintained thereafter, proved unhelpful. The American owner of an adult cinema chain passing through London and enticed into Dean Street shook his head. It would not do, he thought. The days of costume drama and all its attendant exoticism had passed. What the American public wanted was straight sex and no messing. Casting sessions, planned in anticipation of his agreement, were hastily cancelled. Later Morty tested older and more durable affiliations in Europe, wires stretching out beyond the censorship laws of the United Kingdom; they were to no avail. Finally, with affected reluctance, Morty decided to sell several of his freeholds in the East End. 'I'll get a hundred grand maybe,' he explained, 'and it's a bad time for property, but what can you do?' In the event the houses in the Bow Road realised seventy thousand pounds. It was a bad time for property. But the money proved narrowly sufficient. A second group of actresses arrived at the loft to take off their clothes and parrot the lines of dialogue I had written for them. The proceedings were enlivened by the presence of Mr Tovacs himself. He sat in a deckchair at the back of the room and seemed flattered by the deference paid to him. 'You would not perhaps think it possible,' he explained, 'but I have some small experience of these matters. In Berlin, before the war. I must say that this seems very tame by comparison.' Mr Tovacs brought another girl with him, not American, who spoke no English. At intervals during the auditions they conversed in an odd, unidentifiable language.

The image of Mr Tovacs hung heavily over these weeks of preparation: interested, amused, inscrutable. He came into Morty's office and sat poring over books he had brought with him, or chatted affably with the cameramen. At other times he was gone, off to attend meetings about the Polish crisis, meetings at which toasts were drunk to the Gdansk shipyards and Jaruzelski burned in effigy. He returned from these gatherings subdued, a little fretful, bored by Morty's talk and the Dean Street chatter. It was Elaine, characteristically, who put this change in temperament into focus.

'They don't like him you know at those *Solidarność* rallies. I went to one once. Very cool. Lots of old ladies looking down their lorgnettes at him. They wish he wouldn't come.'

'Why?'

I saw little of Elaine at these times. It was a routine to which we had become habituated: a routine of snatched conversations, information gathered in the course of day-long absences carefully stored up for future use.

'Tovacs. Not a Polish name. Hungarian. A vicarious attachment, don't you think. And then there's the question of the money.'

'Plenty of wealthy Hungarian émigrés in London, surely?'

'Not like Tovacs. Tovacs is properly rich. I went to a party at his flat once. Expressionist paintings all over the walls. Real expressionist paintings, not copies. Sideboards full of silver. They don't like that, the Poles. You talk to them about how they got here and you hear about abandoned castles, all the stuff the Nazis took. "My father was a prince and I live in a bedsit on the Bayswater Road." You saw the ones at the Wigmore Hall. They might look like royalty in exile – some of them are – but they're as poor as churchmice really. Moth holes all over the court dresses. Tovacs brought all his with him. No commissars to get rich on what he left behind.'

'When did he get out?'

'Nobody knows. Nobody says. I'll tell you another thing. Get Tovacs to talk about the Jews. Tovacs is good on the Jews. Tovacs lived in Germany. Don't ask me how I know. It just came out once. Not what you'd expect.'

So I had another pastime in these days of waiting and desultory preparation. As Morty fretted over cashflows and storyboards, as negotiations were set in hand to hire a country house where *Resurrection* might be filmed, and as Elaine retired yet further into herself, I set about investigating Mr Tovacs.

Even at this early stage I found Mr Tovacs a figure of consuming interest. The literary affiliations, the hint – conveyed in the story about Walesa – of exalted connections in quite another sphere, what Elaine had said about the Jews, an overwhelming appropriateness to his environment. Each of these factors, unremarkable in themselves, combined to provide a purposeful air of mystery, a series of minor conundrums brought together in a single acrostic of intricate design. Though the specific enquiries which arose about Mr Tovacs – his relationship with Morty, his interest in Morty's operations – might receive satisfactory answers, a greater puzzle remained, one whose bearing on our own lives could not be ignored, whose capacity to threaten a far from impregnable position promised future disturbance. Absorbed, engrossed, giving the impression of being caught up in a dozen careless intrigues, there was something about Mr Tovacs which set one's teeth on edge: a tiny intimation of disquiet rising up to disturb the expressions of amity, which only constant surveillance might keep in check.

The trail led in many directions. From an antiquarian bookseller in Cecil Court I purchased, at exorbitant cost, an early number of *Pages*, Mr Tovacs's literary magazine. Printed in the late 1940s, a Picasso nude on the frontispiece, the endpapers a design by Henry Moore, its theme was the reconstitution of European culture. There were poems by Tambimuttu, Spender and Maurice Sachs, none at their best. Mr Tovacs contributed a queer, billowing editorial, extending to several pages, in whose resonant periods and lapidary phrasing I detected the mark of the polyglot. There were winsome marginalia, messages of support from Shaw, Sartre and Edith Sitwell. It was a wholly exotic production, un-English, a whiff of high European culture blowing across the straitened domestic landscape. There was an air of cultivated modesty about the introductory notes, with their references to 'Mr Eliot' and 'M. Proust', as if the writer were determined to demonstrate that he was merely an impresario, one who had assembled this august company, but was scarcely fit for inclusion within their ranks; here and there an odd tart remark suggestive of some long-dead literary controversy. At no point did the writer reveal anything of a personal nature.

The catalogue in the London Library listed a dozen items: books, pamphlets, a Proust symposium printed in Paris on the thirtieth anniversary of the writer's death. Many of these had now disappeared from the shelves, but after persistent searching I secured a further three novels – *Columbine*, *Harlequin* and *Pierrot*. Published in the 1950s by an obscure English firm, these were handsome productions, finely bound and with engravings by Augustus John and Felicien Rops. *Columbine*, in particular, attracted my attention. A long short story, scarcely more than a hundred pages in length, it concerned a woman known only as 'C' at large in a fantastic world of ancient castles and perilous mountains, and her efforts to avoid 'the enemy'. The model, clearly enough, was Kafka, but the incidental descriptions of landscape and scene had all the glamour of the fairy tale. The book's conclusion, too, suggested fable, a fable gone horribly wrong, perverted out of its original course: C, imprisoned by the enemy – sinister, black-coated men – becomes their willing ally, betrays her family and lover and is fêted by her pursuers.

Mr Tovacs himself was a more elusive quarry. There were several references in the more gossipy memoirs of the period, many of them contradictory. His age was variously estimated as 72, 65 and – bizarrely – 90. He was supposed to have been Matisse's pupil, to have collaborated with Moholy-Nagy and been the friend of Sylvia Beach. I suspected immediately that such descriptions had an apocryphal quality, that Mr Tovacs was no more than one of those busy minor figures who attach themselves to any cultural landscape, moving on from city to city, from salon to salon, steadily accumulating their rows of footnotes in the cultural gazetteers. I found him everywhere, in Stravinsky's *Collected Letters*, in the correspondence columns of *Horizon*, even – impressively – in the *Fontana Dictionary of Modern Thought*, polite, knowledgeable, suggestive. But still amid this wealth of allusion, resplendent among these exalted connections, there was no trace of his essential nature. In the company of men and women whose lives now lay documented to an infinite degree, he had somehow managed to evade the biographer's grasp.

And then, quite by chance, I discovered a work by various hands, published in London in the 1950s under the title of *Émigrés.* Compared to the elevated productions to which Mr Tovacs customarily put his hand, this seemed every inch a commercial undertaking: a series of essays in which foreigners now resident in the United Kingdom reflected on the circumstances of their arrival. Their tenor – ambassadorial, Anglophile – was not wholly dispirited. Mr Tovacs's essay was the exception. In contrast to optimistic titles such as 'Why I came to London' and 'Land of opportunity', his own was headed simply 'Exile'. It began, conventionally enough, with a résumé of the theme of exile in literature: Adam and Eve, the Exodus, the Greek myths, Viking sagas, moving on to medieval themes of loss and estrangement. A short coda seemed to strike an autobiographical note.

> The exile [Mr Tovacs had written] takes with him to his new life not only a sense of dispossession, of removal from a land that is rightfully his, but the sense of grievance. This grievance takes many forms. It is directed, most obviously, at whichever agency ordained his departure, at a social or economic force, at an ideology, at an individual, but it is also directed at himself. For the exile views himself as one cast out from some roseate, primordial garden, as one who has fallen from grace. And like those expelled from an original Eden, he is conscious that in a large measure the blame lies with himself rather than with those who expelled him. Looking back he can only reproach himself for his failure to compromise, to conciliate, to become as one with those who dismissed him. We are all, in a certain sense, born in exile, spend long ages working our passage back over uncharted seas. But the true exile is one who lives with his anxieties, to whom the older world, with its sense of infinite promise, is now more real than that which has taken its place.

Kay says, 'I thought you come from London at first. I thought you were really strange. But you're from round here, aren't you? I can tell it sometimes when you talk to him.'

Early afternoon in Fat Eric and Kay's cluttered lounge. Bobby Dazz on the record player, the sheen of sunlight reflected off the abandoned lager cans. Shuffling in from the kitchen, tray balanced precariously on one hand, Kay stops to look at me, a momentary shrewdness suffusing the peasant features.

'I'm a Norwich boy, Kay. Always will be. Colman Road Primary and the Grammar. You know, the boys in the blue blazers.'

'I know. The Spuds, we used to call them. King Edward potatoes, you know. Now Eric, he used to *hate* the Spuds.'

It's a private school now, gentrified by the Labour government. Kay reminisces on, 'Used to hate them. When he was fifteen, you know how it is with those grammar-school boys, he hit this kid in the mouth with a hockey stick. You never saw anything like it.'

Kay. For some reason I get to see a great deal of Kay these days. I see her sidling past in the gloomy forenoons on her way back from the shops in Unthank Road, I glimpse her staggering back from the off-licence under the weight of Fat Eric's carry-outs. We meet in the newsagent's, in pubs, takeaways. Skulking back from long, cross-city trawls in the late afternoon there comes, inevitably, a time when I stop and register the identity of the figure under the tree, smoking the cigarette. There are, it should be said, very good reasons for these encounters, splendid reasons. Why, Kay is buying a newspaper, a drink or a takeaway, or simply 'out for a walk'.

Fat Eric's impedimenta lie nearby: over the sofa and across the floor, giant spoor left by some gross, untidy beast. Duty-free Marlboros, still in their cellophane, videos, a sheet torn from the *Eastern Evening News*, bearing the legend 'Kevin Flack signs new contract'.

Kay goes on, 'I used to think you were making it up at first, all that stuff about Bobby Dazz and the Glasgow Express. But you're not, are you? Making it up, I mean?'

'No, Kay, I'm not making it up.'

'When I was a kid,' Kay says absently, 'I used to like the Express. I mean, *really* like them. This girl and me, right, we used to dress ourselves up in the gear. Sew tartan flares into our jeans and that. I often wondered what happened to them.'

Died. Went mad. Vanished. 'Show business is a funny thing, Kay. People come into it and then they leave it, and sometimes nobody knows why.'

'Uh huh.' Kay opens one of Fat Eric's cigarette packets and scoops a Marlboro into her mouth. She smokes with peculiar intensity, in bitter, angry puffs. Looking at her as she sits there on the sofa, legs drawn up beneath her teeming haunches, pudgy forearms dangling, I realise that this is what is known in local terms as 'letting yourself go'. Suzi uses this expression sometimes. For her it means not washing your hair three times a week and drinking too much on your birthday. For Kay, alas, it means not washing your hair at all and drinking too much all the time.

Outside a skateboard clatters on the concrete. The wind lifts. All day it has been blowing in from the coast, from Yarmouth and Cromer and Sheringham, bringing the gulls and that odd smell of salt. Later, as the unprompted monologues grow longer and the cigarette smoke rises, Kay grows confidential. She says, 'Oh, he's a wrong 'un, Eric is, a right bastard. I don't mean he'd do anything really bad – he wouldn't break into people's houses, he wouldn't hurt them or nothing – but he's a wrong 'un just the same. Where do you think he gets the videos he sells in the pub and the cigarettes? And that stall on the market. Him and that Ron. You didn't ever meet Ron, did you? Proper pair *they* are.

'. . . I suppose I should have told him to go away. Can always do that, can't you? Tell them to go away. I don't know. I was seventeen. I didn't know anything. And then I'm in this pub in Earlham and this bloke comes up, and he's got the money and he's got the chat and reckons he can get me a job. Got this place we can live in, I didn't think about it. Eric weren't like anyone I'd ever met before, not in Fram. After I came down here this boy used to ring me up, just friendly like, you know. I honestly don't think he were interested. Anyway, Eric smashed him with a glass one night in the Gates . . .

'. . . He don't do that so much now. I mean fighting's for kids, isn't it? That lot you see on the park, the Steins. Eric isn't one of them real nutters, you know, the ones you see at the match, the ones who'll hit anyone just to see what happens. Not like that.' Using the cigarette like a magnet to draw the room towards her, Kay smiles for a moment, like the terrorists' mothers one sees on the television, the relicts of the brave boys in Long Kesh, still doling out their foolish charity, and the certainties of life with Fat Eric, of life with this terrible shiny beast, painfully unroll.

'You're tough, Kay. You can take it.'

'That's what Eric says. "You can take it," he says, when we're in the pub with Woody and that lot, making me drinking that Pernod. The fucker,' Kay says.

Later, when I get up to go, she says, 'I meant to tell you: it don't mean anything, you know. Oh, I know you and Eric're mates, and he buys you drinks and goes after your money, but it don't mean anything. He's sly, Eric is. I can see the way he looks at you in the pub. He'll have Ron round to talk to you next, that's what he'll do, and then you'll have Ron ringing you up, wanting you to do things. Just little things at first. You know, twenty quid for repairing the van because you're mates and they're hard up. Once that starts you won't hear the last of it. It'll be bigger things after that. You know, two hundred quid for a trailer and "You got any contacts?" and getting asked round Ron's for meals. Big house up Thorpe way he's got; I been round there once and it's full of stuff you'd want to ask questions about. And then you're one of Ron's mates and where are you? Got Ron sitting on your neck, asking you to do things.'

'So long, Kay. Thanks for the coffee.'

Kay shakes her head. 'You don't know anything about it,' she pronounces. 'Eric now, he's a hard case. He doesn't care about people and he doesn't care about me, but he don't mean any harm. Ron, he's something else. Eric's scared of Ron. Says he isn't, but he is. I can see it. Eric, he might talk big now and again, but Ron, he's a real *villain*.

'I reckon Ron's really hurt people,' Kay says.

Outside the street is grey and sad. The privet hedges are covered with a watery film. I go back to the house – no Suzi and the flies scuttling over the unwashed plates – and think about some other *villains*, about Morty and Terry Chimes, Crazy Rodney and Charlie Scaduto. Did Morty ever really hurt anyone? I don't know. Like many another small-timer on the way up Morty was skilled in the art of frightening people – the well-intentioned word that, obscurely, prompted some rival to start another business in another town – but I don't think he ever really hurt anyone. I go to the hidey-hole beneath the staircase, take out the video from its sleek box and juggle it from hand to hand, wonder about the person who sent it. Did he ever really hurt anyone? The light fades and the dark moves in through the uncurtained windows. Eventually Suzi arrives, lets herself in, and finds me half asleep on the sofa.

'Nice dreams?' she asks, scarlet-faced and wearing her tennis gear.

'No,' I tell her, 'not nice dreams. Not nice dreams at all.'

Later in the evening Kev Jackson telephones, a pleased, proud Kev Jackson, whose voice tingles with self-importance. He says, 'I have that information you wanted. Like to hear it?'

'Where did you get it from?'

'Been asking around,' Kev says affably. 'You remember Tony Winder, that guy Morty used to hang out with in the early days? Well, I took him out to lunch and . . .'

'Fine,' I say, cutting short this recitation of source material. 'Just fine, Kev. What did you find out?'

'It's all on file,' Kev says. 'Just listen a minute, will you? Okay: Elaine Keenan. Born County Kerry, Eire, 1953. Around in London late '75, early '76. First starring role was in *Girlschool Janitor* with Frank Fellatio. Played the governess in *Stately Lust* . . .'

'I know all that.'

'This is just background,' Kev concedes. 'Ten or fifteen films with Morty. You can still pick them up in Soho. I watched a couple the other week at some video store in Brewer. Quite hot, even now. An inspired performance in *Mother Superior* . . .'

'I know all that too. What about later on? After *Resurrection*, all that early-Eighties stuff. What about then?'

There is a pause. Paper rustles faintly down the wire. 'Yeah, well that's when things start getting confused. Terry Chimes – I talked to him last week, he says to say hi again – reckoned she went to Berlin, starred in that Color Climax series, *Chambermaids*. You ever see any of those?'

'No.'

'Well, take it from me, Martin, it would make your hair curl. Show that on a screen anywhere in the UK and you'd have the Vice Squad round to breakfast, dinner and tea. Hard-core and then some. Couldn't see if it was her or not, though. All the girls were blondes and they didn't have a castlist . . .'

He prattles on and I look away out of the window at the dark hump of the park rising up above the hill, back to the desk where there is a photograph of Suzi, a very young Suzi with half-formed, snowball breasts swelling out of a halter-top bathing costume, a memento of God knows what teenage saturnalia.

'. . . Then I talked to this other guy I met at the *Adult Video World* party, used to work at one of the model agencies, reckoned she was in Manchester working for some PR outfit.'

Suzi's face in the bathing costume picture looks absurdly flat, like dough rolled up into a slab, features stuck on as an afterthought.

'Look, Kev,' I interject, 'this is great. I mean, I appreciate what you've done and everything, but you have to get me an address.'

'An address?' He considers this for a moment, wide-eyed Kev in his writer's flat, somewhere in teeming London. 'That could be difficult.'

'A phone number then. Just a phone number and I'll tell you everything. Morty. Terry Chimes. The money. All of it.'

He rings off after this. I pad down to the lounge where Suzi is marking essays in a vague, bovine way.

'Who was that?' she enquires.

'Just a friend.'

We look at each other for a while reflectively. Eventually Suzi turns on the television and I sit down with the *Eastern Evening News* to relish again its cheering quota of tree-bound cats, confectionery shop break-ins and Kevin Flack's groin strain, and there is harmony of a sort.

It happens on the way back from the Manchester United game. Woody and the others have disappeared somewhere, vanished into the early-evening maelstrom of the city, peeled away to fish and chip shops, to pubs and pizza joints. Just Fat Eric and I plodding away on our homeward route, through the boarded-up walkways of the market, up past the City Hall, over the dark expanse of Chapel Field Gardens. It happens there in a dense patch of shadow, the streetlamps buzzing away imperfectly above us, where the path descends towards the subway. Fat Eric, subdued by the excitements of the previous three hours, Norwich having miraculously contrived a 2–1 victory, is discoursing soberly on the topic of Kay. 'A real *alki*,' he deposes courteously, 'a real *boozer*. I come back from the stall the other day – Ron and me, we'd put in a good twelve hours – and there she is on the sofa, pissed out of her head . . .' It happens when the four boys, all curiously resembling each other – vee-neck pullovers, short hair, trainers, white, moon faces – ease out of their lair somewhere in the murk beside us and come galloping on. It happens so fast that I don't even appreciate what it is. I even apologise as the first one stumbles into me, say 'Excuse me' in a mildly puzzled way as he veers round and shuffles into me again. Even at this point, as numbers two and three cannon purposefully into Fat Eric's *embonpoint* stomach, the feeling is less that of fear than slightly aggrieved bewilderment, the thought that somebody will shortly explain what this is about, that there is some perfectly convincing reason for this odd circuitous sequence of push and shove, pantomime blind man's buff, like a children's game I used to play at primary school where you stand on one leg, fold your arms and try to barge your opponent into oblivion.

Fat Eric? Fat Eric is magnificent. I once saw a television nature programme in which a solitary, determined moose fought off the onslaught of a pack of starving timber wolves, tossed them on his antlers, ground them remorselessly into the dirt with his hooves, stamped viciously on their pinioned skulls, until the wounded remnant slunk miserably away. This is a fair approximation of Fat

Eric's fighting technique. Grim, resourceful, steel-eyed, he wheels backwards, comes down hard with his foot on a rashly extended instep, takes out a second assailant with a flailing forearm, goes to corner a third up against the subway wall. The pale boys look worried now. This wasn't what they expected, wasn't what they wanted at all. The fourth one, who has been scuffling with me in a half-hearted way, thinks better of it and sets off at a run, disappears into the silence of the park. Fat Eric, by this time, has got his quarry in an arm-lock, whips a massive knee up into his face and sends him sprawling on to the tarmac. 'Bastard,' Fat Eric is muttering in a detached monotone. 'Bastard, bastard, bastard.'

It stops soon after this. The first two of Fat Eric's victims limp away. The third lies in an untidy heap propped up against the subway wall. Fat Eric kicks him a couple of times for good measure and then strides on. 'Them kids,' he says, 'ought to be more careful who they have a go at.' Later he says, 'Fucking Steins. You can tell it from what they wear. Them purple vee-necks. Dead giveaway they are.'

We plod on through the subway, emerge on to silent, empty streets. The incident is never referred to again.

In addition to his flat in Kensington, Mr Tovacs had premises in Red Lion Street: a set of rooms above an émigré bookshop which sold newspapers in a variety of languages and displayed portraits of exiled Eastern European royalty. It was here that Mr Tovacs conducted the editorial business of *Pages*, from here that he addressed his contributions to the correspondence columns of weekly magazines. A Polish relief organisation, supported by several MPs and prominent *literati*, operated from offices on its upper floor. It was here too that, one evening late in November, the various collaborators in *Resurrection* were bidden to assemble.

Rain, sweeping in sharply from the direction of High Holborn, gave a menacing aspect to a landscape with which I was already familiar. The old *Spectator* offices, where I had peddled articles six or seven years ago, were a stone's throw away in Gower Street. Here too Roger Garfitt and I had once come in search of vacation jobs with a news agency in Red Lion Square. The glamour model, I remembered, had rented a flat in Coram Street, handy for the

Daily Mirror building in Holborn Circus. Each of these associations bore its own fatal quota of distress: memories of overlong waits in gloomy reception halls, fruitless self-advertisement – the news agency found to be bogus and offering only unpaid 'experience' – silent recrimination. Turning northwards from High Holborn, the lines of traffic immediately diminishing into a single vehicle twenty yards ahead of us, apparently proceeding under some constraint, this sense of unease became almost tangible: a pressing reminder of past uncertainty and enduring hurt. The rain continued to fall. Elaine said, 'Did anyone tell you to expect a party?'

'No. Did they tell you?'

'I found out,' Elaine said inscrutably. 'Nobody told Morty or Terry either.'

'Will that make a difference?'

'I shouldn't think so. But it might cramp Morty's style.'

'Who'll be there?'

'Writers. The Polish lot. Tovacs's women.'

'Tovacs's wife?'

'No. Definitely not Tovacs's wife.'

I was used to this compartmentalising of professional and private lives. Morty's wives, their number now settled at three, were brought out annually at parties held on New Year's Eve. There was supposedly a Mrs Chimes living somewhere on the Suffolk border. Nobody I knew had ever seen her. Looking at Elaine as she stood in the reflected glare of the streetlamp, I realised that this revelation explained various peculiarities in her get-up: it explained the beret, worn rakishly at an angle on one corner of her head, and it explained the gleaming definition of her features. She seemed nervously expectant, I thought, the possessor of a store of secret information which might be doled out during the course of the evening.

'Have you been to these things before?'

'Once. About a year ago. That time you were in Amsterdam with Morty.'

'What happened then?'

'Not much. There was a string quartet playing mazurkas, and Tovacs talked a lot about Picasso.'

The bookshop stood halfway along Red Lion Street, between a silent restaurant and a boarded-up newsagent's. Its frontage, previously reserved for a display of unpromising-looking titles, was now dominated by a huge *Solidarność* banner, extending across almost the entire width of the room. Noise – music, indistinguishable voices – drifted down from an upstairs window. The car which had slowly preceded us along the street stopped abruptly and a brooding, bulky figure emerged.

'That you, Martin?'

'Over here.'

Terry Chimes said, 'Thought it was you when I turned into the road. Couple of cunts holding hands under a streetlamp. Thought it was you.' He cast an eye briefly over the window display. 'Fucking awful place to have a party, don't you reckon?'

I turned and looked at him. Boisterous and unimpressed, Terry Chimes seemed an incongruous visitor to Mr Tovacs's lair. He was wearing what he sometimes called his 'cunt-hunting' suit, a garment in outsize red check, its trousers flared to the point where they resembled Oxford bags, a white shirt with wide, drooping collars. He carried a bottle of whisky, lodged stiffly under his elbow like a swagger stick.

'Any sign of Morty?'

'Left him at Dean Street. Still fixing up that place in Suffolk for the shoot.'

'Suffolk, is it now?'

'Sure. Aldeburgh, or Southwold, or somewhere. Some country house somebody told him about. In the middle of a field of sugar beet and five miles to the nearest boozer.'

He seemed disinclined to talk. By now it had begun to rain even harder and we clustered beneath the overhang of a small porch to the right of the shop. Here, beyond an illuminated glass door, steps rose sharply into darkness. Elaine pressed the buzzer. On the far side of the glass, legs, weirdly truncated by the angle of the staircase, slowly descended. A voice said indistinctly, 'Welcome to the bat-cave.'

It was the American girl, Jerry. She gave no sign of recognising any of us, or being particularly interested in our identities. Dressed in a black body-stocking, the general air of gloom brightened by a scarlet sash tethered around her waist, her attitude suggested someone constrained by higher authority into a role she considered entirely beneath her.

'The party's upstairs,' she said.

As we filed past she lay back against the banisters and examined us critically. Elaine and I seemed to pass muster. As Terry Chimes drew level with her on the stair I heard her mutter, '*Not* fancy dress.'

Beyond, a dark corridor opened out to reveal a long, angular chamber, high-ceilinged and brightly lit, the further end widening into a recess dominated by a broad trestle table on which lay wine bottles and plates of sandwiches. That this was a place of business recently converted along lines thought suitable for entertainment seemed clear from a general air of untidiness. There were cardboard boxes all over the floor, bookshelves pushed back to the walls and draped over with cloths, a pile of stamped envelopes pressed into service as a doorstop. Thin, unidentifiable music, apparently coming from some fixed point high above us, was finally located in a wind-up gramophone placed on an occasional table by the door. As Elaine and I stood uncertainly by this humming relic Mr Tovacs, previously unseen behind a knot of guests, detached himself and moved hastily towards us. Showing by the alignment of his body that he spoke to Elaine, he said, 'I am delighted to see you again. It was good of you to come. No doubt you have brought Mr Goldstein with you?'

'Still at Dean Street,' Elaine said. 'He'll be along later, I shouldn't wonder.'

Mr Tovacs nodded. The transformation in his appearance was, I realised, complete. Seen in the unfamiliar setting of the Wigmore Hall a month before he had seemed uncertain, ill at ease, unable for the most part to defend himself from unwelcome questions and chance insinuations. Here, on what was presumably his home territory, he looked entirely in his element, a creature of infinite resource, concealing reservoirs of expertise that would enable him to deal with the unlikeliest contingency. He wore predominantly the clothes that I remembered from our first meeting, but there were quaint and somehow wholly appropriate additions – a spotted foulard scarf, a buttonhole, odd, parti-coloured shoes, the whole adding an extra, resonant dimension to the earlier portrait. It was a dandy's get-up, I thought, not many miles distant from the music hall comedian. In fact, if Mr Tovacs suggested a prototype it was Archie Rice in *The Entertainer*.

There was a sudden press of new arrivals: two girls of about Elaine's age, a venerable Pole in a greatcoat whom Mr Tovacs kissed decorously on both cheeks and then directed toward the drinks table.

I said, 'Are all these people connected with the Solidarity campaign?'

'A number. They are also artistic people, literary people.' Mr Tovacs looked cautious as he said this, as if he would have preferred an explanation of my interest in the Polish situation before going any further. 'After all, we are in Bloomsbury, are we not? A very suitable place for *a salon*?'

'A very suitable place. I suppose you must have entertained many celebrated people here?'

It was obviously the right thing to have said. Whatever doubts Mr Tovacs might have had about my interest in him were immediately dispelled. He said, 'You are kind enough to say so. There was a man here last week from a newspaper asking the same question. He wanted to know about Eliot,' Mr Tovacs went on, a shade petulantly. 'An ignorant man. It is no use talking to such people. What is it to them that Cocteau sat in that chair, or that in this room I took dictation from Maurice Sachs?' He paused. 'And yet today I find that I have achieved distinction in quite another sphere.'

'What sort of distinction?'

Mr Tovacs fished carefully in the inner pocket of his jacket, at length emerging with a crumpled press cutting. Taken from the 'Pseuds Corner' column of *Private Eye*, it was an extract from an obituary Mr Tovacs had written of a recently deceased Bulgarian poet. I ran my eye over the quaint, orotund phrases: 'An embodiment of the *Zeitgeist* . . . The inhabitant now, alas, of that remote, nether pantheon . . . Plangent, crystalline verses . . .' To the casual reader it was a pretentious enough piece, certainly, but there was something oddly authentic about Mr Tovacs's eloquent memorials. Overstated and absurdly phrased, the motivation that lay beneath them seemed more or less genuine.

'It's a bit unfair.'

For some reason I supposed Mr Tovacs to require consolation for this indignity. Paradoxically he seemed delighted by this exposé of his literary style. 'No, you misunderstand me. It is the English sense of humour. Always, it has never ceased to amuse me. Art. Literature. Always, I have thought, these are closed doors to the English mind. But the English sense of humour? It endures. It is a constant. Somehow it is a compensation for these deficiencies . . .'

A mounting babble of noise from the far end of the room now exploded into crescendo. 'You must excuse me,' Mr Tovacs said, 'we will talk later.' I watched him ease his way off through the throng until he disappeared into the press of bodies, then turned – Elaine nowhere to be seen by this stage – to consider the room at large.

Looking at the scene of Mr Tovacs's party, some fifty people now, crammed into a space adequate for perhaps half that number, it was possible to locate echoes of an older age. The literary odds and ends, the boxes of magazines, 'artistic'-looking women with untidy fringes – all this suggested a Connolly/*Horizon* gathering along lines parodied by Evelyn Waugh. But there were other, decidedly unliterary, parallels. The sound of upraised, foreign voices, the gesticulating elderly men, the sense of angry, embittered exile: this seemed to belong to a yet more distant past, to evoke images of clandestine plotting, the secret police waiting at the door, frustrated hope – like a painting of the Paris Commune. The presence of so many women – young women dressed in black like Jerry, slightly older women in evening gowns with their hair scraped back across their foreheads, a few elderly gorgons of the type seen at the Wigmore Hall – all without exception attendant upon and observant of Mr Tovacs, introduced a third element, that of the seraglio.

Amid this throng, a gathering in which no one age or nationality predominated, a single figure stood out. Terry Chimes sat on a chair in the middle of the room cradling the bottle of whisky in his lap. He seemed hopelessly out of place, someone not up to the demands placed on him by his milieu, his appearance – the bizarre suit somehow appropriate – suggesting inner resources which he did not actually possess, like a Christy minstrel brought on to play Othello. As I stood watching him, Jerry came up. Mysteriously, all trace of her previous neutrality had vanished. She said, 'You were the guy who turned up at the Wigmore, right?'

'Right.'

'Uh huh. I heard you giving Tovacs all that soft soap about the fucking magazine.'

The note of aggression, trailed faintly in the first question, deepened in the second. She went on, 'All that stuff about Eliot. I heard. And taking dictation from Maurice Sachs. Has he told you about Picasso yet?'

'Not yet.'

'Uh huh. Look up there.'

At eye level on the wall beside us there were innumerable framed photographs, sketches, drawings in sepia and pencil, caricatures: Eliot seated on a footstool, one knee hoisted over the other, staring gloomily into space, a tall curly-haired man who might have been Stephen Spender standing beside him. Above, figures from an older, foreign era predominated: the Countess de Noailles, de Max in Pierrot costume. Among this profusion of portraits, theatrical scenes, aggressively posed literary groupings, was a framed drawing, notionally sketched in black ink, of a single, unidentifiable face, executed on what appeared to be a paper napkin. Beneath it ran a line of type: 'A gift from Pablo Picasso, Paris 1958.'

'Picasso drew this?'

'Uh huh. Do you know what he did it on?'

'No.'

'It's a piece of toilet roll. Straight up. Tovacs followed him into a public lavatory one time and asked him for a contribution to *Pages*. Caught him with his pants down. Literally. Picasso was so surprised that he just tore off another sheet and scribbled on it.'

'Did he get a lot of contributions like that?'

'Tovacs? Tovacs would dig up somebody's grave – some Nobel prizewinner's grave, that is – if he reckoned there was an unpublished short story buried along with the corpse.'

I had heard hints of this before. A recent issue of *Pages* had contained a *Times* crossword allegedly completed by Graham Greene at a public dinner in the 1960s and detached by Mr Tovacs while his fellow-guest was out of the room. Though it was good to hear these stories corroborated they did not detract from Mr Tovacs's allure as a personality. There was something ridiculous, certainly, about his pursuit of Picasso into the public lavatory –

what exactly had he said, I wondered? How had he introduced himself to the startled artist? – but also something dogged, a persistent unwillingness to settle for second best.

Jerry said, 'Looks like your friend could do with some help.'

'Which friend?'

'Medallion man. The guy you came with.'

In the centre of the room Terry Chimes stood talking to one of the girls in black, a younger and more appetising version of Jerry herself. The contrast in their attitudes was marked: the one cheery, confidential, insinuating, the other puzzled, laconic, suspicious. The conversation – animated on one side, reluctant on the other – stopped when Terry Chimes put a hand on the girl's shoulder and whispered something in her ear. The girl raised her eyebrows and marched off. I moved across.

'Chat-up lines not working?'

Terry Chimes prodded the carpet resentfully with his foot. He said, 'Thought I was on to something there. Right little prick-teaser if you ask me.' His manner changed abruptly and he raised his head. 'I can't stand those arty girls. Always wanting to talk about fucking music.'

'I should have thought that would be right up your street.'

'*Classical* music. Mozart and Wagner and all that crap.'

'What did you say to her?'

'I told her,' said Terry Chimes mournfully, 'that she ought to take a look at the size of my oboe.'

At close quarters, the bottle of whisky brought with him now, I noted, a third empty, he seemed unusually gloomy. It could not, I thought, be on account of the rebuff – after all, Terry Chimes was used to accumulating five or six of these in the course of an evening. I guessed that there was some deeper malaise.

'Some of these girls,' he went on, 'just can't take a joke.'

Simultaneously we found ourselves caught up in one of those periodic, wide-scale displacements of people that characterise large parties held in small rooms. A line of women who had been grouped around the trestle table suddenly detached themselves and moved resolutely forward. Two men, one of them the elderly Pole in the greatcoat, who had been innocently grouped in front of us were now spun out at right-angles by the force of this assault. In the confusion I caught sight of Elaine standing in the doorway talking to Mr Tovacs. Then, inexplicably, the movement stopped, the lines re-formed and Terry Chimes and I found ourselves together again.

'How's business, Terry?'

I had never known how to talk to Terry Chimes, what way in which to address him, which subjects might be likely to amuse him. Sex, usually a reliable standby, might only depress him further. Business seemed a suitably anodyne topic.

'Business is bad. Bloody bad I'd call it.'

'The Express anniversary tour wasn't a success?'

'Fucking disaster area.' He made a small, menacing movement with the bottle. 'Nobody's interested in a load of thirty-year-olds wearing tartan trousers. Not even the Glasgow Apollo. Plus the LP didn't sell.'

'*Songs from Auchtermuchty*?'

'That's the one. We've tried giving it away with soap powder, but that didn't work either.'

'What about Bobby Dazz?'

'Fucking his secretary, last I heard.'

'And those new young groups you were going to sign up?'

'No good. No good at all. Do you know what worries me about pop music now, Martin?' There was another abrupt change of gear; Terry Chimes's tone became declamatory. 'It's that I just can't keep up with it any more. With the changes, I mean. Ten years ago you knew where you were. Girl groups. Guitar groups. Kids from America. Novelty records. You knew what the fucking categories were. Find some bunch of Irishmen singing in a pub in Romford, put them in matching suits, give them a flash name, buy lunch for a tame DJ and Bob's your uncle. But it's not like that now. The styles used to change every year or so. Now it's every three months. Take New Wave . . .'

I could see Elaine signalling to me through the crowd. There was no way of knowing how long this monologue might continue. Terry Chimes hastened on, '. . . Take New Wave. I could cope with New Wave. Chug-a-chug guitars and kids in leather jackets singing flat. Might smash the place up once in a while, but you could sell stories to the papers about how they were good boys really and went home every weekend to their old mums in Lewisham. Trouble was it didn't last. And then there was this Two-Tone thing. Pork-pie hats and sunglasses. Uncle Rastus and his Swinging Six, that sort of thing. Trouble was that didn't last either. You remember that nigger saxophone player I signed? Fucking disaster. Now it's all New Romantics. I had this geezer in my office last month wearing a fucking *ruff.* Course I turned him down flat. Next week he signs to CBS for a quarter of a million.'

He paused to brood for a moment on this ripe fruit that had evaded his grasp. Then he said, 'Morty here yet?'

'I haven't seen him.'

'I need to talk to Morty.'

'What about?'

'Money.' Terry Chimes gave me a faintly exasperated glance, as if this was an obvious answer. He looked across to where Mr Tovacs, supported by two or three of the black-clad girls, had begun a monologue involving elaborate gestures and tossings of the head. 'Arty parties I can just about put up with, so long as the money's there. Put up with anything,' Terry Chimes went on, 'so long as there's some folding stuff at the end of it. The question is: is there?'

'Morty said he'd had a cheque.'

'Development costs,' Terry Chimes said contemptuously. 'Rehearsal rooms. Camera-hire. Getting those cunts at Starfinder off their arses for a bit. Mr fucking Teasy-weasy to do the hairstyles. Isn't anything else. I dunno what Morty's up to. Off hiring actresses, booking the site – this place in Suffolk is costing the fucking earth – like there was no tomorrow. Question is: who's going to pay for it? The old pantomime dame over there?' Something in the corner of the room caught his eye and he drew himself up to attention, like a drunken NCO upbraided by a superior officer. 'I'll catch you later, Martin.'

The faint air of unease that had characterised Leisurevision's dealings with Mr Tovacs had not until now been given such coherent shape. Left abruptly to my own devices I thought for a moment, as I had thought several times before, about the impulse that had driven Morty, usually the model of circumspection, into this unlikely partnership. Awareness of artistic potential (Morty had a naïve admiration for what he called 'real artists')? Desperation?

There was a small case of books directly in front of me, from which the cloth had slipped away. A half-filled wine glass, balanced precariously in a delta formed by two of the larger volumes, looked as if it was about to topple over. Having rescued it, I stood looking at the books. They were volumes of Ezra Pound's speeches, the broadcasts made on Rome radio in the early 1940s. I flicked through the first of these for a moment in the same half-intrigued, half-disgusted way that I occasionally examined the hard-core magazines Morty brought back from the Continent. Odd sentences stood out from the lines of solid, leaded type: '. . . The Jew must realise, if he is to realise anything at all, the consequences of his actions . . . The fate of the Jews of Eastern Europe we already know about. The Jews of America we can only warn . . .'

A voice beside me said, 'Pound was a very great writer, you know.'

I turned and discovered Mr Tovacs looking at me with an expression in which pride and embarrassment were uncomfortably mingled, rather as if, I thought, I was a schoolmaster who had chanced upon an exercise book full of his adolescent poetry. Several plausible enough replies suggested themselves.

'You knew Pound?'

Mr Tovacs looked pleased. There was, as I had realised by now, an immediate, fail-safe way of appeasing him whenever the conversation turned to literature. This was to suggest that he had known personally, or at any rate had some lesser connection with the writer being discussed.

He said, 'Only a little. Towards the end of his life, and then only a little. He was not,' Mr Tovacs paused, as if weighing the words carefully, 'he was not, what is the word you would use, a *sympathetic* man. And he had made that fatal mistake for the intellectual, for the artist, in Anglo-Saxon countries, of engaging himself in politics. An interesting phenomenon: the artist as man of action. It is not something which is . . . encouraged, perhaps?'

'I suppose not.'

I remembered what Elaine had said: 'You should hear Tovacs on the Jews.' It seemed safer to change the subject.

'Do you know Suffolk?'

'Suffolk?'

'Suffolk. *Resurrection* may be filmed there, I think?'

Mr Tovacs's eyes, which had narrowed markedly during the conversation about Pound, now resumed a blander look. 'There is a place on the coast, is there not, where musical festivals are held? Aldeburgh or some such name? I went there once as a guest of Ben's.'

It was typical, I reflected, of Mr Tovacs to have known Britten. He looked as if he might be about to say something else about the Aldeburgh festival, but then, raising his hand in an odd sort of benediction, thought better of it and began to shuffle away. His figure receded, was caught up again in a knot of elderly women, and then disappeared. I looked about the room for Elaine, last seen in the area of the trestle table, but there was no sign of her. As I watched, Morty appeared in the doorway, wavered slightly as he caught sight of the press of people and then moved determinedly on. There was, I saw, something peculiar about Morty's appearance: beads of moisture on his forehead; the left side of his face seemed violently contorted. I guessed that this late arrival was the result of an unscheduled visit to the dentist. He had come only a yard or so into the room when Terry Chimes bore down on him; they stood talking animatedly. I strained to hear what was being said – from the look on Terry Chimes's face these were not ordinary pleasantries – but another burst of music, this time identifiable as a Schumann *lied* played very loud, drowned out the words. Elaine materialised, apparently from nowhere, at my elbow.

'I want to talk to you.'

'Go on then.'

'No. Not here. Somewhere you can hear what I'm saying.'

I looked at her. The beret hung at an even more rakish angle, so much so that I wondered whether she had secured it there with hair pins. Her hair, previously coiled up and tamed beneath it, had begun to stray outwards; an entire hank cascaded down one cheek. She looked prodigiously bored.

'There's a room upstairs at the back we can go to.'

Reflecting that Elaine seemed to know her way about Mr Tovacs's premises, I followed her out into the corridor, past Terry Chimes who, glancing over his shoulder, winked in a marked manner, and towards a second staircase set at an angle to the one by which we had first entered the building. Here the press of people had lessened, although there were one or two couples – European-looking girls, men in parodies of evening dress – arranged on the lower steps. Elaine pushed past these onlookers with the air of someone intimately concerned with the management of the party who might at some not very distant point turn dictatorial and start to evict people. At the top of the staircase there was a single door which at first sight appeared to be locked. Elaine twisted the handle a couple of times, put her shoulder to it and finally succeeded in wrenching it open.

'In here.'

We found ourselves in a small, sparsely furnished attic – the single window looking out into blackness – which seemed to be used as a storeroom. A few chairs stood at right-angles to one another next to a battered sideboard along whose surface ran a line of carved South American figurines – parrots, crocodiles, squat grinning homunculi with wildly overproportioned eyes. Beneath, in decaying cardboard boxes, reposed elderly copies of *Pages*, some of them as much as thirty years old. I inspected the title pages: 'A Laforgue Tribute; Ginsberg at 50'. Elaine, who had been staring angrily at a further display of photographs and framed memorabilia, turned back from the wall and said with an effort, 'I wanted to tell you that I'm clearing out.'

'Clearing out?'

'Clearing out,' Elaine said. She lit a cigarette, something she rarely did except at moments of personal distress, and drew nervously on it once or twice. 'Leaving.'

'Leaving here? Leaving Leisurevision? Leaving me?'

'All of them, probably. I can't stand it any more and I just wanted to tell you.'

There had been declarations like this before. The trick, I had learned, was to accept them matter-of-factly, as the prelude to a neutral discussion of logistics, contingencies and obligations.

'Any particular reason?'

Elaine gave me a look which suggested that it might be unwise simply to humour her. 'The usual ones. What am I doing with my life? What am I doing with you? And don't think any explanation you can come up with now is going to be especially satisfying. It's quite simple, Martin. I just don't like what I'm doing any more. Not now. And you don't help, Martin. You just sit there and you don't ask the right questions.'

'Which questions?'

'Oh . . . I don't know. Hasn't it ever struck you, Martin, just how weird all this is? I mean, *what are Morty and Terry up to*? What is Tovacs up to? This isn't Tovacs's usual thing. Not his usual thing at all. Why does he want to put money into one of Morty's dodgy films? What does he think he's going to get out of it?'

'Have you asked any of them?'

'That's another thing. Morty and Terry are up to something. I don't know what it is, but I don't like it at all and I want out.'

'Now?'

'Maybe not now. Maybe not until *Resurrection*'s over and we get paid. But I want out.'

There was a silence. From below came the hum of conversation, the sound of something – a glass? a bottle? – smashing on the floor, somebody's voice – I guessed it to be Terry Chimes's – raised in protest.

'Look,' said Elaine, 'don't take it personally, okay? We can talk about it some more when we get home.'

It was impossible not to take it personally. Looking at Elaine now as she leant back against the sideboard, one arm apparently about to detach a large, stylised representation of a panther, I realised how unfathomable I had always found her, that this realisation, for which I could not be said to be unprepared, was simply the culmination of a great deal of wayside incomprehension in the years we had known each other. That common ground which authenticates a relationship, so often hinted at in a gesture or apparent understanding, had simply failed to materialise. I continued to stare at her, thinking of all this, until the silence became intolerable.

'Come on,' Elaine said, 'let's go downstairs.'

As we descended the narrow staircase, the loitering couples now mysteriously disappeared, it became clear that some sort of minor crisis had arisen to disturb the even tenor of the party. The music had stopped. From beyond the doorway came the clamour of raised voices. Moving into the room, several clues as to what had happened swiftly presented themselves, the whole suggesting a tableau that might have been captioned 'Wounded Dignity' or

'Honour Spurned', a tumult of activity frozen suddenly into sharp relief by our own arrival on to the scene. Terry Chimes stood in the centre of a group of people which included Morty and Jerry, nursing his right hand and glaring stonily at a second group made up of several other guests, whose leader seemed to be the girl whom Terry Chimes had previously tried to pick up. In the middle of this assembly sat, or rather half-stood, supported by the girl, a man whom I had not seen before, clutching his fingers over the upper part of his face. Fragments of a bottle, Terry Chimes's bottle of whisky judging by the label, formed an odd symbolic barrier on the floor between these apparently opposed forces. At once everyone began to talk again very loudly, the girl in black giving out two or three piercing screams before being silenced by one of the older women. I moved over to where Morty stood with his arms clasped protectively around Terry Chimes's waist.

'What happened?'

Morty shrugged. He was obviously extremely annoyed, though whether with Terry Chimes, or the man now sitting on the floor was difficult to tell. 'Christ, I don't know. I only just got here and my teeth hurt like fuck. Boy meets girl. Girl isn't interested. Somebody interferes. Terry takes a swing at them. Don't ask me.'

Mr Tovacs stood a little way off. He seemed not so much disapproving as nervous, fearful perhaps that what appeared to be no more than a minor scuffle might yet inspire more alarming conflict. He said to no one in particular, 'I really do not know what to say. It is all most regrettable. But perhaps Mr Chimes was provoked in some way?'

Whatever might have been the cause of the fight, it was a signal for dispersal. The two participants were helped away. Two girls who had been helping to serve drinks came and swept up the broken glass and conferred in undertones with Mr Tovacs about a chair which Terry Chimes might or might not have broken. There was a slow but remorseless drift of people towards the staircase, down to the lower floor in search of coats and handbags. Elaine had disappeared, either in the company of Morty and Terry Chimes, or off on some errand of her own. As I stood uncertainly by the door, wondering if I should say something on behalf of Terry and Morty to Mr Tovacs, wondering whether if I went home immediately I should find Elaine, wondering even if it were worth going home to resume that conversation, Jerry moved purposefully towards me.

'Still here? What happened to your girlfriend?'

'Gone already, I think.'

'With medallion man, huh? Boy, that was a scene.' Jerry looked animated, I thought, as if the events of the last ten minutes had somehow provided the high point of the evening. She was holding a half-empty glass which she now put down on a side table. 'Jesus. After that I could do with a drink.'

'Plenty of wine left.'

'Not wine. A real drink. Tovacs doesn't keep spirits on the premises. Have to go someplace else. You want to come?'

I considered. It was barely ten o'clock. The probability was that Morty, Terry and Elaine had gone back to Dean Street. There would be no one at the flat until eleven.

'All right.'

'Attaboy. Why don't you wait downstairs while I go fetch some things?'

At the bottom of the staircase a kind of *mêlée* was in progress in which various guests, enraged by the smallness of the cubby-hole in which they found themselves and the inaccessibility of the coats – piled up on a distant ledge – were arguing with each other. I stood and watched this for a moment until Jerry reappeared. She was wearing a long, shapeless dufflecoat and had exchanged her ballet slippers for a pair of fur bootees, this suggesting a store of clothing kept on the premises from which suitable items could be extracted when necessary. Together we stepped out into the street.

'Do you live here?'

'Sometimes.' Jerry set off at a rapid pace. Used to Elaine's notoriously laggard saunter I had trouble in keeping up. 'There's a camp bed upstairs I use when I'm hanging out with Tovacs. Otherwise I go back to Kentish Town. Jesus,' she said, 'Tovacs's parties never work. Always something like that happens.'

'Tovacs seems to enjoy them.'

'Tovacs is an egomaniac. Tovacs would enjoy a party on a desert island with a couple of cannibals so long as it was him doing the inviting. First time we've had a fight though.'

'What happened?'

'The usual thing that happens. You were upstairs, right? Well, medallion man started sniffing round that girl in the black, the one who gave him the brush-off before, and the guy she was with told him to cool it. Next thing you know medallion man goes for him with a bottle of bourbon. Does he always act like that?'

'Sometimes.'

'Uh huh. I figured him for a meathead. You get that in the States. I was at a book launch once in Madison Avenue when Norman Mailer loafed this guy with a wine cooler. I never saw that sort of thing happen here before.'

I considered this information. As well as demonstrating Jerry's familiarity with literary society on both sides of the Atlantic, it suggested that she thought the British way of doing things feeble by comparison, and that a certain degree of violence might actually be necessary in promoting a suitable atmosphere. We pressed on rapidly towards High Holborn.

'Where are we going?'

'A little place I know about just along the street. American beer too; I can't stand that English stuff. Don't worry,' she added, as if these attractions might not have been sufficient. 'It's not far.'

She continued to talk in a desultory way as we crossed the main thoroughfare – deserted now except for taxis – and walked on towards Southampton Row: about Mr Tovacs, about her landlord in Kentish Town, about difficulties with a work permit. I had the impression of a hard, sharp intelligence, oppressed by its dealings with the people it ran up against, but allowed insufficient room for any manoeuvre which might have turned the tables on them.

In Southampton Row she turned sharp left into an alley connected in some way with the shops in Sicilian Avenue. Whatever illusions I might have had about our ultimate destination – I had envisioned a drinking club along the lines of an American gangster film, a speakeasy peopled by burly, hard-faced men in suits – vanished abruptly.

'This way,' Jerry said.

A single outer door, painted in black and white stripes, gave way to a flight of stairs descending into a small, hollowed-out cavern strewn with bar-stools. Here a few people sat individually and in twos and threes drinking in a subdued way. The atmosphere was determinedly American. A sign on the wall, the neon beneath it barely flickering, read 'Sam's bar and diner'. Uncle Sam himself glowered from the wall in facsimile. Curiously the decor reminded me of Morty's club: an air of seediness narrowly kept at bay, the suspicion of people with nothing better to do. Jerry, however, seemed very much at home.

'Ah,' she said. 'Simpatico. You want a drink?'

'Do you come here a lot?'

'Now and again. I get tired of Red Lion Street. Everybody working their asses off just because Tovacs has some French poet coming to tea that no one's ever heard of.'

'How did you get to meet Tovacs?'

Jerry frowned, as if the question was an unwelcome one, reminding of some part of her life that was better forgotten. 'Back home. Some bunfight to launch a book. I used to work for Scribner's in New York. Tovacs gave me his card. A bit later I started sending poems in to *Pages.* Then when I came over here I got in touch again.'

'Did the poems get printed?'

Jerry frowned again, a yet rawer nerve obviously exposed. 'A few. Anyone can get printed in a poetry magazine, you just have to know the editor. Jesus, I was so green in those days. Coming to England. Thinking Tovacs was the big time.'

'Which he wasn't?'

She lit a cigarette and stared at it irritably. 'There are two types of hangers-on: little hangers-on and big hangers-on. Little hangers-on are people like me: people who write poems and hand out the wine at parties. Tovacs is a big hanger-on. Hasn't got any particular talent – not now, at any rate – but he knows people. People like that can make major nuisances of themselves.'

'How do you mean?'

'Tovacs is a real bloodsucker, a real manipulator. You let him into your life, even professionally, and you can spend all your time letting him out again. I'll give you an example. That guy who won the Nobel last month, Milosz. He's a Pole, so of course *The Times* rang up and asked Tovacs to do a piece. Naturally Tovacs jumped at the chance. And then he started asking for things: a plane ticket to Stockholm; someone to help him with the typing. Got hold of *The Times* guy's number and started ringing him up at home. There are easier ways of filling a newspaper.'

'They could cancel the commission.'

'An old man of seventy-five with a heart complaint who knew James Joyce? No, Tovacs doesn't lose spats like that. Once you've got him in your address book he stays there.'

There was a minor diversion as a man wearing overalls and carrying a guitar emerged from a side door and seated himself on a stool by the bar. Having looked rather nervously around the room once or twice and struck a few preliminary chords he began to sing in a put-upon, doleful voice:

In a one-horse town I know so well to the west of Abilene
There's a little girl who waits for me, the best I've ever seen.

Jerry brightened. 'That's Chet,' she said approvingly. 'He plays here most nights.'

We sat in silence for a moment listening to the tale of Mary Lou who had sent a steely dart into the bottom of this poor cowboy's heart. I realised with a kind of belated intuition, that Jerry was drunk. She gazed raptly at Chet for a while longer and then without warning grew sulky once more.

'I expect you just want to sleep with me, isn't that right?'

'No. What gave you that idea?'

'Uh huh. Most of the guys you meet at Tovacs's do. "I read your poems" just means "Flap your tits in my face."'

It seemed a good time to revert to an older topic.

'Tell me about Tovacs.'

'Uh huh.' Jerry considered this for a moment. Chet, having finished his account of the girl from Abilene, looked expectantly around the room: there was a very faint scattering of applause. 'What do you want to know?'

'For a start, how did he get involved with Morty and Terry Chimes?'

'I told you. Tovacs collects people. People who might be useful for Tovacs.'

'But why does he want to put money into one of Morty's films?'

'Actually,' Jerry said, giving the impression that the topic was best approached obliquely, 'Tovacs has had quite a career already in films.'

'He has?'

'Sure. You know all that stuff about *mon ami Jean Cocteau*? All the stuff about the references to him in *Le Passé défini*? Well, practically the only thing Tovacs did do with Uncle Jean, so far as I can make out, was to help him make his films.'

'*Les Enfants terribles*?'

'Not that sort of film. A bit more specialised than that. Hunky *matelots* and that sort of thing.'

I thought about this. The picture of Mr Tovacs which it conjured up seemed, in the light of all that I had so far assembled about him, perfectly credible. Somehow each of Jerry's remarks had the ring of authenticity. The way she conducted this exposé, implying that I could take it or leave it and that she herself could not be bothered either way, seemed to confirm this. Something of what I was thinking must have passed through Jerry's mind for she said quite quickly, 'Sure, I could spill some beans about Tovacs. Maybe I will before I clear out.'

'When will that be?'

'Who knows? This month. Next month. Between you and me I've had just about as much of Tovacs as I can stand. Washing up wine glasses and fending off old roués with bad breath who reckon you might be impressed because they once met André Gide. Not my idea of a great night out.'

Here the conversation stuck. Jerry looked sulkier than ever, eventually announcing that she had to go to the 'bathroom'. While I waited for her I thought about Elaine, whose own plans had been stated in curiously similar terms. It was nearly eleven. Perhaps, after all, she would have gone back to the flat? Perhaps, on the other hand, I could collect her from Dean Street? While I weighed these possibilities against each other, Jerry returned. She seemed faintly surprised to see me, uncertain for a brief moment, I thought, as to my identity. Recovering herself she said, 'Look, don't think me rude, will you, but I want to talk to Chet here.'

I looked over to the bar where the singer, his repertoire apparently complete, sat drinking with his back to us.

'I have to go anyway.'

'Tear your girl away from medallion man? That's the spirit.'

'Yes.'

At the door I turned and waved. Jerry, now seated at the bar, her farouche, pointed features creased into a smile by some remark of Chet's, barely looked up.

In the taxi I pondered on the events of the previous four hours. Oddly, the memory that endured was of Jerry's threatened exposure of Mr Tovacs, the grounds not even guessable, a threat that seemed potent and immediate, hedged about with indications that it would actually take place. Elaine's statement of intent, by contrast, seemed flimsy, uncertain. I had no doubt at this stage that she would once again change her mind. On a broader canvas, the sense of some mystery, involving Morty, Mr Tovacs, the film and all manner of issues scarcely hinted at by Jerry's denunciation, grew stronger. As Kensington gave way to the Fulham Road, the long lines of traffic breaking up now and disappearing, bafflement was replaced by uneasy anticipation.

There was a light on in the flat. Elaine sat in the front room, her feet raised on a stool. She stared at me unblinkingly.

'You were home early?'

'There wasn't anything happening at Dean Street. Terry thought he might have broken a knuckle, so Morty took him to hospital.'

'Had he?'

'No. Terry's such a *jerk*. He wanted to go back there with Crazy Rodney and take out the guy who hit him.'

'What did Morty say?'

'He got tough. You know that way Morty gets when there's money involved and someone's not taking it seriously. It was quite funny in a way. They stood there in the Out-Patients shouting at each other until the security guards thought they were a couple of drunks who'd come in off the street.'

I thought for a moment about this all-too-plausible scene. Then, without warning, two things happened. First, the floodlights from the adjoining tennis court were switched off: the numinous haze outside the window fell away into darkness. At the same time the phone in the hall rang urgently.

'It'll be for Mr Solomon.'

But it was not for Mr Solomon. At some remote point in the history of the flat it had been owned by a Mr Kreutzner. It was for this man, a vague, shadowy figure to whom bills and circulars were still occasionally addressed, that the call was intended: a woman's voice, high, querulous and resentful. Halfway through the lavish monologue, I put the phone down. Elaine lingered in the hallway.

'You want to know what I think about all this? About all this *filming*?'

'Tell me.'

'I think it sucks. I don't think it'll ever happen. Not really. Tovacs is always going on about putting money into things. Fancy editions of crappy poetry. Paying some publisher to do his memoirs. Wants to be the big impresario, you see, and give parties where people nudge each other when he comes into the room. But it never comes to anything. The crappy poetry just lies around in proof and the publishers, well, the publishers aren't exactly queueing up.'

'Morty seems to think it's okay.'

'Morty's just desperate,' Elaine said with unprecedented hostility. 'All these years of doing his arty porn and thinking he's some sort of libertarian into the bargain, and all of a sudden the money isn't there any more and over in Europe they've just discovered real filth for a change and suddenly all this prick-teasing stuff doesn't cut it.'

'And what about you?'

'Oh, I'm desperate too. Incredibly desperate. Do you know what I found the other night when I was cleaning up, Martin? I found that copy of *Ireland's Own*, with that picture of me my dad sent in when I was fifteen. And it just cracked me up. I mean, I haven't got a lot of shame, but I can tell you seeing that was much worse than anything we ever did with Morty Goldstein. Much worse.'

Often in the ensuing weeks I found myself remembering this conversation; not so much for the warning it conveyed as for the sharp hint of vulnerability. This was not a quality I had previously associated with Elaine. Now, extracted at long last from a mass of unpromising detritus, it became central to my conception of her, something capable of redeeming the indifference and the casual neglect. When I came to reckon up the balance of our relationship – a process I conducted every so often in a phantom ledger – this knowledge acted invariably as a trump card, sweeping away the opposing catalogue of hurt and embarrassment. The air of delusion hung irremovably over my dealings with Elaine, but I knew that it would be fatal to acknowledge it. Only this bright, consoling fantasy kept my own desperation at bay.

In the event Elaine's pessimism was unfounded. Slowly but inexorably, like some Heath Robinson contraption always surmounting the apparent certainty of failure, the juggernaut of film production creaked forward. There were further meetings above the shop in Red Lion Street and further lunches at Morty's club. A country house near Southwold on the Suffolk coast was hired for filming and a date set in early February. Morty, alone of all the various people involved in the enterprise, remained unmoved by this evidence of progress. 'I feel like the guy in the story,' he said on more than one occasion, 'the guy in the story who was told that he couldn't marry the girl. So he goes out to drown his sorrows and ends up in the town brothel and gets a dose of the clap. Next week the girl rings him up and tells him that she's changed her mind.'

This morning Suzi says, 'I'll need the front room tonight. You remember?'

'No. What for?'

Suzi gives me one of those intent, sorrowful looks in which she specialises these days. 'I did tell you. For Terry's coaching.'

'Yes.'

Terry's coaching. Generally in the course of her professional life Suzi concerns herself with nine- and ten-year-old boys, but there is a sideline in after-hours encouragement for exam-chastened adolescents, hulking sixteen-year-olds needing to be dragged through *Dombey and Son*, or helped to devise a plausible account of M. Jambon's *vacances*. Such sessions are a more or less unavoidable consequence of Suzi's job, her school being one of those swindling private establishments aimed at the dullard progeny of the comfortably off. Gross, lymphatic farmers' sons from the Norfolk plain, pallid mannikins whose parents have profound doubts, don't you know, about the value of a comprehensive education, an actual half-wit or two – these are the types who turn up here early on winter evenings with their expensive atlases and shiny calculators, all the hapless paraphernalia of the scholastic loser. I think about this as Suzi chunters on, looking up as she reaches her peroration.

'So if Terry arrives before I get back you'll let him in, won't you, and give him a cup of tea?'

'Sure.'

Terry is the likeliest of several likely lads whom Suzi is trying to coax through their O-levels. Seventeen and a half – already failed them twice – and from the roving, knowing eye he turns on his instructress you get the feeling that he'd rather be doing something else. Poor Terry. He ought to be out there bringing in the hay, or manhandling bags of fertiliser, but no, the horny-handed satrap of some farmhouse out Reepham way has decided that he needs *qualifications* and the result is this shambling, tongue-tied display of ignorance twice weekly in the front room.

'See you later then,' says Suzi. I check the post on the mat, find nothing alarming, look up. 'See you later then,' Suzi says again, 'after rounders.'

After rounders. In recent weeks Suzi has stepped up her schedule to an unprecedented degree: a ceaseless round of marking, administering, conferring with the parents of her delinquent brood. I ask her about it sometimes.

'Why do you do all this?'

'All what?'

'All the stuff nobody pays you to do. Running the PTA ceilidh. Making the punch for the staff party. Helping the dimwits to get a grade seven rather than a grade eight in their CSEs.'

'It's my *job*,' Suzi says with apparent sincerity. 'I mean, that's what I'm there to do, isn't it? Take Terry . . .'

'He's a half-wit.'

'. . . He's just a bit slow, poor kid. And if I can help him to do a bit better than he would have done otherwise, then he'll feel that he's achieved something.'

There is more to it, though, than the marking and the PTA meetings. In the past month or so Suzi's social life has undergone a decisive change in gear, grown suddenly hectic and indiscriminate. I come home sometimes and find her crouched happily over the telephone talking to women with names like Jackie and Debbie, girls she knew at school, it turns out, transformed by the years' caress into bustling mothers of three with bungalows at Cringleford and serious husbands who work in insurance. They come round here occasionally: rosy Norfolk girls with wide hips and solemn offspring already dulled by the weight of parental expectation.

Suzi goes out. The day assumes its characteristic focus. I play the window-cleaner tape through again, marvelling at my pitiless, unremembered dexterity. Outside the familiar processions soldier by: the files of schoolchildren, the old women out shopping, the restless unemployed. Later on, in the afternoon, as the mist rises over Heigham Park, I slip out in search of Fat Eric, find him immersed in the purposeful chaos of his lounge, ponderous and inert, but prepared to discuss business plans and hint at the alleviation of his chronic, plenary indebtedness. There is no sign of Kay. 'Nice to see you, squire,' Fat Eric intones, and the time slips effortlessly away, gone in a spiral of cigarettes and instant coffee, in silent autumnal frowsting. Kay comes back, a brace of carrier bags dragging sadly behind her, and we take tea wedged together on the shiny sofa while Fat Eric stares wordlessly at the blaring TV and I wonder idly, the thought stealing up on me unawares, quite shocking me with its insidiousness, how long this can go on, this quiet burrowing life, here in the corner of this quaint, frozen world.

Later still the light of the streetlamp glimmers through the dark, uncurtained room, as Kay falls asleep on the sofa, one arm twisted awkwardly over her face, jaws unclenched. Fat Eric has disappeared on some unexplained errand: I can hear him upstairs moving ceaselessly from room to room, a giant antediluvian lizard slapping his tail on the floorboards. I wander out into the musty hall where half-full packets of Marlboro are strewn about over the carpet and there lie accumulated on the strip of lino that serves as Fat Eric's doormat a winded football, two Sindy dolls in cellophane wrappers and a pram filled with what looks like cement.

Back at the house Suzi and Terry are already ensconced in the front room, a fact brought home to me when I blunder in to discover them regarding the piled textbooks, hear Terry's voice – that slow, clueless voice – stutter off into embarrassed silence.

'I'm sorry,' I say, 'I didn't think you'd be here.'

Suzi looks up from the pad of paper spread across her lap. 'I did *tell* you,' she says. I look at Terry, over whose pitted, knowing face there is already rising the ghost of a smirk. 'Stay if you like,' Suzi goes on, equably. 'We've nearly finished as it happens. Terry doesn't mind, do you, pet?'

'*I* don't mind,' Terry says negligently. I sit down and affect to study the sports pages of the *Eastern Evening News* with their alarming intelligence about Kevin Flack's depressed cheekbone fracture, and the lesson proceeds, intently fascinating in its intimation of warped communication lines, its chronic bewilderment.

'Terry was just telling me about *The Mayor of Casterbridge*,' Suzi goes on. 'It's his set book.'

'Fine,' I say. 'Don't mind me.'

'Don't mind Martin,' Suzi says. 'Just carry on with what you were saying, Terry.'

Terry makes a few laboured observations about *The Mayor of Casterbridge* that are quite startling in their lack of conviction. I gaze at him as he does this, brow furrowed, forefinger tethered rigidly midway down the page, get a sudden inkling of the epic contempt in which he holds this inexplicable ritual, something devised, apparently, with the express purpose of boring and disconcerting him, his bemusement at whichever fate ordained this monstrous thraldom which he has no power to escape or alter.

Suzi's voice drifts in above the drone, 'You see, Terry, the point about this man is that he's a corn-factor. Now, if you were in his position, how would you feel? How would you feel about all the things you've just been telling me?'

I catch her eye as she says this: there is not a trace of mockery, not a shadow. Terry says something about it all being mechanised anyway these days and Suzi nods at him professorially, worlds away from me in my chair, lost in some elemental world of Honest Effort, Hard Work and Just Rewards. Getting up, sauntering back to the hall, I am struck by the dreadful realisation that her humanity shames me.

And then out in the hall, at the foot of the staircase, drenched in artificial light, something very odd indeed happens: out of the tail of my eye I catch a glimpse of my father staring out over the topmost banister. A late-period incarnation of my father, the hair neatly Brylcreemed back over his scalp, the eyes unfocused but alert, a split-second framing between the strips of wood and the billowing space beyond. Blinking slightly, I repeat the glance. He isn't there. I press on upwards. Down below the voices echo.

I heard the news of Mr Tovacs's death – a month ago, in a Paris nursing home – quite by chance, on a radio news programme sandwiched between fat stock prices and an interview with a government minister about export credit guarantees. Subsequently a number of weekly magazines printed obituaries, Channel Four screened a programme about him made thirty years before and he became for a brief period a subject of interest to the arts sections of Sunday newspapers. There was talk of '*Zeitgeist*' and a serious young critic devoted nearly a page of the *Daily Telegraph* to the suggestion that he represented 'a link between the ferment of early modernism and the less confident art-forms of our own age'.

I read these memorials with interest. Many of them, hastily composed and presumably compiled out of reference books, gave the impression of having been written by people with little or no knowledge of Mr Tovacs's personality. He was widely and erroneously spoken of as the friend of Diaghilev (Mr Tovacs's published work showed a marked distaste for the *Ballet Russe*), the patron of Beckett (he had abominated *Godot*) and the amanuensis of Joyce. There was the inevitable confusion over his age, variously located in the mid-sixties, early seventies or late eighties. Several newspapers had produced more or less relevant illustrations: a charcoal drawing by Augustus John of a Sitwell dinner (no figure recognisable) which he was thought to have attended, a *Horizon* frontispiece (his name, on close inspection, not listed among the contributors), a dubious Sutherland caricature. *The Times* notice, alone among these respectful *éloges*, appeared to be the work of someone who had known him at an earlier period in his life and had some conception of what it was that he might have been thought to represent. Its tone was quaint, leaving one to suspect that it had been written some years before.

> With his death, [*The Times* obituarist wrote] the world of European high culture has lost not so much a genuine creative force as a potent impresario. Even more, it has lost a living relic of one of the most turbulent and exciting periods in its recent history. There are few enough men of whom it can be said that they knew Proust or saw Firbank plain, but Tovacs was one of this rare breed. Inevitably, perhaps, his affiliations and his gift for friendship took precedence over his own literary output. His novels are now perhaps no more than period pieces, exotic blooms out of a landscape long barren

and fruitlessly retilled, although in such works as *Harlequin* and *Columbine* we may note an early attempt to link the symbolism of Apollinaire with the brooding introspection of Kafka . . . *Pages* is his enduring memorial. In it he forged a literary vehicle that was truly international in its scope. Gide wrote for it, Moore and Sutherland decorated its covers. In its half-century or so of precarious existence it played host to a galaxy of talent composed of stars as varied as Ginsberg, Creeley and Mishima. And it is in *Pages*, this refuge from the grasp of a less tolerant world, that Tovacs is at his best. His prefatory notes, lush arboreta of hothouse prose, where the shades of the great departed meet and talk, where Rabelais is invoked to examine Baudelaire and Fragonard walks with Rothko, are notable not only for the suggestiveness of their conceits, but for their self-effacement. In the cavalcade of lustre and *éclat* which Tovacs assembled, it was his nature to see himself only as a minor attendant . . .

There was a great deal more of this. Accurate, perhaps, in its assemblage of names, it gave no hint of the knowing, confidential tone with which Mr Tovacs had invested his editorials. He had hobnobbed with his authors, I thought, taken Eliot and Rimbaud out into the compendious, book-lined study of his mind and subtly patronised them. Milton's shade and Rabelais's grosser spectre might have wandered through these brightly lit corridors, but it was for Mr Tovacs's benefit that the diversion had been staged. Reading through this stately summary of his life and achievements I was left with the very faint suspicion that, in defiance of probability, through aliases, perhaps, or complex channels of inducement, Mr Tovacs had written it himself.

Christmas came: a chill and desolate feast. Grey clouds moved west over the bare South Norfolk landscape; the Caistor-by-Norwich road where I walked on Christmas afternoon was aflood with icy water. Within the house at Glebe Road lay equal desolation. A year ago there had been a pine tree, strings of coloured lights and a certain amount of conviviality. Now there was only quiet unease. Stray flames of conciliation which had sprung up unexpectedly in the previous week had been damped down or extinguished. Early on Christmas morning Suzi departed to Bungay to spend the day with her parents. I ate my lunch alone in the dining room.

Over the years I had grown accustomed to these solitary meals. My father regarded Christmas as an institution got up for the exclusive benefit of the retail trade. 'A hundred and fifty years ago,' he used to say, 'Christmas was a civilised festival. But then a lot of shopkeepers, encouraged I regret to say by the Prince Consort, got hold of it and invested it with the vulgarity of commerce. Paper hats,' my father said severely, 'extravagant decoration and over-eating. All quite unnecessary.' But there was a second line of thought commonly brought out at this time to justify the absence of hospitality and excess. 'A lot of people,' my father would say, 'simply make Christmas the excuse for holding a sort of open house to acquaintances they very probably dislike and would certainly avoid at other times of the year. Well, we are a big enough unit as it is.' Such stringency could not be gainsaid. Later on there had been other Christmases – Christmases with Morty and the current Mrs Goldstein in Essex, Christmases with Elaine in country hotels – yet the tradition remained. It was here, I thought, here in Norwich amid rain and recrimination that the true spirit of the season resided.

Suzi returned late in the afternoon. The present from her parents – a vast bottle-green smock – lay gleaming from the back seat of the car. Looking at her as she stood in the hallway, face crimson from the wind, booted feet moving up and down in an exaggerated military step, I wondered at the impulse that had brought her back. It was, I realised, part of an engrossing ritual. What was it she had said about Nick and Tony and all the others? 'It wasn't working out . . . Thought we'd carry on for a bit and see . . .' I was familiar with the words, their casual evocation of emotional fracture. Each of Suzi's relationships, I saw, had followed this pattern: a build-up of expectation, a year or so of pleasure, a slow fading away. There was, I thought, a predictability about them which she found consoling. It was, for her, how a relationship worked. In a month, or a week, she would leave me. Until that time she was content to hang on, precariously, in the face of ever-diminishing returns.

A single custom survived from former Christmases. Suzi, I had discovered early on in our relationship, was an inveterate player of indoor as well as outdoor games. Cardboard boxes containing Scrabble pieces or Trivial Pursuit cards lay everywhere over the house. There was also in her room a tea-chest filled to the brim with relics of her childhood – spillikins, Cluedo, a complicated pastime which involved spearing small translucent fish with a kind of metal spatula. It was to this treasure trove, late on Christmas night, that we repaired.

Suzi said, 'I'd like to play the memory game, if you don't mind.'

'I don't mind.'

And so we played the memory game, which of all the diversions with which Suzi occupied her leisure hours was the one she favoured most. In essence it was an aural version of Kim's Game, the tray and its random collection of objects replaced by a tape recorder. Each player selected a cassette – Suzi had a vast array of old Light Programme comedies specially recorded for the purpose – and, having listened to it for a certain period, was asked a series of questions.

'*Hancock's Half-Hour*?'

'Too easy.'

'We haven't listened to it for ages.'

'If you like.'

Long years of practice had made Suzi adept at the memory game. She knew by instinct which pieces of information might attract my questions, precisely the level of recall necessary to win points. As the tape recorder played – it was 'The Blood Donor' – she wrote tiny, indecipherable notes on the back of an envelope.

'What does Hancock say when they tell him they want to take a pint?'

'He says, "But that's an armful."'

'Correct. What is the name of the nurse . . .?'

It was to no avail. Whatever strategies I had thought to confuse her with, whatever technicalities I had dredged up to confound her, none had the slightest effect. She won handsomely.

'It's a question of technique,' Suzi said. She frowned at the scrap of paper. 'There comes a time when you begin to see it in your mind.'

She was generous in victory. Later when we moved on to other games, to Monopoly and then to a complex re-enactment of the

Second World War which I remembered playing with my father, the result was the same. There was something pitiless, I thought, about this absorption, something that lifted it on to a higher level than an exchange of playing cards. Occasionally, when I made some spectacular blunder, or was detected in some flagrant lapse from the rules, I caught her staring at me. It was an odd look, in which righteousness and contempt were neatly blended, as if these were real banknotes being passed across the table, real ships being inveigled across the Atlantic to eventual sabotage. In this, as in so many other things, I had been found out.

After lunch on Boxing Day I walked through the wet streets to Eaton Park. In the pale light of a winter afternoon the place had a gloomy air. The grass had grown wild and untended on the bowling rinks; there were weeds creeping up through the tarmac of the tennis courts. I wandered on through an avenue of moulting trees to the bandstand. Here too there were signs of decay. The boating pond had been drained: strange detritus, lumps of stone and wooden fence posts, lay across the concrete floor. The roof of the bandstand sagged uncomfortably. Beneath, a small area had been cordoned off and there were workmen's tools propped up against the pillars. A few children on bicycles or carrying shiny plastic toys roamed around the gravel pathways.

Beyond the circle of changing rooms and the boarded-up tea-shop with its advertisements for ice-cream and Seven-Up a turfed incline led down to the soccer fields. There the ground was soft and wet; in the distance three small boys were taking desultory shots into an empty goal. I had played on these fields myself as a child. The teams still ran in my head: Buckingham Rovers, Avenue Rovers, South Park Albion; each name taken from a street adjoining the park.

On the western edge of the fields there was a stone gatehouse where, entombed behind barred windows, extravagant model yachts could be glimpsed. As I walked towards it a figure emerged out of the shadow beneath the gate and moved hesitantly forward. I became conscious of a sidelong glance, a faint straining after recognition. A voice said, 'It's Mr Benson, isn't it?'

I turned and found Mr Robey. Removed from the confines of his office and the bar of the Maid's Head he seemed a diminished figure. He wore a flat check cap of the kind affected by middle-aged men in situation comedies and a shiny oilskin jacket. There was a small cigar smoking in the fingers of his left hand (he explained the cigar in the course of the evening by saying, 'I don't usually smoke, but somebody gave me a packet and it seemed a pity to throw them away'). It was two years since I had seen him, but he fell in beside me and began talking in the manner of one who resumes a conversation broken off a day or so previously.

'It is Mr Benson? I never forget a client. It's an advantage, isn't it, for someone in my line of work?'

'I suppose it is.'

'But you'd be surprised how many people do. I've seen solicitors, professional people, walk past clients in the street a day after they've shown them out of their offices. That sort of thing looks very bad.' Something seemed to strike him and he turned towards me. 'That was a good evening we had, wasn't it? I always say you can't beat a good evening with people you've got something in common with, people you've been to school with. Did you go to the old boys' dinner this year?'

'No.'

'No, I don't remember you there, now you come to mention it. It was a good evening, though,' Mr Robey said defiantly, as if I had somehow called the event into question. 'A great success. We had a civil servant who was something high up in the Foreign Office. I can't say I'd ever heard of him, but everybody said it was very good.'

By now we had reached the outermost limit of the park. Here stunted trees lay in clumps, following the curve of South Park Avenue. Behind us a fiery orange sun cast angular shadows across the playing fields. It was growing dark.

At the gate Mr Robey stopped. 'I say. You'll think this awfully forward of me, I know, but what would you say to trying to find a pub somewhere? Somewhere we could have a bit of a drink and a natter?'

I remembered the family portraits on his desk. 'Won't your wife be expecting you back?'

Mr Robey looked uneasy. 'Between you and me, my wife's taken the children round to her mother's in Thorpe this afternoon. So this excursion is rather in the nature of a breather.'

'While the cat's away?'

'*Exactly*,' said Mr Robey, with unexpected fervour. 'That's exactly what it is.'

There was a pub at the very end of South Park Avenue called the University Arms where on rare occasions I had accompanied my father. It was here, driven by some unspoken mutual instinct, that we repaired. Inside, dark wooden beams and a single, flickering striplight combined to produce a sub-aqueous effect. Two elderly men sat playing dominoes by the fire.

Mr Robey brightened. 'Well, this is a find,' he said. 'What will you have?'

'A small whisky.'

'Nonsense. Always drink doubles at Christmas.' Mr Robey advanced on the landlord. 'Two double whiskies if you please.'

This was a new and unexpected version of Mr Robey, a bright, capering figure come to confound the anonymous wraith of the solicitor's office. He came back from the bar carrying the drinks in outstretched hands and laid them with an odd little flourish on the table.

'Actually,' he said, 'I used to come here before. Back in the old days. It was handy for the university, you see.'

'You were a student at the UEA?'

'Not me. Keele,' Mr Robey said sadly, as if this explained any later misfortunes to which he might have been subject. 'No. UEA girls. When I was in the sixth form at school we used to take them here.'

'I don't remember that happening in my day.'

'You'd be surprised,' said Mr Robey sagely. 'You'd be surprised at what went on.'

There was an expression which my father had used with reference to a decayed crony of his from the Norwich masonic club. 'Mr so-and-so,' he would say, with infinite contempt, 'was rather a dog in his day.' Mr Robey, I saw, had been such a dog. I remembered his kind from school: loud, confident teenagers who drove their fathers' cars, who spent summer weekends at beach parties on the coast at Bacton and Cart Gap and could be seen arm-in-arm with busty sixthformers from the Norwich High School for Girls. This early superiority had rankled. Monitoring the reports of their later careers – accountants, estate agents, insurance salesmen – I had always felt a keen sense of reparation.

Something, plainly, was preying on Mr Robey's mind. Presently he said, 'Extraordinary stroke of luck us meeting up like this, wasn't it?'

'I suppose it was.'

'To tell you the truth, it was a bit of a godsend you turning up like this. In fact, if I hadn't seen you when I did there's no knowing what I might not have done with myself.'

Years spent with Morty's entourage had accustomed me to confidences of this sort. 'What on earth is the matter?'

'Christmas,' said Mr Robey bitterly. 'I can't seem to get through it any more like I used to. It was all right in the old days. I could go down to the rugby club, play in the Boxing Day game with some of the old crowd and we'd have a hell of a time.'

Another piece in the jigsaw puzzle of Mr Robey's dog-days clicked neatly into place. Above our heads the lighting flared suddenly into life and then receded again. 'Couldn't you do that now?'

'Crocked. Dodgy cartilage. If I run more than ten yards my knee gives out. Happens to us all, I suppose,' he went on. 'But it's not the same, you know, just standing on the line and watching the others. You feel you're missing out.'

'What does your wife say?'

'Barbara? She's a grand girl, Barbara, but she doesn't understand. Not about sport. Women never do. I never knew a woman,' said Mr Robey, as if defining some incorrigible sex-wide deficiency, 'who really cared about sport. But she's a grand girl, Barbara. I wouldn't like you to think that I was doing her down.'

It was what men said about women they had grown tired of, or of women they suspected had grown tired of them. Suzi, I realised, was a grand girl. It meant imperfection, resentment, that fatal waning of interest.

Mr Robey's eye, which had been ranging nervously around the bar, now fell on our empty glasses. 'Look,' he said, 'I know it's a terrific cheek, but would you mind just talking to me for a bit? You're a man of the world – you've done some interesting things, I can see that. Solicitors notice things about their clients, you know.

I could tell that from the moment you walked into the office. I'd take it as a great favour if you'd just talk to me for a bit.'

An idea which had previously existed only in outline suddenly assumed coherent shape in my head. 'Mr Robey . . .'

'Geoff.'

'Geoff . . . Now you mention it there is something you could give me your professional opinion on. Would that be agreeable?'

'I'm all ears,' said Mr Robey. 'Go right ahead.'

And so I explained about the telephone calls, about the photographs and the video cassettes. And as these people also had their place in the story I explained about Morty, Terry Chimes and Elaine. It was a considerable monologue. Throughout it Mr Robey listened with an expression of rapt interest. When I had finished he said, 'This is way above my head, I don't mind saying. Someone unknown to you has been sending you pictures in which you appear, but you don't remember anything about it?'

'Nothing.'

'Extraordinary,' Mr Robey said. All trace of his depression of spirit had now lifted. 'I think we'd better have another drink and put our heads together about this. You see *technically* nobody has committed any crime, except of course sending obscene materials through the post. Even if you could find out who was responsible there wouldn't necessarily be any means of bringing them to court.'

We had another round of drinks. 'I acted once in an obscene publications case you know,' Mr Robey went on. 'Shocking business it was. Married couple out at Thetford used to sell photographs of themselves by mail order.'

'What happened?'

'Let off with a caution. All to do with freemasonry, if you want my opinion,' said Mr Robey moodily, 'but then it's all a question of knowing the right people, isn't it?' A sudden flash of belligerence lit up his face. 'Between you and me, Barbara's dad is high up in the masons.'

Later, when we were very drunk, we found ourselves outside in the darkness of South Park Avenue. Light gleamed from the surrounding housefronts. Mr Robey said, 'Do you know what we could do? We could get a taxi and go into town. Go to a night-club and have another drink. A proper drink.'

'Do they have many night-clubs in Norwich now?'

'Dozens. Samantha's. CJ's. Danny's Den. We could go to one of those and have a proper drink. Lot of trouble they have in the city these days, fighting and so on – always having people in my office charged with causing an affray – but so what? I'm pretty quick on my feet. I can take it. Let's go to a night-club.'

We wandered unsteadily along South Park Avenue for a while. On the rare occasions when a vehicle passed us Mr Robey leapt into the road behind it and shouted 'Taxi' very loudly. Then abruptly, his mood changed.

'It's no good. Better go home. Wouldn't do, would it? "Respected local solicitor charged with causing affray in night-club." It was good of you to suggest it, but we'd better not.'

'You could come back to my place and have a drink.'

'It's kind of you, but no. I've enjoyed our little chat,' said Mr Robey decisively, 'don't think I haven't, but no.'

And so on the corner of South Park Avenue we separated, he to move purposefully along Colman Road past the grey expanse of the infant school, I to walk less confidently through the succession of alleyways and side roads that led to Glebe Road. There was no sign of Suzi. I threw myself fully clothed on to the bed. Hours later I woke to find the light on and the telephone ringing downstairs in the hall.

A voice said, 'Merry Christmas, Mart.'

It was Morty. He too was drunk.

'Where are you?'

'Christ. At Terry's. Someplace in Essex. Saffron Walden, Great Dunmow, I don't remember. Full of fucking cows and fields of cabbages. You want to speak to Terry?'

'Is he there?'

'Hang on.' There was a flurry of remote, disconnected movement. 'No, he's fucked off somewhere. Went to the off-licence with Rodney or something. Hey, I got something to tell you though. That business of the pictures, those photos you keep getting sent. Terry heard something about it the other day.' There was a silence. 'You still there, Mart?'

'Yes.'

'Where was I . . .? Yeah, that business of the pictures. Well, somebody Terry was talking to reckoned it's some mad chick that's doing it. Some mad actress that must have got pissed off with you in the past. Wants to get back at you and that sort of thing. You got any ideas?'

'Have you?'

'No. There was that Lynsey Laguna didn't like the way you monkeyed about with her scripts . . . Jesus, she earns two hundred grand a year in the States now, she wouldn't want to do a thing like that. It beats me, Mart, it beats me. I should just sit tight if I were you, just sit tight and Terry and me'll see what we can find out.'

'Yes.'

There was another long silence. Dimly in the distance I could hear Morty's heavy breath panting down the line. Finally he said, 'Look, it's Christmas, Mart, Christmas, and Terry and me were thinking we ought to see you. Old times' sake and all that. Why don't you, why don't you just come on over?'

'Jesus, Morty, it's seventy, eighty miles away.'

'Yeah, I know that, I know that. But Terry's got some tame mini-cab firm. Reckons they owe him a favour. They could be over in an hour.'

'It's almost midnight, Morty.'

'Yeah, I know that. You know something?' Morty said evenly. 'You disappoint me a lot.'

'I'm sorry.'

'Yeah,' Morty said. 'But I'm still disappointed. Lots. You remember that, Martin. So long.'

The line went dead. I stood for a moment in the hallway considering the vague air of menace with which Morty's words had been attended. Then I went back to bed.

Much later in the small hours I woke to hear the sounds of Suzi moving about below: a faint hum of voices, clicks of dislodged crockery. The television rasped noisily for a few moments and was then switched off. Outside it began to rain. From the distance, beyond the dark rooftops and the scudding clouds, came the sound of thunder.

On New Year's Day Kev Jackson calls again. Coming back from the City Gates, awash with festive bonhomie, I hear the phone ringing outside the house, dash in and pounce on the receiver just before it expires. Kev is brief, businesslike.

'I got that address you wanted.'

He mentions a domicile somewhere in Greater Manchester.

'That's great, Kev.'

'Don't mention it . . . There's a phone number as well.'

I convey the proffered digits to the message pad. Key Jackson goes on, a touch nervously now. 'Good Christmas, Martin?'

'Can't complain, Kev. What about you?'

'Actually,' Kev Jackson says quickly, 'I got an invitation from Morty Goldstein. Over to Terry Chimes's place. Near Saffron Walden. That farmhouse he built after RCA bought him out of Grunt.'

Out in the street I can hear Fat Eric making a raucous, vagrant progress back to his front door. 'Glad to hear it, Kev. I thought Morty wasn't talking?'

'Oh well.' Kev Jackson turns nonchalant and unassuming. 'It's not so much about the book . . . Well, I don't want to give too much away at this stage, Martin, but Morty and me, we've got interests in common.'

Interests in common. Morty and I have interests in common. Elaine and I, wherever she is, have interests in common. Whoever it is who's sending me these pictures and I have interests in common.

'Too bad you couldn't make it yourself,' Kev Jackson goes on. 'At Christmas and that. That reminds me, Morty sent you a message.'

'He did?'

'Sure. He said to say, "Wait and see is best." '

'Just that?'

'Just that. "Wait and see is best." Now, I have a few questions here I want to ask you.'

I turn the words over in my head as Kev Jackson chunters on about a tedious and negligible scandal involving some purloined tapes and the *News of the World*. Outside there is a tumultuous crash which, experience suggests, is something to do with the beery pageant of Fat Eric's return, then silence. I put down the phone, stand by the window looking out in the empty streets.

A bit later I dial the number Kev Jackson gave me. It rings on endlessly. Several times over the ensuing days I try it again. No one ever answers. I wonder about writing to Elaine, I wonder about bombarding her with a torrent of allusive postcards, wonder even about taking a train to Manchester, confronting her on her doorstep. Eventually I do none of these things. Prompted by mounting inner disquiet I do, however, pay a visit to Norwich Central Library and, adrift amongst the pale students and the restless flotsam of the reading room, take a look at a Greater Manchester street directory. There is, as I suspected, no trace of Elaine's address.

Rain, slanting in from the west, came suddenly out of sky the colour of slate. Above, a group of sea gulls, jerked upwards by a gust of wind rising from the head of the dunes, hung motionless for a moment, squawking plaintively, before flapping slowly landward. Becalmed at the point where blocks of charred, unidentifiable wood lay half in and half out of the water they regrouped, heads low down against white pelts, feet balanced uneasily on this precarious perch. To the left choppy, gravy-coloured sea rose and fell inexorably, empty except for one or two low, solid shapes far away on the horizon. Dusk, which had stolen up unawares in the last fifteen minutes, drew nearer.

Elaine said, 'Do you think we ought to turn back?'

'It's only a mile to the town.'

'A mile back to the house if it comes to that.'

'There's four of us,' Jerry said. 'We ought to take a vote, at least.'

Back along the beach at the point where the coast began its slow curve in the direction of Lowestoft, mist was rising in dense, vaporous trails, partly obscuring the woods where we had walked only an hour or so before. I reflected on the inconsistency of the human spirit when presented with even the mildest obstacle of climate. The walk had been Elaine's idea. It was she who had instigated the route, she who had assembled the accompanying party, she, even, who had rummaged around in old cupboards and cloakrooms to procure suitable clothing and footwear. Now, by a strange but compelling twist of logic, it was she who seemed the most anxious to turn back.

Jerry said, 'We could at least walk up to the top and take a look at the place.'

Beyond and to the right, past outcrops of sandstone, shoreline bric-à-brac of rotting spars and plastic containers, a path rose shakily to the cliff top. Here there was further evidence of human debris: cigarette packets stamped into the sand, discarded fishing nets, salt-encrusted onions – a characteristic piece of east-coast jetsam – beaten into pulp. Looking back, the pattern of the rain increasing now to produce tiny indentations in the sand, I was struck by older associations: M. R. James's ghost stories, invariably set in this part of East Anglia, in which tatterdemalion wraiths rose up unexpectedly out of the sedge and demons capered beneath the sea wall; a painting by Wilson Steer of fog hanging over a marsh near Walberswick, folk tales of black, phantasmagoric animals said to haunt the coastline. In these circumstances – late afternoon in early January, twilight rapidly descending – it would not have been surprising to see Black Shuck or one or other of the local spirits loping hungrily up the beach.

Something of this feeling seemed to have occurred to Elaine. Pausing at the foot of the steps, where the overhang of the cliff face combined with encroaching shadow to create an atmosphere of unusual gloom, she said, 'I wouldn't like to come here after dark.'

'No one's asking you to.'

Crazy Rodney said, 'I know what you mean. Gives me the fucking creeps.'

Reaching the summit of the cliff, the wind gusting horizontally against the outcrops of sea grass, it was possible to hear echoes of an older world. Mist rolling away in queer clumps and hillocks over recently tilled fields, now breaking up in wispy, striated patterns, suggested something bordering on the prehistoric: Saxon coastguards, perhaps, staring anxiously out to sea, a vista of archaic battledress, beards, 'noble' expressions, in the manner of one of those fanciful paintings of the pre-Raphaelite school. Obscurely the town, a mile away, its outlying flanks discernible in the grey sea defences, bore out this impression. Church spires, rising out of the fog, a few lights already shining, the distant houses towards Blythburgh disappearing into shadow, it seemed as remote and self-absorbed as any medieval encampment. You imagined gate-keepers, venerable constables of the watch, Shakespearean paraphernalia of curfews and cock-crows.

Remote, dense, engrossed: I had always visualised the East Anglian landscape in these terms. History supported this sharp, austere conception: longboats nosing into the Suffolk creeks, dark sails along the river Wensum, King Edmund, his chest shot full of arrows like a pincushion, dying at Hellesdon, the monks scurrying westward from the sea. This feeling was strengthened by the experiences of the past week: fog, a constant feature of the terrain, rolling up at a moment's notice to obscure harsh views of sedge, bracken and scrubby pasture; rushing wind; cattle seen dimly through the mist like ghostly monsters out of a primeval landscape. We had descended into an older world, I thought, regressed into some elemental amphitheatre presided over by remote, clangorous gods.

On the cliff top serpentine pathways rose and fell: up to distant, vapour-shrouded fields, down to the low walls of shale and concrete. Ahead lines of tangled fencing, torn paper flapping heavily on the wire, enclosed nondescript pasturage. Sheep, huddled up against the posts, stirred anxiously at the intrusion. Here we lingered for a moment, stamping our feet against the cold, lighting cigarettes, in silence broken only by the wind and the skirl of the gulls.

Crazy Rodney said, 'So what happens there?'

'What happens where?'

'Down there. Sarfwold or wherever. What happens?'

'It's a town, Crazy Rodney. People live there.'

Hunched in his greatcoat, looking neither to right nor left, tendrils of cigarette smoke obscuring his pinched, watchful face, Crazy Rodney cut an incongruous figure. Massive inner resentment, narrowly kept at bay over the past week, now welled up uncontrollably.

'But what the fuck do they do?'

'Watch television. Look at the sea. Make money out of the tourists.'

Crazy Rodney shook his head. 'Carrot crunchers,' he said. 'Fucking carrot crunchers.'

'We'd better go back,' Elaine said. 'See whether Morty wants to retake that last scene.'

Jerry said, 'I never came any place like this before. Never.'

Another gust of wind whipping up from beyond the face of the cliff set the issue beyond doubt. It was now raining very hard indeed. Two-by-two, Jerry leading with Crazy Rodney, Elaine and I following close behind, we set off cautiously along the coast path.

Kessingland Manor dated from the early nineteenth century. Here at around the time of the Napoleonic wars some newly married Suffolk squire had built for himself a capacious family dwelling: two long vault-like reception halls, a low, draughty kitchen, a warren of bedrooms and servants' quarters. Later inhabitants had added on billiard rooms, gun rooms and out-houses; the whole constructed in greying limestone, taking on the character of an impregnable and faintly Gothic-looking fortress.

Terry Chimes proved to be unexpectedly knowledgeable about bygone domestic arrangements. He said, 'A hundred years ago there'd have been three, four, half-a-dozen horses, probably a coach as well. Kept them in the barn next to the courtyard, I shouldn't wonder.'

'What makes you think that?'

'Nearly bought a place like it myself once. Fucking estate agent – bright bloke he was, been to Oxford and that – told me what to look for.' Later he said, 'Bloody great barrack and all. Wouldn't surprise me if we had to do all the shooting outside.'

However the interior had proved surprisingly amenable to Morty's design. Arc lights had been rigged up in the second reception hall towards the back of the house; one of the gun rooms was a mass of electrical equipment. Actresses, parcelled out three or four to a bedroom, had so far voiced only minor complaint.

'In any case,' Morty had said, 'if they don't like it, they know what they can do. Plenty of other girls ready to flap their tits about and they know it.'

Returning to the house, one proceeded by a complicated series of landmarks. Paths through coils of dense, wet bracken gave way eventually to a precarious back road, bordered by ravines of mud, finally a dirt-track overhung by sere, dripping elms. By now darkness had fallen. In the drive, where cars and vans lay drawn up in a haphazard semi-circle, a flashlight hovered for a moment and then moved haltingly towards us. A voice said, 'Who's that?'

We identified ourselves. Morty's face loomed up suddenly out of the murk.

'Sorry, Martin. I thought you were those American girls.'

'Which American girls?'

'The two the agency were supposed to be sending. I've been expecting them since lunch-time. I suppose the fucking trains are out again.'

There was a railway station at Halesworth, ten miles away. At intervals over the past five days it had disgorged a succession of new arrivals: exotic, gaudily dressed girls, bewildered by the unpromising terrain in which they now found themselves; sharp-faced men in suits, old allies of Morty's from distribution agencies and cinema chains, come to check on progress. In this ceaseless shambling to and fro across the level East Anglian countryside there had been casualties: actresses stranded in anonymous Suffolk towns where there were neither buses nor taxis; one of Terry Chimes's Grunt Records understrappers finally run to earth in Dunwich some miles down the coast. It was impossible to predict what might have happened to the American girls.

'I'd better go and have a look,' Morty said.

We left him standing uncertainly in the beam of torchlight and moved on towards the house. Here there were signs of recent activity. Packing cases, their tops prised open, their contents – pieces of unfamiliar lighting equipment – strewn about, lay in the vestibule. Two members of the film crew, vague anonymous men who had not been heard to speak during the course of the shoot, straightened up as they saw us, as if expecting some rebuke, then resumed their work. Mr Tovacs sat alone in the hall, his legs angled towards an electric heater, reading intently. Seeing us he rose noisily to his feet and gave a mock salute.

'You came upon me unawares,' he said, 'wholly given up to literature. Is that not always the case?'

In the interval since the Red Lion Street party Mr Tovacs's character had undergone a decisive shift in orientation. Previously he had given the impression of being no more than an interested spectator in the plans for filming *Resurrection*. Now, gradually, yet with increasing confidence, he had emerged into the role of patron, someone intimately involved with each twist of a complicated piece of machinery, fearful lest his own interests should be ignored. Taken round the building by Morty, made party to various technicalities, he had the intent but slightly suspicious look of a tourist, conscious amid much communal diversion that responsibility for settling the bill lay with him alone. There was something ominous, I thought, about his continual presence on the edge of scene and conversation, his quaintly phrased questions: the scent of trouble.

The girls disappeared to their rooms, Crazy Rodney to the kitchen where, fires kept burning throughout the day, there was a promise of warmth. Mr Tovacs seemed disposed to talk. I examined the book he had just put aside. It was a paperback of *The Spoils of Poynton*, an appropriate choice in the circumstances. Much of Kessingland Manor's furniture and ornaments had survived the house's transformation into an upmarket holiday home. There were a number of superior knick-knacks lying about on tables, stout sideboards, a profusion of oil paintings dominated by a large, square portrait of an elderly patriarch in stock and side-whiskers. Mr Tovacs surveyed all these benevolently, his gaze finally resting on the portrait.

'He is a splendid fellow, is he not? A fine old *bourgeois*? One could make an interesting study of the social attitudes of Victorian portraiture. Art as the handmaiden of imperialism. I expect he gave people a terrible time in his day.'

This remark, unexceptionable in itself, gave another clue to the change in Mr Tovacs's character. He had, so to speak, moved up a gear, ascended to a new level of self-absorption and invulnerability, what the Victorian novelist – James himself, if it came to that – would have called a 'high demeanour'.

'Have you been here all afternoon?'

Mr Tovacs frowned at the painting, as if finally deciding that it did not match up to the exacting standards he required of portraiture. In one way or another he seemed extremely pleased with himself.

'Very little has happened. I believe there is some problem about transport. Earlier on your Mr Goldstein made an attempt to film some scene in the barn behind the house. It grew very cold so I ventured indoors.

'It is none of my business,' Mr Tovacs went on. 'The technicalities that form a part of this project. Though naturally one has one's opinions.

'There has been an *argument*,' Mr Tovacs said.

Snow fell later that night. I watched it, sitting up in bed, the curtain undrawn: a grey expanse of parkland, darker clumps of trees and shrubbery, all steadily obliterated by a pale, relentless tide. Snow falling over the wide East Anglian plain, descending to swell the mutinous sea, confirmed the impression of antiquity. I thought of wolves roaming through the frozen thickets, horses' hooves scraping the ice, old, unsanitised fairy tales of cheerless hearths and evil visitants. Beside me Elaine slept noiselessly, one arm flung out over the white sheet, hair spilled out across the pillow, so that she too seemed somehow a part of these unreal landscapes, lost and transient, like the wolves ripe for dissolution when the storyteller snapped his fingers and brought an end to his tale.

When I woke at dawn the room was empty. Outside the landscape had taken on sharp, unfamiliar outlines: fence posts running across snowy fields like the piping on a dress; a line of rooks rising suddenly from the woods and moving in formation away inland. I was dressed and sitting on the bed by the time Elaine returned.

'You poor baby,' she said. 'You were supposed to be asleep.'

'Where have you been?'

'Where do you think I've been? Out for a walk? Playing strip-poker with Terry Chimes – there's no point by the way, he always cheats. Jesus, Martin, I suppose you'll start talking about *loyalty* in a minute and mature relationships.'

'Who is it then? Is it Morty?'

'No.'

'Terry?'

'It doesn't matter who it is. What matters is that you shut up about it.'

'Or is it Crazy Rodney? He always has to have at least one actress a shoot. He told me once.'

'You poor baby,' Elaine said again. Mockery and faint, derisive sympathy could not be disentangled. 'I treat you so badly, don't I?'

'No worse than you always did.'

'I treat you so badly,' Elaine went on. 'So badly. And do you know what the joke is? The real joke is that you never do anything about it.'

The American girls emerged for the first time at breakfast. Sullen and fractious, they spoke only to each other.

'Too fucking cold to work. If Goldstein wants me to work he'd better lay on some heating.'

'But honey, you got a contract.'

'Yeah and I got a weak chest as well. No heaters, no nude scenes.'

Later in the kitchen Cindy, the second American girl, said, 'You have to excuse Mary-Beth. She's had a lot of disappointments lately.'

'What sort of disappointments?'

'The usual sort of thing. I mean, you wouldn't believe it to look at her, but she used to be a serious actress. Her pa used to be head of East Coast production at Universal: she got a lot of parts that way. Supporting roles, nothing you could write home and tell your folks about, but, well, serious. She got to screw Rod Steiger once in a motel scene. Can you imagine that? Screwing Rod Steiger in a motel scene and it's the high point of your career. But then her pa died and she ended up in the skin trade. It just goes to show, I suppose.'

Traces of Mary-Beth's earlier respectability remained. She pronounced the few lines that the script allowed her in an odd, strangulated parody of an English accent. Cindy shook her head. 'All on account of when she was a kid,' she explained, 'and her pa used to show her these tapes of Edith Evans playing Lady Bracknell. Right from the start, right from when she was in high school drama proms, she thought that was the way actresses were supposed to speak.'

In the intervals of filming, members of Morty's cast emerged on to the meagre terrain of the surrounding countryside. Here they loitered unhappily in the snowbound lanes or took buses to Lowestoft, ten miles along the coast, in search of amusement. Numbers of them descended on Southwold where they could be seen staring moodily from the windows of tea-shops, or pondering the newspapers in the sailors' reading room. An undercurrent of mutiny, never quite allowed to rise to the surface, was narrowly kept in check by these relaxations.

Meanwhile I had plenty with which to occupy myself. Even in its revised and attenuated form, *Resurrection* had proved unmanageable for the limited resources with which Morty now found himself provided. Substantial cuts would be needed. I made Sir George a housebound invalid, his dissipation confined to voyeuristic eavesdropping on kitchen maids innocently exploring each other in the hayloft. I invented a makeweight subplot in which two of Sir George's grooms competed for the attentions of a buxom cook.

Though Morty approved these alterations, his mood remained grim. He said, 'You're doing your best, Martin, I can see that. It's just that . . . Christ, we've got to lose that scene at the wedding breakfast.'

'The one where they drink the bride's health and it turns into an orgy?'

'That's the one. We haven't got the costumes. Well, not enough of them. Didn't have enough money to hire them.'

'Well, shoot the whole thing nude then. As a sort of joke. You know, Sir George starting where he means to go on. Or have them all wrapped in blankets. I don't know.'

'Christ, Martin, sometimes I don't think you're taking me seriously. Sometimes I . . . Look, I'm sorry, Martin, I'm not getting at you. It's just that . . . Look, Martin, I've got problems like you wouldn't believe.'

'Tovacs?'

'No, not Tovacs. I can handle Tovacs, specially as he's come up with most of the money now. Keeps putting his nose in, keeps asking for things. Always asking for things. When he got here he wanted a phone put in his room. Yesterday he wanted a car to take him back to London for the night. I soon told him to fuck off about *that*. But it's not Tovacs, it's his girl.'

'I hadn't noticed anything.'

'You wouldn't. Glued to the fucking typewriter, aren't you? Well, there's something going on there. You just take a look and tell me if you don't agree with me. And fix the fucking wedding breakfast. I need to get it on tape.'

In the intervals of fixing the wedding breakfast – reduced eventually to a sober foursome involving Sir George, his bride, the best man and the head bridesmaid, a horde of imaginary guests continually spoken of as being 'in the other room' – I monitored the relationship between Jerry and Mr Tovacs. Outwardly all was as it had been before. They appeared together in public, sat next to one another at meal times, retired at night to a bedroom on the upper floor. But Morty's surmise was, I realised, correct. There was a sharp flavour of animosity about their dealings, the hint of Jerry's deep reservoir of resentment only now being allowed to seep out into the clear water around it. Once, passing their room late at night, I heard the sound of voices raised in recrimination: sharp, unmistakable voices in which Jerry's predominated. I dismissed them as of little account: a diversion, perhaps, running in parallel to my own greater disquiet, faint echoes of a wider and more personal anguish.

In retrospect I recall this period as a series of potent but scarcely reconstitutable images: smudged portraits on the crackling tape, random, blaring soundtrack. Crazy Rodney on the cliff top; Morty, serious, aggrieved, casting his eye over a tableau of naked actresses; the American girls bickering in their dressing room; a memory of Terry Chimes met unexpectedly on a walk in the lanes and flashing me a smile whose significance I was not then able to appreciate; Mr Tovacs ambling pointedly from room to room in search of an electric heater; playing card games with Jerry in the dull forenoons. Later these pictures fade away, replaced eventually by the single figure of Elaine: Elaine in her role as *ingénue* bride, swooning on a sofa when faced with the first unignorable evidence of her husband's designs; Elaine cavorting with whoops of bogus lust over Sir George's recumbent body; Elaine backstage, wrapped in a towel, staring fiercely into space.

Time dragged.

Weather conditions, which had improved with the disappearance of the snow, rapidly worsened. Thin rain falling steadily across the barren fields alternated with winds rushing in from the coast. Crazy Rodney, who penetrated as far as Southwold harbour, reported waves as much as twenty feet high and the threat of flooding. At night absolute blackness descended, a blanket of cloud and mist impenetrable even by torchlight. It was in these conditions that Terry Chimes, returning late one evening from a pub in Kessingland village, tumbled into a roadside ditch and broke his ankle.

In the evenings Jerry and I played Scrabble.

'"Yapok". Five letters. That's seventy-eight points.'

'"Yapok"?'

'It's a South American water opossum,' Jerry explained. 'Your go.'

When I had taken my turn she said, 'We ought to take a look at the score. Go ahead and add it up, will you?'

'Two hundred and seventeen against sixty-five.'

'I like a close game,' Jerry said, without apparent irony. 'Now, where'd we get to? "Zydeco". That's twenty-two points, plus the triple word score which makes sixty-six.'

'Don't you mean "zodyco"? A type of Afro-American dance music played in the southern states. With an "o"?'

'Not in Alabama.'

Mr Tovacs hove into view, hoisting his way carefully around the long kitchen table as if he doubted his ability to walk unaided. He said, 'I have just been reading the scene in which Owen and Feeda are interrupted by Mrs Brigstock. I recommend it to you.'

'For Christ's sake,' Jerry said, without looking up from the board. 'Go away.'

Unexpectedly Mr Tovacs's attitude changed. He seemed suddenly detached, quite unable to cope with this dismissal. He said, a shade peevishly, 'I am not feeling at all well. It is probably the cold. I wish you would come and talk to me.'

After he had gone I said, 'Shouldn't you go and see him if he isn't feeling well?'

'Later,' Jerry said, 'later I will, maybe, if I feel like it. Maybe I won't, who knows? . . . "Xylitol".'

'"Xylitol"?'

'There's a dictionary if you don't believe me.'

I read: 'A sweet, crystalline, pentahydric alcohol derived from xylose and present in some plant tissues.'

Upstairs in the master bedroom Morty was hard at work.

'Okay. When it comes to the bit where you take your clothes off I want you to take your time over it. I know it's fucking cold, but Rodney here'll make sure the heater's turned up. Then when you come out from behind the screen you get the feeling there's somebody there. Stare around a bit, look under the bed if you like. Then scream.'

Mary-Beth, got up in a passable imitation of a Victorian parlourmaid, stood with her hands on her hips. Sir George, a mustachioed figure with terrific check trousers, lingered unhappily in the corner of the room. She said suspiciously, 'Let's get this straight. You want me to take my clothes off behind the screen while he hangs around looking like an old man in a park? I never did a strip show where I stayed out of sight before.'

'You wouldn't understand.'

'What wouldn't I understand? I happen to be a fucking *actress* and don't you forget it.'

'Just do it,' Morty said wearily.

Silence descended, broken only by the whirr of the camera. Eventually Mary-Beth said, 'Listen, Rodney or whatever your name is, you can take your fucking hand *off*, okay?'

Even in these later days, harassed by inadequate resources, supported by inferior talents, Morty's sense of irony had not wholly deserted him. Two or three years back a screenplay such as *Resurrection* would have produced a range of extravagant responses, stirred him to contrive a number of delicate conceits, each somehow capable of assimilation into the flamboyant overall design. Actors in punctilious period costume would have found themselves weaving rare and subtle patterns in a remote and inchoate tapestry, cameramen resigned themselves to picking out individual threads in a grander mosaic kept for the most part out of reach by its creator. This desire to exclude collaborators in his films from all but the most cursory knowledge of their aims and intentions was an essential part of Morty's temperament. He maintained that his employees – actors, cameramen, technicians – gave their best performances when set to work in isolation, wholly ignorant of the wider mechanisms whose component parts they were instructed to engineer. Allied to this characteristic was a second Goldstein trait: an element of surprise, introduced at the most improbable moment, with the connivance of a bare minimum of those involved. There is a moment in *Stately Lust* which perfectly encapsulates this tendency. An early Leisurevision effort, notionally derived from *Lady Chatterley's Lover*, the film depended for its apogee on the tumultuous coming together of Lady Maud (played by Lila St Claire) and her manservant Hodges. This liaison took place in a potting shed, featured a wide range of Edwardian corsetry – a subject on which Morty claimed to possess specialised knowledge – and relied for its incidental effects on views of a garden party taking place outside the window, the absence of Lady Maud and her lackey becoming steadily more flagrant. At a crucial moment in the proceedings, and without warning, Morty introduced a live ferret into the shed. He continued to film throughout the resulting confusion: Lady Maud snatching up her garments and fleeing into the garden; Hodges, puzzled, alarmed, finally seizing a pitchfork and preparing to do battle; the ferret, predatory and beady-eyed, eventually attaching itself to his leg; bolder guests clustering round the doorway; the result a bizarre mixture of flailing limbs, rapid, unsynchronised movement, the vague hint – amid much ancillary humour – of menace.

Later Goldstein productions refined this technique to a startling degree: the moment in *Frenzy* when Sheri La Grange and Frank Fellatio, frozen in mid-coitus, are suddenly entombed beneath a falling roof, emerging amid clouds of rising dust and fractured plaster; the scene in *Scuba Girl Dive Dive Yes* when Corona d'Amour and Barry La Boeuf, wrapped in an underwater clinch, are suddenly prised apart by the sight of a barbed black fin coursing through the water towards them. Chance, random contingency: it amused Morty to direct these gusts of sharp, realistic air throughout the stylised, hothouse landscape of his art. 'Basically, Martin,' he would remark, 'basically what your average punter doesn't understand is that pornography is funny. A girl and a guy pretending to fuck each other. It's a scream. Might be a turn-on for a bit, but how do you take it seriously? That bit in *Night Nurse* where Mitzi says to the guy, "Okay, big boy, let's see if you can rise to the occasion." You'd have to be pretty stupid not to laugh at that.'

'Some people are pretty stupid, Morty.'

'They'd have to be pretty stupid to take *me* seriously.'

Despite these disavowals there was much in the Leisurevision *oeuvre* to delight the cinéaste. Self-aware, reflexive, ceaselessly turning in on themselves in frequently alarming ways, Morty's productions displayed a healthy awareness of their own artifice. Generally this emerged as a minor twist on the cinematic thread – a sudden cutting away from the main action to a window or a polished surface, a split-second reflection in which the eye of the camera was briefly revealed, a mirror hung at an oblique angle behind the set – but there were hints of a grander subterfuge: *Casting Couch*, for instance, shot in 1976, a film about the making of a pornographic film, the deceit only disclosed in the final moments when actors, cameramen, onlookers mingle unexpectedly in the centre of the stage.

In contrast *Resurrection* ploughed a humbler furrow. Odd juxtapositions of the family portraits in the opening sequences; a queer moment in which the camera moves from a shot of Sir George grappling with his bride to linger on a vase shaking perilously on the edge of a nearby sideboard, its final collapse, descent and explosion into fragments coinciding with a dramatic off-stage moan. Its highlight, perhaps, was Mary-Beth's protracted striptease, a divestiture prolonged with the aid of screens, decorousness and protruding furniture, to six or seven minutes of camera time. Even here though, there were signs of approaching dissolution: Mary-Beth, bewildered, uncertain as to what was required of her, struggling with her unfamiliar armature; Sir George, embarrassed and unhappy; Morty preoccupied, offhand in his directions. Watching a rough cut some time later I was struck only by the gap between design and execution, a proud glamour irretrievably compromised.

Elaine said, 'Tomorrow, the next day, whenever Morty finishes filming, then I quit.'

'Where to?'

'I don't know. London. Somewhere in the country. Somewhere I can have a rest.'

'You,' I said, 'have the greatest capacity for self-deception of anyone I have ever met.'

'Fine. If that's the way you want to remember me, then just go ahead. Fine.'

'Look, Elaine, it's not a question of wanting to remember you. It's a question of . . .'

'Listen, Martin,' Elaine said wearily, 'four years I've spent doing this, doing these films and being with you and watching you being so superior about the *irony* of what you do for a living, and that's it, forget it. While we're at it, I'll tell you another thing. In case you're wondering where I was last night and the night before and the night before that, it was with Terry.'

'Terry Chimes?'

'Why not? Terry's pathetic really. He wants to do things Morty wouldn't even dream of filming and that's only when he stops talking about his mother, but I can understand Terry Chimes. I've known a lot of Terry Chimeses. But I can't understand you.'

'I can tell you if you want.'

'It's a bit late for that,' Elaine said. 'About three years too late. Now, why don't you go and do something useful? You could go and find out who's making all that noise for a start.'

Screams, dimly discernible from somewhere in the lower region of the house, now rose in crescendo. Footsteps, audible a long way off, could be heard drawing nearer, mixed with other, less insistent, voices. At the foot of the staircase, Mr Tovacs cowering in a pained and resentful way before her, Jerry was shouting, 'Nazi, Nazi, Nazi,' each repetition increasing in volume and causing Mr Tovacs to shrink further back against the banister. Morty, emerging from a side door, moved swiftly towards them and grabbed her arm.

'Look, if you're going to have a fucking row, there are places where . . .'

'He's a Nazi,' Jerry said, 'he's a fucking Nazi. Go on, ask him. You're a Jew. You ought to be interested, of all people. Go on, ask him what he did in the fucking war.'

Mr Tovacs spoke for the first time. 'This is all most unnecessary. I will not allow you to speak to me in this way.'

Jerry said, 'I'll tell you what he did in the war. He was a fucking collaborator. Don't ask me how I know, but he was a fucking asshole collaborator. Stuck in Poland after the Occupation . . .'

'You are making a very great mistake . . .'

'Loading Jews into railway carriages . . .'

'You had better stop this now . . .'

'In the fucking ghettoes . . .'

'*Stop it now . . .*'

Simultaneously three things happened with astonishing rapidity. Mr Tovacs, who had been opening and closing his mouth noiselessly, suddenly began to topple down on to his knees. Jerry burst into tears. Onlookers – Crazy Rodney, the two American girls – now came forward to attend to Mr Tovacs's collapsing form.

'And another thing,' Jerry said to Morty as these actions continued, 'you shouldn't believe anything he tells you about money. Not a word.'

Mr Tovacs was helped to a sofa in the hall where he lay without speaking, his face in repose an odd compound of bewilderment and fatuous content. Later ambulancemen, diagnosing a mild heart attack, came and took him away to Lowestoft hospital. Morty went off to telephone. Jerry, who had declined an invitation to accompany the ambulance, sat on a chair in the kitchen smoking furiously. She said, 'You know how you get intuitions about people? Well, I used to get them about Tovacs. Little things. He'd talk a lot about what he did in the Thirties and he'd talk a lot about being in Paris after the war. Never about anything in between. So I thought, never mind, perhaps he doesn't want to talk about it, perhaps it was all too harrowing. My dad was like that. He was a fighter pilot in Germany in 1944, but he didn't want to talk about it. Wouldn't ever say. But Tovacs couldn't stop dropping hints. Going on about the Jews. Going on about Ezra Pound being misunderstood. In the end I wormed it out of him.'

'What did he do?'

'Nothing you could put your finger on. Nothing you could even say was a war-crime, not now, not forty years later. From what I can make out he was some sort of Nazi stooge, somewhere in occupied Poland. You know, pretended to be sympathetic to the resistance and all the time he's supplying information to the other side.'

I remembered the plot of *Columbine* with its hints of divided loyalties, eventual betrayal. 'Then what happened?'

'Who knows? Nobody knows. Poland gets liberated. Tovacs disappears. Turns up again in Paris with a literary magazine and a nice line in introductions to Eliot and Stravinsky. People die. People forget. People move on. I don't suppose anybody knows what really happened.'

'People could find out.'

'Maybe people did. I remember once Tovacs being terrified when some old Polish guy he hadn't seen in decades turned up at Red Lion Street. I don't know what they said to each other, but it was like something out of a Victorian novel. You know, when the brother everybody thinks died thirty years ago comes back to claim his inheritance. Old, grim faces and the dread hand of the past. That sort of thing.'

'What about the money?'

'I don't know,' Jerry said. 'Who knows? Who can tell what the old buzzard's done about the money?'

Later I walked down through narrow, uneven pathways to the beach. Storms had blown up the previous evening, persisted long into the night, and left queer relics on the greying sand: more strings of onions, a fraying mauve jersey wreathed with seaweed, spongy accretions of cotton wool. Along the horizon, grey sea rising to meet the scarcely less grey expanse of sky, long ships – four or five of them, almost amounting to a flotilla – moved in a slow, inch-by-inch progress. In the distance, at the point where the beach curved into a promontory of dunes, odd formations of rock and sandstone jutting out almost to the limit of the shoreline, there were figures moving hastily in and out of vision, the effect resembling a complex game of concealment and revelation, oddly enticing. There were footprints in the sand, two sets, the second hemmed in by furrows and pockmarks, suggesting a walking stick, impeded movement. I followed them for a while, head down against the wind, until they veered hard left towards the dunes, the trail lost in softer, shifting sand, clumps of sea grass. Simultaneously it began to rain. I gave the beach a last, fleeting inspection – gathering clouds, the dark shape of a dog or some other animal nosing far away amid the strewn jetsam – and turned back towards the house.

Morty stood disconsolately in the driveway. He said, 'You seen Terry?'

'There were people down on the beach. It might have been him.'

'Trust Terry to piss off at a time like this. I just phoned the bank and we're seriously fucked.'

'How seriously?'

'Seriously seriously. That last big cheque of Tovacs's – the one that covered the letting fees, the one that was going to pay for the promotion – well, you can take it from me that it never got through.'

'What are you going to do?'

'What can I do? There's two or three scenes left to film – we can cut that last bit in the hayloft. If I finish shooting at least there's a product at the end of it.'

'How long will it take?'

'Four, five hours. Terry said he was going to organise some sort of piss-up. At least we can all get drunk after I wrap.'

The rain came in more fiercely now, plastering the strands of sandy hair over Morty's forehead. He looked doleful, enraged, uncomprehending.

'What did you tell the girls?'

'The girls?' Morty stared wonderingly. 'Fuck the girls, Martin. Just fuck them.'

Twelve hours later at 4 a.m., bright arc lights burning furiously into the night, the wind blowing noisily against the uncurtained windows, the actresses red-eyed and exhausted from lack of sleep, Morty wrapped.

'You couldn't possibly understand,' Suzi says.

'No?'

'You couldn't possibly understand what it's like. When you're about fourteen. First you have to have been kissed. Not just on the mouth: everywhere. And if you haven't, then you have to say you have. A bit later you have to sleep with somebody. Properly, so you can tell the other girls about it. A bit later you don't have to just sleep with somebody, you have to sleep with them a *lot*.'

'You do?'

'*You have to have a boyfriend*,' Suzi says fiercely. 'You just have to.' She recites the prurient enquiries of long ago, like some easily remembered catechism. '"What did you do last night?" "Oh, I did my homework and then Barry rang." "What did you do at the weekend?" "Oh, I watched television and then I went round to Barry's." "How many times did you do it?" "Three or four times, I don't remember." And the thing was,' Suzi says, 'that the boys didn't really want to do it at all. They'd have sooner been mending their bikes, or playing football. It was just something they had to do so they could go and talk to their mates about it as well.'

Early evening in Glebe Road, warm mellow light diffusing through the room and another discussion of the vexed question of Suzi's past. Suzi, it has to be said, is behaving oddly these days: no longer irritable, distant, combative, but watchful, conciliatory, solicitous. She makes a habit now of cooking me dinner when she comes home, standing over me as I eat it. But there are signs, tell-tale signs . . . Last night, for example, she was up in the loft, the repository, among other bulky items too large to be stored in her bedroom, of her suitcases. This evening comes another cautious hint of what lies in store.

'I went and saw Christopher after work today,' she says.

'How was he?'

'He was all right. He lives in this bungalow up Eaton way. Very posh,' Suzi pronounces.

'I suppose he would. Being a manager.' The irony rises up, is considered, rejected and goes away again.

'We had a long talk,' Suzi says. 'A long talk. And we agreed that it would be nice to see each other again. Just as friends.'

There is a silence.

'It's funny,' Suzi says. 'But all the time I was sitting there on the sofa – he's got this new sofa, he's ever so proud of it, he bought it at Debenham's – all the time that I was sitting there I couldn't think for the life of me what it was that I used to see in him.'

We have a mild, complicit laugh over this that extends, unusually enough, to a short-lived necking session on our own sofa, before the telephone rings and Suzi clambers up to answer it. I add this to the other bizarre portents that the last week has yielded up. Two days ago I lent Fat Eric three hundred pounds, three hundred pounds in five-pound notes extracted from the building society and conveyed to him by way of a brown-paper envelope at lunch-time in the City Gates. Oddly, this was received not with wild and fulsome gratitude, as one might have expected, but with what amounted to indifference, Fat Eric merely looking rather glum and stowing the envelope hurriedly away in the pocket of his jeans.

Yesterday, having devised further enticing bait on the subject of Morty and Terry Chimes, I rang Kev Jackson. The phone rang for a long time before he picked it up.

'Kev. Martin Benson.'

'Yes.'

'I was thinking . . . about what we were talking about the other day. I've got some more information that might interest you.'

'You have?'

'About Morty and Terry Chimes. The stuff you wanted for your book.'

I could hear Kev Jackson breathing heavily down the line for a moment. Then he said, 'Look, Martin, let's forget about it, shall we?'

'About Morty and Terry Chimes. About that girl you were interested in.'

'Let's just forget about it, shall we?'

'But what about your book? What about your ten thousand from the publishers?'

'Let's forget about that too. I'm sorry, Martin, but it's all finished. It's *all over.*'

After that he rang off. When I redialled, the phone rang on endlessly, was picked up and then sharply replaced.

Meanwhile Suzi comes back into the room. She looks thoughtful, preoccupied.

'Who was that?'

'Just a friend,' I say. 'Just a friend.' She goes upstairs after this. There are more shiftings and scuttlings in the loft.

And then one day I come home and find her gone. Five o'clock on a steely January afternoon, four hours back on the road from Brooke, I return to discover that certain aspects of my life are irrevocably changed, altered out of recognition, fallen lamentably away. The harbingers follow an odd, cumulative pattern: the shoes gone from inside the door, a queer emptiness from inside the hall finally revealing itself as the absence of the occasional table. The telephone lies on the carpet, message pad stuffed haphazardly underneath it. The note on the top is a day old: 'A man rang. Said he'd ring back later.' I press on upstairs into Suzi's bedroom, bed stripped and vacant, wardrobe thrown open and gaping, stop for a moment on the landing – a white untarnished square where the Monet poster used to hang – head downwards again into a kitchen where the miniature bottles of herbs are gone, the cupboards ransacked and some pitiless intelligence has gone through the cutlery, removed its own and left the rest in a shiny pile on the draining board. There is a peculiar angriness to the chaos, I note: cups lie shattered in the sink, chairs skewed over on to their sides, the contents of a bag of flour rises like ghostly dust from beneath my wary feet.

Another prowl through the upper regions of the house, in the hope of finding some faint departing trail. The bathroom has been cleaned out, only a box of aspirins and a packet of disposable razors left to decorate the top of the cabinet. In a drawer of the bedside table I find a heap of tampons and a copy of *The Friendship Book of Francis Gay*, nothing more. I go to the lounge last of all. Here the absences are more fundamental: the row of glass animals on the mantelpiece gone capering off to some lusher resting place, snooker videos gathered up and taken away. Still no note, still no explanation. Even here, amongst all the unpromising evidence of emotional fracture, the potent symbols of accumulated resentment, one would like it in writing.

The photographs lie on the carpet beneath the TV. I don't notice them at first, so preoccupied am I with the reproach of the empty shelves and the vanished invitation cards. When I do, I sidle up gingerly, as if it might be possible to take them by surprise, catch them unawares, somehow anaesthetise the hurt that they undoubtedly contain. For a long time, seated there with these celluloid rectangles on the floor beneath me, I notice only incidentals: the white envelope they came in ('Miss S. Richards' firmly typed on the front), the tiny imperfections of shade, shadow and misalignment, the fuzz of unexpected movement confusing the camera's eye. Blurred, dog-eared snaps. As the inspection proceeds, this air of remote detachment hypertrophies. Finally, when I come upon myself, note the painful activities I appear to be engaged in, it seems nothing more than an embarrassing memento from childhood, brought out twenty years later by indulgent grandparents. This is not real. Real life disintegrated some time back, went away beyond recall, and in a moment or two the Queen of Brobdingnag will saunter airily by with a sabre-toothed tiger straining at its leash. I snap out of my trance, switch on the TV, move over to the drinks cabinet, find a bottle, bring it back.

Later on when I wake up from this wretched, drink-fuelled sleep there is still no sign of Suzi; the television blares wordlessly on. I scoop up the pictures from the carpet where they lie undisturbed and look at them again. They could be fakes, of course, just about. The one in which the girl stares up anxiously at her brooding pursuer, the one in which the dreadful implications of what is going on are so neatly apparent, it could just be a masterly contrivance, stills blended expertly together, only the faint, blurred foreground suggesting artifice, a tiny unevenness in the way the whole is constructed trailing the thought that perhaps it didn't happen, that perhaps somebody made it up. And the ones shot in shadow, in which the faces disappear into a background of jittery limbs and sharp, reflexive movements, it might have been anyone. At any rate, it might not have been me.

Eight o'clock. Three doors down Kay will probably be waiting, hoping I'll be round. And all of a sudden I want very much to be sitting in Fat Eric's front room amid the sprawl of lager cans and discarded trainers, beneath the watchful gaze of *Norwich City: The Division One Story*, I want very much to sit there listening to Kay impart more homely details of life with Fat Eric, about how he hits her and won't let her go out in the evenings. I want very much to tell her some more gilded lies about Bobby Dazz and Barbie. Outside it's dark, the streetlamps loom up and I have this nasty habit of bumping into things – the gatepost, the hedge, a skateboard which some conniving infant has left in the road – but in the end I find myself trembling by the fence that adjoins Fat Eric's porch.

The house is dark, just a faint glow deep in the shadow of the upstairs window, but I press on. I ring the bell emphatically a couple of times and then, for good measure, I slam my fist against the wide expanse of the door. I shout, 'Kay,' once or twice fairly loudly. I wonder about flinging some gravel up at the window. People wander past, dim outlines caught in the tail of my eye, but, bless you, they don't notice, they don't care. Round here you don't interfere in such circumstances. Finally there are minor, reluctant noises from within, uncertain footsteps that start and stop, go away and come back again, and Kay opens the door.

'I was upstairs,' she says, 'I didn't think you were coming.'

'Kay . . .'

She doesn't look well, Kay doesn't, or happy, or particularly pleased to see me. What with the bruised temple, the slow, animal stare and the nightdress clutched absently around her, I get the impression that Kay would rather be somewhere else, somewhere miles away from myself and Fat Eric and all these other cunning tormentors.

'I can explain, Kay,' I tell her, 'I can explain everything. I only want to talk to you.'

'You'd better come in,' Kay says.

Inside, the chaos is more random, more purposeful than ever. Pictures hang drunkenly in their frames. One of the ducks has disappeared from the wall, leaving a gout of dislodged plaster, and the contents of the video shelf have been upended over the floor where they lie like scattered dominoes. A broken bottle. Smashed ashtrays.

Kay says, 'Eric done that. He come home at dinner-time and done it. Him and that Ron. Well, not Ron. Ron just stood there and looked as if he was somewhere else. I've been sitting here since then wondering why he did it.'

'Why did he do it?'

'I don't know. Come home at dinner-time, and tells me I'm a tart and he isn't going to stand for it. You want to see the kitchen,' Kay says. 'He put a chair through the window in there.'

'Kay . . .'

'It was that Ron. Ron put him up to it. Just at the end, before they went, Ron takes me to one side and says, "Eric's very upset. You want to remember that next time, remember how upset Eric can get." The fucker!'

In the kitchen smashed glass gleams palely from the floor. A pool of something white and viscous glistens from the table. I arch a finger over it and taste: milk. At once I realise that I've been here before, back in the old days, in the East End, when I once went to examine a house Crazy Rodney had smashed up at Morty's behest. Crazy Rodney had done a thorough enough job – fire irons through the patio window, television set lobbed out into the back garden, electrical fittings dangling brokenly from the ceiling – but what had struck me was how unconcerned the family had been. Perhaps, having had long-term dealings with Morty, they were used to having their home smashed up? Perhaps when they went to switch on the television and instead found it lying in the garden with its entrails spilled out on to the grass, they simply shrugged their shoulders and opted for some other diversion? Perhaps it really didn't matter any more? As I remember it they ended up making me a cup of tea while Crazy Rodney stood with his hands behind his back looking guilty and eventually unbent sufficiently to replace one of the light bulbs.

No such nonchalance here, though. I look at Kay: a fat girl in a nightdress crying in a wrecked kitchen. Kay looks at me. Outside in the distance I can hear the cars on the ring road, cars heading off to Dereham, or Wymondham, or away over the Suffolk border to Ipswich. Smoke drifts in from somewhere near the park and suddenly it feels very autumnal here in the kitchen, very played out and dying.

I say, 'Leave it. Get up and go away.'

Kay flops her head down on my shoulder. 'I wish I could,' she whispers. 'Tell me how.'

There is a swirl of movement behind the door, the sudden hint of an intent, purposeful passage, the light goes on and, 'What the *fuck*?' Fat Eric says.

A tradition of post-filming parties went back to the early days of Leisurevision, back to the time of *Capital Pick-up* and *Stately Lust*, films shot in single rooms in a matter of hours with tiny budgets and minuscule casts. Later the celebrations had expanded to the point where they became recognised marker flags on the social calendar, eagerly anticipated by people with only scant connection with Morty Goldstein, prolonged to almost unprecedented periods of time and only reluctantly allowed to reach any sort of point of dispersal, their main incidents kept alive in any case by an endless process of orgiastic reminiscence. These were lavish entertainments. Two hundred people had assembled once at Dean Street after the completion of *Sex Riot* in the late 1970s. A squadron of American investors had flown in from Cannes on a Lear jet to witness Morty putting the finishing touches to a film called *Girl Hunt*. Such conspicuous expenditure was painfully absent from the present scene, where crates of supermarket wine, brought back by Terry Chimes from an expedition to Lowestoft and lying about on chairs and tables in the main hall, provided a single point of focus.

Bright, scary light. Cigarette smoke rises in dense, vertical clouds to the ceiling so that we shoo them away with our hands. The people stand around in small, discontented groups warming themselves at the big storage heaters. Morty prowls aimlessly among them, stops for a moment at the foot of the staircase to look at them, moves on upstairs on some mission of his own.

In the corner Terry Chimes, propped up against the wall with his crutches jammed under his arms, says to Crazy Rodney, 'Of course, with the dogs you're not talking big money, not at all. Catford. White City. Romford. Used to go there five, six years ago when I'd got a good tip, try and put thousand-pound bets on. Bookies wouldn't look at you. Thought you were up to something.'

Crazy Rodney says, 'I used to go to Romford with my dad. Late Sixties when I was a kid. Had a dog as well, Satan's Pride. You ever hear of that? But dad reckoned it was all fixed. Used to stand by the side of the enclosure, the other trainers did, trying to stamp on the dogs' legs.'

Terry Chimes says, 'But you're not talking big money, not these days. Me and me mates set up this queer bookie once, for a laugh. Queer bookies. Had these runners called Cedric and Quentin, right? We set him up. Had this other mate who was in the know. All of us went and put five-, six-hundred-quid bets on this 50–1 outsider. Course, after a while he realises there's something going on, starts dropping the price, but by then it's too late. It won by a length. We cleaned him up for twenty or thirty grand. Last queer bookie ever turned up at Catford.'

Mary-Beth says, 'Yeah, I hung out with the best of them in my time. Belushi. Aykroyd. Billy Murray. All that *Saturday Night* crowd. They'd see me sometimes in the street and they'd say, "Hi, you doing anything?" and I'd just smile, you know, the way you do. Or we'd go off and have breakfast someplace and they'd tell me how screwed up they were. But, yeah, I hung out with the best of them in my time.'

Cindy says, 'Don't worry yourself, hon. You had a good career ahead of you and then you fucked up. What's so bad about that?'

Terry Chimes hobbles back from the kitchen, a champagne bottle wedged tightly under each arm. Still grasping his crutches he lets the bottles bounce down heavily on to the table. He says, 'First bankruptcy party I ever came to. Make sure you don't leave anything.'

There is a smattering of polite, nervous laughter.

Morty stands in the centre of a crowd of wary spectators. His mad eyes swivel crazily in his gopher's forehead. He says, 'What beats me is why he did it. I mean, did I ever show the guy any disrespect? Did I ever tell him to get the fuck out of my studio?' He takes another swig from the bottle. 'I spend two hundred grand making a film and then they turn round and tell me the money isn't there.'

In the bright light the room swells to gigantic proportions. The walk back to the table is a hike past grim, swaying giants, through intense searing heat. I look for Elaine amid the vast untidy throng – so many sad, gaping faces – fail to find her. Only the violent contending voices.

Mary-Beth says, 'You wouldn't think it, would you, but I was very strictly brought up. My pa was a Baptist before he got into Hollywood. I remember when I was seventeen, going to an audition for the first time, and this director puts his hand on my tits. Boy, did I give him something to remember me by.'

Cindy says, 'I just lay down and opened my legs, honey, I didn't have your strength of character.'

Everybody seems very drunk now, very boisterous and unhappy and mad. I go and stand in the corner of the room, beneath the brooding portraits, and listen to Morty and Terry Chimes bawling at each other. Terry Chimes says, 'The thing about music now is that you don't even have to pretend to be talented. That's why it's changed. When I signed the Express, right, everybody knew – well, everybody in the industry knew – that they couldn't play, but it didn't matter. They just *pretended* they could. That's all over. The gimmick now is that you don't even pretend. I got this band Grunt's going to launch in the summer. They're going to go on *Top of the Pops* and just fuck about, play football and smash up their instruments. And the thing is, the record's going to be like that too. Just three and a half minutes of fucking about . . .'

Morty says, 'What annoys me, what really pisses me off, is all the pictures I never got to make. That remake of *Ben Hur*, the film about the World Cup. All the pictures I never got to make.'

Terry Chimes says without interest, 'You'll survive. You'll make it.'

Mary-Beth says, 'And then you hit thirty-one, thirty-two, your tits start to sag and your face looks like a crocodile-skin handbag and what the fuck are you supposed to do with the rest of your life?'

Cindy says, 'I had this girlfriend saved up enough money for a silicon implant. But then the stuff solidified or something, and they reckoned if you could have cut the tit off you could have gone bowling with it.'

Everything seems very played-out and dead now, very dead and played-out. I notice small things: Morty's neck as he bends over to whip the cork out of another bottle, glistening like red tyre rubber, Terry Chimes's blackened toes sticking out of the plaster cast, Crazy Rodney's eyes narrowing as he tracks the path of the American girls. Terry Chimes wrestles with the wire cage of another champagne bottle and then gives up, smashes the neck against the fireplace. I monitor the expressions of the family portraits, note how they seem to change, one moment remote, the next interested and companionable. Elaine arrives suddenly in the room, looks severely around her once or twice and then marches over.

I say, 'Where have you been?'

'Packing my things. Packing my things to leave in the morning. To get out of here,' Elaine says angrily.

'Do Morty and Terry know?'

'They know enough. Jesus,' Elaine says, 'none of you three *owns* me. I don't have to ask anyone's *permission* before I clear out.'

Bright, scary light. There is something very wrong here, some irrevocable fracture shot through the burnished glaze. I remember odd things: I remember Elaine spreadeagled beneath Frank Fellatio – game Frank, swept away now in the clutter of time – that vanished morning in the loft; Crazy Rodney on the towerblock stairs. Those conversations with Morty upstairs at Dean Street, burrowing on into the grim dawn. A blinding summer's afternoon in Glebe Road with my father seated in a deckchair under the tree and the sun beating in from over the park. Low flat fields under the pale East Anglian sky. I wave my arms from side to side and it seems for an instant that I am on the ocean floor, blundering on through thousands of cubic feet of water, bemused by the ghostly light high above me.

Elaine says, 'Are you okay?'

'Perfect. Fine. I need to talk to you. *I need to tell you things.*'

'What things? What do you need to tell me about?'

The people in the pictures look as if they're about to walk out of their frames, skip out and come tumbling into the room. The voices, retreating now, flying up to the ceiling where they buzz and hang, are coming from a long way off. Elaine paces towards the far door and the corridor and I follow shakily, uncertainly, losing my way on the shortest of journeys, off through the low, flat fields.

Morty says, 'I could have been an *artist*, that's what it is. But it's a class thing, isn't it? That Tovacs, knowing Picasso and everyone, what would he want to be doing with someone who makes dirty films for a living?'

Terry Chimes says, 'Couple of working-class tossers, you and me, that's what we are. Couple of working-class tossers, and proud of it.'

Crazy Rodney says, 'Never worried me. Not with girls and that. Get some flash piece, pearls and daddy's got an estate somewhere. Me, I'm a breath of fresh air to a girl like that. Eat out of your fucking hand they will if you ask them.'

Mary-Beth says, 'That East Coast thing, it works against you, you know. I had a good education. I could have gone to Ivy League, married a lawyer, or somebody in real estate.'

Cindy says, 'You once got to screw Rod Steiger in a motel scene. How many people can say that much?'

Bright, scary light. The room somehow rolling off its hinges, shaking from side to side, lurching out of kilter. Remembering the first time I slept with Elaine. The narrow bed in the room in Hammersmith? That grim resolve. The faint slipperiness of yielding skin. Elaine rising above me, fading away again. We wander off through the sparse, empty rooms, into the kitchen where one of the sound men lies fast asleep in a chair with his tongue hanging out, fat and lumpy like a mollusc, on through pantries and gaping corridors.

Elaine says, 'I used to wonder about you, what it was that made you so different from everybody else. At first I thought it was just detachment. There are people like that. You don't come across them very often, but there are people like that. Then I thought it was fear, I thought it was just that you were frightened of people, Terry and Rodney and people like that. But I was wrong about that too. Now I think it's just superiority. I think it's just that we're all really beneath your contempt. Something Terry said, "All the time he looks at me it's as if he's surprised I can actually talk." '

Vague, distant noises. Scuttlings and shufflings. Sharp, intrusive movements. Somewhere away in another room the sound of breaking glass. Elaine stands in front of me, pale and indignant. Carefully, doggedly, patiently negotiating the obstacles, the heavy shifting air, the monstrous furniture of this cartoon world, I move towards her. I watch her expression change, from anger, to consternation, to wide-eyed incredulity. The room lists, shudders, explodes.

When I wake up, daylight, bright intense daylight, is streaming through the high windows. The room is cold, empty. Terry Chimes, a grotesque, staring figure, stands at the foot of the bed.

'Elaine . . .' I say.

'Gone,' Terry Chimes says. 'Packed up and gone away.'

'Where?'

'Not where you'll find her,' Terry Chimes intones. 'Not where you'll find her.'

What happens? Amazingly, perhaps, he doesn't hit me. In fact he doesn't touch me at all, merely stands to one side in the wrecked kitchen as Kay and I awkwardly disengage, looking anguished and formal. It is, I realise, a *feudal* look, the look that the ancient family retainer gives his lordship's scapegrace brother over the pilfered silver, the look that the gamekeeper lavishes on the squire's son discovered in bed with his wife, a gaze of shattered illusions, old confidence pitilessly fractured.

'Fat Eric,' I say, 'Fat Eric, I can explain. I can explain everything.'

All of a sudden everything is quiet, very undramatic. Kay, seated now on one of the tiny, elfin chairs, snivels silently to herself. The moon shines in through the uncurtained window, is lost immediately in the coruscating light. Fat Eric broods solicitously above me for a while and finally says, 'It don't matter. Just get out, that's all.'

'But I can explain.'

'Just go away, will you?' Fat Eric says thickly. 'Don't want you round here no more.' He shuffles towards Kay, fists raised, and I think, oh God this is where we see some real violence, this is where we see some proper action; but no, Fat Eric merely places one arm protectively around his weeping doxy, swivels round to face me again.

'Don't want you round here no more,' he repeats with surprising dignity. 'Just go away, will you?'

I leave them there amid the wreckage, steal out as guiltily as any adulterer into the pale streets, back to the silent house.

Half an hour later a small package lists gently through the letterbox. I turn the contents out on to the kitchen table, shrink back in incredulity. Sixty five-pound notes.

Slipping upstairs at midnight, drunk, fearful, shot by both sides, I come across Suzi's departing gesture. Sauntering into the bedroom, twitching back the coverlet, I discover Elaine staring up at me from the white sheet, Elaine reclining in the white rose backdrop of the *Virgin Bride* poster. There are other pictures there too, burnt and curling at the edges: Morty and Terry Chimes arm-in-arm, Crazy Rodney in his lank frightener's overcoat. Lila St Claire and Talia Silk and Corona d'Amour in all their pneumatic glory, a glistening sea of bogus smiles and eerily juxtaposed flesh. I breathe heavily, shaken by the familiar scent. Pornography has a smell all of its own: that shiny, heavy odour of expensive art paper put to nefarious use. Morty used to claim that he could identify a copy of *Upfront* concealed in a pile of *Radio Times* with his eyes closed. I scoop up a handful of torn pages and the paper coverlet shifts and lists, breaks up and flutters limply to the ground. Skeleton leaves on the forest floor, dark, ocean-floor eyes.

The tape comes at 9 a.m. I knew it would. I sat waiting for the postman's knock. I take it to the video, slam it into the sleek, accommodating holder.

Filmed on an eight-reel. Monochrome. Grainy, with smudges on the tape: a crackling soundtrack. There are initial establishing shots: a long, low coastline, surf crashing down on grey sand, a high aerial view of distant woods, before the camera moves down, burrows inward through trees, fantastic traceries of foliage, dense scrollworks of fern, to the house. Potent rural symbolism: a weathercock swinging idly on a vane, a horse sweeping away through rising meadows, cut short by sharp detonations of static, thin black lines that veer across the screen, weave together and break apart. The camera moves in on a wide, featureless room, without windows. Seated on a chair, dead centre, knees pulled up to her chin, is a mournful-looking girl with abundant dark hair who, without further preliminaries, begins to take off her clothes, garment after garment, folding them neatly over the chair and then sitting down beside them. The tape crackles. A silent expressionless man – early thirties, perhaps, with receding hair – approaches, also naked. What follows is standard hard-core, something you could see at any hour of the day in one of the Triple X shops at Frankfurt airport, except that, except that at the height of this passionless frenzy the man brings both his hands up sharply from the carpet, as if performing a complicated piece of physical jerks, and clamps them purposefully around the girl's throat. The last thing you see before the screen goes blank is that rictus of glaring agony.

Elaine. Myself. What more to say?

When the telephone rings I pick it up instinctively. An unknown man's voice: subdued, apologetic.

'Martin? I take it you got the tape?'

'Who are you?'

'Never mind. I take it you got the tape?'

'I got the tape. What do you want me to do?'

'Nothing. Just sit there and wait is best.'

There are other voices away in the distance. I strain to catch them.

'Who are you? What do you want?'

'Wait and see, Martin,' the voice says. There is the first faint hint of mockery. 'Just wait and see is best.'

Ten o'clock on a January morning. Outside, real life is grinding remorselessly into gear. A milk float rattles into view. Fat Eric's Hillman surges past up the hill in a cloud of exhaust fumes. Infant voices blown back on the wind. Last night's photographs still lie accusingly on the carpet. I fetch a brush and dustpan from the kitchen and, wondering a little at the nature of the task, start to sweep them up.

Later I will remember. Somehow, in the end, you always remember. They fall down when you hit them. Somehow I never envisaged this, that they might fall down, sprawl headlong across the floor, prove incapable of revival . . . Although Morty distrusted such elementary techniques of crowd pleasing, from time to time a Leisurevision production would climax in a fight sequence. These were elaborately staged: Frank Fellatio in *Stately Lust* picking up an antique cuirass the better to engage his wife's seducer in combat; a fight between Lila St Claire and Cindy Lu Win in *Maneater*, set in a kitchen, in which volleys of crockery were hurled unceasingly across the narrow valley of a table. To these stylised incidents could be added more straightforward bouts of fisticuffs: an epic punch-up at the conclusion of *Roadhouse Stud*, the episode in *Furore* where Barry La Boeuf, shirt torn across his chest, arms flailing, standing triumphantly athwart the prostrate body of his paramour, sees off the pack of bicycle-chain-wielding hoodlums. Such scenarios allowed Morty to indulge his pronounced taste for parody, engage in a wholescale mockery of the conventions of the on-screen rough house. He examined typical episodes of cinematic violence with something amounting to disdain. 'Ridiculous,' he would say. 'One guy punches another guy in the mouth. It's the sort of punch that would knock out Muhammad Ali. I mean, have you ever been hit in the mouth, Martin, really hard? Take it from me, you don't get up. But no, the other guy just rolls over, shakes his head, picks up a table and throws it back. Just popcorn.' Leisurevision fight scenes reproduced these conventions to an improbable degree: fountains of gore spurting from mute, uncomplaining orifices, incidental scenery – chairs, tables, bicycles – pressed into service as weapons. There is a bizarre twenty-minute sequence at the end of *Satan's Slaves*, shot in distinct imitation of Kubrick, where whole limbs are torn away, but the protagonists – their faces, torsos, arms gouged out of recognition – still fight invincibly on. More characteristic than this – Shakespearean even in its mockery – was Morty's unwillingness to allow any sort of natural termination to these scenes. Thus in *Stately Lust* the villain, stabbed, pounded, lies inert in a pool of blood while Frank Fellatio and his wife embark on a passage of tender reconciliation, only to be interrupted, moments later, by a yet more ferocious onslaught, ending when Frank entombs his attacker beneath an up-turned grandfather clock. The film's conclusion, cutting away from the final, remorseless coupling, depicts a bloodied hand twisting inexorably from beneath the splintered wreckage.

But in real life they fall down when you hit them, they fall down and don't get up. The head jerking back against the too-solid floor, the pained expression – half annoyance, half bewilderment, the arms drawn up protectively around the sagging, lumpy torso, eyes aslant. And afterwards: no movement, no straining after revenge, no laboured return to the war zone, no resolute picking-up of teeth from the carpet, just silence, the odd, awkward arrangement of limbs beneath the bright, merciless light.

* * *

And afterwards, after the crash. What happened then?

We move on now: history comes loitering out of the rest-room, idles at a snail's pace through the long, trackless days. I sell the place in Bishop's Park, dull now and expensive, buy another one in Cricklewood. I sell the other place in Winterbourne – I wish I could afford to stay there – and don't replace it. I sell the Ferrari and buy a Ford Escort. I lose heavily on all these transactions and it matters, it matters a great deal. 'Go easy on the money, Martin,' Morty breathes, whenever that increasingly vital subject is mentioned, 'the money . . . the money's a bit tight at the moment.' And the money is a bit tight. Morty and Terry Chimes, by this stage, are sadly straitened beings, weekend in Suffolk cottages, think about selling their timeshare apartments, sports stadium executive boxes, Wimbledon concessions. The third Mrs Goldstein sits tight in Ongar and nags Morty about her allowance. There are accountants, lawyers, estate agents, stockbrokers, telling us to save money, cut back on expenditure, minimise our investments. Not to be outdone I take away the cheque book and the Peter Jones expense account I gave to Emma, Elaine's replacement, but come home twenty-four hours too late to find the flat strewn with gift-wrapped parcels – CD players, microwaves, freezers, clothes – and Emma sitting amid them like a child in a toyshop. 'What did you buy all this for?' I ask angrily. 'I don't know,' she says. 'I just wanted to. Do you mind?' 'Of course I bloody well do,' I tell her. Later I haul the collection into the meagre hallway, inventory it and calculate the bill. It comes to £18,000. Two days later I take it away and sell it.

I do other things. I bring home travel-agents' brochures and instruct Emma – a resentful, tight-lipped Emma – in the catechism of the low-powered domestic weekend-awayer. 'Scarborough?' 'No.' 'Great Yarmouth?' 'No.' 'Isle of Wight?' 'If you like.' I don't like, I don't like *at all.* Overcoming this initial reluctance we go on short, purposeful, rain-swept excursions. We traverse the North Yorkshire moors, we sidle through the clotted streets of out-of-season Blackpool, stare at the smoky industrial towns from the gangway of a coach speeding back down the M6. It is all very expensive, all very odd. Sometimes in these anxious trawls through flyblown English cities I explore the business angle. I go to

Liverpool and check out the black-windowed cinemas and the Private Shops in Shaw Street. I traipse through the street markets in Manchester where you can buy old Leisurevision videos from the Seventies at three quid a time. I attend cheapskate promo launches in Midlands drinking clubs, nod my head sadly over the on-screen thrash and regret that it won't do for the foreign market. They all know Morty, these amateurish Brummie pornographers with their C&A suits, these wrecked Glasgow filth merchants with their thick accents and their fetid breath. 'Morty Goldstein,' one of them tells me at a trade convention in Macclesfield, 'is fucking bad news just at the moment.' I listen to the chatter about the latest council closure, the latest firebombed rubber shop, nod my head, collect my rail ticket, slink back to a newer, scarier world.

I do fewer things, the same things. I give parties, cheap parties, *cost-conscious* parties. At the place in Cricklewood, mostly. Hardly anybody comes. Morty, Terry Chimes and their predictable women – the corkscrew curls, the ravaged complexions – they don't come. Other people come: friends of Emma's, hard-faced girls who work for PR agencies in the West End, broken-down cameramen, Crazy Rodney. They are subdued, reflective little gatherings. And suddenly it is all hardly affordable, suddenly it is hardly there. It is at this point in my life that, for the first time, I am unable to comprehend just how little I am earning. This fact is visited upon me one Friday evening in November 1981 when I open the top drawer of the bedside table, in which I am accustomed to store loose change, IOUs, red-stamped electricity bills. Down beneath the swirl of incriminating paper there is a handful of five-pound notes and silver. Taken out and counted – a surprisingly easy task – it realises £37.50. 'What do I do with this?' I demand of Emma, marching into the lounge where she sits staring vacantly at the television and depositing the coil of notes on a sofa cushion. 'You can give it to me.' 'No, I'd better keep it.' 'No, you don't want it. I'll have it.' We compromise by spending all of it. On dinner. In the Kilburn High Road.

Quiet, trammelled months. I sell the place in Cricklewood – I couldn't meet the mortgage payments – rent another in West Hampstead. I sell the Ford Escort and don't buy anything at all. Morty and Terry Chimes, by this stage, are fabulously reduced beings, weekend at home, think about selling their domestic appliances, their gardening equipment. Where has the money gone to? Sometimes, during the course of snatched, ten-minute breaks Morty, Terry Chimes and I ask ourselves this question. There seems no ready solution. We fail to make *Housewives' Party*, *Schoolgirl Affair* and *Frenzy*, projects of Morty's from way back, as no one will give us any money. And in the intervals of this tense, low-key existence, there is Emma.

I do mad things with Emma. I recall a conversation from about this time. Late autumn. Early evening. The night gapes before us.

'So what do you want to do? Stay in and watch a film?'

'No.'

'Go and see what there is in the video shop?'

'*No.*'

'There's fifteen quid in the drawer. I could go down to the Indian takeaway.'

'*No.*'

Try again, more circumspectly.

'There's a new night-club in Harlesden Crazy Rodney got me membership of. We could take a bus over there and check it out.'

'No.'

'We could go and see your mum and dad in Ealing.'

'*No*, for fuck's sake.'

Try again, more cravenly.

'So, tell me what you'd like to do. Tell me what you'd like to do and we'll do it. Anything. Anywhere. Think about it.'

She thinks. I wait. Eventually she says, 'I'd like to get a cab, go into town and have dinner at Boulestin's. Four courses. I'd like to go to Paris for the weekend and stay in a decent hotel. You can take me.'

Incredibly, we try to pursue this, of late, unprecedented course. We take a cab and proceed at a gentle pace down the dark, noisy streets towards Covent Garden. Unflustered, we march past welcoming doormen, negotiate the complex Boulestin menu. We order champagne cocktails, smoked salmon, Dover sole and fresh English strawberries. The fantasy of wealth, opulence and abandon persists until the end of the meal when my Masterclub card is returned to me, grimly, on a plate with the news that I am no longer creditworthy. Eventually, with the maximum display of resentment and outraged female propriety, Emma pays. Later we take a bus back up the Kilburn High Road to attend a cramped bedsitter party held by two of Emma's venomous attendants; the excursion takes on otherworldly shapes and contours, becomes wreathed in mystical trappings, an Alice-in-Wonderland trip deep into some wholly fantastic bolt hole. Another time. Another world. The incident is never referred to again, largely owing to the fact that, shortly after this, Emma left me. Two days later I came breezily back to the flat, after a crate of lager taken incontinently in the company of Crazy Rodney, and simply found her gone. There was no note – there seldom is in such circumstances – merely the evidence of a precise, tidy mind in retreat: the bedside drawer plundered of its stock, the stack of clothes cleared from the wardrobe, the electric heater even. Two days later there came a postcard which claimed that 'I gave you the best of me and what did you give me in return? Anyway, you never had any fucking money.'

What did I do? I remember standing uncertainly in the lounge for a while before swaying off to search for fresh signs of Emma's departing spoor. I even remember crying a bit, not for Emma, certainly not for Emma, but for the sense of passing time which loomed up briefly in front of me and then slowly receded. In the bedroom I found at last a tangible reminder of her going: carrier bags of mementoes from the Dean Street days spilled out randomly over the bedspread. There were rows of videos in their black plastic boxes, the odd copy of *Bouncers*, *Flesh*, that sort of thing, scuffed black-and-white photographs, a few of Morty's old business cards. Surmounting it all, curiously enough, was a photograph of Elaine. I looked at it for a while – it was an early one, the gesture unconvincing, the abandon suspiciously feigned, the general effect not in the least erotic, simply a bored and not particularly happy girl taking her clothes off in front of a camera – before settling down to gather up the sprawling detritus.

A week later, the rent unpaid and the furniture sold off, the threatening bills lying piled up in the hall, the stray messages from Morty and Terry Chimes unanswered, I left London for good.

* * *

Nearly dark. Outside in Glebe Road the streetlamps are going on, singly and in twos and threes, up the hill to the distant horizon of bunched cars and clustered rooftops. Rain coming in over the dun East Anglian sky. Below there is dense, uneasy silence.

Wait and see is best. The car arrived about an hour ago. It sits there still, ten yards down the street, wedged up against Fat Eric's day-glo Hillman. I wouldn't have noticed it were it not for the two figures in the front, narrowly outlined in the lamp-light glare. Occasionally they light cigarettes and I can see the tiny orange glimmers rise and fall. What else? Earlier on Fat Eric and Kay went past arm-in-arm, the former clutching a stupendous carry-out from the off-licence: I don't think they saw me. Twice in the last hour the telephone has rung. I haven't answered it. The second time it rang on uncontrollably for three or four minutes until at the end, just before it stopped, it was like a drill boring into my ear canal, a circular saw biting into the blameless trees.

I pad across to the window, steal another look at the car. Shadows obscure the watchful faces. Two hours back I had a mad idea. Pack a suitcase, head off to the city centre and find a bus. A bus to anywhere. To one of those gaunt, windswept villages on the coast: Bacton, Sea Palling, Mundesley. Winter out in a fisherman's cottage behind the dunes, walk along the empty beaches, watch the glistening sea and think about it all. But then a queer, paralysing inertia set in. What if there wasn't a bus? What if there wasn't a cottage? By the time the car arrived it had reached the status of a pleasant daydream, something to occupy the mind in the face of more pressing contingencies, nothing you would actually do.

I have always dreaded a deliberate step.

Morty had strong views about how a piece of cinema should end. He disapproved, instinctively, of films which erupted into a single, mighty conclusion – the couple, after much incidental tribulation, ecstatically reunited, the flaming car disappearing over the cliff top, the sudden remorseless shifting of circumstance. This is not to say that he distrusted the working out of inexorable fate, merely that he had a dislike of finality imposed for its own sake, of lines drawn randomly at the foot of a page when the interior logic of what had gone before suggested endless turnings over and re-evaluation. His own films occasionally ended with a single potent image: a figure fixed unalterably in the camera's eye; a tangle of moving limbs; a face transfixed suddenly by exultation or despair. More often they suggested a process that was destined to continue, the camera apparently removing itself at some quite arbitrary point, interrupting a scene whose climax might reasonably appear to take place at some time in the future. So a Leisurevision production might end in the middle of a conversation – the following remarks tantalisingly absent – with two lovers taking off their clothes, with a couple, enigmatic, their intentions by no means clear, striding hesitantly towards one another.

Just as Morty believed that there was no such thing as a finite beginning, so he believed that there was no such thing as a finite end. It suited him to allege uncertainty, to leave his audience at a crossroads of plausible exit routes, each somehow hinted at, or at any rate not discounted by what had gone before. This characteristic invested even his most trivial productions. An example of this was a short early film erected around a girl's inability to decide between the contending attractions of twin brothers. A plot of exquisite tergiversation, each shift in allegiance swiftly cancelled out or overthrown, it ended with the girl confronted simultaneously by both men and compelled to make a last, irrevocable choice. As she opens her mouth and begins to speak, silence descends: the credits roll. Each of her attendants remains impassive. Or there was the use of telephone calls, in Morty's hands transformed into a device of unparalleled complexity and confusion. Numbers of Morty's films ended with telephone calls: with buxom women crouched anxiously over cradled receivers, sudden intimations of emotional fracture or despair. I remember in particular a film called *Embracing the Slaughterer* – the Brechtian title chosen by myself – in which the technique received its most systematic application. An erotic thriller, a genre in which Morty excelled, its motif was the reparation exacted upon a venal anti-hero by his former associates. Invested with every kind of deception, involving complicated snares and ruses from which the stooge was quite unable to extricate himself, it concluded with the man entombed in a silent house with a single sinister familiar. Quietly, with only the briefest flurries of Kafkaesque dialogue, an air of desperate menace was built up: references to 'them', a message which 'they' will ultimately deliver, a destiny which is in 'their' hands. Finally, a state of maximal anxiety having been sustained almost to breaking point, the telephone rings. The familiar answers it, his expression ambiguous, remote. As he puts down the receiver and turns to his companion, the film ends.

But I digress . . . Outside there is movement in the street, car doors slamming, footfalls on the pavement, a muffled undercurrent of conversation. And thinking about it, I would have liked to be in Bacton or Mundesley, staring out across the mutinous sea, in a world without redress or retribution. The rain gusts against the window, the mad, unappeasable rain. Beyond, a blanket of cloud hangs across the line of the park and the naphtha glow of the far-off streets. I look out of the window: the car is empty now, the figures are gone and the wind surges up through the road's dead corridor, uncurls itself and taps its fingers against the pane. Somewhere in the distance glass shatters, and I remember other glass breaking long ago, Terry Chimes standing over the broken bottle in Mr Tovacs's studio, the bulbs exploding in the Dean Street loft. There is pandemonium in my head, the telephone begins to ring again in the hall but I pay it no heed, sit here tensed and expectant, waiting for whatever will happen to happen.

[illegible] they would [illegible] [illegible]
[illegible]
[illegible] to bringing [illegible] the [illegible]
[illegible] and at the [illegible]
[illegible] and went to the country [illegible]
[illegible] more [illegible]
[illegible]
[illegible] the [illegible] and [illegible]
[illegible]
[illegible]
[illegible] the [illegible]
[illegible]
[illegible]
[illegible] the [illegible]
[illegible]
[illegible]
[illegible]
[illegible]
[illegible]
[illegible]
[illegible] for whatever will happen [illegible]

TRESPASS

I've taken this extravagant journey
so it seems to me
I just came from nowhere
and I'm going straight back there

Howard Devoto, 'Boredom'

Family likeness has often a deep sadness in it. Nature, that great tragic dramatist, knits us together by bone and muscle, and divides us by the subtler web of our brains; blends yearning and repulsion; and ties us by our heart-strings to the beings that jar us at every moment

George Eliot, *The Mill on the Floss*

Dream not of other worlds what creatures there
Live in what state, condition or degree

John Milton, *Paradise Lost*

Prologue

Waking at five, in near darkness, I often used to experience that feeling of complete detachment which is characteristic of the overstretched mind. The properties of this sensation were always the same: the noise of the sea boiling away in the distance, a faint glow of light from the street, the low and slightly sinister hum brought on by the Caradon's eccentric heating arrangements. Proof of identity lay everywhere around – in my reflection in the cracked mirror, a foot away on the bedside table, in the copy of *La Nausée* lying next to it – but for quite a long time I would literally not know who I was. In this disembodied state, the people and incidents I thought about – they were seldom contemporary events, usually from fifteen or twenty years before – seemed profoundly alarming. My uncle standing in the wide boardroom; the big house at Sunningdale with the French windows open to let in the air; older pictures from the Redbridge days and beyond – all were both recognisable and full of a kind of horror I had never associated with them in life. Perhaps half an hour would pass in this way, mounting languor always balanced by the sense of impending doom, until, like a fast-working anaesthetic, sleep would come again.

On this particular morning sleep did not come. It was about half-past six. Beyond a patch of uncurtained window, rain fell over the grey streets. From below, somewhere deep in the bowels of the hotel, there came a sound of odd and somehow furtive movement, as if the person making it feared detection in every step that he or she took. Nearer at hand, someone else – almost certainly Mr Archer – was singing in a high, sad voice:

'Beans won't get no keener reception
In a beanery
Bless our mountain greenery home
Ta-ta, ta-ta . . .'

Long-standing residents sometimes said that the Caradon looked at its best in the early morning. The front lobby, reached ten minutes later – you could never be sure of hot water at that hour – bore this out. Sunk in grey light, which bobbed and glinted off odd protrusions of glass and chrome, it looked vaguely welcoming: austere, maybe, but not despicable. Standing on the lower stairs, at the point furthest away from the reception area, it scarcely resembled a hotel – more an exceptionally badly furnished domestic house or antechamber to some public room. Nearer at hand the place's true identity was revealed in a high, formica-covered reception desk, a green baize square set into the wall and pinned with notices, and a blackboard covered with unclaimed envelopes. As I stood looking at all this – a scene inspected twenty times before but forever fascinating in its seediness – a light went on in the office behind reception and there was a furious scrabbling noise: boxes being thrown about, heavy feet wandering. Eventually Mr Archer's face and upper body appeared from behind the hatch.

'Up early?'

'That's right.'

'Off to get a newspaper?'

'Probably.'

'We can get them delivered, you know.'

People going out to buy newspapers was an old grievance of Mr Archer's. I looked at him while he pronounced this rebuke. In the yellow early-morning light he seemed more ghastly than ever: livid, his face cut while shaving and dotted with tiny plugs of tissue paper. The clothes he wore – an infinitely old and battered dressing gown covering a lemon-coloured vest – reinforced this effect. Thinking perhaps that it was bad policy to criticise a guest at such an early hour of the morning, he said in a more conciliatory way:

'Another ashtray went last night.'

'Did it?'

'That's right. Seven in the last fortnight. I shall have to start chaining them to the tables if this goes on.'

I moved on towards the door, which was unlocked as usual. Someone had left a pail of water, half full, on the topmost step. Narrowly circumventing this, I stepped down into the street.

'Not bad for –' Mr Archer would sometimes say, naming whichever month the calendar had reached. It was not bad for February. In the eastern sky, where, far distant and invisible, lay the Hook of Holland, crimson streaks were emerging out of a slate-grey surround. Nearer at hand there were gulls crowding over the rooftops and the lighthouse tower. A few cars chugged by.

A hundred yards down the street, at a crossroads within sight of the sea, there was a shop which sold newspapers, cigarettes, cream cakes of a kind I rather liked. Here a minor crisis presented itself. Owing to a mix-up in the delivery arrangements, the teenager at the counter proposed, nothing had so far arrived at the shop except the local papers – the *Eastern Daily Press* and the *Waveney Gazette* – and a single copy of the *Financial Times*. I chose the *Financial Times*.

It was still hardly seven o'clock. A few of the town's early risers – old women walking their dogs, a couple of men who worked at the brewery – straggled past, bodies angled against the wind. Imperceptibly, I felt another tug on the thread of memory: first the pre-dawn reverie about my uncle; now the purchase of a newspaper with which I would always associate him.

Beyond the headland, to the north of the town, the sun was rising over the wet grass and the endless fields of sedge. In the distance the sea boomed. The Caradon's foyer was deserted, except for a pile of post that had appeared on the lino inside the front door. I picked it up, thereby infringing another of Mr Archer's private ukases, and began flicking through it. There was a letter to Mr Archer from the bank: that would cause trouble; nothing else of interest. I moved off into the silent lounge, reached by way of a corridor that snaked off along the left-hand side of Mr Archer's office. Here it seemed even colder than the street, each exhaled breath rising dramatically to the ceiling like an orc's spout. I settled myself in a frayed armchair underneath a reproduction of Dürer's 'Praying Hands' and began to examine the paper.

Reading the *Financial Times* alone in the residents' lounge of the Caradon, raw Suffolk air seeping through the thin glass, raised mixed emotions. A feeling of pleasurable recognition – like finding a school magazine describing the doings of your contemporaries – was quickly cancelled out by regret that everything you read described a world from which you were eternally debarred and could only monitor from afar. I turned over a couple of pages and read a report about joint venture agreements in Vietnam and a column in which somebody worried about the effect of Finnish depredations on the Eurobond market. The lines of level, even print, broken up with their advertisements ('*as a matter of record only*') ran stiffly away on all sides. In these circumstances it was the merest chance that I saw the two paragraphs about Huntercombe Holdings, the merest chance, in fact, that those two paragraphs had ever been included by some dutiful company news editor, for they recorded only the barest information: the final disposal by an administrator of the assets held by a collapsed unit trust. There it was, though. There was no getting away from it. Huntercombe Holdings had been only the tiniest fragment of my uncle's empire – in its original form no more than a shell company through which he intended to channel various off-shore profits – but for some reason I remembered the day on which it came into being with vivid accuracy: my uncle in the great boardroom; the blue company proposal books; the lunch ('Let's have lunch, George,' I could hear my uncle saying, 'Simpson's or the Ivy or somewhere').

The smell of cooking was beginning to pervade the room. Somewhere in the distance someone was striking a gong. I sat back in the chair. There was more of this, I realised, a whole lot more. Laying the paper carefully down across my knees like a travelling rug, I began to brood over past time.

In the six years since the crash I had lived a vagrant existence. Did you ever know a time when you hadn't the faintest idea what to do with your life or where to live it? That was me since the day the DTI inspectors moved in on Chell Holdings, and my poor, browbeaten uncle embarked on what was to prove his final journey. At a stroke that old life, that spangled existence I'd somehow imagined would go on for ever, was blown into smithereens. Even then I knew that there would be no point lingering in the rubble. The world had changed, and all that remained was flight.

Some instinct took me east. Not to Norwich, where I'd grown up – which would have been a rather symbolic admission of defeat – but to the coast. Enough money had survived the bust-up to allow me a competence, and for a couple of years I lived a frugal, solitary kind of life in bed and breakfasts and cheap flats. The oddest things kept me in one place or sent me on my way again: the way a cat sauntered across a farmyard in the early sun; the slant of a line of trees down from a railway embankment. I couldn't explain these sensations, or the contradictions they produced – the wish to settle down countered by the need to be moving on; all I could do was to react to them. Predictably, I've scarcely any memory of those early months. What there is is queer fragments: smoking a cigarette at Lowestoft station; watching a dog stalk a hare once in a field outside Woodbridge (he did it in an odd, delinquent way as if he feared that at any moment an invisible hand might fall on his collar); a sunset somewhere near Orford that seemed to go on for hours, burning off the rock and the distant sea. I don't know if I enjoyed any of this: I think I was numb in a way. There was also a sense that I was entirely alone, what with my uncle gone and the business closed down, and somehow without the resources to find a new kind of life. And yet I didn't grieve for him, because I knew he was vanished and there was no chance of bringing him back.

After a while things improved. As the money held out – I rarely broke into the capital sum and aimed to live off interest – I gave up the bed and breakfast shacks for small hotels: gaunt seaside premises along the Suffolk coast in Southwold, Felixstowe and Orford Ness. Here, curiously, there was society of a kind: grim old ladies abandoned by their families, wayfaring middle-aged men, 'travellers' in confectionery and fancy goods who survived on twenty-pound orders from the corner shops. All the jetsam of English society comes to rest in a seaside hotel out of season. There were even women of a sort, and a series of tense, fugitive relationships conducted in badly painted rooms that echoed to the cry of sea gulls, and an ominous third presence – the long grey arm of the sea, always visible from the window. It is impossible to convey the dreariness of those days – wind blowing in across the flat, the subdued chatter of the lounge, the stinking corridors – so much so that I think at an early stage they became external to me, routine appendages to a proper life lived out somewhere else, away from the sandy carpets, the bridge fours and the eternal reek of salt. At the same time I don't believe I was unhappy. I was treading water out here in the narrows, half-submerged, head bobbing above the surface, the big ships far away, grateful to have avoided the deep water below.

From time to time the older, bygone world intruded. Sometimes letters came: I threw them away unread. Outside the context in which I knew them, their writers seemed scarcely to exist. Once Kippax himself arrived unexpectedly at a hotel I was staying at in Great Yarmouth and we walked up and down the front for an hour or so: two courteous ex-businessmen, each of whom knew more about the other than he cared to let on. I never liked Kippax, and I was glad to see him go. All the same, he had revealed something to me, something that the paragraph in the *Financial Times* had brought home with greater force: that it was all still there, that life, still constant and enduring.

And now, I realised, I had a purpose. There was an attaché case in the back of a wardrobe at the Caradon that had lain unopened for years. That evening, greatly daring, I took a safety-pin – the key had long since disappeared – picked the lock and shook the contents out over the bedspread. There wasn't much – less than I remembered. A few press cuttings from the late Seventies. A letter from the DTI people. Some salary chits. One photograph stood out. In it my uncle, dressed in an expensive suit but still contriving to look faintly shabby, ambled nonchalantly up the steps of a great building – the immediate resemblance was to the Bank of England, but this seemed unlikely – his expression somehow combining several, though not all, of the elements I associated with him: good humour; candour; puzzlement; mild enquiry. I stared at it for a long time as the wind blew in against the high windows and the bulb danced in its shade.

Later that night, tumbling in above the noise of the sea, the voices began:

Do you think, later, you could explain it somehow?

I might . . . Yes, of course I will.

. . . All of it, I mean. Right from the beginning.

The beginning? Where's the beginning?

The very beginning. Do you think you could do that?

I could try.

I promised him, you see.

Part I

In those days the council houses stretched all over the western side of the city: row after row of huddled, dingy dwellings in orange half-brick or pale white stucco, exotic street names – Fairfax or George Borrow – that weren't at all suggestive of the people who lived in them. In summer the chemicals from the May & Baker factory two miles away came and hung round the doors and gardens with an indescribable smell of sulphur, and the most common sight in that part of Norwich early in the morning was a paperboy wrinkling his nose in disgust as he negotiated somebody's front path.

Most of this early life I've forgotten. But there is a memory of sitting, or perhaps balancing, at any rate precariously, on some vantage point near an upstairs window, and looking at the houses as they faded away into the distance, and my mother – a vague, hectic presence – sweeping me up and carrying me away. Later on there are other phantoms – faces that I can't put names to, my mother, again, ironing towels in the back room of a house that I don't think was ours, snow falling over the turrets of the great mansion at Earlham – but the houses remain, a vista of sagging blue walls and sandpapered outhouses, propped bicycles and scuffed-up lawns. The Norwich council tenants were proud or disdainful of their backyard plots by turns, and a bandbox Eden was generally followed by a cratered dustbowl.

Into these early memories my mother habitually intrudes. I remember her as a small, precise and nearly always angry woman, the source of whose anger I never quite understood, and consequently couldn't do anything to appease. Even as a child, though, accompanying her to the small shops in Bunnett Square or on longer excursions into the city, I'm sure that I had some notion of the oddity of her personality. She was, for instance, quite the most solitary person I have ever known, as alone in a room full of people as on a moor. To this solitariness was added a fanatic adhesion to a kind of propriety uncommon on the West Earlham estate, which occasionally broke out in furious spring-cleanings or handwashings and instructions to 'behave proper'. As a moral code this was completely beyond my comprehension: even now I'm not sure that I understand it. To particularise, behaving proper meant not straying into neighbours' gardens or jeopardising their rose bushes as you walked down the street; it meant sitting for long half-hours in a silent dining room, with your hands folded across your chest, listening to radio programmes that my mother liked; it meant – oh, a hundred proscriptions and prohibitions and adult blindnesses, and I never could get on with it or believe in its prospectus or deal with the directors who offered its scrip.

In time other figures emerged on to these grey early landscapes. For all her aloofness and her tart disparagement of the gossip of the street corner or the garden gate, my mother wasn't without her cronies. There was an old, faded gentlewoman with hair that might have been made of patent leather who came silently to tea on Sunday afternoons, with whom my mother talked ambiguously about certain 'old days' – horribly ancient and remote they seemed to me – that I later discovered to be a time when my mother had worked in domestic service. There was a decayed and entirely honorary uncle named Jack Carstairs, who rode an antique bicycle and had something to do with a hire-purchase firm, with whom she conducted faintly embarrassed transactions in the kitchen. But above all there were the women who came to the house on Friday evenings, and together formed a kind of sorority of the back-kitchen. There were three of these women: Mrs Buddery, who was fixated on the Royal Family; Mrs Winall, who said exactly nothing, except for grunts supporting the main speaker; and Mrs Laband – livelier than the others, and of whom they vaguely disapproved. To me – of whom these ladies took scarcely any notice – they seemed grave, awful people, unsparing in their censoriousness and ghastly in their obsessions. A specimen conversation might go:

MRS BUDDERY: They do say that Prince Charles is going to Gordonstoun. I wonder what his mother's thinking of.

MRS WINALL: (*thoughtfully regarding her teacup*): Ah . . . um.

MRS LABAND: Now, girls, what about a go at cards. Canasta or gin rummy?

MRS BUDDERY: My *Daily Mirror* said that Her Majesty – the old Queen, that is – likes a game of Black Maria. Though I must say I never held with it myself.

MRS WINALL: Oo!

MRS LABAND: Alice! That chap I was telling you about as works in the post office. Not the chap as was being talked of with her from Stannard – you know, the one that serves Saturdays in the Romany Rye – the other one, well apparently . . .

MRS BUDDERY: And when I heard the news about that Rhodesia leaving the Commonwealth, I said to myself *the idea* . . .

MRS WINALL: (*with a satisfied air*): Ah . . . hah!

MRS LABAND: . . . married a black man from Birmingham, as I'm a sinful woman.

MY MOTHER: This tea's stewed. I'll put the kettle on.

It was only later that I comprehended how stupendously, how blissfully, how incorrigibly ignorant this triumvirate were. Poor Mrs Winall! She couldn't have told you whether the earth went round the sun or vice versa, the name of the current Prime Minister, what fid. def. meant on a penny, any of those inconsequential pieces of information that give pattern and substance to our lives. Once, when I was in my teens, I came across her reading a newspaper – lip-reading, that is – with a kind of baffled, bovine stare, and I watched her with a profound interest and contempt. As for the others, they formed a depressed and depressing sisterhood, a little dribble of inconsequent talk about bad legs, obstetric horrors and the perils of ingrate children, a category in which I nearly always felt myself included. Looking back, it was as if a giant paperweight, composed of the West Earlham houses, my mother and her cronies, the obligation to 'behave proper', lay across my shoulders, and that it was my duty immediately to grow up and start the work of prising it free.

Growing up in West Earlham at this time followed a well-regulated pattern. Until you were five you simply sat at home and got under your parents' feet (I can just remember awful trackless days, when I must have been about four, playing on a rug in the front room while my mother sat frostily in an armchair). Then, the September after your fifth birthday, you were packed off to Avenue Road infants' school, half a mile away in the direction of the city. If you were lucky your mother would have a rickety bike with a child seat – these were extraordinary contraptions in cast-iron with improvised safety-straps. As far as I recall, my mother consigned me to the care of other children in the street. At seven, unless you were exceptionally stupid (in which case there was a remedial school called the Clare) you stepped up to 'primary', which had a proper playing field. and a school football team, and – so the rumour went – the teachers were allowed to hit you on the hand with a ruler if you misbehaved.

If I remember anything about these early years it's the summer holidays, and the endless days spent roaming the parks or lounging by the roadside in Lound or Stannard listening out for the ice-cream vans. A cornet cost threepence in those days, and a Sky-Ray lolly was even cheaper – twopence, maybe, or even a penny-ha'penny. It was in the holidays, too, that you caught occasional glimpses of the world that existed outside West Earlham, a horizon that wasn't bounded by your mother's disapproval or the gloomy Bunnett Square shopfronts: a vague old man who lived next door to Mrs Buddery in Stannard and told stories about his time in the Merchant Navy, who would have invited me to tea if my mother hadn't worried about my being 'interfered with', stepped in and snuffed out our intimacy; a charity fête, once, held at a house far away in Christchurch Road, where a motherly woman doled out lemonade and tried to get me interested in something called the League of Pity – a kind of junior version of the NSPCC, I think – only for my mother, to whom subsequent application was made, to dismiss the scheme on the grounds that its organisers were 'only after your money'.

Mercenary motives were a familiar theme of my mother's conversation. To hear her talk you would have thought that the entire administrative world existed merely to take pecuniary advantage. Education, though provided *gratis*, was a conspiracy to charge you money for supernumerary pairs of gym shoes. The church – there was a friendly curate from St Anne's who sometimes called at the house – 'never paid for itself'. Politicians my mother held in the deepest contempt. If she thought of the House of Commons – and I am not sure if her mind was capable of such an unprecedented leap of the imagination – it was as a kind of opulent poste restante where plutocrats ripped open letters stuffed with five-pound notes sent in by a credulous public. No doubt I exaggerate my mother. No doubt I ignore her virtues and magnify her frailties. But I can remember when I first came across the Bible marking the appropriate passage with a glint of recognition. There was no milk of human kindness in my mother: it had all been sucked out of her, sucked out of her and thrown away.

Such a queer life! Hedged round and bound up with suspicion, like one of Houdini's packing crates that I saw once in a book, so criss-crossed with thongs and chains that it seemed a miracle that the prisoner could ever free himself. There was a cathedral in Norwich – you could see its spire from the top of Mousehold Heath, triumphing over the skyline – but I never went there; there was a university rising up across the golf course to the west of Earlham Park, in great tessellations of concrete breeze block, but it might as well have been a sewage works for all the notice my mother took of it. To do my mother justice she wasn't unconscious of her role as the guardian of my education. On Sundays occasionally, when the furious 'tidying' mood was on, she would hustle me into my 'good' clothes – tight little jackets and pairs of drooping flannel trousers – and take me on the 85 bus to the Norwich Castle Museum. Here, hand-in-hand, suspicious, but mindful of the free admission, we would parade through roomfuls of paintings by Watts and Alma-Tadema and the painters of the Norwich School. My mother wasn't, it must be known, altogether averse to this recreation, which she called 'doing the pictures', and eventually almost got to have opinions on the various subjects presented for her edification. I can remember her stopping once in front of a painting by Lord Leighton of a gauzily clad Greek girl reclining on a balcony to remark, 'Well, she must have been able to count her goosebumps.' I recall this as a solitary instance of my mother attempting to make a joke. At other times, her mood painfully resigned, she would go off to the museum's restaurant – where they served grey-coloured tea at threepence the cup – leaving me to traverse the empty galleries alone.

Of explanation – who we were, where we came from, what we were supposed to be doing – there was none. And yet it seemed to me that my early life, lived out in the confines of the West Earlham estate, in a dark little house in a fatally misnamed terrace called Bright Road, was crammed with mysteries that demanded explanation. There was, to take the most obvious, the question of my father: a supernatural being, presumably, as he was never referred to or otherwise mentioned. There was the grey-headed gentleman who glared at us from the wall of a back room my mother described reverently as the 'parlour' and who some vague presentiment of ancestry suggested was my grandparent. There were occasional letters, which my mother took from the postman with the most terrific gravity and sat over grimly for a moment or two, and whose by-product, I dimly understood, was a marzipan cake from Oelrich's, the bakers in Bunnett Square, the following Sunday, or an extra-long bus-ride. My mother sometimes imparted little confidences to Mrs Buddery about 'doing her duty by the boy', but I could never get her to divulge what that duty was, or how she came by it. Once in fact – emboldened by some children's book in which He Came Back After All These Years – I came straight out and asked her. It was in the kitchen at Bright Road, on a seething August forenoon, with flies buzzing sadly from the strip of flypaper hung in the topmost window, and damp clothes from the wash lying in baskets under the table. Occupied with the contents of the sink, straightening up from some negotiation with a tea-towel, my mother only half-heard me.

'What's that you're saying, George?'

'I suppose,' I proposed innocently – I was ten years old and thought of myself very much in the manner of those pattern juveniles in children's books – 'that Father's coming back soon. Seeing he's been away so long. And I just wondered . . . *when* exactly?'

My mother had a number of stock phrases designed to quell irruptions of childish spirit. They included 'Don't give me any of your nonsense', 'Don't start' (pronounced with duosyllabic emphasis, so that the word sounded like *star-art*) and – conclusively – 'That's enough of that, *young man*.' On this occasion she simply gaped, so that as I had no other words in which I could frame the question there was no knowing how long we might have gone on staring at each other, until finally, hoping to move matters forward, I venture again:

'About Father. And when he's coming back.'

'Don't give me any of your *non* . . .' my mother began mechanically, and then stopped, and I saw her looking at me, not unkindly, but with an air of dreadful foreboding. 'I may as well tell you,' she said, picking up a flat iron and beginning to apply it with huge, angry strokes, 'your father's dead.'

So that was it. Wondering a little, I imagined a pale and somehow melancholy-looking man supine on a hospital bed.

'What did he die of?'

'Die of?' By this stage my mother was thoroughly exasperated. 'What does it matter what he died of? The *idear*! He's dead and gone and we've got to make the best of it.'

At this distance I can't quite recollect the tone in which this information was conveyed to me. Annoyance, certainly – as if I'd disturbed long-dead ghosts which had been better kept in their vault; alarm perhaps, in that I might have asked questions which would have been altogether beyond my mother's ingenuity to deal with.

Curiously I received the news, which might have distressed a less sensitive child, with a certain amount of complacency. The divorce laws had got as far as West Earlham by the early Sixties and there were other children at school, several of them, who had absent fathers. Not having a father at all seemed to place me in an exclusive category, and I can remember several pitying looks from my mother's cronies at around this time, or rather pitying looks that now bore some sort of explanation. It would be true to say, also, that the mere fact of my mother's unburdening of herself in this way lent a kind of complicity to our relationship, that each of us was aware in the last resort that there was a great deal more to be said. Even my mother, capable at other times of the most fantastic silences and duplicities, was prepared to acknowledge that. What precisely was said about my father on this occasion I don't recall, but the abiding photographic image I have of him – a small, faintly put-upon figure with greying hair cut *en brosse* – dates from this time, as do the few odd talismans that my mother had preserved in commemoration of him: some postcards sent from Occupied Europe during the war; an RAF pay book; a carnation pressed into a music hall programme.

As relics, though, they were hugely unsatisfactory, if only because no imaginative life seemed ever to have attached to them. My mother, for instance, though she wasn't above displaying them to me on odd occasions, never talked about them or cared to be drawn on their ultimate significance to her life. The consequence was that I found them arbitrary and faintly inhuman, difficult to connect with the living entity of my father and better forgotten. I can remember once or twice putting some direct question – it may even have been about the postcards, which contained queer little ironic protests of affection – and despairing at my mother's absolute refusal to become involved. After which the mystery of my father simply took its place among the many mysteries that lay behind my childhood; something that I imagined I would come back to but knew that I didn't possess the immediate resources to make my own.

I've said that my mother was ignorant. This isn't completely true, as her knowledge of West Earlham lore – in particular its social demarcations – was encyclopaedic. Even at a distance of thirty years I can remember something of this litany. Bright Road was 'better' than the adjoining thoroughfare of Stannard, though neither matched, in terms of desirability and *éclat*, their near-neighbour George Borrow. Ideally one would eschew council accommodation altogether – everyone I knew, even Mr Hopkinson, whom my mother worshipped as a kind of god because he worked for the Norwich Union Life Insurance Society, lived in a council house – but you could mitigate this disgrace by renting one of the 'double bay fronts' along Earlham Road. As a small boy, to whom social hierarchies existed simply as 'poor people' and 'rich people', I consumed details of this kind like bread-and-butter. Then there was the vexed question of what one produced to eat at the Sunday-afternoon high teas that were the high point of neighbourhood social life. A few society hostesses provided crab meat, which my mother thought was ostentatious. She herself served tinned salmon, bought in two-shilling tins from Davies's, the grocer on the square, but there were families known to make do with sardines ('The *idear*,' my mother scoffed) and Mrs Winall, whose husband was unemployed and whose children sometimes hovered on the brink of raggedness, incurred lasting ignominy by regaling a select band of intimates with a tin of frankfurters. Most important of all, though, was what you did for a living. My mother liked the idea of a schoolteacher, could have tolerated a reader of electricity meters, but regarded the average motor mechanic as a Morlock from the depths. Several other talismanic phrases remain in my head: that such and such a person was 'no class'; that such and such a family's children 'had no backsides to their trousers' – which was social conservatism, if you like, but of a peculiar and contradictory kind, in which envy and humility came curiously blended together, certain hierarchies were meekly accepted and others sharply resented, the whole thing bound up in mysterious wrappings of divinity, royalty and precedent, and never experienced again from the moment I left the place for good.

I'd like to think that in the course of this humdrum early life, those sequestered parlour Sundays, those prematurely shortened evenings, I was kind to my mother, I conciliated her, tolerated her, did my best to please her, but I don't think I did. It was all too far gone for that, too broken up and irreclaimable. And also because, in the intervals of wondering about the curious and insoluble position in which I found myself, I was too busy doing all the things that being a boy in West Earlham at this time involved: going after horse chestnuts in the woods near Blackdale School, joining the Cub Scouts (which my mother vaguely approved of until she found out about the weekly subscription), running Saturday-night errands to the fish shop or the off-licence, saving up for bicycles and pairs of 'longs' and the first Beatles LP.

Curiously, I retain only half a dozen extended memories of these preliminary days, by which I mean memories that aren't simply fragments but follow some proper and didactic path. The incident engraved on my mind, as forming the quintessence of West Earlham and West Earlhamite prejudice, concerns a boy named Mark Farrier. Everything about this boy – a young god of eleven with a snub nose and a shock of tow-coloured hair – was wonderful: that he lived far away from West Earlham in the paradisal splendour of Unthank Road; that his father wore a white coat and performed surgical miracles at the Norfolk and Norwich Hospital; that somehow I'd come to know him; and that – the most wonderful thing of all – he invited me to his twelfth birthday party. My mother pooh-poohed the party. She suggested with the most awful lack of tact, that it 'wouldn't do'. To counter my enthusiasm she devised half-a-dozen little embarrassments and obstacles. There was the present, for example, which would no doubt be expected of any celebrant of Master Farrier's nativity: how were we going to afford that? There were, in addition, the other boys, whom I 'might not know' and 'might not get on with'. Above all there was the mile-long journey to Unthank Road (this was the reddest of red herrings – she sent me further on her own errands) which might be 'dangerous'.

In the end she forbade me to go. I went anyway – it was the first rebellion of my eleven-and-a-half years of existence – stepping boldly out of the house in my 'party clothes' – grey sweater, long black trousers and sandals – only to find that each of my mother's predictions had been accurate. I knew no one except the host, who seemed somehow amazed and a little discomfited by my presence, and who grinned at my present of a Matchbox police car. In the end, after an hour, I slunk home. At the gate in Bright Road I met Mrs Buddery. This lady, folding her mottled arms together across her chest, regarded me with distaste. 'I've heard about you and your disobeying,' she said as I approached. Then 'I'm surprised at you, considering the circumstances . . .' Then 'Break your mother's heart one day, you will.' Finally, as I made no move to acknowledge her presence but continued head down along the path, 'Well then, I've no patience with you!' In fact Mrs Buddery was wrong. It was I who had no patience with her, and all the dismal, stifling orthodoxies that she and her kind and the whole dead weight of West Earlham represented, and from that day I began to plot and scheme and reassure myself that whatever happened, and whatever misfortunes I might be subject to, my future would lie elsewhere.

'You'd be surprised, sir, at some of the people who've stayed here in their time. Famous people, I mean. Actors and actresses and so forth. I've a number of letters of thanks that I keep together in a folder, if it would interest you to see them. Quite fulsome, some of them are.'

Outside the rain fell smartly against the misted-over windows. In the distance gulls cried over the boom of the sea. It was still quite early in the morning, and the overhead lighting had a sickly, unnatural quality. At intervals above our heads the telephone rang.

'In fact on one occasion a whole television crew came and stayed a week to make a documentary. Naturally I was glad of the money, but in the end so many people complained of the electrical equipment they left in the lounge that we had to ask them to go.'

'I can see that being a problem.'

Sitting in the kitchen listening to Mr Archer as he peeled potatoes was a good way of spending time at the Caradon. All the same it was hard to establish how the definite feeling of relaxation came about. Cramped, airless, always bitterly cold, never seeming to contain any food, the Caradon's kitchens were horribly cheerless. Mr Archer, too, was not at his best within their gloomy confines. Early morning – the only time of the day when he could be run to earth in these freezing depths – found him irritable, preoccupied and liable to take offence. On this particular morning, though, he seemed strangely talkative.

'Look at that now,' he said, holding a pale white object out for inspection on his palm. 'Isn't that a beautiful thing? Don't you think that's a beautiful thing?'

'Beautiful.'

'That's right. It's a shame to eat them, you know. I've often said as much.'

Sometimes I tried to reckon up the elements of this tableau – the spirals of exhaled breath rising above our heads, Mr Archer's keen pleasure in his task, the delicate white globes on the marble table top – but it was never any good. Deconstructed, the picture not surprisingly fell apart: the chill walls of our sunken cavern drew imperceptibly nearer.

'Of course,' Mr Archer said unexpectedly, 'being in the hotel trade, you always find yourself thinking about the past. I don't know why it is. Many's the time I've been sitting down here working or upstairs making out a bill or something of that nature and the queerest things have come into my head. The queerest things. Don't you find that?'

'What kind of things?'

'People who've stayed here. Curious things that have happened. You won't perhaps credit it, sir, but odd things happen in hotels. Very odd things. It's something I always tell my staff: "Expect the unexpected. Plan for the unplanned." '

It was one of Mr Archer's habits to deal out the most banal observations as if they were Johnsonian epigrams. Here, though, I rather sympathised with him. It stood to reason that a life like Mr Archer's, lived out among two dozen other people, none of whom he was particularly intimate with, would contain its fair share of surprises.

'You mean police raids, things like that?'

Mr Archer bent over the large, upright freezer and tugged hard several times on the handle. At the third or fourth pull the door flew violently open, in the way that a door in a situation comedy might have been expected to. Breathing heavily, he said:

'I was thinking more of exorcism, sir. I'd be obliged if you'd keep the information to yourself, but when I first came here, after a month or so had gone by – just time to get ourselves settled and think about new furniture – I found the place was haunted. Footsteps on the stairs at night. All the lights suddenly going off. A woman's voice screaming sometimes. It upset the guests no end.'

'What did you do?'

'I started out trying to make light of it, sir. You know, used to say, "That'll be Mad Mary again" – we always called her Mad Mary – whenever the bulbs dimmed, but it was no good. People used to laugh, but I could see they didn't like it. In the end I had to get a clergyman to come from Lowestoft and cast it out.

'Cost me twenty pounds as well,' Mr Archer said.

The gulls swooped in at the windows once more. Upstairs the telephone rang again, and Mr Archer bent his head rather sorrowfully over the potato bucket.

In the afternoon I walked across the common to the harbour. Here, out of sight of the sea, a few cows huddled together in the briny fields. Passing cars threw up sheets of water from the heavily rutted road. At the harbour's edge an outcrop of small buildings – tiny houses, ships' chandlers – backed on to the riverbank. A plaque at shoulder height on the nearest house recorded the level of the 1959 Eastwold flood. I thought about Mr Archer's assertion that keeping a hotel made you think about the past. Staying in a hotel, especially of the kind Mr Archer kept, did that too. There was a sense of having slipped backwards, ebbed away downstream on a slack, uneven tide. Such voices that called were far back in time.

The collapse and dismemberment of Chell Holdings – half a decade ago, now – had stirred prolonged media interest. Two national newspapers, half-a-dozen publishing houses, the London end of a Hollywood film company – all had made lavish offers for the story of my uncle's life. All had been repulsed. At the time I'd seen these emissaries of stage, screen and print as no more than intruders, dustmen arrived to rake through the ashes of a shot, spent world. There had been a queer, ineluctable pleasure in turning them down. Five years on, the trail had gone cold. From the publishing houses and the newspapers came printed intimations of regret. A letter sent to the London office of the film company was returned marked 'Address Unknown'. Finally a literary agent with whom my uncle had had vague and inconclusive dealings – one of his many unrealised schemes to produce an autobiography – wrote expressing an interest, and I travelled up to London to see him.

As the train rattled west towards Ipswich, the coast behind it turning grey in the uneven autumn light, I thought not about my uncle but about my destination. It was four years since I'd been in London, ordered to attend the final day of the DTI enquiry. Curiously, I remembered this only for its incidental detail: Kippax outside in the street afterwards looking as if he might be about to faint, someone who claimed to have lost money in the crash – there were always such people hanging about the building – shouting 'That's him, that's one of them!' as I walked through the thinning crowds. They were bitter memories. By Colchester, though, and later as the carriage rushed forward into the familiar hinterlands of Romford and Shenfield, my uncle's shade had risen up to displace these thin, insipid ghosts.

MacCready & Sergeant had premises in a nondescript building in New Oxford Street. Treading the polished corridors that led through the rows of offices, I remembered similar journeys made fifteen years before in a London that had seemed less subdued. Outside pedestrians walked between the skidding cars. Rain beat against the windows. I'd descended into an older world, I thought, sunless and subterranean, that bore no relation to the revels of my youth.

Mr MacCready received me in his private sanctum. Fat, sandy-haired, in late middle-age, he seemed remote from popular conceptions of the literary agent.

'Chell Holdings,' he said. 'Remember it well. In fact I don't mind telling you a cousin of mine lost money in it. Got badly stung. Wasn't there someone did it at the time?'

'That journalist Myerson. And then Kippax wrote something.'

'Kippax, was it? The confidential secretary? I think I remember it now you mention. Any good?'

'Not really.'

'No,' said Mr MacCready, 'I don't suppose it was. What'll your line be?'

'My line?'

'Your line. What makes you better than Kippax?'

It was a good question. What was my line on my uncle? That he'd been misrepresented? That there were sides to his character that had never been brought to the public notice? That he was much better than the popular conception of him or much worse? Somehow none of these statements seemed wholly true, or even particularly useful. In the end I settled on personal knowledge.

'I knew him better than anyone else, I think. We spent five years in the same office.'

Even that, I realised, posed all manner of unanswerable questions. Had I really known my uncle better than anyone else? Than Greta, for instance, who'd spent upwards of ten years living with him. Than my mother? Than Kippax even? While I thought about this Mr MacCready made notes on a jotting pad. Eventually he said:

'I need to think about this one. You've got documents, I suppose?'

'What kind of documents?'

'Old school reports. Wedding photos. Human-interest stuff. That kind of thing.'

I thought about the box files under the bed at the Caradon. 'Oh yes,' I said, 'I've got documents.'

'And what about the writing? Could you do that?'

'Doesn't everybody?'

'I've had people in here,' Mr MacCready said savagely, 'wanting to do books about themselves who could barely write their name. If you wanted some help, I dare say we could find it.'

He made further desultory squiggles on the jotter pad. Behind the desk, ascending in rows almost to the ceiling, were shelves of books: old paperbacks wedged together in little clumps; squat, hardcover editions of film stars' memoirs in powder-blue jackets with titles like *From Vermont to Vegas*. The vision they conjured up of literary endeavour was hugely dispiriting.

'Don't mind my asking,' Mr MacCready broke in, 'but were you wanting to make a lot out of this?'

'Not specially.'

'Depends whether there's a lot to be had, of course. Normally I'd say you were wasting your time. I mean, no disrespect, but old bankrupts are ten-a-penny, aren't they? But I remember old Chell in the papers. Wasn't he a bit of a lad? Night-club hostesses, that kind of thing?'

'He had a colourful personality, if that's what you mean.'

'Going to take more than a colourful personality,' Mr MacCready suggested, 'to sell a book about him. Any of his associates still in business?'

I selected a couple of names at random from the Sunningdale guest lists. Mr MacCready's mouth made a small O of appreciation.

'Point taken,' he said. 'I'll see what I can do. Is there anything on paper yet?'

'Not really.'

'Publishers like a synopsis,' said Mr MacCready, as if he had just divulged some momentous trade secret. 'Just put down half-a-dozen paragraphs or so. Your uncle as you remember him, that sort of thing. Something I can send round. Now, is there anyone we could get to write a foreword? Some ex-Governor of the Bank of England or someone?'

'I wouldn't have thought so.'

'Maybe not then . . . I'll get Angela to show you out.' But there was no sign of his secretary, or indeed of anyone else in the glass-panelled cage that backed on to his office, and so Mr MacCready escorted me down the empty corridor himself. Standing by the lift shaft, watching his ponderous figure in retreat, I felt a sudden sense of misgiving.

Outside the rain had diminished into a steady drizzle. There were a couple of hours to kill before the train. I headed east towards more familiar lands that my uncle and I had colonised years before: along New Oxford Street to High Holborn, down into Chancery Lane and Fleet Street, on past Blackfriars Bridge towards the City. Here, strangely enough, traces of my uncle's presence still lingered. The old premises in Carter Lane had been rebuilt and turned into a travel-agent's parlour, but the office in Lothbury where Roper the fat commissionaire had stood loftily inspecting the passers-by were more or less unchanged. Round the corner in Throgmorton Street I found a pub which Kippax and I had sometimes patronised on summer evenings – evenings that seemed a long time ago, quite remote and vanishing – and sat outside watching the traffic.

Back at Liverpool Street, on the Ipswich train, I thought about the encounter with Mr MacCready. Only two hours gone, it seemed completely unreal. I wondered what my uncle would have made of Mr MacCready, whether he would have been overawed by his profession, or contemptuous of his lack of 'practical skills'. It was never very easy to judge how my uncle might behave to people of the MacCready type. The train rolled on through the Essex suburbs, and I realised I was no nearer to solving any of the problems the day had thrown up. Outside grey East Anglian dusk rolled up to the track, the cattle in the fields receded into wavy swirls of ectoplasm, and I thought about Carole and Helena, my mother and her cronies, the grey stone sweep of Bunnett Square and the serious faces of long ago.

The Caradon, reached at half-past six, was sunk in early-evening torpor. The lights were on in the residents' lounge and there was a smell of stale cigarette smoke. Mr Archer, alone behind the reception desk, was making entries in one of the vast, red-backed ledgers that he habitually carried about with him. Hearing my footsteps in the hall, he looked up and nodded.

'Been away for the day?'

'To London.'

Mr Archer considered this information for a good half-minute, as if he were not quite sure whether he approved. Then he said: 'I'm always telling myself that I ought to have a proper day out in London. See the sights. Go places. The Tower. The Palace. Soho. Now there's a wonderful place. Have you ever been to Soho?'

'Occasionally.'

'I often think of the days I used to spend in Wardour Street. There really isn't anywhere else like it.'

I walked slowly upstairs over the broken stair-rods. Dinner that evening was fish and creamed artichokes. In the morning another ashtray was found to have disappeared.

Beyond Bright Road, the West Earlham streets spread out in a geometric pattern: Stannard to the south, Lound – not much more than a dogleg of three or four houses – to the east. After Lound and the back of St Anne's church came Colman Road, which if you crossed it took you to the branch library, and if you followed its course downhill for a hundred yards across The Avenues brought you as far as Bunnett Square which, with its dozen or so shops, post office and pub, was the centre of the West Earlham world.

Apart from her weekly bus-trip into Norwich, and an occasional Sunday-afternoon stroll to hear the band playing in Eaton Park – another half-mile away down Colman Road – I don't suppose my mother ever went fifty yards beyond these narrow boundaries. Once, I remember, there was a terrific upset because she had to visit someone in Bungay, fifteen miles away on the Suffolk border: it could have been Borneo for the trepidation with which she approached the four bus-rides and the half-hour wait in Bungay market square that the journey involved. Another time she won a competition run by the local paper where the prize was a trip to Newmarket races. My mother flatly refused to go. It was 'too far'. There was 'no point'. What was she supposed to do when she got there? Even Mrs Buddery, who generally supported my mother in her vagaries, thought this was overdoing it.

Curiously, these anxieties, which extended to bank accounts, official forms of any kind, even unexpected letters, were symbolic of much more fundamental timidity. Like most of the West

Earlham housewives my mother kept her front door locked and bolted, on the principle that anyone she knew automatically went round the back; feet moving up the front path were simply ignored. Travelling salesmen, who infested the estate in the run-up to Christmas, were dealt with from out of an upstairs window. Even here, though, extraordinary gradations of social terror came into play. Gypsies, whom she called 'didakois', my mother wouldn't open the window to, and once when a negro – the first black man I had ever seen – came round selling clothes pegs she locked the back door and literally went and hid in the lavatory.

It was into this tight, circumscribed world that my uncle arrived.

For my mother not to give any warning of what was, practically speaking, an uprecedented visitation was to be expected. In fact in nearly any arrangement concerning my welfare she was – to use another analogy from later life – like the chairman of an ailing company who, to lessen the chance of anyone attending its annual meeting, stages the event on Boxing Day at a hotel in Cardiff. My mother justified these *faits accomplis* by maintaining that I 'wasn't old enough to know my own mind' and that I was in any case 'lucky to get' whatever it was she had arranged for me. And so, dawdling home from school one day, a scuffed satchel lofted over one shoulder, I realised that her first words, looking up from the *Eastern Evening News*, which she read each afternoon from cover to cover, were:

'I b'lieve your uncle's coming to see us tomorrow.'

'Uncle Jack?'

'Hah.' My mother sniffed disparagingly. 'Thinking Jack Carstairs was your real uncle. The *idear*. No, your Uncle Ted.'

I was thirteen years old by this time and, so it appeared to me, a person of some consequence. I had a paper round, three intimate friends of my own sex, and had taken part in a dare that involved shouting the word *fuck* very loudly late at night outside the house of the school music teacher. All the same, the idea of possessing an uncle, even an uncle who had blown in, so to speak, from nowhere and might just as easily blow out again, strongly appealed to me. I could have glorious times with an uncle, I thought – confidential and revealing times. My mother caught something of this anticipation and went on hurriedly:

'He won't be staying long. Just a flying visit, he said.'

The vision of an uncle who led such a vagrant and wayward existence that he could only pay flying visits was even more enticing.

'What does he do?'

'I b'lieve,' my mother said, bitterly, 'I b'lieve he sells toys.'

As it turned out, this was pretty near the truth. Once, a long time later, my uncle sketched for me the unenviable routine that brought him to Norwich in what would have been the winter of 1965. 'I was eastern area rep for Palitoy in them days, George. Model aircraft kits and soldiers and stuffed animals, *you know*. Devil of a job that was. Train out of Liverpool Street. Another train from Norwich out over the flat to Yarmouth, and stand in the shop while some sniffy little tobacconist gave you a ten-bob order. Anyhow, happened that a department store at Lowestoft had gone broke all of a sudden. Left me with a spare afternoon, so I reckoned I'd look you up.'

In a locale where the employed male population worked in the boot and shoe trade, or at Jarrold's printworks, or for the electricity board, selling toys had a conspicuous air of novelty. Such was my absorption in this alluring figure, I remember, that I asked a question which no right-minded person who knew my mother's habits or temper would ever have dared.

'Will Uncle Ted be staying the night?'

'Stay the night?' my mother repeated. 'Certainly not. *The idear*.'

I cut the last hour of school next afternoon to be home early (nobody noticed) but he was already there. He sat with my mother in the two worn leather armchairs by the fireplace smoking cigarettes – everyone smoked in those days, even downtrodden Mrs Winall fished packets of Park Drive out of her handbag and consumed them while the others talked across her – a small and faintly nondescript man in a dim grey suit with a chalk pinstripe, the face above it disproportionately large and a bit humorous, surrounded by receding and strangely perky tufts of grey-brown hair. Any ideas of drabness and restraint suggested by the suit and the scuffed suede shoes, one of whose heels was about to part company with its sole, were somehow cancelled out by a canary-yellow waistcoat that protruded from the folds of my uncle's jacket. The waistcoat was obviously a source of pride to my uncle. He caressed it occasionally when it rose over the mound of his stomach, like a cat, and he was forever polishing its buttons with a scrap of handkerchief.

My mother, I noticed, followed the movement of the waistcoat with a suspicious eye.

'So this is George, is it?' said my uncle easily as I came into the room.

'Yes, that's him,' said my mother briskly, as if she were identifying a suspect in a police parade. 'Say hello to your uncle, George.'

My mother had been smoking too: inexpertly, so that four or five cigarette stubs in varying stages of decomposition smouldered on an ashtray at her side. She looked faintly embarrassed and, I thought, skittish, as if I had intruded on some intimacy she would have liked to keep from me. My uncle, meanwhile, was looking at me keenly.

'So this is George, is it?' he said again, and the canary waistcoat slid sinuously out of the fold of his jacket. 'I'm very pleased to meet you, George.'

'I'm very pleased to meet you too, Uncle Ted,' I ventured, quite sincerely.

'Goes to th' grammar school, does he?' he enquired of my mother.

'Didn't pass the exam,' my mother whipped back triumphantly. 'Anyhow, you know I don't hold with grammar schools.'

Oddly enough, I agreed with my mother about the grammar school. At thirteen, the idea of dressing up in a bright blue uniform and cap six mornings a week and walking a couple of miles to a scattered outcrop of buildings near the cathedral seemed to me absurdly juvenile and meaningless (there was a solitary grammar school boy on the West Earlham estate whom we occasionally chased home from the bus-stop and, if caught, flung into hedgerows). My mother, on the other hand, seized on the notion of caps and exams and masters in gowns and mortar boards in a spirit of furious utilitarianism. The *idear* of teaching huge great boys Latin and Greek when they could be doing something useful. The result of the 11-plus exam, consequently, in which I meditated a story about an Angevin crusader, lost the thread of it and sat staring at the page with a kind of irritated complacency – there was a small part of me that had wanted to make something of the crusader – was a joint relief.

'Grammar schools never mattered to a boy with brains,' said my uncle unconvincingly. He was sitting back in his chair now, chewing at an unlit cigarette with his lower lip and disclosing a row of variegated and discoloured teeth. It was then, I think, that I got the first hint of the chronic restlessness which seemed almost to inflame him, and which I now believe to have been at the root of his troubles. Using the cigarette as a phantom toothpick and massaging his scalp with his other hand he threw a series of sharp glances around the room, at the brown holland rug which covered the area of the floor in front of the gas fire, at the antiquated wireless that my mother kept in a cabinet under the window, and a bookcase which contained miscellaneous volumes of Arthur Mee's *Children's Encyclopaedia* and a work called *Spirit Hands Have Touched Me* in which my mother sometimes impressionably browsed.

'Snug little place you got here,' he said eventually.

'It is and it isn't,' my mother said enigmatically.

'I mean,' said my uncle, suddenly becoming animated, 'you could really make something of it if you liked. Get one of those hanging lamps – what are they called? *You* know, kind the big department stores sell, and put them in over the mirror. Then take out the sideboard – nasty heavy piece of wood – and put in a chaise longue . . .

'Elegant,' my uncle said, coming to an unexpected halt. We regarded him silently: myself with growing respect; my mother with an astonishment bordering on exasperation. It was clear that nobody had spoken to her like this for many years.

'And then . . .' my uncle began, waving the tip of his cigarette above his head and somehow drawing the length of the shaky ceiling into a new and original focus, but something in my mother's eye deterred him and he subsided.

From outside the customary five o'clock West Earlham noises were starting up: footsteps drumming down the street, a breathless voice or two, a woman shouting, 'Jimmy, where '*ave* you gorn again?', at first angrily, then with increasing plaintiveness, bicycles skidding from road to pavement.

'George,' my mother said decisively, 'why don't you take your uncle for a walk? Take him round and show him a bit. And then when you come back, p'raps we can give him his tea.'

For some reason I expected my uncle to jib at this, but instead he put the cigarette back into his coat-pocket – they were Woodbines, rather to my surprise, a cheap brand which people said were made of powdered horse dung – and rose meekly to his feet.

'*I* don't mind a walk, Jane,' he said. 'That's if this youngster doesn't mind accompanying me. What do you say, George?'

My mother mumbled something on my behalf, but I lost it in the wonder of hearing somebody address her by her Christian name. Indeed, I'm not entirely sure that I knew it myself until that moment. The sorority of the back-kitchen always called her Mrs Chell, and it was the same on the rent books and the hire-purchase agreements. Thinking about this, and about my uncle's apparent dissociation from this kind of life, its evasions and its secrecies, thinking too about the cavalier way in which he proposed to redesign my mother's sitting room, I stepped out into the street.

There were two principal walks that you could take in West Earlham: the picturesque, which led you along the wide, tree-lined thoroughfare of The Avenues towards a school and a glimpse of ragged countryside; and the prosaic, which went along the cemetery railings for half a mile or so before plunging downhill towards the Dereham Road. I chose the prosaic. As we threaded our way along Lound Road through the groups of children playing hopscotch at the kerbside – girls with their hair in bunches and stringy woollen cardigans, squinting, crop-headed boys – past the shunted-up cars and the worn grass and into the mournful highway of Colman Road he looked enquiringly about him.

'Lived here a long time, haven't you, George?'

'Thirteen years . . .' and something prompted me to add a courteous 'Uncle'.

'That's right. Just you and your mother, eh?'

The cemetery gates loomed above us. Here, instead of following the path northward, my uncle wandered diffidently inside and stood examining a painted notice-board offering details of crematorium opening hours. In the fading late-afternoon light the place had an unbelievably dreary aspect, a vista of great, gloomy catafalques crumbling into uncut grass, unpruned trees which drooped and wept over the palings.

'Famous old place, ain't it, George?' my uncle remarked at length. 'Just imagine what it would be after dark, eh?' He paused. '*I* once spent a night in a cemetery when I was your age.

'For a dare,' he elaborated.

Something seemed to strike him and he said: 'Get along all right with your mother, do you, George?'

'Not really.'

'No, I didn't suppose you did . . . Bit of an item I should think, your mother . . .

'I could tell some tales . . .' he went on.

And so we strolled around the cemetery as the light began to fade and a blood-red sun sank starkly in the western sky, my uncle commenting on little details that took his fancy: a cracked angel's wing fallen drunkenly over a gravestone, a stupendous family mausoleum in black granite, other things. So practised was this commentary that I suspected it was merely one of his idiosyncrasies, that long years of solitude had accustomed him to talking to himself, that he scarcely noticed I was there. Eventually we turned out of a side gate and plodded back along Colman Road.

The confusion that Uncle Ted's visit had brought on in my mother's mind was sharply apparent on our return. It was fairly obvious that she had been torn between the contending notions that a tea in his honour required lavish preparation or none at all, equally clear that she had compromised by choosing an elaborate menu and presenting it with maximum slovenliness. Luckily my uncle appeared not to notice the fraying bread and butter or the glint in my mother's eye as she dispensed it. He ate a huge amount of pickled herrings and boiled eggs in an abstracted way, occasionally cocking his head at me as if to acknowledge that we shared some exquisite private joke.

Finally, standing in the doorway buttoning up his overcoat, he produced a black attaché case, very battered and worn, and took out a long, rectangular parcel.

'Got a present for you, George. What do you say to that, then?'

Unwrapping the Action Man from its nest of tissue paper – such things were for children, as any self-respecting thirteen-year-old knew – I caught my mother's glance: half-censorious and yet half-gleeful, as if she wanted to rebuke my indifference while somehow exulting in the failure of my uncle's gesture to hit its target.

'Thanks very much, Uncle Ted.'

'Glad it's what you wanted,' my uncle said affably. 'G'bye now, you people.'

'Huh!' my mother said, after the door had closed and we heard the sound of him whistling – whistling with an odd and somehow laboured jauntiness – along the darkened street. 'Giving you something like that. The *idear.*'

And so, leaving only the memory of a dozen sentences or so of fugitive conversation, my uncle slipped out of my life for the next six years.

Early on these winter mornings, often before the light had properly come on, I used to walk along the beach. At dawn, the rows of beach chalets locked up and silent, empty even of the old women walking their dogs, the place had an attraction that it rarely regained at other hours of the day. Fog hung low over the sand and the escarpments of the sea defences, so that the cries of the gulls seemed curiously disconnected, lost somewhere in dense clouds of vapour; the sea was the colour of gravy. Coming back along the high street it was sometimes possible to buy a cup of coffee at the baker's shop in the square. At other times, though figures could be seen vaguely through the misted-up windows, the door mysteriously stayed shut.

Part of the interest of these excursions lay in what you might find on your return. Mr Archer was subject to early-morning fits of restlessness. These bursts of energy sometimes prompted him to embark on lightning schemes of refurbishment, so that it wasn't unusual, entering the lounge at seven a.m., say, to find the carpet up and trays of tools scattered over the bare floorboards. At other times, however, a peculiar sluggishness overcame him: on these days breakfast would be served by the maids or, very occasionally, not served at all. Mr Archer affected ignorance of the physical cause of this behaviour. He said: 'I've never been able to explain, sir, why my body should behave in the way it does. You wouldn't believe it. Sometimes I wake up at dawn just bursting to run a mile, and other times I feel as if I couldn't lift a teacup. Several doctors, sir, have commented on this peculiarity in me.'

Negotiations about the book dragged. Two or three encouraging letters, written by Mr MacCready at an early stage in the proceedings, were followed by a long period of silence. Then he telephoned out of the blue to say that a small imprint of a substantial Anglo-American firm had made an offer. 'Not very much money,' he explained cheerfully, 'but there might be a newspaper deal.'

'Is that likely?'

'You never know.'

In the course of the conversation Mr MacCready explained how books of this kind got written. 'Best thing to do,' he said, 'is to speak it all into a tape recorder, and then tidy it up afterwards. You need to be careful, though. I had a bloke who'd known Ronnie Kray fill seventeen cassettes once. The other way is to do a collaboration. Get a journalist to come and ask you questions, and then work the raw material up into manuscript.'

'Can you arrange that?'

'I could try,' Mr MacCready said. 'Leave it with me.'

I left it with him. Several weeks passed. Mr Archer disappeared for three or four days, reappearing dressed in a checked suit and looking faintly pleased with himself. It was rumoured that he had been racing in the Midlands. More than once I took a pen and paper and tried to follow Mr MacCready's instructions about the synopsis. It was a futile exercise. Momentarily pinned down on the page, my uncle immediately took wing again; laid out in recognisable planes and angles he changed shape, metamorphosed into a completely different object. In the end I was reduced to choosing words that I somehow associated with him: *fat*, *generous*, *secretive*, *curious*, *irritable*, *tenacious*, and *overbearing* were some of them. I put the pieces of paper in the box file and left them there.

Then one afternoon towards the end of February as I sat in the residents' lounge brooding over *Quentin Durward*, Mr Archer summoned me to the telephone by the reception desk. It was Mr MacCready.

'That chat we were having the other day,' he said. 'I think I've got just the person.'

'A journalist?'

'*Writer* she calls herself on her CV,' Mr MacCready went on. 'Not that I mind that. Woman called Frances Eccles.'

The name meant nothing to me. 'Is she at all well known? Should I have heard of her?'

'Let's see.' From the pauses at the other end of the phone I deduced that Mr MacCready was reading from a handwritten sheet. 'Editorial assistant on *Vogue*. Along with half of London, I shouldn't wonder. Two years out of the profession travelling. Occasional book reviews for *Good Housekeeping* . . . Editorial work for a variety of small publishing firms . . .'

'Does she know anything about the City?'

'I dare say she could pick it up,' Mr MacCready said. There was an uneasy silence. On the other side of the desk Mr Archer was polishing wine glasses, blowing fiercely on their upturned rims and burnishing them with a hank of tissue paper. 'Look,' Mr MacCready went on, 'didn't you say you lived in a hotel? Why don't you book her in for a fortnight? As a trial arrangement. See how it goes.'

'All right.'

Later on, when Mr Archer had finished the wine glasses and begun on a row of filthy brass candlesticks, I made the arrangements for Frances Eccles's visit. Mr Archer recorded these details with absolute impassivity, his eye fixed on the barometer six feet behind my head. When we had finished he said:

'Will the young lady be wanting a cooked breakfast, do you suppose?'

'I've no idea.'

'Well, perhaps you could let me know nearer the time, sir. Only it will be more convenient from the catering point of view.'

'I'll try.'

Later that afternoon the wind blew in violently from the sea. It would be a wet spring, Mr Archer said, because winter storms usually meant weather of this kind.

To get to Eaton Park you went down Colman Road, turned right into South Park Avenue past the Esso garage and the row of shops and walked a hundred yards to the point where the railings began. Inside were two dozen acres of bowling greens, football pitches, a circular edifice of tea-huts and changing rooms put up by an unemployed workers' project in the 1930s, and an ornamental fish pond into which – this was a famous local legend – someone had once introduced a pike. In the winter of 1963 the snow lay over the fields for six weeks, and I helped to build an igloo that took half a ton and stayed there for a fortnight until a rival gang came and knocked it down . . .

I'm sure that I must have forgotten a great deal of these old West Earlham days. Sometimes I can find myself remembering some odd particle or fragment – Bunnett Square at dusk, say, with the lights flaring up inside the shopfronts, or the bus-stop on Colman Road opposite the church and the Scout hut – but the rest somehow escapes me. Which is to say that I recognise its elements, its shapes and substances, but that the whole thing hangs a little way off, and beyond my power to call back. It seems to me, too, that this is simply the essence of West Earlham seeping in and stifling me, like a pillow held over my head, so that it was only many years later, with these scraps and oddments as materials, that I could begin to reconstruct this early life.

I don't recall that my schooldays were unhappy – in fact I recollect a good deal of undivided fun. At the same time I wouldn't care to live through them again, and I know I couldn't wait for them to stop. Education in Norwich at this point was divided into three. There was a superior grammar school of ancient foundation, whose pupils wore blue blazers and whose prize day was elaborately reported in the *Eastern Evening News*; two inferior grammar schools, less ancient and less elaborately reported; and several 'secondary' schools of a mixed and ambiguous character. I landed up at a school even more mixed and ambiguous than its rivals called Bowthorpe High. Later on, if I wanted to remember what Bowthorpe High was like, I could remind myself by walking through the corridors at Lothbury early in the morning, just after the cleaners had left, and smelling the disinfectant. Most memoirs of schooldays go on about the smell of the food or the chalk-dust – with Bowthorpe High it was the disinfectant that hit you in the face whenever you walked through the main door.

Despite the purdah in which my mother had raised me, I got on well with the rest of my classmates – they were great, hulking louts from Northfields and the Larkman Estate, which had a bad reputation even by the standards of West Earlham – and if you were to show me a school photograph from those days I dare say I could identify most of the people in it. Apart from this, though, the place was a disgrace, just a kind of sink aimed at preparing teenagers for the local factories. Beyond a few implausible mathematical formulae and certain geographical suggestions, I don't recall that we were told anything that might have a bearing on our future lives. The masters who taught us – we called them 'sir' in a feeble imitation of 'good' schools – were practical people. They wanted us to be quiet, they were keen that we shouldn't fight each other or boys from other schools (West Earlham was famous for gang warfare of this type), nor plunge the place into public disgrace, and on the whole I think they just about succeeded.

Happily – for I wouldn't have wanted it otherwise – my education didn't diverge from this elemental pattern. At the age of fourteen I believe I knew that density equalled mass over volume; that there existed a startling and limitlessly divisible number called 'Pi'; and that the capital of Ecuador was Quito – that was the kind of thing they taught you at Bowthorpe High. Beyond this all was darkness. And yet at the same time I was conscious that something, some vague kind of interest and intent, had begun to point me in quite another direction. Where they came from, these faint glimmerings of sensibility, I can't imagine, and I can remember trying to ignore them, to batten them down, and yet always failing to suppress them. I remember discovering Norwich Central Library – no one took me there, the building simply presented itself to me one Saturday morning as I climbed back up the market steps from Jarrold's department store – and moving with a kind of sacramental awe along its miles of shelving. Even my mother could see the point of libraries, though she hardly ever set foot in one. She was intimidated by the stacks of books, still more by the birdlike middle-class ladies who presided over them, and I've an idea that she was slightly suspicious of reading in general. If she looked at a novel it was usually a gloomy family saga with a death in the first chapter and the heroine forced into an unhappy marriage by her scheming parents.

But books were only one of the odd yearnings I cultivated in these teenage years. It was the same when I discovered a copy of the Bible in the bookcase in my mother's room next to an illustrated edition of *Foxe's Book of Martyrs* and some old copies of the *Friendship Book of Frances Gay*. Naturally we'd had pieces of scripture read out to us at school, but this was the first time I'd sat down and taken it in, and the effect was electric. For about a year I walked the streets of Norwich convinced that I was in communication with God, a God who looked something like the Almighty out of Blake's designs for Job, and had pronounced views about the length of my hair and my personal deportment. I even once, nodded at by the friendly curate, went to a service at St Anne's church and sat expectantly in the front row, entertained by a baying elderly choir, until the mysteries of the communion rite drove me out.

It disappoints me sometimes that I gave up this association with God . . .

The result of all this brooding was that I went through my adolescence in a kind of ceaseless ferment. I was forever picking up things and putting them down. I planned schemes of reading out of useless old books that I found in secondhand shops in St Benedict's and then discarded them. I wrote poems in the back of an exercise book – very bad poems they were – and tore them up.

I cultivated a passion for a meek little English teacher at school who read to us once out of *The Lord of the Rings* and thought me 'promising' which only died when she invited me home to tea and I sat round a table with three adenoidal children and a husband who washed up in a flower-patterned apron and never said a word. The English teacher was thrown over for a brief flirtation with an archaeological society, whose excursions involved much sieving of powdered Norfolk earth and a great deal of dark tea dispensed by elderly ladies, followed by a gang of West Earlham skinheads who lurked under the streetlamps at Bunnett Square, insulted park keepers and once murdered a cat by cornering it in the cemetery and pelting it with stones.

It turned out that this restlessness wasn't unique to me. Gradually I worked out – and the revelation was comforting but at the same time vaguely shocking – that an identical ferment had begun to excite the world beyond the Bright Road back-to-backs, that it had a tendency to break out in demonstrations and marches, its generating spirit endlessly dividing and redividing like a colony of amoebae under the lens. Some of its more innocent manifestations could even be witnessed in the humdrum backwaters of West Earlham. The first West Earlham mini-skirt, which appeared on Bunnett Square in the summer of 1966, was greeted very satirically by my mother and her cronies ('The *idear*', they pronounced, 'of those women showing off their legs like that') but within a year the Colman Road bus-stops were full of bolster-shaped women displaying their thighs. My mother and her friends took mini-skirts very hard, as they did all the inventions of that era, from contraceptive pills to decimalisation, as a kind of personal snub. They saw them – and I suppose they were right to see them – as the death knell of all the things they valued and held dear. For years they'd gone on imagining that life would always be the same, that until the end of time vague, put-upon middle-aged women would take the bus into Norwich to do their shopping, read *Woman's Journal* for its cures for bad legs, and sit round their kitchen tables trading scandal – and now suddenly it was all gone in an explosion of strikes and love-ins and women's rights. I can remember Mrs Buddery, once, drowsing in an armchair in our front room while my mother fussed about infusing tea, and picking her way with a moistened forefinger through a newspaper report about some period freak – Lennon's 'Bed-in for Peace' perhaps – and finally declaiming, in a kind of incandescent fury, that 'it shouldn't be allowed'. By 'it' I was shrewd enough to realise that Mrs Buddery meant not merely John and Yoko but everything – kaftans and beads and long hair and Harold Wilson, the protests against Vietnam and all the rest of it.

The sorority of the back-kitchen was breaking up in any case. Mrs Laband had decamped to Wymondham and, it was rumoured, an interest in spiritualism. Mrs Winall, poor vacant Mrs Winall, was dead of a long undoctored stomach complaint (none of the West Earlhamites 'held' with doctors) belatedly diagnosed, after God knows what agonies, as abdominal cancer. My mother, too, seemed somehow less solid, less liable to take offence, more likely to stop whatever she was doing and stand staring out of the kitchen window or sit rather sorrowfully in the front room with her eye fixed on the complex imbrication of light and shadow thrown up by the window frame. In fact there were times when my mother became practically confidential. I can't remember much of what we talked about, not because I lacked interest, but because my mother had a trick of collecting up whatever lay in her head and depositing it in so many fragments around more general conversation. But if there was no narrative with my mother, only allusion, it sometimes seemed to me that she was on the brink of some startling communication that might radically transform the view that I took of her, and our life here in West Earlham, and perhaps of myself, something that might lead away from the dull Norwich skyline and the reek of the May & Baker factory. On these occasions I strained very hard to interpret the queer code in which my mother communicated, convinced that revelation lay only a sentence away, but it was never any good, and I might as well have been talking to a fence post.

Sometimes the figure of my father was present in these conversations, or if not present then dimly visible on their margins. It wouldn't be true to say that my mother never talked about my father, as I got older, but when she did it was bound up in extraordinary vagueness and imprecision. Beneath these shutters of concealment a few fragments of pale light seeped through. In particular, my mother had a habit of apostrophising 'a certain gentleman' who could only have been my father. 'A certain gentleman liked mustard on his sausages . . .' 'A certain gentleman used to say . . .' What a certain gentleman used to say had a hard, didactic edge. *Never a borrower or a lender be*, for instance, or *Blessed are the peace-makers.* I was depressed by these allusions, as they seemed to bestow on my father a glaze of irretrievable banality. Only the novelty of hearing him discussed kept the tediousness of the reportage at bay.

There were other fragments here and there: odd bits of china hoarded over the years from which occasional shaky mosaics emerged. Books in the front room turned out to contain his signature on the flyleaf. Once a little bundle of photographs came tumbling unexpectedly out of a tea caddy, and my mother looked at them impassively for a moment or two. Another time she started talking about a holiday they'd taken in the North of England – the only holiday she seemed to have taken in her entire life – which could only have been her honeymoon. Mrs Buddery, too, was not averse to mysterious confidences, whose import it took me some time to appreciate, and I have a memory – not a very precise one – of a conversation in the dark of an October evening, when my mother was out somewhere, full of gloomy hints about rows and departures, at the conclusion of which Mrs Buddery solemnly swore me to secrecy, like a great black witch looming up in front of the grim fireplace.

The upshot of all this was that by my mid-teens I'd built up a reasonable portrait of my parents' life together. Much of it was the purest speculation – I had an idea that my father might have been some kind of commission agent, though I've no idea where this suggestion came from – but I knew they'd got married in the late 1940s. I'd been born in 1952, and I think there'd been some sort of separation before my father's death, which Mrs Buddery, thought (and even she seemed slightly alarmed at transmitting the information) might have been in 1953 or 1954. Having assembled these data, though, there was nothing I could do with them. Confronted with any direct question about my father, marriage, even her own early life, my mother simply clammed up or resorted to evasions that would have disgraced a child. What do you do in such circumstances? It was a kind of mental treasure trove, which

I brooded over and polished up all through my teenage years, but knew that I could never bring out on public display.

At long intervals my uncle communicated. He had a habit of sending comic postcards from holiday resorts on the east coast: Skegness, Scarborough, Whitby, Wells-next-the-Sea, each with a line or so of corroborative detail. My mother read these effusions aloud, without comment. There was something about them, I thought – perhaps the flagrancy of their humour or the sparseness of their messages – that displeased her, though she would never confirm that this was the case. And so our lives dawdled on in what I had already come to recognise as the approved West Earlham pattern: incurious, sequestered and remote, with only one question hanging over my head, and that the entirely mundane and familiar one of what I was going to do for a living.

At sixteen I hadn't any pronounced view of my destiny, other than a desire to get out of Bowthorpe High at the earliest opportunity. In this it seems to me that I was perfectly imbued with the West Earlham spirit, which sent boys into factories and girls into corner shops and looked down on 'cleverness' as the moral equivalent of leprosy. My mother, as it turned out, had certain vague longings for clerkish respectability. I think she had an idea of me working for the Norwich Union or in one of the offices in Exchange Street: at any rate for some time the words 'collar and tie' had featured largely in our discussions, and I remember her lingering once over an advertisement in the *Eastern Evening News* in which an auctioneer offered £10 a week to a smart boy who could write a fair hand and didn't object to rail travel. In the end, though, it came to nothing and, application being made to Mrs Buddery – who had watched over the clerical plans with secret scorn – I found myself apprenticed to the latter's brother-in-law, who kept a newsagent-cum-tobacconist's shop in Bunnett Square.

I think my mother regretted the collar and tie and the other seductive appurtenances of clerkdom. She looked unconscionably wistful when Mrs Buddery produced the figure of her brother-in-law and further alleged that I was 'just the kind of lad that would do'. For my own part, I was perfectly indifferent. It was how things were done in West Earlham, how life was arranged. You don't believe me? In every house in Bright or Lound or Stannard where there was a teenage boy, a tribe of relatives would sit in judgment on his prospects in this way, before bundling him off into some frightful apprenticeship: picking up scraps of leather off the floor of one of the boot and shoe factories, say, or manhandling boxes at Jarrold's. Even at the time I used to marvel at the oddity of these attitudes. The West Earlham people voted Labour in their thousands, 'couldn't abide' privilege or pretension, but still allowed themselves to be quite thoroughly downtrodden, or, rather, allowed themselves to have all their decisions made for them by prosy little patriarchs who smoked pipes, looked knowing and were invincibly ignorant of every topic that was suggested to them. The inanities I imbibed in that dim backyard society! The barefaced untruths about science, religion and human feeling! All this I remember very clearly – the ineffable stupidities and complacencies, the unkindness that was actually a kind of fundamental, dimwitted incuriousness.

Mrs Buddery's brother-in-law, Mr Blessington, was quite wonderfully representative of these attitudes. I've never had a chance to correct the brief impression I received of him, and he exists in my mind as a kind of dreadful caricature of incompetent self-righteousness. His newsagent's shop, which lay in the farthest corner of Bunnett Square squeezed up against an off-licence and a vague emporium that sold bicycle 'spares', was a queer, dingy place: a gloomy rectangle of premises with a corridor behind, crammed with all kinds of insalubrious clutter: bales of newsprint never returned to the wholesalers, cheap plastic toys hanging in rows off the vending spindles. Mr Blessington dominated this unpromising landscape in the way that a goldfish dominates its bowl, endlessly digging into old cupboards at the back of the shop, hobnobbing with favourite customers or standing in the window with his hands in his pockets metaphorically preening himself. He was a small, grim, desiccated man, balding and slightly stooped, so that in peering upwards from behind the till with the light shining off his wrinkled forehead he bore a faint resemblance to a tortoise, and in the six months I worked for him I don't believe I ever heard him make an original remark. His conversation was of the most stupidly querulous type, a kind of perpetual lament about the Church Commissioners (who owned his freehold) and his fellow-tradesmen in the square, with whom he enjoyed chronically strained relations. Poor Mr Blessington! I suppose I should have felt pity for him, for like my mother and Mrs Buddery he was simply another victim of the pressing modernist tide, but at the time I merely thought him ridiculous and dull, and longed for a chance to outwit him.

It was clear to me from an early stage that Mr Blessington and I would fall out.

Mr Blessington (Mrs Blessington, Mrs Buddery's sister, lived a strange, isolated life in the flat above the shop, in which eyrie she could occasionally be heard lumbering back and forth, and I don't suppose I saw her more than twice) ran his establishment on individual lines. Essentially it was an old-fashioned 'paper shop' that sold cigarettes and confectionery and other uncategorisable items like string and baking foil, but made its money out of delivering newspapers, morning and evening, to around five hundred households within a range of three square miles. The opportunities for upset which this presented to someone of Mr Blessington's limited organisational powers were immense. He was forever devising 'schemes' for the greater efficiency of the delivery boys – there were a dozen of them who assembled blearily in the shop's backyard at six every morning while Mr Blessington regaled himself with tea inside – forever changing his wholesalers, or forgetting to change them, so that on one memorable morning the entire day's supply of newspapers arrived in duplicate.

One of the most bizarre of Mr Blessington's 'schemes' entailed the display of material that was not actually for sale. And so, one afternoon early on in my tenure behind the antique gunmetal till, ducking to avoid the hoops of suspended bicycle tyres (the result of some mysterious 'arrangement' concluded with the shop next door), I looked up to find him advancing surreptitiously on the shelves – shelves filled with knitting pattern-books, women's magazines, odd partworks about photography and sailboat construction – with a peculiarly thoughtful and satisfied air.

'George?' (Everyone called me George these days, rather than the 'Georgie' of my childhood.) 'You sell that copy of *Homes and Gardens*?'

In fact I was rather proud of this sale, to an unknown woman whose ten-shilling note formed a quarter of the afternoon's receipts.

'Yes, Mr Blessington.'

Mr Blessington prowled stealthily along the shelves for a moment more. 'Y'didn't ought to have done that, George,' he said mournfully. 'Didn't I ever tell you y'shouldn't be doing that?'

'No, Mr Blessington.'

I never could resist a smile at Mr Blessington's locution, with its blithe disregard of vowels and its utilitarian truncations. He had a habit of pronouncing his 'sh' sounds in a lazy, sibilant way that sounded like a bottle-cap being drawn.

Abruptly Mr Blessington changed tack. He picked up a copy of *The People's Friend*, leafed through it solemnly for a moment, and then straightened up. 'Let's get this straight then, George. There's this copy of *Homes and Gardens* gone missing, that you say you've been and sold.'

'That's right.'

'Well' (impressively) '*that magazine was on special order.*'

Brooding over the episode years later – and it seemed so starkly revealing of a certain kind of human temperament that I often reflected on it – I decided that it grew out of a primordial wish to have one's cake and eat it, that Mr Blessington in the last resort could not bear to have a ten-shilling magazine for which he had paid a wholesaler six shillings and twopence lying idle on the customer order shelf when it could be proudly displayed in his window. In fact Mr Blessington had countless idiosyncrasies of this kind – 'notions' about selling newspapers at half-price a day after their publication, and a devious scheme whereby customers got a third off if they brought their papers back in the evening, thereby allowing him to send them back the next day as 'returns'.

I decided to get back at Mr Blessington over the copy of *Homes and Gardens*. For a week, whenever anyone attempted to buy anything in the shop – even a packet of cigarettes or a fourpenny cigar – I'd sing out respectfully, 'Is it all right for me to sell this, Mr Blessington?' It seemed to me that the customers rather approved the joke – they said I was a 'scream' or a 'funny young feller' – but it mortified Mr Blessington as I think no other failing of mine had ever done.

In its own curious way Mr Blessington's shop was one of the hubs on which West Earlham society turned. People came to gossip there, and hold fierce little arguments while they turned over back numbers of *Cage Birds* and the *Angling Times* in the bargain box next to the window. Gangs of small boys came and stood staring at the display cases of toy soldiers, or 'cheeked' Mr Blessington until he lost his temper and drove them out. The highlight of the day in Bunnett Square, though, came at four o'clock in the afternoon when the delivery van arrived with its three hundred or so copies of the *Eastern Evening News*. Standing in the shop doorway sometimes, while Mr Blessington fussed over the delivery books or conducted laborious inventories of the contents of cardboard boxes, I used to watch the square preparing for this event. By twenty to four there would generally be two or three women with prams or shopping trolleys starting to congregate on the concrete esplanade, or outside the front of Oelrich's bakery, three doors down. By ten to, middle-aged men in collarless white shirts with unlit cigarettes stuck in their mouths would be tethered restlessly at vantage points near the pelican crossing or by the Romany Rye pub in the square's far corner, whole half-a-dozen paperboys crowding their bikes into a circle on the pavement. The sight of the van charging down Colman Road to veer left into the sliproad before the row of shops galvanised these disparate groups into action: the men shifting purposefully forward, the paperboys thronging round the shop door, Mr Blessington on his knees at the roadside hacking at the bundles of newsprint with a kitchen knife, people flinging sixpences at him as they swooped on the first copies. Even my mother used occasionally to stalk down to Bunnett Square to 'wait for the papers' as she put it, and march proudly home to brood over the flower show reports and the small ads offering secondhand trailers and cheap radios. The *Eastern Evening News* was a proper local paper. When Robert Kennedy was assassinated – something I particularly remember, as it happened just after I went to work for Mr Blessington – it was reported halfway down page three, next to a story about a cat that had been rescued from a tree in Christchurch Road and a picture of a prize-winning vegetable marrow.

To go back to the question of the delivery arrangements, which were my undoing and in some sense the reason for my departure from West Earlham and the close of this chapter of my life: Mr

Blessington's connections, 'worked up' over a period of thirty years, were extensive. His delivery routes – there were about a dozen, some of them taking as much as two hours to complete – snaked out all over the western side of Norwich, inward as far as the top of Avenue Road, outward up to the gates of the University. To extend, refine and command this network was Mr Blessington's obsession. He had an enlarged Ordnance Survey map of the city on which the limits of his empire were picked out in red poster paint, and he was forever colonising extra streets, 'taking on' additional customers from rival newsagents and generally making himself objectionable to the Norwich paper trade – they had a poor, run-down trade organisation and were always sending him lawyers' letters accusing him of breaking some protocol or other. For a short time I shared this fascination. There was to me a magic in the way Mr Blessington deployed his battalions, rallied them and sent them out. Even today, passing a newsagent's shop with a fleet of big iron-panelled delivery bikes gathered up at the door, I get an indescribable feeling of youthfulness and purpose. But there was also – this being Mr Blessington and West Earlham – ineptitude that a child of ten would have cried over. For a start Mr Blessington had a habit of transporting his stock from the backyard, where it was delivered each morning by the wholesaler's lorry, to the interior of the shop, from which vantage point he parcelled up the rounds to be taken back again by the delivery boys to the yard where the bicycles were kept. For a long time I used to wonder what benefit Mr Blessington derived from this half-hour or so of superfluous labour, but it was no good, he *would* start his day in this way. Far more injurious, though, was the business of the delivery books. There were a dozen of these: fat red notebooks in which the details of the rounds were set down in Mr Blessington's crabbed and allusive hand (thus FR – 17 DT, 19 DM, 21 DE XS34, which meant *Fairfax Road, Number 17 Daily Telegraph, Number 19 Daily Mirror, Number 21 Daily Express third and fourth week of September only*). Mr Blessington's idiosyncrasy in the matter of the delivery books was a habit of recording each change to the round occasioned by a customer cancelling his order, going on holiday or taking a different newspaper, by hand the previous evening, thereby ignoring the delivery boys' habit of memorising the contents of the book and referring to it only in extremity. When, on my own initiative, I devised a system of supernumerary slips, enabling the delivery boys to note changes at a glance, Mr Blessington was simply furious. Sighing through his teeth – a curious sound, suggestive of cataracts, which I couldn't hope to reproduce – he submitted me to a long, fragmentary monologue of complaint.

'Ju see what I tryin' to tell y'George . . . On'y way y'can manage these things is to have a *system* . . . Dessay you're a bright enough lad in y'way but . . . no cause to go *interfering* in what don't concern y' . . .'

Struck dumb by this tide of long pent-up exasperation, I could only stare at Mr Blessington – head peering up from his bowed shoulders, hands clenching and unclenching as he delivered it. He was, I could see, genuinely shocked by this minor intervention in his affairs, and alarmed by the implications for his business. So bewildered was I by this unexpected rebuke that I took the unprecedented step of taking the matter back to Bright Road. My mother, stirred from contemplation of *Coronation Street* – we had a television set now, on the instalment principle – was doubtful ('Telling that Mr Blessington how to manage his own shop, the *idear*').

Among other things my mother confirmed that Mr Blessington had a 'hot temper'.

Matters came to a head one morning in November, the unexpected early return of Mr Blessington from a jamboree of the East Anglian Confectioners' and Newsagents' Guild revealing that this intrusion into his livelihood persisted. It was seven a.m. An early customer or two stood at the far end of the shop browsing through the magazine racks. To the right of the till assorted newspapers lay in piles awaiting the delivery boys. On each, tell-tale pink slips protruding from their tops, lay a red delivery book. Mr Blessington came noisily into the shop through the front entrance, altogether failing to conceal the impression of a man who has driven seventy miles through the dawn to detect an employee in some minor act of disobedience. When he saw the notebooks he stopped dead, picked the nearest one up and brandished it furiously in front of him.

'You . . .' he said. 'You . . . *shithouse*!'

There was a recognised West Earlham expression for losing your temper. It was called 'putting your parts on'. Hitherto my experience of this irruption had been confined to juvenile acquaintances. The adult version, I divined, was infinitely more fascinating and dramatic.

''Nearth d'y think y'doing?' Mr Blessington shouted, advancing on the till.

In an instant the shop seemed full of people. A middle-aged lady with a dog who came in every morning to buy the *Guardian* stared at us from the doorway; a wide-eyed delivery boy flattened himself against the shelves as Mr Blessington rushed past. The customers by the magazine racks began saying things like 'Here!' and 'Now then!' and, more menacingly, 'Now *then*!' and something hard and flat (later identified as a black account book from the stationery shelf) flew past my head and shattered a glass display cabinet. There was a confused impression of screaming, feeble grasshopper fists beating at my chest, an astonishing rictus of scarlet skin, popping blue eyes and peg teeth that was Mr Blessington's face in close-up, and an almighty thump as his head suddenly fell out of view, descended rapidly on to a pile of *Daily Mirror*s and ceased to move.

Whereupon we all – myself, the lady with the dog, the delivery boy and the two customers from the magazine racks – came and crowded round him with very grave and proper expressions of alarm.

Though it was later agreed that I hadn't hit my employer, whose sudden collapse was attributed to his feet having given way beneath him, my disgrace was absolute. Mr Blessington, very shaky and querulous, his forehead bound up with strips of sticking plaster, pronounced my dismissal within the hour. Two policemen, summoned by the lady with the dog, were entertained with cups of tea but then discharged (nobody in West Earlham liked involving the police in anything) and my mother arrived grim-faced from Bright Road to take me away. There was no question, I was informed, of Mr Blessington taking me back, or of anyone else employing me, and I should sit in my room until it was decided what to do with me.

That night my mother and Mrs Buddery held a council of war. I could see that what I'd done had badly frightened them – it was so beyond their experience, so alien to all the dismal West Earlham precepts they had grown up on. Mrs Buddery, I gathered, was all for enlisting me into the army, or the navy, or the air force, or anything that might make me 'realise my responsibilities' (the frightened, stupid gravity of Mrs Buddery's expression as she said this!). As for my mother . . . Even now I don't really know what my mother thought, although I have a suspicion, based on certain remarks made in Mrs Buddery's absence, and a vivid, picturesque framing of the incident in the shop ('The *idear* of him falling on the floor like that . . .'), that the thought of Mr Blessington's discomfiture wasn't wholly distasteful to her.

It might be wondered why I put up with this – Mr Blessington, Mrs Buddery, my mother's meek acceptance that I should 'realise my responsibilities'. But it was what one did in those days, in that kind of life, and in fact I've subsequently wondered whether such attitudes may not have been central to the West Earlham mind. Together they constituted a kind of smug resignation, a sort of wistful stifling of talent or enterprise, a grainy levelling down of expectations. You were always coming across 'promising' seventeen-year-olds jerked out of their education and put to work in a bank or found sheepishly stacking trolleys at one of the city centre supermarkets. Now and again some surly individualist would break out of this strait-jacket, win a place at university, say, or take 'a funny kind of job' (i.e. non-clerical) in some alien city. The direst forebodings greeted these divagations from the eternal path, and the West Earlhamites went to extraordinary lengths to recapture their escapees. I once knew a family who were so concerned at the probable dissipation of their son, a student at Leicester University, that they made a habit of visiting him every second weekend.

And so it might have been with me, had Mrs Buddery not overplayed her hand, my mother not had her private doubts, and the whole affair not been complicated by an unlooked-for revelation. By the end of the week that began so memorably in Mr Blessington's shop parlour I'd started to hear about a sum of money 'left' to me by my father, hitherto kept 'in trust' (my mother was vague about this), to be put into my hands on my eighteenth birthday. It was about £300, perhaps a shade more. And though I can't reassemble the exact details, I recall that a day or so later there was a definite feeling in the air that I ought to be given the money to 'go away somewhere' (Mrs Buddery) and 'make something of myself' (my mother). I was all for the idea, particularly as to 'go away somewhere' could only mean one thing. Once as a fourteen-year-old on a school trip I had spent a day in London. It remained with me as a confused impression of crowded streets, policemen in white bands directing traffic, great bridges perched above grey-coloured water and smoke hanging over distant, endless rooftops. And by this stage I'd read enough literature – mostly novels out of the West Earlham circulating library – about wide-eyed young men who had set off from dull provincial towns towards the bright metropolitan grail to make the prospect of London seem not simply enticing but somehow necessary and inescapable.

And so, incredibly, the business was fixed. The £300 ceased to be a mysterious secret of my mother's and became an actual blue-grey building society account book made out in the name of G. R. E. Chell in a faint and unrecognisable hand. But even here it seemed to me that the limitations of the West Earlham scheme of things stood pitilessly exposed. My mother and Mrs Buddery (between whom and myself there now existed a kind of armed truce) had not the faintest idea of what I should do when I arrived in London. My mother, who I suspected had never been there in her life, suggested that there were such places as a 'temperance hotel' or a 'Rowton House' where I might stay until I 'got myself settled'. Mrs Buddery, I remember, was full of vague but profuse recollections of relatives who had 'done well for themselves' in London, and at one point unbent sufficiently to make me a present of an A–Z guide to the capital printed in 1937.

West Earlham begins to fade from my mind now, become inconsequent and strange, merely a synthesis of drab little streets and asphalt. I spent the time which remained to me there in a condition of profound euphoria. It was late September, and I recall that I occupied myself in walks: back and forth across Eaton Park, where the dead leaves lay carpeted across the terrace, to the great house at Earlham, whose thoroughfares plunged this way and that through fantastically overgrown shrubbery, out into the byroads near Brooke and Poringland. I don't think that my motive was nostalgic, or even elegiac: I believe it was simple restlessness, an urgency to be off, to assert myself, among unknown circumstances and people. And finally there came a day when I placed myself and my belongings into a taxi – a measure of the journey's importance, as I'd never travelled in one before – and was driven away to Norwich station along roads lined with late-flowering lime trees, sunk in the shadow of an autumn sun. My mother declined to accompany me to the station. She was altogether quiet and good-humoured that morning, I remember, a morning in which I found myself noticing all sorts of odd little things about her: the movement of her jaw as she ate, the slightly distracted way in which she arranged her thin, straggling hair on top of her head, her lists and tabulations – all things I'd seen a thousand times before but had somehow never remembered or assimilated into the idea I had of her. At the gate, as the taxi driver nodded over the suitcase and flocks of children roamed past on their way home from school, she gave me a very odd look.

'You better kiss me, George,' she said at length. And so I dabbed my lips in a general way in the region of her cheek – something I hadn't done for ten or even a dozen years – which was cold and leathery and smelt somehow of face powder, although this wasn't something with which my mother ever adorned herself.

'That's right,' said the taxi driver, who had begun to take a fatherly interest in the proceedings, and by this time I was in the rear seat, looking back at my mother's small, impassive but still faintly forlorn figure, unable to work out if she was in the grip of some violent emotion or really wished me gone, until the cab moved away, the housefronts receded, and she disappeared.

To this day I wonder what my mother thought of my leaving Norwich.

That is all there is to say about West Earlham. I sometimes wonder whether I've been truthful about the place, whether there were things – kindnesses, sensations, warmth – which I missed, and that prejudiced me against it. But there is a way in which it has never left me – the reason, no doubt, why I have spent so long in describing it. It stands in my mind as the representation of everything that I fought against, all that blinkeredness and vague stupidity that propelled me and determined my course in life.

I went back there once years later, at the height of the Boom, and wandered round Bunnett Square calculating how the place had changed. Everything seemed smaller, as if the intervening years had somehow shrivelled and diminished it. Blessington's was long gone, of course, transformed into a big shop that sold videos and computer games as well as the rows of newspapers; the bicycle repairer was an Indian takeaway, and the field outside the Scout hut had been colonised by a municipal office. I saw no one I knew, except a very old lady who might have been Mrs Blessington tottering on sticks across the square, and whom I studiously avoided. Eventually I took a bus into Norwich down the same green avenue of lime trees and sat in the bar of the Maid's Head Hotel – a place I wouldn't have dared to enter ten years before – drinking beer and watching the sky darken over the cathedral.

West Earlham! It seems odd to me that the place exists, so fantastically conceived was it, so warped and generally misshapen, so defiantly out of kilter with the quickening passage of time. But it launched me and is, I suppose, in some way responsible for all that followed, and if someone were to ask me, 'What began it all?' I could truthfully answer.

Well – that's all I have to say about West Earlham.

In the afternoons, when I was tired of reading or Mr Archer's presence became unusually wearing, I used to wander through the town centre. As well as the brewery there was a second hotel, more expensive than the Caradon, to the extent of displaying printed dinner menus, a bookshop that sold prints of old Suffolk and a tea-shop with unusual opening hours. All these premises were congregated around a small square on which market days sometimes took place, thronging the hotel entrance and occasionally giving rise to quite severe disturbances.

Mr Archer incubated a violent dislike of this rival establishment. He said: 'Of course, in a town this size you end up seeing rather a lot of your fellow-businessmen, but nothing on earth would ever induce me to eat a meal in that place.'

Coming back from one of these walks I found Mr Archer waiting expectantly in the hall. He said: 'The young lady's arrived, sir.' Then, as if there might be some doubt over the visitor's identity, he continued: 'The young lady you said you were expecting.'

'She's a day early then.'

'Quite all right, sir,' Mr Archer said. He was obviously enjoying himself hugely. 'No trouble accommodating anyone at this time of the year.' He rubbed his hands together obsequiously. 'You'll find her in the lounge then.'

Frances Eccles sat in an armchair by the unlit fire. Further proof of Mr Archer's high good humour appeared in the pot of tea that lay on a small occasional table at her side. In the past week I had spun various fantasies around her appearance. These ranged from blonde of a certain age to the kind of harassed girl you saw presenting news reports on the local television channel. None was in the slightest degree accurate. She was a pale and faintly sullen woman of around thirty, with dark circles under her eyes and badly chewed fingernails.

'I know I wasn't meant to come until tomorrow,' she said stiffly, 'but there was a bit of a mix-up.'

'It doesn't matter.'

'Actually,' she went on, with a faint air of wanting to unburden herself, 'I got thrown out of my flat. It was either that or spending the night at my parents'.'

'How did you get here?'

'Train to Lowestoft and hitched. Had to walk the last mile carrying my bloody bag.'

There was a battered suitcase, tied together with a pair of elasticated grips, lying in the corner of the room.

'I'll leave you to get on with it then.'

'Okay. But tell that goon on the desk I don't need any more tea. He's already given me two cups and both of them were foul.'

'I'll tell him.'

At dinner that evening, as the rain beat against the window and the candles waved in their saucers, she was more forthcoming.

'To be honest with you, I've never done this sort of thing before. Helping someone with a book, I mean.'

'What do you do?'

On the far side of the room, cut off from us by a solitary old lady and an exhausted-looking commercial traveller, Mr Archer was ostentatiously carving a chicken. He glanced at me for a second, his face radiating curiosity, and then went back to his work.

'All sorts of things. Book reviews. Features. Sex research for the women's mags.'

'What's that involve?'

'Oh, it's not as awful as it sounds. You know every month *Cosmo* or whatever has a piece on "Men fake orgasms too" or "Why bondage is back"? And there are always lots of quotes: "Alan, 31, a journalist, says 'I like my girlfriends to tie me up' " – that kind of thing. Well, I have to ring people I know up and get them to say things.'

'It doesn't sound very difficult.'

'So anyway, I thought, I needed a change from all that, and when Eddie said he'd got someone needed help writing his autobiography, naturally I jumped at it.'

There was a silence while Mr Archer served us plates of chicken, cut up into odd, square cubes. It was hard to know what to make of Frances Eccles, harder to know if the way she talked about her career should be interpreted as gauche or impossibly knowing. Hardest of all was to work out whether she would be any use in the project we contemplated. For a moment I wondered whether I'd simply made a mistake, whether the whole apparatus – Mr MacCready, the publisher's contract, Frances – would be better abandoned.

'Do you know much about my uncle?'

'A bit. No thanks, go away.' Abashed, Mr Archer hoisted the dish of chicken off to another table. 'I mean, I remember it happening – when everything fell apart, that is. But I went to Hendon and looked at the newspaper files. It's quite interesting in a way.'

'In what way?'

'I'm sorry. I keep forgetting he's your uncle. You look terribly like him too. No, it's interesting because of what people said about him. I mean half the journalists who wrote about the enquiry obviously detested him, even when what happened couldn't possibly have been his personal responsibility. The other half are always making excuses for him. *Always.* Putting it down to naïveté or foolishness, whatever.'

'What do you think about him?'

'I don't know. Does liking come into it with someone like that? I mean they're just there, and they do things, and someone has to work out the impact.'

By now the dining room was nearly empty. Brenda, Mr Archer's maid of all work, was grimly spooning pieces of uneaten potato into a kind of funeral urn held tightly against her waist. From the residents' lounge, not far away, came the noise of a television switched up very loud. Frances said:

'Is there anything to do here? In the evenings I mean?'

'Not really. They sometimes play bridge at the Conservative club. The nearest cinema is Aldeburgh, but it shuts for the winter.'

'There must be some pubs or something.'

'I'll take you to one if you're desperate.'

There were three pubs in Eastwold: the Nelson, which was always full of crab-pots and fishermen in blue pullovers; the George, whose landlord was notorious for having married a Nigerian woman; and the King's Head, which was nearly always empty. We went to the King's Head. Here a solitary barman stood polishing the horse brasses. Light from the fruit machine flickered erratically through the gloaming.

'Very quiet tonight,' the barman said.

'Very.'

'I'm afraid if you were wanting food this evening there isn't any.'

The barman at the King's Head, if not in Mr Archer's class, was thought to run him close at times. We took our drinks to a secluded area near the fireplace.

'Do you like living here?' Frances asked.

'Yes, of course.'

'But why?'

I thought about this for a moment. It was difficult to explain Eastwold's attraction. And yet there was an attraction: something to do with absolute predictability, solitude, opportunity for reflection, those kinds of things. In the end I said:

'There's something about a seaside town as the autumn comes on. First the tourists disappear. Then the lights start going on earlier. Then the Salvation Army mission shuts down, and then they close up the putting course. Then one morning you go out on the beach and you don't see a soul. Except that you know life is still going on all around you, the difference being that you can't see it.'

'It sounds awful. I don't think I'm going to like it. I don't think I should have come.'

'You said you didn't have a choice.'

'Did I? Well, there are choices and choices.'

There was still no one else in the pub. The barman had finished the horse brasses and moved on to rearranging the beer mats. Frances said:

'God, you wouldn't believe the day I've had. What with having the row with those bitches at the flat, and then getting down here.

I think I'm going to bed. I suppose you'll want to start in the morning?'

'How long are you planning to stay?'

'I don't know. A fortnight? Three weeks? I've got nowhere else to go.'

'Are you sure you won't have another drink?'

'All right.'

After Frances had had some more gin she cheered up a little. She said: 'That man who runs the hotel, Mr Archer, he's a scream, isn't he? When I turned up at reception and asked for you he looked, well, almost shocked. As if I were a tart or something. And then when I'd explained everything he suddenly went all polite. I think he even called me madam.'

'You obviously made a good impression.'

'Did I? Well, it's a change for me to make a good impression, I must say.' She said this with an odd, selfconscious wistfulness, and then made a meditative little prod with her forefinger at the gin glass.

As we made our way out the barman had begun to polish the framed engraving of the Battle of Sole Bay that hung over the fireplace.

'Sure you won't have another?' he asked.

'No thanks.'

'All right then.'

Back at the Caradon Mr Archer was arranging the typed notices on the green baize notice-board. When one of the notices fell off he picked it up off the floor and replaced it with an expert twist of his index finger. He said:

'A gentleman rang for you, madam. He didn't leave a name.'

'Must have been Eddie wanting to know if I got here all right.'

'A most interesting-sounding gentleman. We had quite a long conversation.'

'Christ,' Frances said.

Imperceptibly over the next few days a routine established itself. In the mornings we sat in my room – the residents' lounge if there was no one else about – tape recorder between us, and discussed my uncle's career. After lunch, eaten at the Caradon or one of the tea-shops in the High Street, we went for walks over the common towards Walberswick or inland to Blythburgh church. Sometimes it rained and we took shelter under the great beech trees or huddled in the lee of the dunes watching the silent landscape of reed and sedge. Occasionally during these interludes I asked Frances questions about herself and her life, never with much success. She had a habit – as in the story about being thrown out of her flat – of revealing some faintly lurid detail about herself and then refusing to elaborate, however much pressed. In this way I heard about a man she was supposed to have married, a house in Walthamstow of which she was supposed to have become part-owner, and a holiday that she was supposed to have taken in Goa – queer, subjunctive fragments, whose ultimate design lay out of reach.

Little of her life seemed to have followed her to Eastwold. Sometimes in the evenings Mr Archer would summon her to the telephone; a letter or two came in the morning post; nothing more. Once, going up to her room on the upper floor and finding the door open, I stood for a moment or two taking in the contents. A white, sprigged nightdress lay on the pillow, and there was a copy of *Mansfield Park* on the bedside table.

Twice in the first week Mr MacCready rang. 'He just wanted to know how we were getting on,' Frances reported, coming back from the phone. 'What did you tell him?' 'I said we were getting on fine.' 'And are we?' 'Are we what?' 'Getting on fine?' 'Of course.' Most of my conversations with Frances had this odd, rudimentary quality, the sense of nothing more being given away than was absolutely necessary. Trying to draw her out about her life, health, opinions, anything, you met only an impenetrable wall of monosyllables. 'Do you know Suffolk at all?' 'A bit.' 'Constable Country's not far away. We could go there if you like.' 'All right.' As a result of this exchange we did in fact, one bitter afternoon, pay a visit to Flatford Mill and Copdock: it wasn't a success. At the time I sometimes wondered why I made such an effort with Frances. I think it was because I sympathised with her. The solitude, the disagreeable task, the bleak surroundings of the Caradon – these were all factors to be taken into account. Frances divined something of this sympathy, but did not resent it. 'You don't have to feel sorry for me, you know,' she said once. 'You don't have to *make me feel at home.* I've had worse jobs than this.' 'Such as?' 'All right. Hat-check girl in a night-club.' 'Tell me about it.' 'I might, sometime.' But the night-club, like the husband, the house and the holiday, lay deep in the bran-tub of her conversation.

There was one subject, however, in which we were in complete agreement: this was the fascination of Mr Archer. If anything, Frances's interest in Mr Archer's more bizarre pronouncements exceeded my own. 'You were right,' she said on the afternoon of the third day after her arrival, 'Archer's a real find. I've never met a bore like him. I mean, they could make a radio programme about him: "Archer Talks" or "The World According to Archer". He could make a fortune.' In fact Frances's most animated moments tended to come at times when Mr Archer was in the room – presiding over the supper table, perhaps, or dilating on holidays he had taken in France.

Mr Archer reciprocated this interest. 'A very polite young lady,' he told me once. 'It was odd, wasn't it, how interested she seemed about the cathedral at Arles. Do you think it would amuse her to see the photographs I took? There are a great many, and I should be delighted to show them to her.'

Q: Why did you come here? To the seaside?

A: I always liked this part of the world. 'Silly Suffolk', Norfolk people used to say when I was a boy. I never thought so. Curiously, my mother once brought me here when I was a child – I say curiously because my mother hardly ever countenanced any kind of excursion or holiday. But I think she liked it here. It was all much livelier in those days, of course. I mean, there was more going on on the pier, the local church used to hold a beach mission – that kind of thing.

Q: Those days being?

A: 1963, 1964. I have a vivid memory of walking back along the front towards the High Street, where the buses left from, and hearing 'I Want to Hold Your Hand' being played on somebody's transistor radio. That would be 1963, wouldn't it?

Q: But you couldn't have stayed in London?

A: I don't know. I suppose I could have, though in the circumstances it would have been difficult to find work. Despite the unconditional discharge. People in the City have long memories. Also, you see, by that time it had all ended. I had no affiliations. There was just my uncle. One or two others, perhaps: Kippax, who was his main associate, a man named Grundy who ran the administrative side. So when it all fell apart, after the mess had been cleared away, there were no threads to pick up, if you see what I mean. Just an absence. Also, I think I probably wanted to distance myself from it all.

Q: And you like it here?

A: I don't dislike it. Wilson-Steer used to come here to paint because of the light. Unfortunately that doesn't mean anything to me. But I like the sea. And I like the contrast between public and private perceptions. The sense of nothing ever happening on the surface, but a great deal seething away below. It's not really a tourist resort any more, you see. Not since Dr Beeching took the railway away, and the sea started eroding the cliff. There are a few diehards, not many. So the local people mostly have the place to themselves. So yes, I like it.

Q: The solitude doesn't bother you?

A: I live in a hotel with an average of fifteen residents: I don't call that solitude. But, yes, I see what you mean in principle and, no, the solitude doesn't bother me. I led a very restricted childhood, literally seeing no one, certainly hardly anyone of my own age. My mother was one of those odd working-class people – there were many more of them in those days – who really did believe in keeping themselves to themselves. *My* self too. It was a kind of religion with her. I can remember, well, one could only call it the delight with which she turned down the very few invitations she received. I think a great deal of what followed stems from that.

Q: What exactly?

A: That sense of restriction, deliberate limitations. Actually I'm a great believer in restrictions. But that was restriction for its own sake, unconsidered, simply a kind of meaningless private treaty with oneself.

From Norwich station the tracks head south under a few blackened bridges, past the cattle market and the distant floodlights of the football ground, on through the back gardens and allotments of Trowse and Tuckswood towards open country. Five miles out in the direction of Diss the landscape settles into its characteristic pattern and you see only flat fields, the square hedgerows falling gently away across the horizon and the rooks circling in the empty air.

I came to live in London, as I'll tell you, a few weeks after my eighteenth birthday. Norwich grows very small now, very meagre and distant, and West Earlham altogether remote, like a fairy kingdom of legend rolling into view every so often through the mist: I don't suppose that during the next five years I thought about them consecutively for more than a few minutes. In any case the memories of these days are dominated and superimposed by the figure of my uncle – which is odd in a way, as I didn't fall under his spell until at least a year later – as well as being inextricably bound up with the experience of London. In fact in a strange way the two have grown inseparable, and when I think about a certain part of the south-western city – Fulham, perhaps, or the streets round Putney Bridge – it's always my uncle who rises up to paint the memory in his own idiosyncratic colours.

All this is anticipating things, though. I remember that, before I arrived there, I had ludicrously distinct ideas about London. I saw it, I believe, as a wide, interminable landscape of grey, angular squares and monuments, a little ragged, perhaps, at its edges but stretching away into enticing suburbia. Later on, when this vision had been blown away, I still tried very hard to understand London, to map it out in my mind and to establish how it grew and functioned. Did you know, for instance, that with the exception of the central zones, London postcodes run alphabetically by district? Think about it: SE2: Abbey Wood; SE3: Blackheath; SE5: Camberwell; SE6 Catford . . . I was always coming across information like this and storing it away in my head with a kind of glee that I'd never dreamed of bringing to the West Earlham back streets.

For all that, I don't think I ever really understood London, or imagined it to be anything more than a chaos of streets and people. At the same time there were definite paths that I carved out through the rock, and several tunnels that I constructed through the green and populous moss. South of the river was a foreign country, but I knew North London pretty well, and there was a point in my life when I could probably have gone from Canning Town to Ealing Broadway without the aid of an A–Z. And of course there were all the curious places that I stumbled upon by accident – queer old museums found down alleyways in the heart of the City, wild little gardens discovered in the middle of Chelsea. They were refashioning the place then and the bulldozers were out uprooting the old Victorian terraces, but the bones of the old city shone up out of the dirt. It was here, oddly enough, that I came upon occasional reminders of West Earlham and the West Earlham system: a newsagent's shop in a square in Islington run by a man who might have been Mr Blessington's brother; a patch of small stucco houses somewhere off the North Circular that I remember examining curiously for a time in the dark of a Saturday evening, so sharply did they conform to the Bright Road pattern.

All this, though, was in the future. The London glimpsed out of a railway carriage that November afternoon was a very different animal. It was raining gently, and this, added to the drifts of fallen leaves that lay about in the streets and the grim little parklands, gave everything a silent, smoky and beaten-down quality. Churches, patches of waste ground, serpentine red-brick terraces – everything ran off into the distance in the same undifferentiated way. And yet sitting at the back-end of a second-class carriage – the only other occupant was an old man with bad teeth browsing through the *Daily Mirror* – I was perfectly happy. I felt – I don't know to any degree of certainty what I did feel, apart from a pervading loneliness, a huge dissatisfaction with everything that had previously been given to me, and the thought that for the first time in my existence there might be things I could look forward to. In those days the journey from Thorpe station to Liverpool Street took a couple of hours, but everything had a profound novelty, and I looked out contentedly at the grey expanse of the Stour estuary outside Manningtree, read the graffiti that gleamed up from the iron-work bridges of the East End and even got up a conversation with the old man with bad teeth, until the light began to fail, the passing stations – Ingatestone, Romford and Shenfield – came bunched together and the train rolled into Liverpool Street.

It was six o'clock on a Friday evening, the height of the rush hour, when I descended to a great grey concourse thronged with all manner of human traffic: rushing middle-aged men in mackintoshes with briefcases clutched to their chests, gangs of dawdling girls, silent youths loitering under the lamps. I can remember being so intoxicated with the scene, so desperate somehow to become a part of it all, that I carried my suitcase into a pub on one of the upper levels and sat at an empty table drinking a pint of bitter while the crowd swarmed around me. It was, I realised, like nothing I had ever witnessed before, almost like being set down in another country. Later on I wandered east through Whitechapel and Stepney, along cramped roads strewn with rubbish and splintered packing cases, and eventually fetched up at a men's hostel in Bethnal Green where for the sum of £3 I was presented with a single room, a batteryless transistor radio and the promise of unlimited hot water.

And so, for the next three months, the pattern of my life was established.

It was the oddest kind of life. I lived all over east and north-east London: in Bethnal, Hackney, Shoreditch, Bow, as far east as Leyton, as far north as Stoke Newington; in lodging houses, 'commercial hotels', furnished rooms taken a week at a time. Once, I remember, I spent a week in a YMCA in the Kingsland Road populated entirely by Nigerian students and marvelled, on coming down to breakfast on the first morning, at hearing the tables resound to language that wasn't English. It took me perhaps a month to discover how little I could survive on, even in London in 1970. You could live on £10 a week then if you were careful. Trying to piece together this time I find that all the intimate details have simply eluded me, and that I only remember the wayside oddities: sleeping on Hampstead Heath one winter night (it was the merest freak – I had the price of a bed in my hand), or a fantastically cheap café in Dalston where a plate of eggs and bacon cost two shillings and the old woman who helped with the washing-up claimed to have watched Queen Victoria's funeral procession.

Looking back, I can scarcely believe the loneliness of those first few months. I used to get into conversations with complete strangers sometimes just to hear the sound of another voice, spend money that I couldn't afford in pubs simply for the sense of company, and travel miles on the off-chance of free entertainment. One Sunday, I remember, I took a bus from Leyton to Hyde Park and ended up at Speakers' Corner, where I listened to a man in a battered morning coat explaining that his marriage to the Queen Mother was to be postponed 'for reasons of state'. Another time in a pub in Whitechapel late on a Saturday night a gang of Irish road builders took a fancy to me, stood me drinks and even held out the promise of a job if I turned up at their depot on the Monday morning. I never went – it would have been the easy way out, or rather the wrong solution to the problems I was setting myself. I wasn't, I regret, particularly chaste or particularly scrupulous. I have a recollection – an awful guilty recollection – of waking up in a dismal garret of a room with frameless windows and a bare boarded floor, that contained only myself, two piles of clothing, a bed and the woman with whom I had spent the night, and of silently leaving the building – it was an abandoned house, colonised by squatters – feeling half-ashamed and at the same time faintly satisfied at the thought of a difficult task finally accomplished.

I might have gone to the dogs altogether during that first winter in London, if it hadn't been for a kind of bedrock shrewdness, a certain awareness that the kind of life I saw practised around me, the busy brooding life of the cheap lodging houses and the squatters' encampments, wasn't indefinitely sustainable. I don't give myself any great credit for this. It was simply that I knew that there were other kinds of experience that I badly wanted to appreciate. I had a huge book jag when I first came to London. In some ways the thing I remember most about those early times is reading paperbacks out of the bargain bins in Farringdon Road, or illustrated nature books in the upstairs room of Holborn public library. I hardly ever bought a book in those days. I once read the whole of *The Grapes of Wrath* in a dozen half-hour instalments at Foyle's in the Charing Cross Road, and I can never look at a copy of *New Grub Street* without thinking of the musty secondhand shop in Cecil Court where I first came across it and the silhouettes of the people outside passing by the green glass windows. In fact all I have to do is look at the cover of the old Penguin edition – the one with Whistler's *Nocturne* on the front – and suddenly it's 1970 again, the newspapers are going on about England's chances in the World Cup and Harold Wilson's in the General Election, and I'm eighteen years old, standing on the pavement of Charing Cross Road staring at the crowd.

By a mixture of economy and mental discipline, I managed to keep the practical realities of life in London at bay for nearly four months. It was only when my father's money had dwindled into single figures that I steeled myself to take drastic action. Oddly enough, it wasn't that hard to find a job in London in those days – every café would have a 'help wanted' sign on the wall or a handwritten advert for builders' labourers. For a fortnight I washed up in a café on the Old Kent Road which opened at dawn to service the passing lorry trade. A bit later I helped deliver milk on a council estate in Holloway where the walkways were always scattered with glass and mad old women negotiated their requirements from behind locked doors. Curiously, despite my temperament and the hold that all the West Earlham nonsense about a fair day's work for a fair day's wage had on my mind, I found the business of earning money in this way unexpectedly satisfying, as well as being an absolute stop on the notions (what kind of notions they were I could still barely put into words) I'd begun to conceive for myself and my destiny. I knew, you see, that it was something of which my mother and Mrs Buddery would have broadly approved. They'd have hated the notion of working in a café

('Nasty, dirty places' I could hear my mother saying) but the idea of eight hours' back-breaking labour for starvation wages would have deeply appealed to them.

It was at this time, in the foothills of these great ideas, that I encountered Ekwall.

I can remember precisely where I met Ekwall: on a Saturday morning in April at a pavement café near Camden Lock where we'd both gone independently to read books and look at the people. I haven't seen him for ten years, and I haven't the least skill as an artist, but I think that if you gave me a pen and paper I could make a stab at drawing Ekwall. He had one of those long, thin, horsey faces that look down on you from immensely stooped shoulders – rather like Doré's illustration of Don Quixote or, nearer at home, an early photograph of George Orwell. In no other respect was Ekwall the least like Orwell – apart from a curious, drawling upper-class-cockney voice – but he liked having his attention drawn to this resemblance. He was a tall, pale, faintly ramshackle creature, a year or so older than me, with a permanently hang-dog look, who'd been thrown out of Oxford for some escapade that I never quite got to the bottom of, and was living in his parents' house near Regent's Park (again there was some mystery about his parents, who were hardly ever in London) while he, as he put it, 'looked around for some inoffensive way to exert myself'. Ekwall was always saying things like this.

I never properly established what Ekwall was doing that Saturday morning in Camden, but I suspect that he'd simply gone there on the off-chance of a pick-up. Up until then – I was coming up to my nineteenth birthday – I don't suppose I'd exchanged a word with a genuine homosexual. We'd had them in West Earlham, of course – faintly epicene middle-aged men who lived on their own or with doting mothers, whom my own mother referred to contemptuously as 'nancy boys' – but this was my first experience of one at close quarters. In ordinary circumstances, I suppose, all my mother's prejudices would have come into play, but Ekwall was so painfully inoffensive, so utterly unlike the accepted caricatures of inversion, that I never dreamed of mocking him. There was also the fact that he appeared to take no pleasure from the furtive, predatory kind of life he led. I got the feeling that he regarded it all as something routine and unavoidable, and appalling even to himself. Once or twice, later on in our relationship, I got to meet some of Ekwall's 'boys' – he called them that – and they were always waiters or shop assistants who stared at their drinks while Ekwall prosed on about Dickens or Eliot: he'd been studying English, you see, until they threw him out. I remember once asking him why he couldn't find someone of his own type (by which I meant someone who was well-off and knew about books) but he looked grimmer than ever. He'd tried all that, he said, and you simply stayed at home all night having supper and arguing about who did the washing-up.

If all this makes Ekwall sound like an object of pity, that wasn't the case at all. In fact I admired him unreservedly and relished the time I spent in his company. As for Ekwall, I think he was a bit amused – not just because he'd found someone who liked listening to his talk, but because I was so obviously such a different person from the kind he was used to. Used to socially, I mean – in other respects I could have been taken, in fact probably was, for one of his boys by anyone who saw us together. To do him justice he was quite unselfconscious about this, and when he drew attention to differences in the way we talked or behaved it was with a kind of disinterestedness, like an anthropologist. He used to walk round the house in Regent's Park – he had a couple of rooms on an upper floor which he'd converted into a pigsty of dirty clothes and scraps of paper – pointing out things he thought I might be interested in. As I remember they had a Landseer and a couple of Hockney prints, and that, Ekwall said, was ignoring the safe in the cellar which he didn't have access to. At the time I couldn't understand his attitude to the house or its contents – he used to tread mud deliberately into the carpets and look the other way if one of the 'boys' stole anything, which they were always doing (one of them walked off with half the silver once, but he hushed it up somehow), and I remember him saying once that he wouldn't have minded if the place burned down provided he wasn't in it at the time. Now I think I understand it a bit better and can comprehend something of the mixture of boredom, unhappiness and resignation with which he approached life. 'The problem with me,' he used to say sometimes – and he did it without a trace of irony, 'is that I've lost my way. As simple as that.'

He drank a huge amount, of course. On the day we met we hadn't been talking for more than a few minutes before he suggested that we go to a wine bar, and later on any arrangement to do something usually began with me dragging Ekwall out of a pub somewhere. Again I don't remember being censorious about this, but merely accepting it as one of the compromises you had to make to spend time with him. Looking back I think I've a great deal to be thankful to Ekwall for. I don't suppose, if you were to reckon it up, that our acquaintance amounted to much more than a succession of nights spent drinking or watching films – we must have seen every film that came on general release in London in those days – but at the time it seemed as if an extraordinary new world had opened up in front of me, full of books and pints of beer and vague talk about 'life'. Oddly enough it was Ekwall who got me the job at Chaffington's. Hopeless about disentangling his own affairs, he could be highly objective about other people's.

'What you need,' he told me, a few weeks after we'd met, 'is something to do. Gainful employment.' (Ekwall habitually talked in these finespun clichés.)

'I've had jobs. I'll have them again.'

'No, I mean a proper job. Not washing-up. Something steady.'

'I get by.'

'But you don't get by, do you?' Ekwall said. We were in a pub in Soho waiting for Ekwall's current 'boy' – an off-duty guardsman from the Knightsbridge barracks – to finish jamming a pile of shillings into the fruit machine. 'You see, it's all right for me. I've got money. I can work this kind of Bohemian racket.' He made a large gesture round a room that included a Dickensian barman, two withered old women wearing cloche hats and shapeless coats that reminded me of the garments my mother put on for Sunday-afternoon excursions to Mrs Buddery's, and a group of fishy-eyed teenagers. 'You can't. Well, not for much longer. Regular money's what you need.'

'Any ideas?'

As it happened Ekwall did have an idea, in the form of an uncle who was a partner in an accountancy firm somewhere north of

High Holborn: 'Fine old firm. Could have gone there myself only it didn't suit.' Introduced by Ekwall in the character of bright lad and personal friend (you could still get jobs like that in those days), I went to an office in Red Lion Square one morning and was interviewed by a diffident old man in a pinstripe suit who seemed to think it would be all right. Why did I do it? I suppose because I had boundless faith in Ekwall and his judgement, and also because I suspected he was right, that I couldn't go on living from hand to mouth for very much longer or continue with the vague, restless life of the past six months.

And so, not without certain private misgivings, I became an articled clerk at Chaffington's in Red Lion Square. It was odd, this transformation. One moment I'd been spending my days lounging in the Charing Cross Road, the next I was one of the tribe of grey-coated men and women who were borne via the Central Line to Chancery Lane each morning, to swarm thereafter in a mournful tide along High Holborn and its multitudinous alleyways and conduits. For some reason my progress becomes clearer now, and the thoroughfares and byways of old Bloomsbury are very vivid to me. There was a particular seat in the gardens of Red Lion Square, stuck between a hydrangea bush and a statue of George Lansbury, where I used to eat my lunch every day, and a bookshop nearby in Sicilian Avenue where the lunch hour could sometimes be prolonged until as late as half-past two. Chaffington's 'went in' for legal work. They audited law firms in Shepherd's Inn and Carey Street and did tax computations for rich barristers with chambers in the Gray's Inn Road, and a veil of antiquated respectability hung over their premises. There were still iron stanchions by the door where, it was suggested to visitors, the link-men of two centuries before had hung their torches, and the partners' offices were done out in mahogany with framed Victorian audit reports on the wall.

Mysteriously, and by degrees, I became habituated to the profession and its regimes. Auditing seemed to me a gigantic guessing-game, played with inadequate materials, in whose satisfactory outcome men of fanatical probity would shamelessly collude. Taxation looked far more pointed and rewarding. Insolvency and some of the more exotic branches of management accounting I never came near to: the firm looked down its nose at bankruptcy cases and an insolvent tobacconist was generally referred to a liquidator's shop in Bedford Row. Despite these limitations there was a logic and an exactitude about accountancy that rather impressed me. In my second year I took a prize for auditing in the Intermediate Examinations of the Institute of Chartered Accountants in England and Wales and was rewarded by the firm with a copy of *Bartholomew's Principles and Practice of Elementary Book-keeping.* I learned to perform reconciliations and deferred profit forecasting, and to enter figures in a ledger opened by the senior clerk with an expression of the most sacramental awe. A sense of propriety was firmly enjoined at Chaffington's here in the early 1970s. The senior partner – I looked him up in the Institute yearbook and found he'd first been admitted in the year of the General Strike – still wore a morning coat to work and the junior clerks – white-faced youngsters from Highgate and Holloway – were famous for the sobriety of their get-up. I've a photograph of myself taken around this time: grey-suited, briefcase under one arm, looking very pale and serious on the office steps.

In the meantime, and in the company of Ekwall, I continued to lead an energetic double life. Mostly this consisted of an activity that Ekwall called 'seeing a bit of things'.

'Look here, George,' he would say over the telephone – personal calls were discouraged, but everyone knew about Ekwall's uncle – as I stared at the leafless late-November trees. 'Friday night tonight. What do you say to Soho?'

'We've had all that before. No fleshpots. By agreement. You remember?'

'No. Not that. Not the delights of Frith Street. *Writers.*'

'What kind of writers?'

'Poets. Novelists. Corporation of the Goosequill. Genius renascent in Old Compton Street. Apparently there's this club called the Colony Room . . .'

And so we went to Soho in pursuit of writers, where, having been refused admission to the Colony Room, we ended up in a room above a pub in Brewer Street talking to a dirty, elderly man who in return for half-a-dozen glasses of brandy and water consented to tell us about the homosexual relationship he'd had with Dylan Thomas or it might have been Julian Maclaren-Ross.

Other times we sprawled in armchairs listening to Ekwall's records and trying to work out their effect on our consciousness.

'Like feeling hot wax dripping over your forehead.'

'No, you're wrong there. Like being whipped *very slowly* with birch twigs.'

'By a man or a woman?'

'A man, of course . . . And what he's singing isn't *Lady in a black dress.*'

'No?'

'No. It's *Layer deer anna black duress.*'

It was at about this time that Ekwall had a poem (entitled 'The Grinding Gears of My Love Forge Upward') accepted by *Encounter.*

And so time went on in that calm and endlessly inviting way that it does in your early twenties when everything is dawns and horizons and promise. I was twenty, twenty-one then, and London was still a source of fathomless interest and amusement to me. The strangest places drew me to them. There was a particular road – called Dombey Street, I think – near High Holborn where I used to loaf in the sun for no other reason than that I liked the look of the shabby Georgian houses and the thought of Dickens walking there with Forster and Maclise, and a particular pub next to some run-down gardens near Doughty Street that I used to drink in because it contained some extraordinary specimens of taxi driver and Billingsgate porter. 'Half-past seven and an empty street' is a phrase that sticks in my head from these days. Together with half-a-dozen freer spirits among the articled clerks I founded a society called the Chaffington Irregulars and went with it on evening excursions to odd pubs and wine bars between Fleet Street and the river, or to quasi-official celebrations of completed audits known as 'drink-ups' held in the upstairs room of a big old railway hotel near King's Cross station. Even now I could give you thumb-nail sketches of the Chaffington Irregulars: a red-faced boy called Martingale whom I afterwards knew as the magnificent director of an insurance company in Eastcheap; Savage who went into traded options and died a bankrupt; Jenkins whom I last saw getting out of a Daimler near the Bank of England. Sometimes if I think very hard I can imagine myself back there in Red Lion Square, with the sunlight falling across the ancient pavements and the statue of George Lansbury, back in the days before my uncle's hectic reappearance in my life, before the shadows closed in around us.

My mother died in 1972, suddenly and according to Mrs Buddery – it was she who telephoned Chaffington's to tell me – inconveniently. In a subsequent letter she enclosed a list of items purchased by her for 'the dear departed' in the days before her death. They included a transistor radio, several pounds of oranges and, oddly enough, a pair of shoes. I took a day off work and travelled down by train to the funeral.

In the years since I'd left Norwich I hadn't stopped thinking about my mother. I'd thought about my father too, but he was remote and unquantifiable. The grey-haired man in the photographs, the postcards from Dresden and Cologne; it was my mother who moved most sharply through my consciousness. She reared up at me in the most unlikely circumstances: late at night in Soho with Ekwall, hunched over my desk in Red Lion Square, in the tiny bedsit I'd begun renting in Belsize Park. Now, as the train rolled through Chelmsford and Colchester and the sun hung low over the silent estuaries, I thought of her again: a lean and slightly exaggerated figure, her features sharper and more pronounced than I remembered. In particular, I cast about in my mind for my earliest recollection of her and emerged once again with the white houses streaming away from the window and the sudden apparition gathering me up in her arms. And I have a distinct memory of repeating the word 'dead' to myself several times.

I'd assumed the funeral would be held at St Anne's, a stone's throw away from the house in Bright Road. In fact it took place at another church out along Earlham Road where Mrs Buddery had some vague influence with the vicar. I remember taking a particular interest in a memorial tablet to the left of me recording the accomplishments and progency of a certain Josiah Garbutts Esq. and in the difficulties of the undertaker's men who knocked the coffin against a pew and ended up pushing it before them like a supermarket trolley. In the pew behind me Mrs Buddery, swathed in black vestments, vigorously intoned the responses.

There was a black-crape bouquet stuck to the door-knocker of Mrs Buddery's house in Stannard. Inside, the dining table had been dragged into the centre of the front room and spread with what the sorority of the back-kitchen had liked to refer to as a 'cold collation'. Here various more or less recognisable people in badly fitting formal clothes introduced themselves to me. In their vanguard was a shabby and slightly worn-looking figure in a crumpled serge suit. It was my uncle.

'I'm glad to see you here, George,' he said, shaking my hand with an odd effusiveness. 'Sorry of course, in the circumstances, but glad. Very.'

'Were you at the service, Uncle Ted?'

'Couldn't get away in time,' said my uncle vaguely. 'Spent half an hour sitting in a train outside Diss. But I'm here *now* and I'm very glad to see you. We can go back together. Have a bit of a talk.'

There was something proprietorial and faintly ominous in the way he said this, and at the same time something reassuring in his large, humorous face – the tufts of hair not quite as pronounced as they had been, but still in some way efflorescent and perky. Together we became part of a circle attending on Mrs Buddery, now in a state of advanced emotion.

'I don't know what I *shall* do now Jane's gone. They say the Good Lord takes the best ones first and I'm sure that's right. There never was a one as helpful and considerate as her for errands or helping a body with shopping and such . . . I'm sure I *shall* miss her,' Mrs Buddery ended defiantly and, I thought, a shade unnecessarily. Later I found myself in the centre of a small crowd made up of a diminutive man and woman, both looking extraordinarily like one another, and a brood of noisy, round-faced children, anxious to ply me with reminiscence and advice. 'Fred and Eileen Allman. You won't remember us, but your mum used to bring you to see us when you were a baby. Out Blofield way. And if I were you' – Mr Allman lowered his voice – 'I'd take a look in the cupboards to see what the old cat's walked away with.'

I've only the vaguest memory of what happened in the next hour or so. But I do recall collecting the key from a tearful and in some way reluctant Mrs Buddery and, my uncle accompanying me in the role of close and interested relative, walking the forty yards to

Bright Road for a last look at the house. Something in its silence, broken only by the sound of dense Norfolk air rising against the windows, conveyed to me what I hadn't even in the train chosen to consider – that my mother was dead, that whatever I thought about her I should never see her again, and that she had indisputably and according to her lights cared for me – and I roamed around the place for a while and my uncle stood sympathetically and it seemed to me a bit oddly by the stairwell. My mother's bedroom was quite empty. Somebody had cleared the wardrobe that stood by the bedstead, and there was a little scattering of hairpins and disturbed dust on the carpet.

I went back downstairs to find my uncle grown animated in the way that I remembered from our first meeting. 'Rare old place this is, George,' he said, standing in the tiny room and rattling his fingers on the window casings. 'I remember when these houses were built. One. Two. *Pop!* Blink your eyes and another street would've gone up. They didn't waste time in them days.

'Or money,' he added.

Then, on the instant, his mood changed. 'Of course, y'could stay here if y'like. A word to the council'd settle it. What do y'say to that, George? Live in Norwich and get a job eh? – a job that'd pay.'

I shook my head. 'I already decided, Uncle Ted. I'm not coming back.'

But my uncle was by now looking at a featureless picture of a country lane in winter that my mother had hung from the wall next to the big gilt mirror. 'Now this, this is a piece you could do something with. If I were you, George, I'd take this back with me and no mistake.'

In a cupboard by the fireside my mother had left what she called her 'heirlooms': old brooches with damaged catches, a photograph or two, silver threepenny bits that had once decorated a Victorian watch-chain. These I scooped into a brown paper envelope.

'Things to remember her by,' said my uncle approvingly. 'That's right.'

A moment later I shut the door on the house in Bright Road for the last time.

As we wandered back along Stannard, where the guests had by now debouched into the street and Mr Allman stood agitatedly calling his children to order, and thence to Colman Road, where there were buses to the station, I found myself wondering again about my mother, not now in relation to my own distress but in terms that were exclusive to her. What, I wondered, had my mother wanted? Had she ever been ambitious? Happy? The fact that I couldn't come up with answers to any of these questions seemed shameful and inexcusable.

I began to wonder, too, about my uncle. Clearly his work now took him to London, as there was a return ticket sticking out of the breast pocket of his suit. In the train, despite the promise of 'a bit of a talk', he seemed forlorn and ill at ease. He had a battered and very rusty old umbrella that he placed point downward on the floor before him, the handle balanced in the groove of his chin, and in this attitude he passed the journey as far as Ipswich. Then, as the train picked up speed beyond the Essex flats, he seemed ready for conversation, or if not for conversation then for the reflective and interruptive monologues which, I later came to realise, were his means of communicating to the world.

'A hard kind of a woman, your mother. I don't mean to criticise, I suppose we're all of us hard enough if you did but think about it, but . . .

'It was all a long time ago,' he said conclusively.

'What was?'

My uncle appeared not to have heard. 'I can remember during the war buying her a hat, and her not liking it. Y'd be surprised, George, the fuss there was about that hat.'

This was interesting. In fact it suggested sides to my mother's life and temperament that I'd never stopped to consider. Wanting to tap this vein of reminiscence, I asked straight away:

'Did you know my father at all well, Uncle Ted?'

My uncle looked uncomfortable. 'He was older than me, eight years older. That's a big difference when you're a kid. And then when I was growing up he was always away somewhere. But I remember him being good with his hands,' my uncle said cautiously. 'Remember him once making me a rabbit hutch out of a pair of old orange boxes. Extraordinary thing it was.'

Some odd fact about my father's family, remembered from the conversations with my mother years before, stole into view. 'Was that when you were living at Thorpe?'

But my uncle shook his head, a terse gesture that immediately established him, I realised, as my mother's confederate in any sortie in pursuit of my father's memory: unapproachable, evasive, shifty.

Grown suddenly restless once again, he began to ask me questions about myself. What was my job? Did I like it? Did I have a high opinion of my employers and they of me? Did I save money? Where did I live? There was a touch of shrewdness in these interrogations that I hadn't previously noticed in him, and his advice had an autobiographical flavour.

'Biggest mistake *I* made when I came to London, George, was to overdo things. 'Spensive lodgings. Three-course dinners. Football matches. Thing to do is to gather your resources and live cheap . . .

'No one ever did any good by overdoing it.'

I had a sudden vision of my uncle a quarter of a century ago: spruce, dapper, hair slicked back, wearing black and white co-respondent's shoes, slipping along the thoroughfares of London.

'How's business, Uncle Ted?'

He looked thoughtful. 'Not so good as it might be . . . In fact I'm thinking of making a change, young George.'

'A change?'

'That's right. Getting a bit tired of carrying boxes of toys round the country in the back of a car. Been thinking of setting up on my own,' my uncle announced proudly.

He paused. 'There's got to be more to life than selling toys,' he said.

'Not that I haven't done all right out of it,' he added hastily, as if I'd hazarded a career in the toy trade myself and this might be construed as dissuasion.

'. . . I might be talking to *you* about it one of these days,' he ended decisively.

More than this he wouldn't say. By this stage, tired, emotionally overstretched and in any case not specially interested in whatever commercial plans he had mapped out for himself, I didn't press him. It strikes me in retrospect, though, that perhaps the great Chell empire, with all its lustrous satrapies and satellite kingdoms, took root in this conversation, that in all probability its outline had never been put into words before, even in the few halting sentences that my uncle allowed himself here in a three-quarters empty train shuttling over the East Anglian fields in the twilight of a January afternoon. Looking back I can see that, far more than our later conversations – either in Putney or at the house in Sydenham – it had a prophetic quality, a sense of sharp, shrewd intelligence taking hold of itself in a way that it had perhaps never done before. At the time, though, I'm certain that I marked it down merely as another of my uncle's 'notions', sketchy daydreams of the kind he'd already hinted at in the graveyard conversation of nearly a decade ago.

Liverpool Street, reached at five, looked even more like an ant-heap. My uncle stared at it from the train window, gravely but with a definite enthusiasm, as if in moving towards it he knew very well what he was about. We said goodbye on the steps of the underground station, after I'd refused his offer of 'a bite to eat'. Part of me was simply exhausted. Another part of me had had rather more of my uncle in the past four hours than it could decently take. But a third and much greater part had been struck, suddenly and inexorably, by a sensation that had nothing to do with the other two, though it may in a small way have been pushed to the surface by them. The sensation, which required silence and solitude, and couldn't have been approached in my uncle's company, was that I had fallen in love.

Q: Did your uncle ever talk about his early life?

A: About his private life, nothing. About his business career, a very little.

Q: Didn't this strike you as odd?

A: Not in the context of my family. The Chells are famously secretive. Even now, I don't know who my grandfather was. There was something disreputable about him that caused my mother never to mention his name. Obviously I inherited this tendency, because it never occurred to me to ask awkward questions – well, hardly ever. I think even when I was very young I respected these silences. *Especially* when I was very young. These hulking gaps in your family history weren't unusual in our part of the world. Nearly every family I knew as a child – and there weren't many – had some unexplained scandal fraying its edges, some delinquent brother or illegitimate child who was never mentioned. My family was an extreme example of this tendency.

Q: And your uncle began as a travelling salesman?

A: In toys, that's right. At least, that's what he was doing when we first met. Before that it may have been something else. I don't know. He always gave the impression that the travelling job was unimaginably awful – hanging around in tobacconists' shops on the off-chance of selling thirty shillingsworth of stock. And extraordinarily badly paid. A basic salary of a few pounds a week – this would have been the mid-Sixties – the same again in commission, maybe, if you were lucky.

Q: The register at Companies' House has two mentions of him in the late 1950s. The first as director of a toy-manufacturing concern in

Harrogate; the second as director of a small printing firm, also in Harrogate.

A: Then the register at Companies' House knows more than I do! No, I was aware that he'd been involved in one or two business ventures before this. Very occasionally people would turn up at the office who'd known him from that time in his life, usually as a result of having seen his picture in the paper. It was all presented in a spirit of good fellowship, but inevitably they all wanted to touch him for money. My uncle had an absolute horror of these people – no, perhaps horror is the wrong word. He was embarrassed by them and at the same time faintly sympathetic – I mean, they could always be sure of getting something from him.

Q: Why embarrassed?

A: I think because all this represented a part of his life that he wanted to forget. Both businesses failed, I think. He used to hate it when newspapers ran 'profiles' that went in for this kind of sifting through his earlier days. I remember him once nearly issuing a writ against the *Daily Mirror* in that respect. In the end the lawyers advised against it. On very good grounds.

Q: Which were?

A: That most of what the *Mirror* said was true. That he had been appointed director of a certain company in 1950 – whenever it was, that two years later that company had failed, and that a dozen or so people had lost their jobs. There might have been something odd about the ensuing liquidation too – the directors managing to retrieve their goods by way of third parties, something like that.

Q: Were you curious about this part of his life? Did you ever ask him about it?

A: A little. Not much. If people don't want to talk about things, then they don't want to talk about them, do they? *Won't* talk about them in some cases. Certainly a quality I associated with my mother. As I say, I collaborated to some extent in the air of mystery she put about, but at the same time there were some things I did want to know very badly, and she would never tell me. I spent a lot of time with my uncle, a great deal of time, but that didn't mean he was approachable. He would *confide* things sometimes, the oddest things, but there were great stretches of his mind that I could never penetrate.

Q: What kind of things did he confide?
A: Financial things. What he thought about other people.
Q: What he thought about you?
A: We were both Chells. Chells don't tell other Chells what they think about them. They leave them to find out.

In the evenings, when the sea could be heard in the distance beating against the esplanade, Mr Archer liked to talk about the things that had attracted his attention during the day: the peculiarities of the postal service, news heard on the radio, Brenda's inability to clean the upstairs corridors without leaving pools of water behind her. He delivered these observations in a high, breathless monotone, usually while carrying out some domestic chore – buffing up a caseful of fish knives, perhaps, or itemising a bill on scraps of paper torn from the margins of that morning's *Daily Telegraph*.

Occasionally this monologue became entirely personal.

For example, Mr Archer once said, 'I don't know if it would interest you to know, sir, but I once wrote a book.'

'Did you? What kind of a book was it?'

'A lot of people have asked me that question, sir – people who knew about my literary ambitions of course – and, do you know, I've never known what to say to them. It began as a kind of autobiography, but I always feel, at least when I read other people's books, that to write an autobiography you need to have had an interesting kind of life, and I don't believe that's something I could truthfully say that I've done.'

'What kind of a book was it then? A novel? A kind of memoir?'

'Oh there were no *characters* in it, sir, if that's what you mean. Just a lot of thought.'

It was impossible to draw Mr Archer out on the subject of his book, or indeed on any other topic to do with himself. I saw that his was the comparatively rare kind of egotism that takes its pleasure from concealment rather than revelation, offering up tantalising glimpses of some shadowy life which investigation would probably show to be duller than the listener supposed. At the same time Mr Archer specialised in rather lurid confidences. Once, when there was no one except ourselves in the silent lounge, he said unexpectedly:

'I believe you know Brenda, sir.'

'Of course I know Brenda.'

'The red-haired girl who cleans here in the mornings,' Mr Archer went on, ignoring my reply. 'The one I had occasion to complain of when she left the floor polish stuck all over the upstairs landing. Well, it's not something I like to ask one of my guests, but what would be your opinion of Brenda?'

This was a tricky question to answer, seeing that Mr Archer was thought to be obsessively interested in Brenda. Hinting that you liked her might be entirely the wrong thing to say – it might simply inflame Mr Archer's jealousy. On the other hand, saying that she fell short of whatever standard you or Mr Archer looked for in a chambermaid might be just as inflammatory.

'She seems fairly capable at what she does.'

Oddly enough, this answer seemed to throw Mr Archer altogether. He put down the pile of napkins he had been folding into neat isosceles triangles and stood for a moment rocking backwards and forwards on his feet. When he spoke at last it was in a lower and more subdued tone, as if what I'd said had been so unexpected that he needed to make a considerable effort to reply.

'Capable? I suppose you could call her capable . . . Do you want to know what I think of Brenda, sir?'

'Tell me.'

'I think' – there was no mistaking the absolute sincerity in Mr Archer's voice – 'I think she's the kind of girl *that will come to a bad end*.'

'What makes you say that?'

'Seen her type before, sir.' Mr Archer lowered his head. 'The way she scrimps on her work. Way she looks at me. Why, only the other day in her room . . .'

But the sentence was extinguished by the arrival of another resident in the lounge, and I never discovered what Mr Archer had found in Brenda's room, still less how he had come to be there in the first place. Frances, to whom I reported this conversation, had her own theories.

'I expect Archer lets himself into her room with the master-key and goes through her underwear. I can just see him sweating over her knicker drawer, can't you?'

'I don't know. I wonder if Archer has any sex-life at all.'

'Bound to. Those pale, red-haired types always do.'

'How would you know?'

'Bitter experience,' Frances said.

That evening the rain came in implacably. We heard it drumming on the windows in the small hours. By dawn the concrete yard visible from the bathroom was a brimming lake. An inspection of the breakfast room early the next morning revealed that a further three ashtrays had disappeared.

Part II

It is odd that I can't remember when I first saw Carole, whom I was eventually to marry and to make more wretchedly unhappy than any other person I have ever met (I was made wretchedly unhappy myself, but then the fault was mostly mine). In fact I only noticed her at first as one among a number of familiar figures – the old gentleman in the Archie Rice pin-stripes, the ambling hippy in the kaftan – glimpsed on my journeys round Red Lion Square and the region of High Holborn. There was a small library set in a recessed courtyard off the Gray's Inn Road where I used to go in my lunch hour, which she frequented with such regularity that for quite a long time I thought she was a student at the University of London. As it turned out she was interested in dressmaking and fabrics and used to use the library to hunt out 'patterns'.

She was a small, plump, blonde girl, but industrious and somehow indefatigable-looking: one of those girls who look as if they would be equally at home fell-walking in the Lake District or swimming the Channel. In those days my ideal of female beauty was somewhere between an Alma-Tadema portrait and a picture of Jane Asher I had taped to the wall of my bedsit in Belsize Park. In the summer Carole played tennis on a court in one of the Bloomsbury squares and it was here, I suppose, that I first became aware of her. In those days she had very fine, long hair and it was this, bouncing off her back like the mane of a pony, that immediately distinguished her from the other players. There was a coffee shop, too, on the corner where High Holborn meets the

Theobalds Road, where I used to see her after the tennis matches, pink-faced and animated between a brace of nondescript friends.

A piece of good fortune brought us together. Paying for her coffee once, as I sat a dozen feet away pretending to read a book, she began fumbling nervously in her handbag and then in the pocket of her coat: she had left her purse behind.

Luckily I had some money.

She accepted it with a minimum of fuss – at any rate nothing like the degree of relief I had wanted – and also with a kind of knowingness, as if the transaction was almost a private joke between us and she'd expected me to leap up from my seat and suggest it. After that we started seeing each other in a low-key and rather desultory way. There was another meeting at which the three or four shillings I'd lent her were restored (the money came concealed in a white envelope which seemed to me strange and utterly intriguing, revealing a social protocol I hadn't previously encountered) and a conversation in the library. We talked about books, I remember, and what we did for a living, and I discovered what I might have guessed if I'd thought very hard about it, that she was a legal secretary in one of the big offices on the Gray's Inn Road. Curiously I recall that first talk very well: the light from the open window shining off her hair in odd glints and softenings as she discoursed seriously about lunch hours and overtime. We discovered, too, that her firm had some vague connection with Chaffington's – in fact most of the professional firms in the area were connected with each other and did little bits of business on one another's behalf – and rejoiced in what seemed to us a symbolic coincidence. Later, in what order I can't now recollect, we went to a cinema, an exhibition at an art gallery somewhere near the Tottenham Court Road, and – a tremendous excursion, this, that involved booking seats and chartering taxis – a musical in the West End.

The relationship was a source of frenzied excitement and bewilderment to me. Starting the day's work at nine, knowing that I would meet her at one, I used to divide the morning into sixteen quarter-hour phases, each one ruled on to a sheet of graph paper, and tick them off as the clock advanced (I still have some of these sheets, their backs scrawled over with calculations in my uncle's hand). And yet our conversation, squeezed out over sandwiches in a street café or seated next to each other in one of the Square gardens, was hugely unremarkable. If there was one characteristic I associate with her in these early days, it is determination. There were various little battles involving colleagues at work which she fought with the greatest persistence, and a woman called 'Collie', pointed out to me once or twice from a distance in the street, who I gathered did not treat her with complete cordiality.

I was very loyal on the subject of Collie, and hated her profoundly.

But I was excited and bewildered by Carole, and also hugely respectful, for it was clear to me that she knew a great deal more about the world than I did, and in fact was far more at home in it. She was, for instance, the first person I'd met of my own age who had any political opinions, who preferred Mr Heath to Mr Wilson and could explain the advantages of the Common Market, and she was very knowledgeable on such subjects as the tax registration of cars or who to complain to if a bus ran late. This feeling was only slightly lessened by a visit I paid to her parents' house one Sunday. The Bansteads – that was the family name – lived in Redbridge, at the far end of the Central Line, in a road off one of those great thoroughfares that snake out of London to the Essex suburbs; the noise of the traffic was everywhere. Her parents were small and somehow dusty people, united and in my eyes distinguished by the pride they took in their daughter. Their house, halfway along a pre-war terrace of identikit semis, seemed the most perfect and conscious extension of their personalities: full of dark little rooms crammed with ancient furniture, the walls hung with pictures of Carole at various stages of her teenage life. But they were hospitable to 'Carole's friend', as they made a point of calling me, and disposed to be chatty. Mr Banstead, in particular, was greatly impressed by my apprenticeship at Chaffington's. He talked once or twice of his own business affairs in such a vague and disinterested way that it wasn't until long afterwards that I found out that he was a clerk at the Eagle Star Insurance office in Gants Hill.

For my own part, I was hugely fascinated by the Bansteads. Together with their house and their daughter, they were my first exposure to a kind of lower-middle-class suburban life which I hardly knew existed. My mother, I am sure, would have examined Mr Banstead, with his row of *Reader's Digest* condensed books and his *Radio Times* in its leather cover, and Mrs Banstead – she was a pale, straggling woman irresistibly like a goose who appeared to do nothing but sit at home all day – and said something highly disparaging. To me, though, they represented not so much culture – even I wasn't taken in by old Banstead's pose of 'knowing something about books' – but a peephole on to a kind of life, that intimate Redbridge suburban life, that I knew nothing about. The Bansteads, for instance, went to church on Sunday mornings (arriving there that first Sunday I found them, prayerbooks in hand, divesting themselves of their coats in the cramped vestibule that Mrs Banstead called the 'hall'); they went on summer holidays to resorts on the south coast. These were both activities that I regarded with a kind of wonder. Even more wonderful – their trump card, so to speak – was the fact that they were Carole's parents. They were talkative people, and consequently I learned from them more about Carole than she told me herself – how she'd turned down a place at teacher-training college (Mrs Banstead thought privately that this was a mistake, Mr B. wasn't so sure) and her broken engagement to a printer's representative living two streets away ('which I can't say I ever approved of', Mrs Banstead enigmatically pronounced). And at the same time I became aware, without ever making any strenuous effort to find out, of the sort of life they lived together as a family, and the oppositions that occasionally underlay it. The Bansteads deferred to their daughter in everything, but they sometimes declined to do it without a struggle and even on that first Sunday I witnessed several bitter little engagements about the disposition of the tea-things or the scope of knitting patterns.

Oddly, the Bansteads were the subject of our first disagreement, a very minor one, but enough to rob the walk back to Redbridge station that night of its sheens and surfaces.

'You mustn't mind about Mother and Father.'

'I don't mind about them.'

'I mean . . . They always take over everything.' She bit her lip.

'I don't mind. I like them.'

'You don't *understand*,' she said. 'The times they try and spoil everything . . . As bad as Collie sometimes.'

Queerly, but not I think without all reason, the Bansteads liked me. At a time of student protests and long-haired dissent, they appreciated my deference and the way in which, as Carole informed them, I applied myself to my work. I think they thought, in their curious middle-class way, that I was a salutary influence on her. I took to spending weekends at Redbridge, interminable trackless wastes of time spent watching *The Morecambe and Wise Show* or eating fussily served but wonderfully indigestible meals. Once, I remember, I even took old Mr Banstead to a football match at Leyton Orient, where he smoked a pipe, commented knowledgeably on the game and, coming back on the bus, became highly confidential about the insurance office at Gants Hill.

And constantly, throughout all this, there was the thought of Carole springing up at the unlikeliest times and in the unlikeliest places. I used to think about her sometimes in the room at Belsize Park – a sparse, shabbily furnished room looking out over a row of perpetually weeping trees – as the night wore on, and the stock of shillings I kept for the gas meter dwindled away to nothing, and my face – glimpsed in the cracked shaving mirror – turned white and ghastly from want of sleep. At other times her presence became so tangible and unbearable that I took to leaving my desk, hurrying to a pay-phone on the corner of Red Lion Square and breaking an absolutely savage proscription on telephoning her at work. I don't know what I thought about her. I think even at this stage I'd worked out all the disadvantages that any kind of life with her would mean, and I'm certain that by then I'd already divined the glimmerings of everything about her that was later to exasperate me: her tendency to domineer, and her ineffable complacency about almost every aspect of her not very remarkable life. But it took no effort of will to ignore these conclusions: it was all, so to speak, part of the business. Mr Banstead and Mrs Banstead, *The Morecambe and Wise Show* and the endless traffic, it was all somehow inescapable and undeniable. I suppose I must have seemed particularly thoughtful at the time, because Ekwall swiftly established what was afoot. 'No doubt about it, my boy,' he said one night as we queued in the foyer at the Albert Hall, waiting to see a concert by Captain Beefheart, 'you're in love. Now is she – I'm presuming it's a she, you see – blonde or dark, eh? And are you going to tell me about it?' So I told him about it – not everything, which was perhaps an ominous sign – but with a fantastic cheerfulness that I'm confident was what I was experiencing at the time.

Curiously she never took to Ekwall, never quite saw the point of him or his function in my life. Quite early on in the affair I convened a grand meeting with the object of introducing them, of allowing Ekwall to bask in admiration of her and vice versa, but it hadn't the slightest effect. Afterwards she embarked on one of those brisk, impartial analyses which I remembered from the Redbridge supper table.

'I'm sure he's very clever and everything . . .'

'He writes poetry,' I suggested. 'Very good poetry, some of it . . .'

'I wonder how he lives,' she speculated. 'That is, what does he live *off*?'

'I think his parents give him a bit.'

'Still, it's not as if poetry was a job or anything.'

We were sleeping together by this time. In retrospect I don't know how we managed it. We did it at Belsize Park, in the house at Redbridge when her parents were away. They were joyless interludes: tense and furtive episodes which bore no relation to the feelings that I incubated about her. I don't think she enjoyed them much. Once, I remember, the Bansteads disappeared for a whole weekend to visit some relatives in Suffolk and we spent the time together. I recall waking up in her parents' bed, very late, with autumnal rain breaking against the window, as she snored gently beside me, and ghastly, embarrassed meals around the family table under the big old pictures in their frames.

Occasionally we had disagreements, intense, passionate disagreements that I could no more accurately reproduce than my childhood dreams. The following is a specimen:

'Do you love me?'

'Yes.'

'You shouldn't say things like that. After all, we hardly know each other.'

'Yes we do.'

'. . . Mother and Dad were engaged for three years before they got married. So she could be sure, she said. And then he took this woman at the office to a dance, and she nearly broke it off.'

For some reason I never believed the story about Mr Banstead and the woman at the office. I knew Mr Banstead wouldn't have had the guts.

'Anyway, I do love you.'

'There are some nice houses,' she said, 'out Wanstead way.'

And so you'll understand, perhaps, how the first great crisis of my young life came about. My mother dying, Ekwall, Carole and the queer, semi-genteel world of Redbridge – all played a part in the predicament in which I found myself. My work fell off, I shirked around the place at Red Lion Square and the various people who had congratulated me on my prize for auditing were heard to remark that none of the young men Chaffington's got these days was reliable any more. Worse than this, though, was the curious sense of listlessness that infected my life, and which had the effect of rendering the brightest experience pale and humdrum. I remember spending a whole long Sunday – my twenty-second birthday, as it happened – sitting in the room at Belsize Park staring first at the grey flock wallpaper, then at the rows of books on the shelves – a miscellaneous collection that included *Zen and the Art of Motorcycle Maintenance* and *Tolley's Tax Guide*, finally at the weeping trees in the street, and then going out to wander dejectedly through the twilight into Hampstead and Kilburn and a great stretch of north-west London.

All this finally became clear to me in a melancholy interview conducted with one of the Chaffington partners. He was a polite man (all the Chaffington partners were polite – they could sack an articled clerk without batting an eye) and the sedative effect of his smiles and periphrases was such that it wasn't until the very end of the interview that I began to understand his insinuations. I knew, didn't I, that my conduct was, well, not of a kind of which the firm could approve? I realised, didn't I, the implications for my future? I appreciated, didn't I, how greatly it pained Chaffington's to convey these kind of admonitions? (I remember nodding seriously at each of these suggestions.) Even then, the old gentleman diffidently proposed, they might have felt able to make an exception, had it not been . . . And here he produced a certain ledger which I vaguely remembered looking at in a fit of late-afternoon depression two days before. I understood, didn't I, that Chaffington's prided itself on its professional standards, and that the ledger's inaccuracies had only by the merest chance been kept from reaching the eye of the client himself? Twenty minutes later I found myself sitting under the tree in the Square carrying my briefcase, a copy of *UK Generally Accepted Accounting Practice* and an envelope containing four weeks' wages in lieu of notice.

Oddly enough I didn't then – and don't now – bear the old gentleman any malice, for he was only acting according to what he imagined were the best interests of us both. Even more odd, perhaps, I wasn't at all cast down by this reverse. So far as I remember I walked airily into Soho, watched a film in one of the afternoon cinemas, ate a pound dinner at a wonderful restaurant called the Stockpot in Panton Street, and ended the evening in an advanced state of intoxication with Ekwall somewhere in Somers Town.

Carole, understandably, was aghast.

'You don't mean to say you've lost your job?' she said when I told her. 'What *are* you going to do?'

'Get another.'

'How? They'll want references, and who's going to give you one? How could you be so *stupid*?' She was genuinely distressed, far more so than I was. I didn't then know of the fear of 'the sack' that still hung over the sequestered world of Redbridge.

'But you said yourself that you were thinking of leaving Halperin's . . . That you couldn't stand any more of Collie.'

'That's different. That would be my decision. You've just been thrown out into the street.'

There was a lot more of this. By the end of it I understood that I'd been shamefully negligent in allowing myself to be sacked, that the law required firms like Chaffington's to follow set procedures in these cases, and that I'd allowed myself to be made a fool of. I have a vision of Carole, very red-faced and tearful, lecturing me on this topic in a café near Chancery Lane, and ending rather lamely but perhaps ominously that 'Mother and Father will be so disappointed'.

I suppose I could have averted nearly everything that followed by giving up there and then – repudiating Carole, avoiding Ekwall, looking upon the old gentleman in Red Lion Square as a disguised saviour. Very likely if I'd been older or wiser I would have taken this sensible course, packed my bags and gone back to Norwich where at least there existed a world that I knew about and where I certainly wouldn't have starved. But I was twenty-two, and self-willed in a way that is now entirely beyond my comprehension. Worse, I felt that I'd by no means exhausted the pleasures that London, which continued to fascinate and startle me, could offer. And so rather than admit defeat, and with a kind of circumspection that now rather alarms me, I put the four weeks' wages, together with various other small amounts that lay to hand, in a Post Office savings account and resolved to live modestly until such time as I could find another job. Feeling a need to tell someone other than Carole or Ekwall of this resolve, but finding that no name came immediately to mind, I wrote to my uncle at an ancient address that fell out of an old pocket book informing him of my intentions. It was 1974 and I had been in London four years.

In the event the Post Office money stayed untouched, as I found another job almost immediately. Travers & Peabody occupied four rooms of an upper storey in Hatton Garden, advertised incessantly in the trade press for 'part qualifieds' and were the kind of small accounting firm whose clients feel the need of someone to persuade the Inland Revenue of the legitimacy of spending four-fifths of your income on 'personal expenses'. They acted mainly on behalf of commission agents – weather-beaten middle-aged men who arrived on the premises bearing sample cases – and small jewellers, and maintained a fluctuating staff of five. There was no agitation about references.

I had been warned, on my departure from Chaffington's, about firms like Travers & Peabody.

Travers & Peabody I discovered on my arrival there that first Monday morning to be purely nominal. In their place I was inducted into the business by the firm's general manager, Mr Holroyd, a sad-looking middle-aged man who wore a pair of striped trousers so old that they shone, rather in the manner of black satin. He cheered up, though, on learning that I'd been articled to Chaffington's. 'Very superior firm, I b'lieve. Senior partner comes in at eleven and lunches out, I dare say. Accounts at twenty-eight days and that sort of thing. Well, you won't find much of that here, I can tell you.' He was right too: Travers & Peabody offered up their invoices at seven days' grace, and penalised defaulters by adding two per cent interest for each succeeding week. 'A highly equitable system,' Mr Holroyd proposed innocently. 'At any rate we always find that it works.'

What else to say about Travers & Peabody? The staff divided neatly into cheery and profoundly anonymous youths of about my own age and broken-down old men superannuated from the big firms. There was a dreadful old wreck of about sixty, I remember, whose first act on arriving at the office was to remove his false teeth and place them on his desk, the better to drink his tea. Mr Holroyd looked benignly upon this person. 'Does us no end of good,' he would say, 'having someone like old Powell here. You see, *he worked at Coopers & Lybrand once.*' At times when Mr Holroyd was out of the office, and the rest of us grew boisterous, Powell would occasionally remonstrate that it wasn't quite the thing'. I had a desk looking out in an easterly direction along Hatton Garden, which afforded interesting prospects of sloping rooftops, gleaming frontages under striped awnings, and black-coated Jews going about their business.

In the middle of this induction my uncle telephoned, using the number of the pay-phone three flights down from the bedsitting room, and I was summoned by another lodger to speak to him. My uncle was mysterious, vague and allusive. Unprompted, he issued an open invitation to supper. The address was somewhere in Putney. On the next evening, having nothing better to do, I went to visit him.

It was about eight o'clock when I arrived at Putney Bridge and set off south across the river. At night the water was as sluggish and unparticularised as ink. Eastward towards Hurlingham and Chelsea Harbour a few small craft clanked together in the shadows. My uncle inhabited a dank little street by the river's edge, one of several dark and silent thoroughfares somehow giving an impression of recent inundation. The house, grave and remote beyond black shrubberies, lay sunk in shadow. Somewhere deep within, orange lights glowed and a radio was playing. Eventually, after a noise of plodding footsteps and a painful exhalation of breath, my uncle opened the door.

There was no light in the doorway and he looked at me with a kind of abstract moroseness – he was still champing his tea and held a pint glass full of beer in one hand – until faint recognition dawned and he opened the door a shade wider and grinned hugely.

'I b'lieve it's young George. Who'd have thought it, it *is* young George. You'd better come in. Greta, it's George! George, as I was telling you about.'

At the farther end of the passage in which he stood a light went on and I became aware of a plump, blonde woman of the type infallibly characterised by my mother as 'brassy' standing in an inner doorway. She, too, bore evidence of an interrupted meal, in this case the remnant of a sandwich clasped between the finger and thumb of one hand, but she was smoking a cigarette, negligently and almost insouciantly out of the corner of her mouth, and seemed highly amused by something.

'I told him, "Put your drink down before you open the door," ' she said equably. 'You never knew anyone like Ted for rushing about things. I've seen him go to the post office with a dinner plate in one hand.'

From the doorstep I made a vague, temporary stab at assimilating the aspects of my uncle's character and temperament which this tableau revealed. The house, I now saw, was substantial and not badly decorated: there were sporting prints on the wall and a coatstand draped over with an immense sable jacket. Greta, now revealed by the light to be about forty-five, with an extremely pink complexion and carmined fingernails, was further evidence of the way in which my uncle seemed to have moved up a gear, become in some mysterious way a more substantial figure. Something of these inferences seemed to have occurred to my uncle, as he transferred the pint glass from right hand to left and gripped my forearm in a savage grasp.

'I b'lieve,' he said, 'as we've just about finished supper, why don't you come back here, into the office, and we can talk a bit?'

He led me off along the passage, past the open door from which the noise of the radio buzzed – I had a momentary vision of a flaming orange carpet, piled newspapers, Greta's face under the lamp – and towards another room, again in darkness, to whose centre he gently propelled me before switching on the light. The effect of this reversal of the ordinary processes of hospitality was bizarre: dazzled by the blinding light, I took several seconds to register anything of my surroundings. The first impression was of extreme untidiness: of papers stacked haphazardly over chairs and carpets, a filing cabinet disgorging its contents over the floor, and a pile of addressed but unstamped envelopes. The second, oddly enough, was of a photograph of my mother in a cracked gilt frame above the fireplace.

'Found that in Bright Road after the funeral and took it,' said my uncle easily. 'Didn't think you'd mind.'

It occurred to me that I'd never seen my uncle on his own territory, so to speak, and that previous encounters with him had always been in Norwich or on the neutral ground of trains or railway stations. Later on, in the big house at Sunningdale, or even in the hotel suites from which my uncle sometimes conducted his business, I didn't find anything to diminish this first assessment, which was of an overwhelming obsession with clutter, a complete inability to distinguish between the usefulness, or otherwise, of any item that came into his hands. Or, worse, an actual relish for huge quantities of junk and the problems of taxonomy that it posed. He was never so happy, I discovered, as when attempting to impose some order on the squalor of his abodes – inventing a new filing system, say, or storing things in a collection of plastic refuse sacks.

'Famous old place this is, isn't it, George?' my uncle exclaimed. 'Got it through an ad in the paper. As easy as that. Rang a man up, signed a piece of paper and we were in. Pictures. Furniture. You should see the bedrooms! Everything just as you'd like. And no expense spared on the fittings. Just look at this now.'

He picked up a flat, oblong canister which turned out to conceal a cigarette lighter and lit a cigar with it. The flame, held for a second close to his face and combined with the dark of the window, gave it an odd, Mephistophelian glint. I recognised immediately another side of my uncle's character, which I remembered from our graveyard interlude: that fusty, impressionable, antiquarian side, delighting in knick-knacks and trumpery rubbish that 'something could be done with'.

So many descriptions were written of my uncle in the period immediately after this time – the period when he began on his startling ascent through the social and commercial world – that it's important to me to set down an account of what he looked like at this early stage in his career, before photographers and public relations men and assistants took him up and worked on him and changed not a little of his external character. It seemed to me, looking at him then, that he'd shrunk somewhat since the day of my mother's funeral, grown even less tidy and presentable. The hair was mostly grey now, thinning over the peak of his scalp and forming a cluster of exiguous curls at the back of his neck. He wore an ancient shirt, devoid of buttons but reined in, if not wholly subdued, by a lavishly styled but extremely dirty waistcoat, out of whose pockets protruded items such as handkerchiefs, elastic bands and what looked like a packet of contraceptives. This impression of deep, residual shabbiness which no amount of tailoring or sprucing up could repair was heightened by a pair of faded trousers and the black gym shoes – a very shiny black, almost like ballet pumps – that my uncle wore on his feet. The overall effect was very close to absurdity – and I'm sure that if I'd come across my uncle in a shop or in Travers & Peabody's office I would have laughed – but at the same time there was something jaunty and confiding about him that redeemed this unpromising exterior. His face had grown more humorous, more droll and apparently animated by some private joke. His eyes . . . I never did reach any satisfactory conclusion about my uncle's eyes. They were vague and impressionable and whether they concealed something else that was calculating or devious I never quite worked out. Nevertheless, I've set all this down as a corrective to some of the absurdities that were later printed about him.

'Here, George,' he said. 'No need to stand on ceremony. Sit down now. I've bin wanting to talk to you. Sit down and have a chat.'

And so I sat in a small room at the back of the house on a wide, stiff-backed chair whose feet rose out of a carpeting of business papers, next to a window beyond which light glinted off the surface of the river and trains passed back and forth across the bridge, and we talked desultorily about my job and my prospects and all that happened in the year since we'd last met. It isn't an exaggeration to say that my uncle hardly listened. He was preoccupied, I saw, with something that clearly gave him deep personal pleasure but wasn't without its attendant cargo of anxiety. Wanting to uncork this reverie I asked:

'How's the toy trade, Uncle Ted?'

He looked up sharply. 'Oh, I've given all that up. Working on my own, so to speak. Doing my own thing, you might say.'

There was something in the way he said this – something resolute and nearly defiant and to a certain degree complacent – that made me pay more attention to him.

'That's right,' he said again. 'Doing my own thing now, I am. And b'lieve . . . I *b'lieve* . . . I'm going to make my fortune.'

God help me, I nearly laughed at this. Perhaps, in retrospect, I should have done – who knows what embarrassments and indignities might have been avoided? But again, there was something in his voice – conviction? assurance? – that stopped me. Instead I contented myself by saying, half-ironically:

'Going to make your fortune, Uncle?'

'That's right. You ever hear of Sandy?'

I shook my head. My uncle rummaged enigmatically in a cardboard box that lay on a large, square desk towards the back of the room, brought out a couple of nondescript pieces of packaging, looked at them rather sorrowfully, in the manner of a conjurer who has been betrayed by some renegade assistant, plunged his hand in again and extracted a small, pink-limbed doll with a kind of straw hat angled down over her forehead.

'Seen one of these before?' my uncle enquired.

'No.'

'No? Well, it'd be surprising if you had. W'd be most surprising.' (In moments of excitement my uncle scalloped conditional clauses away to nothing.) 'Sandy. Came on the American market in summer 1973. Sandy doll. Accessory sets. Sandy at the beach. Sandy at the barbecue. Sandy's beauty parlour. They were thinking of making a boy doll too – called Randy, I b'lieve – but I haven't seen one yet. Anyhow, total sales so far are ten million units, going on ten million five.'

'What's the attraction? Why do people like it?'

'I don't know. The thing is, they do. D'y'know,' my uncle said, 'they got a Sandy club in New York, with a hundred thousand members. Plus the President's granddaughters have them.'

I listened to this efficient recitation of statistics – so practised that I imagined it to have been aired many times before – in silence. Outside a train rumbled noisily over the bridge; we waited for it to pass. At the same time it was difficult to work out what my uncle proposed to do about a doll favoured by American girldom.

'Will it come out over here?'

'Oh yes.' He looked thoughtful. 'Give it time. A year. Two years. Always takes time for people to pick up on things like this. Thing is, George, I've got a feeling about this. Don't quite know about it yet but I reckon someone could make a mint if they went about it in the right way.'

'But you're not a toy manufacturer.'

'Oh, that's all by the way,' my uncle pronounced loftily. 'Someone else can do all that. I'm talking about merchandising rights.'

'Merchandising?'

'Spin-offs. Authorisation. Think about it, George! Colouring books and chocolate bars, handkerchiefs maybe. Get in on the TV, I don't know – anything! But whatever you do you stick "Sandy" on the label – it's trademarked, by the way – and whoever does it pays you forty per cent. Look!'

He produced, out of the same cardboard box, a letter, typewritten on the gorgeous, embossed notepaper of some American conglomerate, announcing that in respect of monies paid to the above-named proprietor, Mr Edward Chell of London SW had been granted merchandising licences in the product styled 'Sandy' and registered etc. for a period not exceeding three years with the option of a two-year renewal, providing that etc., etc. My uncle watched me beadily as I read it. He was sweating, I noticed, and the cigar drooped out of his underlip.

'Cost me . . . Well, I won't tell you how much it cost me, George, but I never felt safer about anything . . .

'Only needs thinking about, and we can make business *hum* . . .

'Can't think of a better proposition anyone could consider . . .'

I realised dimly that my uncle was offering me a job. As he made these vague and in no way seductive comments, I went through a gamut of emotions: the sense of being flattered, gratitude at the thought of someone I barely knew offering to help me, and a deep assurance of my uncle's innate unreliability. To the temporising that seemed the only prudent response, he proved surprisingly amenable. Remarking that in any case he had 'sprung it on me' and that 'a thing like that needed thinking about' he announced that we should go into the other room where Greta might find us something to drink.

We went into the other room – the big 'family' room I had descried beyond the half-open door – to find Greta in the act of uncorking a bottle of wine. At close range she looked less like a barmaid and more like one of the women I remembered from the Norwich department stores – Jarrold's, say, or Debenhams – whose hankering after perfume and face powder was tolerated by captious onlookers such as my mother and Mrs Buddery as being an unavoidable part of the shop assistant's life.

'I didn't think you were ever going to finish that talk of yours, so I started opening this myself.'

Though I'd been brought up to be temperamentally suspicious of women in middle age whose hair stank of perfume I took an immediate liking to Greta, which persisted throughout the years that I knew her, although I never did succeed in finding out how my uncle had met her or the origins of their long association (I believe now that he simply picked her up in a pub or on a train somewhere in the course of his travels). In fact my uncle never spoke directly to me about her, and treated her merely as a fact of his existence which, like his job and his personal habits, anyone who came into contact with him should necessarily accept.

I don't remember what we talked about that first long evening, as the mist rolled up the river and the lights from the Thames houseboats shone from the Middlesex side (the house's location appealed to my uncle and he spoke more than once of us watching the start of the Boat Race from the bridge). But I do recall my interest in the room, which was large, gaunt and crammed with an impenetrable confusion of objects, and in my uncle's treatment of Greta. They had an odd, noisy Box and Cox routine, which involved long silences and mock chastisings, but I got the feeling that Greta might be a tough customer in any serious disagreement.

She had a way of regarding my uncle (whom she addressed as 'Teddy') with a curious mixture of tenderness and exasperation. My uncle, for his part, darted back looks of unfeigned benevolence.

I came back from the house in Putney in a state of colossal perplexity. Part of this was to do with my uncle and his altered state – I wasn't then at all accustomed to the idea that the condition in which one first encounters a human being is not necessarily the condition in which he will remain. But far more of it concerned questions exclusive to myself – Carole, Travers & Peabody, destiny – all of them in some way knocked to the surface by my uncle's fervent chatter. It seemed to me that I had answers to none of them, nor to the wider generalities in which they reposed, and for the next week or so this knowledge tore and irked me.

'What do women want?' I asked Ekwall once. It was a Saturday afternoon and we were sitting in a pub in Covent Garden drinking brandy while Ekwall read the arts pages of the *New Statesman* and considered whether there was a film worth seeing.

'More than they get, that's for sure.'

'No, but what do they want? Not the obvious things. Rights and so on. But deep down?'

Ekwall turned down the corner of the page he was reading, put the magazine in his coat-pocket and swivelled slightly in his chair.

'I don't know. What the rest of us want. Love. Security. A roof over their heads. Those are the big things. The rest is just temperament. I mean, wanting men to like you. Or wanting men not to like you.'

'But why would a woman want to get married? In this day and age?'

'Look at it the other way round. Why wouldn't a woman want to get married? I mean, most of them do. The odds are stacked against the single woman. Think about it. Sniffs in the queue at the grocer's. From the other women, that is.'

'What about from the men?'

'An offensive interest or complete indifference, depending on age and taste . . . You must realise,' Ekwall went on, vaguely interested now, 'that I have no experience of this. Absolutely none.'

'Not ever?'

'There was a girl at college who thought we might go to bed together. And in fact we did – physically get into bed, I mean. But nothing actually happened . . .'

'. . . Leaving aside children,' I went on.

'But you can't, can you? Leave aside children, that is. You can be as liberal-minded as you like, the biological clock will go on ticking.'

'I don't understand the maternal instinct . . .'

'What man ever did? Look at it this way, George. You're living in a century that's witnessing the break-up of the nuclear family. At least the *Guardian* thinks it is – I never met anyone else who did. And then there's the pill and, I don't know, all kinds of things. But the trouble is, it's not going to make any difference to the way you live your life. Not now. I dare say in 2010 we'll all live in communes and no one will know who the children belong to. But for the time being . . .'

Q: What do you think your uncle believed in?

A: That's rather a large question. I think, more than anything, he believed in stereotypes. No, *archetypes.* He genuinely did believe in the existence of entities like 'distinguished nobleman of large estates', 'starving poet', 'corrupt trade unionist'. Quiddity was quite beyond him: in fact his divisions of human society were almost medieval. Then, of course, there were class distinctions. He believed emphatically in those.

Q: In what way?

A: Oh, it was very odd. Or not odd. You have to remember that my uncle was a working-class conservative of a highly intransigent kind. But all this, curiously enough, was combined with a sort of personal rebelliousness. Perhaps you could define it by saying that he thought people ought to know their places, but he was damned if he was going to know his. This put him in a rather odd relation with the people he knocked up against. Anyone worse off than him was 'no class', as he put it, but he was always terrified that the City men he met were patronising him. He could be bitterly satirical about what might be called 'society'. I remember once going to Covent Garden with him and in the interval some well-bred lady was discussing – rather loudly – the relative advantages of ear-piercing. And for years after this, whenever he heard what he called a 'woff woff' – that is, an upper-class voice – he would do an absolutely brutal imitation of this woman: *Dahs wan have wan's years pee-arsed?* Like that.

Q: Social archetypes and social class. All very secular.

A: Oh, he believed in God of course. Absolutely. And he had fantastically bizarre notions of an afterlife. For example, he always believed that his mother was watching what he did, remonstrating with him when he did something she disapproved of. And he was very keen on what you or I would regard as the most laughable speculations. For instance, I once heard him ask a bishop whether he thought there would be cars in the next world.

Q: It sounds like a joke.

A: It may well have been. One of my uncle's characteristics – his distinguishing mark, if you like – was that you could never work out whether he was being completely serious. It was the same when you came to race. Now, my uncle was fond of making little jokes about Blacks and Jews. For example, if he switched on the television to watch *Songs of Praise*, and they had a choir, and that choir contained a single black singer, he would *always* say, 'Seems to be able to follow the music,' something like that. But if you introduced him to a black person he would always be scrupulously – and, as far as I could make out, genuinely – polite.

Q: You don't make him sound – in this respect at least – a particularly nice person.

A: I don't? Well, I don't mean to. I can give you an example of how someone behaves, but I can't convey their essence. I enjoyed his company, luxuriated in it. I thought that in most respects what he did was admirable – how do I get that across? In Norwich, where I was brought up, he would have been known as a 'character'. And that meant, oh I don't know, eccentric, whimsical, slightly louche perhaps. But kindly, you know? I wouldn't want you to think that I didn't like him, or admire him, for all the stuff about cars and the next world.

It was Frances who put the sense of permanent unease which living at the Caradon entailed into some kind of context. 'Archer gives me the creeps,' she said, about a week after she had arrived. 'He reminds me of one of those serial killers you read about. The Stockwell Strangler or someone.'

'What makes you say that?'

'I don't know. Just the way he looks. I wouldn't be at all surprised if he picked up a carving knife at the dinner table one Sunday lunchtime and stuck it into somebody. Just to see what would happen.'

'Why a carving knife?'

'It would be just Archer's style. Dramatic but ineffectual. One of the things about carving knives is that you can hardly ever cut anything with them.'

Two incidents from around this time provided a revealing gloss on these insinuations. As it happened I was elsewhere in Eastwold for the first of them, known between us as 'the telephone incident'. That didn't matter: Frances described it as soon as I came back.

'It was about half-ten at night. Not later. There were still one or two people in the lounge. The old ladies watching *Newsnight*, you know. I'd just turned the light out when the phone started ringing. Quite near at hand. At first I thought it must be one of the ones in the residents' rooms. Then I realised it had to be the one in the office. That has a distinctive ring. Anyway, none of my business, I thought. Only it kept on ringing. At least four or five minutes, on and on relentlessly. You know how noise that continues at the same volume always sounds louder? Like the noise in that Kafka story?

The one about the subterranean that goes mad from paranoia? By that time it was like an electric drill about a foot from my ear. In the end I got up, put on my dressing gown and went downstairs.

'Quite a little crowd had gathered. The old girls that sit and knit in the foyer. That bloke who tried to borrow a tenner. One or two more. You could hear the phone ringing through the office door, but of course nobody would do anything. We had one of those absolutely archetypal English conversations about it. "That phone's been ringing for a long time now." "It has, hasn't it?" "Do you think one of us ought to answer it?" No sign of Archer of course, or any of the maids. In the end I simply marched into the office, where there was a dreadful smell of smoke but nobody about, and picked it up.'

'What happened?'

'That's the funny thing. A man's voice. At least I think it was a man's voice. The exact words were *Games are cancelled.* Just that. *Games are cancelled.* I said something fatuous about could he speak up or what did he want, but then the line went dead. The others were all standing in the doorway by this time, all very pleased at getting a sneak view of Archer's office, when suddenly along comes the man himself, wearing a kind of leather coat over his pyjamas, with his eyes rolling out of his head. Well, I was still pissed off about being dragged downstairs, and what with the Greek chorus hanging about in the background it was just too good to miss. So I put down the phone and simply said, "Mr Archer, Games are cancelled," just like that. And do you know, he started sweating? Uncontrollably. A split second later he'd absolutely grabbed the phone out of my hand and started shouting into it. "Who's there? How dare you disturb me at this time of night?" Blustering kinds of things like that.'

'What happened then?'

'Oh, the usual thing. People started filing away. Archer looked incredibly embarrassed and started muttering something about wrong numbers. But I could see all the time he was staring back over his shoulder just willing the phone not to ring again. Which it didn't, of course, but you had a dreadful feeling that it might . . .'

The second and even more unnerving episode took place a night or two after this at dinner. Evening meals at the Caradon were strictly regimented, presided over by Mr Archer, who made a point of carving whatever meat was on offer, from a kind of wooden dais at the far end of the room while the waitresses handed round vegetables. Usually Mr Archer carved the meat on his own. On this particular evening, possibly because there was more than one joint available, he was allowing Brenda to help him. The two of them stood side by side at the dais, Mr Archer slightly in front, each armed with a carving knife and fork. From time to time Mr Archer would turn his head and say something in an undertone. Brenda, on the other hand, stayed impassive, head lowered above the serving dish.

I was halfway through the meal when I realised that this arrangement had broken down. In fact the tableau at the dais showed a striking juxtaposition of attitudes. Mr Archer, head bent a little forward, and therefore unable to see his assistant, was still carving industriously, while continuing to mutter instructions of some sort back over his shoulder. Brenda, alternatively, had stopped attending to the meat and was standing stock-still, eyes staring in front of her, the carving knife raised in one hand, like a mechanical toy that had reached the limits of its sphere of movement. As I watched she focused her gaze, which had been fixed on some unknown obiect in the middle distance, and directed it at Mr Archer. No one who saw it could have been in any doubt that Brenda loathed Mr Archer, had reached the end of her tether with him, and that there was even a kind of insanity about her. For a minute perhaps, or even two minutes, the figures stayed in this attitude – Mr Archer carving, Brenda brooding over him like Clytemnestra – the expression on Brenda's face reaching such a paroxysm of fury that I was about to shout a warning, when suddenly Mr Archer glanced back over his shoulder and rapped out a command. Instantly Brenda's face relaxed. She gave a little start, looked round wildly, and then went back to the task in hand.

Later I said to Frances, 'Did you see the look on Brenda's face when she was standing next to Archer?'

'Too busy eating. What was it like?'

'Murderous.'

'There you are,' Frances said. 'Archer's a man who arouses strong emotions. What did I tell you?'

In the end, against all the odds, we got married. To this day I still don't know why we did it. Did you ever do something – back a lame horse, maybe, or buy a badly fitting suit of clothes – in the certain knowledge that you were making a hopeless mistake? That was the spirit in which Carole and I approached the business of getting married. We'd known each other about two years – two years of television watching, endless journeys along the Central Line, snatched intimacy and bitter argument. Towards the end the rows began to turn on the question of marriage. I remember one extraordinary one in a tea-shop somewhere near Chancery Lane that reached such ludicrous heights that even now the words stick in my head.

'I want to get married,' I told her. 'Don't you see? I want us to live together under the same roof.'

'I can't see why you're so set on it . . . I mean, I sometimes think you don't even like me.' During these disagreements, I noticed, she looked at me with an air of anxiety, a sort of subliminal worry that the world she'd picked out for herself was running dangerously out of kilter, sharpened by the feeling that she lacked the power to change it.

'Anyway,' she ended rather lamely, 'we don't earn enough. Not enough to buy anywhere. We'd have to rent.'

'There are always places.'

It was here, I suppose, that I betrayed my fundamental ignorance of what girls like Carole were like. Told that their daughter intended to get married and move into rented accommodation, the

Bansteads would have been horrified – it would have been like having an illegitimate baby; worse, in that an illegitimate baby implied some element of chance or misfortune.

'If we could get a proper house, something out in Essex say, would you marry me?'

'I might.'

'What's the matter?'

'We can't go on like this,' she said.

'Why not?'

'We just can't. Sneaking upstairs after Mother and Dad have gone out . . .' She brooded over the complexities of sex in a disapproving suburban household. 'You should see the look Mother gives me sometimes when they come back in the evening. And then, thinking all the time you've made a mistake.'

'Well, let's get married then. Make it legal.'

'You don't *understand*,' she said. 'You just don't.'

It was late autumn, just beginning to turn sharp: outside the traffic was crowding down the wet streets into High Holborn. We sat there in silence while a waitress cleared the tea-things away and the door banged open and shut in the wind. The lights were going on in the law stationer's windows across the way, and I watched what had previously been grey silhouettes turn into the outlines of human figures.

'We're going to get married,' I said, 'so you'd better get that into your head.'

She gave me an odd look then – not exactly fear, but a kind of awe mingled with exasperation, as if by making it she surrendered up all responsibility for whatever future decisions I might take involving the two of us.

'Right then,' I said, almost jauntily. 'We've decided then. We're going to get married.'

'I suppose we are . . . If that's what you want.'

We didn't go back together – she was meeting a friend from work somewhere. I remember going to look for Ekwall, not finding him, and then wandering the streets in an odd, half-exultant half-apprehensive state, exultant because I'd got what I wanted, apprehensive because I wondered if what I'd got was worth the having. Amid all this, I comforted myself with a series of complacent domestic visions: Carole sitting in a spacious, well-lit kitchen with floral wallpaper while I cooked her breakfast, the two of us doing unimaginable things like spending the day in bed or walking round the house naked. It was very late when I got back to Belsize Park, one or two in the morning perhaps, but I don't remember feeling tired. Amongst the stack of post piled up inside the front door there was a postcard from my uncle that said *Full steam ahead! Watch this space!* but I didn't give it more than a glance. I was revolving all kinds of schemes in my head: Carole, house, promotion at work. Even now, writing this, I feel it again – that odd excitement of life somehow beginning afresh, those crenellations spun out of freezing North London air.

After this things happened very quickly. The Bansteads greeted the news of our engagement with a weary satisfaction. In the two years they'd known me, the hundred or so Saturday nights I'd sat in their front room and watched *The Morecambe and Wise Show*, they'd been too polite, too tethered in the protocols of their class, to ask me outright how long this protracted courtship was going to go on, but I could see from an occasional glint in Mrs Banstead's eye across the teacups that the thought was in their minds. They used to leave property gazetteers around the place too – seriously. They genuinely believed that a good way of administering a hint to a man that he ought to marry their daughter was to decorate an armchair with copies of the *Redbridge Advertiser*. In the end, when there was a ring and talk of an engagement party, they came down very handsomely. Mr Banstead produced £300 for furniture and Mrs Banstead provided carrier bags full of confidential items hoarded across the years against 'Carole's bottom drawer'. At the time I fancied I could separate out the mixture of emotions they displayed: relief, at having measured up to some exacting social yardstick; satisfaction, at having found someone whose good opinion of their daughter confirmed their own; and faint condescension. Now I'm not so sure. I think they were simply proud, unassertive middle-class people who wanted to do their best by their family, even if it meant welcoming into it interlopers of whom they didn't really approve.

For some reason I'd assumed that the wedding itself would be the least troublesome part of the business. I couldn't have been more wrong. In fact the six months or so of our engagement were the first real eye-opener on the kind of life I'd stumbled upon out here in the east London suburbs, and in particular on the rituals around which people like the Bansteads conducted their lives. I saw that the skirmishes around the supper table, the bewildering ordinances about thank-you letters and 'seeing people', were only a preliminary to the really serious business that lay ahead. Almost from the start, for instance, there was a determination to emulate, if not surpass, something called 'the Harrison wedding', which turned out to have involved a cousin of Carole's some years back. Photographs of this event – its marquees, its dappled lawns, its morning suits and its charged glasses – were passed round by Mrs Banstead with a kind of reverential fervour. There was talk, too, of a 'carriage' to take us to the church, half a mile away in Redbridge, and 'favours', which I'd assumed to have died out sometime at the end of the nineteenth century. But no, they were all going strong here in Essex in the mid-1970s, and one of Mrs Banstead's first decisive acts on learning of our engagement was to send out for half-a-dozen caterers' catalogues.

Why did I go through with it? On the one hand, I suppose, because it was something I had brought into being and thought I ought to have the conviction to follow through; on the other because I genuinely had no idea of the willed complexities in which I'd mange to entangle myself. Each stage of the preparations, I remember, involved an argument: about where we should hold the reception, about who should be invited, about what they should be given to eat, with Carole and Mrs Banstead goading each other to frenzied heights of expenditure. I remember above all a discussion about morning coats – there was a particular style then offered by Moss Bros called 'Mr Darren' that Carole wanted me to wear – but . . . In any case, the details aren't important. It was the general air of being caught up in something immensely serious and profound and at the same time wholly inexplicable that frightened me, and which I could never quite subdue (Mr Banstead, I noticed, just kept quiet and looked miserable while these arguments were going on: he confided to me once that he thought 'the ladies were rather, h'm, overdoing it'). Something, more to the point, that only women could come to terms with. I watched Carole going about the preparations for the Great Day – it was called the Great Day, without a hint of irony – and she did so with the grimmest determination, brow perpetually furrowed, lost in some impenetrable world of bridesmaids and 'proper' orders of service. There was a particular moment once – it may have been during the argument about the morning coats – when she said, rather sorrowfully, 'You only get married once, you know' – and she said it with absolute seriousness: in fact I think it was the most seriously meant thing that she ever said to me. What do you do in such circumstances? I suppose that if I'd had any gumption I'd have given the whole thing up there and then, but I didn't. And in any case I could see the preparations going on around me, and the money being spent, and I believe that I was actually rather scared at the violent social forces that I'd nudged into being, and concerned to propitiate them as best I could. I don't think anyone suspected what I really thought, but I caught Mr Banstead looking at me once or twice – he was a shrewd old file in his way – and wondered if he had an inkling of what I was going through. Not that it would have mattered if he had. The Bansteads were decent enough people, but you couldn't talk to them, not about anything proper. I once asked Carole if either of her parents had ever volunteered information about sex or money and she said no, not ever. And that was the thing about them, really, the sense of a world governed by private codes, where nobody asked anybody a question because they knew the answer in advance. I went out for a stroll once with Mr Banstead, a week or two before the wedding, while the women were ensconced at Berkertex Bride, and there was a brief moment when he looked as if he was going to say something relevant to the topic of marriage, what you might expect from it, even his own experiences in the field, but then something else came up and the subject was dropped as quickly as it had arisen.

Of the day itself I don't remember very much, except that it rained and that I had a furious headache as a result of the previous night's carouse with the people from Travers & Peabody. In the event 'carriages' were unprocurable, and we went to the church in hired cars. Ekwall was best man. We hung about together in the porch smoking cigarettes, with rainwater dripping off the gables on to our silk hats, and even then I was still wondering whether I could get out of it in some way. I'd seen a film once where the bridegroom just disappeared, leaving a church full of guests, and went and spent the night in a pub. But the logistics were impossible. And I knew that even if I were to pursue this course somebody would find me out, track me down and punish me. I had a vision of Mrs Banstead coming upon me in Travers & Peabody's office with a raised umbrella, or Mr Banstead mowing me down on a pelican crossing in the family car. Something of this disquiet seemed to have occurred to Ekwall, because he said at one point:

'Do you seriously want to go through with this?'

'No option.'

'Seriously though. Have you thought about it? Really, I mean? The country cot and the pot of pink geraniums. The *wifey*.'

'Do you know her father's spent fifteen hundred pounds on this?'

'It's just money.'

'To you, maybe.' I remember being adamant about this as I said it. 'Not to him.'

'Well, have it your own way,' Ekwall said. And for perhaps the first time in our friendship he looked slightly pained.

'Car's coming,' somebody said as I stared back. 'Better get inside.'

After this I lose track. I remember my surprise at seeing Carole advance along the aisle of the church – surprise because her face, shining with make-up beneath the veil, bore no relation to the one I knew; Ekwall dropping the ring and an inglorious scramble to prevent it falling into a grating; grave middle-class voices singing 'Jerusalem'; fleeing through the porch in a hail of confetti. In the car, as the driver surveyed us tolerantly in the mirror, she became violently proprietorial: sprucing up a limp Moss Bros cravat, fastening an undone button. Slightly absent and certainly not pleased.

'Are you all right?'

'Of course I'm all right.'

'You look very nice.' This was a lie. She looked tired and harassed, and the make-up had robbed her features of any distinction.

'So do you.

'I *did tell* Mother about that hat,' she said bitterly, a moment later. 'That it wouldn't go with the green. But she never listens.'

'No need to worry about that,' I said, mock-jauntily.

'I suppose not . . . It's just that I did tell her.'

The reception was at a hotel annexe somewhere near Gants Hill. There were two surprises. The first was the spectacle of my uncle, whom I hadn't remembered signifying his intentions of attending, sitting on his own at one of the side tables. The second was the presence of Collie, who turned out to be a meek, soberly dressed little woman of fifty and not at all the dragon of Carole's accounts. My uncle laughed uproariously during the speeches, which were facetious and feeble: he wore a pair of half-moon glasses now, I noticed, which made him look slightly owlish. Sweat coursed over his red, shiny forehead. Towards the end I found him lingering next to a sideboard littered with half-drunk cups of coffee, dirty plates and smoking ashtrays, and making vague little motioning signs with his forefinger. He seemed very knowing and confidential about the whole thing.

'Nice affair, George. Service. Reception. Hospitality. Everything.'

'I'm glad you could come, Uncle Ted.'

'Couldn't stand by and not see my own nephew get married. Wouldn't do at all.' He looked round the hall for a moment – at the wilting bundles of streamers and the knots of elderly ladies comforting themselves with tea, a general air of exhausted good fellowship – a shade critically, I thought, as if he felt that his initial summing-up might have been premature. 'Cost a fair bit, I shouldn't wonder?'

'I didn't ask.'

For some reason he was delighted by this. He gave a little whoop of amusement and had to rescue the glasses from the bridge of his nose with a whisk of his pudgy hand.

'You done well with the girl too, George. I was watching her earlier on. A big, *capable* kind of girl, I reckon?'

'I suppose so.' Something from the past grabbed at me, and I said: 'Do you remember my parents' wedding, Uncle Ted?'

He seemed a bit taken aback by this, took a sight on the throng of people and a clump of adenoidal bridesmaids – they were remote Banstead cousins, dredged up from God knows what tangle of ancestry, whom I never set eyes on again – and nodded. 'Quiet affair, George. Very quiet. I was best man. Made a speech and all, though I don't think your mother wanted me to . . .'

'Why not?'

'Oh, I couldn't explain it in twenty minutes, George. Not in an hour.' Mr Banstead, I noticed, was lurking a yard or so away, obviously on thorns to impart some confidence or other.

'I suppose so.'

'Ah well.' And here my uncle paused suddenly, lost in some peculiar reverie of wistfulness and bygone satisfaction. 'Anyway . . . I got to be going now. Things to do. Business. I'll be in touch.'

I watched him go shambling off through the throng of guests towards the door and out into the dark Essex night.

And that is nearly it about the wedding. Several hours later we found ourselves in a hotel in Kent, en route for Calais. I remember looking out of the window to inspect a churchyard full of ghostly moonlit gravestones that abutted the hotel grounds, while Carole padded exhaustedly and resentfully around the room, and the sight of her fat, white haunches in the shadow.

'What do you think about being married?' I asked her at one point during the night.

'I don't know.'

'Are you happy?'

'I don't know. I'm very tired, George, and there were all sorts of things I thought I'd put in my case that I think I've forgotten, and . . . *I didn't think it was going to be like this.* But perhaps it'll all look differently in the morning.'

'Perhaps it will.'

When I woke up it was a half-hour or so after dawn. For some reason I didn't feel like sleeping any more, so I put on my clothes and went downstairs through the dead, empty corridors, found a side door that was unlocked and wandered out into a tiny, overgrown sliproad – it was no more than a farm track – overhung by great drooping trees. In the distance fields ran uphill towards a line of woodland drenched in mist. A vague white snuffling presence grouped behind the hedge turned out to be cows huddled together in the wet grass. The air had a raw and curiously bitter taste, and I stood there for a moment breathing it in and wondering what to do. Even now, I supposed, there was nothing to prevent me leaving, no real force that could compel me to stay, to go back to that dreary hotel bedroom and pretend that I hadn't made the wrong decision. Reaching into my pocket I found the two tickets for the Channel ferry. I could simply throw them away if I wished. Suddenly and dramatically it began to rain. The cows bellowed dejectedly behind the hedge. Northwards, beyond the trees, mist was streaming down over the damp fields. Still clutching the tickets, I began to walk back.

And so we went off on our honeymoon, came back from it, began on our married life and were about as thoroughly unhappy as two people can be who have made a calamitous mistake and realise that it was in their power to prevent it. We lived in Redbridge at first, in a ghastly two-bedroom affair half a mile away from her parents which Carole thought had 'possibilities'. Mrs Banstead didn't visit more than three times a week. I used to come back in the evenings and find them sitting on either side of the fire like a couple of malignant sibyls. It was 1975 now, 1976. Amazing how quickly time passed, back then. One moment I'd been a boy of twenty boozing with Ekwall in Dean Street whose only problem was whether I could afford the bus fare back to Belsize Park; the next I was a married man with a Woolwich Building Society mortgage account and an obligation to eat Sunday lunch with my parents-in-law fifty weeks of the year. Sometimes, doing the washing-up in Redbridge or during one of our rows – mostly during the rows – I used to wonder where all that past life had gone, why I hadn't appreciated it while it was there, made better use of it, until something – a voice, a phone call, soft Essex rain on the window – recalled me to the aching present.

What went wrong? After we'd come back from the honeymoon – a fortnight of low-spirited sightseeing and dismal semi-intimacy – and my initial bad temper had subsided, I decided that I ought to make the best of it. I used to bring her back little presents from the City, spend weekends decorating rooms she thought 'needed seeing to', take her out for meals, but it was never any good. Somehow marriage had knocked all the wind out of her, left her spiritless and morose. I'd lie there at night watching her lying there next to me in a fat, bovine kind of way, and want to reach out and shake her, so acute was my distress at the great weight of inertia that seemed to sit upon her. Everything about her irked me: the grim determination with which she set about 'getting the house right', a systematic campaign of refurbishment in which there was no joy, simply a resolve to effect change for change's sake; the Bansteads, who monitored these developments with a pious satisfaction; the evening parties of work colleagues and their husbands which were her idea of entertainment. Fundamentally, I suppose, all our perceptions of life differed. I can still remember the patient, sedulous way in which she 'arranged' the front room in Redbridge, filling it up with pretentious knick-knacks and absurd little piles of pottery, the arguments we had about pictures or television, or fifty things that weren't important in themselves but betrayed the deeper malaise. She knew nothing, I realised, about books or art – just a few vague but tenaciously held opinions picked up at school and buttressed by her parents. As for Mr and Mrs Banstead, they haunted our house like a pair of ghouls. Once we began on the decorating, Mr Banstead took to coming round at odd hours with lengths of plywood and paint samplers: I think he saw me as a kind of surrogate crony that he could have man-to-man chats with, but I always fended him off. Oddly enough, his is the image that stays with me most from those days – fiddling about with a tape-measure in the kitchen or wandering from room to room with a hammer in one hand and a couple of rawlplugs sticking out of his mouth.

It was a queer kind of life, those old Redbridge days: sitting on my own late at night in the front room reading *Vanity Fair* or *Jude the Obscure*; hearing Carole roaming about in the bedroom above my head; taking her on dismal Sunday-afternoon 'drives' to Ingatestone and Brentwood; staring out of the kitchen window on endless weekend afternoons at the backs of the adjoining houses; and it took only a few months or so to establish that it had all been a terrible mistake. In the end I simply took to spending as much time as I decently could out of the house – going to the football at Orient or West Ham on Saturdays or working late at Hatton Garden. I was still at Travers & Peabody, which was precarious if you like – the Institute was forever talking about closing them down or suspending one of the partners – but in a strange way I enjoyed it. At Chaffington's there'd been this great illusion of gentlemanliness, that 'commerce' was conducted by silver-haired chaps in pinstripes at desks in EC2 who'd all been at school with each other. Working for Travers & Peabody you saw business as it really was: shifty-eyed commission agents worried that the Revenue was chasing them for three years' unpaid tax; half-dead 'family' concerns in moribund parts of the East End where the profits were sliding, the leases were running out, but the old father still believed that some miracle would enable him to transfer everything to a layabout son just itching to squander the money on women and the dog track. I was an audit manager by this time, too, which meant that I had a couple of trainees to order about and a table of my own to sit at and smoke cigarettes while the junior brewed tea and looked out back numbers of *The Accountant.*

Most of this time, when I wasn't worrying or wandering around Redbridge, and quite a lot of the time when I *was* doing these things, I spent thinking about Carole. Her spectre visited me with unfailing regularity: swooping down over the steps at Chancery Lane station, looming up over the streetlamps at the day's end. At first I thought about her with a seething, irrational fury, later with a colder, more calculated anger, finally with a kind of intrigued neutrality, but she was always present, more present, in fact, than at the times when I was actually talking to her. What I suppose I wanted was some kind of explanation: to know how the person I'd been obsessed with had turned into the kind of woman who agonised over fabric patterns or marked down the night's TV viewing with a series of Xs in the *Radio Times,* but I supposed, too, that in trying to procure it I might simultaneously uncover the roots of my obsession. Well, I never found it, never really worked out why so many years' desperation had finally broken themselves here on this plump, cross-grained and imperious girl who in the end I could hardly bear to speak to. Curiously, the idea of being unfaithful to her scarcely occurred to me, not so much out of loyalty – though I did for a long time maintain that loyalty, if only because I knew it was all my fault – as from a feeling that all that side of my life was over, closed off and shut down. Whatever

Carole thought about this I never found out. She used to look at me sometimes in that puzzled, faintly scared way that I remembered from the night I'd asked her to marry me, and once, right out of the blue, when we were out somewhere with her parents, she asked me, 'Did you get what you wanted?' – so matter-of-factly that I thought it was something to do with the afternoon's shopping. It was only later that I realised she'd probably raised a question – the only question – about marriage and what I expected from it. Oh, but I couldn't sketch it out for you if I tried: the silences, and the mean, shrivelled conversation.

Sometimes I'd get a brief, tantalising glimpse of the world I'd known before Carole, the Bansteads and Redbridge. The Sandy dolls were in the shops by this time: you saw knots of them grinning at you from supermarket windows, a bit later children marching down side streets with them tucked under their elbows. My uncle sent occasional postcards – old pictures that had taken his fancy or holiday resorts in the Mediterranean – with unintelligible messages scrawled on the back. I never replied. I had a feeling that what I'd done would mark me down as a failure in his eyes; a suspicion, too, that my uncle, whom I'd always regarded with tolerant disdain, was drawing away from me, spiritually reinventing himself in a way that I could never hope to follow. And yet for some reason I kept the cards. Left in desks, propped up on dusty mantelpieces, they occasionally resurfaced to remind me of the life I'd left behind.

Time dragged. The hot summer of 1976 came, and the house turned into a sun-trap of boiling surfaces and dancing motes. Ekwall had gone off in a van on the hippy trail to Afghanistan or somewhere by this time, but in any case I'd hardly seen him since the wedding. I used to get up at dawn and sit in the lounge listening to the early traffic and riffling through old books while Carole slept on above me. In the evenings, when she disappeared to sports clubs or her parents, I'd drag a chair out into the dusty yard, where in the distance children scuffled and Alsatians barked, and drink my way through a six-pack of lager. Sometimes it would be gone eleven before I went in, with the din of the yard reduced to the hum of television sets behind curtained windows, the firefly lights of the Essex suburbs fading away into gloomy darkness. There were other people who did this, I noticed: baffled fathers of six who sat in deckchairs surrounded by their romping broods, who crawled and toppled over them like swarming bees; morose younger men tethered to transistor radios while their wives washed up indoors – a whole community of silent, solitary husbands cast down by the destinies they'd fashioned for themselves.

The circumstances of my removal from this slough – or if not removal then the first glimmering of another life that might be lived out elsewhere – are still extraordinarily vivid to me. It was late on in that summer – very late on, as there were leaves blowing over the pavements in Hatton Garden and a breeze disturbing the distant pennants and garage bunting – about half-past twelve in the morning, and I was lounging in the outer offices of Travers & Peabody talking to a couple of the clerks when, from twenty feet below us at the foot of the staircase, came the sound of the street door being turned. This in itself wasn't unusual. Travers & Peabody suffered perpetually from 'callers' – travellers in office stationery with trays of paperclips, insurance salesmen who sat uninvited on the one easy-chair trying to wheedle an interview, clients who 'needed a word' with the senior partner. In fact, so determined was I not to have to deal with whichever representative of these species the footsteps now resounding on the wooden stair turned up that I was bending deviously over a filing cabinet when the door opened, and so heard rather than saw the person who entered.

'Name of Chell,' a breathless but companionable voice announced to the room at large. 'That's who I'm after . . .' And then, as I straightened up, 'Why, there you are, George. Knew I'd find you!'

I hadn't seen my uncle for two years. Framed in Travers & Peabody's seedy vestibule, where shadows crept over the distempered wallpaper, he seemed an incongruous figure. Suit, carnation, black and white co-respondent's shoes – each gave notice of a visitant from an altogether grander commercial universe than the one which we inhabited. Something of this discrepancy occurred to the younger of the two clerks, who immediately jumped up and demanded:

'Will you have a cup of tea, sir?'

'Eh?' My uncle looked vaguely round the room for a moment, taking in the guttering ashtrays, the cheap suppliers' calendars on the wall and the shelf of dusty reference manuals, and then turned back. 'No, no tea. It's George I want. You busy, George?'

There was no point in pretending otherwise. My uncle nodded. 'Got something I specially want to talk to you about, George. Thought about ringing you at the weekend, but reckoned it wouldn't keep. You free to have lunch with me, George?'

'Yes, Uncle Ted.'

'Right then.'

While I pulled on my jacket and combed my hair – Travers & Peabody inclined to informality about the office – I stole a closer look at him. My uncle, feet planted squarely before the glass-fronted bookcase, was evincing the greatest interest in a volume called *Taxation of Foreign Nationals in the UK*. Clothing apart, it took some time to work out the definite change that had come over him. The hair had mostly gone now, hands, face, stomach were fatter, but there was a kind of sheen about him, a self-possession even, that I hadn't noticed before. We descended the small flight of steps to the street in silence. Outside on the Hatton Garden pavement he immediately took charge of the situation.

'Lunch, George. Where do you like to lunch?'

'There's a place in Chancery Lane I usually go.' For some reason I said this with a kind of timidity.

'No, I didn't mean that . . . Where do you *like* to lunch? Savoy Grill? Simpson's? Tremendous steak and kidney they have at Simpson's,' said my uncle reminiscently.

There was a taxi edging by that looked as if it might be about to pick up a fur-coated woman with a clutch of carrier bags, but which, seeing my uncle's raised hand, stopped suddenly alongside us. Wondering a little, I followed him into its interior and was borne away along High Holborn and towards the Strand.

'You're looking very well, Uncle Ted.'

'I am well, George. You'd be surprised. Want to know what I've been doing this morning? No? I'll tell you. Got up at five and read some prospectuses. Dull things they are, but you have to do it. Breakfast at six. Then I had Jarvis – Jarvis is my driver – bring me in. Early meeting over in Finsbury Square. Property company I've had a punt with in my time, but I'm not sure about this one. Left them at ten and went and took a walk. Do you ever go and walk round the City, George? It's the strangest place. Lothbury and Bucklersbury and those funny little streets near the Bank. Full of churches, too, that you'd never know were there. Got to the office around eleven and signed some letters. Then I thought I'd step round and look you up.'

'Where's your office?'

'Carter Lane, EC4. Know it? Handy for the trains, but it's a bit poky. We shall have to be moving soon.'

There was a briskness about the way he said 'moving soon', like a general giving orders to break camp, a tracker sniffing the air and deciding that his quarry had gone. By this stage the taxi had halted. Still trying to come to terms with the idea of a travelling salesman who had himself chauffeured around London and attended meetings with property companies in Finsbury Square, I was carried into the depths of Simpson's, where black-liveried waiters stood in little knots beneath the winnowing fans. It was here in the tiled entrance hall, caught up in the lunch-hour traffic, that I think I understood the transformation that had come over my uncle. There was a polish in the way he dealt with the waiter, a kind of habituation of gesture, that the old, battered figure from the West Earlham days could never have brought off. My uncle seemed to have realised the effect of this new manifestation of his personality, for he said, almost naïvely:

'Bit of a change, isn't it, George? Coming to eat at a place like this? Do you know, when I first came in here and looked at the wine list I was *scared*? Frightened I'd make a fool of myself, I dare say.'

A waiter approached, bearing an ice bucket from which the neck of some unknown vintage protruded.

'Not that,' my uncle said affably. 'Not that old stuff . . . Now why don't you see if you can find something you fancy, George, while I deal with the wine?'

And so I sat in the wide, gleaming room, while the last of the summer sunlight spilled in through the high windows, and did as my uncle directed. Looking back, I remember the surroundings rather than the conversation that passed between us: the damask carpet and the rolling draperies, big, red-faced men brooding over solitary meals, a general sense of self-absorption and well-being and calm, unhurried time. While we ate, my uncle talked. He did so in a curious, rambling way, pulling out scraps of information that he thought might interest me, making queer little allusions that I altogether failed to understand, discussing his business affairs as if I were an associate who'd been with him from the first. I had a sense of numberless schemes and plans, at once vast and vaguely conceived.

'What happened about the dolls?' I asked at one point.

'Oh, I got out of them,' my uncle said. 'Asked for a price. *And* got it. There's no money in toys, not on this side of the Atlantic. Thought of going into model aircraft kits – you remember those Airfix models, George? – but it's not the coming thing. No, I'm putting my money to work, George. Speculation. 'Vestments. Who knows how it might turn out? You know anything about gilts?'

'A bit.' Travers & Peabody had once possessed a client who had dealt, with catastrophic lack of success, in gilts.

'Interesting things they are, George. I've been making a study of them. All down to mathematics, you know. Working out what your profit's going to be. And when to realise it. Of course, I don't do that. But I can pay people to do it for me.'

Even at this stage I didn't know whether to believe everything my uncle told me. There was a moment, I'm afraid – somewhere during the speech about gilts – where I decided he was simply an impostor, one of the hundreds of people who in those days floated around the City on a tide of self-delusion and a smattering of technical jargon. But it was only a moment. Somewhere, I divined, my uncle had acquired knowledge, information, about the world he proposed to inhabit. This absorption in milieu became painfully apparent when the talk turned to my own affairs.

'Travers & Peabody . . . Not a good reputation, George.'

'No?'

'I've been making enquiries. Oh, I dare say they're not *a bad* firm, but you're never going to get on if you stay there. Besides, I happen to know that the next time that senior partner of yours gets brought before the Institute he won't be let back into practice.'

There was a silence while my uncle lit a cigar, a great fat thing that quivered beneath his fingers like a miniature rolling pin.

'It won't do, George. Not now. Not when there's *opportunities*.' And here my uncle looked embarrassed, as if he'd revealed something that prudence counselled him not to reveal. 'What I mean is, George, I'm in a position where I could do something for you. Now I dare say you don't b'lieve the half of it. "Here's old Uncle Ted," you're saying to yourself, "dressed up in a pinstripe suit and talking about investments." Well, you can think what you like, George, but there's a job waiting for you if you want it. Least you could do is come to my office and take a look.'

'What kind of a job?'

My uncle made a cascading motion with his hands that suggested champagne bottles detonating, or doves taking flight. 'Bright lad like you. Accountancy training. You qualified yet? Well, that's worth an extra thousand for a start. Can be my right-hand man if you like, George.'

While I thought about this, my uncle brooded over a glass of red wine the colour of blood. Then he came suddenly to attention and examined his watch. 'I got to go, George. Meeting to attend. Anyway, you just think about it and let me know ... You remember that time in Putney when I said I was going to make my fortune?'

I nodded.

'I dare say you didn't believe me. Well, I never spoke a truer word. Never did.'

For all the incongruity – and even as he spoke I had a memory of the toy salesman seated nervously in my mother's parlour – there was something irresistible about these words, something about their perky confidence, their self-assurance, that excited me. 'That's right,' my uncle said vaguely, and I realised that each of us was operating by means of some private vision that we had of the other: that my uncle perhaps thought of me as a combination of likely lad and unignorable connection; that I for my part regarded him as potentially unreliable, three-quarters comic but, above all, something known. And that, of all things, was something I knew myself to be profoundly in need of.

Afterwards we walked out into the street, where there were jacketless students loitering outside the gates of King's College and newspaper vendors selling the *Standard*. 'Start Monday fortnight,' my uncle said emphatically. I watched the taxi bear him away towards Fleet Street, aware that the world was not the same in his absence as it had been half an hour before, and that for the life of me I couldn't put my finger on the change.

There remained the business of telling Carole. I'm quite ready to admit that I was unkind about this, that I could have chosen a time when she might have been prepared to consider the idea, but did not, and that, when it came to it, I simply went home and told her. I'm not proud of it, but then I'm proud of scarcely any of my dealings with Carole. There was so much that I could have done, and so many ways that I could have mitigated the damage I caused her. Just to make matters worse, I made an extra mistake, which was to attempt to convey to her something of the romance of that lunch-time in Simpson's, my uncle and his cigar and the wine that looked like blood. It didn't work.

'What do you mean, he offered you a job?' she asked.

'What I said. In his business.'

'But doing what?'

And then it struck me that, apart from a few hints about investments and gilt-edged securities, I had no idea what my uncle wanted me to do for him.

'He said he wanted me to be his right-hand man.'

'How much is he going to pay you?'

For a moment I wondered about inventing a sum larger, but not improbably larger, than the £3,500 a year allowed me by Travers & Peabody, then I realised that the consequences would be too grave.

'I don't know.'

She started crying after that, noisily and reproachfully, sitting on a chair by the kitchen window and refusing all attempts at consolation. I gathered that I'd done something unprecedentedly foolish and wilful, so wilful in fact that I could only have done it to spite her. A bit later she said in that decisive and impassioned way women have at these times:

'You must go and see Mr Holroyd first thing tomorrow and say that you've made a mistake. Say you want to withdraw your notice.'

'I won't do it.'

'I don't understand you,' she said. 'You have a perfectly good job. With *prospects*. And now you want to throw it all away for some, some . . . With a man who sells toys . . .

'. . . As if you were doing it deliberately.'

I'd stopped listening then, but that wasn't the end of it, not by a large measure. She had the Bansteads on the case within the first half-hour, of course, and over the next few days I had a series of exhortatory visits, singly and jointly, including one dreadful episode when the two of them simply harangued me for an hour in the front room. Funnily enough, of the two it was Mrs Banstead whom I couldn't tolerate. Mr Banstead was merely cross. He knew that I'd made a decision I wouldn't be talked out of, and he just wanted to tell me what he thought of me. Mrs Banstead, on the other hand, simply chipped away relentlessly, like water dripping on a stone: couldn't I *see* how foolish I was being; didn't I *realise* how upset her daughter was, etc., etc. What made it worse was that I don't think Mrs Banstead even knew what it was that I was doing – just being told that it was a bad idea gave her an excuse to whine on in that depressing lower-middle-class voice. It was an odd experience, because it showed me what people of the Bansteads' sort were really like when the chips were down: all the sham politeness went out of the window, and you weren't left in any doubt about what they thought of a jumped-up proletarian from a council estate who'd presumed to marry their daughter. There was one awful moment – following on from the argument in the front room, as it happened – when Mrs Banstead took me on one side and frostily informed me that she wouldn't have her husband spoken to like that 'by the likes of you'.

The Bansteads! I never think about them without remembering Mrs Banstead's piteous, complaining, *good* kind of voice, or Mr Banstead bristling up in that scandalised but still painfully inoffensive way he had. In the end, of course, they knew there was nothing they could do about it, and I can recall Mr Banstead shaking my hand on the hearthrug and announcing that he intended to 'let bygones be bygones' – whatever that meant – but I knew I'd disgraced myself irretrievably in their eyes. In any case it was all slipping away, that kind of life – the clatter of the Redbridge traffic, grim dawns at the tube station, Carole's face in the summer twilight – and while one part of me regretted its passing, another was looking ahead to a new world in which my uncle appeared at the top of dusty staircases, cowed waiters with a flick of his hand, and was borne away by taxi into the heart of the mysterious City.

Q: Did you ever see her again?

A: Oddly enough, yes. Quite by chance. I was in one of the big West End stores around Christmas time, a year or two later, and literally walked into her.

Q: Did you speak?

A: Of course. After all, she had been my wife. Still was, in fact, at that point, as we hadn't been formally divorced. And I didn't feel any anger towards her. I was more afraid she'd feel anger towards me.

Q: And did she?

A: Not really. Some, perhaps. I remember she said she'd had trouble selling the house in Redbridge. I think that annoyed her.

Q: What did you talk about?

A: I don't know. What do people who haven't seen each other for years talk about? I remember her being interested in my uncle's business. We'd had a fair amount of publicity by this time, to the extent of getting our pictures in the paper fairly regularly, and I imagine she'd noticed this.

Q: Did she have any regrets about what had happened?

A: Again, I don't know. There may have been another man on the scene by this time. There certainly had been in the past. I think we swapped phone numbers and talked about meeting again, but I never tried to contact her. Or her me. Later I remember trying to get in touch about some legal thing, but she'd moved by this time and I had to send the letters care of her parents.

Q: What feelings do you have about her now?

A: Whatever feelings I have about her are coloured by the fact that it was all my fault. Well, mostly. (*Pause.*) Obviously it takes two people to contract a marriage, but it need only take one to ruin it (*laughs*). It was my fault because I stuck out for something I already knew it was foolish of me to want. That it could only end in tears. I think she was slightly stunned – and a bit anaesthetised – by my persistence.

That aside, I think I thought that she was rather complacent in the way that middle-class people of that kind sometimes are. She assumed that people like her parents and herself had a kind of God-given right to have comfortable jobs and live in comfortable suburban houses, and watch ineffable TV programmes, and not really care about anything else. But I also thought that she was slightly angry, and that the anger was to do with all that not being enough. I suppose that was part of the attraction.

Q: The rest being?

A: You have to remember that, with the partial exception of my mother, she was the only woman who had ever taken an interest in me. I mean, taking an interest to the extent of wanting to know what I thought about things, and not seeming to mind spending time with me. You can put up with quite a lot on the strength of that.

Q: But it was all your fault?

A: Oh yes. Well, at least I think so. I mean, it would be very odd if it weren't.

Idling in the residents' lounge one evening, and prompted by a pack of playing cards that somebody had left lying about, Frances volunteered to tell my fortune. She did this in the most ingenuous and amateur way, simply taking cards at random from the two or three piles placed face-down on the table before and making plausible suggestions based on what she knew or suspected of my own life. Flattered by the exercise, I was also intrigued as I imagined – correctly as it turned out – that Frances would use it as a way of projecting various hypotheses or conclusions about my character that she would never have wanted openly to discuss.

Several unexciting cards were turned up, then the Queen of Diamonds. 'There have been many women in your life,' Frances proposed. 'You have liked some and hated others. Some have hated you.'

'I don't think that's very original.'

'You don't know whether you want them to like you. If they like you, you sometimes want them less.'

This was much more interesting. I was just about to suggest that the opposite could be the case, thinking of all the women I had very definitely liked and whose complete indifference had only made me want them more, when I noticed that Mr Archer had come into the room. Normally we would have ignored him: in fact life at the Caradon largely consisted of ignoring Mr Archer and the pervasive interest he took in his guests. However, it took no more than half a minute of his presence by the door – he began by making a feeble pretence at tidying some newspapers, then merely stared at us – to demonstrate that the gleam in his eye was more than simple curiosity. Eventually he said rather wistfully:

'I could do that for you, you know.'

'Tell fortunes?'

'If you like.'

Curiously, there was something enticing in the idea of having your fortune told by Mr Archer. Everything about him suggested that as an experience it would be out of the ordinary. I looked enquiringly at Frances. The same thought had obviously occurred to her, as she winked back.

'Do you tell fortunes often?'

'It depends.' Seeing that he was being asked to perform, Mr Archer had cheered up immensely. 'Now and again. It depends who it is. Some people don't approach it in the right spirit.'

'What makes you think we will?'

'Instinct,' Mr Archer said, decisively. 'Always rely on instinct in my line of work. Now, do you want me to do you first or the young lady?'

Frances tapped her finger twice against her forehead. Mr Archer nodded. Seating himself next to me at the table he began to shuffle the cards in a practised manner.

'This is very exciting,' Frances said. 'I don't think I've had my fortune told since I was at school.'

'Ah,' said Mr Archer. 'But I expect that was a lot of silly girls, wasn't it? Wanting to know about boyfriends and exam marks?'

There was something definitely professional in the way he leaned forward over the table, gripping the pack lengthways between finger and thumb. Turning over the first card with a great flourish of his wrist and cuff, he produced the Jack of Hearts.

'What does that mean?' Frances asked. 'Something to do with love?'

By way of an answer Mr Archer raised his forefinger in front of his mouth. Taking up the cards had transformed him, I saw. Staring thoughtfully at the table he seemed a completely different person, wiser perhaps, more resourceful.

'I can see a tall man,' he intoned. 'No, two men. A tall one and a short one. The short one has gone away.'

'That must be Conrad,' Frances said. She was amused rather

than animated, but I noticed that her hand shook slightly as she reached forward to light a cigarette.

There was quite a lot more of this: a dark man about whom Frances couldn't make up her mind; a sum of money that might be anticipated, possibly from abroad; nothing definite. Listening to these generalisations, I felt mildly disappointed. Somehow I'd expected something better from Mr Archer. something more idiosyncratic.

'That'll do nicely, thank you,' Frances said, a moment or two later. 'Lots to think about. You can do his now.'

We swapped places at the table. Mr Archer gathered up the cards again and divided them. Abruptly, I noticed, his mood seemed to have changed. With Frances he had been genial, even a bit patronising, obviously enjoying himself in doling out patter. Now he looked worried. The first card was the Ace of Spades.

'Don't worry,' Mr Archer said, without much conviction. 'Often starts like this . . . I see a group of men, several men. You are one of them. There's money, but you are not happy. Another man comes . . . It is very confusing. Somebody is warning you, warning you about something. The woman is not there.'

'Is it as bad as that?'

'Difficult to say.' Mr Archer didn't seem in the least put out by this catalogue of ill-fortune. 'You see, a warning could be anything. Could be an income tax demand, TV licence reminder, anything.'

'And the woman?'

'Anyone. Wife. Mother. Someone you came across.'

For some reason I was horribly depressed by this. The first part of Mr Archer's monologue had described so accurately the events of the previous few years that for a moment I wondered if he knew more about me than he wanted to say. Perhaps this whole episode was an elaborate act of revenge, the cards left out with the deliberate intention that Frances and I should come in and start telling our fortunes? This, I reasoned, was nonsense. The cards, I knew, belonged to another of the hotel's long-term residents, an old lady who amused herself on winter afternoons by playing patience. And Mr Archer's face was devoid of the irony that might have been expected in anyone who had manufactured a practical joke.

'It all seems a bit depressing.'

'It does.'

'Not a shade of hope anywhere?'

'It's only a pack of cards,' Mr Archer said, rather brusquely.

'Even so . . .'

'Oh, for God's sake,' Frances broke in, 'will you shut up about those fucking cards? I wish I'd never suggested it.' Turning to look at her for the first time since Mr Archer had begun speaking, I discovered she was close to tears.

'Are you all right?'

'The young lady's a bit upset,' Mr Archer remarked sententiously. 'I think it's time for me to say goodnight. Dare say I've said more than I should have.' He left the room in a dignified way, while still managing to suggest that his feelings had been badly hurt. Frances and I sat and stared at each other.

'What's the matter?'

'Why do you have to take everything so bloody seriously? Why couldn't you just have treated it as a joke?'

'It didn't sound like a joke.'

'But that's the point, don't you see? Not letting things get to you.'

'I suppose so.'

Outside wind whipped sharply against the high windows. There was a storm brewing. You could always tell when a storm was brewing, Mr Archer maintained, from the way the wind came in from off the sea. I realised suddenly that he was a person of some consequence. First the business about the weather; now this. Perhaps Frances appreciated this expertise more than I had. It was hard to tell. In the distance the sea boomed. Frances was more composed now. She said:

'I think I'll go to bed. I've had enough excitement for one night.'

'So have I.'

As we passed through the foyer on our way to the staircase I stopped by the reception desk. The front door was open and a stream of cold air poured into the foyer. Outside rain was falling at an angle against the brickwork. I watched for a moment or two, wondering whether I ought to close the door or otherwise investigate, when a shadow loomed up suddenly from beneath the light and Mr Archer appeared in the doorway. His hair was plastered back across his scalp; rainwater fell in runnels over his face towards an already sodden jacket.

'Always like to go outside if there's a bit of a storm,' he explained. 'This time I got caught right in it.'

He shook himself vigorously, like a spaniel, so that water cascaded over the ochre linoleum. 'Very sorry about the business in the lounge, sir,' he went on. 'My fault entirely. Should have stopped when I had the chance.'

'It couldn't be helped.'

'I suppose not. Still.'

'I must go to bed.'

'That's right.'

Climbing the staircase, which was unlit and made hazardous by defective stair-rods, I wondered what my uncle would have made of Mr Archer. There was certainly an affinity between them, to do with self-possession, the sense of something hidden behind an unpromising façade. Whether my uncle would have welcomed this resemblance was something else. Like many people, he had a habit of disliking in other people the qualities that were his own.

'Something odd is going to happen,' Frances said when we met at breakfast the next morning. She looked curiously bedraggled, as if she had slept the night in her clothes. 'I know it is. I just know.'

I don't think I quite knew what to expect on the day I started working for my uncle. I suppose I thought I'd immediately be inducted into a gleaming universe of attentive secretaries and private sanctums, and I'm fairly certain that I imagined there would be a repeat of that ambrosial hour at Simpson's. In the end I spent the first three weeks in my uncle's employ in the basement of an office in the City Road itemising a packing case full of documents that he'd acquired as part of some queer transaction whose nature I never really determined. It was a damp, unheated room with a strip of glass at head height looking out through a dismal area towards the entrance to Old Street station, and the work would have been intolerable if it hadn't been for the company of an ancient clerk called Ridgebird whom I discovered already knee-deep in paper on the first morning I arrived.

For some reason I took to Ridgebird. He was a fantastically weather-beaten old man of about seventy, who claimed, among other exploits, to have witnessed Neville Chamberlain arriving at the Bank of England in a tailcoat for a meeting with the Governor, and to have fire-watched from a chimney stack on top of the Stock Exchange during the Blitz. The work was of the dreariest kind. The packing case mostly contained defunct share certificates, but here and there would be a discounted bill or a building society pass book dating from the 1950s, which Ridgebird seized upon like a boy pilfering eggs out of a bird's nest: he had a kind of genius for appraising the worth of a financial document in a couple of seconds. The packing case, according to Ridgebird, harboured the paper assets of a brace of liquidated companies that my uncle had bought in a fire sale, a purchase whose prudence depended on whatever we turned up. He was a talkative character, with a pair of striped trousers so old that they shone like the surface of oily water, and a passion for Victorian novels. We spent our lunch hours in companionable silence, drowsing over *Pendennis* or *Beauchamp's Career* while the rain fell over Old Street and pairs of legs, weirdly truncated at the knee, passed by the area steps.

Throughout this early and, I suspect, probationary period I saw my uncle several times. He had a habit of 'looking in', as he put it, late in the afternoon to see what the day's researches had amassed. On these occasions I sat meekly at my desk in the corner of the room while he and Ridgebird – a galvanised Ridgebird, grown suddenly brisk and respectful – conferred over the lists of salvaged scrip. I was amused by Ridgebird's grave deference to my uncle – I can remember him once setting out a chair and then dusting it down with his handkerchief in a gesture straight out of drawing-room comedy – but also intrigued, for it confirmed the picture I had built up of my uncle as someone who had transcended his origins, established himself, through some mysterious and unguessable process, into a figure of consequence. I can recall him bending over a sheaf of foolscap that Ridgebird offered him and murmuring, 'United Textiles. Lemme see. Not paid a dividend in ten years, but there's no reason why they *oughtn't* . . .' and marvelling at the stock of lore he had acquired from somewhere.

His attitude towards me in these days was approving but distant. 'Getting on all right, George?' he would ask as he rolled into the room, or 'Found anything interestin' for me today?' but I could see that it was Ridgebird he was really interested in, Ridgebird and the contents of the packing case. By rights I suppose I should have been distressed by this indifference, but I fancied my uncle was applying what his curious and idiosyncratic mind conceived of as a test: if he were to employ me in his business, whatever that business might be – and I was wholly, shockingly ignorant of what it was that my uncle *did* – then it would be wise to know what I could do. That was how I reasoned, throughout these long, autumn days, yawning in the basement and watching Ridgebird unearth a

Liverpool and District Coal Company share certificate from 1953 or poring over the Everyman edition of *The Return of the Native.*

And then on the Friday afternoon of the third week, when only a handful of documents remained to be docketed and filed, I received from a motorbike messenger – a delivery channel that I later found to be characteristic of my uncle – a summons to meet him that night at an address in Sydenham.

Chronologically I suppose the Sydenham days are only an interim in my uncle's career, a brief resting space before he moved on to grander and finer things – and I don't imagine that he stayed more than a couple of years there – but somehow they are very vivid to me: much more vivid than my married life in Redbridge or the gloomy bedsitter evenings in Belsize Park, though even those have a kind of retrospective charm that I wouldn't want to deny or minimise. At any rate I have a strong recollection of that first evening in the big dining room with the parallelogram of garden descending to a little copse of trees, light splintering off a brace of cut-glass chandeliers, and the attitudes and complexions of the people with whom my uncle had populated the place. At a decade and a half's remove I realise that they were the dowdiest kind of suburban gentry – partners in accountancy firms with their desiccated wives, small solicitors and golf club loungers – but at the time I wandered through the wide rooms listening to their conversation (they talked about school fees and the Callaghan government) with an unmitigated respect. Without stating the fact in so many words, the house stank of money. There were flowers all around, in heart-shaped vases on top of a piano, piled up in baskets on the tables and all manner of knick-knacks – miniatures and silver snuff boxes and cigarette cases – that I couldn't imagine my uncle buying on his own account. Dazzling white rugs stretched across the far end of the room and a couple of life-size stone leopards guarding the fireplace represented the limits of taste in this ornate but somehow slapdash and infinitely chilly setting.

What my uncle's guests made of all this I don't know. There was a kind of homogeneity about them, I now realise, that rather betrayed them and, though they talked knowledgeably enough about the latest West End play or exhibition, I doubt that many of them ever attended these entertainments. There was something unfeigned, too, in their interest in my uncle, the way that they appraised his house and its decorations. But to me, who had known only the middling stuffiness of Redbridge, they seemed very grand people indeed, and I was rather afraid of them. My uncle hovered in a little alcove apart from the main room, broaching bottles and directing a pair of waitresses in black cocktail dresses. He had picked a couple of cronies out of the throng, I noticed, demure little men of about his own age who called him Teddy and made what were to me incomprehensible remarks about the City. Outside rain fell over the neat, rolling garden, and I found myself, glass in hand, wandering through the rest of the house: into a wide hall where a personage in grey trousers and a dinner jacket was storing coats in a cavernous cloakroom, past a smaller apartment containing a desk, a row of box files and an engraving of the *Cutty Sark*, on again into a long, low kitchen, rather like a ship's galley, with a round glass table at the end. A plump, yellow-haired woman, discovered smoking a cigarette at the table, jumped up (half guiltily, I thought) when she saw me, and then gracefully subsided.

'Why, it's young George,' Greta said. 'Gone and got married too, by all accounts, since we last met.'

'You should have come to the wedding. Uncle Ted did.'

'Oh, we were having one of our disagreements,' she went on. 'Would have stuck pins in each other, I dare say, if I'd come. Anyhow, what's she like, this young lady of yours?'

I explained as much as I decently could about Carole and our life in Redbridge, while Greta ate olives from a saucer positioned in her lap. Outwardly as jolly as ever, she seemed faintly irritated about something.

'Happy throng not to your taste, Greta?'

'Oh, him and his parties. "We ought to entertain, Greta," he says. "Ask people round and see them enjoying themselves." Well, I'm all for that when it's friends and suchlike. Where he gets this lot I don't know. Goes round to the golf club and asks anyone he finds there, I shouldn't wonder.'

'I didn't know Uncle Ted played golf.'

'He doesn't. Well, he does, but it's the funniest thing . . . Oh, I don't *mind* if he enjoys himself. But I draw the line at asking them back to the house. If he wants to entertain them he's welcome to, but I'll just sit it out here, thanks very much.'

'I like the house,' I said, truthfully, and thinking to find a less controversial topic. It was obviously the right thing to have said, for Greta's face immediately broadened into an admiring grin.

'That's right. I've known him take trouble about things before, but never so much as he's taken over this. Do you know he had the decorating done twice because he didn't like the way the first lot had done it?' "No point in having something you don't like," he said, "even if it does cost money." Look, I'll show you.'

And for a quarter of an hour or so, with an immense gravity and seriousness that was delightful to watch, she conducted me round the house: its wide staircases and half-dozen bedrooms, its marble baths and box-rooms full of queer old lumber – dusty suitcases labelled *E. Chell* and old toy catalogues. From time to time we encountered other guests on the look-out for lavatories or cloak-rooms. On these occasions Greta bristled up furiously.

'They probably think I'm one of the waitresses,' she said. 'Wouldn't surprise me. And the joke of it is five years ago it would have been true. Used to do waitressing work back in the old days before I met Ted.'

We were back in the kitchen now, seated at the glass table with a bottle of white wine Greta had produced out of the fridge. 'How is he?'

'Ted? He's all right. Always off on some scheme or other. Goes all over the place, too. Birmingham, Bristol, Manchester. Paris it was, last week,' she exclaimed as if it were incredible that anyone should travel to another country in pursuit of business.

'What kinds of schemes?'

'Oh, this and that. Sometimes he tells me about it, sometimes he doesn't. I don't mind. Been the same ever since he sold up the toy business. One long rush. And then coming here . . . It's a funny time, George.'

I didn't quite know what to make of this, whether it was a reference to my uncle or something more obscure. Greta went on:

'Reminds me of just after the war. Everybody terribly excited and tired at the same time, and with money they hadn't had before, but desperately worried about what was coming at them over the horizon. Anyway, that's enough of me. You'd better go and see your Uncle Ted, George. He'll be wondering where you've got to.'

'I like sitting talking to you.'

'I mean it, George. He was set on you coming. "We must have young George," he said. "There's things I want to say to him." You don't want to go and disappoint him.'

Looking back, I suppose that was one of the longest conversations I ever had with Greta, but it's surprising how many of the phrases that remain from those days turn out to be hers. *Fussing and fretting over nothing* (of some business anxiety of my uncle's). *Dressed up like a pox doctor's clerk* (a particularly lurid suit he persuaded me to buy at this time). Even then, I think, I knew there was more that I could have found out about Greta, and which might have done me good if I'd discovered it – and I don't mean things destructive of her privacy or our intimacy, such as it was, but things that might have helped me to understand myself.

I wandered back into the hall to find most of the guests gone, the grey-trousered butler drinking sherry at a green baize table, and the waitresses clearing up a dismal array of half-empty wine glasses, plates streaked with cigarette ash and dirty cutlery. The air was dense and smoky. My uncle stood slightly to one side, fidgeting his hands in his pockets and looking rather red and creased, with his chin low down in his collar.

'Wondered where you were, George. Thought you might have got lost somewhere. Hah!'

I explained about finding Greta, and the tour of the house. My uncle looked vaguely discomfited.

'Greta's not stuck on these occasions. Says they're a waste of time. Can't say that I blame her, I suppose.'

'I suppose not.'

'*You* know how it is, George,' said my uncle loftily, and I saw at once that I was being appealed to in a discreet way, so discreetly that anything I said would have been gathered up and trampled on as a rebuke to my own lack of discretion. 'Have to see your friends. Once in a while. Social duty. Do it in style. If you want. Why not?'

There was something faintly querulous about the way he said this, something remote and rather peevish. I saw him look me up and down once or twice, as if he couldn't quite work out whether I counted as Greta's ally in this argument, then thought better of it.

'Glad you're here anyhow. Sorry your young lady couldn't make it.' (There had been a polite fiction about Carole's absence from the gathering.) 'Wanted to talk to you, George. Did indeed.' In the outer reaches of the hall more waitresses were removing crockery, Greta a distinct, cynical presence in the background, and we moved through them like a couple of proud, confidential kings – not, as I'd supposed, to the room with the box files and the engraving of the *Cutty Sark*, but to a lofty sitting room at the very top of the house which I didn't recall Greta having shown me, strewn with books and newspapers, where a decanter and a pair of brandy glasses stood on a tray.

'Been doing a bit of reading,' my uncle apostrophised the books. 'Extraordinary thing, reading.' They were miscellaneous volumes. *Don Juan*. A manual of dairy farming. *Crockford's Clerical Directory*. As I watched he seized some of them in his arms and began slotting them at random into the long, low bookshelf. 'One of these days, George, we'll have a good long talk about books, you and me.'

Later it would become difficult to distinguish between the various conferences that my uncle held with me in the big house at Sydenham. They concertinaed into one another, blocking out the intervening days or weeks, so that what remained was a continuous stream of conversation – or rather monologue, as it was my uncle who did most of the talking. Sometimes they began in the evening and went on late into the night – I can remember once hearing a faint snatch of birdsong and glancing out of the window to find that dawn had come up over the grey Kentish gardens and there was pale sun shining over the distant weald. On other occasions, back early from the City, they started after lunch and continued into the afternoon, until Greta, exasperated, would knock on the door and ask if she should wait with tea any longer. As far as I can recall, the tea always waited. But for some reason I have a strong memory of that first night and its properties: the books spilled out over the Turkey carpet, the brandy, which was of a particularly old and fiery sort, owls out hunting in the dusk, and my uncle prowling the room as he talked. He was cagey but affable, congratulated me on the work I'd done with Ridgebird –

apparently there'd been a couple of title deeds he'd been specially pleased with – digressed about a property concern he had some interest in, but always I could see that he was holding something back, some extra information that he wanted to surprise me with. At other times he launched on great commercial ruminations, all of which, I later saw, were to have some bearing on what followed. I can see him as he did so – a short, squat man standing four-square on the rug with one hand anchored in his pocket, savouring his reflection in the brandy glass.

'What do people want, George? Money, of course. But they want security as well. Now, how do you get security?' And he paused for a moment to look reprovingly over the top of his spectacles. 'In my day it used to be savings. But what good's savings with all this inflation, eh? Say you're retired and such, with a few thousand in the bank, how are you going to get by on savings? No, that's what the politicians don't realise. They think if you're earning then you don't mind spending. But what if you're not earning? You want a guaranteed return on your money, that's what you want.'

It occurred to me that my uncle was talking about gilt-edged securities and the advantages of trading in them, also that he – or the people with whom he worked – had devised some exceptional way of performing this trade. And, though I don't make any claims for my intuition, this, curiously enough, was how it turned out.

'You ever hear about bond-washing, George?'

'A little. Not enough to tell you what it is.'

'Kippax'll tell you about bond-washing. He knows all about it. All to do with Capital Gains Tax. Say you buy a gilt just after it's paid a dividend? Well, the price'll be lower because there's just been the payment, don't you see? Now, say you hold the same stock until just before the next dividend payment. The price'll be higher, because it's going to take into account the money due. Now, what would you do if you wanted to get the maximum return?'

'I don't know. Collect the dividend, I suppose.'

'No. There you're wrong, George.' And here my uncle looked very serious and knowing. ''Stead of keeping the stock and getting your divvy, you sell them at the higher price. That way you're not receiving a dividend payment – which is taxable – you're making a capital gain. And a capital gain up to the value of five thousand pounds isn't taxable.'

'I'm still not quite sure I understand it, Uncle Ted . . .'

'Let me spell it out, George. You're a pensioner, say, with a bit of money. A bit of money you want to make work for you. Well, this'll give you a guaranteed income and you won't have to pay tax.'

There was a great deal more of this, ebulliently dealt out as beneath us the noise of the house receded and fell away into silence, stuff about transfers, abstruse financial instruments that I couldn't comprehend without a copy of the Stock Exchange Handbook. Much of this, I suspected, my uncle had learned by rote at someone else's instruction, but here and there a pet phrase would show how he'd taken the material to heart.

'It can't lose,' he said at one point. 'That's the thing about it, don't you see? It can't lose.'

Travers & Peabody had dealt with the aftermath of many a crazy scheme of this kind over the past three years: the man who claimed to have invented a 'scientific' method for predicting the movements of penny shares; the firm that worked out an infallible way of playing the Chicago Futures Exchange. Each of them Mr Holroyd had happily delivered to the bankruptcy court. I shook my head.

'What about the capital? What about the intermediaries? What about the banking regulations?'

'Don't need capital, George. This is clients' money we're handling. All we do is take commission. The intermediaries – those little chaps as call themselves independent financial advisers – they'll come quick enough when they see our ads. As for the banking regulations, no one quite knows if we need a licence, but Kippax says there's nothing in the rules that stops us commencing to trade.'

He had it all pat, of course. Clients. Business. Profit. And such was the pitch of his enthusiasm, such were the surroundings – that it was impossible not to be caught up in it, not to feel flown, exalted and expectant. In this spirit I learned that I was to become my uncle's personal assistant (at a salary to be agreed), that a glorious future awaited me, that my life – I remember these as my uncle's exact words – had just begun, and that there was no knowing, no knowing at all, where it might end. Later, I remember, we descended to the huge, empty drawing room, where Greta sat soberly and pale-faced over the fire, and discussed what to do with me, it now being one a.m. and the last train long gone from Sydenham station.

'Can stay here if he likes,' my uncle ventured. 'Make up a bed for him upstairs.'

'Of course he can stay here,' Greta said sharply, and I got a sudden glimpse of the old days back in Putney to which I'd been a witness, back before the arrival of money and the trackless schemes which my uncle had devised, or had had devised for him, about bond-washing. We contrived a bed in a room on the first floor: I climbed into it to the sound of my uncle's footsteps rising in a series of crisp detonations to an upper storey.

And so began that unforgettable period when I laboured as my uncle's personal assistant, was party to his monetary secrets and his dearest wishes, lived cheek-by-jowl with him in the big house at Sydenham and half-a-dozen other places, and moved with him among great people in the great world. I suppose it must have lasted six years, but it seems both shorter and longer: hectic, indiscriminate, infinitely drawn out, but at the same time containing a number of dominating pictures, endlessly repeated – my uncle at his desk, outside his offices at Lothbury (formerly inhabited by a defunct metal-broker), consulting with Kippax and his henchmen. My uncle looms very large now, very bright and purposeful. When they wrote about him in the newspapers, which they did profusely and incessantly, he was always photographed at the big desk in Lothbury, cigar balanced in his thick fingers like a wand. The promotional literature issued by the firm was always in the end about him, and came in homely little paragraphs about security and the rainy day, tailed by his sprawling signature.

You mustn't think, through all of this, that I was merely a passive observer: even then, at the very beginning, I had my own ideas about things, and my solutions to the many problems with which my uncle was daily presented. In the days that followed the journalists sometimes gave the impression that I was only a tiny cog in the vast, imponderable machine that my uncle had set in motion, but I like to think that I helped him. It was I, for example, who conceived the preliminary set of advertisements, the giant ones that filled half a page of a broadsheet newspaper, in which my uncle demanded of his audience: did they want to lie awake at night agonising over an uncertain future, or sleep the sound sleep of those who knew that their money was prudently invested? It was I, too, who devised, and in the end administered, our commercial network. I spent nearly a year in the late 1970s travelling round the country from one provincial town to another meeting small accountants and financial people and urging them to recommend us to their clients. For some reason these meetings usually took place over lunch, in the back rooms of gloomy carvery restaurants, and if I try to piece together that time it dissolves instantly into a sea of pinched faces guzzling their way through plates of roast beef and potatoes. And yet I don't think, even amidst the endless plates of roast beef and the damp salt cellars, that I was unhappy. For one thing I'd never seen England before, never once in my life travelled through the place or thought that it had anything to offer me beyond the West Earlham back-to-backs or the Redbridge traffic. There was romance, consequently, in these train rides across the Lincolnshire wolds or the western marches and their endings in grey-brick termini and run-down Midlands stations. I remember once discovering Salisbury and spending a rapt half-hour between appointments looking over the cathedral and its precincts; another time riding through Suffolk very early on a November morning and watching a pair of eager grey horses come loping forward through the mist. English cities: Oxford, Cambridge, Lincoln, Gloucester. It took me until my twenty-fifth year to find them and the things they contained: cathedral closes and old stone, cobbled streets and shops selling prints and secondhand books. I used to wonder about living there when it was all over.

But I'm advancing matters, losing sight of the true march of time. Kippax belongs to this period, there are even glimpses of Helena and Lord Charlesworth and the lunch tables of Belgravia, and my uncle's manoeuvrings after the football club, when the great world lay before us, defenceless and inviting. Somehow, though, in my imagination all these things belong to the future, to another part of life, and all that remains is a confused mixture of cathedral spires, the stink of diesel and the grey horses moving silently through the fog.

Q: How well do you think your uncle handled money? I seem to remember a TV programme concentrating on, how shall I put it, conspicuous consumption?

A: I take it you mean the ITV documentary in the early Eighties? Naturally I think that was regrettable.

Q: Regrettable?

A: A good opportunity gone to waste. I seem to remember that when the idea first came up – and the TV companies were always hugely keen on my uncle – we advised him not to do it. On the grounds that it would make him look foolish. And then when he wouldn't be talked out of it, we tried to get him to send it up ... You know, allow the camera in to one of his dinners and simply have baked beans and a glass of water. In the event, it didn't turn out like that.

Q: You mean that it made him look foolish?

A: Oh, immensely. That kind of thing brought out the worst in my uncle. The very worst. If the producer suggested that he ought to do a particular scene drinking a glass of champagne and smoking an eight-inch cigar, then he'd do it. He couldn't see that he was being sent up. And this was a pity, because that was a side of my uncle that he indulged very rarely. It was almost as if it needed to be licensed by a TV producer or a newspaper.

Q: Like the 'America with Chell' thing?

A: Exactly. All dreamt up by a newspaper editor, and for some reason my uncle bit. As far as I can remember, it was some competition whereby the winners got a free flight, first-class, to

New York – with him actually on the plane – and a certain sum which they could invest with us. It was all very successful, but I don't think in the long run it did us any good.

Q: Why not?

A: It made him look like a spiv. Which, to do him justice, I don't think he was. Also it made him look as if he wanted money just to be able to spend it on rubbish. In fact my uncle was very serious about money. It was something that brought you security. Not to be thrown away on trash.

Q: Even so . . .

A: As you say, even so. And I wouldn't attempt to deny any of the stuff the newspapers came up with afterwards. I mean, it was all *there*, wasn't it? The yacht and the debentures and everything else. But I think I'd want to stress that this wasn't a normal part of my uncle's life. There were just times when he couldn't stop himself.

Q: Such as?

A: Oh, at public functions. In restaurants sometimes. You know that photograph of him drinking champagne out of Cilla Black's slipper? I was there. I never knew why he did it. But so much of it was the child-in-a-toyshop mentality. I mean, I remember once being with him at, I don't know, perhaps it was the Connaught, when they brought the wine list. Normally he would simply have ordered a bottle of house red, or a medium claret. But somehow – it may have been that he'd pulled a particularly adept stroke of business that morning – he got it into his head that he'd like the most expensive bottle they had. Just to see what it tasted like. And of course they produced something that cost £175.

Q: What did it taste like?

A: Warm raspberryade, so far as I remember.

Q: Did he mind?

A: I don't suppose he noticed. As I say, the mentality was that of a child in a toyshop. And he had this quite naïve idea that something was always worth what you paid for it. Also, at times like these, that all economies were false. I remember him once ordering two half-bottles of something when, inevitably, it would have been much less expensive to buy a single bottle. That kind of thing . . .

A highlight of life at the Caradon was Mr Archer's periodic rebukes of his staff. These took place at unexpected moments. You might go downstairs late at night to fetch something from the residents' lounge and find him haranguing Alison, a girl who worked in the kitchen, as she made her way out of the foyer towards the hotel door. Alternatively, it was possible to come across him at unearthly hours of the morning upbraiding the chambermaid as the two of them moved in and out of empty bedrooms. Undoubtedly Mr Archer enjoyed these occasions. The oracular nature of what he had to say, and the length at which he said it, suggested that he had composed and memorised the words in advance. Comfortingly, there was no embarrassment in breaking in on one of these scenes, if only because none of the Caradon's employees gave the slightest sign that they listened to what Mr Archer was saying, much less intended to take any notice of it. It was as if both parties realised that allowing Mr Archer to let off steam in this way was a necessary part of employment in his hotel. Certainly nobody bore any malice about it. The exception, perhaps, was Mrs Bennidge, who 'helped out' in some unspecified way upstairs. Mr Archer's treatment of Mrs Bennidge showed an interesting side to his character. With the other members of his staff he was simply irritable: there were specific failings that he wanted to address. With Mrs Bennidge it was clear that these public rebukes had a kind of moral dimension, that it was Mrs Bennidge's whole attitude to her work, to the hotel and to life in general that upset him. For her part Mrs Bennidge made it just as clear that she resented these pep talks, but was too frightened of crossing Mr Archer to make a serious protest. This gave their dialogues a touch of unease that other disputes lacked.

Usually these arguments took place in the foyer. Mrs Bennidge, a burly, eternally put-upon woman who was said to 'give her husband a time', normally stood with her arms folded on one side of the reception desk, while Mr Archer prowled round her. His tone was exhortatory. In fact, in lecturing Mrs Bennidge Mr Archer served notice of a moral vocabulary that was absent from other aspects of his life.

'The thing is, Mrs Bennidge, I know you could try harder. I know you could really make something of the work you do for us. And yourself, of course. That goes without saying. Surely you can see that it would be better for all of us if you pulled your weight? Surely you can?'

'Perhaps I can.' In answering Mr Archer, Mrs Bennidge gave nothing away.

'And I don't want you to think, Mrs Bennidge, that it's just me who thinks you could do better. Everyone thinks so. Geordie in the kitchen. Brenda and Alison . . .'

'Nasty little tarts, they are.'

'No, we're all of us the same mind. All of us. As I'm sure you are too, when you really think about it. So that's why I'm going to ask you, on behalf of us all, to make an effort. So that we don't have to go on having these conversations. Now, don't you think that's a good idea?'

'If you say so.'

The glance Mrs Bennidge gave Mr Archer at this point was one of the purest hatred. On several occasions I almost thought she was going to hit him. For his part, Mr Archer obviously found these conversations a strain. At the same time you could see that he thought them something he was morally obliged to go through.

'The only reason I don't give that Bennidge the sack, sir,' he once told me, 'is that I feel sorry for her.'

The idea of Mr Archer feeling sorry for anybody was a novel one. 'Why do you feel sorry for her?'

'Lives in a rubbish tip down by South Green. Husband's a waster. Two idiot sons. The kind' – Mr Archer paused savagely –

'that make you glad you never had children. But it doesn't matter what you do with people like that, sir. I know. I've tried. Treat them badly and they just accept it. Treat them well and they take advantage. What am I supposed to do?'

Curiously, my sympathies were with Mrs Bennidge. It was not that I liked her – for as far as I could see everything Mr Archer alleged about her was true – simply that I agreed with Mr Archer's diagnosis that it didn't matter what you did with people like that. If you dealt with Mrs Bennidge, it seemed to me, you accepted her on her own terms. Anything else would merely store up trouble.

Frances was interested by this aspect of Mr Archer's personality. 'Why doesn't he just get rid of her? If what I hear's true, she's already been sacked from half the hotels in Suffolk.'

'Maybe he sees her as a challenge.'

'That's what people always say about other people whose thought processes they couldn't begin to comprehend.'

'I feel sorry for Mrs Bennidge.'

'So do I. So would anyone . . . It's her that takes the ashtrays, by the way. I came into the lounge one day and saw her stuffing one up her skirt. What people like Archer never realise is that there'll always be other people like Mrs Bennidge. It wouldn't matter if you paid her £50,000 a year with ten weeks' holiday, she'd still come in and steal the ashtrays.'

'So what do you do about people like her?'

'Tolerate them, I suppose,' Frances said. 'And nail down the ashtrays. But the last thing you do, the very last thing, is to read them lectures on moral usefulness.'

I had always known I would find the second lot of photographs. It was one of those things to be counted on in advance, like a rotting tooth that would eventually have to be pulled. They came to light at the bottom of one of the box files, wedged between old bank statements, company prospectuses, odd bits of artwork that my uncle had commissioned on a whim and then forgotten. Finding these smudged black and white mementoes of past time was both comforting and the exact reverse, each warm association somehow cancelled out by a memory of what had followed. There was no getting away from this. These feelings were symbolised by a picture of my uncle, Kippax and myself standing outside the office in Lothbury in what must have been early 1983. In retrospect, knowing what had happened six months later, it was impossible not to translate our satisfied expressions – my uncle's peculiar gleeful gaiety – into the grimmest of grim jests. It had not seemed like that at the time. There was a photograph of Carole, taken outside her parents' house in Redbridge: plump, red-faced, mouth half-open, hair fanning out behind her in the breeze. This conjured up a bewildering range of sensations: memories of dense traffic heading east towards Essex; fields seen from a train; Carole's wedding dress thrown over a bed; a weekend spent decorating; odd remarks let fall by her father; evenings taken up playing cards with her parents. There was a lot more of this: painful, immediate, difficult to push aside.

Beneath the photographs there were other odd souvenirs: football programmes from the early 1970s; press cuttings; notes in a slanting feminine hand written on the headed paper of a City PR firm; queer fragments of my uncle's handwriting sprawling across scraps of card; dinner menus; even a paper napkin on which were inscribed the words *Mem: buy 25,000 pref. TTW, Consolidated to query?* It was impossible to work out what they meant. Why had I kept them, I wondered? Not for information. What then? My uncle had been keen on the talismanic aspects of business life – renting office space previously tenanted by a famous venture capitalist, engaging a chauffeur previously employed by the chairman of Lloyd's. He felt that in some way the qualities of their former owners rubbed off on him. More curiously, he may even have thought that material success depended on some magic wrought by the possession of symbolic artefacts of this kind.

All this was beside the point. Having found the pictures, it was difficult to know what to do with them. Keeping them would be painful. Somehow, not keeping them would be worse. I knew, for example, that if I tore up the photograph of Carole I should instantly regret it, would probably even try to retrieve the pieces from the wastepaper basket half an hour later and reassemble them. What was to be done? In the end I thought of the strongbox Mr Archer kept welded to the floor of his office, and in which were stored his own items of value. The knowledge that the bag in which

I had put the contents of the box file lay in a locked safe, and that someone else had the key, would be an adequate hedge against temptation. Mr Archer was intrigued by this transaction. 'Used fivers, I shouldn't wonder,' he remarked as he placed the bag inside the strongbox, which contained in addition a watch and, for some reason, a set of false teeth. 'And I hope, sir, that you've written down the serial numbers.'

Oddly, Mr Archer supplied a twist to the dilemma of the photographs. A couple of days later, entering the residents' lounge at a furious, headlong pace that suggested he was trying to retrieve a hat carried off by the wind, he said:

'I expect you've often wondered, sir, about the photograph that hangs on the wall to the left of the reception desk.'

As it happened, I had occasionally wondered about this photograph, if only because it was next to impossible to stand in the foyer for any length of time – usually kept there on some pretext of Mr Archer's – without your eye coming to rest on it. It was a black and white studio portrait of a youngish, not specially attractive woman – over-large nose, slightly protruding teeth – dressed in the fashions of the late 1960s.

'Who is it?'

Mr Archer seemed pleased by this interest. Baring his teeth obsequiously, pausing to give greater emphasis to what followed, he said:

'The lady in question was my wife.'

Given Mr Archer's habitual silence about his past, this was a startling revelation. I fought for something to say.

'I didn't know you'd been married.'

'It wasn't for very long, sir. All most unfortunate. Between you and me, I wouldn't want to go through that again.'

'Why? What happened?' By this stage I was seriously interested in Mr Archer's marriage. It seemed a subject of consuming importance.

'Not something I'd like to talk about.'

'Go on.'

What followed was an elaborate but disconnected monologue, which had clearly circulated in Mr Archer's head for many years but was only rarely brought out on public display. 'Difficult to say what I didn't like about her . . . Dreadful habits she had, I may say . . . When all's said and done, just a question of incompatibility . . . The *personal* side I shouldn't care to go into . . . Could have thrown the crockery at her sometimes, just sitting there at the dinner table . . . All a terrible mistake . . . Talking about it somehow makes it worse . . . Misunderstandings . . . Terrible sense of relief when it was all over . . .'

This went on for some time. Once or twice Mr Archer seemed about to draw the proceedings to a close, only to rattle on at an even faster rate. In the end he wound things up with a final, dramatic flourish.

'To tell the truth, sir, it cast a blight over my young life.'

It was difficult to know what to say. Compliment Mr Archer on his altered state? Ask him for further details (it might be that he wanted to make further revelations but needed some kind of prompting)? Fortunately, the photograph itself offered an exit route.

'But why do you keep it on the wall?'

'Keep what on the wall?'

'The picture of your wife. If being married to her was such a hell on earth, why remind yourself of it every day? Every hour even?'

Mr Archer thought about this for a moment. He looked worried, more worried that I ever remembered seeing him. In the end he said:

'Well, the way I look at it, sir, is that it's a part of your life, isn't it? Something you can't get away from. Not even if you tried. I did do that for a time, you know. Pretended that I never had been married. Whenever I had to fill in a form that said "Marital status" I *always* put down single. It became quite a habit with me. But then I thought I ought to face facts. After all, you've got to face facts, haven't you?'

'Do you think your wife – your ex-wife – feels the same? I mean, does she have a picture of you on her wall?'

'I wouldn't know, sir,' Mr Archer said, a shade stiffly. 'The young woman's habits are of no interest to me.'

For the first time during my stay at the Caradon I wondered whether I had been entirely wrong, whether there wasn't something admirable about Mr Archer. The story about his wife cast him in an unexpected light: resolute, tenacious, obdurate. Some of us hid pictures of people we had loved and who had made us unhappy in locked safes; others placed them in a position where they might see them a dozen times a day. Did this make Mr Archer a better man than me? I felt a powerful urge to find the ex-Mrs Archer and hear her side of the story.

'Do you want to hear what happened on the last day we were together?' Mr Archer asked, less formally than before.

'I'd like to very much.'

'It's harrowing stuff. Are you sure?'

'Go on.'

'It was about this time of the year. We were living in Frinton in those days, keeping a boarding house. Quite a nice little business it was. Funnily enough we weren't getting along too badly. A few disagreements. The guests used to joke about it. And then one morning I came down to the dining room and the guests were all sitting there complaining they'd had no breakfast. And about the smell, of course. She'd locked the kitchen door, but I broke in and found her.' Mr Archer paused impressively.

'Do you mean to say she . . .?'

'Oh yes. Those were the days when mains gas could kill you. But do you know what was worse than that? She'd left a note. Pinned up on the notice-board, too, so that everyone could read it. *You have ruined my life.* Just that. *You have ruined my life.* I often wonder,' Mr Archer said, 'what I did to deserve that. Wouldn't you?'

Frances refused to believe the story of Mr Archer and his wife. 'I don't think he was ever married. I think he just made the whole thing up.'

'What makes you say that?'

'I don't know. Yes, I do. He's too selfconscious about women ever to have been married to one. Have you ever seen the way he looks at me when he comes into the breakfast room? Now a married man might look at me – well, he might – but he wouldn't do it in the way Archer does.'

Frances was caustic that morning. There had been a letter from the magazine she wrote for, returning an article as in some way 'unsatisfactory'. But I was intrigued by this idea of the married man's unselfconsciousness about women.

'What about me? Where do I fit in?'

One of Frances's agreeable characteristics was her ability to discuss her own and other people's lives with something like objectivity. She said:

'I wouldn't say you were selfconscious about women. I just think you're the silent type. Most men who've been married – even when it was a long time ago – talk about their wives *all the time*. It doesn't matter if they hated them. Then it becomes a war story, only the bullets are all plates, and the sentry duty the night you spent outside in the car.'

'But Archer talks about his wife. Where does that leave him?'

'Archer talks about a picture of a woman on the wall. It could be anyone. He could have had a wife who committed suicide – and I never knew anyone whose wife committed suicide who was prepared to talk about it – but the picture could be someone else. I just don't think you should believe everything Archer tells you just because he tells it to you.

'Anyway,' Frances went on, 'why are you so interested in Archer? He's just a dreary little man who owns a hotel. Not a very good hotel either, if it comes to that.'

Later, when Frances had retired upstairs to read a book called *Iris Murdoch: The Relativity of Guilt*, I thought about this. For a start, it seemed to me that Mr Archer was the reverse of dreary. Sinister, perhaps, overbearing in the way he pressed his company upon his guests, but not dreary. Fortune-telling, speculation about the lives of his staff, a wife who had killed herself: none of these qualifications might have shown Mr Archer in a favourable light, but he wasn't for that reason uninteresting. There was also the Caradon itself. Without seriously exerting himself, Mr Archer had managed to impress his personality on every aspect of the hotel. It flared up at you when you walked through the door; waited on the doorstep to usher you out. This was an achievement too. Then there was the question of the late Mrs Archer. Here Mr Archer had seemed to speak with absolute conviction. The story had a kind of practised quality. I thought about this for a long time as the sky darkened and rain broke in across the eastern sky. Later I went up to

Frances's room. The door was open. *Iris Murdoch: The Relativity of Guilt* lay face up on the bed. I read a paragraph which began: 'Murdoch's characters aspire to freedom, but there are times when these aspirations are confounded by their very articulacy. In analysing their various predicaments to their own satisfaction, they are more likely to be constrained by the emotional patterns revealed than released. This reining in of temperament can sometimes have dramatic consequences.' There was no sign of Frances.

Coming back from my early-morning stroll along the beach, I found the letter lying in a pile of envelopes recently delivered by the postman and stacked up inside the front door. Inside the buff rectangle, postmarked 'London WI' and with a typewritten address, a single sheet of paper had been folded into a tiny square the size of a small coin. Unravelled and smoothed down, it turned out to be a piece of lined foolscap on which, printed in letters of differing size cut from pages of a newspaper in the manner of ransom demands, ran the message GEORGE CHELL IS A SWINDLER.

There was no point in taking something like this in to breakfast. Instead I carried letter and envelope up to my room and sat down to examine them. There was no clue, though, as to provenance. The individual letters looked as if they might have been snipped from a copy of the *Daily Telegraph.* No other incriminating details emerged.

In the years since the crash I'd received a good many hostile letters. Some were anonymous. Far more, unhappily, had been signed by the former investors who had written them ('As a pensioner in my seventies, I wish to place on record my disgust . . .'). There had never been anything like this. I decided that I was intrigued rather than alarmed. Whoever had sent the message clearly knew where I was, even down to the final letter of the postcode. Anyone meditating violence would presumably have done something by now. You could only wait and see. I put the envelope in the box file and went downstairs.

At breakfast Mr Archer was particularly good-humoured. 'Do you know, sir,' he said as he offered toast from the Caradon's curiously elongated toast-racks, 'I'm sure I felt a touch of spring today. Of course, we never really get the decent weather here until May, but I must say it cheered me up no end.'

Part III

For some reason I remembered that evening in the big house at Sydenham four or five years later in a boardroom high over EC3 as warm, late-afternoon sun streamed in through uncurtained plate-glass. In itself the memory was odd, because the Sydenham house was long gone by then, replaced by a grander and yet more luxurious mansion at Sunningdale, and the sensations it stirred up might have belonged to a previous era rather than a matter of a year or two since. What pushed it to the surface, I think, was the sound of my uncle's voice rambling on in that vague and faintly repetitive way he had as he talked to Kippax, the two of them craned earnestly over a sheaf of papers. Without warning, as I turned to look at them, the scene acquired a kind of mythical, eternal quality: light falling over the long, elliptical table, other people – a pale-faced clerk or two, a plump factotum from the firm on whose premises the meeting was taking place – reduced to the status of minor attendants, the two sharply contrasted figures absorbed in their discussion. Louder perhaps than the circumstances warranted, the voices – my uncle's bland and ruminative, Kippax's wholly deferential – came drifting across the room.

'Have to do something about that chap in the Midlands as wrote the piece in the *Post* . . . Wouldn't do if any of the London papers picked it up. D'y' suppose we should talk to him? Ask him to lunch or something . . .? What is he anyway? You know I don't go much on them journalists . . . But the people do read them, drat them.'

Kippax, as this monologue continued, made notes on a small, ring-bound jotter balanced on his knee and jealously guarded by an outstretched arm. He was a tallish, lean man with bristling russet-coloured hair that stood up straight on the top of his head like a sanitary brush, and an ability to project his voice into a variety of non-human personae. Dealing with a mislaid document, when his voice rose to a kind of strangulated bark, he could look distinctly foxy. Just now, inclining his head in a way that emphasised his over-large ears, and resting his protrusive front teeth on his lower lip, he resembled an exceptionally nervous rabbit.

'Of course, it's all part of communications generally . . . Sure you think that just as much as I do. In fact I don't wonder if it's time we had a proper PR campaign . . . Y'know, something *understated* and that . . . All very well advertising y'self in every blessed newspaper in every blessed town and then finding there's folk that's never heard of you . . .'

Kippax, hand moving at speed across the page, looked slightly cross at this. As head of the firm's marketing department, in addition to his task of advising my uncle on investment strategies, he was ultimately responsible for any press coverage, favourable or unfavourable, that we did or did not get. Lowering his head still further, so that it was almost at the level of my uncle's knee, he spoke several muttered words in a tone of comparative urgency. If this was intended to stop or divert the flow of speech, it had exactly the opposite effect.

'In fact, what we ought to do, K, is to get up a circular . . . Something we can send out to the chaps in the regions . . . Perhaps you'll do me the kindness to investigate. And while we're doing that, *while* we're doing that, there's a whole heap of other things we ought to be considerin'. Treasury paper on capital gains and a statement expected. Now, what do we think about that, I wonder?'

My uncle sounded querulous, a bit exhausted. That was to be expected. Two years or so as a public figure had taken their toll of him. Physically enlarged – his stomach jutting out over the table, face lost in an accumulation of chins – he seemed at the same time slightly diminished, fallen away into some odd world of mental torpor, disinclination to act. Kippax, to do him justice, was usually the victim of my uncle's 'moods' as he called them. I watched the two of them for a moment longer, as the wide oak doors at the back of the room swung open, admitting another pair of functionaries, and someone else approached with what might have been a jug of Pimm's, wondering how long the afternoon would go on and whether it might be allowable to go and call Helena.

Outside, on a church tower a hundred yards away, clock hands moved towards five. The sound of the chimes, a few seconds later, seemed to galvanise the occupants of the room into action. The two functionaries – senior members of the merchant bank whose office we were attending – sat down abruptly at the table end. Kippax advanced on them sternly, his fountain pen held out in front of him like a duelling poniard. My uncle gave a sigh of weary resignation, flicked his spectacles up from their descent along the bridge of his nose, and swivelled round in his chair. In the two years spent attending gatherings of this kind I had become grossly over-familiar with these rituals: Kippax's nerves; my uncle's sulks; stalled negotiations kicked into gear. Here, as so often in his undertakings, my uncle wanted money: specifically several million pounds to fund expansion of the side of his business that targeted overseas investors. As security he was offering the lease of the building in Zurich where Chell Holdings carried out these transactions. Interested in principle, the bank was querying my uncle's ability to dispose of this lease under Swiss property law. Here the matter had stuck.

The clock finished striking. Ten storeys below, on the pavement beyond Threadneedle Street, shirt-sleeved hordes were already in flight. It was a Friday on the last day of July. Nearer at hand, sonorous, formal voices met, broke apart: Kippax, my uncle, a banker together. Then Kippax and my uncle. Finally Kippax alone.

'Think the bank may not have considered the true implications of such a scheme . . . Collateral offered *in addition* to the extremely beneficial interest rate . . . Can think of many similar arrangements concluded in the past . . . Would like to draw the bank's attention to identical instances in its own recent history . . . Bona fides not in doubt . . .'

Fluent, grave, vaguely clerical, Kippax usually got his way on these occasions. For a moment I concentrated on what he had to say, half in admiration, half disapproving. If the truth is to be known, I never liked Kippax. His deference, which my uncle accepted at face value, I thought simply obsequious. But there was something worse than this. Kippax, in fact, in some distinct way, was sinister. I could never put this dissatisfaction into words, but it was always aroused at times like this: by the flat, accentless plod of his voice, the surreptitious glances at my uncle, his habit of appearing to read off what was actually a blank sheet of paper.

'A question of arriving at a *modus vivendi* . . . Identical arrangements entered into by ourselves, both here and overseas . . . National jurisdictions in no way an impediment . . . Not at all disagreeing with the need for a full and frank exchange of views.'

Putting Kippax on to perform in this way was, I suspected, my uncle's idea. He had a theory that long draughts of undiluted Kippax induced a sense of panic or hopelessness – bitter despair at the tedium of time passing – in his auditors. My uncle, needless to say, revered Kippax, whom he called 'K' and consulted at every opportunity.

'A surveyor's report *not* necessary in the circumstances . . . In fact surprised that the bank should think . . . Elementary safeguards of property law . . . Subterfuge . . .'

There was no telling how long this would go on. I settled down to brood about my uncle and his affairs. We had been living this kind of life – Kippax, city boardrooms, ever-increasing sums of money – for upwards of three years now. It showed no sign of diminishing, calming down. Newspaper journalists who wrote about my uncle sometimes stated that he had become a millionaire 'overnight' on the foundation of Chell Holdings. This was hardly true. A good week's takings in the early days might have been £2 million, but this of course represented only the sum in which my uncle dealt, not the ultimate profit. All the same, this must have been a reasonable amount. There were bank statements piled up in the office at Lothbury to which only my uncle and Kippax had access . . .

Was Kippax reaching the home straight now? He had a trick of repeating himself in the last stages of these exhortations, running through half-a-dozen pet phrases in an effort to round things off. Punched out of his mouth with an effort, the words seemed to bounce back from the opposite wall.

'. . . Lay this before you with confidence . . . *Unreservedly* commend these details to your attention . . . Clear that . . . Urge you . . .'

Nearer at hand my uncle was shifting his bulk uncomfortably from one area of his chair to another. Catching my eye, he winked. For all the veneration in which he held him, and the licence he allowed him in administering the affairs of Chell Holdings, my uncle wasn't above treating Kippax with a certain amount of irony: proposing some absolutely ludicrous business scheme, for instance, in an effort to see how far Kippax could be gulled into supporting it. What Kippax made of these jokes at his expense, which he received with indefatigable good humour, was anyone's guess.

There was a violent clashing of furniture as Kippax dried up, a kind of prolonged clanging of wood on metal, like a prison riot about to begin. My uncle said 'Yes' quite loudly to no one in particular. One of the City moguls leant back wearily in his chair and had to clutch at the table to regain his balance. Two or three people started speaking at once. It was too good an opportunity to miss. Nodding at my uncle, I wandered out through the swing doors into a corridor that backed on to a communal area where secretaries stood round gossiping or rifling through open handbags. Here I found a telephone and dialled Helena's number.

'Is that you?'

'We're practically finished. Kippax has been giving them the third degree.'

She laughed. 'Will he win, do you think?'

'Should do. If not, I'm sure they've got something else planned. Where can I meet you?'

'The train goes at 6.10. Say six o'clock at Paddington. Platform three.'

'Okay.'

For a moment I wondered about returning to the meeting. Then I decided against it. Kippax would get his money. In any case I should be seeing my uncle that night, spending the weekend with him for that matter. Standing by the lift I thought again about Kippax's slow smile, my uncle winking delightedly across the table, the dust motes hanging in the warm summer light.

If I've dramatised this scene it is because it is so vivid to me – infinitely more vivid than most of the events that preceded it. West Earlham seems very small now, very insignificant and meagre; the early London period is a forgotten glow, and even the Sydenham days appear somehow trivial and preparatory. I can't work out what caused this transformation, only mark its effects, and it's a fact that I can recall the conversations and the faces of this time in a way that still surprises me. Kippax's speeches to the moneymen, my uncle truffling his way through their ponderous dinners – all this is very real to me, and very poignant.

Imperceptibly, we had become great people. There was no doubt about this. I think it must have been about the time my uncle took the house at Sunningdale that I became aware of the fact of our greatness. He was on advertisement hoardings by now, asking worried investors if they thought they were getting the best rate of return on their money, and in newspapers waving a fat finger at a column of dubious figures. At the time we thought the advertisements were an inspired stroke – the mild, homely-looking man, the unanswerable demands – but looking back I don't think they were: they unsettled him, and they brought him too near to the people whose money he took. They may have raised the confidence of the public, but they lowered his own.

'Can't say as I like it, George,' he told me once. 'Why, it's like turning up in someone's front room and trying to sell them something.'

'It gives what we do a personal touch,' I explained. 'That's what Kippax says.'

'Too personal for me,' he said. 'Too personal by a long stretch.'

All the same, I think he liked the sensations of great persondom. If I've a predominating memory of the great house at Sunningdale, with its half-dozen reception rooms and endless conservatories, or of our final offices in Lothbury, it's of the sacks of correspondence – great shoals of letters addressed personally to my uncle and begging his assistance in the most unlikely matters. To settle a marital dispute, invest £100,000 in a lemonade bottling plant, stand for Parliament, present himself at a certain address in Bolton, Lancashire on a Thursday afternoon in November 'so that myself and a few friends can express our appreciation of your efforts' – all these demands it was assumed that my uncle would fulfil in the free-handed style that was thought to characterise his business dealings. In the wake of the letters came the visitors – fierce, mustachioed men with trackless and unfeasible schemes in their heads for manufacturing cars that ran on electricity, or raising Spanish galleons and their trove from the Bristol Channel, or equipping polar expeditions. Some of them my uncle received in his sanctum at Lothbury, but he was rarely taken in. I think he listened to them – I was about to write 'spoke' – because he felt sorry for them, or recognised in them something of himself, or – less frequently – because their imaginings contained the kernel of something that could be put to his own use.

'George,' he would say ruminatively as I came upon him sometimes in the big office, where sacks of unopened post lay over the sideboard and a man in a baize apron might be seen hanging a painting on the farmost wall – buying 'pictures' was one of my uncle's passions at this time – 'George, got a chap in here this morning talking about a new distilling process. You ever hear anything about that kind of thing?'

'What sort of a chap?'

'Poor suit,' my uncle would say reminiscently. 'Looked as if he could do with a square meal. Damn it, I nearly asked him out to lunch only I had an appointment with them corporate finance people. Said he'd been in the loss adjusting trade. Think there's anything in it?'

'Could be.' (I had no idea.) 'Don't whisky manufacturers say the industry's fifty years out of date? Did he have any apparatus?'

'No. Just drawings. Such a sad-looking chap, too.'

None the less, he made a number of shrewd speculations in this period. A couple of estate agencies in the suburbs that paid pretty well, a secretarial bureau in High Holborn and a Carshalton printing works found themselves shuffled into my uncle's grasp and placed under the notional control of Kippax and myself. Do you remember a literary paper called the *Monthly Bookman*? I still have one of the specimen covers they sent to Lothbury when the first approaches were made.

KINGSLEY AMIS – THE ENGLISH BREUGHEL?

THE STATE OF FICTION; A SYMPOSIUM

FLECKER'S DEBT TO HENLEY

MARGARET DRABBLE IN HER LIBRARY

A NEW POEM BY SIR JOHN BETJEMAN
THE DECLINE OF THE BELLES-LETTRIST
AN EXTRACT FROM THE LYTTELTON/HART-DAVIS LETTERS

'Extraordinary how these things carry on,' my uncle remarked as he signed the deed of purchase (I think he paid a sum in four figures) before relaunching the magazine with colour advertising and incendiary essays by Clive James and Anthony Burgess.

As I say, we became great people by degrees. Sometimes, lunching with my uncle in the City, I'd overhear people at adjoining tables considering his prospects. 'Isn't that Chell?' 'What, Chell Holdings?' 'Looks an ordinary little chap to me.' 'Well, he could have *my* money to lay out and welcome.' My uncle was unabashed by these salutations. 'Never does any harm to have people talking about you, George,' he remarked. 'You and me sitting down to eat in a restaurant, why it's as good as a free advertisement.' He was right, I suppose, but I never liked these occasions, never cared for the spectacle of my uncle blandly shovelling food to the accompaniment of these oblique murmurings. There was something shameless about it, I think, which he didn't quite appreciate, or perhaps I'm misjudging him, and the joke was really on the prurient throng that studied him.

But it was the house at Sunningdale that cemented our position as great people. I can remember my first sight of it, out of the nearside window of my uncle's Jaguar, as we motored down out of the Surrey hills towards the plains of Berkshire one hot summer forenoon: a little townscape of buildings and a rolling lawn like a billiard table, gravel moats, the infinite surround of gable and red-brick terrace. The spectacle was so extraordinary, so unlike anything that either of us had seen before, that my uncle stopped the car at the side of the road and stood silently on the kerb peering down through the heat haze. Later on as we prowled about the grounds, inspected the grottoes of funerary statuary and the spotless pathways, he seemed slightly shamefaced. 'I s'pose you think I'm a fool, George, buying a place like this, though you're too polite to say so.' 'No. Not at all.' 'I mean' – and I could see his mind working at the thought without reference to what I had said – 'who *lives* in places like this? Who lives in them, eh? Dukes?

Duchesses?' 'Dukes and duchesses couldn't afford it,' I suggested. 'I s'pose not. No, they couldn't.' He looked worried for a time, as if the prospect of dukes and duchesses being unable to share in this good fortune troubled him somehow, but then he brightened up. 'We must find out who the neighbours are, George. Find out and invite 'em round.' Later still, as we sat in the biggest drawing room and were served tea by a grave and awful butler, he revealed something of his purpose. 'This'll be good for us, George, a place like this. Make people take notice, you'll see.' He was right in a way. The newspapers pronounced him vulgar, hopelessly vulgar, but they were fascinated by the house, its regiment of staff, its platoon of gardeners, its heated swimming pool and its lustrous neighbours, who turned out to be a Lloyd's underwriter and an absentee Saudi prince. Myself, I never found its vulgarity annoying. In fact of all the places I associate my uncle with, I think I remember the fort at Sunningdale with the greatest fondness: not for its company days, but for the rain-swept afternoons when Helena and I used to wander the great paths or watch the leaves falling on the virid lawns. At other times the house was full of people. My uncle entertained there: he had 'little dinners' for two dozen, served up by a chef poached – if you will excuse the pun – from the Dorchester, with wines sent up by the case from Berry & Rudd. And it was here, too, that, coming upon my uncle in conversation with a group of persons on the vast Turkey carpet – persons whom inspection revealed to be the Chief Financial Secretary to the Treasury and the editor of the *Daily Telegraph* – I realised just how far this frantic and overpowering progress had taken us.

I shared only intermittently in these social experiences. Often my uncle used to introduce me to the circle of grandees on the Turkey carpet, with an odd, knowing glint in his eye, as 'my nephew . . . works with me in the business, y'know', but I disliked these occasions and tended to avoid them. If I've a memory of those evenings at Sunningdale it's of a dozen silent bald heads bent over the grand dining table while I sat with Greta in an ante-room watching the dishes go in and listening to my uncle's laugh rising and falling in the distance. All the same I used to wonder about the kind of company we saw, here amid the Berkshire granges and the dappled lawns, here at the tail end of the 1970s, wonder where it came from and what our own part in it might be. Above all it seemed to me that there was a change in the way my uncle regarded the people who thronged his house, and whereas in the past he'd welcomed anyone who was prepared to be received by him, now he had begun to discriminate in a savage and yet subtle way. Characteristically, my uncle confirmed these observations.

'Always plenty of people want to know you, George,' he said. 'Question is, do you want to know them?'

'That depends. It depends what you want to know them for.'

'Right,' my uncle said thoughtfully. 'But we got to be thinking of the future. Moving the business forward . . . Can't stand still for a moment, y'know, not in this day and age . . .

'. . . They're nice fellers,' he said. 'Some of them, anyway . . .'

At this distance I lose track of many of the celebrities he consorted with. Canforth the industrialist was there several times; Geoffrey Howe dined there once. If I ransack my impressions of this time I find a great uneasiness. I saw politicians outside the debating chamber, magnates detached from their boardrooms, all sorts of eminent and significant people, and their shared characteristic was fear. They had no answers to the problems that confronted them, and they assumed – with what now seems to me a startling naïveté – that my uncle could help them. They had committees on which they wanted him to sit, funds that they wanted him to manage, even a parliamentary seat, once, that he could have had by lifting a hand, or rather writing a cheque. I can see him now, standing before that fireplace, a small, brisk, fat figure crowded in by those heavy, distinguished faces, laughing at his jokes but not, I think, liking him or appreciating the fact of his dominance over them.

To do him justice, my uncle was quite aware of the position he filled in relation to those great people. 'Of course,' he told me once, 'we shouldn't really be here, George.'

We were standing in the big entrance hall at Sunningdale, and he made an expansive gesture around the swooning staircase and the glossed panelling to emphasise the remark.

'Why not?'

'Not our style. Not what we're used to,' said my uncle affably. 'Mind you, who's to say what a person's used to? But no, it isn't really our kind of thing, talking to big people . . .' His voice pattered off into silence. 'We're trespassers really. Found the gate left open and decided to walk inside.'

'Is that what you think?'

'Certain of it, George.' And then, 'Goodness gracious, look at the time. Due at Lothbury at three, we are.'

More than once in the months that followed I thought about that exchange, but I never reached any firm conclusion about it. For what the observation is worth, I think my uncle exaggerated his singularity. In fact it seemed to me, the more I examined the world in which we found ourselves, that England was full of trespassers, people who had come from nowhere to somewhere, and basked in a glow of their transit. There was Barnstaple the insurance broker, who had started life in a corner shop; Walsh the Barnado boy who floated his property company for £100 million. Curiously, there was no confraternity between these commercial meteors, and my uncle, who met them at dinner, was very scathing about Barnstaple's social peculiarities and Walsh's Devonshire accent. 'It's not where you come from, George,' he told me, coming back gloriously from one of these occasions, 'it's how you behave.' He was wearing a new suit, in elaborate pinstripe, and smoking a Havana cigar, and he looked like a little fat man whom the gods have suddenly decided to take pity on.

I am not mocking my uncle here: at least I don't think I am, for I continued to esteem him in all sorts of ways. He 'saved' a pre-Raphaelite painting for the nation at about this time, and he made legendary contributions to charity. I suppose my anger wasn't directed at him, but at the people who surrounded him. I remember a conversation from this period that I had with a Tory MP met on the fringes of a Sunningdale party.

'So you're old Chell's nephew, are you?' he said. 'Delighted to meet you. There are people say that you and that chap what's-his-name Kippax are the real powers behind the throne. No, don't misunderstand me. It's just that people occasionally wonder how your uncle does it.'

'Does what?' He was a portly, twinkling character who sat for a farming seat in the south of England and was later supposed to have lost half a million pounds at Lloyd's in the Eighties meltdown.

'Oh, keeps it all up. Do you know how much this place is worth? Of course you do. I had lunch the other day in Lothbury, a whole gang of us. Couldn't have been fewer than sixteen sat down. Champagne. Lobster. Hired waiters. Couldn't have cost under a thousand, that lunch. Does he do them often? I mean, I'd like to come again of course, but why *does* he do them?'

'We're gilts traders. We need to inspire confidence.'

It didn't sound very good, and I knew it didn't.

'Of course you do. Don't worry, I know all about it. But gilts traders put ads in the newspapers, don't they? They don't give thousand-pound lunches to, well, anyone with a handle to their name. And those buildings your uncle goes after, those mansion blocks in South Ken, where's the money coming from, eh? It's all right, I know all about it, but you're not gilts traders, or not *just* gilts traders.'

We were standing, I remember, in a recessed window in the big drawing room, looking out on to the teeming terrace. Scarlet-faced, dressed in a striped jacket and flannel trousers, my uncle wandered through the throng like some gorgeous, preening butterfly.

'Quite a phenomenon, isn't he, your uncle?' my companion went on. 'Shouldn't wonder if he does very well when we get back again. Herself approves, you know. All the same, nobody quite knows what to make of them, do they? And I'd be a lot happier if I knew where the money was coming from. Or where it was going to, just for the sake of argument.'

'We pay a fixed interest rate quarterly to all our clients,' I told him. 'Thirty days withdrawal notice for anyone who's not satisfied.'

'I don't doubt you do. All the same . . .'

For quite a long time I wondered whether to tell my uncle about this conversation. In the end, though, I decided against. He had reached a period in his life when he fretted about trifles. If a financial journalist, writing in a daily newspaper, came out against one of our products he would write exasperated rebuttals. If a gossip columnist printed teasing nonsense about him he would bombard the editor with endless letters of rebuke. The psychology of these irruptions quite escaped me. I don't think, in the last resort, that my uncle minded what people said about him, but I believe he resented the suspicion that he was being got at.

'There's people out there,' he told me once, with a kind of wonder that even then I couldn't wholly believe, ''ll write bad things about you just for the fun of it.'

'It's the first principle of journalism, Uncle.'

'But it's not right,' he said. 'It's not right, do you hear me? They ought to be ashamed of themselves.' It was the most outraged I ever saw him.

It was odd how my uncle retained this touching, archaic naïveté about people and things . . .

And so our lives went on in this queer, irresistible way: a high and dizzying trajectory that there was no way of quantifying. I tried to keep a diary at odd times, but it was no use. The days spun away beneath my hand, went careering across the horizon and out of view. But I remember the night of the 1979 General Election, in front of the television at Sunningdale, in the company of a red-faced and exulting throng, and, a little later, the visit of a very grand and eminent person indeed (I recollect the exact words this lady spoke to me, as she turned a hard and stony blue eye, and they were 'Very hot, isn't it, for September?' and it *was* very hot). He was summoned to a Downing Street reception not long after, where he stood uncomfortably in a crowd of entrepreneurs who were supposed to represent the economic spirit of the age, but I don't think he was very happy. In fact I sometimes wonder whether he was very happy generally in these days. He would disappear for days on end to European capitals with Kippax and his advisers and come back tired and spiritless and somehow uneasy in himself. He became hypochondriacal, inflicted dull, insipid diets on himself and worried Greta with fish-oil and ginseng tablets. And while he talked all the time, he seemed to communicate less of himself. He was always, or so it seemed to me, hovering on the brink of some revelation, some mighty confidence that would astound me and bind me to him for ever, but the step was never taken.

Sometimes, quite unexpectedly, he used to talk about the old days, the very old days. We'd be lingering in the office at Lothbury, as the streetlamps flickered over the empty pavements, waiting for the car to bear us away, when I'd catch him looking at me – poised over his desk with a pen in one hand, say, or leaning back in his chair, hands behind his head, staring at the damask-coloured walls.

'George,' he would say – and he would say it in the tone of a man who is determined to inflict some damage on himself, whatever the consequences – 'do you remember the old times? Norwich, I mean, and such?'

'A little. Different things at different times.'

'What kind of things? I mean, what comes into your head when you think about it?'

Curiously, I found these questions embarrassing: an old, tightly policed world of the imagination now penetrated by an intruder. 'I don't know. I remember my mother of course. All sorts of things. Norwich cathedral. Seeing the houses out of the upstairs window.'

He looked slightly disappointed at this, as if he'd fed me some obvious and unignorable clue which I'd failed to grasp.

'I'll go and see where the car is,' I said. 'Baker' – Baker was the chauffeur – 'may have gone round the side entrance by mistake.' I was half out of the chair, but he waved me back.

'No. 's all right. Nice to have a bit of a chat for once in a while. Don't worry about Baker. Now, where was I . . .? I mean, Jane, your mother, what did she use to talk about?'

It was a good question. What had my mother talked about? I recalled a few censorious remarks about neighbours, stock phrases of one kind or another. Obviously my uncle had something more elevated in mind. It was difficult to know exactly what might satisfy him.

'It's hard to say, Uncle Ted . . . I can remember her being very upset when I went away to London.'

At this rather disingenuous account of my departure from West Earlham, his face brightened. Mystifyingly, I had said the right thing. 'Upset? Of course she would be. It's what any mother would feel.' For a moment he looked almost triumphant, as if a point had been proved to some invisible audience. 'Did she write at all . . . when you were in London, I mean?'

'Hardly ever.'

'Not much of a one for writing letters,' my uncle said, in a rather subdued way. For a second or two something hung in the air between us, something remote and quite unguessable. He opened his mouth and closed it once or twice, looked as if he might be about to speak, and then shook his head.

'Doesn't do to be harping on that kind of thing,' he said vaguely. 'Doesn't do at all.' A moment after that the car arrived.

I dare say I should have pursued my uncle on this topic – this mystery of his connection with my mother – drawn him out and established what he meant, but somehow I never did. It was all too remote, too far away, and in any case I was irretrievably caught up in my own concerns. I was leading a strange life then: intent days in the office at Lothbury, the long evenings at Sunningdale (I had a flat in Kensington at this stage, but I don't suppose I went there more than one night in three), curious weekends at country houses where my uncle's celebrity had purchased us an entrée, solitary vacations in Continental towns where I wandered about without the faintest idea of how to conduct myself. I don't think I understood. No, let me be honest, I don't think I even tried to understand.

Q: How near before the crash do you think it was before he realised that things were going wrong?

A: Very near. Or maybe not at all.

Q: Not *at all*?

A: It's difficult to say. Have you studied the careers of the swindlers in Victorian novels? Merdle in *Little Dorrit*, Tigg in *Chuzzlewit*, Melmotte in *The Way We Live Now*. There's a tremendous inner conviction about them, an extraordinary sense of believing in their own myth, to the extent that they couldn't distinguish what was real from what was patently illusory. That feeling of carrying on in the face of overwhelming odds.

Q: You're suggesting that your uncle was like a character in a Victorian novel?

A: No, not really. Besides, they are bad men, I mean through and through bad men, which I don't think my uncle was. I think he just had a naïve belief that if people could go on being paid, then everything would work out in the end. It's fair to say that people like Kippax encouraged him in this belief.

Q: The following is taken from the *Observer* special report on the collapse, dated 27 May 1985: 'A premeditated plot to defraud, in which it is hard to know whether the cupidity of the fraudster, the negligence of the regulatory authorities or the naïveté of the investing public should take precedence.' Do you have any comment to make?

A: That's nonsense. Well, two-thirds of it is. The 'naïveté of the investing public' is simple patronage, as most of these investments were made under the auspices of independent advisers. 'Negligence of the regulatory authorities' is definitely right. None of this would have happened if they'd realised and done something about it when they did realise – that we needed a licence to trade gilts in this way. Which, in fact, we never obtained.

Q: Going back to the first question, surely he must have had an inkling that everything was falling to pieces.

A: I think he had an inkling. But not much more than that. You see, we'd had these mini-crises before, and always managed to survive them. Always the authorities' fault. Someone would ask a question in the House, or in the newspapers, as to whether we were trading legally, there'd be a few hostile articles and certain investors would ask for their money back, but the regulators would simply prevaricate. Make a few enquiries of the kind that a first-year audit trainee would have thought inadequate. It was only when the DTI was talking about outright closure that anyone became alarmed.

Q: You'd been investigated by independent auditors before this of course?

A: Twice. And very respectable firms they were too. But you see, an independent audit doesn't mean anything. An auditor just wants – or wanted at this stage – to see that the books balanced. Now anyone can make the books balance. You do it by shifting money from one bank account to another. If you're clever. And this is what Kippax did, I imagine. The account books showed that *x* million had been received from investors, so the auditors needed to find *x* million in a certain bank account. And they found it. Later it got more complicated.

Q: How?

A: In the end, as you know, the DTI sent insolvency specialists in, meaning that they thought the firm was insolvent and would need to be wound up. Even then Kippax had ways of throwing them off the scent. For example, there were several million pounds lying in a deposit account that hadn't come from gilts trading – they'd come from a property deal, which according to the letter of the law was illegal – so Kippax had to find some way of accounting for them. He did this by inventing and retrospectively recording in the books thousands of non-existent transactions. It very nearly worked.

Q: And your uncle remained ignorant of everything that was going on?

A: I think he could feel which way the wind was blowing. But he was able to dramatise it in terms of his personal myth – the little man up against the big battalions – and this comforted him. He got very broody, though, those last few months. He was always starting vague and faintly melancholy conversations about the future, which I now see to have been rather more ominous than I thought at the time. But there was never a sense that 'the shadows are drawing in' or 'the game's up', at least not until the very end.

That evening Mr Archer complained of a headache. Standing by the fire in the residents' lounge, one foot crossed over the other in an odd, balletic stance, he discussed his symptoms with hypochondriacal fervour.

'Of course, this is not what you might call a proper headache. Not on the general scale of things. If I were going to quantify it, I'd say three point five on a register of ten. Not like some of the headaches I've had in the past.'

'A kind of reminder, in fact, of past unpleasantness?'

'That's it. That's it exactly.' Mr Archer shifted the position of his feet slightly in an even more balletic shape, so that for a moment I thought he was about to spring up on to the mantelpiece. 'Many's the time I've been prostrate with pains in the head. Had to lie down in a darkened room with a wet flannel over my face.'

'But you don't feel like that now?'

'It's difficult to say. Of course, I'm not someone who complains about illness. I can't abide those people who go on endlessly about every ache and pain they have. But I should say that it felt like having something rustling inside your head, somebody walking on leaves a long way off. You understand what I'm saying?'

'Perfectly.'

It was clear that Mr Archer found the condition of minor illness gratifying not because it encouraged him to talk about himself but because it allowed him to ventilate various theories he had about illness in general. Later that same evening he said:

'I've always thought that being ill is all in the mind when you come to think about it. For example, I once had a great-aunt who was always taking sick. "Taking sick" – that's a good old-fashioned expression, isn't it? It became a regular thing with her. On high days and holidays, whenever anyone in the family wanted to go out anywhere, she'd lie there in bed. I used to go in and see her sometimes – I was only a small child, you understand, but I could see the truth of things – and I'd say, "Aunty, there's nothing wrong with you, you must get up." I was thought very forward for doing so.'

I had been reading the *Gesta Daemonorum* of Abbot Wulfric, which some long-departed guest had left in the Caradon's meagre bookcase. In those days – though written in the 1400s the book purported to describe events at the end of the ninth century – the Suffolk forests had stretched for thirty miles, from Newmarket to the sea's edge. Here the ancient kings of East Anglia had hunted lynx and bear. A wolf six feet high had been dragged out of a pit near Iken. At Rendlesham the royal hunt had brought down a fabulous wild boar in whose eye sockets red rubies glittered. Mr Archer, I now saw, was another of these mythical creatures, something set down arbitrarily in these bleak landscapes, ancient, elemental and rare.

Mr Archer's illness worsened by degrees. For some days he was not seen about the hotel, and was assumed to be keeping to his room. Then he rallied, and could be heard below stairs having a furious argument with the chef. People about the Caradon began to say that it was quite like old times, and that Mr Archer's having an argument with the chef was a sure sign of his return to health. All the same, he continued to look unwell, and could be seen sometimes examining himself in a large mirror that hung in the hotel foyer when he thought no one else was looking. I found him doing this one evening on my way down to dinner.

'How are you?'

Mr Archer looked round rather furtively. He seemed absolutely wretched. Never at all healthy-looking, his face had the colour of putty. All the same, his reply was completely characteristic.

'I'm very well. A bit tired, but you have to expect that when you've spent a day or two in bed. It's what I always told my aunt when she complained of depression. I'm glad to say nothing of that kind ever affects me.'

'Pleased to hear it.'

'It's a funny thing, though, lying there on your own when you know you ought to be up and stirring. You have *premonitions.* For instance,' Mr Archer explained, 'I had this dream about a funeral. Big old-fashioned affair, like you see in picture books. Horses. A carriage and four. What do they call those black drapes that mourners used to wear?'

'Weepers.'

'That's right. Huge coffin inside the cart. The hearse, I suppose you'd call it. No idea whose it was, though. None at all. Do you ever get dreams like that?'

'No.'

'Now, my aunt, she was *always* having dreams like that.'

That night, browsing through Abbot Wulfric, I came upon an arresting paragraph. This described the character and habits of a thegn or associate of the East Anglian royal house named Eorpwald, in effect a tenant who paid tribute for his land and was obligated to provide military service when required: '. . . a very mournful, jealous knight. And if his liege should command that he doeth, or that he goeth, Eorpwald would wax great in his wrath, saying "I know more than the king knoweth" or "In that matter I have the advantage," so that his majesty did greatly wonder at the thegn's spirit . . . His haunt was ever the chase: bear, wolf and beaver did he harry. And yet here his fancy knew no bounds, and he would beguile his majesty with tales of a hart that he had taken which dropt golden blood, or a wolf that spake to him, so that at length his majesty disbelieved his account, and put him from him . . .' There was no doubt about it. This, surely, in an earlier incarnation, was Mr Archer. The exaggerated humours. The wish to be affable contending with a hauteur that was manifestly unsuitable to his position in life. Above all, a complete inability to know where to stop. Eorpwald, I suspected, had spoiled a very good hand (royal favour, appreciative audience) simply by not knowing how far he could go. Mr Archer was the same. Or perhaps in both their cases, the line between fact and fancy had become irretrievably blurred. It was difficult to know.

* * *

Work on the book, which had slowed for a couple of days, mysteriously quickened its pace, only – just as mysteriously – to fall away again. Reporting this lack of progress to Mr MacCready over the telephone one afternoon, Frances came back shaking her head.

'He says there's no hurry. Apparently the editor's just been fired . . .'

'What for?'

'Rationalisation or something. Eddie says he thinks they're going to be taken over again.'

'Will that make any difference? To the book, I mean.'

'Probably not. But you can never tell in publishing,' Frances said cheerfully. 'Ten to one they'll just forget about it until somebody finds the contract in a file in six months' time.'

Curiously, I refused to be dispirited about this. For some reason working out what I thought about my uncle and the pattern of our life together had taken on an independent existence, quite removed from its eventual appearance in print. Frances, though, seemed slightly depressed.

'I suppose I'd better stay for another fortnight.'

'If you want to.'

'If it comes to that,' Frances said, 'there isn't anywhere much else to go.'

Whether it was based on sympathy, appreciation of our joint predicament or the wish to make the best of a bad job, Frances's interest in me dated from about this time. She took to coming back from the town with little gifts: a bar of chocolate, a jar of home-made marmalade from the charity shop. These offerings were always handed over with utter nonchalance. Another time she said unexpectedly:

'You ought to do something about your room.'

'What in particular?'

'Make it look as if a human being lived in it. More welcoming.'

And so under her direction I bought a couple of pot plants which sat on the corners of the dressing table and a strip of yellow carpet that lay over the Caradon's regulation drugget like a rash.

'Much better,' Frances said, in the wake of these adjustments. 'It's never going to be cosy, but it might as well be habitable.'

She was especially interested in the anonymous letter.

'You mean to say you really have no idea who sent it?'

'Not a clue.'

'Nobody you can think of who'd know your address here?'

'No one.'

'So what are you going to do about it?'

'Nothing. If it was seriously meant I don't think whoever sent it would have stuck to letters, do you?'

'Maybe not.'

But there was something about the letter that vaguely impressed her. In some strange way, I could see that it gave our exchanges over the tape recorder and the phone calls to Mr MacCready a seriousness that they hadn't previously possessed.

By degrees Frances became a fixture in the daily life of the Caradon. She could be seen writing her pieces of journalism at a table in the residents' lounge, or taking calls from the phone on the reception desk. At other times she stood in the foyer reading the notices on the green baize notice-boards, or hovered irresolutely in the doorway with her coat on, trying to judge if the weather was safe to go out in. For my own part, I never quite knew how far to involve myself in these extra-mural activities, had no idea whether she wanted to be taken out for a drink, invited to watch TV or otherwise entertained. The upshot was that we existed in a permanent state of silent semi-intimacy, forever bumping into each other on the main staircase or nodding across the foyer.

Mr Archer greeted the news that Frances would be staying at the Caradon for a further fortnight with huge enthusiasm. 'A highly intelligent young woman,' he told me once. 'It makes a nice change to have her about the place, sir, I can tell you.'

And so we became great people, and I met Helena.

I've some confused early impressions: a coil of blonde hair framed by a car window; strewn pairs of court shoes caught in sunlight; the entrance to her flat, one of those ornate mansion blocks in Earl's Court with a porter and double glass doors; effortful and unsatisfactory sex in a hotel along the Thames at – would it have been Goring?; a voice saying, 'And I really am leaving *this moment*.' I never did tie down that voice and work out just exactly what it was made up of: a hugely embellished upper-class drawl with flattened a's ('I wish you *hed*') and gross syllabic absurdities ('That would be *mah*vellous') but in the last resort idiosyncratic and unquantifiable.

Curiously enough, I have Kippax to thank for Helena. Towards the end, when the newspapers were getting to be a problem, he and my uncle grew obsessed with bringing in a high-class City PR outfit to represent us: 'raising our profile in the market-place' (Kippax); 'proper interviews *with pictures*' (my uncle). For some reason they settled on Egremont & Baker, where Helena worked, and consequently my first exact memory is of her sitting very primly halfway along a thronged elliptical table while Kippax prosed on about capital gains and my uncle ate boiled sweets surreptitiously out of a dirty paper bag. Three-quarters of the way through the meeting I stole a look at her jotter pad and it contained the words *Ravel, Rimsky-Korsakov, Rachmaninov* and *Rossini* ('Composers beginning with R, darling,' she explained subsequently, 'only I was so *bloody bored*'). Later there was a dreadful lunch at Egremont & Baker's offices in Fetter Lane, culminating in an interview for the *Money Programme* somebody had managed to fix up for my uncle. Then an encounter at some Moorgate Place cocktail party. Then dinner. Then a whole range of absurd little meetings in pubs and theatre foyers in which neither side quite managed to articulate what it wanted from the other, climaxing in a series of guarded declarations and the weekend in Berkshire, whose other abiding memory is of Helena complaining about the sheets ('Nylon, darling, and none too freshly aired either').

Already I'm conscious of somehow failing to do Helena justice, of making her too hard-boiled, which she wasn't, generic, *brittle*. I remember once making an inventory of her as she lay asleep on the sofa at Earl's Court, stark naked with one arm flung out behind her, and being quite unable to fathom the intensity of the attraction she had for me, how much greater the whole was than the sum of its parts. It was late on a Sunday afternoon, with long shadows already rising up the mulberry-coloured wallpaper and the answer phone blinking away in the corner of the room, but I sat there in a kind of trance, endlessly running my eye over her body – head, neck, breasts gathered up in shadow, pale thighs, feet – and then beginning again, like a big-game hunter who can't quite believe in the existence of the felled tiger that lies in his path. Oddly it was the imperfections I liked best: a tiny cicatrix on the edge of her cheek, freckled shoulders, a tracery of shot veins on the back of one calf. She was – and how do I say this without exaggerating or diminishing the emphasis? – a big, tall, gay, smiling girl with one of those Lady Diana page-boy haircuts (it didn't suit her, but this was 1981 and everybody had them) who moved elegantly in and out of rooms, never seemed discomposed, and had an address book the size of a small bible.

Inevitably I compared her to Carole. There was something premeditated and cruel in the way I did this, even once writing down a list of their characteristics on opposite sides of a piece of paper, but I don't think it did me much harm. For one thing it taught me an immensely sobering lesson about my own shortcomings and reaffirmed to me how much I had been to blame. At the same time it taught me something valuable about Helena, which was that by the time you had reckoned up dim adjectives like *impulsive*, *generous*, and *spontaneous* you were left only with a boundless knowledge of environment and its possibilities. What separated Helena from Carole, it seemed to me, was really only a self-confidence born of superior information. I suppose what surprised me, in those early days, was how much she knew: the connections and inter-relationships of people in the City, ownership of land and property, the source of concert tickets. She was not a clever woman – I never saw her read a book, and any newspaper above the level of the *Daily Mail* was '*much* too brainy, darling' – it was merely that she possessed a stock of interior resources which she knew how to use.

I realise that in describing Helena in this way I shall sound like an anthropologist. All I can say is that I don't mean to, and yet she was so hugely unlike anybody I had ever met that I could only spend the moments in which I thought about her reflecting on this momentous divide. We used to talk about our respective childhoods with a show of reluctance that masked deep, implacable fascination.

'So tell me about a typical day at school.' (She'd been to some extraordinary-sounding boarding establishment, staffed by vigilant nuns.) 'Describe it to me.'

'Oh, I don't know. Get up at six-thirty. Breakfast at seven. See if Mummy and Daddy had written. Then lessons. Monday morning would have been Divinity. Domestic Science perhaps. But I don't know how you can be so interested, darling. Surely a school's a school, isn't it?'

I tried to tell her something about the educational arrangements prevailing in West Earlham in the early 1960s and she listened for a while.

'I'm sure it must have been absolutely ghastly. But you seem to have survived it pretty well.'

Or I would try to get her to talk about her home life.

'All absolutely conventional. I mean, I don't know if you know about those Surrey people, but take it from me, Mummy and Daddy are the last word in stuffiness.'

'But what did they do?'

'When we were little? Daddy was at Lloyd's then. Mummy had her charities. And, of course, there was the house to look after.'

There was a way in which these exchanges made her seem less shrewd than she actually was. All the same I sometimes suspected that the odd, complacent wonder with which she received the stories of my childhood really was no more than that, that for all her worldliness she couldn't believe that there were places like West Earlham and people like its inhabitants. 'After all,' she said to me once, and I never could work out if it was seriously meant, 'if you didn't like it you could always have moved somewhere else.'

I'm trying to be honest about Helena, to be honest, too, about the effect she had on me, and I know that even in the depths of my infatuation there were things about her I didn't like. She had scores of silly, aimless, talkative friends, all exactly like her save for the essential difference that I wasn't in love with them, who enveloped her waking life like a cloud of midges: Henrietta, Sally-Ann, Lucinda – bold, confident women who communicated to each other what seemed to me the most inconsequential drivel. There were men too: short-haired ex-army officers working as trainee merchant bankers, hearty rugby-playing bores from Threadneedle Street and the Exchange with names like Gavin and Piers and Jonjo whom I disliked even more.

'You really mustn't mind Piers,' Helena said once at about this time. 'He really likes you, you know.'

'He's an idiot.'

'Actually, darling, he's *jolly bright*, and he went to Oxford. And you really shouldn't say those things about him.'

'And I suppose he'd have got the job at Lazards even if his father hadn't been on the board?'

'You don't understand, do you?' Helena said with unexpected seriousness. 'If you were the chairman of a merchant bank wouldn't you want your son to work there too? Come to that, if you had a milk round, wouldn't you want your son to inherit it? It's not our fault, darling, if we weren't born with your disadvantages.'

I note this exchange as a rare example of what I can only call class consciousness passing between us.

There was a dreadful irony about these preliminaries, as they coincided almost exactly with my attempts to separate myself legally from Carole. By this stage in the proceedings I hadn't set eyes on her for nearly three years, but queerly enough we hadn't altogether lost touch. Letters came occasionally from the old address at Redbridge: diffident but strangely rambling effusions retailing odd bits of Banstead gossip. By the time the legal hearings began I must have accumulated a dozen of these, and curious documents they were – not accusing, which perhaps I had a right to expect, but somehow doleful and resigned. They seemed to me wholly unbelievable, by which I don't mean that I thought Carole hadn't written them, or couldn't visualise the circumstances in which they'd been composed, merely that I couldn't believe in the world they conjured up: that fretful suburban world of traffic, gloomy evenings in the Essex twilight, Mrs Banstead's voice rising querulously from the sofa. It was all burnt up and gone, like so much firewood. In the end, most of the business was conducted by Mr Banstead, who began our transactions determined to hate me, but stopped when he saw that I was prepared to agree to practically anything, so that I saw Carole only once, when we were called in to sign papers. She seemed subdued but at the same time watchful and disappointed, as if she had come to make various dramatic statements but found them not worth saying. There was a moment towards the close out in the hallway of the solicitor's office – they were a biggish firm on the outskirts of Covent Garden who'd once advised my uncle on a property deal – when I found myself alone with Mr Banstead.

'Is she all right?'

He bristled up immediately, and I saw that all the credit I'd accumulated in our half-dozen meetings had vanished on the instant. 'No thanks to you if she is.'

'There's no need for that,' I told him. 'What does she do with herself?' For some reason we'd barely touched on this.

'Not a lot,' he said fiercely. 'She thought the world of you, you know.'

I was going to say something then, but I thought better of it. It was impossible to work out what Mr Banstead meant by this: whether he was being ironic, poking bitter fun, whether some extraordinary act of will had enjoined him to make the best of things, whether he seriously did believe that Carole had projected these emotions on to me. On balance, I concluded later, the truth was a combination of alternatives three and four: that whatever he might have thought of me privately Mr Banstead had decided that it was appropriate for his daughter to 'think the world of' whomever she married and once the fact was accomplished had managed to convince himself that this was the case. There could be no other explanation. All this occurred to me later. At the time I simply stared at him, there in the arid vestibule, conscious of Carole's bulky figure moving towards us through the double door, trying to think of something that would be simultaneously emollient, accurate, sparing of Carole's and his own feelings, but somehow conveying how dreadful and dispiriting life with his daughter had been.

'Perhaps she did.' It seemed absurdly inadequate to me, but Mr Banstead just shrugged, not unkindly, turned back to the doorway to gather Carole up as she passed (she glanced at me solemnly for a second) and shepherded her down into the street.

And so the Bansteads passed out of my life, perpetuated only in a photograph of the house at Redbridge with the two of us standing shyly in front of it, which I kept in a drawer somewhere and the occasion on which, interviewed in one of the tabloids, Mr Banstead revealed that he'd always had the greatest respect for me personally but couldn't speak for the probity of my business affairs.

Meanwhile my uncle had contrived to find out, at an early stage, about Helena. At this point in his career – rather like Helena herself if it came to that – my uncle sat at the centre of a complex web of personal intelligence. Data of this kind enabled him to pull off what were to me astonishing strokes of connection and influence, but were, I suppose, only the way in which a resourceful businessman conducted his affairs. In the matter of Helena he was characteristically circumspect.

'Nice-lookin' girl I saw you with the other night, George. It was you, wasn't it? At Hennessy's or somewhere. So many blessed places I go to, I can't remember.'

'She's called Helena. Helena Charlesworth.'

'Know that name,' my uncle said. He was reading the business pages of the *Daily Telegraph*, held at an angle away from his face. 'Charlesworth. Tall feller sits on the board of Associated Life. Met him. Met him somewhere. Sure of it.'

I nodded.

'Now that, George,' my uncle went on, 'is a concern I'm interested in. More than interested. Next time you see that young lady, you ask her how her father is. Or bring her to dinner. That's right, bring her to dinner. Ask Greta and set a date.'

And so I took Helena to dinner at Sunningdale: an extraordinary meal eaten alfresco in gathering dusk on the terrace, now illuminated by strings of coloured lights, and Mortimer, my uncle's newly acquired butler, handing round ices on a tray and the smoke from my uncle's cigar rising evenly into the calm summer air. I wish I had a tape recording of that night, something that could convey the full extent of my uncle's roguishness, his garrulity, Greta's ironising, Helena's laughter, my own silence. What did my uncle talk about? Racy City talk, mostly, anecdotes picked up on his travels around the Square Mile, society gossip that I marvelled he had access to.

'Nice girl that, George. Enjoyable evenin',' he said pompously when we met the next morning.

'You keep that up, d'y hear?'

I kept it up.

A great deal has been written about the zenith of my uncle's trajectory, the boom years and their traffic: my uncle's extravagance, the private jet he was supposed to have chartered for holidays in Tenerife and the Algarve, the lavish entertainments he sponsored, the matchless glamour of his ascent. You can read about it in the book Myerson the journalist wrote not long afterwards. 'A Fine Excess', 'The Shadows Lengthen', 'Countdown to Tragedy' – these are only the chapter titles: you can imagine the rest. For myself, I rather liked Myerson, whom my uncle took pains to cultivate at this time and whose account of his enormities, despite a certain tendency to exaggeration, was, I imagine, a more or less accurate résumé of what went on. So much of these last acts took place in the public eye – how my uncle and Kippax tried to borrow the money to buy Associated Life, how they bargained with the regulatory authorities, the accumulations of capital piling up in Gibraltar and Grand Cayman – that the only gloss I can add is either corroborative or faintly mitigatory. And even this carried its cargo of doubt and speculation. My uncle's affairs had branched out now into all kinds of uncharted territory, much of which I neither penetrated nor understood. I never did comprehend the reason why we needed to buy Associated Life, although it was explained to me often enough, in the big room at Lothbury with my uncle's pudgy hand tapping at the sheaves of printed foolscap.

'It's capital we need, George. Capital and contacts. Get hold of Associated and we get both. Two hundred branch offices to bring in the business. Sell on the property portfolio when the market picks up. Kippax has got it all planned. Respectable concern too. Two MPs and a baronet on the board. Just the thing to get the regulators off our backs and stop those blessed accountants asking questions.'

I don't know when exactly it was that my uncle began to lose my sympathy, but it must have been about this time. And again, I don't quite know what precipitated it. But I was aware that I thought he was behaving foolishly, and that sooner or later this foolishness would be flung back in his face. He gave silly, careless interviews full of little bits of indiscretion. He embarked on grandiloquent and unrealisable schemes: the Chell Award for Young Entrepreneurs, which ran for a year and was eventually bestowed on a hairdresser's shop in Brixton; a plan for bigger, purpose-built offices on a site in Docklands. He had vainglorious arguments with a newspaper proprietor that led to a series of incendiary exposures of the state of Chell Holdings and its finances. The offices at Lothbury had lost their air of quiet, sober efficiency and became a kind of caravanserai of human traffic. Those offices at Lothbury! Someone should have painted them towards the end – some modern-day Frith, I mean, not an interior decorator. Double doors leading down into the street, before which you could be pretty sure of finding a couple of mysterious old men in mackintoshes, a harassed commissionaire, a vestibule containing perhaps two dozen persons connected in one way or another with Chell Holdings: foreign investors talking in unknown mid-European languages; messenger boys from the City chatting together as they loafed by the marble pillars; a corporate finance team from one of the big accountancy practices seated proudly along a bench; fat, pompous men in pinstripes, with attaché cases under their arms, with appointments; nondescript characters in shabby serge suits without;

clerks issuing all the while from interior rooms with messages for the receptionists, rebukes for the serge suits or merely to stand by the desk staring complacently at the throng. And my uncle arriving suddenly in the doorway, very red-faced and out of breath, with perhaps an attendant behind him or a factotum carrying a case of files, to be assailed on all sides by looks, salutations, even importunate figures clutching at his sleeve, before the commissionaire bore him away to his sanctum and the series of private audiences that followed. I cornered him in there once, on a morning when I'd been made furious by an interview he'd granted to the *Evening Standard*, thereby forcing an emissary from the Bank of England to kick his heels for twenty minutes on the bench outside. He was smoking a cigar and drinking a glass of tonic water in which a couple of dyspepsia pills clinked and fizzed.

'Hell of a stomach I've got this morning, George,' he said mildly as I strode in. 'Can't think what's caused it.'

'Have you seen this?' I demanded, throwing the paper down on his desk, where it came to rest amongst a pile of company prospectuses, several chocolate wrappers and a gilded invitation to drink cocktails with the Worshipful Company of Dyers.

'Read it first thing,' he nodded. 'Didn't seem too bad to me.'

'It's a disgrace,' I told him. 'Makes you look an idiot. And the firm look as if it doesn't know what to do with its money.'

'Now you look here, George . . .'

'Just look at it. Did you really take him to Claridges? And give him oysters?'

'His idea, George,' my uncle wailed piteously. 'You know what those journalists are like.'

'Never mind that. All this business about a new building in Docklands. You know we can't afford it. And the two hundred extra staff. Where are they coming from?'

'Prospects, George. I was talking about prospects.'

'You're going round the City looking for money. You've got a corporate finance team from Price Waterhouse sitting out there *this minute* waiting to talk to you about venture capital. What do you think they're going to make of this?'

I was ready to carry on for another five minutes, but by this time my uncle had stopped trying to answer and simply sat staring rather vacantly in front of him. The cigar smouldered away against the invitation from the Worshipful Company of Dyers.

'I'm tired, George,' he said.

'Is that all?'

He blinked once or twice in a vague way. 'Well, that's the truth of it. I'm tired, George, and . . . and I don't like you going *on* at me.'

'And the political stuff? The things about the unions and the benefit cheats. How do you think that's going to go down?'

'Twist things,' he went on. 'Twist things, those journalists. Just to make you look stupid . . . You know how it is, George.'

There was an urgent knocking at the door then, and the voice of a factotum murmuring something about the Bank of England and kept waiting, and an ominous rattling of cutlery and tea trays, so I got up and left. That evening, though, I drove down to Sunningdale – he was dining in the City, I'd made sure of that – determined to see Greta. It was nearly dark when I arrived. Devoid of my uncle's presence, the big house took on an odd, sepulchral quality. There was a light burning in the courtyard but the rest of the place was plunged in darkness. In the wide hallway I fell over a henge of parcels, all propped up on their ends like standing stones. Further inside, pale half-light fell over the furniture in the giant reception rooms and glowed off the great square mirrors. There were white invitation cards neatly drawn up across the mantelpiece and I took a look at them: *The chairman and directors request . . . Lord and Lady FitzMaurice at home . . . Sir Robin Charlesworth* . . . Sir Robin Charlesworth was Helena's father. Higher up the wall numberless representations of my uncle stared out of their gilt frames: dazed and unhappy in a morning coat and striped trousers on a green lawn somewhere; leaning conspicuously over the rail of somebody's yacht; shrewd and interested in the Ascot paddock; at his desk in Lothbury, looking up sharply over the half-moons of his spectacles. I prowled on towards the back of the house, peering through doorways, negotiating the long track of bristling carpet. I found Greta in the kitchen, reading the evening paper by lamp-light. She stared up vaguely as I came in.

'I knew it was you,' she said. 'Saw your car in the drive. Have a drink?'

Looking at Greta in the arc of light, yellow hair piled up on top of her head like candyfloss, I wondered how old she was. Fifty?

Fifty-five? There were huge fissures down the side of her cheeks. She moved off purposefully to the cupboards and returned with a bottle of gin.

'Thought you'd be in the City still. At that dinner at wherever it is.'

'No one asked me.'

'I expect you could have gone if you'd wanted. Isn't that right?'

It occurred to me that Greta had perhaps had more than a little to drink. There was no visible evidence of this – no glasses, paraphernalia or physical manifestations – merely an odd sense of increased volubility.

'What do you do in the evenings, Greta? I mean, when Uncle Ted isn't here?'

'What do I do most evenings, you mean?' She smiled, but not fiercely. 'Oh, I look after myself, George. Mrs Cann the housekeeper lives in, you know, though she's off tonight visiting her sister, and we generally have supper together. And there's always the TV, only I don't really like it so much as most people. Sometimes I think I'll just sit down and write my memoirs.'

'What would you put in them?'

'Oh, you'd be surprised, George. Not things about *him*, perhaps. I had a life before that, you know. A good long one.'

There was no doubt about it. Greta was emphatically drunk. I wondered how often she did this, and whether this information about Mrs Cann was accurate.

'Did you see those parcels in the hall?' she went on hastily. 'Expect you're wondering what they're for.'

'No idea.'

'Garden chairs. Seventy garden chairs. His idea. "Ought to have a party in the summer, Greta," he says the other day. "People sitting out on the lawn and such." I told him there's dozens of chairs in the old summer house, but he won't listen. Goes off to Harrods the next morning and orders them.'

'You could send them back.'

'I could, couldn't I? I don't suppose he'd notice. It's in the head one minute and out of it the next with him.'

'How is he, do you think?'

Greta's features relaxed immediately. 'Says he's tired. Always. And he is tired. You should see him sometimes when he comes back here after one of those dinners. Face as white as chalk. But he doesn't sleep, not much. And then he worries all the time.'

'What about?'

'Business, stupid. He gets in a terrible state about Kippax and whether he'll leave the firm. Time last year when Kippax went on holiday, he was dreadful. Kept on sending telemessages to his hotel and got a car to fetch him at the airport. Never seen him so bad.

'I don't like that Kippax,' Greta went on. 'Don't know why, and I don't like to speak ill of anyone, but I just don't like him.'

After this she would say nothing more about my uncle's affairs: in fact there was a faint impression hanging in the air that she had said too much and regretted it. We went through into one of the smaller rooms off the big dining chamber, where there was a piano and sheet music lay scattered about on the floor.

'Been learning to play,' Greta said, with an odd, dreadful humility. 'Gives me something to do in the evenings. Afternoons too.'

I picked up one of the books. It was called *Mozart in Easy Steps.*

Half an hour later, turning into the asphalt drive that led to the main road, I saw headlights moving towards me. Pulled into the verge, I sat and watched a chauffeur-driven Jaguar glide by. My uncle sat in the back, face dropped into the shadow, presumably asleep. By rights I should have turned and followed the car back to the house. Instead I moved off again through the inky Berkshire night.

Q: What about Greta?

A: As I think I've tried to convey, Greta wasn't something my uncle talked about. As to how they met, your guess is as good as mine. It's perfectly possible that he simply picked her up in the street.

Q: Implying that . . .

A: Implying nothing. Not the least shred of evidence. It was just that Greta seemed to know a great deal about a certain kind of life in which street-walking formed a definite part. I remember once being with her in some quite respectable part of London – if not Belgravia then somewhere like Pimlico – when a modestly dressed but somehow conspicuous woman stalked past, and Greta said something like 'Cold day for it,' and I think I was rather startled that she'd been able to identify the woman as a tart. I don't think this was a reflection of her own previous life. But she'd certainly, I should say, worked behind a bar for a long time. Or maybe in a big hotel. Something like that.

Q: And she got on with your uncle?

A: Oh, invariably. They were like an old married couple. Except when she thought he was 'lording it' – that was her expression. Or perhaps that just made them more of an old married couple. I don't know. Actually Greta was kept very much in the background – never came out with him in public and so on. I don't think this was deliberate policy on my uncle's part: I think Greta preferred it like that. She had a kind of horror of being conspicuous, looked at. It was a pity in many ways, because she would have been – was, when she was there – a good restraining influence.

Q: You make it sound as if your uncle badly needed a restraining influence.

A: Do I? Well, he did. Not always. Just occasionally. Greta was very good at that: don't have the extra glass; put your cheque book away; come home – that sort of thing.

Q: Do you think he was faithful to her?

A: Almost certainly. Yes, undoubtedly. If experience has taught me one thing it's that pronouncements on other people's emotional lives are completely valueless, but in so far as I can judge, yes.

Q: There was a certain amount of newspaper gossip . . .

A: I'd never seen one of the girls who made the allegations, literally never heard of her. Also, the locations were – well, let's just say implausible. The other one was a secretary who got fired for petty theft, which I think answers your question.

Q: Nothing else?

A: My uncle had old-fashioned attitudes about women. Unreconstructed. I mean, he used to talk about 'bints' and 'bits of stuff' and 'hot tomaters'. Quite unselfconsciously. And he always had a dinner party list.

Q: Which was?

A: Oh, an elaborate fantasy of a dinner party at which he would be the only male guest, surrounded by the kind of women he found attractive. In the early days this meant people like Julie Andrews or Joanna Lumley. A bit later it extended to Mrs Thatcher and Joan Collins. But it was quite innocent. I mean, there was no harm in my uncle about women, certainly none that I could see. It was all done on a kind of music hall level. You know, jokes about newly married couples, and lodgers.

Two more messages came that week, both with typewritten addresses and W1 post-marks, both constructed from letters cut out of the *Daily Telegraph*. The first simply said JUSTICE WILL BE DONE. The second, a shade more elaborate, ran VICTIMS OF CHELL UNITE TO FIGHT.

'Doesn't this worry you?' Frances asked.

'A bit. Not very much.'

'You ought to try and find out who's doing it.'

'It could be anyone.'

'How many people in London know your address?'

I thought about this for a while. Kippax maybe. One or two of the Lothbury hangers-on. It was difficult to think of anyone else.

Mr Archer, I noticed, had developed an interest in these communications. He brought the third one to me on a plate – an archaic flourish that made him resemble a Victorian footman.

'Another letter, sir.'

'Thank you.'

'From London.'

'The correct postcode too.' (Inaccurate postcodes were one of Mr Archer's favourite grouses.)

'Wonders never cease.'

Mr Archer's expression, as I said this, was quite extraordinary – furtive, flushed and pop-eyed. Then, without warning, the light bulb above our heads – we were standing in the residents' lounge at the time – fizzed and went dead.

For some reason the effect on Mr Archer was electric. He went chalk-white and dropped the plate on to the floor, where it promptly cracked into several pieces.

'Are you OK?'

'You'll have to excuse me, sir.' With an abasing gesture, Mr Archer dropped to one knee and began to pick up the fragments. 'My nerves are something awful this morning. It could almost have been Mad Mary back to haunt us.'

'I hope not.'

'You've dropped your letter too, sir.'

'So I have. Thanks.'

I left him kneeling on the carpet, sweeping up the pieces of china with a wholly unnecessary fervour.

If I remember that weekend in Wiltshire so vividly, which began underneath the clock at Paddington on a Friday evening in July after a day spent in the boardrooms of Threadneedle Street, it's because my uncle, too, was there. At this distance I don't properly recall what compulsion it was that forced him to descend on the big, manorial house a mile out of Westbury, where a driver delivered him with two suitcases and a parcel of wine late on the Friday night. I remember Helena explaining to me, with her habitual precision, the exact connections that drew him to our host and our host's acquaintance, but I was more interested by the spectacle of him, aloof and comfortable, in an armchair at the back of the drawing room, or taking solitary rambles among the rose bushes. My uncle had a way of imposing his personality on a house, of being found in remote rooms where guests seldom penetrated, rooting through bookshelves, taking baths at odd times of the night. For a day or so our paths scarcely crossed, although I had half-a-dozen opportunities of watching him at a distance: playing croquet with fantastic ineptness on the lawn, reading the *Daily Mirror* in a chair after lunch, sitting up late with a couple of cronies (I remember coming into the room unobserved and seeing their three bald heads glinting together under the light). But on the Sunday morning he sought me out.

'Nice sort of place, George,' he said offhandedly as we moved towards one another in the garden.

'I like it. Helena likes it.'

'Often thought about it,' my uncle ventured. There was a weak sun shining over the chimney pots, and the eaves gleamed under the Wiltshire sky, and he shaded his eyes with his hand as he stared up vaguely towards the rooftops. 'But you'd miss London. Think about it in winter, too, with the roads frozen and everybody stuck waiting for a train.'

'I didn't know you were coming.'

'Neither did I. Last-minute thing. Thought I'd talk about it here instead of on Monday morning.'

'Important then?'

My uncle looked mournful. 'There's something up, George. Don't quite know what it is, but there's something up. They're ganging up on me, George. Out of *spite*. Associated Life. And some others. All quite above board, you know, but . . . ganging up.' He paused impressively. 'There's a question goin' to be asked in the House on Tuesday.'

'Who by?'

'Some Labour chap. Always a Labour chap asks questions like that. Ability to meet payments. Government licence. That kind of thing.'

'What does Kippax say?'

'Kippax? Kippax?' My uncle smacked his hand suddenly against his ribcage. 'Kippax ought to take a holiday. Kippax is getting nervous. Starts seeing trouble when there isn't any. That's what I think of Kippax.'

We took another turn round the grass, my uncle blowing stertorously as he came up to the gentle incline before the croquet lawn. There was something worrying him, I saw, that had nothing to do with people ganging up on him or Labour chaps in the House. Eventually he said:

'Come a long way, haven't we, George?'

'A very long way.'

'Where do you think it'll end?'

'I don't know.' I really didn't know, had no idea where my uncle's frantic, inexpressible ambitions might take him. 'Buckingham Palace. The Guildhall. Chairman of a building society. Who's to say?'

My uncle listened to this with absolute seriousness. 'Some of those chaps,' he went on – and I suppose he was referring to the kind of people who were knighted, became Lord Mayors of London, or sat on the boards of building societies – 'had to struggle a bit in their time. Not just up, I mean. Envy. People out to get them.'

'Bound to have.'

'That's right,' he said. 'Well, I'm not going to give up. They'll see.'

The lawn was becoming crowded now, with old gentlemen in striped jackets and red and yellow ties ('MCC,' my uncle had intimated proudly when he first saw these decorations) and freckled elderly ladies in sun-hats, and one of the cronies of the previous night loomed up and swept him away. An hour later I asked Helena:

'What's happening about the Associated Life deal?'

'I don't know. Daddy did say something the other day. Something about the money not being there.'

I related the conversation in the garden.

'I really don't know anything about it.'

'Nothing?'

'Nothing at all.'

At lunch-time my uncle had cheered up. He sat at the far end of the table and ate a Melton pie with gusto. 'Extraordinary good idea,' he was heard to say, 'putting all those things in it.' But there was a phone call early in the afternoon, and by tea-time the Jaguar had come and gone and only the wine-parcel – my uncle's present to his host – lay on the broad windowsill next to the door as a reminder of his visit.

I think it was during that weekend that I first became aware of the peculiarity of my position in the world to which my uncle had introduced me. It was my first experience of living in, as opposed to watching or speculating on, an exclusive social group, and I don't think I much liked it. In fact my strongest impression is of a kind of confidence – of red-faced men sitting round a table laughing, cigars winking through the twilight, casual orders communicated to domestics – which I could never hope to reproduce. I don't want to emphasise this sense of apprehension, for I know that I was perfectly capable of holding my own with Helena and anyone else to whom I happened to be introduced, simply to say that I was always aware of it, and that it was constantly with me.

At the same time, if I try to isolate the things that separated me from that world I can only come up with a kind of emphasis, a sort of self-asserting boosterism that disturbed me because I couldn't see its use. They were very kind, those people, but I was an attendant on the scene in which they moved and deliberated, and I knew there were great areas of their world that I could never hope to penetrate or understand, invisible doors and frontier gates that would always hold me back. Perhaps in the end it was collective memory that did this, the perpetual invocation of 'Do you remember?' and 'the time when', a bruising solidarity of schools and shared upbringings. I tried explaining this to Helena, without success.

'The odd thing,' I told her, 'is how well you all seem to know each other. I mean, right back to when you were children. The time Jonjo fell off the pony. When Hermione had to wear braces and what the other girls said.'

'It all seems very normal to me. You make friends, and they stay your friends. I know you grew up in a kind of leper colony somewhere in East Anglia.'

'You're missing the point. You all know *about* each other. Where you went to school. What your fathers do. You may live a hundred miles away from each other, but you're a real community. Shared assumptions. Shared ideals.'

'I dare say it's the same on any council estate.'

I have a feeling that Helena thought there was something rather regrettable about this curiosity, and wondered whether she ought to conciliate it. She said once:

'I think you have the wrong idea about people like me. Like Daddy. And the rest of them. You think, I don't know, some kind of oligarchy that runs everything and *decides* everything. But it's not like that at all.'

'You mean, if it was then I wouldn't be here?'

'Oh, I wouldn't put it quite like that. But I can see you bristling up every time you sit down to eat a meal. In case there's more than one fork and you don't know which comes first. Your uncle doesn't worry about that. He just gets on with whatever he's doing. You see, it's just how people behave, what they do. I mean, you must have had rituals of some kind when you lived with your mother?'

'I remember she always screamed if I put a milk-bottle on the table instead of pouring the milk into a jug.'

'There you are . . . Would she have approved of me?'

It was a good question: would she have approved of Helena? For that matter, would she have approved of anyone? For a moment I imagined my mother appraising Helena's knee-length skirt, bobbed hair, heavy earrings.

'I expect,' Helena went on, 'she'd have thought I was a corrupting influence on her darling boy.'

In fact it was doubtful that my mother had ever thought of any relationship in these terms. I remembered her once disparaging the idea, apropos a piece of gossip conveyed to her by Mrs Buddery, that you could 'ever know what made some people like other people'.

'What about your uncle? Did she approve of him?'

Questions of this kind were unanswerable. 'Not really. At least, I don't think so.'

'Well, that surprises me,' Helena said. 'I think he's a sweet old man.'

Some highlights from Helena's vocabulary:

This chappie – any unknown man of working-class origin

Wet – variety of definitions, most consistently ineffectual but also obtuse or even ignorant ('It's very wet of you not to know')

Civilised – expensive

Nice – all-purpose commendatory adjective, used ironically in descriptions of female acquaintances ('She's very *nice*, don't you think?')

Presentable – expensive

Oomski – dirt, mud, surface of a ploughed field, etc.

ETs – Essex tarts (of secretaries)

Clever – commendatory when used of clothing or other inanimate objects ('That's a clever tie/map, etc.'), deadly insult when applied to people ('They say Julian's very clever')

SHAH – So Hurt and Humiliated (of minor inconvenience)

Solid – clever (of a weekly magazine, 'Is it solid, darling?')

Expensive – ostentatious, in poor taste ('You seem to be wearing a very expensive suit')

* * *

What else is there to say about Helena? I met her parents once or twice, at weekends in a grim old house in Gloucestershire. They were polite, brittle, distant people whose affectation it was never to have heard of the most innocuous manifestations of popular culture. This pretence was elevated to such an awful level as to prohibit nearly any conversation. They even did it with Helena, I noticed. 'Is he an actor?' 'I'm afraid we don't read the Daily–.' 'Is that something on the television?' They had a TV set in the corner, neatly fenced off by a kind of embroidered screen, on which Lady Charlesworth occasionally watched nature programmes and afternoon racing, and pictures of horses lay all over the place: photographs in heavy gilt frames athwart mantelpieces and pianos, a great painting of a stallion in oils that hung over the fireplace. On Sunday afternoons we put on waxed jackets and wellingtons and tramped laboriously around the country back roads or over the low Gloucestershire hills, heads bowed against the wind. I don't know what the Charlesworths thought about it all, but I was conscious of them watching me: I remember once vaulting over a stile on whose further side the three of them clustered in an intent, staring huddle. In Gloucestershire Helena became an exaggerated and at the same time slightly ghostly version of her London self, trading gossip with her mother in an impenetrable shorthand. 'But didn't she marry old Newbridge in the end, post-Harry I mean?' 'Jonty had to sell Heveningham for DDs' (DD stood for 'death duties', I found out). My memories of this time are woefully thin and partial: Helena curled up beside her mother on the sofa, flicking through an illustrated magazine, in riding gear once on the gravel forecourt, exclaiming over the paper-board invitations on the mantelpiece.

But it was all falling away by now, all disappearing into some black hole from which I could never extricate it or check its descent. My uncle was fuddled by lunch-time these days, flushed and voluble, ready for a chat – a good old chat – give Kippax the slip – have something sent in on a tray hay? – anxious to talk – the weather in the Mediterranean – thinkin' of going there for a bit – the old days in Norwich, my mother, anything except the state of his business affairs. Kippax begins to fade a little from the picture now. No doubt he was still there, but I don't remember him. In the photographs which remain from that time it's always my uncle who dominates: shaking hands with a first division football side whose kit someone had induced him to sponsor; addressing a fringe meeting at the Conservative Party Conference; silk-hatted and stripe-trousered in the Ascot enclosure. In each of these representations he looks the same: petulant, preoccupied, defensive. There was a profile of him in the *Sunday Times* around this period that greatly upset him: not, I think, because it cast any doubt upon his business dealings, but because it depicted him as dull and stupid ('even his intimates recognise that Chell has no social sparkle . . .'). I arrived at Lothbury on the Monday morning to find him deep in it, the cigar in his hand dangling two inches of ash.

'What is it about these fellers?' he asked. 'Now, if I'd written a book or something, that this chap didn't like, and he thought I was a fool for writing it, then I could understand. But why say I'm stupid? Why say I don't fit my clothes? Not as if I ever *met* the chap.'

'It's not worth bothering about,' I told him. 'Forget it. Burn it.'

'But you don't understand, George,' said my uncle slowly. 'It is worth bothering about. Never was anything more worth bothering about. Here I am, respected businessman, worked my way up, created employment – don't forget that, George, given people jobs – and now I'm to be abused for wearing a decent suit and liking a drink. It's not good enough.'

The upshot of this was an injurious episode in which, in the vicinity of a Press Association photographer, my uncle attempted to hit a journalist being presented to him by the President of the Institute of Chartered Accountants in England and Wales at a reception held at the Institute's premises in Moorgate Place. The picture – my uncle's wattled face, glasses slipping down the bridge of his nose, fist flapping weakly before him – made most of the next day's papers. There was talk of a court action, but my uncle's lawyers settled it behind his back.

One other incident from this time sticks in my head. It was late on a Friday afternoon, so late that the Lothbury receptionist had gone home, when the phone rang in the outer office. Picking it up I heard a woman's voice in which alarm, vexation and curiosity were uncomfortably blended.

'I need to speak to George Chell.'

'This is him.'

'Name of Edward Chell mean anything to you?'

'Uncle.'

'Thank fuck for that. You'd better come and get him then.'

'Where?'

With extreme gracelessness, as if it was exceptionally stupid of me not to know, she named an address in south-west London. I took a taxi through the dense, early-evening traffic to a drab little street on the south side of Clapham Common where estate agents' boards jostled each other for space on the frontages of a cramped Victorian terrace. Halfway along, a woman standing in a doorway flagged us down. I left the taxi idling at the kerb.

Inside the house was a small hallway where coats hung on a row of stark metal hooks. Camphor pervaded the air. The woman stood at the foot of the stairs, passing one hand aggressively through a thatch of bleached yellow hair. She would have been about forty.

'Well, I'm fucking glad you got here,' she said. 'At least I'll say that.'

It was difficult to know how to respond to this, where to begin. The first task, obviously, was to establish my uncle's whereabouts. The woman looked me up and down once or twice, decided I was harmless, and half turned on the stair.

'Up here.'

At the top of the stairs the landing widened out into three or four bedrooms with their doors ajar. Each contained no furniture other than a bed, a chair and a side table. Outside the furthest was another chair on which lay a ball of wool, stabbed through with two knitting needles, and a half-finished pullover.

'Go *on*,' the woman said.

I have a fleeting memory of white-washed surrounds, a window looking out over the South London rooftops, a picture of a lachrymose Victorian child in a sailor suit fixed to the wall. My uncle lay on the bed, fully clothed, his arms drawn up over his chest, wallet and keys neatly stacked on the bedside cabinet. He was snoring loudly.

'Is he all right?'

Having got me into the house, and to a certain extent established that I was prepared to accept responsibility, the woman seemed slightly mollified. At any rate she lit a cigarette, leaned back against the doorframe and looked at me thoughtfully.

'I don't know. He'd only just got here – been here five minutes maybe – when he says he's tired, can he have a bit of a rest? That was three, four hours ago. I got your number out of his diary.'

I saw immediately that there was no point in asking what my uncle was doing here, the identity of the woman or the nature of the premises: in any case all three answers were perfectly clear. The important thing was to remove him as quickly as possible.

'Have you tried waking him up?'

'A bit. He just goes back to sleep.'

There was a bathroom back along the corridor. Filling a tooth-mug with water, I threw it in his face. My uncle continued to snore. After a second application he opened his eyes. Of all the memories I have of my uncle, I remember particularly that look: resigned, hang-dog, instantly aware of the position in which he found himself.

'I've been asleep, George,' he said, staring up from the pillow.

'Should think you fucking well have,' said the woman, not unkindly. 'Hours and hours.'

'Are you all right?'

'Tired,' said my uncle indistinctly. 'Heavy night. Lot on my mind. Glad to see you though, George.' I helped him down from the bed and he rested for a moment in my embrace, breathing deeply.

'George,' he whispered, 'I got to go to the *toilet*.'

'Are you sure you're all right?'

I watched him lumber off along the corridor. Some time later there was a sound of running water. Back in the bedroom the woman was smoothing down the disordered bedspread, cigarette twisted at an angle so that the smoke avoided her eyes.

'Does he often come here?'

The woman considered this with her head on one side, left hand pummelling the pillow. 'Now and again. Twice a month maybe. You his son?'

'Nephew.'

'Never said anything about a nephew.'

Any further revelations were silenced by the sound of footsteps proceeding back along the corridor, a door slamming. My uncle appeared in the doorway, breathing hard.

'I'm not feeling too good, George.'

'You want an aspirin, Ted. That's what you want,' said the woman, with faint animation. 'To pick you up. Put you on your feet.'

'I b'lieve you're right, Jennifer. I think that's what I do want.'

Watching from the doorway, I found these exchanges – the sudden use of Christian names, air of complicity, the hint of some fairly long-standing relationship – wholly sinister. What had he done in this room, I wondered, what had been said, and for how many years? If it came to that, what business was it of mine? Jennifer produced a couple of aspirin out of a packet concealed in the bedside cabinet, and my uncle crunched them up, looking round rather timidly but with a perceptible renewal of confidence.

'There any drink in the house?'

'Not that *you'd* want. Half a bottle of gin and some lager maybe.'

'Not gin,' my uncle demurred. 'Not that blessed rot-gut. All right, George.' He stared at me for the first time since his reappearance. 'Better get off, I suppose.'

'You get an early night,' Jennifer instructed, almost affably. She was lighting a second cigarette off the stub of the first. 'No staying out now.'

Fetched up in the tiny hallway, briefcase clutched against his midriff, eyes red and blinking, he made an attempt at jauntiness, lifted his feet once or twice in an exaggerated military step, winked at me over his shoulder as Jennifer pulled open the door. As we trailed off towards the taxi, she stood watching us: expressionless, self-absorbed, mildly amused perhaps. Then the door slammed shut.

'I'm sorry, George,' my uncle said, as soon as we were seated in the cab. 'Truly sorry.'

'It doesn't matter.'

'Doesn't matter! All very well saying that,' my uncle went on. 'Doesn't help though. Can't think what came over me. Ought to have spared you that at least. And Jenny ringing you up like that! Can't think what got into her.'

'She thought you were ill. You wouldn't wake up.'

'I was tired, George.' His voice rose to a high, spiritless whine. 'You don't know what it's like. Being badgered from morning to night. Kippax always interferin'. Newspapers. I can't stand it, George, and I won't.'

'Where's the taxi to go?'

'Anywhere. The office. Sunningdale. No, better make it the office. I got an evening meeting.'

'You ought to go home.'

'Don't get *on* at me, George,' he said in exasperation. It was what the West Earlham women, leaning at gateposts, shouted at their husbands. But when I directed the driver to Sunningdale he raised no objection. By the time we reached outer London, where mid-evening sun drenched the lines of traffic queueing for the motorway, he was asleep again. For the rest of his life my uncle never referred to my rescue of him from the Clapham terrace, but I don't think he ever forgot it. I believe he thought that I never really forgave him for it. In some ways I believe he was right.

Q: When did you first think your uncle might be doing something illegal?

A: I don't know. I suppose when I found out about the gilts market, and the kind of returns it was capable of producing.

Q: Not before?

A (*giving the impression of having rehearsed the words*): I had a boundless confidence in my uncle. Limitless. When I'd first known him he'd been – well, I suppose the word is a very *humble* figure, living in very unassuming circumstances. And now . . . he'd managed to reinvent himself in what was, to me, a startling way. He'd acquired this expertise, which I was greatly in awe of.

Q: But you are a qualified accountant. It can't have taken very long for this *expertise* to seem dubious.

A: It took long enough. For one thing, I wasn't working on the purely financial side, at any rate not on a daily basis. And then gilts accounting is extraordinarily complex – multiple transactions, staggered interest rates, floating commission to intermediaries. It's not really comprehensible, even to the financially literate.

Q: So when did you begin to suspect that something was wrong?

A: Not until late on. Very late on. And largely as a result of the allegations. That was when I sat down with the books – in so far as one could sit down with the books in a business like Chell Holdings – and did some serious investigation. But no, if I thought about it I suppose I'd have to say that I always had one or two doubts.

Q: Why?

A: Because I couldn't see how we could pay the interest rates we advertised and still make a profit. For example, a security might pay a thirteen per cent annual rate of interest. Now, we were offering thirteen per cent – sometimes even fourteen – to our investors. That would have meant paying no commission to our intermediaries – the people who recommended clients to us – and taking no profit ourselves. Yet we were declaring profits, *and* buying stakes in other companies. Corporate raiding. All that kind of thing.

Q: Did you express these anxieties to your uncle?

A: In the end. Up to a point. It was very difficult to pin him down. Essentially his position was that if we were paying the advertised rate of interest to our investors then our legal obligations were being met.

Q: But in fact you were paying the interest out of capital held on clients' behalf. Rather than investing that capital?

A: Absolutely. And effectively risking much of it in speculative stock market ventures. Robbing Peter to pay Paul.

Q: And what was your reaction when these facts were finally known to you?

A (*a long pause*): I don't know. A mixture of things. As I say, it was very late in the day. There was a definite sense that things were slipping away from us, that we'd lost whatever limited scope we had to amend matters, to set them to rights. But then again, I had boundless confidence in my uncle's abilities. Even at the end I thought he'd find some way out of the situation, that he'd manage to carry it off. I think a lot of other people in the financial community thought this too.

Q: Even though it was all illegal?

A: Even despite that.

Spring came slowly to these bleak hinterlands caught between the sea and the fields of sedge. In the afternoons fog rolled up from the marshlands and hung low over the town, so that a journey from the Caradon to the esplanade became a laborious trawl through twists of dense, unyielding vapour. A dead whale, washed up on the shore, lay and rotted there until the local fire brigade came and dragged away the remnant of its carcass with nets. Sitting in the residents' lounge in fading light as the mist rose outside the window, Mr Archer sometimes talked in a vague way of his troubled finances. He said:

'I'm a disappointed man, and I don't mind admitting it. All down to money of course. You wouldn't believe it, sir, the things that have gone wrong with me on account of money.'

'What kind of things?' I thought for a moment of all the ways in which money could make things go wrong. 'Legacies you expected not arriving? Losses on the stock market?'

Mr Archer shrugged. 'I sometimes think, sir,' he said, 'that it was all *fated*. Even when I was a child, you understand. I was always getting into trouble about money. I can remember my father telling me, in fact: "Money will be your undoing." I would have been ten or eleven at the time.'

'But how has money disappointed you?'

At these times Mr Archer sat at the head of the larger table, resting his hands on a small pile of items that he liked to carry with him around the hotel. They included a copy of that morning's *Daily Telegraph*, a pair of scissors, various pens and pencils. Moving these backwards and forwards with the tips of his fingers, he went on:

'Oh, it was all a long time ago. And it wasn't so much to do with the money itself. More the advice I was given.'

'Somebody gave you bad advice about money?'

'In a manner of speaking.'

More than this Mr Archer wouldn't say. But it was clear from the number of times he referred to the subject that money remained one of his deeper grievances.

Hurrying back to the hotel early one evening after a walk across the common, I came across Frances sitting on a chair in the foyer. There was no one else about: Mr Archer had gone to Lowestoft for the day. Seeing me at the door, she said unexpectedly:

'Are you doing anything tonight?'

'Not specially.'

'You can take me out to dinner if you like.'

'Now?'

'Half an hour. I'll meet you here.'

Standing in the reception area half an hour later, I wondered what Frances would wear for an evening meal outside the Caradon. It would be interesting to see if there were any variation on her usual dress of pullover and jeans. Seven o'clock came. I read the notices on the green baize notice-board, none of which had changed in the past fortnight. At ten past Mr Archer stalked in, swathed in an enormous greatcoat, the points of his ears sticking out from under the brim of a fedora hat. He looked rather wildly around for a second, saw me and said:

'As cold as charity out there, sir.'

'That's right.'

'I could drink a pint of brandy, I don't mind telling you.'

As Mr Archer disappeared into his office behind the reception desk, I saw Frances coming down the stairs. She had chosen a compromise between her usual get-up and its opposite. In fact she was wearing a kind of long skirt, so long that it reached nearly to her ankles, and a shapeless top.

'Where are we going then?' she asked briskly.

'Where would you like?'

Prospective diners-out in Eastwold between the months of October and May had a limited choice. Essentially it consisted of the rudimentary pub fare of the Nelson, the fish-and-chip shop or a restaurant staffed by harassed middle-aged women called Martha's Pantry. We chose Martha's Pantry. Here an enormous paraffin heater sat in the middle of the dining room and two or three couples hunched close up to it effortfully conversed.

'Eddie rang this afternoon,' Frances said, as we ate eggs hollandaise. 'I meant to tell you, but you were out.'

'What did he say?'

'Still nothing from the publishers. He sounded a bit gloomy.'

None of Mr MacCready's low spirits had rubbed off on Frances. In the month or so of her stay at the Caradon, I couldn't remember a time when I had seen her so animated.

Wanting to keep the ball in motion, for some reason, I asked: 'Who was the person you were talking to earlier on?'

'When was that?'

'Ten, ten-thirty this morning.'

'Oh, that. That must have been Conrad.'

'Conrad?'

'Oh, just some man.' Frances didn't seem put out by this enquiry. In fact the look on her face suggested that she was quite keen to be asked. 'Just some man you meet at a party and see for a month or two, and then can't work out why you bothered only they keep on ringing you up and there really isn't anything you can do about it. Actually, Conrad's something special. Do you know, he's been researching a thesis for eight years? That's right, *eight* years. Eight years in the British Library writing notes about some balls like the cult of the child in early-Victorian literature.'

The reek of paraffin was almost overpowering. 'I thought you liked books. Literature.' For an instant I remembered how Carole had pronounced the word: *lit-ratcher*.

'Sure. Sure I do. But he just does it to look smug, I think. You know, here we are in the late twentieth century, in the middle of a technological revolution and a demographic nightmare, but no thanks, I think I'll just work out what Dickens thought of pre-teenage sexuality, and that's all that's important, Jack.' She brooded about this for a moment. 'Listen. Can I ask you something?'

'Whatever you like.'

'Something personal.'

'Go on then.'

'All right . . . All that stuff about Carole. The Bansteads. Redbridge. *The Morecambe and Wise Show.* I mean, what did you think about her?'

'I don't know. Half of me was completely obsessed with her, while the other half always knew what the consequences of that obsession would be. But there wasn't any way of stopping it.'

'You see, I never felt like that about anybody,' Frances said. 'Certainly not dreary Conrad with his special seat in the BM and his four-foot card index.'

It was here in the revelation about Conrad that I realised a certain kind of courtship ritual had moved into gear. Always, in any relationship with a woman, I'd been able to establish the precise point when some tiny spark of attraction ignited. With Carole it had come in an unexpected solicitousness about my health, instructions to put on my overcoat, things like that; with Helena a determination to finish a book I'd lent her. I thought about other glances, other hints given and received. Frances said:

'This wine is completely disgusting. Let's go back.'

'All right.'

Outside, wind was careening down the high street, stirring the surface of the pools of water. In the distance the beam from the lighthouse broke into view and then disappeared. In an odd, flustered gesture, Frances took hold of my hand.

Half an hour later she said: 'I'm sorry. It's not going to work.'

'No?'

'I'm really sorry. I just don't think it's a good idea.'

Somewhere beneath us Mr Archer – it could only have been him – was singing along dejectedly to a radio playing 'When Your Old Wedding Ring was New'. The room was dark except for the illuminated hands of the clock and orange light seeping in from beneath the door. Frances's pale shoulders gleamed through the dusk.

'Is it always like this?'

'Mostly. Look,' she said, 'if there's anything you want to do, why don't you just go ahead and do it?'

'Don't be silly.'

'Why not?' She was close to tears now. 'That's what Conrad used to do. Corpse fucking, he used to call it.'

'Will you shut up about Conrad?'

'I think I'm going back to my room,' Frances said. 'Don't come up, please.'

'All right.'

I watched for a second as she struggled into her clothes. Downstairs, now sounding even more melancholic, Mr Archer was accompanying 'You Can't Get a Man with a Gun'. The door slammed shut. I thought about the previous twenty minutes. It was difficult to get them into focus. Above my head footsteps pattered away into silence.

Next morning Frances sat at the breakfast table without speaking. The post brought another anonymous letter, this time an amateurish drawing of a gallows with the words JUST DESERTS assembled beneath it. In the corner of the room Mr Archer buttered toast with firm, decisive strokes. Once around this time I asked her, 'Do you think this is going to be a good book?'

'Not really. No.'

'Why not?'

'It's hard to say. Sometimes I think you're not telling the truth. Other times I think you are telling the truth, but a bit selectively. Or that you're telling the truth but you're not really sure about the important things.'

'But isn't not being sure about the important things a point in my favour?'

'It might be. I don't know. But I think you could have worked it out a bit more in your head before you sat down and started this.'

'What do you suggest?'

'It's not really for me to advise. I suppose I'd say, stop trying to do everyone justice. If you didn't like someone or something they did, say so. I mean, what did you really think of Helena? She sounds like a dreadful upper-class bag.'

'Does she? What if I genuinely don't know?'

'This is *history*,' Frances said, quite sharply. 'Nobody ever got anywhere with puzzled incomprehension.'

* * *

Mr MacCready's letter arrived a day or so later. It conveyed the news that owing to what Mr MacCready called a 'reassessment of priorities' arising from their recent take-over, the publishers no longer wished to continue with the book and were, in effect, cancelling the contract. In the circumstances they would not press for return of the advance. Mr MacCready added that he was prepared to approach other companies with the project, but that there was no guarantee of interest.

'Figures,' Frances said when I brought the letter to her. 'Happens all the time in publishing. Some American corporation moves in, pensions off the directors and starts writing off anything it doesn't like the look of.'

'Do you think there's a chance anyone else will want it?'

'You want me to be honest? Not really. For a start it's old news. And then your principal villain – here – whatever, isn't around any more. If he was in prison or on a Caribbean island somewhere it would be different. As it is, he's just in a cemetery in Oxford somewhere. I'm sorry,' Frances went on, seeing my expression, 'but these things happen.'

We sat in the dining room for a while where a couple of waitresses – chivvied in Mr Archer's absence by Brenda – laboured sullenly over the rows of plates. Outside light was shining off the housefronts.

'What are you going to do?'

'Do?' She seemed surprised by the question. 'I'm going to pack up my things, climb into a taxi and head off for Halesworth station.'

'And when you get back to London?'

'Go and see whether I can get back into my flat. Ring up Eddie and see if he's got any more work for me. Go round to the *Guardian* and see if that balding swot who edits the books pages will give me a novel to review.'

'What about if I came with you?' I said desperately.

'No. I'm sorry, but it's just not going to happen, is it? I mean think about it. We can try and have a fuck for old time's sake if you like, but this is as far as it goes.'

I had a sense of things slipping away, of long-meditated plans suddenly snapped apart.

'Archer will miss you,' I said, half-joking.

'Oh, *fuck* Archer. Look, why don't you leave Archer alone? I mean, interfering in his life, cooking up all those little fantasies about him. It's just a kind of trespassing, when you think about it. Feeding off someone else's world. A pretty sad world, if it comes to it.'

We sat there a while longer. I remembered similar scenes with Carole, Helena, other women, my complete inability to say anything that would mend the situation, relief even at the inevitable outcome.

'I'm sorry,' Frances said after a bit, 'but I don't think I can go through with the fuck for old time's sake. And I didn't mean what I said about Archer.'

'No?'

'There's a way in which people like Archer just lay themselves open. Like the fat girls at school. You must have known some. I mean, *why* did they look like that? Who was ever going to let them off?' She opened her mouth to say something and then stopped. 'We'd better just say goodbye, I think.'

She left half an hour later. I watched the taxi move slowly along the high street towards the bend in the road where it would take the Halesworth turn. Then it disappeared.

And so I come to that confused and inchoate period of my life which even now seems hedged about with uncertainty, the period of my uncle's final distress and abandonment. Often in the succeeding years I set out to reconstitute some of its fragments – my uncle's white face glimpsed through the car window, the newspaper headlines, the flight over the Indian Ocean – but the final mosaic always escapes me. I can remember sections – our conversations in the Cornish cottage in the rain, the path through the fields to the village, the fretful ascent of my uncle's breath above the bedclothes – never the whole. In fact there is a more prosaic explanation of my failure to distil the essence of this chain of events, for my imbrication in them began nearly four thousand miles away, in Sri Lanka of all places, and much of what I saw was at second hand. Other people have written accounts of that week: Kippax and several journalists. Reading them, I suppose I feel as Napoleon might have felt if shown a cartoon dramatisation of Waterloo: trivial things magnified, mighty episodes diminished, the whole somehow exaggerated and underplayed at the same time. And yet I've no reason to suppose that Kippax and the others didn't set out to tell the truth according to their lights, merely that, not having seen where our story had begun, they were incapable of imagining how it had ended.

What was I doing in Sri Lanka with Helena? You'll hardly believe me, perhaps, when I say that we were on holiday, and yet we were. Don't even business executives have holidays? And wasn't this a good time to take one, it being the slack summer season in Lothbury and elsewhere? It was mid-August and the Square Mile slept. People used to take month-long vacations in those days: the partners' offices in the big accountancy firms in Fetter Lane gathered dust in the sun and the secretaries sat and idled at their desks. Most of Chell Holdings' business, consequently, was in suspension, and while there were a brace of acquisitions pending and rumours of a government enquiry into the gilts trade, no one anticipated any movement until September. 'City's dead,' my uncle pronounced one morning early in the month as we met in the Lothbury entrance hall. There was no one about. The receptionists were fanning themselves with rolled-up magazines; the plump commissionaire stood uneasily fingering his collar in the sunlight, and a solitary messenger boy lounged in the vicinity of the marble pillars. 'If you and that young woman of yours were thinking of a holiday,' my uncle elaborated, 'you should get on and take it now.' He looked more cheerful than in recent weeks, redder-faced and with an immense stuttering cough that erupted out of him at unexpected moments. 'Summer cold,' he gasped as the final words ended in a paroxysm of wheezing. 'Don't seem to be able to get it off my chest. Go on. Take a fortnight. Kippax'll be back next week.'

I studied Helena's travel preparations with interest. A great family suitcase in scuffed leather, a gazetteer of pre-war Ceylon that had belonged to a colonial grandfather, a pair of ancient field-glasses that weighed nearly half a stone, half-a-dozen packets of digestive biscuits: all this accompanied us in the cab to Heathrow and the Air Lanka flight out over the Gulf. At Dubai, where we landed an hour or so before sunrise, it was 90 degrees in the shade and the water in the airport lavatories was boiling hot: I sat in the arrivals lounge talking to a couple of tea-brokers on their way to a tour of the plantations while Helena trawled the duty-free shop for perfume. Thirty minutes later we flew on into the purple dawn.

It was an immensely dull and pompous excursion, redeemed only by a few incongruities of scene: a decayed country club, like something out of Kipling, with leopard skins on the walls and elephant's foot waste paper baskets, where we ate roast beef and Yorkshire pudding in the midday glare; a beach hotel next to the ocean, populated by sun-cured old women who lay all day on the sun-loungers smoking cigarettes; a mongoose suddenly frisking over my feet in the botanical gardens at Kandy. I record these experiences if only because they are something hard and tangible to set against the accompanying silences and resentments.

From time to time, in amongst the queer, staring faces and the dusty roads, came glimpses of the life we had left behind. The island newspaper had a page each day devoted to English county cricket. On the wall of an old colonial hotel outside Colombo I found a framed photograph of some visiting American film stars, taken in 1940. Canny, amused, the face of the current American president stared out. Once, from a modern establishment near the airport, I tried to phone the office at Lothbury, but my uncle was away and the receptionist's voice was so faint as to be indecipherable. Two days later we went north to Kandy, to a hotel where there was only a single telephone, connected to the main exchange in the south of the country – or so it was said – for a bare three hours a day. Why I was so alarmed at the idea of losing contact with the outside world I don't know, but I used to loiter about in the reception area. Helena, too, was forever making fruitless calls home, calls that never got beyond the Colombo exchange or perished somewhere in the ether above the sea. We used to discuss our predicament desultorily in the evenings, out on the terrace watching the firefly lights from the town below. 'Have you heard anything?' 'No, have you?' 'Daddy said he'd ring, but I expect the lines are down.' 'I expect they are, yes.' Neither of us could ever quite put into words the news we expected, but a sense of foreboding infected our conversation like a distemper.

Two days after this, Helena succeeded in getting through to her father. It was early evening in the hotel lounge, deserted except for a gaggle of German tourists, silent except for the occasional thud of a stag beetle hitting a window, and she glided back into the room like a thin, white ghost.

'What's the matter?'

'Daddy says there's something happened about your uncle.'

'What do you mean, "something"?'

'Something about an investigation. An official enquiry . . . I couldn't quite get it all, but he says they've been forbidden to trade.'

'Is your father involved in any of this?'

She gave me a sharp look. 'What do you mean?'

'Only that the Associated deal was still pending. It's not inconceivable that he had something to do with it.'

'I don't know. What would I know about it?'

'Do you think we ought to go home?'

'I don't know.'

That night it rained. While Helena slept I flung open the shutters and sat staring out at the dense sheets of water, seeing my uncle's face through that downpour and the gloomy sky. Twenty-four hours later I saw it again – in a two-day-old copy of the *Daily Mail* bought at Colombo airport. The story took up most of page two. Helena wandered by my side as I read it, looking over the scarves in the tourist racks. Half an hour before the flight, from a telephone in an airport security room, watched by a wide-eyed functionary bribed with a twenty-dollar bill, I managed to get through to Lothbury and Kippax.

'It could be worse,' he reported. 'The DTI got here at nine the morning before last. Fortunately I'd got wind of it the night before and took the precaution of removing some of the files. They'll have to come back, of course, but for the moment everything's nicely confused. It's the full works. Independent investigating accountants – there's four Price Waterhouse partners shovelling print-outs in the basement *this minute*; all trading suspended, balance account reconciliations in progress, that kind of thing.'

'What about the off-shore accounts?'

'You tell me. They might find out about them, they might not. If they do, there's a chance we can claim the money's for – I don't know – software sales through a subsidiary, something like that.'

'How's he taking it?'

'Ted? Difficult to say.' (It struck me that this was the first time I had heard Kippax call my uncle by his Christian name.) 'He made a speech to the TV cameras when they caught him outside the office yesterday, that was on the lunch-time news. But the first Price Waterhouse meeting was a disaster.'

'Why especially?'

'Wouldn't talk. I was there. They asked him to comment on some discrepancy – just a few thousand, gone out of some holding account – and he sat back in his chair and said "I have been betrayed," just like that. He's gone back to Sunningdale now, gone back and switched the phone off, and I haven't seen him, but there's talk of a search warrant.'

There was a kind of jauntiness about Kippax, I realised, unexpected and yet wholly welcome. Confronted with the prospective loss of his livelihood and a great deal of unfortunate publicity, he was more animated than I'd ever heard him before.

'What did he mean by being betrayed?'

'He thinks someone at Associated tipped off the DTI. Someone who didn't fancy being taken over.'

'Is that likely?'

'Could be, could be not. When are you coming back?'

'Twelve hours' time.'

Kippax's voice faded away into the warm air. I put down the phone and walked out into the departure lounge where Helena sat appraising a batik print. 'I think,' she said, 'that this will be a bit much for Mummy, but you can never tell . . .' They were the last real words that she ever spoke to me.

These Sri Lanka memories stand by themselves: a little cranny of time whose deeper recesses contain a lot more that I've never cared to take out and examine: watching Helena stride towards me, once, through outcrops of rock on the outskirts of a ruined temple, and understanding the hopelessness of it all – realising, too, that I suspected her of something that I could barely put into words but was somehow central to my own and my uncle's existence.

We landed at Heathrow at dawn, to find the newspapers, the placards and the television screens of the duty-free shops full of my uncle's bankruptcy.

At Heathrow I took a taxi to the City, stepped out of it on the corner of Eastcheap and went to Lothbury on foot. Outside the office a scrum of people converged on the door – I could see Roper, the fat commissionaire, in the entrance hall feebly trying to repel them – monitored by a television crew encamped on the far side of the pavement. As I approached, somebody shouted, 'That's him, that's young Chell!' and there was a general movement of the crowd towards me. Someone took my arm. There was a dim sensation of someone else pulling at my legs, a woman's voice shrieking insults. Roper's face, white and exasperated, loomed up through the throng.

'Mr Chell's not here, sir. There's no one here at all.'

'Where is he, do you know?' I bawled back.

'At home, they say. Mr Kippax . . .'

But whatever he was going to say about Kippax was cut short by a sudden surge and redistribution of the crowd. There was another taxi idling at the kerbside fifty yards away, and I ran to it pell-mell through an obstacle course of flapping raincoats, briefcases held up like shield walls to bar my path. It was raining hard by the time I reached Sunningdale, and the water ran in little rivulets over the gravel drive and the stone porch. The house looked infinitely gloomy and tragic: black creepers had grown round the marble porticos and two of the window panes were out. Inside Greta stood in the entrance hall folding and refolding a mournful black tablecloth. When she saw me she stepped back a little way and put her hands up to her face.

'We didn't think you'd be back. Kippax said . . .'

'Where is he?'

She jerked a finger back over her shoulder. 'In the back room there. Unless he's gone upstairs somewhere out of the way. There was police here this morning.'

In the end I found him in the small room near the kitchen which I had once assumed to be his study. Shirt-sleeved, his face red and perplexed, he was opening box files and scattering their contents over the desk-top. When he saw me he stopped and stared sorrowfully at the mess, the sea of torn papers and the disarranged shelves. He looked tired, I thought, tired and bewildered, and the colour of his face was fearful.

'George! We thought you were abroad still, George. Ceylon or somewhere.'

As I explained the circumstances of my return, my uncle stood carefully drawing in his breath and letting it out again in great wheezy rasps. Long before I finished he said: 'I've been done, George. Done, by Christ! You seen the papers?'

'Some of them.'

'Associated Life. All those journalists. Not wanting our money and running to the Department. Independent auditors coming in and trying to reconcile the balances.'

'What do they say you've done?'

'One thing you've got to remember, George,' my uncle said heavily, 'is that we always paid our investors. Every penny of interest. Everyone always got paid.'

'But what do they say you've done?' I think in my heart I knew the answer to this question, but somehow I still had to ask it.

'It's bad, George. Oh, it's bad. I don't deny it. Fraud they're saying, misappropriation of funds. All the files gone from Lothbury . . .'

'Kippax said he's saved some.'

'Kippax?' My uncle brooded savagely for a moment. 'It's my belief Kippax knows more about this than you'd want him to.'

What he told and insinuated and speculated to me over the next hour, as the rain rushed against the window and the telephone rang on unheeded in the distance, I can't begin to remember: about Kippax and Lord Charlesworth and anonymous letters and the three-hour grilling in the senior partner's office at Price Waterhouse, assurances received, accepted and then removed.

'I've been done,' he said again. 'By people I trusted. It's hard, you know.'

'Did you . . .?'

'Oh yes. I rang Her. Quite early on. Wouldn't speak to me. Some dratted private secretary saying he'd pass on a message. Told *me* he'd pass on a message.'

After this he grew quiet. We sat down, the two of us, my uncle at the desk, myself on the floor with my back propped up against the wall, and he brooded again for a while as the rain fell. There was a cigar lying amongst the scrambled papers, a huge Havana like a small bludgeon, and he lit it, puffed uncomfortably for a moment and then lapsed into a fit of spluttering.

'Are you all right?'

'Chest infection,' my uncle gasped. He looked, I thought, much worse than when I'd arrived, shaky and unnatural, like an animated representation of himself. 'Got some antibiotics somewhere. Don't care for them.'

He wandered off vaguely into the hall and I heard him shouting for Greta. In his absence I turned over some of the papers. They were bank statements: terse, uncommunicative documents concerning companies I had scarcely heard of. Some were addressed to my uncle, others to Kippax. He was gone a long while. When he came back he was carrying a mug of tea and a big accountant's briefcase, out of whose unfastened pockets more papers bulged.

'George,' he said absently, 'we got to go.'

'Go where?'

'I've been talking to Kippax. Got him on the phone just now, and there's a warrant out. They were at Lothbury twenty minutes ago, he says. So we got to go.'

I thought about this for a second or two, considering other possible courses of action, Helena, Kippax and betrayal, if that was what it was. There was a kind of congruity in what my uncle proposed, I realised. He wanted to flee, to remove himself from the mighty elements that oppressed him. What was wrong with that?

'All right,' I said. 'Where do you want to go to?'

'West Country,' my uncle hazarded. 'Devon, Cornwall someplace. Somewhere out of the way. Sit tight and weather the storm. Just you and me. Greta won't want to come, not her. Just you and me.'

He had it all planned, I realised. Even in his hour of extremity, his mind was still revolving in a way that was at once idiosyncratic, calculating and curiously naïve.

'All right. The West Country then. Devon or Cornwall. How do we get there?'

'There's a car round the back,' my uncle said wheezily. 'The Jag. Can drive a Jag, can't you?'

'I can drive a Jag.'

And so, watched by a stern and quite unyielding Greta – who I think disapproved completely of what we were doing – I loaded a couple of suitcases into the back of the Jaguar, while my uncle hunched miserably under an umbrella. When this was done, he stood uncertainly by the open passenger door and tried vainly to release the umbrella's catch until Greta snatched it away from him. She was, I saw, hugely annoyed and at the same time deeply solicitous. Busying myself with the seat-belt and a road map I discovered in the glove compartment, I heard him say:

'You'll be all right, will you, Gret?'

'I dare say I shall.'

'I'll phone, you know,' he suggested. The water was splashing down his face now, and collecting on the point of his chin. 'Let you know about things.'

'That's right,' Greta said, giving him a strange look. 'You let me know.'

And so we moved off in a wide semi-circle around the back of the house, silent and gloomy in the downpour, and along the side road that led to the front drive, past the great gates, out into the wider world.

Thinking about it now, I remember a considerable part of the first day of our flight, and while incidental vignettes occasionally supervene – eating lunch in a wayside restaurant near Stonehenge, with my uncle managing to interest himself in the weight of the stones ('Curious business how they must have got 'em there'), watching the sun rise up again as we entered a wide, sloping vale in Wiltshire – what remains is the memory of the road, like an endless conveyor belt, and the restless, unhappy figure beside me. For an hour or so, until we were well embarked on the A303, my uncle slept. Waking, he talked in a vague, jittery way, which suggested that his mind wasn't wholly in kilter.

'When you turned up at Sunningdale,' he said, 'could you see what I was doing?'

'Tearing up papers, it looked like.'

'That's right,' my uncle harangued. 'True enough. And what if I was?'

'It's illegal, for one thing.'

'Illegal,' he said. 'I'll thank you, George, not to tell me what is and what isn't illegal.'

A little later he said: 'That Lord Charlesworth, that chap whose daughter you were so friendly with. Come across him ever, did you?'

'Yes.'

'Queer chap. I'm not talking about business, George, not that. D'y'know, we once got talking about sport, and he'd never seen a game of football in his life? Not ever. Even when he was a kid . . .

'What d'y' do with people like that?' my uncle wondered seriously.

Once or twice I tried to draw him out on the subject of his shattered finances, but it was never any good. He had a number of pet phrases – 'I shall have my say in the end, George,' 'You'll find it'll all come out in the wash,' 'There'll be others that sink while I'm still swimming' – designed to plunge any enquiry into a fog of dissimulation. In the end I gave up.

It was mid-afternoon by the time we reached Exeter. At five, crossing the Tamar into Cornwall, the rain came on again and we sat in a lay-by listening to the radio news. The Chell Holdings story featured third on the roster, but there was no mention of my uncle's disappearance. Then we drove on towards Bodmin, as the moor rolled away dismally on either side of the road.

'I'm tired, George,' my uncle said. 'Want to sleep a bit.'

'We'd better put up somewhere for the night,' I suggested. 'Find somewhere proper to stay in the morning.'

In the end we got as far as Truro, and found a bed and breakfast hotel in the shadow of the cathedral. I had incubated the most absurd fears of our arrival, but the people weren't in the least bit interested in us. In the evening my uncle dozed while I walked nervously round the town: there was a picture of him on an advertising hoarding in the high street, a remnant of the old campaign six months back in which, forefinger extended, he demanded of the public if its money was safe.

We were sharing a bedroom. Still lagged from the flight, I was woken in the small hours by the sight of him lurching unsteadily over my bed. Behind him, moonlight streamed through the gaps in the curtains.

'What's the matter?'

'I don't feel well, George.' In his pyjamas he looked frail and wasted; his hands moved listlessly in the region of his chest. 'Got this *feeling* in my stomach. Cough's bad too.'

'Are there any of the pills left?'

'Disappeared somewhere. In the car maybe.'

I remember him standing by the window as I drifted back to sleep, while the light glowed around him, staring up at the cathedral spire.

It was in the morning that I first realised there was something badly wrong. Coming back to the hotel after a journey to enquire about holiday lets I found him sitting wretchedly in the front room beneath a faded poster advertising the Cornish Riviera and a bookcase filled entirely with back numbers of the *Reader's Digest.* Cheered by the sunlight, our remoteness from trouble and the ease with which I had managed to acquire a cottage near Falmouth, I was making light of this distress when he cut me short.

'George,' he said soberly. 'I'm not well, George.'

'You're exhausted. You said.'

'No, it's not just that, George, there's something I've got to tell you.'

'What is it?'

'I can't get up, George. I can't. I've been sitting here trying to since you went out and I can't seem to manage it somehow.'

'Do you want me to get you a doctor?'

'No. Just help me get up. Please. Just help me get up and get me into the car and I'll be all right.'

I did as he told me, and left him slumped against the window while I went to settle the bill. I suppose that if I'd taken him to a doctor then and there I might have saved his life: why didn't I choose to do so? I suppose because I still maintained the conviction that he was indomitable, that somehow he would survive these batterings, that everything, ultimately, would fall away, leaving him exhausted but essentially the same. When I came back to the car he'd rallied a little, and was even conning over a copy of that morning's *Daily Mail* which I'd left on the driver's seat, but there was a film of sweat over his puffy, unshaven features and his hands shook as he turned the page.

'Hot today, George,' he said plaintively as I got into the car.

It was quite a cool morning. Then the last of his self-possession fell suddenly away and he beat the newspaper with his fist.

'I *can't* be bothered with this,' he whimpered.

The cottage was a mile out of Falmouth at the end of a farm track lost in clumps of rhododendrons. A farmer's wife living halfway up the hill gave us the keys and was helpful about bedding. While I made the beds and stowed away the food we'd brought from Truro my uncle sat blearily in an armchair rubbing his ribs with his hand.

'Got this pain,' he said, thoughtfully, once or twice. And then: 'Would be all right if I could sleep.'

In the end I put him on the bed, fully clothed, and he slept through the afternoon, while the flies buzzed in the doorway and bored announcers – I had discovered an old transistor radio in the kitchen – unveiled thirty-minute theatres and afternoon stories. Later I went and walked in the woods, blundered through yards of tangled foliage and emerged into rising, verdant pasture, where a herd of cows regarded me wonderingly. In the distance yachts tacked back and forth across the wide estuary. When I returned my uncle was sitting bolt upright on the bed massaging his scalp with both hands.

'Just woke up, George,' he said. 'Such dreams I've been having. Actors and actresses. All kinds of people. Like being in a film . . .'

I brought him a glass of water and he looked at it rather in the way that the cows had stared at me twenty minutes before. '*Such* dreams,' he said again.

Did he know that he was dying? Maybe. Maybe not. I remember him being bewildered rather than frightened; peevish, regretful. As his mind wandered it tracked steadily backward, moving rapidly beyond Kippax, Lord Charlesworth and the embarrassments of the last week to distant memories that were barely intelligible to me.

'Always served my country, George. Then and now. Wireless operator in the war, did you know that? Wanted to be air crew, to fly you know, 'stead of sitting on the ground . . . Glad I never was . . . Not that you were safe, mind. Once saw a man killed by a bullet from a Messerschmidt. Came straight through the side of the truck, through the wireless, through the operator, out the other side. Extraordinary thing.

'. . . Public works, that's what I started on, George. If you couldn't get a job fifty years back, that's what you did. Remember them buildings in Eaton Park – the changing rooms and the café? Spent three months working on them in 1937, with a barrow and shovel . . . Nothing else to do, George, nothing else to do . . .'

Occasionally his imagination soared to quite exalted flights. Where he'd got the information I don't know, but it poured out of him like water from a leaking reservoir.

'Napoleon, George. Did you ever hear about Napoleon? Saw a film once, all about him . . . Years ago. "I shall ride a white horse.

I shall ride at the head of my men." And Ney and the others. And the gates at Elba like a fairground show . . . Would have been good to see him, George. Would have been good.'

Once something he said coincided so exactly with my own memories that I sat and stared at him.

'White houses, George, going down the hill . . . Remember them . . . Bright. Stannard. George Borrow. And then the fields running down to Earlham Road . . . Old farmer who kept sheep. Came back after the war and they were gone . . . Just houses going on to the roundabout . . . Always wondered what happened to those sheep.'

I can't remember how long this went on for. A day? Two days? At intervals other people came and went from his bedside: a doctor, whom I summoned from the farmhouse telephone; the farmer's wife, intrigued and appalled at the prospect of death. By this time there was no doubt as to our identities. In fact I saw the doctor looking at my uncle with a kind of wonder, prior to taking his pulse. At noon on the second day a police car bumped down the farm track, idled by the gravel surround and then went away.

There was a general consensus that he was dying. A move to transfer him to hospital was shelved when his condition worsened. Three or four times I went back to the farmhouse to telephone Sunningdale, but the phone rang on endlessly. All this time my uncle lay barely moving on the bed, small grey head at an angle, wisps of hair flung out against the pillow. He had lucid moments. Once he said: 'Sorry to have given you all this trouble, George. Would have avoided it if I could.'

'I believe you.'

'And I'm grateful, George. Wanted you to know it.'

'Of course.'

There was something greatly animating him, I realised, something that disturbed him even more than the pain. Once or twice he tried to say something about money, but the thousands transformed themselves into millions and back again and it was impossible to construe. Then, on the evening of the second day, standing over the gas ring in the kitchen, I heard him mumbling dejectedly to himself.

'What is it?'

'Something I want to tell you, George. Something you ought to know.'

I sat down in the chair. 'Tell me.'

I have no means of reproducing exactly what he said. This is only the barest impression.

'You remember when you were a kid, George? Back in Norwich?'

'Some of it.'

'Times I used to come and see you' (with an effort). 'Time we walked round that cemetery.'

'I remember.'

'Well, the thing is . . . the thing is, *I'm your father, George.*'

I remember only an odd feeling of impersonality, a sense of looking into the room from above, staring interestedly at the figure on the bed and his attendant, but with a comfortable conviction that nothing there concerned me.

'It's true,' he said, after a half-minute or so had passed. 'Truer than true. Don't you believe me?'

Again, there was nothing to say. I sat and looked at him, thinking about the picture of my mother on the wall of the house at Putney and the years of surreptitious glances.

'Don't you believe me?'

'Why should I?'

'I'll prove it, George,' he said weakly. 'That case I brought with me. Full of old papers and stuff. You'll see.'

The big accountant's briefcase lay on a chair in the sitting room. I went and fetched it, placed it on the floor at my feet and, following his directions, began to unpack quantities of folders and single sheets of paper.

'Look in there,' he directed. 'In the big envelope.'

Delving into it, I brought out a thin pile of ancient documents: old, flimsy paper that stuck to my fingers, some of it folded and refolded into grimy packages. There was an RAF identity card made out in the name of Leading Aircraftsman E. Chell, a book of W. & H. O. Wills cigarette cards depicting notables of stage and screen and beginning with Jack Buchanan, finally some bundled pieces of blue cartridge paper. Unfolded and smoothed down, these turned out to be letters – ten or a dozen of them – in my mother's handwriting. I glanced at them for a while, taking in their odd, forceful phrasings, their dramatic underscorings, occasional protestations of a kind that it was impossible to connect with the silent woman in the house at Bright Road.

'When were these written?'

'1952, 1953,' he said feebly. 'I was out on the road. Up north, travelling in confectionery. You were about by then, of course. She used to send me pictures sometimes.'

'And how did you . . .?'

'I don't know. I never could work it out. Ever. Me. Her. The two of them. They never did get on, her and Jack. Didn't matter what they did, what promises they made, couldn't get on. All news to me. I'd been away a year or so after they got married, came back to find Punch and Judy. And of course in those days you had to put up with it. No saying you'd made a mistake and trying for another go like they do now. Your grandad and grandma were dead by then, and I hadn't anywhere to go, so I used to stay with them a time or two. Not in Bright Road – they had a place over near the Fiveways roundabout then. And then I came back one day – he was out somewhere, he was always away in those days – and it just happened.'

I thought about this for a while: the house in West Earlham, my mother looking up, my uncle luminous in the doorway. What had he looked like then, I wondered? Fresh-faced? Knowing? Irresistible?

'Did he know?'

'No one ever said anything, but he was a sharp-eyed one, your dad. I reckon he guessed which way the wind blew. Then again, I never knew what your mother told him. Or didn't tell him. And she was a great one for not saying anything, your mother, for keeping things bottled up. But, whatever, he'd gone soon after that, and then he was dead, poor feller, in a cottage hospital out Attleborough way – just after the Coronation it was – with your mother and me coming over on the bus to see him.'

'But how can you be sure he wasn't my father?'

My uncle stirred himself slightly and clawed at his face with his hand. 'I can't. Nobody could. I'm just telling you what she told me, George. You can make what you like of it.'

'Why didn't you . . . I mean, after he'd died, what was to stop you . . .?'

'Often wondered that, George. Often wondered that. Then and now. But she wouldn't have it. Don't know whether she felt bad about your dad dying, or ashamed about it all, but it was never the same. Flaming rows we used to have. Not about anything in particular, just for the sake of arguing. I used to come home and stay a night once in a while – little chap you were, you wouldn't remember – but it never worked. In the end I took to putting up at the pub over the way, the Romany Rye. And pretty soon after that I stopped coming at all . . .

'. . . d'y think about it, George?' He was wandering again, in and out of sense. 'Think about that for a temper? Goes to her grave, and . . . and never tells you.'

'You never told me either. Not until now.'

'Tried to . . . I was always going to, George. Times I was going to . . . That night in Putney when you came over. Times at Lothbury, Sunningdale . . . Used to mark dates on the calendar. *June the third, tell George* – that kind of thing. Christmas Day, birthdays . . . So many things to tell you . . . but you're an odd fish, George. Didn't know . . . whether you'd be pleased.'

Was I pleased? I remember being intrigued, charmed, mournful, furiously angry. Other than experiencing these emotions, I had no idea how to behave, no idea of how he expected me to behave. Looking down at him, I saw that he was regarding me wonderingly, half affectionate, half curious.

I took his hand.

We talked a little more after that, mostly about my mother. Later, when he slept, I heard him murmuring phrases that could only have been about her. '. . . Time on Thorpe station . . . In a blue dress . . . Took the car and on up the hill, up the hill towards the sea, the bloody sea . . . Waves in the distance . . . Yarmouth and Lowestoft and the bloody waves . . .'

It was getting dark. The doctor, who came again at ten, reported that a police car was on the track, and a television crew, the former keeping the latter at bay. As I was making him a cup of tea in the kitchen he said:

'Extraordinary thing him turning up here like this.'

'Oh yes.'

'My wife had a couple of thousand invested. It just goes to show.'

'It does. It goes to show.'

In the doctor's absence the cottage seemed bigger and more desolate. Outside I could see lights winking in the distance beyond the overhang of foliage. There was no sound except his breathing, rising and falling in the inner room like the ebb and flow of the tide. All night I sat in the chair compiling a list of questions I could ask him: questions about my mother, their relationship, his job, life, other particulars. When I woke it was dawn and he lay there huddled against the coverlet, the only proofs of our conversation the small stack of paper spilled over the floor, like spent cartridge cases, I thought, rising up to transform the innocuous Flanders mud.

I have written all this down because I thought it should be recorded.

Q: Do you believe that the allegations made against your uncle are true?

A: If you mean by that 'Do I think that he acted illegally and deployed his investors' money in ways that he was not entitled to?' then, obviously, yes. If you mean 'Did he know that he was acting wrongly?' then I'm not so sure.

Q: You think that distinction can be made?

A: It's very difficult to quantify. Especially at this distance. But I think a lot of the time my uncle didn't know what he was doing, whether he was breaking the law or not. Perhaps this gives an impression of incompetence, but in fact he was a very competent man, and so were the people he employed. You have to be in this kind of world.

Q: It's difficult to conceive of a chief executive of a firm of investment brokers 'not knowing what he was doing'.

A: I'm expressing it badly. For example, he always gave the impression of being utterly sincere. Sincere in what he thought was his duty to his investors, I mean. He genuinely had this vision of himself as a kind of saviour of elderly people on fixed incomes, whom he could help by making their money go a bit further. For instance, he used to love speaking engagements. An intermediary would fix up for him to go and talk to three dozen pensioners at a lunch-club somewhere. He relished anything like that.

Q: Why so much? Why pensioners?

A: I think because they were small people, not well off, making do. My uncle really believed in those clichés about 'struggled all our lives to get by', 'saving for a rainy day' and so forth. And he thought that people who had lived their lives according to these principles had suffered at the expense of big people. Corporations. Big business. As I say, I never found the smallest reason to doubt the sincerity of this. There was a moment, towards the end when the press were on the case, when some elderly people turned up at some function he was leaving, and an old lady shouted 'Swindler' at him, something like that, and he was hugely, deeply upset. He wanted to invite the whole lot of them to Lothbury, explain the situation to them, reassure them. I remember having to talk him out of it.

Q: Why?

A: I don't know . . . Because I didn't think things were explicable by that stage. Because it wouldn't have helped, might have made things worse in fact.

Q: Small people and big people. Saving for a rainy day. It sounds – how shall I put it? – rather a simplistic view of life.

A: All I can say is that it made perfect sense to him. He was from the last generation who grew up before the war, you see. I think that made a big difference. He didn't understand inflation or asset-stripping or any of the financial things we take for granted. Or rather he did, but they annoyed him. He thought they were just wicked tricks, that's right, *wicked tricks*, designed to hurt the small man. I'm sure his business activities reflected this.

Q: And yet – you have acknowledged this, I believe – he was a corporate raider. I mean, there are several well-documented cases of him buying small concerns with a view to fattening them up and selling them off . . .

A: There came a point, I think, when it became very difficult to distinguish between reality and its opposite. Buying a football club, or a shop, or a fashionable restaurant – these were all things that he wanted to do, with varying degrees of success. But he did them, I think, because it was what he thought people like himself ought to do. There were times when he really did see himself as a kind of commercial buccaneer, taking risks just to see what taking risks might be like.

Q: Did you approve of this?

A: I wonder how much my approval or disapproval meant to my uncle. Or anyone's for that matter. He could be very self-willed.

All to do with the small man standpoint, I think. No one had ever helped or advised him – or at any rate done so disinterestedly – and so he thought he could do it all himself. *Think things out.* But perhaps this is an exaggeration, because sometimes he would buy really good advice, the best – get a firm of solicitors from London Wall to advise him on some legal point – and when he did this he could be very deferential . . . But going back to the question proper, I don't know that I actually approved, but I remember being very excited about it, very disbelieving at first, but very excited. And this excitement persisted, even though I could see that in some very important respects his judgement was seriously flawed.

Q: His business judgement?

A: His business judgement, obviously. But there were personal things, ways in which he dealt with people that were inappropriate, *grand gestures* I suppose, which could sometimes be offensive. I can remember once – he used to support a great many charities, particularly those for the elderly, and he got invited to a Christmas party at an old people's home. Now my uncle was very concerned that he should give something away, distribute presents. He agonised over this. Nobody would have minded if he'd taken boxes of chocolates, bottles of wine even, but my uncle took it upon himself to bring a wad of ten-pound notes and simply press them upon people. I can remember very vividly him going along this line of old people, sitting in their chairs, and giving them money . . . I thought that was horrible, distressing; I didn't want anything to do with it.

Part IV

And then Mr Archer died.

The news was communicated to the Caradon's guests at breakfast one morning by the younger of Eastwold's two doctors, a melancholy man who looked rather like the Prince of Wales. Though suitably euphemistic, the doctor did disclose that Mr Archer had been in a 'depressed state' and that 'things had become too much for him'. Close cross-questioning of Brenda revealed that Mr Archer had been discovered sitting up in bed, dressed in his pyjamas, one hand clutching an empty bottle of sleeping tablets. An incoherent note was found in the drawer of his bedside table.

Mr Archer's death was thought highly inconvenient by most of the Caradon's guests. 'That's all very well,' an old lady was heard to say after the doctor had left, 'but what about us? Are we simply going to be thrown out into the street? Somebody should say something.' For a while a number of people hung round the reception area in the hope that there would be an 'announcement' of some kind, but when it became clear that nobody knew what arrangements had been made to carry on the business in the event of Mr Archer's death, they slunk away.

It was difficult to know what to do in the circumstances. To stay in the hotel might seem prurient. An offer of help with the myriad arrangements necessitated by Mr Archer's death might be misunderstood. In the end I walked over the common to the creek, crossed over the Bailey bridge and sauntered round Walberswick for an hour. Here it was raining and none of the shops was open.

Back at the Caradon I found Brenda standing by the reception desk. White-faced, with her hair fantastically disarranged, she had obviously borne the brunt of Mr Archer's death. Seeing me in the doorway she said:

'Could I have a word with you, sir?'

'What about?'

Brenda made a small, confidential movement with the fingers of one hand. 'It's a bit difficult to explain, sir. Perhaps you wouldn't mind coming into the office?'

I followed her round the desk and through the door of Mr Archer's private sanctum. Here some mysterious agency had been at work, for the papers which Mr Archer usually left over the floor and the mouldy teacups had been taken away. As well as this the tear-off calendar on the wall now registered the correct date. Brenda shut the door with a terrific rattling noise. She said:

'It's about his room.'

'His room?'

'That's right.' Brenda looked as if she might be about to say something, thought better of it, and then began again. 'Did you know that it was me that found him?'

'No. That must have been a shock.'

'I've had worse. It's surprising how often people die in hotels. But it's not about that. The thing is, his sister's coming over in the morning, from Peterborough, to go through his things, and I just wondered, seeing how friendly you and he were – I just wondered whether you'd mind looking round the room.'

'You want me to look round the room?'

'That's right. Just to look round it.'

'Now?'

'If you wouldn't mind.'

I wasn't surprised that Brenda had brought this request to me. The idea seemed perfectly reasonable. Mr Archer, whatever you thought of him, had been a highly unusual person. It was on the cards that his living quarters would contain some unusual items. He and his sister could not have been close: in fact this was the first I had heard of his having a sister. For Brenda to want to prepare the way by sending in an advance party showed tact. All the same the task filled me with unease. For a second I wondered about making some excuse, but Brenda, I now saw, was looking at me with an expression of unutterable relief. Clearly some unimaginable burden had been lifted from her shoulders.

'I'll go up then.'

Brenda nodded. 'You'll find the door's open,' she said. 'I didn't see any point in locking it after the undertaker's men had been.'

Mr Archer's room was at the very top of the house, practically under the eaves. The corridor was sunk in gloom: cleaning materials – bottles of bleach, a bucket or two – lay scattered about. As Brenda had promised, the door was slightly ajar. There was a strong smell of ammonia. I grasped the handle and moved forward. Inside, the first sensation was of light falling gently over the surrounding furniture: a double bed with a thin white counterpane, a couple of chairs, wardrobe, Victorian dressing table. The walls were bare except for a reproduction of an Alma-Tadema portrait that looked as if it had been torn out of a magazine. Beneath the window, which looked out over the common towards Walberswick, Mr Archer's shoes were drawn up in a long, wavy line. It was difficult to know what Brenda meant by 'looking around', for the whole air of the room was resolutely impersonal. Somehow this feeling of anonymity was symbolised by the wide double bed. It seemed impossible that anybody had ever made love in it, laughed in it, cried in it. Perhaps this was doing Mr Archer an injustice. I examined the drawer of the bedside table and found a packet of aspirins, a ball of cotton wool and a pair of false teeth. Downstairs someone was hoovering: the floor vibrated softly beneath my feet. It occurred to me that I ought to investigate the wardrobe. This was an immense wall of mahogany, six feet high and prevented from falling forward into the room by little plywood plinths. It was unlocked. Here at last some trace of Mr Archer's character displayed itself. There were rows of stiff, ancient suits, a striped boating blazer like a Neapolitan ice-cream, a dinner jacket in a plastic dry-cleaner's carrier. Lower down, at knee-level, half-a-dozen cardboard boxes lay in a heap. Transported to the bed and drawn open they revealed a cache of boy's school stories from the early years of the century: *Shandy of the Shell*; *The Liveliest Term at Templeton*; *The White House Boys*. On their covers fresh-faced teenagers punted rugby balls back and forth or stood poised to dive into swimming pools. There were thirty or forty of these at least.

Nothing much else remained in the wardrobe except an unlocked Gladstone bag, much scuffed and dented. I hauled it out and inspected its contents. There were old letters tied up in bunches – Mr Archer's sister could look at them if she wanted to; a pile of miscellaneous papers, old tax demands, telephone bills, pages of notes in Mr Archer's thin, spidery hand. I examined a paragraph at random . . . *think that if you considered the position, you would appreciate the very real embarrassment to which . . . Notwithstanding these efforts, I submit that this evidence entitles . . .* Drafts of business letters? The ground-plan for an experimental novel? It was impossible to say. I got a sudden inkling of what must have been the awfulness of Mr Archer's life: the silent brooding in the Caradon's kitchen; the solitary letter-writing; reading Edwardian school stories. There were a few photographs wedged into the side-pocket of the bag: flyblown family groups; a picture of a small boy on which the vague hint of Mr Archer's adult features might just have been discerned. An envelope, on which these rested, turned out to contain six or seven pictures of Brenda. They were all shot from odd angles or distances: Brenda walking towards the Caradon's front door or bending over a table in the corner of the dining room. It struck me that they had probably been taken without the subject's knowledge. I put the Brenda photographs in my pocket. At the very bottom of the bag there was a flat package of commercial documents bound together with elastic bands. Something about the way these papers were arranged drew you towards them. I rolled off the bands and shook them out on to the bed. All at once there came over me that sensation sometimes induced by seeing a familiar object – an image from a well-known painting, say – out of context, a violent shake to the consciousness that immediately sends you searching for that broader framework. In this case the stimulus was a folded half-sheet of white cartridge paper hedged about with green scrolls. *Dear investor*, it began, *I should like to thank you for your very welcome enquiry. There has never been a better time to invest in gilt-edged stock. Why is this? Because the market conditions are such that gilts represent by far the most attractive proposition for the prospective investor. There has never been a better vehicle for your investment than Chell Holdings. Why is this? Because our analysis of the trading environment is unparalleled . . .*

There was no point in reading any further. I knew the letter by heart, knew it because, ten years ago, in the office at Lothbury, while Kippax fussed over a Securities and Investment Board memorandum on advertising, I had written it. My uncle had signed thousands of them in his time, sitting in the big office, a fountain pen sticking out of his fat hand like a cudgel, looking out of the window at the crowded skyline and the dawdling traffic. Transfixed by this vision – my uncle seated in his room, the pile of documents, the signed letters being borne away – I went hastily through the rest of Mr Archer's papers. There was everything I might have expected – more letters from Chell Holdings, many more letters, some signed by Kippax, others with a great, sprawling facsimile of my uncle's signature in purple ink. Some of these listed dividends; others solicited Mr Archer's interest in other investment opportunities. A third category simply congratulated Mr Archer on his choice of investment ('Cheer-up stuff' my uncle had called this type of letter). Later came letters from the insolvency firm who had taken over the company, interspersed with copies of Mr Archer's replies. I read only the first of these before stuffing the whole bundle of papers back into the bag.

There was a small chest of drawers next to the wardrobe. For a time I went through one or two of the compartments, which revealed nothing more than that Mr Archer had possessed a lot of winter underwear. But this and a search in the wastepaper basket proved fruitless. In any case, I was almost sure that Mr Archer had manufactured the anonymous letters.

Oddly, my uncle seemed very close to me then. I could see him, practically, alongside me in the room, and I could smell the distinctive combination of cigar smoke, sweat and expensive aftershave, could almost hear him coining one of his bland but curiously perky epigrams about life or money. There was rain coming in against the window and I watched it for a while, thinking about all this – my uncle's unexpected presence, Mr Archer's unlooked-for embroilment in the story of my life. There was nothing to be done, I realised, nothing at all.

Downstairs the noise of the hoover stopped suddenly as I walked into the lobby. Brenda was coiling the flex into long, shiny hanks, like licorice. She looked up enquiringly.

'It's all right, Brenda,' I said. 'All perfectly in order. Nothing anyone could worry about.'

Brenda nodded. 'Always best to be on the safe side,' she said. It was clear that Mr Archer had confirmed her low opinion of him by not leaving something outrageous in his wardrobe to embarrass his executors.

There was something strange about the reception area, I realised. It took a moment or two to work out that the green baize notice-board had been taken down and replaced by a painting of some roses that had previously hung in an obscure corridor, also that the picture of Mr Archer's wife had disappeared. Brenda noted my interest.

'I never did see the point of that board,' she said. 'All the things on it people seem to know anyway.'

'I suppose you're right.'

The front door was open. I wondered what would happen to the Caradon. Brenda's enthusiasm suggested that perhaps she had a part to play. As in so many aspects of his behaviour, Mr Archer's posthumous intentions could only be guessed at. In any case I shouldn't be there to see. Outside the sky was growing dark. Eastwards, towards the common, the lights were going on. Wind blew in from across the tops of the houses. Head down, hands plunged into the pockets of my jacket, I set off towards the sea.

There was a recognised procedure for leaving West Earlham in times of crisis or extremity: it was called 'doing a flit'. Such departures happened literally overnight. Harassed by the hire-purchase collectors or chased by the council for rent arrears, it wasn't unusual for some families simply to disappear, leaving the neighbours to shake their heads and wilfully obstruct any official pursuit. At these times solidarity hung over Bright and Stannard like a fog, and people who hadn't spoken to their neighbours in years would cheerfully tell lies on each other's behalf. Once, as a teenager, I even witnessed one of these upheavals. It involved a family called the Kennedys, who lived two doors down from us and whom I don't think my mother ever spoke to during the three years they inhabited Bright Road, so far did they fall beneath bedrock local standards of decency and sobriety. My mother's dislike of the

Kennedys, whose children she referred to as 'dirty little tykes', stemmed almost entirely from their previous address (they came from Cadge Road on the far side of the estate, which was popularly held to be the worst street in Norwich) rather than any outrageous personal characteristics. As far as I remember, Mr Kennedy was a thin, aimless-looking man who worked intermittently on building sites, and his wife a great vacant slattern who had flaming rows with him outside their house while the rest of the street affected not to notice.

Nobody knew what led to the Kennedys' departure, whether it was unpaid rent, trouble with the moneylenders, some more nebulous dissatisfaction with the milieu that my mother and her cronies wouldn't have been able to comprehend. Whatever the cause – and it may be that the Kennedys were simply the roaming, vagrant kind who arrive at places and leave them merely on a whim – I knew as soon as I turned into Bright Road and saw the van parked outside their house that something was afoot. It was quite late on a Friday night in summer and Mr Kennedy stood on the pavement directing members of his family – there were three or four lymphatic teenage children – as they carried boxes and brimming shopping bags out of the house. He looked slightly hang-dog and furtive but not wholly embarrassed, as if a small part of him rather looked forward to the reputation for defiance, for not giving a damn about whole areas of civilised, mainstream life, that taking a step of this kind would retrospectively confer. I walked past head down – it was considered the height of bad manners to come out on the verge while these manoeuvres were going on – but he wandered over signalling for me to stop.

'It's George, isn't it?' he said. 'George Chell?' (Despite my mother's dislike of the Kennedys, and an absolute prohibition on having anything to do with them, I'd been out once or twice with one of the sons and even been round to the house. It was an indescribable tip – I think the first thing I saw was a dog-turd in the middle of the kitchen floor.)

'That's right, Mr Kennedy.'

'Well, you won't be seeing us again, George.' There was something almost impressive about Mr Kennedy as he said this, resigned but at the same time faintly impudent. 'Leaving in the morning, we are.'

'In the morning?' (Again, it would have been an unforgivable solecism to ask where the Kennedys were going.)

'That's right.'

We stood looking at each other for a bit, neither quite knowing what to do, until one of the children loped up to ask a question and Mr Kennedy said, 'G'bye then,' as he turned away. Mrs Kennedy drifted out to watch the proceedings, and the last I saw of any of them was her standing at the kerbside – she must have weighed twenty stone – staring stupidly at the pile of boxes.

But there was something else about the Kennedys, something else about this incident, that gave it an importance far beyond the admittedly dramatic severing of a casual acquaintance. It was the only occasion on which my mother, to whom I immediately went and related the episode, spontaneously mentioned my father's existence. Even more curious was the fact that she did it mostly by accident. Coming to the end of a string of remarks about the Kennedys and the foolishness of expecting anyone from Cadge Road ever to live respectably anywhere, she stopped suddenly, so suddenly that I see the memory flaring up within her, and said: 'The time your dad left he just took a suitcase with him.'

'Only a suitcase?' I was startled and alarmed, but at the same time determined to keep the ball rolling, to find out all there was to know.

'That's right. A suitcase. Walked off down the street with it under his arm as bold as brass in the middle of the afternoon so that everybody could see.'

'Couldn't you have stopped him?'

'Stopped him?' my mother repeated vaguely. And suddenly the realisation of what she had been saying dawned on her, her face turned scarlet and she began a great diversionary harangue about being seen with the Kennedys and the penalties that would await me if I repeated this sin – all of which was completely unnecessary as we never set eyes on them again and next morning the house was picked and empty.

Standing on the esplanade, as the rain whipped in from the sea, I thought about the Kennedys, West Earlham, my mother, my father stalking down Bright Road (if it had been Bright Road, which I rather doubted) with the suitcase under his arm. Behind, the locked doors of the beach chalets clanked in the wind. Above and slightly to the left a dull red beam pulsed from the lighthouse. There was something to be said for departures of this kind. I thought about my mother and my uncle. Both had loved or at any rate accepted me, but the one had held me at arm's length and the other sought me out on his own exclusive terms. Each had existed in a remote, inviolable world where, it seemed to me, I had barely penetrated, and whose conditions of entry I had hardly ever been able to fulfil. Whether you respected them for this, hated them, or veered somewhere between the two, nothing could be done. Meanwhile there was the question of myself. The rain was growing heavier now, and the flags warning against sea-bathing stuck out at right-angles from their posts. Presumably life at the Caradon would go on. Even without Mr Archer, Frances or the nagging stimulus of Chell Holdings, some sort of existence would be sustainable. For a moment or two I felt ashamed of the way I had patronised Mr Archer, amused myself at the expense of someone whose life I could be indirectly supposed to have upset. I considered Mr Kennedy and the transit van. The rain came again with redoubled fury. I began to walk back along the low greystone wall towards the high street.

Back at the Caradon the front door was open and pale yellow light gleamed from the ground-floor windows. Brenda sat behind the reception desk, pencil poised over one of the thick black ledgers that Mr Archer had liked to carry about with him. She looked much better than she had done earlier that morning: the maid's uniform had given way to a kind of brown trousersuit. When she saw me she looked up.

'Gracious, you must be wet through. There's a fire in the lounge, you know.'

'Thanks. I think I'll go up to my room.'

Brenda made a decisive tick in the ledger. 'I've just been going through some of the books,' she said, confidentially. 'You wouldn't believe the state they seem to have got into. Bookings that were never taken up. Beds you don't know were slept in or not. It's going to take me hours to sort out.'

There was a small pile of ashtrays, perhaps six or seven, lying on the edge of the desk. 'And then coming down after lunch I found these lying in the hall,' Brenda went on. 'Can't think where they all came from.'

I went upstairs. Unusually the bedroom was warm and a film of condensation stretched across the window pane. The transcripts of the last month's conversations lay in a folder on the bedside table. After thinking about it for some time I tore them up and threw the fragments in the wastepaper bin.

Q: And afterwards. What happened afterwards?

A: What usually happens in cases like this. Some people stayed put and tried to brazen it out. Other people left in a hurry. As you know, I was acquitted. They brought Kippax back from Spain. I think he got a suspended sentence.

Q: And the business itself?

A: It took the insolvency experts nearly a year to sort it all out. Think of that! They had to trace every transaction back through the bank accounts and the ledgers, and this was before bespoke computer software. The only equivalent I can imagine is particle physics, where you can literally track a fragment of matter back through time, back to the Big Bang or whatever. Curiously, the shortfall wasn't that great in the end – about £10 million.

Q: Do you still see any of the protagonists? Hear about them?

A: Not at all. Not really. Greta disappeared. I think my uncle had settled some money on her, money that couldn't be got at or put against any of his debts. I saw Kippax's name in a newspaper a couple of years ago, quite respectably. I believe he'd been appointed finance director of a textile firm, something like that. I never liked Kippax, as you know.

Q: Why?

A: Oh, I suppose I felt that he was the one who was leading my uncle on, the one who was truly responsible for all this . . . all this mess. And that's what it was in the end, certainly what offended me about it. It was almost an aesthetic thing. I remember being in the office a day or so before things got really serious – Kippax had already shredded half a ton of paper by this stage, and there were rows of split-open box files all over the floor – and thinking what one would think if one saw the compartments of a vandalised train: here is a mess that someone has got to sort out. Which it was, I mean. The receivers ended up billing the DTI for £2 million over Chell Holdings, which is an enormous amount for an insolvency.

Q: What do you remember about the aftermath?

A: Chiefly bafflement. In that the press reports of the case seemed to bear no relation to the life I'd been leading in the past five years. Also a profound disorientation. In that all the people one had lived this life with were no longer there. Not only no longer there, but quite uncontactable. I remember once, for some quite innocent reason, having to track Kippax down in Malaga – a labyrinthine process that took about six phone calls – and it was like something out of an espionage novel.

Q: You were compelled to attend the trial of course. And I believe you were also present at the DTI enquiry?

A: That's right. I suppose because I was interested to see what the due and proper processes of public investigation would make of it all, whether they would be able to unravel something I'd certainly never come anywhere near being able to unravel. Going back to the remarks about particle physics, I seriously do have this image in my head of a tiny nugget marked 'truth' being dredged out of a primeval swamp, somewhere back in my uncle's early life, back in West Earlham even, certainly somewhere which I could conceive of. But in the end it was all highly unreal, tuppence coloured, *glamorous*, which it wasn't, really.

What I really remember in all this is the funeral. At some tiny church in Oxfordshire which he'd been to once and liked, and written into his will on a whim. They'd kept the press away for some reason, and what with the mass disappearances there was hardly anyone there. One of those bright, cold days when the wind scrapes you like a blunt razor, though it was only early September. The church was on a hill, and I remember coming out and seeing the mist disappearing into trees across the valley, and nearer at hand the undertaker's men with the coffin moving across the churchyard like a huge black beetle. Just that. The mist and the trees. Greta crying somewhere behind me. Turning away because it was all over, quite beyond the power of calling back, and walking away, towards the trees. And the rest of life, I suppose.

I've tried throughout all the story to tell things as they happened. Looking back on it, through the cracked glass of memory, I can only say that most of it astonishes me. Not so much the part played by my uncle – which is verifiable in books and newspaper libraries – as the more anonymous role cast for myself. Why did I do these things, I wonder – leave Norwich, marry Carole, roll through those hectic years in the big house at Sunningdale and elsewhere? All I can say is that I was impelled to do them, swept up by a series of personal and social forces that I couldn't comprehend at the time and am even less certain of now. I don't even believe that there was any pattern, any fundamental tethering in class and outlook. To particularise, I think that in leaving West Earlham I was trying to get away from a distinct and distinctly limiting kind of life, that in marrying Carole I was trying to grasp at what I imagined was a roseate version of that life, that in knowing Helena I was launched in pursuit of something altogether different whose real nature appalled me when I came to understand it. But I doubt whether any of this has any sociological force or validity. And I doubt even more that it comes anywhere near to solving the problem of my uncle.

Even now, I have no idea whether what he'd told me was true. Later, after the fuss had subsided, in the aftermath of the enquiry and Kippax's newspaper interviews and our general vilification, I went back to Norwich and looked into it all. I suppose at bottom I had an idea that even then, forty years on, some of it might be soluble, but there was nothing there. Bright Road had been dug up and rebuilt – even the stink of sulphur had disappeared, I noticed – and the people who'd lived there had vanished, gone nobody quite knew where, to the new estates at Tuckswood or Thorpe Marriot, and were quite beyond the power of tracking down. At the same time it occurred to me that even if I had found them, there would have been very little they could have told me. In the end, by dint of advertising in the *Eastern Evening News*, I turned up an old woman who'd lived in the same street as my parents and attended their wedding. She remembered my uncle as 'a fat chap' who 'made a speech'. That was all: nothing tangible, no indication of how my uncle and my mother had lived together, acted towards each other, fallen apart. Still less was there any explanation of the great wall of silence that descended after my uncle's departure. For some reason, out of shame, embarrassment, some inconsolable antagonism, they'd decided – or rather my mother had decided and made my uncle go along with it – that, their relationship having ended, it should be treated as if it had never been. I don't comment on this: I simply state it as the conclusion of my researches.

Curiously though, being told about the real nature of our relationship – and even now I can't be *certain*, who could? – didn't cause me to revise my opinion of my uncle. The things that I admired about him were still admirable, the annoyances still annoying. And I tried very hard not to colour our life together in a layer of retrospective pathos, because I knew it hadn't been like that, and that any kind of shift in perspective would devalue what I felt for him at the time.

So much of it, too, is quite impenetrable. My uncle's silence after my mother's death, for instance, I don't begin to understand. Did he not want to upset me? Fear the consequences of exchanging one elaborately developed persona for another? In some perverse way enjoy the long – and presumably agonising – years of procrastination? I could never answer any of these questions. And though there was probably other information I could have uncovered if I'd cared to – it struck me that Mrs Buddery, had she still been alive, must have known something – in the end I decided not to pursue it. There was something deeply purposeful in the way my parents – my real parents – had covered up their respective tracks, something ominously deliberate, and I recoiled from the prospect of following them any further. It was only after he'd left my mother, in fact, that my uncle's trail became at all decipherable. I shadowed it for a while through some vague and rather unsatisfactory business ventures in the late 1950s up to the repping for the toy companies. I got an impression of a solitary, faintly aimless life lived out in rented rooms and bed and breakfast hotels. Like father like son, you could say. Nothing in it suggested the remorseless trajectory that was to come.

My mother is gone from me now – it's all too long ago, and my attempts to conjure her into existence are useless – but my uncle is still very vivid in my mind. Scheming with him in the office at Lothbury, those endless nights at Sunningdale with the owls swooping over the silent garden: his voice still rises up at me when I least expect it. Of all this strange accumulation of people there is no one left but me. The rest is old newsprint, dead faces, ashes and dust.

Waking at five, as pale spring light showed faintly behind the curtains, I often used to reflect on the changes that had come over the Caradon in recent weeks. It was now over a month since Mr Archer's death. The funeral, held in Eastwold parish church, had been poorly attended: half-a-dozen local tradesmen, the president of the town's Conservative Association, a few staff and guests from the hotel and Mr Archer's sister, a tall woman in black who bore an uncanny resemblance to a figure from the *Commedia dell'arte.* Whatever this lady had said to Brenda after the service had ended was never made public. At the same time it was clear that some kind of accommodation had been reached, for the life of the hotel went on unimpeded. Unimpeded but not unaltered. A van came from Lowestoft to remove the contents of Mr Archer's room and clear the store-cupboards in the basement, and a painter was hired to redecorate the residents' lounge.

'There's nothing improves the look of a room like a nice coat of paint,' Brenda was heard to remark.

Lying in bed, sleep kept at bay by the gradual accretion of early-morning noises – the faint hum of the central heating, footsteps sounding in a corridor nearby – I thought about all this.

It was surprising how quickly Mr Archer's personality had been effaced from the premises. Going down to the kitchen the day before, for some reason that I couldn't quite put into words, I had been taken aback to find an electric heater installed beneath the streaming window and a sack of frozen, ready-peeled caterer's potatoes lying on the table.

From below, perhaps on the main staircase or in the reception area, someone – almost certainly Brenda – was singing in a high, relentless voice:

> 'I'm just a girl that men forget
> – Just a toy to enjoy for a while.'

Brenda had odd tastes in music.

Three days ago a letter had come from Frances. It contained an article she had written for the *Independent*, entitled 'Why motherhood is back', and a postcard that read *Sorry it didn't work out. Life goes on.* Well, that was certainly true. The noise of Brenda's singing was beginning to die away. I remembered a conversation I'd had with her two mornings ago as we met in the entrance hall.

'Up early?'

'That's right.'

'Off to get a newspaper?'

'Probably.'

'We can get them delivered, you know.

'Rotten weather for April,' Brenda had added as I moved past. Coming out of my room the next morning at seven-fifteen I had found a neatly folded copy of the *Guardian* propped up against the door.

The noise of the footsteps and the hum of the central heating were now moving in counterpoint. For some reason I wondered what my father would have thought about Brenda. He would have called her 'an attractive young woman', perhaps, or even 'a hot tomater'. Sleep came at last.

THE COMEDY MAN

The greater a comedian is, the more gruesomely and helplessly he reduces our stupidity to the comic formula, the more we have to laugh! How people love to laugh! They flock from the suburbs in the bitter cold, they stand in line, pay money, and stay out until past midnight, only in order to laugh a while.

HERMANN HESSE, *Reflections*

To exhibit themselves, perform before a crowd, is the keenest pleasure many people know, yet self-presentation without a basis in art is liable to crumble to dust and ashes.

ANTHONY POWELL, *Temporary Kings*

You can take the boy out of Norfolk, but you can't take Norfolk out of the boy.

ANON.

UPWARD & KING

Arthur Upward (b. 1938) and Edward 'Ted' King (b. 1940) originally met as National Service conscripts. Upward came from Salford, Greater Manchester; his partner was born in Great Yarmouth, Norfolk. Although they were on the road as a comedy act by the mid-1960s – their earliest engagements were in Soho cabaret – the duo's breakthrough came several years later, when ITV commissioned the first series of *The Upward & King Show* (1972). The pair had previously built up a reputation in BBC radio. Several more series followed, and for the rest of the 1970s they were rarely absent from the nation's screens.

With roots deep in the routines of the old-style Variety halls, Upward & King were essentially a cross-talk act updated to suit the modern taste: Upward short, red-haired and combative; King tall, reflective and lugubrious. Though initially seen as 'Northern comedians' – a consequence both of Upward's origins and their long apprenticeship on the working men's club circuit – they quickly adapted their act to a wider audience. Often compared to Morecambe & Wise (q.v.) and, less usefully, to Mike and Bernie Winters (q.v.), Upward & King were perhaps a more abrasive proposition than some of their television material (collected in *An Audience with Upward & King*, 1984) might suggest. Unusually for the period, they were not afraid to tackle political issues, while their odd, if slightly old-fashioned, brand of surrealist slapstick drew comparisons with The Crazy Gang (q.v.).

Off-stage, Upward & King's lives seemed uncannily straightforward projections of their professional guises: Upward extrovert and a staple of newspaper gossip-columns; King more thoughtful and retiring. Almost uniquely for their time, they succeeded in attracting the attention of both the mass audience and more highbrow critics – including, at the start of their career, Kenneth Tynan – who cherished their links to inter-war Variety.

In 1980 ITV declined to renew their contract. There were several ill-advised film ventures, notably *It's Nicer Lying Down* (1981), in which the pair's familiar bantering – a curious mixture of genuine affection and apparent contempt – is ruined by a creaking script (in general they wrote most of their material themselves). They formally separated in 1982, citing Upward's ill-health – he had suffered a minor heart-attack while filming the final TV series – although their popularity had for some time been in decline. There have been sporadic reunion concerts, and low-key, and mostly unremarkable, solo work. Upward's autobiography, *Solo Performance* (1984), provides a somewhat self-serving account of their boom years.

[From *Heroes of Comedy: An A–Z of British Comedy Acts, 1900–1985*, 1987]

Prologue

It was only when they started clearing away the plates from the first course that I realised the thin man was Tracy Jacks.

Until then I hadn't taken much interest in my surroundings. The two old girls on either side of me, each of whom had peered suspiciously at the menu card arranged against my napkin, had been rebuffed after a sentence or two. A woman I'd known in TV twenty years ago had come and pecked me on the cheek, but she was seated three tables away so there was no chance to talk even if I'd wanted to. In any case, I was too busy thinking. Paula's face propped up against the pillows, Shena's voice on the phone, what you gave a ten-year-old boy to eat and how you got him to swallow it. All the time, though, I'd been faintly aware of the thin man sitting at the top of the table two rows away, picking wretchedly at his food and taking tiny sips of water from a tumbler one of the waiters had brought.

Outside it was raining quite hard, so the tops of the buses moving down the Strand were streaked with water. Inside the low rasp of conversation – occasional whoops of laughter as somebody cracked a joke – blended with the street noise. It was difficult to tell where individual sounds came from. Twenty feet away arc lights burned over the top table. Here half-a-dozen instantly recognisable faces – an ex-Prime Minister, an ex-Prime Minister's husband – bent over their food. I'd been staring at them for a bit in that vague, disinterested way you stare at famous people, still thinking of the trip back from Charing Cross and what I'd say to Daniel, when once again my eye caught the thin man. He was coughing a bit over his glass now and clawing at his raggedy moustache with the fingers of one hand. It was then that recognition clicked in. Something else, too. Voices from far back in time.

An Irishman walks into a pub with a parrot on his shoulder. The barman looks at him and says, 'Where did you get that then?' And the parrot says, 'There's hundreds of them on the boat from Sligo.' Twenty-five years ago, in a studio somewhere in the rafters of Broadcasting House, Tracy Jacks had roared over that.

I was staring across the table to get a better look when I felt a pressure on my arm. The old girl on my left-hand side, prawn cocktail neatly disposed of, was wheeling in for conversation.

'Ai have a feeling,' she pronounced, 'that Ai ought to know you.'

She was one of those beak-nosed, aristocratic types, face sinking away into jowls and dewlaps, with sharp blue eyes and what people call 'good bones': the kind of cheekbones that allow you to live till ninety and still look impossibly haughty.

I muttered something about having a good face for memories, but she wasn't going to be put off.

'Have Ai perhaps seen you on the television?'

Tracy Jacks had seen me now: I could tell. He was making odd little gestures with his hands.

'I suppose you could have done.'

'And what is your connection' (*con-nex-ion*) 'with the magazine?'

'The magazine?'

'With *Senior Citizen*. With this *luncheon*?'

I was saved by the intervention of a waiter, who plonked down a wodge of scarlet beef immediately under beak-nose's chin and waved a mustard pot in her face. Hearing the little-old-lady shrieks as she fended him off, and called for 'Anthea' – apparently the name of the other old girl on my right – to pass the horse-radish, I was reminded, of all people, of Father and the genuflexions he'd have made if anyone with a voice like that had ever come into the shop. That brought me back to Dan again, and the look on his face when I'd left him outside the school gates that morning. Happy? Sad? Confident? Petrified? It had been hard to tell.

Outside the autumn afternoon was drawing in. I'd have to leave early if I wanted to meet Dan. In the far corner of the room beneath the high windows a TV camera was roving silently round the tables. The old lady had a point, of course. What was my connection with *Senior Citizen* magazine? I'd been invited and I'd turned up. Upward always used to say – even in his days of fame and prosperity – that you never turned down a lunch.

Beak-nose, who was struggling gamely with the bloody beef, drew my attention to the camera.

'Quite' (*qui-ate*) 'an occasion. Ai believe Ai heard somebody say that Peter O'Toole had won the award. Ai must say Ai've never really *cared* for him as an Ack Tor.'

Already the waiters were hovering again to whisk the plates away. Peter O'Toole. Ronnie Barker. Bruce Forsyth. Denis Thatcher. On the top table somebody tapped a microphone experimentally with a finger, making a dull, thudding sound like a chair being sharply drawn back. Men – oldish, red-faced men in overlarge suits – were getting to their feet, anxious to have a smoke and a chat before the speeches began. I walked away towards a long, white-cloth-covered table in the corner where there were ice buckets and piles of stacked-up coffee cups.

'How've you been, Ted?'

Tracy Jacks's voice sounded completely anguished – worn down, tragic. Turning round to shake hands, I saw that he looked even worse than the glance across the table had suggested: skin drawn back over his face, desperately thin. He couldn't have weighed seven stone.

'Are you all right?'

'Nothing you'd want to know about,' Tracy Jacks said – not angrily, but a bit sadly, as if he'd somehow forgotten how to deal with questions about his health. The noise of the rain droned on. It would have been ten years since I'd last seen him – back in the sports hall at Witham, perhaps, or at the funeral – but there was nothing I could think of to say to connect him with what had happened in the interval. Tracy looked as if he understood something of this. He waved his hand back over the throng.

'Don't ever remember seeing you at this before.'

'Never got asked.' To which could be added phrases like *wasn't here* and *couldn't have gone anyway.*

'Celebrity like you. I'm surprised.'

I let that pass. 'What happens next?'

'There'll be a speech or two. Then they hand out the awards. "Perkiest pensioner", that kind of thing. Then if you like you can get pissed in the bar.'

'I've got Dan to collect.'

Tracy Jacks nodded sadly. I was on the point of asking him if he intended on getting pissed in the bar, but pulled up. Tracy Jacks, I could see, would be going home to bed, to a doctor's surgery or a hospital.

'I was sorry to hear,' he said. 'Sorry to hear. About Paula.'

There was more tapping on the microphone. Around us the waiters were starting to shoo people back into their seats. Tracy Jacks took a small, uncertain step forward, tottered a bit and then regained his balance. He looked out of place among these large, fat, old people, as if he'd got in under false pretences, might soon have his cover blown, be chivvied out into the street again.

'Thanks, Tracy,' I said. 'Thanks for that.'

We stared at each other for a while longer – me in the double-breasted suit in which I could just about pass for an old-style company director or soccer chairman, Tracy Jacks an angry, soured little fifty-year-old furious at being surrounded by health and appetite – but there wasn't much more to say and we knew it. Back at the table I got a sharp look from beak-nose for holding up the proceedings and sat down in my seat just as the first speech began.

The rain was starting to ease off now, and you could see sunlight glinting off the church spire directly opposite the window. I watched it for a moment as the words of the editor of *Senior Citizen*, a gnarled-looking bloke in a corduroy jacket, echoed above my head.

'Distinguished fellow-guests . . . Delighted to welcome . . . Barbara Castle sadly unable . . . Generous sponsorship . . .'

Seeing Tracy Jacks had badly upset me. There was no question about that, Tracy Jacks who, when I'd first met him, must have weighed thirteen stone. Looking up across the tablecloths, I noticed his place was empty, which made me jump a bit. For some reason, though, there were other things moving into the mental space he'd abruptly colonised: Paula, Upward, Father and Mother, even Mary and the woods beyond the Parmenters' farm.

'Pleased that we could come together in this way . . . As young as you feel . . . Age cannot wither, or custom stale . . .'

It was the usual kind of rubbish you get on these occasions. In normal circumstances I might have put up with it. Now, though, it was all too much to bear. At my side beak-nose was staring furiously at the top table through a pair of lorgnettes. It was half-past two. An hour to meeting Daniel. Taking a last look over to where Tracy Jacks had been – there was still no sign – I stood up, murmured something that the nearest half-dozen guests might just have taken for an apology and hurried out, narrowly missing a collision on the stairs with an old woman who, memory insisted, might just have been the Duchess of Devonshire.

Waterfront

Practically the first thing I remember is the smoke billowing across the wheat fields.

They were burning stubble on one of the big farms alongside the Acle Strait, which means it would have been a Sunday morning in September 1945, say, or maybe 1946. In those days stubble-burning was a kind of social ritual, like Easter or the Whit Monday holiday – all the people in Yarmouth and the nearby villages knew when a farmer was going to let his fields blow, and the whole population would turn out armed with fire-irons and hockey-sticks to see if they could get a rabbit. There were never enough rabbits to go round. It's not exaggerating to say that the whole thing sticks in my mind like a painting: a huge, flat field, perhaps half-a-dozen acres square, the farm-lads pouring trails of white spirit round the edges, the farmer waiting on his big horse by the incline where the two fields met, the crowd of people stirring expectantly by the drainage ditches, like a gang of marathon runners waiting for the off. Then, at a signal from the farmer, one of the farmhands would chuck a lit match into the straw and immediately the flames would take and go rushing over the field in a wall four feet high with the people following behind. The trick was to be there when two lines of flame converged and the rabbits – it was usually rabbits, though once or twice you'd see a fox or even a badger – came leaping back towards you.

But the thing I recall most is the noise: the crack of shotguns that one or two of the farmhands and the lesser gentry had, an extraordinary hubbub of raised voices and drumming feet, the odd whistling noise that a newly harvested cornfield makes when you run over it. A dozen times since that day I've dreamed of this scene: the smoke rolling in monstrous black plumes (woodsmoke is pearly grey in colour, but stubble burns black because of the spirit), the lurcher dogs loping in pursuit, the panic whenever a gust of wind from the sea threatened to blow the flames back in your face. Above all, that tremendous, unrepeatable, *buoyant* feeling of running through a field in late summer, not caring about the smoke watering your eyes or the voices of your parents twenty yards behind yelling at you to be careful, your eyes fixed on the shrinking patch of straw where the flames hadn't yet met. Sometimes as you got nearer, if there was a gap in the smoke, you could see a rabbit frozen with terror at the dead centre of the square. Mother and Father were too slow to catch anything, of course, but hanging around a gang of bigger boys who were banging at a smouldering tarpaulin that someone had left out in the field I once turned up a hare that more or less flung itself into my lap and managed to catch it, which everyone said was a splendid bit of beginner's luck. I remember wanting to keep the hare – it was hardly more than a baby and had enormous floppy ears hanging down over its eyes – and being sharply over-ruled by my parents. No one was sentimental about animals in Norfolk, especially in 1946 with meat still on the ration. I can remember Father breaking its neck with a stick – a bit miserably, as he hated inflicting pain – and the odd thud the hare's body made as it fell back on to the ground. That sort of thing hits you when you're six years old.

Most of my early memories, though, are to do with the war: the sound of bombs exploding out beyond the harbour, and Mother's face framed in the doorway of the Anderson shelter; a group of black soldiers – the first negroes anyone had seen – from the American army base loafing in the market square (people talked about 'these here niggers' and said it was a shame the US government couldn't find white troops to send); Father taking me to see the bones of a Dornier that had come down on the beach near Gorleston. Yarmouth had the guts knocked out of it in World War Two. Most of the bigger streets had gaps where bombs had hit. One night in 1942 an incendiary came down on the grocer's shop on the far side of the square, and Father, who was out fire-watching on the roof of St Nicholas's church, said it went up like a blow-torch. My parents had mixed feelings about the war. Father used to say that it was a necessary evil as it taught 'that there Hitler' a lesson. Mother wasn't so sure. I think that at bottom she thought it was a costly conspiracy dreamed up by a gang of men with the aim of inconveniencing their wives. Certainly I think the idea of war being expensive worried her more than anything, and I can remember her being very cross once when Father read out a newspaper article saying that it took a gallon of petrol to move a tank a mile. 'But who's going to pay for it, I'd like to know?' I can remember her saying once or twice in a vague, frightened way. Sometimes, thinking about this twenty years later, I used to wonder whether it wasn't one of those rare instances of a simple person making a genuinely prophetic remark. In the end I decided that it was simply the small tradesman's inability to see the world as anything other than a gigantic shop. And perhaps, when you think about it, this wasn't such a stupid idea at all. Poor Mother! God knows what she'd have made of my life if she'd lived to see it. Father, too, if it comes to that. I can still hear their voices sometimes – Mother's slow and faintly querulous, Father's more patient and with a deference that came from standing in the shop all day – blending in with the noise of the gulls, the sea booming and the endless rush of the wind. Loud voices in small rooms, wind pouring over the high dunes. That was my childhood, more or less.

To get to the shop from the sea front you headed south past St Nicholas's church, turned left across the market square, took a sharp right through one of the side streets that bordered the quay and went over the bridge that led to Southtown. Here the road fetched up in a longish, greystone square with a few beech trees fenced round with a railing. There were about a dozen shops and small businesses ranging in size from Wedderbury's, the gentleman's outfitter, which extended over two floors and had a frontage ten yards long, to a bicycle shop run by an old man in a collarless shirt and a muffler, who opened up when he felt like it and was cut dead by the other tradesmen out of sheer snobbery.

Father's shop was on the far side, squeezed up between the sub-post office and a tiny baker's. In terms of the square's complex commercial hierarchies it was a small affair. Wedderbury's employed half-a-dozen shopwalkers, chivvied about by an overseer in a black coat, but Father made do with just himself and an occasional errand boy, although sometimes Mother could be got to 'mind the counter' if he had to go out. There was a dusty shopfront – the paint on the window frames had originally been green but it had cracked away to nothing – with a plate-glass window displaying a few fake boxes of chocolates and cigarette packets (the stuff you see in a confectioner's window is always fake) and a line of chipped white lettering that read S. LUTTERWORTH. This wasn't my father's name. In fact it belonged to Mother's father, from whom he'd bought the business, but the shop was known in the area as 'Lutterworth's' and my parents had got it into their heads that it would be a bad idea to change it.

To get into the shop you made as if to enter the wide porch of the sub-post office and then veered left through a second, smaller vestibule past a miniature grenadier guardsman that advertised some tobacco or other and a quarter-size model of a blind boy holding up a charity box, into which I never in all Father's time at the shop saw anyone put so much as a halfpenny. The first thing that struck you was an incredibly strong smell of pipe tobacco from the big jars of Erinmore and Latakia that Father kept on top of the shelf next to the door. To the left, at knee height, level with the window, were trays of sweets of the kind that have more or less disappeared: sherbet fountains, pink sugar pigs, rosebuds, fruit salad, candy bananas. Sweets were cheap when I was a kid. Fruit salad were a dozen a penny, candy bananas were a farthing, and you could make yourself sick for fourpence. Beyond the sweet trays came the counter proper, with its piled bars of Bourneville and Caley's Marching Chocolate that came from the big factory in Norwich, covering two sides of the room and ending up in rows of cigarette packets. Ardath. Woodbines. Player's Navy Cut. Gold Flake. People said Woodbines were made of horse manure. Most of those brands have simply disappeared. At head height and beyond ran a line of confectionery jars: Mint Imperials, Fruit Thins, Sugared Almonds and a queer kind of shiny coconut squares which I think were called Jap Desserts – and above these huge two- and three-pound boxes of chocolates, which people hardly ever bought except at Christmas.

It doesn't take much to imagine myself back in the shop. The sight of a row of lemonade bottles in an off-licence – the old jars of Vimto that Father used to sell forty years ago that are making a comeback – an old-fashioned corner shop of the kind you still occasionally see in northern towns, even a chocolate-wrapper face up on the pavement, and I'm back there, on a grey autumn afternoon, say, in the early Fifties, with the lights going on across the square in Wedderbury's huge plate-glass windows, rain blowing in with the wind, and Father's head bobbing up from behind the till at the sound of the doorbell. The shop is where I best remember Father, and if I want to think about him I have to start by conjuring up the smell of tobacco and sweet stuff (confectionery has a distinctive, faintly sickly smell) that hung around him like scent. He was a small, spareish man, with a lot of brindled hair going yellowy-grey at the sides like old piano keys, and a permanently cricked back from lifting boxes. At this time Father would have been in his late forties – he was born in 1904 – but he already had that faintly pinched, worried look that I associated with older people. This, of course, was standard for the time. People were matter of fact about growing old in those days. Father and Mother would have been scandalised by the idea of a woman dyeing her hair or jogging to keep herself looking young. They would have thought it 'against nature' or – one of Mother's favourite phrases – 'making an exhibition of yourself'.

Even now I'm not quite sure what Mother meant by 'making an exhibition of yourself'. On the one hand, from my own point of view, it described simple bad behaviour – making a noise in the square, putting more food on your plate than you could eat (there was a terrible fuss once when we went to tea at an aunt's house and I couldn't finish a piece of fancy cake someone had given me). At the same time, there was a huge selection of sub-meanings that usually, but not always, reduced themselves to questions of social propriety or (another of Mother's pet phrases) 'knowing how to behave'. Adding a couple of rooms to the back of your house, which meant having builders' lorries in the street and men in overalls unloading bags of cement, was 'making an exhibition of yourself', but so, oddly enough, was ekeing out your income by taking in lodgers over the summer months when the town was crammed with holidaymakers. There was no logic in Mother's pronouncements. To her a plain girl who refused to have her hair set or 'tidy herself up' was as bad as a pretty one who put on make-up and came to church in high heels. Each was somehow an affront to her odd sense of decorum, rules which it was impossible to avoid transgressing because, in the majority of cases, you didn't know what they were.

And yet by the standards of Great Yarmouth both my parents would have been judged dangerously emotional and volatile types – I've seen Father cry more than once, and Mother, too, was prone to extraordinary public sulks and offence-takings. At bottom, I suppose, they were simply selfconscious. In Father's case this deep personal unease had a social origin; he was a fisherman's son from along the coast at Gorleston who had married a tobacconist's daughter, and the awareness of this transit weighed him down and coloured everything he did. With Mother it was more fundamental, a kind of aloofness and detachment from life that concealed a deep and hugely embarrassing wistfulness. Half-a-dozen times I can remember her turning down some social invitation – joining a group of other women for coffee in one of the big department stores near the front, which she always disparaged as 'a nice thing for people with no work to do' – and then brooding endlessly about the refusal. What was Mother scared of? What upset her so much about the idea of three or four shopkeepers' wives trading scandal in a tea-shop? Well, I never found out, and now I never will.

If my chief memories of Father are from the shop – bowing out a customer, perhaps, or standing in the doorway with a copy of the *Yarmouth Mercury* pressed against his midriff peering diffidently out across the square – then I associate Mother with the room that lay immediately behind it. Along with at least half the shops in the square, Lutterworth's had been converted from the front room of an ordinary house. Walking down the passage that began behind the till, consequently, you came first to a parlour, with a fireplace and peculiarly yellow-papered walls, and then a kind of kitchen-cum-sitting room, with the cooker and a row of cupboards at the back and the foreground taken up by a big deal table and half-a-dozen chairs. Like the shop, the first thing that struck you was the smell, in this case a compound of cooking, damp and eau de cologne (Mother thought women who wore perfume were 'cheap', but she wasn't above sousing herself in eau de cologne). She was a big, untidy woman with a scallop of ash-blonde hair that was flattened down into waves in the week after she'd visited Madame Melos's salon on the far side of the square and then sprang shaggily over her head for the month before her next appointment. Sometimes she'd be doing something vaguely culinary in the tiny scullery that backed on to the kitchen, but mostly she sat in an armchair at the side of the deal table nearest the door doing what she called 'getting on with things': knitting, or restitching the stiff white shirts Father wore in the shop, having what was always described as 'a nice cup of tea' or damping down what even as a small child I could deduce was a pretty relentless appetite (she wasn't above pilfering handfuls of sweets out of the trays although nothing was ever said about this).

About five o'clock, if trade was slack, and with one ear cocked for the jangle of the shop bell, Father would leave the counter and we'd have tea together. If you asked me which times I remembered them best as a couple it would be here in the back-kitchen, Father hunched up in the big armchair with his spectacles balanced on the bridge of his nose, reading out paragraphs from the local paper, while Mother cut slices off a loaf of bread (she did this in the traditional Yarmouth way, holding the bread against her hipbone with her left hand and cutting it with her right) or nagged at Betty, my foster-sister, to stoke the fire. Mother had an inexhaustible appetite for the kind of thing that got printed in the *Yarmouth Mercury*: disasters at sea ('all hands missing' is a phrase I remember from early on), fish prices, visit of the Lord Lieutenant, assault cases from the council estates. I can see the two of them sitting there now, Father flicking the pages out in front of his face in a way he had, Mother looking up from her work in a vague and somehow querulous way as they discussed a shoplifting case or the Lowestoft bigamist who was discovered to have three wives living within ten miles of each other. National events completely baffled them, of course. Mother had been to London once or twice and Father, I think, had spent some time in the Midlands during the war, but the world beyond Great Yarmouth might have been the Borneo jungle for all they understood about it. Neither, for example, could have told you the name of any capital city outside Europe, and I don't think Mother knew the name of a politician beyond Churchill, Attlee and Aneurin Bevan. Later, when I was nearly grown up, I can remember them being furious about Suez and 'this here Nasser', as Father put it, without having the least idea of who Nasser was and what he stood for. But this kind of insularity was standard for the time. Most of the tradesmen Father knew in the square were proud of the fact that they'd never left England except for war service, and in some of the nearby villages, even in the Fifties, you could still turn up old people who'd barely been out of the county.

If this makes it sound as if I disliked my parents, thought them timid and narrow-minded, then it isn't meant to. In fact there are times when I'd willingly swap what I have now to be back in that room in Yarmouth, a mile from the North Sea, with the daylight fading across the square and Mother singing quietly to herself – she liked those tremendously gloomy Victorian ballads where the heroine always dies of consumption a week before the wedding – or drowsing over Ethel M. Dell's *Silver Wedding*, waiting for the last of the late-afternoon customers to drift away and Father to come in from the shop to read her a story about a girl who'd been sent to jail for drowning her illegitimate baby. They were decent, modest-living, God-fearing people of a type you don't come across these days: unambitious, sharp in small matters, easily deceived in large ones. I think they loved me, and I'm certain I loved them, admired them too, or at any rate accepted them and their foibles in a way that's now quite beyond my comprehension. When I remember their faces, which I do with surprising regularity, it's for their fundamental incuriousness, the way they'd look at me when I came into a room with an odd and almost bovine disinterestedness. They were my parents, I was their son, and that was it. What would Mother have said, I wonder, if I'd asked what went through her head? Probably told me to stop making an exhibition of myself and left it at that.

It's 1950, maybe, or 1951, and I'm ten years old, sitting in the small armchair on the right-hand side of the deal table with my forehead creased over my geography homework, which involves memorising the English county towns. King George is at Buckingham Palace, and Mr Attlee – of whom Father and Mother heartily disapprove – is at Number Ten. Outside the gulls are soaring over the square. Mother is thumbing through Warwick Deeping's *Sorrell and Son*, while Father reads her a piece about a dead whale washed ashore on Hemsby beach. God knows, there were worse places to grow up.

Though Father used sometimes to say – without the least hint of irony – that 'we' (meaning himself, Mother and me) were 'a big enough unit', this wasn't by any means the limit of the family circle. Father had tribes of relatives living along the coast – red-faced fishermen from Cromer and Sheringham who appeared unexpectedly in the shop at tea-time and antagonised Mother by saying 'bloody' and dropping cigarette ash on the grey drugget carpet. Grandpa Lutterworth, who for some reason was known as 'Grancher', lived with us for a couple of years after the war, although I don't remember much more than an old man wrapped up in a blanket lolling in front of the fire with his mouth open, and there was an odd cousin of my mother's with some queer job connected with electrical parts who came intermittently to stay, and who I think Mother and Father regarded as a bit of a black sheep.

By far the oddest addition to the row of faces round the kitchen, though, was the arrival of my foster-sister Betty. This must have happened in 1951 and took place literally overnight, which is to say that I woke up one morning to find a strange girl in a print frock eating breakfast while Mother fussed about with packets of cereal and teacups and Father fluttered in the shop doorway, running his hand nervously through his brindled hair. This, of course, was standard Southtown practice. Parents didn't tell their children things in those days, and it was quite usual for a girl to be taken out of school and set to work in a shop at a couple of days' notice. Even Mother, though, must have realised that some kind of explanation was called for, and an hour or so after breakfast, when Father had taken Betty into the shop, she summoned me into the parlour and shut the door behind us.

'Now then young Ted,' she said – I was a big, butter-haired boy, tall for my age, and Mother and Father had stopped calling me 'Edward' about the time I went to infants' school – 'who do you think that is then?'

Curiously enough, I was less interested in Mother's explanation of the strange girl in the kitchen than by the fact that she'd dragged me into the parlour to deliver it. It was a dreary, dingy room with a big horsehair sofa and a couple of armchairs and a faded picture of Grancher wearing a frock coat and a pair of spats, which was scarcely ever used except at Christmas or on occasional Sunday afternoons when there was 'company'. The symbolic significance of entering it at ten o'clock on a Monday morning impressed me no end. Perhaps Mother saw something of this uneasiness, for she waited a minute or two before starting off on a slightly different tack.

'I dare say you're wondering who that girl might be,' she resumed. 'The one that's in the shop just now with Father?'

I nodded. It seemed important, all of a sudden, to propitiate Mother. 'Is that what she's here for? To help Father in the shop?'

Mother laughed. 'Help Father in the shop? Not her. Not likely. She's your foster-sister, Ted.'

I thought about this for a bit, skimming over the pictures on top of the teak sideboard next to the fireplace: Father and Mother on their wedding day in 1936, aunts with gleaming teeth, a brood of windblown children staring out of the back of a charabanc.

'How old is she?'

'Fourteen, I think. Fifteen.'

There was a slightly forced jollity about Mother as she said this, which even then I diagnosed as someone attempting to make the best of a bad job.

'Anyway,' she went on, 'her name's Betty – Elizabeth, I should say – and she's coming to live with us. I don't expect she'll bother you much, but you've to try and be a friend and not aggravate her.'

'Will she be staying long?'

'That's for us all to see,' Mother said enigmatically. 'But just remember she's your sister and you've to be kind to her.'

'All right.'

'She seems a nice, decent girl,' Mother went on, without much conviction, 'but I don't suppose some of her ways will be our ways. Would be surprising if they were, wouldn't it? Just remember that, and we won't go far wrong.'

As if to demonstrate that the interview was at an end, she picked up the fire-irons, gave them an almighty clatter, and then began to take a furious interest in a sepia photograph of an old gentleman with a spade beard stooping benevolently over an outsize vegetable marrow.

Even today I can't begin to fathom the motives that led Father and Mother to import Betty into our household. She was a big, square-hipped, curiously wooden-looking girl – the kind that always look as if they're about to burst out of their clothes – with a habit of chewing on her underlip that made her seem faintly simple, which she wasn't in the least. At this point she would still have been at school – she was fourteen and a half as it turned out – at a back-street secondary where the local social services sent their 'difficult' cases, but within a month or so the school business was mysteriously thrown over and she simply lay around the house eating enormous meals, chewing on her underlip and cheeking Father and Mother. I used to watch her doing it sometimes, with a sort of awe that was mixed with admiration, because it was carried out with such enormous subtlety. Listening to her getting out of making a cup of tea or helping Father bring boxes in from the yard, you could never put your finger on the precise word or phrase in her reply that was meant to annoy, while at the same time never doubting the absolute hatred and contempt she felt for whoever was doing the asking.

From an early stage it was clear to everybody – Father, Mother, me and Betty – that her arrival had been the most tremendous mistake. Beyond this, though, any attempt to deal with her was hamstrung by my parents' inability to agree a united front. Father said that she was a 'poor girl' who'd been 'dealt a bad hand in life', and after a few feeble attempts to get her to help in the shop sensibly kept out of her way. Mother, on the other hand, on whom most of the business of supervising Betty naturally devolved, merely disliked her. She was forever chivvying her around the kitchen, or devising futile little tasks which would 'help her to manage a house', or simply nagging at her. I can see the two of them now, standing there in the back room, with Mother doling out instructions in that faintly querulous way she had and Betty making things worse by getting her to repeat everything or pretending she didn't understand. Looking back, I think Mother was just embarrassed – by Betty herself, Betty's cheek, the situation she'd unwittingly brought about – and also slightly fearful, as if there were some even thornier problem looming up on the horizon which only she could foresee.

Quite what benefit Father and Mother thought they'd derive from having Betty on the premises I can't imagine. It can't have been financial – I think the council paid them twenty-five shillings a week for fostering, which given the amount she ate meant they were almost certainly losing money on her. Probably they'd gone into the business thinking they could procure a quiet eleven- or twelve-year-old who'd be a companion for me and perhaps a bit later could help out in the shop, only somehow to end up with Betty, who smoked cigarettes out in the yard and rolled her eyes at anything in trousers.

To do Father and Mother justice, they did make an effort with Betty. Father brought home girls' comics like *Treasure* and *Princess* which he'd gravely present her with, and Mother occasionally took her out to visit friends. It never worked, though. The magazines, with their curly-haired, fresh-faced girls smiling on the cover, stayed unread; installed at some tea party across the square with half-a-dozen shopkeepers' wives, Betty simply sulked. I can see now that my parents were quite baffled by Betty, that they couldn't understand why she wasn't grateful to them for 'taking her in', as Mother put it, or wouldn't lift a finger around the house. They used to sit in the kitchen after she'd gone up to bed having long, mournful conversations about her various delinquencies, but the thought that she might not have liked living in their house, and resented the entire social process that had brought her there, never occurred to them. For my own part, I don't suppose I had more than a dozen conversations with her. You know how you can be in a house with someone for a year – that was about the time Betty stayed in the square – and never really come to terms with them or determine who they are? Well, that was me with Betty. She had a trick of proposing more or less unanswerable riddles. Catching hold of me early in the morning in the passage, she'd suddenly demand:

'What's a thing the cleverest man in the world couldn't do?'

'I don't know.'

'Eat two dinners off the same plate.'

At other times she'd go on about her family – she came from the East End and talked about 'the Smoke' and 'fellers' – and her mother, who she claimed had given her up for adoption at three. This was another thing my parents had against Betty, the fact that she came from London – Mother, in particular, regarded cockneys as not much better than plague-rats, and shivered whenever she saw a London coach making its way along the sea front.

The only real conversation I recall having with Betty was one time when she'd been with us nine or ten months. It was a grey autumn Sunday afternoon, with the rain coming in across the square, and Father and Mother had gone out somewhere leaving us alone in the house. Betty, I remember, was in a worse mood than usual because Mother had finally begun to lose patience with her and was talking about getting her a job in a shop or even – this was a mark of the depths of despair to which she'd been plunged – making enquiries about cleaning work at the Northgate Hospital. I don't suppose I'd ever been on my own with Betty before, and I wasn't much looking forward to it – there was a grisly 'tea' of ham sandwiches and Bath buns laid out on the table – but no sooner had my parents disappeared than Betty lumbered up from her chair next to the radiogram, fixed me with a look that was kind of calculating and enticing at the same time, and said:

'Here, young Ted. Let's go into the shop.'

There was an absolute prohibition on going into the shop when Father and Mother weren't there. Oddly, though, this didn't bother me. In fact a part of me wanted very much to stand on my own under the gaze of a couple of hundred cigarette packets. There was also the thought that somehow I wasn't responsible for this breach of regulations, that if any trouble came of it I could always put it down to malign exterior influence. Betty seemed to know this, for she said rather meaningfully:

'I won't tell. That's if you won't.'

'All right.'

Together we stole through the passage into the space behind the counter. The Venetian blinds that hung across the front windows had been pulled down, and there was a dust-sheet lying over the sweet trays by the door. When I went to turn on the electric light, Betty whipped my hand up from the switch.

'Don't put the light on. Someone might see.'

There was a stool under the lip of the doorside counter which Father used when he was restocking the shelves. I dragged this out into the middle of the floor, while Betty – who'd clearly occupied herself in planning this excursion – roved around the sweet jars for a bit and drummed her fingers on the till. There was a look of animation on her face that I hadn't seen before. All the same I knew that I didn't really trust her, and was already wanting the adventure to end. Finally Betty flicked a packet of Woodbines off the counter, flipped one out and lit it with a sulphur match that she produced from her shirt pocket and scratched on the sole of her shoe.

'Well, this is bloody boring. Come upstairs and I'll show you something.'

Halfway along the passage between shop and living quarters a wooden staircase led up to a tiny landing, where there was a greeny-grey oilcloth carpet and an aspidistra standing on top of a bamboo occasional table. Father and Mother's bedroom lay directly behind, the door thrown open so that you could see the picture of the two carthorses in a field that hung on the far wall. Further along the corridor was my room, the bathroom and a kind of box-room that they'd done out as Betty's bedroom, basically by dragging in a cheap bed bought from the secondhand shop on the far side of the square and filling the rest of the space with various knick-knacks brought down from the loft that Mother thought would 'do'. It was here that we ended up, sitting on the pink satinette bedspread, kicking our legs back and forth, and staring at the room's only ornament – a picture of a man with slicked-back hair and a moustache that Betty had cut out of *Film Fun* and stuck on the far wall.

'Who's that?'

'He's an actor, stupid. Gregory Peck. I've seen him at the pictures. Your dad hasn't got a moustache, has he? I like men with moustaches.'

The idea of liking men with moustaches seemed so alien to any of the notions I'd conceived about the world, any of the preferences that seemed to govern the way in which things were ordered and arranged, that I simply kept quiet. Betty, meanwhile, was rummaging under the bed.

'You can look at these if you like. As long as you don't tell.'

She arranged the objects carefully on the bed. There were a couple of large, two-pound boxes of Milk Tray, a dozen or so bars of chocolate, several packets of cigarettes, two copies of *The Woman's Home Companion*, one or two other things. Betty sat staring at them for a bit, running her hand gently along the edge of one of the boxes.

'You shouldn't take things from the shop.'

'Go on. *She* does. Always sneaking in there when she thinks there's no one looking. I've seen her.' One of the Milk Tray boxes was half open. 'Go on. You can have one if you like.'

They were expensive chocolates, probably the most expensive that Father sold. I got given them occasionally as a treat at Christmas or birthdays. I shook my head.

'Soft, you are,' Betty said, not unkindly. 'Take a box then, and have it later. Go on.'

With the box under my arm, reasoning that I could slip it back into the shop at some future point, I walked downstairs with Betty following. Half of me, I think, was a bit frightened at the sight of Betty's contraband; the other half was faintly exalted. I was twelve years old, and such rebellions as I'd engineered against Mother and Father had been of the most trumpery kind: not eating my tea, say, or pissing in the wash-basin in my bedroom when I couldn't be bothered to go to the bathroom. In the kitchen the fire had gone out, and the plate of ham sandwiches lay fraying on the tablecloth. Betty stood in the doorway, arms akimbo, one leg hooked over the other, smoking another cigarette. She had a look on her face that I later came to recognise: a kind of end-of-tether, don't-care-what-happens look, altogether alien and remote.

'I've a good mind to smash this bloody place up,' she said suddenly.

After that I can't recall the exact order in which things happened. I can remember Betty throwing one of the plates of ham sandwiches on the floor and grinding it with her foot, and finding a tray of eggs in the scullery – fine, brown eggs they were, too – which we smashed against the wall next to the cooking stove. There was a quart of milk in the cold box that Betty wanted to pour over the carpet, but in the end we compromised by throwing flour at each other and smearing jam over the covers of Mother's library book – it was a copy of J. B. Priestley's *Festival at Farbridge*. That's what children are like, sometimes, when they're sat on by their parents, and never allowed to kick over the traces. To this day I don't know why we did it – or rather I know why she did it, but I don't know why I joined in. I can remember feeling faintly sick and excited at the same time, and also a bit awed at Betty's brazenness. There was a moment towards the end when she stripped off her skirt and paraded around the kitchen in her slip pretending to be Diana Dors, and I stood there looking at her marching up and down between the clouds of flour, with the spilled jam sticking my fingers together and the glass from the smashed jar crunching under my feet, thinking that what we'd done was simple wickedness.

I dare say that if we'd been modern kids we'd have finished the job properly, smashed the shop windows, poured creosote over the floor and been found stark naked in Father and Mother's bed clutching an empty bottle of brandy.

But this was 1952, the kitchen clock had marched round to half-past four and old Mr Hargraves who kept the sub-post office next door was out in his yard casting interested glances through the back window. We calmed down a bit then, and sat on either side of the deal table staring at the mess and at each other. I'd got jam all over my white Sunday shirt, and Betty's hair was grey with descending flour. We were crying, too – me out of genuine shock and contrition, Betty more or less out of surprise.

Somehow we cleaned it all up in time, swept up the flour and the smashed plates, scraped the eggs off the wall and wiped it down. The library book was beyond saving, but we concocted a story about Betty spreading a slice of bread and jam and tripping over the lino. For some reason Father and Mother, when they got back, accepted all this, although I can remember Mother being very suspicious about the missing eggs and asking us several times what we'd got up to in their absence.

In normal circumstances, I suppose, this would have been the start of something between Betty and me – some complicity, even some vague alliance. As it happened, though, it didn't turn out like that, and I don't suppose we ever exchanged more than a few sentences (I remember her once stopping me in the street and telling me that she'd got a 'feller', and me asking who it was and being told to mind my own business). But the only thing that really troubled me about the afternoon was the box of chocolates, which I forgot about in the rush of tidying up and then found I'd left on my pillow, of all places. Slipping it into the shop when Father's back was turned, which had been my original idea, turned out to be more difficult than I'd imagined. For a time I wondered about hiding the box under my coat when I went for a walk and chucking it into a wastepaper bin, but it was nearly a foot long and Mother had sharp eyes for that kind of thing. In the end I simply put it in the big store-cupboard at the back of my old bedroom, hidden under a pile of Father's old shirts, which I knew nobody ever disturbed. But for some reason I was always on thorns to make sure it was still there, turning it over in my hands like a fetish, a perpetual reminder of something which in other circumstances I might have forgotten – that queer, other-worldly afternoon when, like Tom Thumb and Hunca-Munca, the two bad mice in the story book, Betty and I had deliberately smashed up my parents' kitchen. But that was the kind of thing that a place like Yarmouth did to you, back in the old black-and-white world of gulls and factory smoke and bicycling old men – turned you in on yourself, made you sour, unable to yield things up and put them aside. Father and Mother never forgot a bounced cheque or a customer who'd 'done them wrong', and they weren't vindictive people, it was just a kind of elemental reckoning up of the profit and loss account by which they lived. I dare say a kid of twelve worrying about a box of pilfered sweets sounds odd to you, but people took things like that very seriously fifty years ago, and certainly I'd never have dared to tell Father and Mother what had really happened. I knew that they'd never believe me, that it would mean months of awful silences and festering resentments. Poor Father! I can see the look he would have given me – a sort of incredulity mixed with bitter disappointment – and I knew even then that I wouldn't have been able to live with it. Would you?

Beyond the dunes the coastal path tracked north to the seaside villages: Happisburgh, Hemsby and Eccles. Here on a good day you could see as far as Scroby Sands, mysteriously reclaimed from the sea in the Twenties, where great herds of seals basked along the shoreline and the boatmen sometimes dropped holiday trippers. Southwards, not more than a few miles took you past Gorleston and Hopton over the county border into Suffolk. Even then people still talked about 'Silly Suffolk' and told jokes about the Suffolk farmer sent to market to find a wife who came back with his sister. Father had an uncle in Lowestoft, which I can only remember as a cluster of old houses and the fish market, but I don't think we went there more than three or four times. Westward lay the Acle Strait, with the Norwich road running through the middle, and the flat fields – so flat that you could look five miles in either direction and not see anything except the windmills dotting the horizon like enormous scissor blades. I haven't thought much about Norfolk in the past thirty years, but there's a confused impression of long, low acres of sedge and drainage ditches running on endlessly into the distance, knife-edged winds, billowing space and silence. Set down at Yarmouth railway station, disgorged from charabancs in front of the Britannia Pier, the tourists sometimes took fright at what they found. In my teens, once, I was hanging around near the marina when a middle-aged man in an open-necked shirt with the collar pressed back over his jacket and one of those old-fashioned cameras with a saucer-shaped flashbulb hanging round his neck came up and, after a minute or two's conversation, asked what there was to see. It was a good question. How were you supposed to convey the immensity of the Norfolk flat, the extraordinary sensation you got walking back over the marshes that nothing had changed in a thousand years, to a man who worked in an engineering shop in Dudley? In the end I simply pointed him in the direction of the pleasure beach and the theatres, and then watched him go off, camera hanging against his collar-bone, reassured by the horse-drawn carriages along the front and the old men playing bowls on the Marrams.

By this time, of course, the herring trade had been and gone, and Yarmouth was a holiday town pure and simple. Thirty years before the trains had still shipped hundreds of fisher girls down from Scotland every autumn to work the quaysides, they'd unloaded eight tons of cod on South Quay in one month in the Twenties, but now the seas were fished out and the great days were over. Everybody over forty in the town had their memories of the herring trade. Even Father and Mother, who weren't at all poetically minded, used to talk sometimes about the forests of ships' masts clogging up the quayside near Lords' Quay. Everywhere you looked, too, there were memorials to this vanished life: shop-window prints of ships crossing the bar of the town harbour; plaques for trawler boats lost in the heavy seas beyond Scroby. It struck me sometimes, even then, that Yarmouth was really only a kind of ghost-town. The heart had been knocked out of it when the herring boats left, Hitler's bombs had done the rest, and only the sun-cured old blokes who stumped round the place in wading boots wearing bosun's caps and taking little skiffs out in the rough water under the pier had any real connection with what had gone. The rest was simply modern rubbish – marinas and pleasure gardens and candy floss – got up to entice the trippers.

The holiday season in Yarmouth lasted from about mid-May to early September, and began literally overnight. One day the front would be virtually deserted, with all the kiosks shut up and the guest-houses slumbering behind pulled-down blinds; the next the hotels would be sprouting a rash of VACANCY signs and everywhere was a riot of popcorn and Kiss-Me-Quick hats. The local people had horribly mixed feelings about 'trippers'. On the one hand, there wasn't a shop in Great Yarmouth, or the surrounding area, that didn't make half its profits in the summer: even in the square, which was a mile from the front, we'd sell a freezerful of ice-cream a week in July and August. On the other, the tradesmen regarded the Lancastrian mill-workers who thronged on to the beach on summer afternoons and got rowdily drunk on Saturday nights in the streets near the marina with an unutterable contempt. No one, for instance, would eat in a restaurant that was known to be patronised by tourists, and I've seen a shopkeeper spit in the till after serving a gang of apprentices with Yorkshire accents.

Mother was particularly 'down' on holidaymakers. At some point in their lives her parents had kept a guest-house, and she used to tell ghastly tales of defiled bathrooms and general misbehaviour, which even as a child I never really believed. Thinking about it now, of course, I can see my parents' point. Relying on the holiday trade meant that the place was dead eight months of the year, and – for any grown-up person – more or less uninhabitable for the other four. All through the summer season they had a special magistrate's court that sat on Monday mornings to try the drunks.

I don't need anybody to tell me that life went at a slower pace in those days. I know it did. This was before television, before rock and roll. I've stood in the doorway of the shop some afternoons, late on a summer Sunday, and not seen a thing stir for half an hour, unless it was a dog moving from the shade of one awning to another, or a child on a bike nosing through the strewn ice-cream cartons and the torn newspapers flapping in the breeze. The things that really stick about those early days aren't to do with the front in summer and the thousands of people turning lobster-coloured in the sun. They tend to take in the older places here and there that hadn't quite been swamped by the ROOMS TO LET signs, the hot dogs and the threepenny arcades: shrimpboats moored on the Bure just above the north-west tower; crab-pots piled on the quayside; old women on bicycles moving purposefully through the mist to early service at St Nicholas's. And above all, the solitude. In those days you could walk along South Denes, beyond the power station with its monster chimney, and not see a soul except an occasional fisherman with his dog, or a schoolboy with his swimming things in a rolled-up towel under his arm, wheeling his bike out of the dunes. Even the courting couples, whom you were always liable to come upon in out-of-the-way places, didn't get that far. Twenty years later, on TV sometimes or with Upward somewhere, I used to find myself thinking about Yarmouth, and it was always the same thoughts: the shrimpboats, and the quayside, and the queer little shops that sold ships in bottles and pink Yarmouth rock, Father and Mother and what they'd think of me. The last thought was the most futile of all. I was a Yarmouth boy, you see, and I knew they wouldn't have approved in a hundred years.

Northwards, beyond the point where the river Yare flowed into the grey expanse of the Breydon water, lay the marshes: flat-bottomed row-boats upturned on the mud like giant woodlice; strange, smoky huts where old men sat making lobster creels; sandpipers scuttling over the creek beds. Further away, in sight of the sea, the landscape flattened out into a carpet of grey-green marsh grass, broken up by criss-crossing inlets and pools of stagnant water: a kind of lost world of marauding herons, smoke rising from the distant huts, sedge bent backwards by the breeze. In the distance, yachts floated sluggishly down the Bure or performed complicated manoeuvres against the upstream tide.

At this point in my life I spent enormous tracts of time at the marshes. Quite what attracted me to them I couldn't begin to put into words, but I know that I got a terrific kick out of the eeriness of the landscape. Coming back over the wet grass on a winter afternoon, for instance, with the mist rising up around you like ghostly cotton wool, you got an indescribable sense of time having stopped, that it wouldn't seem extraordinary to see a pterodactyl taking wing out of the sedge. Even in summer, sprawled full length in a dry ditch with the midges eating you alive, this feeling never quite disappeared. In the holidays from school I'd spend whole days out there with a packet of sandwiches for my lunch and the *Observer Book of British Birds* in my jacket-pocket (the marshes were a great place for birds – coming back at dusk once towards the river I saw an osprey swoop down over one of the ponds) idling through the tall grass or picking handfuls of samphire, which Father sometimes liked to eat with salad for his tea. It had an odd, woody flavour but wasn't bad if you cooked it with butter. And yet the times I liked best were in autumn – late autumn, say, fading into winter, with the pale afternoon sun sinking into half-light, the chill stealing up from the reed beds and the noise of the birds gradually falling away to nothing. God knows I'm not a wide-open-spacer, or one of those people who'll tell you they're 'at one with nature', but I can see that landscape as if it were yesterday: the twilight coming down over the sea, odd bits of timber that caught your eye by the river's edge, the silhouettes of solitary walkers wandering back along the coast road.

That particular Sunday for some reason I came home earlier than usual. Fine, windblown rain was falling over the square, and the streetlamps were going on. None of the shops was open, of course – Sunday opening was unheard of in Yarmouth except for the kiosks along the front – but, oddly enough, the light was on behind our drawn-down blinds, and Father was standing in the doorway gazing vaguely down the street. For a moment I thought he was looking out for me – like most people in Yarmouth Father and Mother had a thing about children 'spending their time at home', which essentially meant sitting quietly with a book while your parents prosed on over your head – but when he caught sight of me in the murk he just nodded matter-of-factly.

'That you, young Ted?'

Father had got thinner in the last couple of years, and his hair was starting to go. Caught in the flaring light from the shop – he'd forgotten to put his teeth in, too, which gave his mouth a fallen-in look – dressed in his usual Sunday-afternoon get-up of shirt, shabby waistcoat and a pair of old corduroy trousers, he looked a bit parched and dried-up. Something in my stare must have alerted him to this strange feeling of dereliction, because he pulled at the space below his gums where the upper teeth should have been and passed his hand over his face.

'Nasty, cold day,' he said.

No climatic conditions had ever existed that appealed to my parents. Mother 'couldn't abide' the cold, and said the crisp autumn mornings made her joints ache. Summer heat, Father complained, left him 'malted'. They watched the rain clouds assembling over the North Sea like a couple of masochists.

'Perishing,' Father said again.

It was actually quite a mild day. I wandered into the kitchen, hearing the sounds of him locking up behind me. Mother was out somewhere in town. On a plate in the scullery lay the kind of meal she thought appropriate for a growing boy on an autumn afternoon – two slices of luncheon meat, a quartered radish and several lumps of cucumber. While I got through this, Father pottered nervously round the kitchen, straightening the slant of the yellowing envelopes on the dresser – some of these were years old, going back as far as the war – picking up towels and putting them down again. There was something worrying him, I could see, that went beyond the usual anxieties of a wet Sunday afternoon.

'P'raps I'll do some sticking,' he said.

Mother had no hobbies, unless you counted library books. She said flatly that such things were 'a waste of time', and was highly satirical of shopkeepers' wives who sowed fourpenny packets of seed in their flowerbeds or went to raffia work classes at the Southtown WI. Father, though, did have a solitary relaxation. He was mildly fixated on the Royal Family, and kept a scrapbook in which he pasted photographs cut out of the newspapers. One of these books was lying on a chair by the kitchen table, I noticed, underneath a pile of clippings from the *Daily Sketch.* I squinnied at the topmost one, which showed the Queen Mother offering Princess Anne what looked like a plate of rock cakes.

'You seen Betty at all?'

So that was it. Every so often – it might be once or month, or once a fortnight, always, though, at times calculated to cause maximum inconvenience – Betty staged what Father and Mother referred to, with no humour at all, as 'vanishing acts'. Duration varied: three hours, once; half a day another time. Once, I remember, they were called to fetch her from a pub near South Quay where she was being stood drinks by a gang of American servicemen. Father's antennae were finely tuned to these disappearances.

There was absolutely no knowing where Betty might be: this much was accepted. Gorleston. Lowestoft. Hopton. Anywhere along a bus route. Several times she'd come back claiming to have gone as far as Norwich, a thirty-minute train-ride away, but no one was quite sure whether to believe this.

'Perhaps she's at a friend's?'

'No,' Father said decisively, and with what for him was a kind of paralysing bitterness. 'She ain't *got* any friends.'

There was something awful about the way he said this, which even as a child of twelve I think I caught something of – not so much in the anger, of which the dropped aitch was a symbol (Father and Mother normally managed to 'talk proper' as they put it unless they were especially upset), as in the dreadful glimpse it conjured up of the life Betty led, or that Father thought she led. Had Betty got any friends? I don't suppose she had. I don't suppose, if it came to that, that anyone cared either way.

Father looked a bit shocked after he'd said this, and muttered something about Betty probably being along in a minute, but it was no good. It never was. Betty's absences irked Father, jangled his nerves, offended his sense of personal security, in a way that I could never understand. The afternoon wore on, and the light faded into darkness. I can remember the rain sluicing down into the yard from the cracked gutter, and Father sitting hunched up in his chair, sunk in misery, as he tried to take an interest in a photograph of the Duke of Edinburgh inspecting a dead grouse. It was in this condition that Mother found us at a quarter to six, coming back in a bad temper because of the weather, with her newly marcelled hair piled up under a rain-bonnet.

After that things happened very quickly. It took Mother five minutes to establish – something we hadn't thought of doing – that Betty's clothes were gone from her bedroom, and that she'd forced open the tin cash box hidden in the airing cupboard and walked off with three weeks' housekeeping money – about £15, I think. The enormity of what had happened – particularly the money going – calmed Father and Mother down a bit. I can remember them sitting there in the kitchen gloomily discussing whether or not they ought to send for the police, and in the end Father being sent into town to make enquiries at the railway station, which even I could have told them was a bad idea, but was typical of the way my parents went about things. It was no good though, no one had seen her, and in the morning – I think they had a vague idea that despite the £15 and the vanished clothes she'd somehow rematerialise during the night – Father had to put his best suit on and go and explain to the council what had happened, which now I think about it must have taken some doing.

To give them their due, Father and Mother were hugely upset about Betty. The official line was that they'd been let down, and for months afterwards they used to talk in a puzzled kind of way about how they'd tried to 'give her a home', only to have it all (Mother's phrase) 'thrown back in their faces'. Secretly, though, once they'd got over the theft of the money, which on the Yarmouth scale of things was at about the same level as adultery, I think they were faintly ashamed. Eventually, when Betty turned up again – in Skegness, of all places, together with the lorry driver who'd given her the lift there – there was talk of her coming back, but everyone knew it would never happen. It was all too far gone for that, broken up and irreclaimable. In a way I think I sympathised with Father and Mother about Betty. It was as if some mysterious agency whose existence they barely knew about had decided to judge them, and found them badly wanting. At the same time I realised that the whole business had done something fundamental to how I thought about them and our lives together in the Southtown square; had diminished them somehow and left them feebler and less confident. There were other things happening by this stage, of course, which I've yet to tell you about, but even then I had an inkling that the old world, that sedate landscape of back-to-back houses and flyblown tobacconists, was on the way out, there in a Yarmouth back-kitchen with Father biting his nails over his scrapbook and the rain falling over the murky glass.

Q: *Why did the lion get lost in the jungle?*
A: Jungle's massive isn't it?

Actually, I'm still trying to work that one out.

Outside the sky is turning grey on blue. In the distance, over towards Millwall, a pair of police helicopters are buzzing over the clusters of towerblocks. Nearer at hand, between the warehouses and the tumbledown wharves, the river runs into view. Its surface is the colour of gravy. Apart from the helicopters and my hand inching over the page, nothing moves. All comedy, Eric Morecambe once suggested, is based on fear. There are times when I could almost agree with that. Now isn't one of them. Comedy of the kind I propose to inflict on tonight's meeting of the Plumstead Over Sixties is based on comfort, recognition, pleasurable re-encounters – a kind of light-entertainment plane-spotting involving outsize insignia, friendly silhouettes and not a bomb port in sight.

My wife, she's so thin that when she drinks tomato juice she looks like a thermometer.

Actually you have to be careful with a joke like that. Anything too funny just exhausts the audience. I ink a neat little line through *tomato juice*, which is one of the jokes that's made it to the prompt card, and go back to the window, where there are gulls hovering in mid-stream and lights going on in the houses by the shore. It's barely half-past four but already the place is settling down, turning in on itself. The newsagents shut at five round here. Later you can walk for hours round the tide walls and the lock-ups near Woolwich and not see a soul. Two floors below there's the faint hum of a TV. *Playdays, Kidscene* or something. The boy gets back from school at quarter to four, but he doesn't come up when he knows I'm working.

Working. It was Lennie who fixed tonight's gig (they all call them gigs now, even the sixty-year-olds). *Now you're back in the smoke you want to be earning a few quid?* God knows how Lennie survives, in his two rooms up the flight of stairs in Old Compton Street with the old *Carry On* posters still stuck on the walls like it was 1965. Lennie still talks about his great days populating the cast of the Black and White Minstrel Show (*Course, some of 'em didn't want to do it, but I told 'em, 'Who's going to see you under the fucking boot polish eh?'*). Perhaps Lennie is one of the Plumstead Over Sixties. It wouldn't surprise me. Nothing surprises me now.

Replaying Lennie's advice on audience requirements (*Arf an hour'll do it, and not too blue mind*) I do another trawl through the memory store. What does 'not too blue' mean these days anyway? Thirty years ago it meant they didn't like you saying 'fuck'. These days it probably means no incest jokes. I once saw Roy 'Chubby' Brown go on stage somewhere in the north where they were having a big child abuse enquiry and greet the audience with 'I'm surprised any of you lot are here. I thought you'd all be at home fucking your children.' Of course they all *roared.*

I asked my wife the other night, 'What do you think about sex on the TV?' She said: 'I don't know. I've always found it a bit uncomfortable.'

That'll do.

I bought this place back in 1972, around the time we did the first TV series, before Lennie, 'alternatives' and jokes about hurting children. It cost £3,000. Everyone else was going for West End flats and Surrey mock-Tudor; I wanted a bolt hole. I remember Upward coming down here once not long after, parking himself in the front room and saying 'What the hell are you up to, Ted?'

You could never explain anything like that to Upward. Women, for some reason, used to like it. Coming back in a taxi, late at night, they detected romance in the curve of the Thames, the lights moving away downriver. Only in the morning would the illusion fracture.

'Why didn't you tell me you lived in the bloody Far East?' a girl once snapped at me from the bedroom door.

To me, though, it was London: grey streets, the river, the petrol smell mixing in the raw air. Coming back a couple of months ago I was surprised to find how much of myself I'd left behind: the blown-up TV stills on the wall, a pile of comic postcards twenty years old sent back by Upward from holidays in the north. (*'Has that vicar any children?' 'No, they say his stipend's too small.'*) In a box in the cellar, hidden amongst old bikes and petrol cans, there were sheaves of photos, professional ones with agents' stamps on the back: Upward and me in the middle of a dance routine involving a file of statues; in the presentation line at a Royal Variety Show; at some bottle-strewn dinner table stuck between a couple of fellow-diners. I had to look at them closely before I could work out quite what was going on, and who was who – that the fat chap with the gurning smile was Les Dawson, that the younger man in the tuxedo with the ambrosial hair was me.

Later I go out for a packet of fags and an evening paper. The streets round here are sharply segregated now: old dockland terraces and the new estates put up in the last property boom. The new estates have names like 'Heron's Quay' and 'Kingfisher's Rest'. God knows who lives in them. There are men in suits out on the pavement in the early mornings, as vague and rootless as tourists. The real inhabitants – vixens wheeling pushchairs, skinny boys in white tee-shirts, burly crop-headed dads – don't come out till noon. Not having lived here properly for a quarter of a century, the first thing that struck me was how fat the women have grown. You see them on the street corners, stabbing the air with their cigarettes as they gesture, elephant legs splayed under micro-skirts or bulging out of shellsuits, with the shaven-headed child in the buggy looking on. Do they like looking this way? Do they aspire to what the newspapers call an acceptable body image? The talk is always of men. Always. *Cunt wanted to do me up the bum, but I wasn't having any*, I heard one say to her mate the other day. Seriously, too.

Half the houses in the street are empty, I gradually worked out in my first month back. Looking through their upper windows you can see the twilight settling like ink. Officially this is a 'regeneration area', and there are posters in the shop windows to this effect, but I don't think it cuts much ice with the flotsam of the streets. No one knows where the original inhabitants went. Downriver to Dartford and Gravesend? Far away into Essex? In their place have come Bengali shopkeepers, stone-eyed Asians in *mujahadeen* fur hats driving mini-cabs. Like the blokes in suits, tapping at their mobiles as they head out into the dawn, they don't look as if they're settled in. Nobody seems to be permanent. Nobody – not the brown women in saris who look blank if you ask for directions or the mini-cabbers who need an A–Z to get to Lewisham – seems to know where they are. Presumably they're already waiting for the next migration, the next grey street with its blocked-up windows, the next beaten-up Rover with the radio tuned to the Gujarati station playing Bollywood film music.

At the end of the street orange light glows out of the Rashids' mini-market. It's the kind of place where they sell, separately, bags of crisps that have 'Not to be sold separately from multi-pack' printed on them. Through the wire cage that twists over the plate-glass window I can see the sari'd bulk of Mrs Rashid hunched into the tiny compartment between the till and the rows of spirit bottles. Mr Rashid will be at the back of the shop, weeding out the cartons of milk gone past their sell-by dates – or not weeding them out. It's impossible for me to look at the Rashids without thinking of Father and Mother and what they'd make of it all. Inevitably they would have been appalled at the idea of people called Rashid even keeping a shop (Mother once confessed to me that she hated the idea of leaf tea because of the brown fingers that had picked it). What I think would have shocked them even more, though, is the absence of what would now be called customer relations. I used to watch Father sometimes when anyone came into the shop. Even as the doorbell clanged you could see the attentiveness spread into his face. Then, as whoever it was moved into view, he'd kind of hover, not exactly defensively, but giving the impression that the act of purchase was a sort of holy compact in which he was proud to play a part. And that of course was before either of them opened their mouths. I don't say that Father *liked* all this, but he knew that it was his duty. The Rashids, on the other hand, just sit there. You can see their point. Why sell civility as well as the groceries? Where's the benefit? Father went bankrupt, whereas the Rashids, according to local rumour, make enough to afford six weeks' annual holiday back in the Punjab.

Inside the shop a stale, sweetish smell rises off the fake grass mats with their little pyramids of mottled bananas and boxed dates. Further along, in defective refrigerator tanks, the *halal* stuff sits and rots. Sure enough, Mr Rashid is pottering away at the back of the shop. He looks up when he sees me, checks that I'm not a criminal or a basket case and carries on tinkering with the tube of unhooked strip-lighting. Paying for the cigarettes and the *Standard* – the last from the pile – something, probably the memory of Father behind his till, the acknowledgement of some shared heritage, prompts me to nod at Mrs Rashid. She stares back impassively, like a piece of teak.

Back at the house the red eye of the answer phone is pulsing away. As I press the 'Play' button I twist my head round the open door of the front room. The TV is still on, but the boy has disappeared. Upstairs, I suppose. In the first week or two I made the mistake of going after him. Nowadays I leave him be. The answer phone message is a woman's voice, youngish, a sentence or two lost in static, and a number. Actually, Lennie has already filled me in on this one. (*Gel from the radio rang about you Ted. What you reckon then?*) It's a mark of Lennie's out-of-touchness that he still thinks the BBC means money. God knows what he told her. (*I told her you was dead busy, but there was no harm in asking. Okay?*) I transfer the number on to the scribble pad before walking through into the front room and extinguishing the blare of the TV. The boy leaves no spoor. Apart from the blue exercise book there's no sign that he's been here. I pick up the book – a school-issue one with *Daniel King* traced on the front in hulking capitals – and read the opening page.

I live with my Dad in a big house near the river.
Before that I lived with my mum. Not here but a long way off.
On Saturdays my Dad buys me a comic.

In the house across the road, framed in the light from the uncurtained window, a bloke and a girl are shouting at each other. I can't hear them, but I can tell from the look on the bloke's face and the way the girl is squeezing folded arms across her chest, as if it will somehow deflect the yells. Sometimes she opens her mouth and yells back. They do this for a good five minutes and then drop their arms and gaze at each other, either exhausted or abashed.

About comedy and fear. Thirty-two years ago I saw a film of Lenny Bruce performing in a club in Chicago. There weren't more than fifty people there – a few students who'd heard he said 'fuck' a lot and a handful of Beat survivors in sunglasses and suits. I can't remember what the final joke was about except that it went on for ten minutes and had seven or maybe eight interconnected threads. At the end when he suddenly dragged them together (the cop, the dog, the drug-store, the preacher's necktie) in a couple of sentences there was a silence, in which the audience checked it all back in their heads, and then an extraordinarily loud exhalation of collective breath, fifty people sighing out of sheer relief. After that, quite a long time after that, they started laughing.

Come half-past seven I go up to change. London turns dead at this time of night. The white vans and the battered Fiestas are jammed up against the pavement now, the skinny boys are all indoors eating their tea and waiting for the football to start, and the streets are silent. Like I say, I haven't lived here properly for twenty-five years, but the old rhythms creep up on you, steal into your blood. Somewhere down below a car door slams and there's a rumble of conversation. Walking down the stairs, I turn into the boy's room and find him stretched out on the bed beneath the posters of Robbie Fowler, reading a paperback called *Goosebumps.* He shifts when he sees me, draws the book into the shadow of his chest as if it's something he fears my reaction to.

'Are you okay?'

'Fine.'

Another thing I've noticed since I came back here is that whereas the girls look older than their ages, the boys look younger. With his cropped hair and his bush-baby eyes, Daniel would pass for eight.

'What did you have for tea?'

'Same as you.'

'There's sandwiches in the fridge if you get hungry.'

Hastily I shoot through the rituals of the next two hours: what to do if the phone rings (leave it) or the doorbell goes (ditto), what you can watch on TV and what you can't, what to do in an emergency (Mrs Finney in next door's basement). When I say goodbye, he surprises me by hurling himself head first into my stomach and clinging there with his arms wrapped round my waist.

Two minutes later, standing outside the locked door, coat flapping against my legs in the breeze, I put my hand inside the jacket-pocket of my suit. The letter that came last week, the letter from Shena which I still haven't dared open, burns against my fingers.

Interview with Ted King

Did you hear the one about the man who decided to be a stand-up comic? All the sit-down jobs had gone.

When did I get the idea that I wanted to tell jokes for a living? Sometime back in the Fifties, I suppose, listening to the Light Programme comedy shows on the big radiogram that my father and mother kept in the parlour, or going to watch the variety bills at the Yarmouth Regal. Variety's long dead now – it's been killed off by TV and pop music – but in the Fifties it was still going strong: nearly every big town had a theatre that was on one of the touring circuits . . . Essentially it was just a concert with a lot of different acts that ran for a week until the performers packed up and moved on to the next place on the tour. The great thing about it was that you could actually see most of the people you heard every week on the radio – Max Miller, say, or Arthur Askey – and even the occasional film star. Sometime around 1953 – it was right at the fag-end of their career of course – I even got to see Laurel and Hardy. It was a huge disappointment, they barely knew where they were.

My parents didn't like the big-name acts. My mother thought that Max Miller was 'vulgar', which of course he was, although he talked so fast that half the time you couldn't work out what he was being dirty about . . . I liked the kind of acts that these days you'd call 'surreal'. Wilson, Keppel and Betty. Cardew the Cad. The Western Brothers. I don't suppose you've heard of many of them. Cardew the Cad was an immensely tall middle-aged man – I think his real name was Robinson – who dressed up in a blazer and short trousers, with a long scarf wound round his neck, and he did fantasy monologues about the public school he was supposed to be at. The Western Brothers were about the nearest that Variety ever got to satire: a couple of chaps in evening dress – one of them might even have had a monocle – who put on silly-ass voices and sang songs that in a very mild way guyed things like the Royal Family or the Empire. My parents didn't like the Western Brothers either. My mother thought they were 'too clever by half', while my father always said he couldn't see what the joke was. But the real reason, I think, was that they were a bit shocked at the idea that anyone could find these things funny . . .

There's no point in pretending that I was some kind of child prodigy – you know, the kind of kid who tells jokes round the supper table and wins talent contests on the pier. They still had what were called 'concert parties' in those days – old chaps dressed up in pierrot costumes who performed at church socials – but I'd have run a mile from anything like that, and if you'd told me I'd end up spending my life on a stage I'd have laughed at you. It was simply a hobby – listening to *Hancock's Half Hour* or sitting in the back row of the Regal hearing the Western Brothers sing a number called 'Play the Game You Cads' – and I hadn't the least idea – or the desire, if it came to that – that it would ever come to anything. Certainly no one at home ever gave me the least encouragement, and I'm sure that if my father and mother had ever lived to see any of it they'd have been deeply shocked. Appalled even, I don't know . . .

from *Here to Entertain You: The Upward & King Story*,
BBC Radio 2 documentary, 1976

The Man in the Corner Shop

I wonder if you can imagine what it was like to be the son of a small shopkeeper on the east coast of England forty years ago?

For a start, the shop dominated your life. Theoretically opening hours were from eight in the morning to six at night, six days a week, but in practice anyone who rapped on the shutters for a couple of hours after that got served, and Father always ate his meals with one ear cocked for the jangle of the doorbell. My chief memory of him as a child is of a harassed-looking man with greying hair putting his fork down on a half-empty plate and scurrying off to sell someone a threepenny bar of chocolate or a box of matches. I don't suppose Father ever worked less than a seventy-hour week. Worse, it was the kind of business where things were always happening at odd times. At least two nights a week Father used to do the accounts, which as he was 'bad at figures' meant that he rarely got to bed before midnight. I can see him now, sitting at the kitchen table with his head down over a pile of invoices and the big metal spike he used for securing bits of paper, a cup of tea going cold at his elbow, trying to work out what had happened to a stray box of Yarmouth rock, or whether it was worth laying in another half-dozen jars of Erinmore to take advantage of a five per cent discount the suppliers were offering. Shopkeeping life was full of these niggling little decisions. Both my parents, I noticed, referred to the shop as 'it', as if it was a living thing. Father would complain that 'it' didn't get much forrader, or that 'it' was a trial. From an early stage I think I conceived of the place as a kind of dreadful, pestilential growth which had coiled itself around them and wouldn't let go until they died.

Worse even than this – worse than the nagging customers and the gangs of children who came in trying to pilfer sugar mice and sherbet dabs – was the state of cut-throat warfare that existed with the people you saw around you. There were about a dozen shops in the square. I can't remember all of them, and the smaller ones were always changing hands, but the big ones have stayed in my head. On the far side there was Salaman's, the off-licence, followed by a tiny wool and knitting shop and a general hardware place that sold everything, from lengths of plywood to nails and twists of chicken-wire. Then came Wedderbury's, and next to it Dunstan's, the big grocer's, and then a nondescript newsagent who was always closing down, reaching an arrangement with his creditors and then starting up again. I don't remember our side of the square quite so well – probably because it wasn't directly in view from the doorway where I was always hanging about – but there was certainly a fish shop, where Mother sometimes bought dabs and half-pints of cockles, and a bakery. I used to like waking up in the mornings on baking days and smelling the scent of yeast in the air. Most of these shops weren't in direct competition with Father, but there were three or four of them who more or less openly impinged on his trade. Officially this was illegal – all the leases were owned by the Church Commissioners, and there were rules as to what you could and couldn't sell – but the big stores had ways of getting round this: selling cheap cigarettes in what were called 'economy packs', for instance, or giving bars of chocolate away as 'free gifts'.

Father's problem was that he wasn't a big enough operator to compete with the smart shops on the far side of the square. If he'd had the capital, or had been prepared to take risks, he could have undercut, taken a lease on one of the next-door shops when it came up, done half-a-dozen things that would have taken the weight off his back, but the money was never there. All he had was the tiny sum – I think it was about £900 – he and Mother had inherited from Grandpa Lutterworth, and no bank manager would ever have lent him a penny. Not that Father would have wanted him to. He was one of those timid, unadventurous types who regarded borrowing as a kind of sin, and the thought of paying interest on someone else's money filled him with horror. I can remember once, on a Saturday when the bank was shut and some emergency came up, him having to touch the sub-post-master next door for a loan and being so embarrassed that the money was repaid by half-past nine on the Monday morning.

What made it worse was that he had struck up a kind of friendship with Dunstan, who owned the grocer's shop and was his biggest competitor. It used to puzzle me sometimes. There was Dunstan – he was a big, barrel-chested man with popping blue eyes and a habit of swinging his arms as he walked – trying to ruin him, and yet Father scarcely seemed to notice. Two or three times a week Dunstan would stump over from across the square and the two of them would stand talking in front of the tobacco and the packets of potato crisps; or rather Dunstan would patronise Father in a rather conspicuous way about the shop, asking him why he persisted with particular lines or didn't colonise the bakery two doors down, which everyone knew was on its last legs, while Father mumbled about things being all right as they were. I can see them now – the big man in his white grocer's overalls (he called Father 'Alf' or 'old man') prosing on with his hand lying casually over the nearside counter, with Father bobbing his head in a kind of respectful way from behind the till. I once caught a glimpse of Dunstan looking at Father when his back was turned to the shelves, and it was rather like a cook eyeing up a turtle that he plans to make into soup.

All the time I was growing up Father was slowly going bankrupt, and I don't think I even noticed. The only thing I can say in my defence is that I was at the age where what happens at school or on a soccer pitch is more important than whether or not your parents are making a living, and also, curiously enough, that Father and Mother scarcely seemed to see it themselves. They'd had difficult times in the past, I think, and in some ways the evidence of the books didn't worry them as much as it ought to have done. There was a vague feeling that things would 'get better' – I can remember them cheering up when Attlee lost the 1951 General Election as Labour was supposed to be 'against' the small businessman – and that good times were just around the corner. I can't imagine what Father thought those good times would consist of – maybe he simply saw it in terms of selling half-a-dozen extra boxes of chocolates every week – but I'm sure this vision sustained him through the dull afternoons (there was a period between about two and four when hardly anyone came into the shop) and the late-night battles with the account books. Sometimes, in the evenings mostly, when tea was over and Mother had finished her housework, they'd talk in a kind of vague, listless way about their predicament, about how trade was bad, or that Salaman's had started a line in cut-price cigarettes. Once or twice, too, Mother would go and stand in the shop and stare reproachfully at the stock, as if she couldn't quite believe that people weren't coming in to purchase all the stuff laid out before her – the packets of Capstan Full Strength, the piles of candy bananas and so on – but I don't think I took much notice. It was merely the kind of thing your parents talked about. Don't get me wrong about this. If someone had told me at thirteen or fourteen that Father was heavily in debt, I know I'd have been seriously concerned – for a start, unlike many kids at the time, I knew what debt meant – and tried to help as best I could, but the thing was that nobody did. The situation just drifted on in a way that was very common at that time, with nobody knowing what the solution might be or how it would all end.

Meanwhile, I was growing up. At thirteen, I was already an inch or two bigger than Father, with yellowish-coloured hair and a nose bent slightly out of joint after an accident that I'd had falling downstairs as a child. I wasn't clever – although I'd scraped into Yarmouth Grammar School, which pleased Father and Mother no end – but I could play games a bit, which was all that counted at that age, and I was fairly popular. School I don't remember much of, except for a general air of chalk-dust and the eternal boiled cabbage smell that hung over the refectory, and being caned once for exploding a firework in the corridor, which was against the rules but everybody did it. It was an old-fashioned place, with a school song about happy warriors marching through the vale of life, and the boys divided up along class lines: the solicitors' and doctors' sons on one side, shopkeepers' and small tradesmen's sons on the other, and a handful of untouchables whose fathers worked on the buses or in low-grade clerical jobs. (I can remember one boy whose father was a farm labourer walking through the school playground to a huge shout of '*Tractor!*' every morning for five years – that was how seriously we took these things.)

I suppose if anyone had taken an interest in me, made me read the right books and nagged me about homework, I could have made something of school, but they never did, and in any case I was too busy pursuing the infinitely more enticing life that lay beyond the school gates: hanging around outside the local girls' school in search of a 'click' as it was called or taking the train to Carrow Road on a Saturday afternoon to watch Norwich play. I think Father and Mother were quite proud of me then. Father used to straighten up from whatever he was doing when I came into the shop wearing my grammar school blazer with my hair Brylcreemed up into a Tony Curtis quiff, and shoot me a look that was kind of shy, admiring and indulgent all at the same time. Somehow this survived all the rows we had at this time – the usual stuff about staying out late and clothes and going about 'looking like a Teddy Boy'. It's a good feeling, you know, that your parents approve of the kind of person you are, even if – as I did – you then go and let them down.

Sometimes, looking back at this from the vantage point of ten or fifteen years later – stuck in some grimy northern town on a Sunday morning in the Sixties, frowsting in digs with Upward somewhere on the south coast with the rain falling over the terraced streets – I used to wonder about Father and Mother, what exactly they got out of life, what made them tick. In the end I decided that there wasn't any great mystery about it, that they were just quiet, simple people who 'kept themselves to themselves' (Mother) and weren't ever troubled by things that went on outside their tiny orbit, not because they didn't know they were there, but because they took no interest in them.

What I'm trying to say, I suppose, is that my parents had no selfconsciousness, no idea that even the life of a provincial shopkeeper in a flyblown seaside town was something you could take pleasure out of if you tried. For a start neither of them had any friends. There was an old couple called Edgell who sometimes came round to play cards on a Saturday evening, and Father was a member of the Royal Antedeluvian Order of Buffaloes – a kind of sub-masonic men's club that met every Friday night above a pub near the market square – but the idea of spending time with people to whom you weren't related, simply because you enjoyed their company was quite alien to them. Sometimes, talking to Father or picking up stray fragments of conversation, I got a hint that his life before he met Mother hadn't been quite so circumscribed, but it was all quite gone now, and impossible to re-create. As for Mother, I think a part of her was merely frightened by the occasional glimpses of the outside world that she got through the newspapers or the radio. I can remember both of them being very exercised by the Ruth Ellis case (she was a night-club hostess who'd shot her boyfriend, and there was a furious row about whether the death penalty should apply). Father, chewing away on his bread and butter over the kitchen table, said in his mild way that it 'wasn't right' to execute a woman, whatever it was that she might have done. Mother, on the other hand, wanted her to hang.

No doubt all this makes Father and Mother seem like the worst kind of joyless drudges. In fact they were companionable enough. Curiously, evenings are the time I remember best at the square, with the radio playing *Variety Bandbox* or *Your Hundred Best Tunes*, Mother drowsing over the paper, me at the kitchen table doing my homework and Father poring over one of his scrapbooks or getting up to answer the shop door if a neighbour came round wanting a packet of fags. You don't get times like that now – with everybody stuck in the same place, the sense of time passing at its natural speed. Sometimes, when I was in my middle teens and was let out in the evenings for an hour or two, I'd come back and find everything exactly the same as I'd left it – Mother fallen asleep in her chair with her mouth open and her reading glasses low on her nose, Father snipping the newsprint from around a picture of the Duke of Kent. The half-dozen or so photographs I've kept from those days all have this queer, sleepy air: Mother standing outside the shop with her head bent against the sun and the shadows running across the street before her; Father staring vaguely from a perch in the dunes, somewhere near Hopton, with the sea grass sticking up around him like porcupine quills; the three of us taken together – God knows where or by whom – Father and Mother in mackintoshes, me in my school blazer and grey flannel trousers. My smile is quite genuine and unforced. The young Queen's on the throne, Winston's in Downing Street, Germany's a dustbin of bomb-craters, and it's all going to be all right. Christ! If only I'd known.

* * *

Sometimes, in odd moments long after they were dead, I used to wonder what it was that Father and Mother believed in. Well, I never really found out, never truly got to the bottom of what made them the people they were. Given their position at the very bottom of an ant-heap of local tradesmen all strenuously trying to cut each other's throats, you'd have thought they would have incubated the most fantastic resentments about the social order of which they were a part – but no, they were the most rabid conservatives and accepted everything that got thrown at them in the same way that they accepted the three times table. Part of it, course, was that hidebound small shopkeeper's mentality that Mother had had in her veins and Father had acquired by marrying her. When I grew up and found out about Poujade, the French tobacconist who started his own political movement, I understood immediately the kind of things he wanted to achieve. Father and Mother would have been Poujadists, no question. They believed in – to take only the most obvious things – the Queen, the Royal Family, God, the House of Lords, the Conservative Party, capital punishment, gentlemen in evening dress, BBC announcers, cut-glass accents, the Empire, Eisenhower and 'a fair day's work for a fair day's wage'. Father, in particular, used almost visibly to cringe whenever anybody with what used to be called an 'educated' voice bought something in the shop.

Beyond these absolutes, though, a certain amount of equivocation stole in. Mother used sometimes to talk darkly about big business and how it was 'doing the small man down', and she had peculiar moments of irritation at the pyramids of social precedence she supported. I can remember her once gazing at a photo in the local paper – it might have been of the wife of the Lord Lieutenant of Norfolk opening a garden fête – and her expression changing suddenly from mild interest to furious disdain.

'I don't suppose she's ever darned a shirt in her life,' she remarked bitterly.

These outbursts punctuated my childhood. You never knew what was going to set them off: a tax demand; a neighbour in a too-ostentatious dress; a local boy who'd 'made good' – that is, got a superintendent's job at the Norwich Union Insurance Company and had his picture printed in the *Mercury* – any of these could incite her to fury. Of the two of them, I think Father was probably the kinder, the less liable to take offence or be cast down by circumstance. He was a very patient man, who'd go out of his way to oblige a customer, shook his head over the newspaper reports from Korea and thought it was a shame that 'these here blacks' weren't allowed to run their own affairs. Oddly the 'Empire' was one of the few things Father and Mother disagreed about: I think Mother's family had belonged to some queer ginger-group called the Empire Loyalists, and I remember her being very upset – perhaps the most upset I ever saw her – when they put a stop to Empire Day sometime in the Fifties.

And all the while time was passing. 1953. 1954. 1955. The new Queen was crowned and the whole school was given the day off. My class voted to spend it at the home of the solitary boy in the form whose parents had a TV set – thirty of us packed into the front room eating sandwiches out of paper bags and cheering vaguely whenever the procession came into view. 1953 was the flood year, when the tide swept over the sea defences all the way along the east coast and dozens of people got killed. Even in Southtown the flood water was two feet deep, and the floor of the shop stank of salt for weeks after. In 1955 there was a General Election and the Conservatives got in again, which cheered Father and Mother up a bit. I turned fifteen, grew another two inches, discovered Elvis Presley and got myself a regular girlfriend called Marjorie Lovelace, who went to the girls' grammar school and whose parents resided in an altogether higher social league than Father and Mother (she talked about 'lavatories' and 'napkins', which was a sure sign that you were upper-middle-class). They were good times, and even now if you asked me where I'd most like to be it would be back on the dunes out Gorleston way with Marjorie Lovelace on a warm evening in August, bikes chucked in the sand below, watching the sun set out across the sea and then bicycling home through the back lanes with a last snog in the alleyway that ran off the side of the square. All the while, though, I could see that things were changing, that the shop was doing badly, and that the future was rearing up at me in a way it hadn't done before. People started asking me what I was going to 'do', and Father and Mother were worrying about jobs and the School

Certificate. You know the feeling you sometimes get of standing outside your life and watching it happen? Well, that was me back in 1955, wanting to concentrate on Marjorie Lovelace (who though she would have died sooner than let me take her blouse off, didn't mind having her breasts stroked from the outside) and 'Heartbreak Hotel', but conscious all the time of the icebergs of work and money and responsibility looming up before me.

I'm not one of those people who get sentimental about their childhood. Later on I met blokes who'd been to private schools and didn't seem to have done a hand's turn until they were twenty-one who used to talk about their 'lost youth' with enough conviction to make you think that a part of them really had died back on some cricket-field at the age of eighteen. I was never like that. It's what being a lower-middle-class shopkeeper's son does for you, I suppose. Come the age of sixteen you realise that childhood is childhood, and that bills have to be paid. What stockbroker's son ever thinks that? A good half of me was aching to get out of school and get some kind of job that would mean wearing a suit and earning money. When you're sixteen and live over a confectioner's shop, with your parents breathing down your neck twenty-four hours a day, that sort of thing means a lot to you. At the same time I didn't have any illusions about the kind of life I'd been leading here in the Yarmouth back streets in a world made up of Father, Mother and the shop. In some ways it was a kind of cyst that the twentieth century had passed by, a little time-capsule full of fat men rolling out of pubs, and draggled-looking women with broods of noisy kids. The old ways ran on, like black hounds under the moon. Old people died with tumours on them the size of grapefruit because their children 'didn't want to go bothering the doctor'. When I was about fifteen there was a terrible scandal when a girl bled to death giving birth to an illegitimate baby (which also died) in a wooden hut on the marshes. Things happened then that you don't see now. I can remember Father and Mother shaking their heads over the dead girl and her baby when it made the papers. Father thought it was 'a shame' and 'a pity'. Mother, I could see, blamed the girl, although this wasn't something she could actually bring herself to say. But what really struck me was how they accepted that the whole thing was inevitable, that a schoolgirl getting herself pregnant was bound to end in some kind of dreadful tragedy.

1954. 1955. And all the while the shop was steadily losing money, and Father was looking thinner and more worried. Even by this stage I still didn't properly know what was going on. I knew that Father was 'doing badly', because it was all my parents talked about, but I don't think the enormity of the situation had really dawned on me. Things would pick up. Somebody would come in and buy half-a-dozen boxes of Milk Tray for raffle prizes. That was how everybody – myself included – imagined things. They didn't know that it was all too far gone to be reclaimed, that the old life of the square, of Father dusting the shutters prior to taking them down at eight a.m., and the delivery vans parked on the forecourt, would be blown away for ever. Father spent most evenings now doing his accounts, working out if he could save on another order of tobacco, or whether a wholesaler's bill could 'stand' for another week, but even then I don't really think he knew what was hitting him. People in that state lose their ability to fix cause to effect. Gissings, the big confectionery chain, which had branches all over Norfolk, had a shop on the far side of the square now – God knows how they'd squared it with the Church Commissioners – and Dunstan's had started undercutting with cheap ice-cream and bargain boxes of five threepenny bars of chocolate for eleven-pence-halfpenny. It sounds a huge joke, I know, but it was how shopkeepers went bust fifty years ago.

To do Father justice he did make some sort of effort to save himself from the meltdown. Early in 1954, I remember, there was a minor crisis when the delivery vans stopped calling and – this was quite unprecedented – the shop ran out of cigarettes, but some kind of deal was struck and he managed to stagger on. Turner, the newsagent at the far end of the square retired, and I've an idea Father scraped together the money from somewhere to buy the goodwill, because the shop suddenly started selling newspapers, and the shelf behind the sugar mice and the fruit salad was taken down and replaced by a table full of copies of *Woman's Realm* and *Caged Birds.*

It didn't last, though – managing the paperboys and getting up at six to sort out the rounds was a bit beyond Father by this stage

– and there were endless rows with customers about missed deliveries. After about six months the paper idea was given up. Then Father got involved in some swindle run by one of the potato crisp manufacturers, whereby if you put in a big enough order and were prepared to stick up display boards in your window you could have a five per cent discount on the stock. Plenty of people in the square sold crisps, though, and in the end they just lay in the card-board boxes going musty. Poor Father! I can see him there now in that narrow space behind the till, with one hand smoothing his brindled hair back over his scalp and the other adding up a sum on the back of a paper bag, looking up at me in that vague, diffident way he had. God knows what he felt about it all, and how it must have been eating him up. That kind of thing marked you in those days, and for a small tradesman to end up in a bankruptcy court was the moral equivalent of leprosy – an awful public admission that your life had been a failure.

I think what hurt Father most was the realisation that one or two of the people he'd assumed were on his side were actually scheming to do him down. Dunstan didn't call at the shop so much in those days, and I remember one afternoon – it would have been in the summer of 1955 – when Father saw him coming from across the square and quite deliberately shot the bolt in the door and went off into the kitchen. I was standing in the sub-post office doorway at the time, looking on in that half-fascinated, half-frightened way children have when they know some secret adult business is afoot. Old Dunstan tried the door a couple of times, rattled the handle for good measure, and then caught sight of me hovering between the spindles of sixpenny seed packets and plastic combs.

'Where's your dad then?' he asked, a bit suspiciously. I'd always hated Dunstan, and he knew it.

'Don't know, Mr Dunstan.'

Dunstan took a step forward into the sub-post office's interior, cool and aquarium-like in the summer heat, as if he half-expected Father to be cowering in there, beneath the posters advertising government bonds and the Junior Saver's Club.

'Not like him to shut up at this time of day,' he said. 'Anything the matter?'

'No, Mr Dunstan.'

I watched him start back across the square and then slipped down the alleyway, through the yard, and back into the kitchen. Father was sitting glumly in one of the big armchairs reading the *Mercury*. When he saw me he divined instantly what had happened. There was silence for a minute.

Then he said: 'The bastard!'

I watched him as he did it, and there was a kind of disbelief in his face, as if even then he couldn't quite believe what everyone in the square had known for years – that Dunstan was waiting for him to sell up in much the same way that a vulture hovers over a sick antelope.

'The bloody bastard,' he said again – it was the first time I'd heard him swear.

I suppose in a way it was the closest we ever got to one another, standing there in the kitchen on a summer afternoon with the flies buzzing near the larder door and the noise of children's voices coming in across the square, until he got up and went back into the shop, and the spell was broken.

That early part of my life starts to fade away now, turn fragmentary and indetachable from what came afterwards. At some point Father and Mother must have explained to me what was going on, and in particular Father's periodic absences in town, but I don't remember. The School Certificate exams were looming in any case, and after two years idling at school I knew that any chance of a job afterwards depended on what I did in the next month or so. The box-room Betty used to sleep in had been empty since she left, and I worked up there sometimes, stretched out on the bed with a copy of *Hartson's Basic Geography* in front of me, or a list of French verbs I'd decided to memorise. Funnily enough, those days – they were evenings, mostly, in early summer – are peculiarly vivid to me: watching the light fade across the square and beyond the distant church spire, with the sound of Father and Mother pottering about below, and, later on, the noise of the wind getting up (I smuggled Marjorie Lovelace up there once when they were out, but nothing much happened). The rest is oddly out of focus: watching the bulldozers filling in bomb-craters; the train-ride along the Acle Strait to Norwich; the figures silhouetted in Wedderbury's windows as the lights went on; foraging among the rockpools for driftwood and onions, which were washed up from the North Sea trawlers and lay across the beach in great strings; files of elm trees dragging across the bare, level plains; the noise of the sea; solitary people lost in the echoing space and silence.

Every Whitsun bank holiday Monday we went down into Suffolk for the Framlingham gala.

I was in Framlingham – which nobody within a ten-mile radius called anything other than 'Fram' – a few years ago, and it hadn't changed much: a sleepy kind of market square, where dogs lay and drowsed in the sun, two or three streets of shops, the church, and, dominating it all, a huge tumbledown castle overlooking a damp meadow where they held the gala (they shifted the animals out a day or so before, but anyone who didn't keep one eye firmly on the ground while inspecting the stalls and sideshows was liable to end up in a cowpat). We used to get there just after lunch, and spend an hour or so watching the livestock exhibitions, the fire brigade display and the beauty pageant prior to having tea with the Pagetts, Uncle George, Aunt Sheila and their family.

I've never been able to work out how exactly we were related to the Pagetts: I think my mother's mother and Aunt Sheila's mother might have been cousins. Certainly there was a photograph of Grandma Lutterworth amongst the clutter on the sideboard, and Aunt Sheila and Mother sometimes used to exchange excruciating confidences of things they'd done together back in the Twenties. I think Mother was a bit embarrassed by the Pagetts. They were a real old country couple – Uncle George would have been about sixty-five, Aunt Sheila maybe a year or so younger – with flat East Suffolk accents, who pronounced 'have' as 'hev' and the gala, in which they took a benign and incurious interest, as the 'gayla'. Neither of them had ever been out of Suffolk in their lives, although Uncle George may have made it to the Suffolk Regiment's HQ at Felixstowe during the Great War before being turned down on account of bad feet. Aunt Sheila's pre-marital career in service had taken her as far as Ipswich, but that was about the limit of their mental world. Mother, of course, God-fearing shopkeeper's daughter that she was, was privately horrified by the thought of having a second cousin who'd been a parlourmaid, but she managed to grit her teeth at the anecdotes about butlers and anchovy toast and what the master (Aunt Sheila always referred to her ex-employer as 'the master') had said in 1914.

For myself, I always liked Uncle George and Aunt Sheila, and entered enthusiastically into the whole social experience of which a couple of hours spent in their company on a warm summer afternoon consisted. They lived in a queer rabbit-warren of a place half a mile out of the town itself, which was always crammed with people – most of the children were grown up and married by now, but the gala was one of the big social events of the year – with a big, neatly kept backyard where Uncle George, who'd been a market gardener before he retired, grew peas and radishes and delicate little James Greave apples. Inside there'd be a throng of second and third cousins, most of whose names I never got round to discovering, crowded round the tea table, with Uncle George – he was a canny old chap with a red, nut-cracker face, bent nearly double from rheumatism – sitting in an armchair by the fire. They had a fire even in May. Beyond the table was a monstrous sofa piled with knitting patterns and back-numbers of *Reveille*, a lowbrow weekly paper full of pictures of chorus girls' legs, which Aunt Sheila took 'for the coupons'.

When I wasn't gorging myself on Aunt Sheila's home-made jam – which was glorious stuff, as unlike shop jam as a bottle of Nuit St Georges is unlike Rioja – or blushing off Uncle George's requests to know if I was 'courting', I used to amuse myself by sneaking occasional glances at Father and Mother. It was an interesting study in contrasts. Mother, it hardly needs saying, was horribly ill at ease and simply sat there on the sofa barely opening her mouth. Father, on the other hand, who was quite happy to descend to a social level considerably lower than the one he was used to, chattered amiably about football with the Pagett cousins and invariably got taken out into the garden to see how the fruit was coming on. I used to look at Mother sometimes as she sat there on the sofa, nervously guarding her Sunday dress from the hordes of tearaway children, and wonder what it was that kept her from joining in, making the kind of small talk that other women ventured about their children and their husbands' jobs. Later on I realised that it wasn't even class consciousness that did it, but a kind of fundamental aloofness and detachment from the Pagetts' world – a world of teeming children, the *Daily Mirror* and endlessly stewing cups of tea. When she did make an effort, it was always to betray what even I could see was an invincible ignorance about the sort of landscapes that Uncle George and Aunt Sheila inhabited – asking them how much they paid their window-cleaner, or how the younger children were doing at school.

Those afternoons at Fram! With the noise of the brass band drifting in through the window from Gala Meadow, children running in to show their parents goldfish in water-filled plastic bags they'd won on the sideshows, and Uncle George falling asleep over the fire and waking up occasionally to drat one of the kids who'd tumbled under his feet. Forty years later it sticks in my head as a vision of red-faced women shrieking gossip at each other, children skirmishing under the table, half-a-dozen conversations going on at once.

COUSIN WILLIAM: Fa! Hev you bin down to Gala Meadow yit?

UNCLE GEORGE: I hev not. Was intendin' on sittin' here with a cuppatoi.

MOTHER: *Can't* seem to get those dress patterns like you used . . . And I must say . . .

AUNT SHEILA: What's that you were saying, Eunice? Bill, *tell* them children their tea's ready.

COUSIN WILLIAM (*proudly*): *I* bin. Tobied on down there an hour since. Reckoned on looking at that there dicker someone was a showing of . . .

MOTHER: Went into Norwich for the sales in January, but they didn't have a thing.

UNCLE GEORGE (*highly amused*): You keep a dicker! Ha! (*seeing me at the table*) That boy of yours'll be a caution, I'll be bound. All the young chaps is these days.

MOTHER: Not him. Far too much schoolwork to do, I'm very pleased to say.

AUNT SHEILA (*nostalgically*): If you'd a had my mother, you'd hev had to make your own dresses, my dear.

COUSIN WILLIAM: Them old dickers! Just scrunch up the thistles, they does, like there was no hay worth eatin'.

'Dicker', by the way, meant 'donkey', while 'Fa' was short for father.

This particular Bank Holiday, though, something was up. For some reason we got there late, long after lunch. Rain was falling over the castle turrets, and Gala Meadow, where the livestock paraded and they had the children's races, was a sea of mud. Back at the Pagetts' Uncle George sat and sulked in his chair, a pair of cousins idled at the table playing spillikins with their huge labourers' hands, and even Aunt Sheila seemed irritated about something. Father and Mother, too, looked agitated, sitting side by side on the sofa like a couple of cats who've just seen an Alsatian on the other side of the street. It was a bit before tea-time, the rain was easing off now, and since I'd exhausted the possibilities of the Pagetts' front room, turned over the yellowing copies of *Reveille* and glanced at the bookcase, which was full of back-numbers of *Farming Week* and a copy of *Pilgrim's Progress* Aunt Sheila had won as a Sunday School prize, I wandered back into the town. Here the water was still coursing along the gutters and the streets were full of people in their best clothes coming out of doorways where they'd taken shelter, and in the distance you could see lines of draggled bunting hanging over the privet hedge that backed on to the meadows. In ordinary circumstances I'd have gone and walked round the castle ramparts, which was something I always got a kick out of, or hunted down an ice-cream van, but somehow I didn't feel like it. Part of this was to do with Father and Mother and the shop, a bit more with Marjorie Lovelace, with whom, and despite now being allowed to put my hand inside her blouse, I was getting rather bored, but most of it was to do with a feeling of altered circumstances looming up at me, the thought that all this – the square, the long rows of sweet jars, even Fram in the rain – was about to change in a way I couldn't begin to comprehend, much less do anything about. In the end I walked into the churchyard at the far end of the winding main street, found a half-empty packet of Gold Flake that someone had dropped, cadged a match, and sat there under a dripping tree smoking them until an old chap with a shock of white hair, who was probably the churchwarden, danced out of the porch and drove me away. Back in the street there was a crowd of people standing outside the Conservative Club listening to a little man in a morning suit declaiming something or other, and I remember stopping to stare at a second man, some kind of chauffeur or servant I think, who was standing next to him holding up an umbrella to keep off the water from the dripping gables, before heading back to the Pagetts with a feeling of absolutely awful foreboding. My cousin Ernie, William's son, was leaning against the front door when I got there, and winked as I turned in at the gate.

'You don't want to go in there, young Ted.'

He was a big, gormless kid of about my age with one of those vacant, rural faces.

'Why not?'

'Some kind of argyment. I dunno.' He must have caught the cigarette smoke on my breath, because he went on: 'Got a fag, hev you?'

'No.'

The front door was half open, and you could hear the raised voices in the hall. As it turned out there were only four people in the front room – Father and Mother and Uncle George and Aunt Sheila. As I came in Aunt Sheila was halfway through a sentence, but she thought better of it, and the only noise was Mother snivelling faintly on the edge of the sofa. Father sat next to her, looking as if he'd just seen a ghost.

'Hop off out of it, young Ted,' Uncle George said, not unkindly.

For some reason, though, I didn't go – something, I suppose, to do with wanting explanations, an eternal fed-upness, which practically every teenager experienced in those days, of being kept in the dark and generally disregarded. Mother started crying a bit louder, Uncle George looked faintly embarrassed, and by degrees the tableau broke up. Aunt Sheila tossed her head – not a figure of speech, she really did toss it – and stumped off to the kitchen. Father got up from the sofa and began dusting down the sides of his trousers, which was one of his characteristic gestures when he was nervous or otherwise upset. Ten minutes later we were back in the car.

Nobody said a word on the way back to Yarmouth. There was a thunderstorm outside Lowestoft and we had to park in a lay-by, but even then neither of them would say anything. In the end, over the next couple of days, I wormed it out of them that Father had borrowed money off Uncle George – £100 it might have been, certainly no more than that – and not been able to pay it back. Funnily enough, I wasn't particularly shocked by this. What really shocked me was Mother's reaction to my finding out. It was clearly the most shameful thing that had ever happened to her – rather as if, I dimly understood, I'd found her in one of the big hotels along the front in the arms of some fancyman.

Two weeks later the final letter came from the bank, and Father shut up the shop for good.

Apparently the Ngongi tribe of equatorial Guinea can survive on as little as 200 millilitres of water a day. The averagely pampered Westerner needs a minimum 700 millilitres to sustain the basic processes of life, but the Ngongi, habituated to the routines of sunshine, scrub and dried-up wells, can make do with the equivalent of a large tea-cupful. I came across this fact in a newspaper account of two West African teenagers named Yaguine and Fodé who stowed away on a Sabena airbus flight from Conakry to Brussels. Eight days later, after the airbus had completed a further three round-trips between Brussels and Guinea, an airport technician found their bodies decomposing in the right-wing wheel arch. Two or three times in the past few days I've found myself wondering about Yaguine and Fodé. When did they realise the enormity of what they'd done? When did they understand, up there in the freezing night with the engines tearing above them that this was no passing chill but the hand of death? And what did they say to each other when they knew?

In a small way, the people round here have the Ngongi spirit. Not the wide-eyed prospectors' certainty that drives teenage boys to freeze to death in wheel arches, but the ability to make do with what's available, to calibrate effort to likely reward, to create an illusion of well-being that – who knows? – is as sustaining as the real thing. The other day I saw a kid in what looked like a Tommy Hilfiger sweatshirt. Close inspection revealed that it was an ordinary grey top on which somebody had carefully etched the designer's name in black marker pen. Not that you don't see plenty of genuine Hilfiger gear round here – a kind of inversion of the look-after-the-pennies-and-the-pounds-will-look-after-themselves routine, whereby the street vixens wear designer leggings, have mobiles and forty-a-day cigarette habits and still push prams whose occupants look as if they were fed exclusively on lard. For the most part, though, the commerce of the street is fantastically low-level, like the small ads in the local paper: *Girls' shoes £5, My Little Pony playset, hardly used, £7, Abba CD £4.* Who wants to buy a pair of girls' shoes for £5? The same people, presumably, who have mobile phones and underweight babies. All part of the average human being's eagerness to adapt himself to his environment and engage in its commercial rituals. No doubt My Little Pony playsets, hardly used, are the spiritual equivalent of Sotheby's (where I went once and watched Upward spend £5,000). Or the Ngongi on their 200 millilitres of water a day.

Not greatly to my surprise I find Lennie waiting for me outside the club: a small, uncertain figure in a sheepskin coat, tossing his car keys from hand to hand and casting anxious glances at the Cavalier parked two or three spaces up the street.

''Ow're you doing then me old china? You're looking good.'

Lennie, on the other hand, is looking very far from good. Somehow it's difficult to put a finger on Lennie's odd incompatibility with the environment in which he moves. The pat he administers on my shoulder as he falls in beside me seems painfully lightweight and insubstantial.

'I didn't know you were a Plumstead Over Sixty?' I say.

'Ah well, we're none of us as young as we was. And there's some good Jewish boys here, you know.'

Lennie's Jewishness, like the smashed veins on his cheeks and the chunky soccer manager's jewellery decked about his person, dates him irrevocably of course. He belongs somewhere in the Sixties, back in a world of cross-talk comedians, *Saturday Night at the London Palladium* and George Best, whose manager, oddly enough, Lennie once was (*'E was a nice boy, Georgie, but, phew, sooner you than me*).

'How's Mrs M?'

'She's okay. She sent you a message. Said. "Tell 'im it's time we saw you on TV again."'

'Sounds more like a message for you.'

'I know. I know.' Lennie's expression as he says this is genuinely piteous, like a child denied some long promised treat on grounds which no one will explain. Nobody seems to have told him that career opportunities are somewhat restricted for seventy-year-olds whose finest moment was staffing the Bobbie Gentry Show back in 1968.

'What about the stars of tomorrow, Lennie? Where are they?'

'Ah, they're not interested are they? All want to be pop stars and footballers. I got this good boy – my great-nephew actually – plays the harmonica at bar-mitzvahs and that. Now, Moishe, he could be the new Danny Silverstein. I keep telling 'im. But 'e's too busy doing 'is computer course.'

It says something for Lennie's longevity that I don't remember the original Danny Silverstein. Perhaps, on the other hand, he never really existed – just a compound of the various elements floating around in Lennie's subconscious to be arbitrarily plucked forth and given a name.

Inside the community centre orange lights burn off a vestibule dominated by a portrait of the Queen Mother – its founding patron, apparently – clad in the royal fashions of the Fifties. Further inside, through half-open swing doors, a few people can be seen moving about. Lennie checks his watch.

'Still ten minutes yet. Let's 'ave a drink.'

As we prowl along the empty corridor towards the bar I realise what strikes me as incongruous about Lennie. There is an odd, rivery smell coming off him, faint yet perceptible, almost as if he rose up out of the Thames half an hour ago. Watching him move towards me across the tattered carpet with a gin and tonic in each hand, I can still smell it: a mixture of fish, the river at low tide, salt air. The smell rises as he settles in his chair.

'You okay, Lennie?'

'I've been thinking, Ted. You know . . . I was at Lew's funeral the other day.'

'Lew?'

'Lew *Grade*,' Lennie says crossly. ''Im and me went back a long way, y'know. So there I was – no one I knew – thinking, funny, there's no sign of Bernie Cohen or Monty Yadinsky. And then all of a sudden I realised they was all dead.'

Lennie has a weakness for old showbiz troupers. Especially Jewish ones. I doubt his acquaintance with Lord Grade extended much beyond standing in the same room as him at a 1973 Variety Club reception. All the same there is something rather uncomfortable about the images stoked into being: mourners passing this way and that over the wet grass (I've read the newspaper reports, as it happens), mist hanging in the air, and in the midst of it all a seventy-year-old Jewish variety agent who smells of fish grieving for Bernie Cohen and Monty Yadinsky.

'Anyway, I started thinking about Lew and those good boys that were gone.'

Outside, through thick plate-glass, rain falls slowly over the grey highway. Cars whine up the hill towards Abbey Wood and Greenwich. Glimpsed in the glass's reflection, Lennie looks faintly crumpled: limbs too small for the sheepskin carapace from which they protrude. Experience tells me that this is the prelude to a more substantial lament: Lennie's monologue on the death of comedy.

Lennie on the death of comedy? 'I just don't understand what's 'appened. Morecambe & Wise? Now they were funny. Benny Hill? 'E was funny. Mike and Bernie Winters? Well, they was all right. Sort of. But this new lot. 'Alf the time you just don't get it. I once paid twenty quid to see Newman & Baddiel at Wembley Arena. Walked out after 'alf an hour. I saw old Abie Myerscough the other day and do you know what 'e said? "Lennie, mate, it's all fucked – 'scuse my French – they don't want nice Jewish boys as can play the 'armonica and tell some jokes your mother could listen to anymore."'

There are wider implications here. Lennie has failed to adapt. His first wife died in 1974. Her replacement (*Nah, she's a good woman. Devoted to me*) sits at home nagging him about villas in Alicante. Looking at Lennie these days I get a sense of a life becalmed, like the big hulks you see out in the Thames at low tide, marooned in mid-stream with the current flowing round them. Perhaps that's where Lennie gets his peculiar odour.

The fish smell rises again as we move off into the hall. Here about three dozen of the Plumstead Over Sixties have distributed themselves in about twice that number of metal-backed chairs. I have a look at them while a man in a suit takes us through the preliminaries. Husbands and wives, mostly, the men in check trousers straining above cannon-ball paunches, the women in 'costumes'. These are Lennie's people, I suppose, old-stagers who know who Danny Silverstein is and remember the décor of the Crossroads Motel.

Lennie introduces me. In public his accent goes spiralling up into unknown regions of Bow Bells pastiche. No one seems to mind. He even tells a few jokes. *Wotcher girls and boys. Now tonight we've got a real treat in store. No, I'm not going to take me clothes off . . . Seriously, tonight's guest needs no introduction. But I'm going to introduce 'im anyway. Look, I've even got some notes. And as Adam said to Eve in the garden of Eden, there must be another leaf somewhere . . .*

They love it, of course. A little old man in the front row turns purple in the face when he hears the Adam and Eve joke and has to be slapped on the back by an equally plum-faced neighbour. This is a new Lennie, a bright, capering spirit come up from the depths to confound us all. Maybe, thinking about it, this is Lennie's tragedy: that he really wanted to be one of those Jewish boys who played the kazoo and told jokes about the rabbi's beard falling into the gefiltefish soup. Who knows? At the end he even does a little shuffle, hands splayed out on either side of his face, like an arthritic tap-dancer trying to remember the steps, and gets a round of applause all to himself.

I once read somewhere that Ken Dodd used to conduct a minute-by-minute analysis of every live show he ever performed. (This was before the age of video.) Each night when he came off stage he'd collect a tape from the sound man's cubby-hole, take it back to his hotel and sit there until the small hours ransacking the spools for evidence of skewed delivery, lowered applause levels, that faint background whisper which is an audience turning restless. First thing next morning he'd work on his running order in the light of this intelligence. To anyone who saw him again the following night the effect was barely perceptible – a couple of dropped one-liners, perhaps, or a longer sketch slowed down by twenty seconds or so. All this in a two-hour spectacle involving half-a-dozen other people and three or four changes of clothing. At the time I was cautiously admiring of this type of perfectionism. Now I think he was slightly mad.

Not that borderline sanity is a handicap, you understand. Upward, in particular, had original views on comedy that emerged from the realms of minor psychological disturbance.

'Of course,' he used to say, 'it's as well to realise that not being quite right in the head's a positive advantage sometimes. Every time I see one of them bug-eyed blokes in bowler hats lurking by the side of the stage I always think, "There's another one the doctors have let out for the day." That kind of thing has a big historical tradition. You'd be surprised.'

'Like medieval kings laughing at cripples?'

'Exactly. Look at someone like Marty Feldman or Freddie Davies. I'm not saying they're not perfectly responsible members of society, but stick them on a stage and your average audience will start laughing out of sheer bloody nervousness.'

'So what would happen if you had a comedian who was a genuine madman?'

'Naturally it'd depend. Of course, if you just foamed at the mouth I can't imagine anyone would be particularly interested, although y' could probably make a fortune doing it in the States. But I used to have an old aunt who went around picking up burnt matches off the floor and shutting them in the oven. You can take it from me, Ted, that was absolutely hilarious.'

Some golden rules of comedy. Doing a TV cross-talk act you look at the *vis-à-vis.* Opening an end-of-pier show in front of 1500 people you look at the space between the balcony and the back row of the stalls. Working a club, on the other hand, you look at the audience, singly and severally. You have to be careful, though. Once, somewhere up north, Upward completely blew it by playing to a woman with a gatling-gun laugh who ended up having hysterics.

There is little danger of this happening with the Plumstead Over Sixties. Actually I go down rather well. The women smile. The men look on benignly. Lennie, parked in the front row and clearly losing interest, starts turning out the pockets of his sheepskin coat. The sex on TV joke gets a huge laugh. So does a Jewish joke of a kind you couldn't tell outside a place like the Plumstead Over Sixties these days, about pound notes being green because the Jews used to pick them before they were ripe. The little old man in the front row nearly has a heart-attack over that. Oddly enough, I don't get the feeling that anyone is taking much note of what I say. They like having me here, of course, they wish me well, but it's what I represent that's important: a glimpse back into that lost world of the Sixties and Seventies, black and white television, Wilson and Heath and Henry Cooper – all rubbish, of course, but known rubbish, connected to them in a way that the modern stuff isn't. Sensing the mood out there – Lennie, I note, has given up ransacking his pockets and is wiggling a cotton-bud in one ear – I delve into the memory archive for a joke about decimal coinage. It gets a huge laugh.

Curiously enough, there's another act on the bill. As soon as I've resumed my seat Lennie leaps up and announces that after a short interval the Stan Rubinovitz Trio with Titch Johnson on saxophone will be here to entertain us. About half the audience decide to leave immediately. Lennie and I followed them out into the orange-lit foyer.

'Great show, Ted. Seriously.'

'You were pretty good yourself.'

'Funny you should say that actually.' Lennie's face turns over a bit. 'I used to do warm-ups for Frankie now and again in the early days. But it never came to anything.'

'Frankie?'

'Frankie Howerd.'

Another good Jewish boy, of course. 'Shonks' Father used to call them – a name I never found in any dictionary – not out of malice but from an urgent need to classify. 'Look at that shonk,' he would say whenever a picture of Bing Crosby or Liberace appeared in one of the illustrated papers.

'Between you and me,' Lennie goes on confidentially, as an elderly man in a dinner jacket – presumably one of the Stan Rubinovitz Trio – swings past us propelling an electric piano before him, 'that one about the Jews picking pound notes was a mistake.'

Perhaps, after all, Lennie is adapting to his environment. Certainly he's found out about political correctness from somewhere. Looking at the Plumstead Over Sixties as they drift past us into the foyer, I can detect a narrowly overcome reluctance to treat with the modern world. There are mobiles out, dialling mini-cabs. One old boy is even loading himself up in an electronic pensioner's carriage. The whirr of the wheels, the hovercraft glide, returns me to Yaguine and Fodé in their wheel arch. Fodé was fourteen. Four years older than Daniel.

'Lennie,' I say. 'Did you read the stuff in the papers about the kids who stowed away in the airbus?'

Lennie completely misconnects. 'Them asylum seekers? You got to keep them out. There's half of bleeding Europe queueing up at Dover from what I hear.'

Lennie's parents, it should be said, came over from Munich shortly after the Reichstag fire. World history to Lennie is consequently Jewish history: Whitechapel synagogues, Mosley's blackshirts, punch-ups in the East End; a bit later the Stern Gang and Menachem Begin. Oddly enough, the Jewish conspiracy angle on world events is one to which Lennie keenly subscribes. To him, the people who run the globe have names like Wasserman and Berkovitz, sit on Senate committees and own the combines who own the mid-west grain silos. Lennie's never heard of Bill Gates, but if he had he'd be able to tell you that his real name is Finkelstein.

Back inside the hall the Stan Rubinovitz Trio is tuning up. It sounds like a single instrument until you realise that the faint scraping sound in the distance is a snare drum. Lennie's gaze is darting back and forth down the corridor, head rising up out of the sheepskin like an elderly tortoise sniffing the air.

'Actually,' he says, 'I forgot to tell you. Was someone else on the dog wanting you. Not that BBC gel. Some geezer.'

'Did he say what he wanted?'

'Nah. 'Ad some funny name too. You know, initials and that. D.I. Something. I give 'im your number though.'

'Thanks, Lennie.'

Lennie clearly isn't interested in the mystery caller. Neither does it seem to strike him that 'D.I.' is short for 'Detective Inspector'. Outside in the street tiny screaming kids run past, though it's already eight-thirty. Over the noise of the Stan Rubinovitz Trio – now grown to a considerable racket – a voice is jauntily intoning:

I got a girl
in Kalamazoo.
I liked her looks when I carried her books
in Kalamazoo.

Did you hear the one about the old lady who went for a tramp in the woods? He got away.

Later a maniac in a beanie hat with a stereo pumping out what sounds like the noise of a dysfunctional cement-mixer mini-cabs me home. The house is quiet. Upstairs the boy sleeps blamelessly beneath his coverlet, flanked by an empty crisp packet and half-a-dozen copies of the *Beano.* Michael Owen looks on above him. I stand there for a minute or so checking his breathing. Even when they've reached the age of ten you still do this, still assure yourself that they're alive. Down in the hall the red eye of the answer phone winks dutifully away. I go to sleep thinking of Yaguine and Fodé, Lennie, Shena's letter, the Stan Rubinovitz Trio's eerie shuffle.

Teenage Kicks

After the letter from the bank things happened very quickly. As it happened, Father's smash-up was much worse than anyone expected. It turned out that he'd been playing off suppliers against one another, as well as stringing the bank along, and there was money owing all over the place. In the end, when the accountants had been through the books, all the creditors had been paid and the stock disposed of, there was slightly under £200 left, which wasn't much even by the standards of 1956. For a time Father and Mother talked vaguely about 'getting back on their feet' and 'starting afresh', but although Father did go after one or two shop manager's jobs in the town, I don't think their hearts were in it. Everyone in Yarmouth knew that Father had 'failed', which was the word people used for bankruptcy in those days, and that the chances of him getting another job were practically zero. Of the two it was Mother who took it to heart. Father was upset, of course – he'd run a business for twenty years and now it had collapsed round his ears – but he was still capable of functioning in a more or less normal way. Mother, on the other hand, was merely distraught. For her, the shop going was a kind of judgment on her life, and an invitation for the people she knew to mock her.

As for me, I don't remember being particularly exercised by the closed shutters and the chaps in grey suits from Larking & Gowan, the big Yarmouth accountancy firm, trying to fix a resale value on the boxes of pipe tobacco. Naturally I was sorry that Father and Mother were upset, but the wider implications didn't bother me. For a start I knew that one of the consequences of this knock to

Father and Mother's self-esteem would be a loosening of the bonds that tied me to them. Which is selfish, if you like, but that's how you think when you're a kid of sixteen whose horizons up until now have been bounded by a market square, the North Sea and a pair of stuffy middle-aged people whose chief object in life seems to be to stop you doing the things you want. I liked my parents, and if they were somehow to walk into the room tomorrow I dare say I'd be happy enough to see them, but at the time I know that I regarded them as an obstacle to my progress through life and I couldn't wait to push them aside.

We had a month's grace in the shop while the Church Commissioners disposed of the lease. It was an odd, unreal kind of life. Father and Mother had nothing to do except read the paper and conduct sniffy, dispirited conversations with each other. I'd left school – at least it was generally supposed that I wasn't going back in the autumn, but nobody seemed to know what I ought to be doing. Meanwhile there was a ghastly symbolism about the events going on around us. Every time a van arrived to take away some unsold stock or a chap with a ladder turned up to fix a 'To Let' board above the window it was like a nail being hammered into the coffin of my parents' lives. On the day they burned off the S. LUTTERWORTH over the shopfront Mother simply went to bed for the afternoon, so great was her misery, and even Father looked a bit green. Later that night they must have had some kind of conference, because when I came down to breakfast next morning it was to find Father sitting very solemn in the big chair by the kitchen table, with the light gleaming off his bald head, while Mother fussed around near the sink. It was so unusual for Father to make a speech that I can remember what he said practically word for word. He and Mother had been having a talk (*sniff*). They'd been thinking (*sniff, sniff*) and what they'd decided was that they were going to stay with Uncle Ralph for a bit – Uncle Ralph was Father's widowed elder brother – until things 'picked up' (*sniff*) and Father could 'see where he stood'. As for going back to school, no one was going to stop me, but in the circumstances it might be best if I got a job (*sniff, sniff, sniff*). And that, more or less, was that. A fortnight later the shop was shut up, Father and Mother removed themselves to Uncle Ralph's house at Gorleston, and I went to lodge with a family called Enright who lived near the market square and started work at the Sun Alliance office.

Do you remember those old office buildings in the Fifties? With a fat commissionaire on the door, a couple of bored receptionists doing their nails in the foyer and, inside, rows of little cubicle offices stretching away down the corridor like rabbit hutches? The Sun Alliance place was exactly like that. It was the biggest insurance firm in Yarmouth, spread over three floors, with a huge panelled boardroom at the top where the directors met, and it employed about 150 people, most of them men but with a couple of dozen secretaries and typists. This being the Fifties, and Yarmouth, the most exacting protocols applied. As a junior clerk you were expected to call the other junior clerks by their surnames, the senior clerks 'Mr' and anyone over the rank of department head 'sir'. The secretaries were addressed as 'Miss', or very occasionally 'Mrs' (the Sun Alliance wasn't keen on employing married women, but they were prepared to let them stay on for a few months after the wedding), and if they suspected you of 'cheeking' them they'd report you to the office manager, an old bloke named Penworthy who never seemed to do anything except fill inkwells and worry about misplaced ledgers. The clerks' room looked out over the market square, and in winter, with the paraffin heaters on and a pleasant fug rising over the long rows of stools, there were worse places to be. Sitting at my desk, with the gulls flapping outside, listening to the thick plate-glass moving in the wind, I used to measure out the time with squares of chocolate, a square every fifteen minutes, looking up at five to find the bar gone, the gulls vanished out to sea, and the shop windows glowing greeny-gold in the dusk.

As for the work itself, a child of ten could have done it. The Sun Alliance might have had four or five thousand policy holders, and my job, quite simply, was to maintain the eight huge filing trays in which their addresses were kept. Other times, if things were slack, I'd be sent out on my bike with an envelope for one of the local solicitors or accountants who doubled up as our representatives, but all through that first couple of years if you'd asked me what I did I'd have answered quite truthfully 'I do addresses'. And if you think this was a humble occupation, I should say that there was a gaunt old spinster called Miss Cattermole, who'd been at the place thirty years, whose task was to assemble the change of address details *before* I filled them in on the filing cards.

And yet I didn't care about the hours spent over the filing trays, or Miss Cattermole sniffing dejectedly in the background – there was a bit of a frost between us as I gathered I'd been appointed over her head – or the derision of the older juniors who looked down on 'kids straight out of school'. I was sixteen years old, had thirty shillings a week in my pocket that were mine to keep, and within certain broadly defined limitations could do more or less what I wanted. In those days, of course, this kind of freedom was faintly unusual. People watched over their children then in a way that they don't do now – not so much because they wanted to stop them doing things they disapproved of, but because they wanted them to go on being children. I've known girls of eighteen training as typists whose fathers walked them to work every morning and collected them again at night.

What was I like at sixteen? What were you like at sixteen? I was five feet eleven by then, which was a goodish height for the Fifties, and what with Mrs Enright's cooking and the stodgy lunches they served in the staff canteen I was starting to fill out a bit. Inevitably, I was completely selfish and I'd have run a mile rather than do something I didn't want to. If you'd have asked me what I believed in in those days I'd have been hard put to tell you – probably just a watered-down version of the stuff Father and Mother had dinned into me over the years. At the same time, without even thinking about it, I was pulling away from Father and Mother. I used to go over and see them at weekends, of course, but the old life we'd had together was smashed to pieces, and they knew it. All I remember of those times is Uncle Ralph's dark front room, with Mother's face peering through the bad light and Father pottering in with one of his scrapbooks, which he'd balance on his lap while he drank his tea. Neither of them liked living with Uncle Ralph, I discovered – the cottage was too small for the three of them and Uncle Ralph, who was a good ten years older than Father, rather looked on them as his housekeepers – and they were still talking about moving on as soon as Father could get himself 'placed'. Even I could see, though, that Father's chances of getting another job were slightly less than me getting a trial with Norwich City.

And all the while time was passing. It was 1956 now, 1957. Suez came, with people nearly fighting on the garage forecourts for petrol and everybody saying that 'these here Gyppos' ought to be taught a lesson. If anyone tells you that British public opinion was against Suez, then all I can say is that they never came anywhere near Yarmouth. There was a murder case down by the quayside – a woman whose husband had found her in bed with another man – and one of the senior clerks at the office had a heart-attack at his desk. It was a good half-hour before anyone noticed, but what I really remember is them shifting the body on to a stretcher and the bottom of his trousers riding up to reveal long woollen combinations. I'd been at the place nearly a year then and was getting to know my way around. Curiously enough, I made a goodish impression at the Sun Alliance. By the time I was seventeen I'd been taken off 'addresses' and put on to drafting correspondence to customers, or phoning people up to check their personal details. I suppose if I'd had any sense I would have been plotting my future, putting money away and taking correspondence courses in business administration and that kind of thing, but I was seventeen, selfish in a way that horrifies me to think about, and as far as I was concerned the £5 a week that my wages had been raised to was there simply to pay for my principal hobbies, which were listening to radio comedy shows and chasing girls.

Girls! Looking back, I don't suppose there were many times between the ages of sixteen and eighteen when I wasn't thinking about girls, or if not directly then about something vaguely connected to them – clothes, say, or Tony Curtis hair-cuts, or the chances of getting a ticket for some youth club dance or other. This kind of mental preparation was important, because girls weren't at all easy to come by in Yarmouth in the Fifties, and to find them meant putting yourself through some extraordinary social rituals. To begin with you had to haunt somewhere where girls – respectable girls, that is – went: a youth club or a church social. Then, after you'd been seen around a bit, you could ask a particular girl for a date. Usually she'd say yes, although in terms of your chances this didn't mean anything. The protocols for 'first dates' were set in stone. You went with another couple, or, worse, the girl would ask if she could bring a friend, and the three of you would traipse along the front for half an hour before ending up for an entirely speechless tea at one of the cafés in town. The second time, which always took place on a Saturday afternoon, you went on your own on something called a 'pier walk', which consisted of wandering up and down the pier half-a-dozen times before retreating to a tea-shop again. The third time, if there was a third time, you got asked to the girl's house for Sunday tea – the most gruesome bit of all, as it meant being asked questions by her parents. Four decades on I can still remember those questions. What do you do (they'd know this already, but that didn't stop them asking it)? What does your father do? Where do you live? Do you go to church? What kind of church (you had to be careful here – everybody hated Catholics and were sniffy about most of the nonconformist sects)? One of my most enduring memories of those years is of sitting in the front room of some bandbox house, set back from the front, with a cup of watery tea in one hand as a suspicious-looking middle-aged man prosed away from the chair nearest the fire and the girl and her mother sat uncomfortably together on the sofa. The worst thing was that you could always tell from the girl's face how it was going.

The odd thing about these relationships (they used to last about two months, by the way, until one of the parties 'met someone else' or 'didn't think it was serious') was, on the one hand, their staggering formality – no one would have dreamt of going out on a date without being dressed up to the nines – and on the other their almost complete sexlessness. Kissing a girl goodnight too adventurously or making a meal of helping her on with her coat (the trick was to turn her unexpectedly towards you so that she more or less fell into your arms) had you marked down as 'fast' or 'unreliable'. Girls talked openly about 'saving themselves' in those days and thanked God that they weren't factory women who 'made themselves cheap'. Looking back, I sometimes wonder why I went through with it – sat through those sofa-bound afternoons with girls who barely knew whether the earth went round the sun or vice versa, with their parents (who were like my parents only somehow staider and less individuated) conspiring over the teacups – and I suppose the answer lies in sheer loneliness.

Meanwhile the time was passing. 1957. 1958. They were building houses now, all over the outskirts of the town, and in the early mornings you could see the brickdust rising like red fog. 1958 was a hot summer, I remember, and people went lobster-coloured in the sun. A boy drowned in the sea that year out near Scroby and there was a panic about lifeguards and scarlet flags to tell you when the water was unsafe. I'd just turned eighteen, had my wages raised another pound a week, and in the intervals of worrying about National Service was going out with a girl called Julia Betterton, who I was quite mad on – she was a small, very delicate blonde girl who never said anything but simply sat on the other side of the table staring at you for all the world like a china doll. They were good days back then – even at the time I knew they were good days – striding over the market square in the mornings with the sun flooding in over the arm of the sea, rushing out in the lunch hour to meet Julia for a sandwich and a stroll along the Marrams, but I could tell they were slipping away. At eighteen, even in a provincial town bounded by the sea and the marshes I could see that – that life wouldn't always be the same, and that it was beyond my power to change it. I'd stopped living at the Enrights' by this time and had gone into digs at a house on Marine Parade. It was a big place – three or four storeys, with a warren of attics at the top. The old woman who owned it lived in the basement, but apart from a knock on the door on Friday nights to collect the rent you were left pretty much to yourself. Now and again I used to cycle over to Gorleston in the evenings to see Father and Mother, but there was a sense – and I'm sure I grasped a little of this at the time – in which they were fading away out of my life, stuck and motionless while I was moving on. Just hearing them talk depressed me beyond measure. They used to sit by the fire endlessly spinning out the same complaints about Uncle Ralph (who might have been bedridden by this time – certainly I never saw him when I came to the house) and people who'd 'dropped them' since the smash. Poor Mother! It was only later, when I thought about it, that I realised just what a comedown her life must have been after the shop went. As for Father, he had this dreadful trick of forgetting to put his teeth in, so that his face always seemed slightly fallen in and withered.

Other times, when I wasn't seeing Father and Mother or Julia Betterton, I just used to lie there in my room with my hands clasped behind my head and think about things – not out of fear, you understand, but with a huge expectancy, a kind of feeling that in some way I didn't quite understand my life was taking shape, everything around me gathering pace and purpose. Sometimes I used to smuggle Julia up there in the evenings – one of the things I liked about her was that she could see the point of spending time like this – and we would just stare at each other. She had a way of curling up on the bed not quite asleep while I stroked her hair – it was very pale, yellow-gold hair, I remember – or tried to tune in to Radio Luxembourg on the big Bakelite set. Christ! I can't begin to describe what it felt like, lying there on a summer evening with the sky turning blue-black out over the sea, and the noise from the town filtering through the window, and Julia stretching herself out lazily like a cat at my side. God knows what we talked about – jobs, probably, and families (her parents kept a shop too, and they were sympathetic about Father) and pop music – the kind of thing teenagers talked about in the Fifties. And though I can't remember the words, the *atmosphere* is as vivid to me as the room I came out of ten minutes ago.

But, as I say, it was all slipping away, rushing on down the slope in front of me. The letter from the army board in Norwich was already lying on the mantelpiece at Marine Parade. I dare say that if I'd had any guts I'd have sat down and thought about it a bit, about Julia, the Sun Alliance, Father and Mother, and what I might be like, or want to do, in two years' time. But two years is an eternity when you're eighteen, quite unquantifiable, and so I just sat and waited, enjoying what I had while it lasted and not caring about what lay ahead. It was July turning into August now, and blisteringly hot. There was nothing to do at work, and I sat at my desk and idled, cheeked old Penworthy even more than usual, and went on long, leisurely 'errands' to Southtown (the greengrocer who'd bought the lease of Father's shop had already gone bust, I noticed, and been replaced by a general provisions merchant who looked as if he was about to go the same way) and once as far as Gorleston.

Four weeks. Three weeks. It was dark by half-past seven now, the military band had played its last Sunday concert on the Marrams, and the pleasure beach would close in a week. Julia and

I spent the spare time going for walks across the marshes, round Cobham Island, anywhere we could be on our own and talk. All that time there was a feeling – not ever put into words – that something was going to happen between us. Thinking about it now, I can't put it into any definite shape, except that it was to do with sex or the promise of sex. I think I thought that if Julia wouldn't sleep with me – and I had this detailed but curiously unerotic vision of her lying stark naked on the bed like the odalisque in the painting – then she might at least promise that she would at some unspecified future time. That was how people lived their lives in those days, people like me anyway. To get anywhere near a girl then you had to spend months scrambling over an assault course made up of God, money, parental disapproval, what you did for a living and what your father did for a living. Anyway, I had it all planned. On a particular afternoon about ten days before I was due to leave, we were going to take the train into Norwich, have tea at the Prince of Wales Hotel, watch the early showing of a film and then get the mid-evening train back to Yarmouth. Even at that stage, when I'd kissed her hundreds of times and spent a dozen evenings lying next to her in the attic at Marine Parade, I had no real conception of what might happen, and I couldn't have written down what I wanted from the day if you'd paid me.

In the end, of course, it was a complete disaster. That morning I looked up from my desk to find old Penworthy craning over me with a face like grim death and waving me off to the superintendent's office. This in itself was enough to put the wind up me – you were never called to the superintendent's office unless it was the sack or someone had died. As soon as I got there I could tell what had happened. Oddly enough, what I remember of the next few minutes is staring out of the window beyond the superintendent's office where they were trying to put back a shop awning that had blown down in the wind. It turned out that Father had had a stroke earlier in the morning. He was expected to live, Penworthy said, but beyond that they couldn't say. By the time I got through on the phone they'd taken him off to the Northgate Hospital, which was the big local hospital, and I finally got to see him, ironically enough, at exactly the time Julia and I were supposed to be having that tea. I don't remember much else of the day except Mother sitting cheerlessly at the bedside and the look on Father's face, which wasn't pained or vacant but simply a bit dogged, as if he were wandering about underwater and couldn't quite make out what the shapes and shadows consisted of. Over the next week or so I got to see Julia a couple of times, but it was all a frost, just sitting in coffee bars and not knowing what to say. The rest of the time was spent at the hospital, listening to Mother glooming on about the future and watching Father vaguely trying to open his mouth. He never spoke again. A fortnight later I was in Catterick.

The Ngongi continue to haunt me. Yesterday I even went to the local library to see if they could supply further information. Personally I wouldn't recommend the local library to anyone seriously interested in books. Or to anyone seriously interested in anything except Bruce Willis videos and wok cookery. Still, they had some stuff about the Ngongi. Apparently the tribe pursues a classic nomadic existence. No sooner have they encamped at one watering hole, fed their oxen, sung their primordial songs, tapped out their primeval rhythms on the birchbark drum, than the urge to depart becomes uncontrollable. A week is about the longest time the Ngongi remain in any one place. All this has led to an interesting controversy in the field of professional ethnography. On the one hand some experts have proposed a theory of nomadic existence, a kind of internal rhythm of life that forces people to move. Other students think that if you give the average nomad enough pasture for his livestock he tends to stay put. Predictably no one has asked the Ngongi about this. Neither has anyone ever given them enough pasture for their livestock. Despite these deprivations they seem to be a cheerful people, content to inhabit a world of endless horizons and diminishing returns. Once again, the ability to adapt is all.

I have an inkling that the Ngongi would feel pretty much at home around here – this in spite of the British National Party stickers and the *Nigger Scum Out* slogans on the viaduct overhangs. South-east London has its own nomadic existences, its oases, its sparse clumps of pasture. Never mind Mr and Mrs Rashid and the other newcomers from Bengal and Uzbekistan, the white people are on the move too. The old East End – the great grid of identikit terraces that stretches all the way from Mile End to Upney – is breaking up, so they say. The diaspora is based on money. With money you can prospect the flatbeds of Romford and Upminster. Without money you end up somewhere like here. The streets are full of off-white vans unloading, families piled on street corners trying to establish their bearings with regard to pub, chippy and corner shop. Meanwhile the older tribes are disappearing, gathering up their tents and moving on. God knows where they go. There are other bolt holes further down the Thames. *Dartford's not so bad*, you hear people say. Lennie has been seriously investigating a retirement complex near Gravesend. (*Getting a bit too old for this malarky, know what I mean*?) I know what he means. Everyone's moving downriver, borne on the restless tide. As I say, I think the Ngongi would feel at home.

There are real gulls, it turns out. At low tide the mudbanks are a playground for oyster-catchers, terns and razor-backs. The other morning I watched a cormorant perched on a PLA hulk in mid-stream and flexing its wings in odd origami patterns, just as if Yarmouth and Gorleston lay across the way rather than the Beckton towerblocks. Oddly, there was no comfort in this apparition. It was an alien bird, out of place on the mudflats. Like the London pigeons, the gulls look ground-down and unhappy. Something tells them they're in the wrong place, fetched up in this urban backwater, far away from the world they know.

Autumn comes early here. By mid-September the dusk is already stealing in at seven and the wind blowing off the river has an edge to it. Standing on the shoreline in the early evening, the view is like a sepia postcard: derelict wharves rotting into the river, behind and beyond the Dockland cranes. To the west familiar landmarks rise into view. Eastwards, downriver, the mist lifts off the surface of the water in ghostly folds and eddies. Nearer at hand there are odd explosions of light: police launches chugging by in mid-stream, a late tourist boat three-quarters empty and knowing it, heading back to Greenwich Pier and Westminster. Above, the sky fades away into dusky pinks and blues. There's a general sense of things settling down for winter, down into the burrowing world of dark streets, pale faces seen under the arc of the lamps, the flaming lanterns outside the pubs and the mini-cab offices.

Like the Ngongi, I'm busily adapting myself to my environment. First thing I take the boy to the school gates and watch him track his way across the scabbed tarmac to the door. I note that I'm the oldest parent by about twenty years. The other dads are bullet-headed little thugs in their thirties. In the afternoons I go out walking. A mile or so downstream the river loops southward, the houses recede from the shore and a different landscape shifts into view: reservoirs and sewage farms set back from the bank, mean little fields. Like the gulls, what ought to remind me of Yarmouth only reinforces its absence. Not salt hanging in the air but something ranker, more decayed: dark ooze and stagnant water. Apparently on a ship bound for the west coast of Africa there comes a day when the wind has a new smell – the heavy, rotting smell that comes from centuries of mangroves decaying into the swamp.

But perhaps the parallels with the Ngongi have been stressed enough.

Two days ago I took the train into town and headed for the West End. Curiously enough it was Lennie's idea. (*See the sights, me old china! Look up a few mates!*) When it came to it there were precious few mates to look up. The Casbah in Gerrard Street was an escort agency; Pantalino's where Upward and I once performed in front of Princess Margaret sometime in the mid-Sixties seemed to have disappeared altogether. But some odd homing instinct took me to the Empyrean in Wardour Street, where I hadn't been for five years and not played for ten, a month before the crash as it happened.

Fenced in behind stout blue shutters, entry through the same dark glass door set far back in the passageway approach, the Empyrean didn't seem outwardly to have changed. Inside there'd been a certain amount of refurbishment. Perhaps a dozen people were seated at the line of tables, mostly in ones and twos: there was probably a bigger dining area out of sight round the back. It was uncomfortably hot. Fetched up in this austere subterranean grotto, looking over a menu card in the shape of a butterfly's wings, it was impossible not to be struck by a dense wave of nostalgia: Upward, Paula, Ravenscroft in his shiny dinner jacket, balloons descending fitfully to the floor. Carried away on this, beyond the plum-coloured décor and the silver-painted stage into a kind of dream world full of dead but all-too-recognisable faces, I felt massively irritated: change, decay, the past not being able to match up to my expectations of it, all that. In the end I ordered an omelette and a glass of wine.

There was a burly maitre d' standing by an inner doorway, leading out into a kind of gazebo hung with vines. I waved him across.

'Does John Ravenscroft still own this place?'

'No sir.'

'Dan Kavanagh? Tim Jenks?'

'Never heard of them sir.'

'When did all this' – I flicked a hand at the plum wallpaper – 'get put in?'

'Couldn't say sir. All before my time.'

Only the bill brought back the Empyrean's former glories. I paid it and wandered off towards the vestibule. There was no one about. Fixed to the wall of the cloakroom was a panorama of old photographs. These showed the Empyrean in various stages of its development: red-faced men in evening suits brandishing champagne bottles, hawkish women in long dresses, a naked girl climbing out of the wreckage of a giant birthday cake. Three or four of the faces – showbiz people, the odd politician – I knew, or knew of. And then instantly, like a coin falling into the interior of a slot machine, I saw that the short, stubby man in the tuxedo, flanked by two statuesque brunettes got up as Edwardian parlourmaids, was Upward. There was no getting away from it. No getting away, either, from the complete vacuum in which it existed. Some of the photos had dates. Others commemorated significant anniversaries. A riot of blue balloons in one picture looked as if they came from an election-night party. Upward's portrait, on the other hand, was lost in space and time.

The maitre d', now definitely suspicious, lumbered across.

'Everything okay, sir?'

'Perfectly okay.'

Outside the clouds were moving west beyond Oxford Street. A man in an expensive suit loped past at a tremendous pace in the direction of Shaftesbury Avenue. Five yards away vapour rose off a deliquescing block of ice somebody had left out on the pavement. It was barely two o'clock. I wondered about going to see Lennie in his culvert round the back of Old Compton Street, in the small room with the Sid James posters and the box-card index that Lennie's had thirty years and keeps for sentiment's sake (I looked inside once and found Sir John Gielgud's name and address in amongst the rows of tap-dancing harmonica players). Then I decided against it. I have enough ghosts to follow.

Actually I get the feeling Lennie thinks my heart isn't really in it. I can tell this from the way he chides me over the phone. *You got the kid to support now and all ain't you?* He's right, of course. I have the kid to support. Not to mention the small matter of myself. Lennie's latest scheme is that I ought to write my autobiography. Even better, have my autobiography written for me by someone else. (*You could just sit there and spiel it, and 'e could take notes. It's 'ow they all do it.*) I don't like to tell Lennie that the world of showbiz memoirs has moved on a bit since he fixed up for Barbara Windsor and Ronnie Knight to tell all to the *People* back around the time of the three-day week. But every comedian is a hero to his agent. According to Lennie I'm still a 'household name'. But then so, apparently, are his tap-dancers and Captain Ludo and his performing seals, who last appeared on *Blue Peter* in 1978.

Meanwhile, I've had a couple of conversations with the BBC girl. As I might have forecast, Lennie had got it substantially wrong. Just a producer wanting eye-witnesses for one of those social history documentaries. I get the feeling that I might be seventeenth on a list of eighteen candidates, but there's talk of a budget and a vague suggestion that we should have lunch. The girl, whose name is Lucy, says things like 'I look foward to working with you Mr King' and 'Graham will be delighted'. I don't think she has a clue who I am. Or was.

Little Boy Soldiers

We were sweeping for mines out near the Nicosia–Kyrenia road.

In those days, of course, sweeping for mines was a chancy business. I've seen TV documentaries about mine-clearance where everybody wears plastic visors and the equipment can turn up a dropped halfpenny at twenty paces. Back then your only protection was a flak jacket, and the metal detectors worked within a radius of a couple of feet. The trick was to do it in pairs: one of you – the NCO, usually – eyeing up the ground for scuff marks or other signs that the surface had been disturbed, the other inching forward with the sweeper, which wasn't much more than a three-foot-long stick with a kind of soup-plate stuck to the end. There were various theories about how you were supposed to sweep. Some of the older men said you should imagine that you were giving the ground a coat of paint and the sweeper was the brush, but the latest idea was for a kind of criss-cross movement, on the supposition that you'd pick up anything between the interstices as you went. What made the job easier, up to a point, was that nobody really believed there were any mines. But practically every week a report would come through, sometimes from a Turkish village, more often from one on the Greek side, that men had been seen out digging by the roadside, and the unit would get a call from Brigade HQ to investigate.

I don't suppose I went on the mine detail more than half-a-dozen times, but for some reason – probably because I was shit-scared – it seems vivid to me in a way that the rest of that time in Cyprus doesn't. The scenery was always the same – the road stretching on past tiny villages with names like Guanyeli and Autokoi, where a few white housefronts poked up out of the scrub, and the mountains rising up in the middle distance, all framed in the relentless glare of the sun. It was only a few weeks after the Guanyeli massacre, when the Turkish villagers came across some Greek detainees – who'd been left to make their own way home having been taken in for questioning – and literally hacked them to pieces, so there was no one much about. Occasionally you'd see a peasant, usually a very old man with a beard, goading his donkey through the scrub, or a file of children on their way to school, but mostly you could wander through the foothills for hours and not see a soul. Not that you ever did wander very far. The thing I remember best about Cyprus, apart from the endless sweep of the mountains and the heat, is waiting all the time for the flat but curiously malignant thump that meant a bomb had gone off somewhere.

Generally there'd be about half-a-dozen of us out on the road, together with a jeep and a Bren carrier that ferried the equipment and covered us while we did the sweep. Captain Groves, who always said that he didn't believe there was a single mine in the whole of Cyprus, usually sat in the driver's seat of the jeep smoking a cigarette. Upward would be in the Bren carrier. That left two of us to do the sweep, someone else to act as look-out – which meant wandering up and down the road stopping the oncoming traffic and staring vaguely up into the hills – and a final pair of hands to shade in the area surveyed on the local OS map. As it turned out I only ended up doing the sweeping a couple of times, but it wasn't something I'd care to repeat. I used to find myself staring at a particular patch of ground, looking helplessly for odd landmarks that would convince me that I'd already swept it, while the NCO coached me forward. 'Come on Kingy, straight ahead. Just fucking move the thing for Christ's sake' etc. etc. Every so often you'd come across something under the surface and there'd be a ghastly wait until someone brushed off the topsoil to reveal an old exhaust pipe or a metal plate. Once there was a terrible panic when Upward thought he heard something moving in the bushes ten yards back down the road and touched off a couple of dozen rounds from the Bren before anyone could stop him. They left a hole in the dirt six inches deep and converted the goat that had been making the noise into a pile of blood and guts. No one blamed Upward in the least. The NCO swore a bit, but Captain Groves said it was all right, and when he saw how shaken up we were he gave us each a fag – strictly against the rules, but Captain Groves was always doing things like this – and we stood around smoking, looking at the hole in the dirt and the mangled goat, and throwing uneasy glances back down the road. That was what being in Cyprus for any stretch of time did for you.

Though I knew both of them for years after, it's from those days that I remember Groves, and in some ways even Upward most vividly – standing there under the boiling sun, with the sweat running down their faces and the mountains looming up in the distance. All down to fear, I suppose, or perhaps the sense of being involved in something collective in which we all had a part to play: Captain Groves's humorous, rubbery face under his peaked cap and his voice saying 'Cigarette, King?', Upward manhandling the Bren, the dead goat's carcass spilled out over the roadside.

I suppose if I'd wanted I could have got out of National Service. By this stage the plans to abolish it were pretty well known, and people were falling over themselves to fix up deferrals or inventing fake illnesses that would fool the army doctors. There were stories of blokes who'd got excused on grounds of flat feet or chronic acne. Even with Father being ill, though, I scarcely thought about it. I'd spent eighteen years in Yarmouth, watching the gulls out over the sea and never taking a breath that didn't taste of salt, and a good part of me didn't mind the idea of two years on the other side of England, or even abroad. Even leaving Julia – who unsurprisingly stopped writing to me after a month or two – somehow paled beside the thought of this new life lived out in a tent or in a barracks somewhere in Europe. That was how people thought, forty years ago. Because they'd never been anywhere, they believed all the stuff about joining the army and seeing the world, just as they believed anything they were told about the people they'd find there.

Anyway, I was posted to Catterick for basic training, which wasn't too bad. What irritated me, I suppose, was that apart from the seven hours or so you spent asleep there was hardly any time you could call your own. Reveille was at five-thirty, breakfast at six, and by eight you'd be on the drill square under the eye of a vicious little corporal called Slater. What with lectures and route marches you were glad enough to spend the hour or so of free time you were sometimes allowed at the end of the afternoon just lying on your bed staring at the ceiling. Predictably, it was the constant activity that some of the recruits – they were thin, pale boys of about my own age, with a handful of older blokes who'd done three years' university – couldn't take. There was a Jehovah's Witness named Warner who used simply to fall on his knees every morning and pray while, around him, twenty other men washed, dressed and defecated with one eye on the door in case Slater was prowling around to catch people smoking. Curiously, no one taunted the Jehovah's Witness. 'There's that fucking Warner saying his prayers,' they used to say, or 'Put a word in for me, will you mate?'. But at bottom I think they were secretly impressed. As for me, I soon got used to living cheek-by-jowl with twenty other recruits, none of whom I'd ever set eyes on before, and the endless feeling of there never being enough time to do things. I won't say I thrived, but I'm the kind of bloke who *can* always survive in situations like that – laugh at people's jokes and generally keep out of harm's way. At least four of the blokes in our platoon didn't last beyond the first three months. One was a mental case, who'd been sent there as the result of an administrative mix-up, two cracked up under the strain, and the fourth, a Welshman named Williams who used to talk to himself after lights out, blew his trigger finger off with a Lee Enfield out on the range.

But if, like me, you came from a family that knew something about the army (Father had done time in the Norfolks during the war) or even if you'd listened to the forces sketches on the radio, then there was an odd kind of familiarity about Catterick. The most obvious way in which it conformed to the ideas I'd picked up in advance was the air of complete confusion that seemed to hang over every decision concerning your personal destiny. When I arrived I signed up for the Education Corps – I rather liked the idea of loafing around at a desk all day reading books – but it turned out that the university boys had already got wind of this, and all the places were taken. Then there was a scheme for me to join the

Royal Armoured Corps, but for some reason that didn't work out either and in the end I fetched up in the Oxford and Bucks. This had its downside – half the regiment was already out in Cyprus, and the other half was set to follow – but there were advantages, too, one of which was the recruits, who were mostly country boys from the farms around Oxford and didn't think it funny that you came from a place like Yarmouth. The other way in which everything seemed like a scene from *Privates on Parade* was the names you got given. Anyone called White was immediately referred to as 'Chalky', anyone sent on the radio course was 'Sparks', and even at half an inch under six foot I was tall enough to be called 'Lofty', which carried the extra disadvantage of being picked as wheelman during drill. I suppose in the end that's what sticks about the army – the sense of reading from a script which nobody had changed since Passchendaele. That, and the dreadful feeling of futility – spending hours blancoing the webbing on your uniform on the off-chance of an inspection, or making sure the done-up laces on your boots were exactly the same length. None of which had the effect of making people disciplined and methodical – as sergeants would sometimes claim, if asked – but simply left them angry at having wasted their time.

I hadn't been at Catterick more than a fortnight before I met Upward.

Even at a distance of forty years I've a precise recollection of that afternoon – it would have been in October sometime – and the mist drifting in across the moors, the formations of khaki figures moving slowly across the parade ground and the files of recruits sweeping up the fallen leaves. Upward was in my platoon but not in my hut, so although I'd seen him around the place – he was a short, stocky bloke with bright red hair and a set of gappy teeth that looked as if they'd been pegged on with Araldite – we hadn't yet spoken to each other. Some errand or other had sent me to one of the lecture rooms, but the lecturer I was supposed to be delivering a message to wasn't there and I walked back along the corridor poking my head vaguely into doorways and rather enjoying the break in routine, with a cast-iron excuse if anyone wanted to know what I was doing. There was no one much about and most of the rooms were empty, but in one of them I discovered

Upward. He was standing by the big rectangular blackboard with his back towards me, not saying anything apart from a grunt or two, but moving sinuously from side to side. Every so often he'd bang the point of his index finger against the blackboard and make a little hissing sound, flip the piece of chalk held in his fist over his head and catch it with the other hand. It took me about half a minute to work out that he was imitating a sergeant called Barnes who lectured us on Field Studies, but when I did the effect was so overwhelming that I burst out laughing. Upward heard the disturbance and turned round. I couldn't tell if he was pleased or not.

'This one's Satterthwaite.'

Satterthwaite was the mess corporal. Again, Upward didn't say anything – I think once he'd nodded to me he was hardly conscious I was there – he simply minced up and down a few times, stuck his bottom in the air and produced a flawless pastiche of a man plonking down a tray of plates on a table covered with breakable objects. I laughed again, at which Upward grinned, whipped his cap out of his shoulderflap, jammed it on his head, bared his teeth – he looked a bit like the boy in the MAD comic – and saluted.

'The management would laik to state that they will not – ai repeat *not* – be extending Mr Upward's engagement.'

Then he winked and marched out, colliding with a tough parachutist called Sergeant-Major Hardwood who wanted to know what a couple of Other Ranks were doing in a lecture room.

Every platoon had its resident wag, of course. Usually they were oily little blokes who called the sergeant 'Sarge' and crawled to the junior NCOs, but even by the standards of Catterick Upward was something special. There was a story that he'd once held up a formal parade by imitating the noise of the staff captain's car failing to start. I got another glimpse of him in action a week later when about three dozen of us were having an unarmed combat session with a corporal called Faraday. After we'd been through the usual routines of treading on our opponents' insteps and pretending to gouge out each other's eyes, Faraday called us together and announced that he was going to teach us all about 'falling'.

'Now, falling, thass a difficult thing to do, see? Any one of you was to fall straight over on the square here, straight down on your side, you'd break your collar-bone, no question about it. Doesn't matter how careful you do it, unless you know how to roll your shoulder you're talking a fortnight in plaster. Now, watch me.'

We watched as Faraday flung himself dramatically down on to the tarmac. He landed on the point of his shoulder, tried to say something and then fell back into a dead faint. Somebody sent for a stretcher to take him away, and another corporal was summoned to take charge.

'Now,' he said. 'No point in thinking you can skive off just because the instructor's indisposed. Where did you get to with Corporal Faraday?'

There was a silence. Then Upward piped up: 'Please corporal, we'd just got to the part where you break your collar-bone.'

A couple of nights after that I got to talk to Upward in the NAAFI. He was on his own – for some reason wags were never very popular with the rest of the hut – and a bit wary. I think he thought I saw him as a kind of free show you could come up and laugh at. I say 'talk', but you didn't talk to Upward, you just listened. Essentially, being in the same room as him cast you in the role of spectator to an extraordinary monologue that could go on for an hour, provided there wasn't a parade to attend or the mess bell went. I say 'spectator' because it was a visual thing as well, with Upward acting out parts or illustrating points with weird and curiously voluptuous gestures. Once, when I had a pen and notebook handy, I tried writing one of them down afterwards. It went something like this:

'We are all of us lying in the gutter, but some of us are looking at the stars. A man called Oscar Wilde said that . . . Wilde by name, wild by nature (*pause*) . . . Obviously never been to Catterick . . . Reminds me of the carpenter whose cabinets were all crooked. He was banned for possessing an unnatural vice (*pause, nodding to someone leaving the table*) . . . Whalemeat again, as the eskimo said to his wife . . .'

Inevitably, this doesn't do justice to Upward's delivery, or the look on his face, which was complete deadpan. If I say that he was the kind of bloke who raises a laugh simply by walking into a room, then perhaps you'll understand what I mean. And yet the really curious thing was that half the time you never knew whether he thought he was being funny. I can remember another time when they were short-staffed at the NAAFI and Upward ended up serving behind the bar. For some reason an officer turned up – there might have been an all-ranks football match going on outside – rubbed his hands together (it was a freezing night in November), advanced on the wooden counter and announced that he wanted a pint of brandy. In fact, as everyone including the officer knew, they didn't serve brandy in the NAAFI, but Upward merely gave a little bob of his head and enquired: 'Martel, sir?'

There was another time, out on a training exercise, when a container in the process of being winched across a stream unexpectedly snapped back and knocked Upward – an interested spectator on the bank – into six inches of water. Seeing him motionless, the NCO – Sergeant-Major Hardwood, as it happened – jumped anxiously into the stream beside him. Upward opened his eyes.

'Kiss me, Hardwood,' he said.

Again, Upward denied he was being frivolous, claiming that he thought himself gravely injured (in fact he sustained mild bruising) and thought these the right words to utter. The sense he gave off, even when doing something outrageously funny, of being a bit of a dark horse, extended over the whole area of his private life, what he'd done before the army, all aspects of him not covered by khaki, so to speak. Publicly, he gave out that he'd been an engineering clerk in Preston – he had a flat kind of Lancashire accent. At the same time he was capable of showing unexpected flashes of expertise. Once, during a lecture about living off the land, a NAAFI sergeant produced a shrivelled, pink-grey carcass on a tray and announced that he was going to explain the best way of boning a rabbit. Upward, who happened to be at the front of the throng of heads, sniffed slightly and remarked:

'That's cat. Count the ribs.'

It was cat, too. Nobody quite knew how Upward had come by the ability to make this judgement. There were plenty of dark horses in the platoon: Plimworthy, whom everyone suspected of being a failed officer candidate, or Stubbs who had a picture of Khrushchev in his wallet and sat on his bed at night reading Communist pamphlets. None of them was as dark as Upward.

Among other things, Upward had a pronounced, and deeply melancholy, philosophical side. Once when we were cleaning equipment in an otherwise deserted drillroom, he suddenly demanded, with extraordinary force:

'D'you believe there's a God?'

It was difficult to know what to say. The way Upward had brought out the question showed that he felt strongly about it. Support or denial could be equally upsetting to him.

'I suppose so.'

Upward put down the part of the Bren gun he was polishing with a piece of lint and turned towards me.

'Of course there is.'

'You think so?'

'Stands to reason.'

'It does?'

There was a tenseness about Upward as this dialogue unrolled that I can't begin to describe. He was sweating, I noticed, and his fingers shook against the lint.

'Bound to be. If there wasn't a God, how could anyone ever be punished?'

'Is that important?'

'Of course it is. Think of all the wicked things people would do if they thought they weren't going to be punished for them. Think of what you and I'd do.'

'What?'

'I don't know. Something awful, I dare say. But the important thing is, *we need to be stopped*.'

Again, I never worked out if Upward meant this to be taken seriously, as a joke, or as a combination of the two. At any rate he never showed the faintest interest in the religious facilities on offer at Catterick. But the conversation about God was somehow symptomatic of his whole approach to other people, his inability to fit himself into normal channels of communication, and the confusions and resentments that this sometimes provoked.

At the same time this melancholic, unpredictable side went hand in hand with a quite startling jauntiness. Public jauntiness, at any rate. In the context of army routine Upward led an extraordinary charmed life. Countless NCOs 'had it in' for Upward: somehow he always survived, dodged the charge, emerged from the orderly room with the mildest of rebukes. I liked Upward from the first, mostly I think because he was completely unlike me: jaunty, devious, calculating, always one step ahead of the game. There was also, although this is difficult to put into words, an odd sense of familiarity. Something about Upward's gestures, the red shining face, teeth, made me think that in however marginal a way, somewhere deep in time, our paths had already crossed.

It was December 1958 by this time, and snow lay piled up on the moors overlooking the camp. In the evenings even a trip to the NAAFI seemed too exhausting to be borne. I used to be on my bed reading old copies of *Film Fun* or dog-eared paperbacks with titles like *Hard-hearted Sal* that went round the place, while the wind tore in against the side of the hut and the light bulbs danced under the ceiling. Often I wrote home – not because I thought Father and Mother would be interested in the kind of life I was leading, but because I badly wanted to connect myself to something that existed beyond the world of regimental brasses and saluting anything that looked like an officer on sight. Mother's letters weren't very communicative. Father was 'better' but he couldn't do more than sit in a chair and stare at whoever was bringing him his tea, and I got the impression, reading between the lines of Mother's pale, watery handwriting that faded away into the Basildon Bond notepaper on which she wrote, that they didn't really have enough to live on. I know I didn't worry about this as much as I should have done. I was too wrapped up in being on my own, and Upward, and the thought that in a month or so I'd probably be in Cyprus. There was, too, the feeling that, whatever happened, in the end something would be sorted out. This wasn't the Thirties – and I'd heard enough about the Thirties in my time. At any rate Father and Mother wouldn't starve. Somehow the kind of life they were habituated to would go on: sitting in a tiny house a mile or so inland, listening to the wind smashing against the eaves, while Father mumbled over his scrapbook and Uncle Ralph rapped on the floor upstairs with his stick for another cup of tea.

Meanwhile, there was Christmas to be got through at Catterick, which meant concert-parties, carol services and a piss-up of such epic proportions that one of the corporals ended up in hospital with alcohol poisoning. It was the oddest time, Christmas in an army camp. Not only was there a sense that normal rules didn't apply – at tea on Christmas Day, for instance, served up with sticks of celery, we simply stood up at the tables and chucked them back at the cooks – but the place was full of people allowing themselves a kind of psychological holiday. Sergeants you hadn't seen smile since you stepped off the train would suddenly consent to strip down to their underclothes and perform ritual dances, or sing maudlin regimental songs going back to the days of the Sudan campaign. This air of temporary licence wasn't altogether pleasant. On the one hand you had no idea what might happen next. On the other there was a feeling that the old rules would mysteriously snap back without anyone telling you, and that laughing at the sergeant's combinations as he performed the Elephant Dance would suddenly get you put on a charge.

On Boxing Day afternoon they had a concert in one of the lecture halls. It was the usual kind of thing – a couple of song and dance routines, an aspiring tenor singing 'The Sun was Declining', a skit on Cinderella transferred to the sergeants' mess – but all the while there was a ripple of excitement going through the audience over whether Upward would appear. Finally, at the very end, somebody announced that they were going to conclude the proceedings with a really class act: a *prima ballerina* was going to perform the Dance of the Sugar-Plum Fairy. No one quite knew what to expect, but someone put a gramophone record on and in a moment or two a figure in a kind of improvised ballerina's costume marched out on to the stage and began to leap about. It took me at least a minute to work out that it was Upward, not only because the figure was heavily made up, like one of the Ugly Sisters in a pantomime, but because whoever it was could obviously dance. It went on for about five minutes – Upward pirouetting on his toes, gambolling unrestrainedly around the stage, taking giant leaps from one vantage point to another, executing high kicks, but always managing to find his balance. At the end, in a pre-arranged gesture, somebody threw a single rose on to the stage. Upward contrived to catch the stem between his teeth. Opinion was divided as to whether Upward had made a success of this routine. One or two people present complained that they'd thought 'that bugger

Upward was supposed to be funny'. There was a certain amount of confusion over whether he had been attempting to pastiche a *prima ballerina* or merely imitating her. Upward reported that he'd later been summoned before the company commander and congratulated for his part in the proceedings. This, according to Upward, gave rise to the funniest conversation in which he'd ever taken part.

It's not exaggerating to say that this was the moment when I saw the point of Upward, got the hang of him, knew somehow of the extraordinary impact he was going to have on my life, there in the draughty lecture hall, with the wind whistling in from across the moors, the cigarette smoke hanging in the air, Upward's face scarlet under the dancing light bulbs.

A month later we were in Cyprus.

It was on the plane out over the Mediterranean that I worked out where I'd seen Upward before. Not, as it turned out, at the Sun Alliance (for a time I wondered whether he'd been an agent for one of the northern branches that I'd come across in the office) but on the stage of the Yarmouth Regal. Two, or maybe three years back, I'd seen a Variety bill containing an act called Eight Lancashire Lads. In fact, as I subsequently found out, the Lancashire Lads were a famous Variety institution. The original line-up went back at least to the Thirties – Father had seen them before the war and reckoned that one or two of them looked a bit long in the tooth even then. The Lancashire Lads were a clog-dancing act. The show began with the curtain raised a couple of feet above a blacked-out screen, with the boys in front of it dancing in black stockings and gold-painted clogs, so the audience got an illusion of weirdly detached feet. In normal circumstances I probably wouldn't have remembered them, but by this stage they'd started introducing patter into the proceedings. Upward, I soon established, had been the young red-haired feed, butt of various jokes about 'courting' and keeping pigeons in his loft.

A bit surprisingly, given the veil of concealment that hung over the rest of his career, Upward happily owned up to being a Lancashire Lad.

'Oh aye. Did that for a year. Biggest bloody disaster I ever knew. There had to be eight of you, because there always had been – the lead bloke in them days was the grandson of the chap who'd founded them – but that meant there was never any money. Plus there was only about two of them actually came from Lancashire by that time, so you had to be careful if ever you played up north.'

'When did you leave?'

'Just after Suez. You won't believe this. We were on at the Scarborough Hippodrome. One of my clogs came off halfway through the first number. Of course there was a row about it afterwards, but I'd had enough of it by then so I just slung my hook.'

Upward's professional stories were always worth listening to. He had a particularly good one about Morecambe & Wise being received in silence at the Glasgow Kelvin Hall and the doorkeeper saying 'They're beginning to like you lads,' as they came off. Then there were the Pilkington Sisters, who according to Upward actually consisted of a mother and her two daughters. Again, it was impossible to work out whether Upward had enjoyed his time on the Variety circuit, whether it was something he put up with on the grounds of gaining experience or actively disliked.

In any case, all these revelations – if they were revelations – lay in the future. At the time I didn't recognise their significance and certainly had no idea of their implications for me. There were other things to think about. The last letter from Mother, which I remember reading on the flight and in a roundabout way probably brought me to Upward, the memory of the Eight Lancashire Lads crashing their way across the stage of the Yarmouth Regal, the blue of the Mediterranean beneath: all this mysteriously fused in my head as the plane touched down and stayed there, so that even now I can remember the particular things Mother was complaining of – Uncle Ralph's sulks and the hospital speech therapist that Father 'didn't take to' – effortlessly combining with the rows of pine trees set back from the airstrip and the blue-white mountain-tops rising in the distance.

The week before we went to Cyprus, a staff lecturer filled us in on the political situation we could expect to find there. Basically it went like this. The island – I had a vague notion, misremembered from school geography lessons, that it was a bigger version of

Gibraltar – was still a Crown Colony under a British Governor, and the idea was that we were preparing the place for independence as a self-governing part of the Commonwealth. The Greek three-quarters of the population wanted *enosis* or union with Greece, while the Turkish minority wanted *taksim*, in other words secession from the rest of the island in their own enclave, which would then be united with Turkey. The Greek nationalists were split up into factions: EOKA, who were right-wing, EDEK, who were left-wing, and EAXEC, who were out-and-out communists; and when they weren't massacring the Turks or shooting us, they weren't above having a crack at each other. Among other things, this caused endless confusion whenever anything serious happened – a bomb going off at a petrol station could mean that any one of about five things was going to happen, ranging from a pact between the socialists and the communists to a Turkish uprising. Sitting in the middle, of course, with orders to keep the factions apart while somebody tried to patch up a constitution, we were fair game for everyone.

By the time we got there the really serious stuff was over, but that didn't mean you could relax. Most of the time was spent manning roadblocks, hanging around in villages waiting for political leaders to arrive or depart, or simply standing in the road trying to search passers-by. Every now and then there'd be a flap – a trooper out on patrol wouldn't come back, or there'd be reports of an explosion at a village five miles away – and the temperature would go up a few degrees, but mostly it was a case of sitting around waiting for something to happen. Oddly enough, though I must have been there six months, I don't remember anything much about Cyprus, certainly nothing about the people. Everyone hated the Cypriots, who they said were simply peasants, and there were stories of Grivas, the EOKA leader, arranging ceasefires and then leaving booby traps when he knew British soldiers would be going in to attend to casualties. As for the work, one roadblock is pretty much like another. If I've any recollection of those six months, it's of small things: roadside shrines, which I suppose dated from the war, with a few flowers rotting in an old glass above a picture of some teenager sweating under the weight of a bandolier, orange groves glistening in the sun, queer processions of livestock –

a couple of goats, a chicken and pig, say – being herded through the scrub by an old woman. That, and squatting outside the tent first thing in the morning trying to prise open a can of foul-tasting muck called 'self-heating soup' while the sky changed from deep violet into the purest imaginable blue and the dew dried under your feet.

But there were other reasons why I don't remember much about Cyprus. Upward was part of it, of course – Upward legend, Upward lore, Upward's imitation of ricocheting bullets, which could get a roadblock detail looking uneasily over their shoulders from twenty yards away. But the main reason, I think, was the effect that service life had on me as a person. Being in the army – even there in a Crown Colony at the fag-end of the Fifties – did strange things to you. Less than a year before I'd been a clerk in an office a mile from the North Sea whose main concern was whether the girl I was seeing that night would turn up on time, and now I was a crop-haired bloke in khaki who got up at five every morning, could get water to boil over a candle, and was uneasily conscious that the next figure who appeared over the horizon could easily be out to kill me. As for 'teaching you skills', which was something the army newspapers went on about, I once itemised the various things I'd picked up in uniform and they included being able to mix up the kind of polish that would enable you to see your reflection in the toe-caps of your boots, fitting thirty pounds of equipment in a pack meant for twenty, and cooking breakfast for six people in a single saucepan. But that was what the army did to you in a way, got you to expend vast amounts of mental labour on solving problems that anyone with any sense would have made sure weren't there to be solved in the first place. The base at Nicosia was full of people running around trying to find new ways of making butter keep or getting groundsheets to dry in the sun without going discoloured.

Captain Groves's theory was that people needed these distractions to stop them going mad.

'Standard army practice since Waterloo,' he explained. 'Why do you think Wellington never let his men have enough food? Gave them something to do, of course. Tell a man he's got to find himself something to eat and that if he doesn't no one else will find it for him, and he won't have time to wonder what he's doing in the army in the first place, and whether the cause is actually worth fighting for. Plus you give him a feeling of resourcefulness. God knows, I've never seen soldiers so happy as when you tell them to pitch a tent at the bottom of a drainage ditch or halfway up the side of a mountain where there's no purchase for the tent-pegs.'

I suppose I first properly came across Captain Groves – the Honourable Jacinth Mountstuart Elphinstone Groves, to give him his full title – about two months into the Cyprus tour. It was a bright, sharp morning in February with the mist clearing a bit towards the mountains, and we'd been sent out to a Turkish village in the hills to clear up after an EOKA attack. When we got there we found that the damage wasn't as bad as we'd been told – two of the houses had been blown apart with grenades, and there were a couple of casualties – so once we'd dealt with the bodies (one of them I remember was an enormously fat chap, probably the village headman, whose belly literally fell down to his knees) and looked around the approach roads for signs of a repeat performance, there wasn't a great deal to do and the NCO decided we could take a breather. By this time it was nearly midday and Upward and I wandered down to the end of the main street where somebody had said you could buy dates and goats' cheese. We'd got the cheese, tried and failed to get the old woman on duty to sell us some of the local wine, when Upward stopped and said:

'Let's go in here a bit.'

There was a biggish house, set back a little from the road, with a kind of trellis-work gate that was mostly in fragments and hung off the stanchions, with bits of debris lying about on the grass. Beyond this was a second gate, set in a high fence and half-open. In the distance two or three voices – English voices – were borne back on the breeze.

'Probably nicking something,' Upward deduced. 'Let's go and take a look.'

Stepping through the inner gate, we came across a sight that even now, four decades later, is extraordinarily vivid in my mind. On the far side of a ragged, overgrown belt of laurels various people – Captain Groves, two or three other officers – were sprawled over a square of bright emerald grass. Behind them a copse of spruce trees led down to the road. As I looked on, Captain Groves's batman emerged from one end of the hedge carrying a couple of bottles of wine, one of them with the neck smashed off, which he set down on a camping stool next to some loaves of bread and bowls of olives.

'Private party,' Upward murmured out of the corner of his mouth, and then, slightly louder, 'Sorry sir, we'll be on our way.'

For some reason, though, neither of us stirred. Captain Groves, who was propped up on one elbow smoking a cheroot while another private offered various bits of food for his inspection, nodded affably. One of the other officers laughed a bit. I saw that, unwittingly, we'd stumbled on one of the escapades for which Captain Groves was famous. His exploits, occasionally recounted by admiring NCOs, included training a corporal to act as croupier in late-night baccarat sessions and – somewhere in Kenya, where normal rules didn't apply – running a company brothel.

'That's all right,' Groves said. 'It's Upward, isn't it? And King. All cleared up in the village? Why not sit down and have a glass with us?'

I dare say you'll think there was nothing very amazing about a couple of squaddies being invited to drink wine with their company captain on a hillside in Cyprus, but let me tell you that by the standards of the British Army it was more or less unprecedented – like being offered a cigarette by your headmaster or being asked to lunch in the senior staff dining room at the Sun Alliance. The wine was extraordinary, too – God knows where they'd stolen it – like crisp-tasting nectar. The odd thing was that Groves didn't seem at all embarrassed at having us there, simply talked about the morning's operation and the football results back home. From below we could hear the noise of lorries reversing in the village, but it was all somehow irrelevant, too remote and far away to be worth bothering about.

Anyway, this went on for about twenty minutes, and we'd eaten a plate of bread and olives apiece, when suddenly Captain Groves clapped his hands together and said to his batman: 'All we need now is some entertainment.'

The batman was a Liverpudlian conscript called Murphy, and famously slow on the uptake.

'Entertainment, sir?' he wondered.

'That's right, entertainment. Upward, I've seen you in Christmas concerts. Go on, sing us a song.'

Upward sniffed a bit at this, while not looking as if he thought this request the least bit surprising in the circumstances. 'A song, sir?'

'That's right. A song. As filthy as you like. I shan't mind. Go on.'

Upward stood up and looked rather thoughtfully down towards the trees. One of the other officers sniggered.

'I won't sing you a song sir. But me and Kingy here, we'll do you a turn if you like. Look, this is the sergeants' mess at eleven-thirty on a Saturday night, see?'

All of a sudden he was off on an extraordinary monologue about Sergeant-Major Hardwood losing his pay book and someone else complaining about watered beer. I could see it was coming and, sure enough, after a minute or two he threw me a line – something about Hardwood's boots, which he was supposed to spend every Sunday afternoon polishing. Somehow I managed to chuck it back, and Upward went off again, doing an impression of another NCO being chased by a bee. I don't remember much else about it, except for Groves and the others guffawing and Murphy stopping clearing up the lunch-things with his mouth hanging open in surprise.

After about five minutes we stopped and just stood there looking embarrassed but also faintly pleased with ourselves. There was a silence, then a round of scattered applause, Captain Groves starting to say something, but the whole thing was instantly blown apart by an immensely loud explosion, or rather series of explosions, from the village. In the distance, down the hill, I could hear people shouting. There was smoke rising over the trees.

'That was the Bren if I'm not much mistaken,' Captain Groves declared, pulling on his tunic. 'For Christ's sake, Murphy, clear that mess up and let's get out of here.'

And so we sped off back to the village, scared stiff that we'd find a terrorist attack in progress, only to discover that some idiot subaltern had been trying to correct the elevation of the Bren with the barrel pointed towards him and the safety-catch off and succeeded in putting half-a-dozen bullets through his chest. He didn't die, apparently, but his face as they dragged him away on the stretcher was the colour of rice-paper. What else is there to say? A fortnight later I got word from Yarmouth that Father had died in his sleep, and went home for the funeral. When I got back, a week after that, it was to find that Upward, for some reason, had been transferred to another unit. And yet this didn't worry me. I knew, you see, that I'd find him again, that it was the start of something, not the finish, that somehow, out there under the blue Mediterranean sky, with Captain Groves leaning back on his elbows as he lit another cheroot, I'd been given a glimpse of the way my life was going to take shape.

This afternoon, back from the Empyrean, I opted to fetch the boy from school. The rain which fell half an hour ago has a bad effect on the crowd assembled at the gate. Fine weather has them all parked alongside the railings, even straying into the first few feet of the asphalt. Now they're massed under umbrellas on the other side of the road, waiting behind the wheels of boxed-in cars. Reading a book about Sid Field the other day – the kind of showbiz biography Lennie likes, where friends of the subject are routinely introduced as *Mr Comedy himself* or *that big-hearted star of stage and screen* – I discovered that Sid was so loath to tear himself away from the amphitheatres of his professional life that he'd frequently beguile the time spent waiting outside his children's primary school by staging impromptu performances for the other parents. Often by the time his own offspring emerged from their classrooms it was to find their father – still wearing his trademark coat and hat, apparently – halfway through one of his monologues, with a dozen or so fellow-parents egging him on.

Even today these performances are fondly remembered by those who witnessed them.

Hemmed in by the tough girls with their prams, the little bald blokes with hang-dog expressions, the big men who come stalking up out of the side streets with a couple of mastiffs on a choke-chain, I haven't the faintest inclination to follow his example. I can see Daniel by this time, wandering out of the main door, head down, deep in conversation with a pair of bullet-headed acquaintances. What do they talk about? The price of Mars bars? Michael Owen?

I honestly don't know. Catching sight of me at the gate, he slips forward a yard or two and nods gravely.

'I was going to walk back with Justin and Jamal.'

Six weeks here and already he's slipping into the local argot. 'Walk' is coming out as *wawk*, 'with' as *wiv*, while 'Jamal' – apparently the name of the big-eyed black boy a couple of paces behind him – is definitely tri-syllabic.

'Don't worry about it. You'll see them tomorrow.'

'Okay.'

As he falls in behind me I flick the top of his head with the flat of my hand in the way you see soccer managers on the TV mark their approval of promising trainees. He raises his eyes in mock disgust. *That poor old bastard*, I imagine him saying to Justin and Jamal, *what does he think he's like?*

'Good day?'

'It was all right.'

There is a mark just above his eye I haven't noticed before, a reddish abrasion the colour of the pink candy shrimps Father used to sell in the shop.

'Somebody hit you?'

'Just some kid.'

'Anyone I know?'

'No.'

At these times I steel myself for confidences, but they never come. My whole information base on Daniel's school is dangerously short on data. Apparently they have football on Tuesdays and Fridays, and there's a Miss Cox whom everybody likes and a Mr Rees whom everybody hates. Last week somebody threw up in a corridor and you can't bring mobile phones in though lots of kids do. As for his mates, Jamal lives in some Afro-Caribbean family colony on the estate looked after by his three aunties; Justin's dad works on the ferry at Woolwich.

Beyond the school gate and the rows of stalled cars, he keeps behind me and slightly to the left. If you saw us you'd wonder at the exact nature of our relationship. Grandfather and grandson? Middle-aged man tailed by pre-teen stalker? From time to time other children rush past or come loitering by on the other side of the street. He doesn't look up. Psychologists – I boned up on this

– say that the ten-year-old is the most self-effacing of all children. Their aim, apparently, is inconspicuousness. Krieger records the case of an eleven-year-old entered by mistake at the wrong school who spent three weeks happily attending classes on whose lists he didn't appear before anyone found out. Invisibility is all.

'Got much homework tonight?'

'A bit.'

'How's Miss Cox?'

'All right.' Something in the way he says this makes me glance back. 'Actually she had a row with her boyfriend.'

'That's bad.'

'It's all right, though, because she was getting tired of him anyway.'

'Good.'

After a can of Coke from the fridge and a canter through the children's programmes on TV he falls asleep on the sofa. He does this perhaps two or three afternoons a week. At first I worried that it was an early symptom of some ghastly children's disease – leukaemia, maybe, or rheumatoid arthritis. But it turns out – Krieger is very persuasive on this point – that ten-year-olds are prone to nervous exhaustion, particularly when placed in an unfamiliar environment.

He sleeps with one arm thrown back over his head, the other pressed tightly against his chest. An hour now since the last shower, there are shafts of sunlight creeping into the room. His face is quite expressionless at these times, no clue as to what goes on underneath. Every so often the hand thrown back over his head twitches slightly and he adjusts his position, burrowing further into the sofa, curling his legs beneath him. The TV, which I haven't yet turned off, switches from kids' programmes to the early-evening soaps: fat Australians glumly reproaching each other; the other one about the depraved Yorkshire village. While he sleeps I take the opportunity to riffle through his schoolbooks: brightly coloured plastic ring-binders with PROJECT stamped on the outside; tiny blue exercise books of the kind Mother used for her household accounts. The promise of their covers is not matched by what lies within. Miss Cox, whom I take to be the impresario of these exercises, sets essays on 'Who is your favourite footballer?' and 'Write about being at the seaside'. At their foot she provides cheerful encouragement: *Excellent Daniel. This was really exciting.* She seems easily pleased. On one page, under the heading 'Write about a journey you made recently', Daniel has written:

> My Dad and me went on a train. We went from the place I used to live to the place I live now with my Dad. All our things fitted on the luggage rack, except a parcel which my Dad carried. I had a comic and some food my auntie made. When we got to London we took a taxi. It cost £34. When we got to the house I went exploring round it. My Dad didn't, because he'd lived there before.

Beneath it Miss Cox, she of the turbulent love-life, has written: *This sounds like a really interesting trip, Daniel.*

Later I go down to the kitchen. Some time later Daniel appears in the doorway, eyes puffed with sleep.

'Would you like your tea upstairs?'

'Okay.'

His appetite is what Mother would have called 'fancy': a minutely itemised catalogue of likes, dislikes, certainties and not sures. Even with the things he likes you can never tell. In some Persian caliphate, Dan the caliph, myself the venturesome chef, I'd have been a candidate for the bowstring long ago. In the end I cook him sausage, beans, tomatoes and oven chips.

Outside dusk is settling over the street. Back upstairs car headlights bounce off the window panes. Downriver ships' hooters are calling to each other in mid-stream. Daniel lacks my absorption in the cityscape. The questions he asks are all deeply particular. Where's the cinema? Is there a bigger park than the one we go to? The sprawl of London, whose outer fringes we inhabit, is of no interest to him. Or maybe he just needs a sense of perspective. Krieger says that ten-year-olds are like lions in this respect – staking out chunks of territory with remorseless zeal but blind to what goes on beyond their boundaries.

Bedtime is a notional nine. Even this makes Daniel a source of derision to his mates: Jamal who lolls up through the small hours listening to his aunties chat, Justin combing through the satellite channels on the portable his dad lets him have.

'What would you like to do now?'

'Watch my tapes.'

There are half-a-dozen of these: thick three-hour reels of old *Match of the Day* and satellite games that somebody did for him back home. Most of the kids round here support West Ham or Charlton. Dan, for some reason, is a Liverpool fan. I know the names now. Fowler. Owen. Carragher. Pale-faced, adenoidal boys who lope around the pitch as if they're a bit depressed by the weight of expectation that rests on their shoulders. Later, while Robbie, Michael and the others are still darting over the green baize surface, he goes to sleep again. I carry him upstairs in my arms, a bit shocked once more by the slightness of him, the ridges of his back ribs pressing against my hands. Krieger says that this anxiety, this paralysing terror about your children, is common in the older parent. Krieger, I note from the jacket of his book, doesn't have any children himself. How can he know about it? Or anyone?

Several messages from DI Stevens. He tends to call in the afternoon when I'm out prowling the shoreline or doing errands. DI Stevens is a policeman. Curiously, he hasn't openly said as much, but the respectful, dogged and slightly bored-sounding Estuary monotone gives it away. That and the buzzing of routine officialdom in the background. No indication of what DI Stevens wants, or any thought of urgency. Perhaps there will be a time when, mysteriously, our paths converge and whatever the business is will suddenly be contracted. London is full of these missed connections, messages left in limbo, accidental comings together and fallings apart. Lennie is always claiming to have been desperately trying to get in touch with me, leaving instructions that I never picked up. (*Was this BBC thing you'd have been a natural for.*) I don't believe him, but it amuses me to see the sincerity with which he keeps it up. Perhaps DI Stevens is one of those people who simply delight in leaving messages, for whom actual contact is a step backwards rather than a problem solved. Or maybe he simply has faith in our ability to find each other. Apparently this is a characteristic of the Ngongi's journeys across the desert. Two fragments of the tribe, setting off from bases hundreds of miles apart, navigating only by the stars, have the ability to achieve a rendezvous almost at will.

Perhaps we are really only desert travellers marching on through the freezing African night.

The envelopes from Shena – there are three of them now – sit on the mantelpiece. Sometimes I take them down and look at them. Other times I make futile attempts to conceal their existence – push newspapers in front of them or hide them behind the clock. But I never open them. I never get near to opening them.

The day I went back to the Empyrean I woke up with a queer feeling of having passed a milestone, inched beyond some memorial post on the mountainside where a bygone traveller had halted. It took me until the end of the evening, long after Daniel had gone to sleep, to work out what it was, but it was the day I'd outlived Father. Naturally, this set me thinking about him and comparing the two of us, though to be honest there wasn't a great deal you could compare. Father was five feet six and would have weighed under nine stone when he died. Me, I'm one of those tallish blokes with broad shoulders and a red face, the kind of person you'd think twice about pushing into in a pub. All the same, he was a better man than me. Seriously. He had something I don't possess, or only have when it suits me – a kind of decency, a fear of imposing himself, that you don't often come across these days. The easy thing to say was that Father was just scared, but I think it ran deeper than this. I think he genuinely did live his life on the do-as-you-would-be-done-by principle and believed until his dying day that if you do people a good turn then they'll do you one back. The difference between us, I suppose, is that he looked for the best in people and was disappointed when he didn't find it, whereas I expect the worst and am pleasantly surprised on the occasions when it turns out the other way. The other difference is that he died in near-pauperdom, whereas I sit here, if not in affluence, then in a house that's my own and with enough money to get by. I've no idea what Father thought about his life, and whether he reached the standards he must have set for himself, but I'm pretty sure he thought he was a failure. As for me, I'm not at all sure what I think about my life, but I wouldn't put money on its being judged a success.

Talking to a Friend About Girls

UPWARD: So when did you first . . . you know?

KING: When did I first what?

UPWARD: You know . . . when did you?

KING: When did I what?

UPWARD: You know . . . *that.*

KING: Oh . . . *that.*

UPWARD: Yes, that . . . I mean, when did you?

KING: It was a long time ago.

UPWARD: I can see that.

KING: It was that Eunice Braithwaite. Her from Market Street. Big girl, she was.

UPWARD: They all were.

KING: What? You mean there was more than one of them?

UPWARD: So what happened?

KING: Well, I felt a right ha'porth.

UPWARD: I've never heard them called that before.

KING: No, seriously. My mother warned nee. She said, 'You mind what you're up to, Teddy' – she used to call me Teddy in them days – 'We've never had no perspicuity in our family.'

UPWARD: You mean promiscuity.

KING: Nor that neither.

UPWARD: But what happened?

KING: Well naturally I had my best suit on. You know, for a special occasion and that. But it all went wrong when we got on the floor.

UPWARD: On the floor, eh? You didn't hang about.

KING: Oh no. You got points deducted if you didn't get on with it . . . and then we kept bumping into the other couples.

UPWARD (*admiringly*): *Other couples!* Pair of swingers you must have been!

KING: Oh no. This was a foxtrot.

UPWARD: Yes, but afterwards. You know. Did you?

KING: Oh . . . that. I should say so.

UPWARD: You did?

KING: Oh yes. Me mother had told me. She said, 'Make sure you behave like a gentleman should.'

UPWARD: So you did it?

KING: Oh yes.

UPWARD: What? All the way?

KING: Nearly all.

UPWARD: Well, how far did you get then?

KING: How far?

UPWARD: Yes. How far?

KING: Well, I only had one and three, so we had to get off at the Town Hall. She let me hold her hand at the bus-stop, though.

UPWARD: What, all of it?

KING: Well, nearly all of it.

1965

Love Song

South of Yarmouth, down from the marshes and the salt-water creeks, the farming country began: acre upon acre of wheat and flaring barley, criss-crossed by tiny dirt-track roads and here and there a farmstead slanting down in the dip between two fields, or a hamlet of farmworkers' cottages grouped round a pub. In those days mechanisation was still coming in, and even the smaller farms would employ half-a-dozen labourers. Ask me what the difference is between then and now and I'd say it was movement. Modern farms are soulless places. You can climb over a hill-top looking down over a sea of wheat and not see a human being for fifty weeks of the year. Forty years ago the countryside had life in it: old men with faces that looked as if they'd been carved out of teak cycling through the early mists; loitering families come to picnic in the ditches; beet lorries lumbering off into the distance over the flat horizon. That's the other thing I remember, of course, the extraordinary flatness, just the fields going on endlessly beneath the wide sky, with perhaps a file of elm trees every so often as cover from the wind. At Parmenter's I remember once stopping to count the church spires, and there must have been a dozen of them stretching across the flat as far as Acle.

God knows what I was doing at Parmenter's that fortnight in August. It was summer 1960, I'd been out of the army a couple of months, and I literally had no one to spend time with. Father was dead. Mother wouldn't be shifted from Uncle Ralph's. The people I'd known before at the Sun Alliance were friendly enough, but two years had gone by since I'd left Yarmouth and that's a long time when you're twenty. All that summer I'd floated round the place like a ghost, noting the things that had happened since I'd been away, the shops that had changed hands, the people who'd died – and even then it was a weird feeling coming back to a place you thought you knew everything about and then finding it ever so slightly different, like an oil painting the artist has had second thoughts about and retouched. I'd been anticipating a summer in the office. Mysteriously, though, it turned out that there was a couple of weeks' holiday owing, and as I didn't fancy going off on my own somewhere I signed up for a couple of weeks at Parmenter's farm.

It was one of those tiny, family farms that have practically disappeared now – swallowed by the big combines and the agribusinesses, I suppose – about a hundred acres of arable and pasture with a herd of dairy cows that looked as if they'd wandered out of the Ark. As it turned out, the harvest wasn't due to start for another week or so, but there were five or six fields of blackcurrant bushes coming into bloom, so I signed up for a fortnight's fruit-picking. Blackcurrants are a sod to pick at the best of times – they're fiddly things, and you can't help taking a handful of leaves with you as you twist off the bunches – but I didn't care. It was enough to be standing in the sun and not hearing somebody shouting at me to pick up a rifle or read a map reference. That, and having people around you whom you could take or leave as you felt. Most days there would be two or three dozen of us in the rows: farm labourers' wives, mostly, who picked like the wind and knew exactly how much green stuff you could leave in the bucket and not get pulled up for it; families of gypsies making their way up through Norfolk to Lincolnshire for the potato harvest. Theoretically you picked until the light got too bad to see, but even in mid-August it was sometimes nine before the twilight set in. Officially I was cycling back and forwards from town, but it was easier some nights just to roll up in a blanket by the side of the rows. You'd wake up at dawn, just as the mist started rising off the hedges likes strands of greying cotton wool, wash your face in a stream that ran behind the back of the orchard, and then stride off through the dew to the meadow where the gypsies parked their caravans to see if you could scrounge a box of matches to start the fire.

The merest chance drove me to the Parmenters, so slight that for years afterwards I used to wonder whether it was chance. On a farm the size of that you couldn't help walking into the farmer two or three times a day, and by the end of the second week I was on nodding terms with Mr Parmenter – he was a short, grey-haired character in his fifties – and even come across his wife once or twice cleaning out the coops or turning over windfalls in the orchard. The labourers' wives said there was an old grandmother, too, living in the farmhouse, but nobody I knew had ever laid eyes on her. Usually this would have been as far as it went – in those days a farmer would have died rather than be seen fraternising with his casual labourers – but for some reason on the Saturday I was due my wages the Parmenters' overseer had disappeared somewhere and word had been left for me to go up to the house. It was a scorching afternoon towards the end of August and there was no one about. Normally if you so much as set foot inside a farmyard a couple of dogs would come and see what you were up to, but the flagged stone square outside the farmhouse was quite empty. It was about half-past five, I suppose, and inside the house there were odd sounds of tea-things clinking together and a radio playing softly in the background. All this is very vivid to me: the slow tread across the yard, the noise my boots made on the raised concrete doorstep, the sound of the bolts being drawn back as someone opened the big oak door, Mrs Parmenter, who eventually fetched up on the far side of it.

'Keep the front door locked, we do,' she said – she pronounced it *du*, in a way that even then was a bit old-fashioned. 'Parmenter's in the top field, so perhaps you'll sit and wait.'

She was a big, untidy-looking woman in a print dress and apron, with her hair coming down at the back, a bit suspicious at first but not unfriendly once she'd established that I wasn't about to cheek her or steal anything – no middle-aged Norfolk woman in those days would give the time of day to a man under twenty-five. Presently I was in a high, brick-walled kitchen, dominated by an enormous deal table covered with blue and white china (as I'd suspected, they were about to have tea) with a round sepia portrait of George VI – the one in which he looks like an exceptionally frightened rabbit – hanging above the fireplace, being introduced to a gaping old woman in an invalid chair (Mr Parmenter's mother, it turned out) and a loafing boy of sixteen or so. Oddly, I don't even recall that Mary was there for the first few minutes – I think she may have been fetching something from an upstairs room – and when I try to recast the scene it contains only Mrs Parmenter, the old grandmother and the boy, with Mr Parmenter coming in a shade later and hovering a bit uncertainly between the table and the fireplace – they had a trick of arranging themselves in a room that emphasised the family likeness, and even now I try to re-create it it's in terms of those high, curiously remote faces, the eyes deeply set back in the head.

Looking back at the Parmenters I haven't the first idea how to describe them. Even now, forty years later – and it's a subject that haunted me deep into the Sixties and Seventies – I couldn't tell you what went on in old Parmenter's head or what made him and his wife regard the world in the way they did. They were extraordinary people, and the extraordinariness was so much a part of them that it took a certain amount of time to establish just what set them apart from the rest of humanity. Once you'd done it, though, spent an afternoon in old Parmenter's kitchen, say, or helped his wife wash up after lunch, the strangeness of it all rattled in your ears like thunder. For a start, the Parmenters' detachment from what might be called the ordinary world – the world of newspapers, sport, entertainment – was absolute. None of them, for example, had ever opened a bank account, taken a holiday, even travelled over the county boundary as far I could make out. Mrs Parmenter used to talk about Norwich, which I think she'd visited three or four times, with a kind of sacramental awe. As a phenomenon this wasn't unusual. Norfolk in those days was full of old folk who barely knew the Second World War had taken place, or who thought that Churchill was still Prime Minister. The Parmenters, though, were very far from senile. They were simply middle-aged people who'd lived through great stretches of recent time which they now claimed to have no memory of. It used to puzzle me sometimes. There they sat in their farmhouse, employing maybe a dozen people, paying tax, presumably going along with a whole mass of government regulations, and somehow about ninety-five per cent of modern life had passed them by. Once, when I'd got to know him a bit better, I tried asking old Parmenter about the war, and what came out was an extraordinary patchwork. He'd heard about Hitler, and I think he was just about aware of the atom bomb, but the rest of it – Stalingrad, Italy, the Normandy beaches – was completely beyond him. I got the impression that the Parmenters had spent the war years alone in their farmhouse with the radio turned off, closing their ears to the sound of the bombs and pretending that the whole thing wasn't happening.

Predictably, the landscapes they'd created around them faithfully reflected this outlook. Lounging in their parlour at the back of the house, with its photographs of Mr Parmenter's grandfather in a billy hat and sprouting side-whiskers fondly regarding a prize sow, ancient farm implements, old Staffordshire china from the last century, you sometimes got the feeling that you were sitting in a room where time had stopped in about 1913. The most modern book in the house was a copy of *The Lion, the Witch and the Wardrobe* which Mary had been given as a Sunday School prize. Everything else on the shelf went back deep into the Thirties. In the two years I was in and out of the place I never saw a newspaper. The women's magazines Mrs Parmenter occasionally drowsed over on a Sunday afternoon came from a huge, endlessly recycled pile kept by the back door and otherwise used as wrapping paper. Some of them were as much as thirty years old.

It might be wondered, given these circumstances, and that they were rather garrulous people, what it was that the Parmenters talked about. You'd have thought it impossible perhaps to get through an afternoon's conversation without mentioning something as up to date as the Cup Final or the Prime Minister, but somehow the Parmenters managed it. Stuck in the parlour with old man Parmenter one afternoon, I once scribbled down a list of the topics that came up, so fascinated was I by his ability to operate entirely beyond what seemed to me the normal parameters of life. It went as follows:

Varieties of apples and their relative size
His grandfather's funeral
The distance between Cromer and Sea Palling
Next week's weather prospects

An argument Mr Parmenter had had with a local landowner, date unspecified, but apparently some time in the Forties.

All this probably makes it sound as if I disliked the Parmenters, was simply amused by them or thought them simple curiosities, but this wasn't the case. They were friendly people, and I liked them, even the old, mad grandmother who I gathered had last stepped out of the house in 1947, or the teenage boy Horace, who'd rebelled against the family worldview sufficiently to buy a motor-bike on the hire-purchase, which worried Mr and Mrs Parmenter no end. More to the point, perhaps, they liked me. Even now I don't really know why, after I'd collected my money and drunk my tea that first Saturday afternoon, Mrs Parmenter diffidently suggested, amid a tremendous rustling of the copy of *Woman and Home* she held across her knee, that if I happened to be cycling round that way some future Sunday afternoon there was a fair chance I'd find them at home. At bottom I think it was that even the Parmenters had begun to realise something of the sequestration in which they held their children, and saw me as a kind of vague and unthreatening remedy. I'd been in the army, too, which was something Mrs Parmenter had just about heard of and was more or less a point in your favour in those days, and I imagine, when it came down to it, that they were simply entertained by me – a talkative young chap who worked in an office but wasn't above picking fruit as a holiday job.

In the same way, I can't begin to explain the force that drove me out on my bike through the backroads a Sunday or two later to see if the Parmenters were as good as their word. I'd been back in Yarmouth for three months, and everything had changed. Worse, I'd changed too, and I knew it. The time in Cyprus had taken me out of myself in a way that scared me a bit. Half of me wanted to be off with Upward somewhere, swapping jokes or planning out comedy routines – I had a stack of them upstairs in an old army file by now, that I'd written in the past six months – the other half lingered way back in a past I knew it was beyond me to reclaim, back with Father and Mother in the square, sitting over tea in the half-light, with Father springing up from his plate to fawn over a customer who wanted a threepenny cigar. Meanwhile, I drifted through the days at the Sun Alliance, and spent the evenings mooching along the front or lying in bed in my digs listening to the radio. I suppose if I'd have thought about it I could have found ways of getting round this feeling of not belonging, joined some club or signed up to run the local Boys Brigade, which was the kind of thing people did in those days. But I was twenty, going on twenty-one, and I'd seen a bit of life beyond Yarmouth by this stage and I knew the place for what it was – a kind of sink that no one in their right minds would think twice about leaving. And at the same time, short of going to some high-up at the office and asking for a job as a travelling representative, I hadn't the least idea of how I could do it.

Anyway, there I was, on a Sunday afternoon in mid-September pushing my bike along the dirt-track that led to the Parmenters' steading, halting occasionally to light a fag or stop the huge sprays of cow parsley that pushed across the path from jamming in the spokes, and generally nosing around the place in a way that wouldn't have occurred to me while I was picking the Parmenters' blackcurrants. In the fortnight I'd worked there I hadn't registered much more than the acreage and the boundaries, but now it struck me that it was the oddest place – overgrown and wild in a way that you rarely found in Norfolk. Even here on the approach road the cow parsley had been allowed to grow eight or nine feet high, and there were great banks of lavender spreading away towards the wheat fields that clearly no one had done anything about for years. There were toads out on the path – great fat things the size of small cabbages – and I watched them for a bit, while the cow parsley jammed into the wheels again and the bees lofted backwards and forwards over my head towards the lavender. The house was a quarter of a mile away, almost lost behind a clump of rhododendrons, and seeing it gave me the oddest feeling, exactly the sensation I'd had in the Parmenters' front room, of time somehow having stopped, the whole twentieth century – Lenin and Hitler and Winston Churchill – only let in on sufferance, and the people wandering around in it simply ghosts whose real lives had stopped a quarter of a century back.

Curiously enough, when I tapped on the back window – I knew enough by this time not to go round to the front – it was to find that most of the family was out: gone on the bus to see some cousins at Stalham, Mary said, who opened the door after I'd hung about for a minute or two. She didn't seem in the least surprised to see me. Though it must have been seventy in the shade there was a fire going in the kitchen, with the invalid chair pushed up close to it, and I could see the old woman lying fast asleep with her head twisted awkwardly to one side. There was a silence for a bit, and then Mary tapped the basket she had dangling on one arm.

'I've to feed the hens.'

It was more of a statement than an invitation, I suppose, but I tagged on behind as she went off across the yard to the coops and stood there while she plunged her hands into the straw and dislodged a dozen or so pale brown eggs. Later on, when I've tried to think about her, it's always that picture that rises up: a thin, brown-skinned girl with a lot of thick, blondish hair in a cotton dress that looked as if it had belonged to her mother. She would have been about nineteen then, but she had a way of looking at you – gravely, with her eyes wide open – that made her seem a lot younger. When she'd finished with the hens, she said:

'There's a cup of tea if you'd like.'

'Thanks.'

'I'm sorry you'll have to wait for Mother and Dad.'

'It's all right.'

In the event we hadn't been more than ten minutes over tea before the Parmenters were back, dressed in their Sunday best, with the boy Horace even wearing a straw hat, and sweating like troopers from their walk up from the road. Like Mary they weren't in the least surprised to find me in their parlour. Neither were they at all exercised by the thought that their daughter had spent the last half-hour entertaining me in their absence, which most self-respecting parents of the time would have agonised over. They were kind, simple people, I decided.

I was wild about her from the start, of course. I can't explain it. I don't suppose you could. Part of it was the queerness of it all, coming upon this place smack in the middle of nowhere, full of people who probably thought Neville Chamberlain was still Prime Minister, and a strange, silent girl sitting by the fire like a princess in a fairy tale. A bit more of it was simple curiosity, the feeling of walking into a world whose dimensions and rules you could only guess at. The Yarmouth people looked down their noses at 'farmer folk'. Father and Mother would have been scandalised if they'd known I was making eyes at a farmer's daughter – they were shopkeepers, you see, and farms meant pigswill, blood and dirt. But by far the largest part of it was Mary herself. Obviously I wasn't a complete starter with girls – there'd been Marjorie and Julia, and a girl who worked in the NAAFI at Catterick – but this was the first time I'd been really rocked back on my heels. You know that feeling you get when you're about twenty and you realise for the first time that the whole business is horribly serious and dramatic and at the same time completely unavoidable? I suppose the thing that struck me about Mary – apart from her looks – was how completely unlike any other woman I'd ever met she was. That's an obvious thing to say, I know, but it was true. Fat, thin, blonde or brunette – all the girls I'd known at school or at the Sun Alliance had been more or less the same: chatty, super-refined and horribly stupid. And now here was this quiet, curiously *demure* girl, who didn't speak unless you spoke to her first, but was always unobtrusively present in your consciousness – laying down tea-things neatly on a table, standing seriously next to her mother to receive a pail of scraps that had to be taken out to the yard.

When I eventually got to talk to her alone they were the sketchiest conversations, full of strange little inferences and implications that I couldn't begin to explain. And that was when you could find anything to talk about. Films, actors, pop music – all the safe young person's topics of the time were out because she seemed never to have heard of them. Most of our early times together were simply spent in silence, and if I've a memory of those first few Sundays it's of her head down over a piece of embroidery while I mooned around by the fire – they kept the fire stoked even at midsummer and the atmosphere inside the house was like a furnace – or listened to old man Parmenter prosing on about the beet harvest.

After a while, of course, I found out a bit more about the Parmenters – not enough to satisfy my curiosity, but sufficient to understand a very little of the kind of people they were. Oddly enough, they weren't really locals – old Parmenter's family originally came from Cambridgeshire – and every so often one of them would use a dialect phrase that you'd strain yourself to comprehend. There were hulking family secrets, too, that you had to be on your toes to spot, as the Parmenters had a habit of closing ranks whenever one of them looked as if it might be let out of the bag. It took me nearly a year, for instance, to establish that the boy Horace, occasionally stigmatised by Mr Parmenter in moments of extreme exasperation as 'backward', was very nearly simple. I used to watch him sometimes puzzling over a paper that I'd left on a chair, or staring at the letters that occasionally came from Mrs Parmenter's cousin in Canada ('Canady' they called it) and it would have broken your heart to see his face – kind of baffled, resigned and yet hopeful at the same time, as if he somehow thought that in the end, if he stared hard enough, the meaning would miraculously jump into place before his eyes. The Parmenters, I discovered, were deeply ashamed of Horace, kept him out of the way and according to Mary had practically given up on getting him educated from the age of eight. At the time I don't think I found anything shocking about this. It was simply how people behaved forty years ago. Old folk whose faculties had gone could spend years vegetating in some mental home with their relatives cheerfully pretending that they didn't exist, and families would move heaven and earth to stop a doctor writing 'died insane' on the death certificate.

In any case, not one of the great Parmenter family secrets that I eventually stumbled upon – the fact that old man Parmenter was working some kind of tax fiddle with his dairy herd, or that they'd lied about Horace's age to keep the school inspectors off his scent – bothered me in the slightest. It was all somehow incidental, barely visible below the surface of the real pursuit. What the Parmenters made of this fixation with Mary, which would have been evident to a child of five, was anyone's guess. I could see from the look on Mr Parmenter's face whenever I turned up that he knew pretty well what I was about, but all the while there was a polite fiction maintained that I was a friend of the family who just happened to be passing. In these circumstances, and what with Horace, who had the characteristic half-wit's ability to turn up when you least wanted him, it was a wonder we contrived to spend any time together, but somehow we managed it. We used to go off on long, dawdling walks on the pretext of inspecting the fences – something old man Parmenter was obsessed with – or checking that none of the cows had got out into the road. In this way I was able to build up a fairly accurate picture of the kind of life that went on here on a farm that was only six miles from Yarmouth but might as well have been on the moon for all the resemblance it bore to the adolescent lives I'd previously encountered.

Until Mary had been about fifteen, I gathered, things had been relatively normal. After all, even the Parmenters couldn't stop her attending school, and I think that at one point she'd even been allowed to join the Girl Guides in the village, but after that the life of the farm, old man Parmenter, the idiot boy, had simply swallowed her up. I asked her once if she'd ever wanted a job, or at any rate to do something that took her away from her parents, and she gave me a kind of puzzled look, as if she couldn't quite fathom that there were existences other than the one she led. It was as if the idea that most girls of nineteen didn't spend their time collecting eggs or sweeping up the scraps of Mrs Parmenter's darning wool had simply never occurred to her. Once, I remember – I'd told her about my job by this time – she asked me about the Sun Alliance.

'Those girls who work there? What do they *do*?'

'Oh, clerical work. In the canteens, some of them. Or secretaries.'

'What does a secretary do?'

I explained what a secretary did, and she thought about it for a while, and then nodded as if some deep, nagging doubt far within her had been answered. There were other conversations like this: about Marilyn Monroe and Hugh Gaitskell, Little Richard and Donald Soper. Years later Upward and I wrote a sketch that grew out of these exchanges, in which Upward played a middle-aged woman who had to have everything – even how you opened a crisp packet – explained to her. I was never happy doing it, for it seemed to mock something that wasn't stupidity but genuine incomprehension. There's another echo of her, perhaps, in a routine called 'An Anthropologist Calls' – the one where a chap with bifocals and a tape recorder turns up at a house on Tyneside and proceeds to study the occupants as if they're a tribe of South Sea Islanders. ('And this, would I be right in saying, is a piece of *stotty cake*?') All this, though, was in the future. The present was really just a series of endless walks: southwards over the ploughed fields, with the flints gleaming up out of the freshly turned soil and the gulls milling overhead, to tiny villages sleeping in the autumn mists, through the grounds of decaying country houses – empty since the war – where the grass grew up six feet high against the windows and there were pheasants nesting in the smashed conservatories. Norfolk was full of these places – great ruined barracks which no one could afford to keep up any more, where the agent might call twice a year. Once, I remember, we broke into one through a tumbledown side-door and stood in what would have been the hallway. The floorboards were green with mould and there were wild mushrooms growing up the staircase. The kitchen was piled with ancient rubbish, and children's toys and old sardine cans lay under the mouse-droppings.

One of Upward's favourite maxims, often dished out in BBC rehearsal rooms, once at least in the tense moment while we lurked behind the stage-curtain, was that no one ever bides their time. Later, thinking about the Parmenters – something I used to do long after the last traces of reality had been stripped from my memory of them – I realised that the time I'd spent with them was a proof of this, that what I'd imagined to be a kind of treading water was actually a deliberate paddling towards the shore. To have no plans, after all, isn't necessarily to be excluded from plans. I suppose if I'd had any sense I'd have suspected that I was using the Parmenters to compensate myself for something I didn't have, but I was twenty years old, and the implications of what I was doing scarcely occurred to me. It was 1960 now, 1961. Kennedy was in the White House and the papers were full of the H Bomb and CND, news of which had even percolated to Yarmouth (Mother thought they were 'a dirty lot of students', I remember, who could do with a wash) but I hardly noticed. I'd slipped out of life, I suppose, left the real world of the Sun Alliance and wattle-necked dignitaries proceeding to the senior staff luncheon room, for an alternative universe made up of the Parmenters' kitchen, rain falling over the cornfields, rooks soaring through the dead air and old Parmenter mumbling over his seed catalogues by the fire. And in an odd way it was a kind of comfort to know that all this existed, that you could fill the newspapers with dire warnings about Russia and the Bomb and still have people like the Parmenters (I tried Mr Parmenter once on CND and got the usual blank look) who simply refused to take any notice of them. In fact there was something breathtaking about the Parmenters' detachment. You got the feeling that had the news bulletins suddenly announced that there were Soviet warships off Gorleston and a row of nuclear warheads trained on East Anglia, Mr Parmenter would merely have pulled down the blinds, shovelled more coal on the fire and pretended that it wasn't happening. At the time I think I rather admired them for this. Even now a bit of me still sympathises with old Parmenter. After all, how many people who've lived through the last forty years wouldn't admit that it was all so much rubbish? But the problem was that none of these things – rain coming in on the wind, Mary's face in the firelight, Horace pretending to write his name on a piece of paper and then slyly pushing the pen away – were detachable from the others. And of course I never knew. But, then, how could I?

And all this time, of course, I was thinking about Upward. When he'd been transferred to the other unit back in Cyprus, we'd agreed that we'd try and stay in touch. Even at this stage there'd been a vague plan that we should start writing sketches with a view to sending them in to the radio – the Variety halls were dying on their feet by this stage and everybody knew it was the BBC that counted. But then when we were back in England he got posted somewhere on the south coast, and by the time I was out of the army he'd disappeared somewhere and the letters started coming back 'Not known'. I suppose if I'd had any guts I'd have tracked him down, written to the army authorities and asked them to forward letters, but somehow I didn't. It was just a fire that I kept quietly stoked up – the hillside in Cyprus, Captain Groves and the smoke rolling up from the village. The same was true of all the other things that went on outside the Parmenters' front room. Yarmouth, the Sun Alliance, family – it was all still boiling away, just as it always had done, but somehow distant and secondhand, as if whatever happened took place behind a pane of glass, and the words were spoken by voices I could barely hear. Counting National Service I'd been at the Sun Alliance office nearly five years, had my salary raised to ten pounds a week and got promoted to something called assistant supervisor, which basically meant stopping the clerks from flicking paper darts at each other. I can just about remember the person I was at twenty-one – tallish, not bad-looking – the butter-coloured hair I'd had when I was a kid had gone sandy by now – dressed up to the nines in a light-grey suit with the tie gathered up in what was called a Windsor knot, spending my time phoning up people who wanted to cash in their life insurance, nodding respectfully while old Penworthy went on about his pet scheme to update the commission agents' address file. That was the sort of thing you talked about in insurance companies in 1961. I think, though I don't know, and I never asked, that Mother was proud of me. I used to go and see her sometimes on Saturday afternoons – they still made you work on Saturday mornings in those days – and it was never any good. Poor Mother! Somehow in the years since the shop had gone and Father had died she'd grown smaller and less solid – not diminished in the way that people in books are said to 'fade away', but kind of worn-down and querulous. I used to look at her sometimes as she fussed around Uncle Ralph's lounge, scooping up books – she'd taken to reading those ghastly novelettes with titles like *All She'd Dreamed* – or hunting for teacups with feeble, little old lady movements, and marvel at what time had done to her.

Still, even in her dog days, Mother wasn't quite without resource. In particular, she'd got to know an old woman called Mrs Moss who lived a couple of doors away, and the two of them spent long hours frowsting in each other's front rooms or going in to Yarmouth on the bus and turning over the stuff in the shilling arcades. Mrs Moss – she was a tall, gaunt old girl with steel-rimmed spectacles – was a member of some odd religious sect, it might have been the Jehovah's Witnesses or even the Plymouth Brethren, and she was always trying to steer the conversation round to whether Mother was 'saved'. I sat through one or two of these sessions – endless debauches of weak tea and sugary biscuits – and came away with the most terrible feeling of depression: I can remember Mrs Moss, who was perhaps about ten years older than Mother, sitting up to administer the tea, and she looked exactly like a deathshead. I suppose if I'd have been less self-centred I'd have done something about Mother, fixed up to take lodgings together, say, or taken her out to places, but of course I didn't. Even now I can still kick myself for what I know I felt about Mother when I was twenty-one or thereabouts, that she was just a dreadful kind of encumbrance who as soon as she saw me would start sniffing about Uncle Ralph or the pittance they gave her as a widow's pension. But she was lost to me, you see, in the way that most of that early life of Father and Betty in the back room of the shop was lost. Once around this time, I remember, I had to cycle through Southtown one Saturday and for some reason I stopped to look at the shop. It sold woollen baby clothes or something by this stage, and there was a draggled, middle-aged woman standing in the doorway next to the sub-post office chewing her underlip with the kind of look on her face that you knew meant they hadn't had a customer all day. Well, there was the place where I'd been born, spent my childhood, sat poring over the *Eagle* and *Look and Learn*, while Father quietly went bankrupt in the next room, and it meant nothing to me. Or hardly anything. I was much more concerned with the afternoon I was going to spend at the Parmenters' and the walk I knew I was going to take with Mary.

By this stage the Parmenter thing had been going on six or seven months. Probably you won't believe me if I say that I don't have any concrete memories of it. The backdrop is all there in my mind – to this day I could tell you the titles of half-a-dozen books on the Parmenters' solitary bookshelf – but what was said and done has disappeared somewhere. What I remember most, of course, is Mary – coming up the track to the house once on a misty afternoon in the early spring, with the cows clustered up close to the fence and fog hanging over the edge of the fields, and seeing her from a long way off doing something in the yard; another time watching her hanging out clothes to dry on the line, and the wide sweep of her hair dragging away from her forehead. Even by then we hardly said anything to each other. And if anyone had asked me why I felt the way I did about her I couldn't have told them. Just something to do with her quietness, mildness, the idea that you could say whatever you wanted and she'd just smile back, a kind of tremulous, subdued excitement I always felt whenever I was with her. The Parmenters, true to form, were completely matter of fact about it all. In fact there were times when I suspected them of encouraging the affair: ostentatiously clearing out of the house on Sunday afternoons on fanciful-sounding errands, or commissioning us to take Horace for a walk in the fields.

Once, at one of these times, she said: 'You're boiling up on account of me, aren't you?'

'I suppose I am.'

'Dad said you were. Said he could tell.'

I took her in my arms then. She didn't resist, just kind of sagged forward with her head against my shoulders while I kissed the side of her face and watched out for Horace, who could be heard thrashing about in the undergrowth fifty yards away. If I'd had any sense I'd have said goodbye to the Parmenters there and then, gone back to Yarmouth on my bike and never returned, but of course I didn't. I just assumed that because I'd set my heart on something, it would work out. From the point of view of the world I'd been brought up in, this was quite par for the course. People fell over themselves to 'settle down' in those days. A girl who wasn't engaged by the time she was twenty-one lived in terror of being thought on the shelf, and the Sun Alliance was full of earnest nineteen-year-olds saving up for their weddings.

Anyway, I don't recall the preliminaries. I just remember deciding one day – in the way that you decide you need a new suit or your car needs servicing – that it had to happen. The curious thing was that I knew somehow I hadn't really made a decision at all, that I was caught up in something that was impossible to get out of. I remember reading a book once about a hotel cashier itching to leave home and start a new life with his mistress, who suddenly finds that somebody has left the hotel safe open. After what seems like an age, he decides not to take the money, only to discover that somehow the safe is shut and the money lying in his hand. That was how I felt about Mary. I think that in an odd way she knew it too. Certainly that's the only explanation I can find for what happened next. It was sometime in April, one of those bitterly cold days in Norfolk when the wind scrapes against your face like steel wool, with rain coming in from the sea. All that morning I'd been mooching about in my digs, listening to the comedy shows on the Light Programme or trying to read the *Sunday Express*, but mostly just brooding about Mary. By the queerest coincidence the previous day had brought a letter from Upward – the first I'd had in months – from an address somewhere in the Midlands. It didn't say much – Upward's letters never did – just things about sketches he was writing, and I remember sticking the envelope in my shirt pocket as I lugged the bike down the steps of my digs with the idea of reading it properly later. In the end I don't know if I ever did.

I got to the Parmenters about half-past two, confidently expecting to find the lot of them in a coma in front of the fire, but no, there was no one much about, just the old lady asleep as usual in her chair, and Mary folding up newly starched sheets from a pile on the kitchen table, so I had a cup of tea from a pot that might have brewed an hour ago and sat and watched her. After a bit she had to put the sheets away in the airing cupboard, and for some reason, not really knowing what I was doing, I trailed after her. And that's about it, really. When we did finally go to bed about an hour later I don't remember much about it, just a curious look on her face at one point, and then waking from what seemed like a day-long sleep, but was actually about five minutes, and lying there in complete silence except for the sound of the pigeons in the eaves, with the light fading in the distance and the wind rushing at the big, square window.

I don't know if Mary actually went and told her mother what we'd done, but from that day onwards there was never any doubt that we were going to get married. The thought of *not* getting married barely occurred to me. To find myself at twenty-one, married to a girl of twenty and living in a two-bedroom terrace somewhere in Northtown seemed a perfectly reasonable destiny. Even at that age, despite the army and Upward, I didn't have the wit to look beyond the Yarmouth back streets, the sea and the dunes. It was how people were in those days. If you'd have asked any of the clerks at the Sun Alliance what they wanted out of life, nine times out of ten it would have been some moon-faced grocer's daughter from Gorleston, two kids and a semi-detached. I was just the same. About twenty per cent of me still pined for the days I'd spent with Upward and the promise they'd seemed to hold, but by far the larger part of me wanted to marry Mary, live in a house that was my own, wake up next to her in bed in the morning. I suppose that seems a fairly humble ambition. All I can say is that it didn't then. Birth. Childhood. Work. Marriage. Death. People didn't kid themselves they were going to live for ever in those days.

The next six months I can't begin to piece together, mostly because nothing very much happened. Any self-respecting Yarmouth family whose daughter had announced she was getting married would have been falling over itself in excitement by this time, but I knew enough about the Parmenters by now to realise that this wasn't their style. In fact I sometimes wonder whether old Parmenter didn't view the thought of acquiring a son-in-law as about on a par with buying a pig. As for Mary, I never did find out what she thought about it. All I can remember is the silences. We used to sit there in the evenings by the fire, while the Parmenters regarded us in a kind of bovine, matter of fact but I think approving way. Oddly enough, the only person who showed the least animation at the prospect of my getting married was Mother. Somehow, probably through Mrs Moss, who had a county-wide intelligence network of this sort, she'd 'found out' about the Parmenters – who they were, where they lived, who they were related to – enough at any rate to be completely horrified. It puzzled me a bit to think that Mother, who'd greeted any piece of news I'd brought her in the past five years with paralysing indifference, should have been so upset by the thought of me marrying Mary. In the end, though, I realised that she regarded it as a kind of personal insult. I can remember her standing in Uncle Ralph's kitchen – somehow the memory is much more vivid to me than anything connected to Mary – telling me that I was 'throwing myself away' (she actually used those words) and then crumpling up in a way that I hadn't seen since the FOR SALE boards went up in the square. At the time I can remember being mostly indifferent to this – I'd had an idea that Mother was going to be 'difficult'. Now I think that in its way this kind of disapproval was faintly impressive. It showed that for all the horrors of the past five years – and from Mother's point of view they were horrors – she'd managed to keep her dignity. All the same, I know that I didn't take the slightest notice. Maybe if Father had been alive the two of them could have talked me out of it, but Mother was fighting a losing battle and she knew it.

In the end we got married almost a year to the day since I'd first turned up at the Parmenters, to pick blackcurrants. It was the very end of the summer, with the beech leaves already turning gold above the Parmenters' yard, and I remember standing outside the church – it was a tiny affair in the middle of a field a couple of miles from the farm – watching the people stream down the hill from the road while the breeze from the sea ripped over the wheat and Horace, who'd been pressed into service as best man, shambled around in the vestibule sucking boiled sweets out of a paper bag. Getting married is an odd business. It's as if the whole thing was designed to terrify you, or at any rate to leave you with a feeling of huge unease, as if all the people staring at you back in the body of the church were thinking 'It's your turn now you bastard, yes, you, you bastard, and now see how you like it!' Most of the guests I didn't know from Adam – I think they were mostly relatives of the Parmenters – but Uncle George and Aunt Sheila had come up from Fram for the day and there were one or two of the people from work. Mother and Mrs Moss sat at the very back of the church like a couple of ghouls and declined to attend the reception. I remember being exhilarated and cast down by turns, one moment thinking about the two-week honeymoon we were having at Sheringham and the £20 the Sun Alliance had given us, the next feeling a bit annoyed that Upward hadn't bothered to reply to the invite I'd sent him. And all the while the thing simply surging on around us – the rows of stolid Norfolk faces in their pews, Horace quietly shoving another sweet in his mouth when he thought no one was looking, Mary's face under the veil, Mother crying in the background. Oh, it was a proper Norfolk wedding all right, even down to the pony and trap to take us back to the reception, and the set of bells I later discovered – we were staying the first night at the Parmenters' – that some wag had tied to the bed.

From time to time in the Seventies, sparked by a feature in the *TV Times* or a newspaper interview, we used to get letters from people who'd known us earlier on. Occasionally the connections they claimed went back as much as fifteen years. Scriptwriters knocked into in BBC canteens wrote from obscure towns in the north of England to criticise recent appearances and offer 'fresh material'; novelty acts with whom Upward might have exchanged half-a-dozen words backstage in 1965 re-emerged to claim guest-spots on forthcoming shows. Nearly always well disposed, sometimes a bit less so, these letters had one common factor – a kind of telescoping of past time that pushed their writers into areas of our lives where we knew they'd never been. Taken together, the vision they offered was unsettling – a sort of alternative life full of stages never trodden, cues eternally missed, and yet so plausible as to cast endless doubt on your own memories. To put it another way, in a world of vague reminiscence, anything seemed possible. At the same time, I had to admit that my own memories of Upward fell into the same unreliable pattern. Looked at from the point of view of strict chronology, he instantly dissolved away to nothing, popped up again in the most unlikely places. It was only by trying exceptionally hard to re-create these dead landscapes that I could prove he hadn't been there. Somehow the early Sixties is one of these grey areas, a time when Upward is there in memory but not in fact. Upward, Brenda and the Minerva – all of them somehow belong to this period, run in and out of my memories of Yarmouth, Mary and the Parmenters, for all that some part of me knows they were never there. Perhaps this is just a classic showbusiness delusion – *the* classic showbusiness delusion – assuming that whatever touches the centre of your life will always touch the rest. On the other hand, Upward himself was fond of saying – although these mightn't have been his exact words – that glamour would always crowd out the non-glamorous. Whatever the truth, when I think of those days it's always in terms of continuity, things moving forward, worlds in view, not the dreadful kind of half-life I know it to have been.

We started off living in a two-bedroomed terrace in Kenilworth Road in the Northtown, plausibly represented by Mother – who had probably never ventured down it in her life – as the worst street in Yarmouth. Do you remember those old back-to-back terraced houses? Ours cost £200 a year, and the first thing we had to do on the day we arrived was to burn sulphur to drive out the bugs. Kenilworth Road! It's odd that you can live for two years in a place and yet have no idea of what it was like. But I remember the downstairs lay-out, which was simply a front door opening into the main room, followed by a kind of back-parlour, with a tiny kitchen behind. The Parmenters had given us pieces of furniture as a wedding present – huge mahogany sideboards and tables that were too big for the rooms and lay around the place taking up space, as if the Queen of Brobdingnag had dropped them there by mistake. The lavatory was outside in the yard. There was a whole row of them running down the back of the street, and early in the mornings the smell hit you in the face like camphor. We hadn't been there more than a week before the bugs returned, of course, and one of my strongest memories is of cooking something on the rickety gas-stove and watching one fall splash! into a pan of milk.

Later on I tried very hard to re-create that time at Kenilworth Road and work out exactly where it had all gone wrong, but I never quite managed it. It was all too mixed up with other things, from later and before: Mother's face, the view out to sea from my office stool, the Parmenters' kitchen. At first it wasn't too bad. We were only a couple of months married in those days, and I can remember coming back early in the evening with a pint of shrimps or a couple of crabs from the fish market, and having them for tea in the parlour, with the late sun coming in over the rooftops and the lines of washing. The idea was that Mary would look for work, in a shop perhaps or one of the local dairies, and we'd use the extra money to move somewhere better. Beyond that I don't think I envisaged anything other than that we'd be together, and that eventually there'd be children. That was how people thought in those days. Ask them what they thought they'd be doing at thirty and they'd have laughed in your face, because they knew that, more or less, it would be exactly the same: same job, same faces around you, the *Yarmouth Mercury* on the tea table, the crab-boats hauled up on the shale, Cromer, Sheringham and the seaside towns marching on up the coast.

What did we talk about on those evenings in the back-parlour in Kenilworth Road, with the light fading away across the yard and the noise from the street growing fainter and the bugs marching two-by-two across the ceiling? God knows. Quite often we'd just sit there until it was practically dark, not saving anything, until, getting up to fetch the tea or switch on the radio, I'd find she'd fallen asleep in her chair. Other times she used to talk about her family – not informatively, but in a kind of solicitous, anxious way. Were they all right? Was Horace all right? She was particularly exercised about Horace, I recall, worried that the Parmenters wouldn't know how to cope with him now she was gone. I remember once asking her about this, a dreadful conversation full of desperate euphemisms and wool-pullings, but crucial in that it revealed to me all kinds of things about her childhood, and the Parmenters, and the odd enclosed life of the farm.

'I mean, when did you, did anyone, realise that Horace was, well, *different*?'

'When he was five or six. I remember once, they sent a letter saying he should go to a special school.'

'What happened about that?'

'I don't know. Nothing, I suppose. Dad used to say there was no harm in a person being slow.'

'But didn't anyone . . .?'

'You don't *know* about Horace,' she said. 'Not like me. I used to try and help him do his sums. When he was at school. Easy ones, they were. A hundred take away ninety. Seven times seven. And he just couldn't do them. Just couldn't. And won't ever. Do you *understand*?'

Needless to say, once we'd moved in, Horace was a regular caller. He used to turn up after tea sometimes on his motorbike, in that silly, moon-faced way he had, and lounge around the place eating enormous meals or listening uncomprehendingly to the radio. Now and again I'd take him to a football match or the speedway and he'd stand there on the terrace with his mouth half open, never quite able to work out what was going on. At weekends, of course, we spent whole days with the Parmenters – endless tracts of time lost in boozing tea by the kitchen fire or helping old Parmenter with jobs around the farm. Oddly enough, I didn't mind about this. I could cope with the Parmenters, the old mad grandmother drooling over her chair – she'd last made a sensible remark about the time we got engaged – old Parmenter standing in the doorway with his jackhammer swinging in one hand and eyeing me up for an afternoon of fence-mending, the scorching fires and the endless tea, because I knew what to expect. What I couldn't cope with was the life of Kenilworth Road, the silence that hung over it and the tremendous sense of gloom that seemed to infect every activity that took place within its walls. I used to watch Mary sometimes moving around the house – clearing tea-things away from a table, say, or ironing – all the things I'd watched her doing in her mother's kitchen and marvelled at – and she did it with a dreadful, selfconscious gloom, as if I was an ogre whose castle she'd strayed into and no amount of pleading would ever let her out again. It was the same with sex. She was willing enough, I suppose, but she'd lie there with a sort of pained, absorbed look, as if what we were about to do was simple torture. I've a dreadful memory – not always brought out, but there all the same – of simply rutting away at her, slamming down on top of her so hard that she practically bounced up and down beneath me, and then going downstairs and smoking half-a-dozen cigarettes in front of the fire while I waited for the explosion of noise that, mysteriously, never came.

I was furious, of course, furious and puzzled, and also a bit ashamed, of myself, her and the situation we'd fetched up in, but there was nothing I could do about it. Whatever lines of communication had existed between us had simply closed down, and that was that. Occasionally, in the midst of all this, I'd embark on conversations with her, rambling affairs that invariably ground to a halt in monosyllables.

'Are you happy living here?'

'Yes.'

'Is there anything you don't have that you want?'

'No.'

'Do you love me?'

'Yes.'

Once, after one of these interrogations, I lost my temper and hit her. We were in the front room, I remember, around tea-time, with the bicycles flying past in the road outside and children's voices mingling with the noise of the gulls. I can't even recall what she said, or didn't say, only leaning over and slapping her on the side of the head, not hard, but hard enough to made her topple over on to the sofa. It sticks in my mind as one of those terrible, odd moments when everything suddenly fades away into dense, far-off surfaces and colours: the blue of the light outside, a man's figure passing not ten feet away on the other side of the window, bits of furniture turned into standing stones.

And all the while, of course, there were other things going on. For a start I was making serious attempts to find Upward. I'd sent a registered letter to the last address I'd had and even written to one or two of the other blokes in the section on the off-chance they might know where he was. It was no good though: he'd vanished off the face of the earth. At the same time I'd finally plucked up enough courage to go and see one of the high-ups at the office and tell him that I wanted a change. Officially this kind of self-promotion was frowned upon at the Sun Alliance, but curiously enough I ended up being offered a job as what was known as a 'regional agent'. This meant travelling round the area and interviewing prospective life-insurance clients, and I jumped at it – not merely because of the extra two quid a week on the table, but because the idea of getting out of the office, being my own man up to a point, rather appealed to me. Norfolk's a big county. You can travel seventy miles along the coast from Yarmouth and still not be in sight of the Lincolnshire border. And that's more or less how I spent the next year – crawling along backroads near Swaffham or Holt to talk to some shopkeeper who wanted £500-worth of life cover. Long Stratton, Garboldisham. Mundesley. Fakenham. Thurton. Brooke. How many of those places have you heard of, I wonder? I hadn't heard of half of them myself until I went out on the road in what would have been the spring of 1962 – Godforsaken villages huddled in the mist, each with its church and its pub and half-a-dozen shops, and most of the adult population straining to leave for the big towns. Oddly enough, I quite enjoyed the work. It paid commission, too, which was worth having on a biggish policy – or would have been if it hadn't been for the frost that waited for me every night in Kenilworth Road.

I found out about the letters quite by accident, one night when I came home early and discovered some sheets of notepaper lying on the kitchen table. They were headed 'Dear Mother and Dad' and furnished a carefully itemised account of everything she'd done that day, right down to the grocery bill and the conversation she'd had with the man who'd come to read the gas meter, all filed away with love from your affectionate daughter Mary Parmenter. Years later – God forgive me – I wrote a sketch for Upward based on this idea: the newly married wife writing home to her mother – the decisive shift being that Upward set it up north and delivered it with a Lancashire accent: *Dear Mam. How are you and how is little Ernie and the budgerigar? Has our Dad come home this week? Married life is very strange, but I am not letting anything get on top of me. Mrs Ackroyd from opposite says it's up to a husband to take his wife's part, and I said, yes, mine does that all the time . . .* Towards the end it all got a bit edgy – Upward used to speed his voice up in a relentless monotone: *It is 10.15 now and no one has been down the street for a whole minute. No actually, Mam, that's not true because I just saw a cat. Which reminds me, how is Mrs Arkwright from next door?* Upward always liked the sketch, which he said was exactly like the way a particular kind of northern woman behaved. The real letters weren't funny, or tense, just boring, quite devoid of personality or even interest. If she'd spent the time abusing me I could have understood it, but she didn't. It was all shopping lists and what we'd had for breakfast – that kind of thing.

All the same, the letters were much too big a thing to be ignored. Once I said to her:

'What do you write about?'

'What do you mean, what do I write about?'

'When you write home, what do you write about?'

'Oh, just things.'

'What kind of things?'

'Things.'

She didn't seem to mind that I knew. I used to wonder how these despatches from life at Kenilworth Road were received at the farm, whether they piled up unread in the kitchen, or whether the family sat round discussing them. I had a vision of Horace poring over them in secret, tongue hanging out of his mouth with the effort of decoding these weird signals from an alien world.

It was summer 1962 now, and we'd been married nearly a year. One night I came home from work and found her gone. I've never forgotten the stillness of that house, the light pouring in across the step of the open back door – there was a cat sunning itself, I remember, which jumped away when it saw me – the crockery piled up by the sink. I knew where she'd gone, of course, and after I'd had some tea I got back in the car and drove over to the Parmenters, to collect her. They weren't in the least put out – not even by the fact that she'd apparently walked the whole way from Yarmouth – just looked at me in that dull, incurious way they had. Everything there was exactly the same – playing cards all over the table, the old woman asleep in her chair, Mrs Parmenter drowsing over a copy of *Woman and Home*.

And yet I knew that somehow I'd changed my mind about the Parmenters – that whereas in the past I'd found them nice, simple people, now I thought them simply ludicrous. I can't really explain this. I just know that by the time I got back into the car with Mary – she came willingly enough – that I never wanted to see any of them again. Later on, of course, I tried asking her what it was that had made her go, but it was no good, and I don't know that we ever had a proper conversation again. I can remember fragments of those last days, but nothing like the whole. She used to move restlessly around the place turning out drawers and looking for things she could never find, or stand in the front doorway staring vaguely down the street. And then, a week or so later, she was gone again. For some reason this time I didn't immediately shoot off to fetch her. I just sat in the house and waited. I suppose if I'd thought about it I'd have gone over there and tried to reason with her, but at the same time I knew that the Parmenters weren't people you could talk to, not in that way. You could have turned up in their yard and driven a tank through the house and they'd have squared it somehow with the world they knew, gone on playing cards or stirring the fire, and never said anything. In the end, though, about a week after she'd vanished, old Parmenter came to Kenilworth Road – a little red-faced man, dressed in the suit he'd worn to the wedding and looking faintly embarrassed. I gathered Mrs Parmenter had practically ordered him to come. As to what was said, I couldn't begin to re-create it, so hedged about was it with silences and imputations. At the end, though, something seemed to strike him and he rummaged around in the pocket of his suit.

'Got this for you,' he said, handing me a large brown envelope.

I waited until he'd gone before I opened it, though I could see the writing on the front wasn't Mary's, and shook the contents over the carpet. Five-pound notes, forty of them.

And that's the story of my married life.

It's not quite true to say that's the last I saw of the Parmenters. Ten years later, coming down the steps of the Blackpool Winter Gardens where we were doing a summer show, I ran smack into a tall, pasty-faced character wearing a cellophane mackintosh – the temperature was in the eighties, I remember – and carrying a thermos under his arm. It was Horace, who must have been about twenty-seven. I was in a tearing hurry, and, worse, I had a reporter from the local paper in tow to whom I was supposed to be feeding some story about the TV series, but something made me stop and say hello. He was just the same, of course – manifestly not all there, but in a way you couldn't quite put your finger on – and we talked a bit about his parents (who he maintained were 'poorly') and the farm, which was apparently just about functioning. I think he knew who I was, but when I asked about Mary he clammed up altogether and gaped at me. A bit after that he started shuffling off. There didn't seem to be anybody with him, so I never found out what he was doing outside the Winter Gardens on a July afternoon in 1972. I can remember watching him sway off down the parade, with one or two of the passers-by giving him a glance, and thinking that I ought to follow him – who knows? He might have had the rest of the family with him – but somehow I knew it wouldn't be any good.

'Who was that?' the reporter asked, not particularly interested.

'Oh,' I said. 'Just somebody I used to know.'

Yesterday I made a new friend. At least I think I did.

It's quarter to four on an iron-grey afternoon in November and I'm outside the school gates with the usual crowd of parental flotsam: the tough girls with their prams and their stabbing cigarettes; bonehead dads in their scarlet Charlton Athletic tops. A pit-bull or two on a choke-lead twists nervously. It might rain, which means that every eye intermittently rises skywards. Londoners *hate* the rain, I notice. The mildest drizzle sends them fleeing into shop doorways or to the sanctuary of the bus shelters. Daniel, soon glimpsed in the first or second knot of children, looks flustered, scuttling across the tarmac as if trying to avoid something. Or someone. A slightly older kid – not one of the usual ones – is a yard or two behind. He doesn't really hit him, more a flap of fingers on the side of the head, but what do you do? Daniel looks pale and also outraged, as if he can't quite believe anyone could do this to him. By this time I'm between the two of them, one hand on Daniel's shoulder, the other gesturing to the kid – I don't remember saying anything – what the consequences will be if he repeats the action. At this point one of the bonehead dads detaches himself from the silent throng by the gate and comes lurching across.

''Ere you, that's my fucking kid you're talking to.' Impossible to reproduce what he actually says. *Ereyou, thass my fuckenkid yer torkintew.*

About five foot seven. White tee-shirt, jeans and trainers. Shaven head merging into genuine hair loss. There are hundreds of them in this part of London. It's a kind of uniform. 'Who took your purse lady?' 'Oh he was bald and wearing a white tee-shirt, jeans and trainers, officer.' I look at him for a bit – there are other parents taking an interest by this stage – and then, curiously enough, remember a line that Upward once threw out in a sketch.

'That's a pity. Couldn't you part-exchange him for something?'

Bonehead takes a step forward and then stops. Even at fifty-seven I'm not the kind of bloke you take unnecessary liberties with. In the end he thinks twice about it, blinks at his kid, by now a hugely interested spectator, gives him what I take to be a playful cuff but actually sends him staggering over his heaped Umbro bag, and says in a tone of absolute ground-down weariness:

'Leave it out will yer, Neil?' Another glance at me. 'Fuckin' kids eh?'

'That's right.'

Bonehead has his cigarette packet out now, the non-professional's calling card.

'I seen you around,' he says, sweeping his hand across the vista of the school gates, as if this somehow explains our little stand-off. 'Have a fag?'

I have a fag. Daniel and Neil, meanwhile, are looking sheepishly at the tarmac, initial interest in what their dads might be about to do to one another replaced by gargantuan embarrassment.

Bonehead ('the name's Kev') turns out to be a bit of a talker. Also concerned to disseminate information about himself. Apparently he lives on one of the big estates down by the river ('Full of fuckin' kids running around pissed out of their heads of course') and used to work in the freight over in Silvertown until the jobs went east to the Isle of Grain. There are several other Neils and a couple of girls ('gels'), the latter back in the flat under the care of a friendly neighbour. Kev's wife works in Woolwich. Kev supports Charlton, only they're fucking hopeless this season. All the time we talk, or rather Kev talks and I nod or grunt in agreement, I notice him shooting inquisitive little glances at me. Finally at the street corner fifty yards from the school gates, where the road forks and bends round to the river, he says what six or maybe seven people a year say to me:

'Seen you before ent I?'

We bid each other farewell with a great shower of shouts and salutations – 'See yer mate!', 'Take care!' – the way the boneheads do outside pubs. A bit later I say to Daniel:

'Why was Neil trying to hit you?'

'Don't know.'

'Did he do it before?'

Pause. 'A bit.'

'Did you tell the teacher? Did you tell . . .?'

'No,' Daniel says seriously. 'That'd be grassing.'

I'll be perfectly honest. I hate all this: ten-year-olds talking like gangster films, vicious little bastards in white tee-shirts. All the other stuff, too – the sorrowings over wretched princesses, the football nonsense. If I had the money I'd send Daniel to some fearful place full of boys with names like Piers and Jonjo with regulation hair-cuts and proper accents, and have him taught Latin and Greek rather than leave Miss Cox to tell him about her boyfriend. Only you don't, do you? Only you can't, can you? You accommodate yourself to what's there and you make the best of it. Like the Ngongi, arriving at the solitary oasis with its flyblown pond half-full of stagnant water, you thank God that there is a pond rather than simply the parched and treeless desert.

The headscarves the old women wear, not changed in forty years, eyes down over the grey pavements, the bags balanced in either hand, down from the river, the lie of the land set back, away from the warehouses and the pockmarked mud.

Several calls from Lennie. Apparently my evening at the Plumstead Over Sixties went down a storm. 'A knockout' is Lennie's exact description. There's a return engagement waiting if I want it. Plus several other similar outfits are interested. I tell Lennie I'll let him know. Lennie's also very keen on the BBC thing (*Nice girl. Really genned up on you and that*), which he thinks could lead to something. Lennie's optimism is incurable. I wonder if his other clients, those Jewish harmonica players in Bethnal Green and bands of red-jacketed close-harmony singers, are subjected to the same paralysing blasts of misplaced confidence.

Actually I've already been surprisingly proactive – to use a word that's even begun to turn up in Lennie's vocabulary – over the BBC thing, to the extent of having lunch with one of the production people. Lucy, the assistant producer, looked to be about thirty-five. Over the lunch, which took place in a subdued winebar round the back of Langham Place, she filled me in on the series. As ever, Lennie had got it substantially wrong. A series called *The People in History*, full of pre-millennial cud-chewing, with a final programme featuring us in the guise of *The Comedy Men*, put together by way of old tapes and eye-witness voiceovers.

'Who's going to be talking about us?'

'Oh, I dare say you could write the list yourself. Bruce Forsyth. The Ronnies. You could probably give me some ideas.'

There was a slight edge to Lucy's voice as she said 'ideas', which made me wonder if certain aspects of *The Comedy Men* weren't altogether to her taste. Actually, meeting people like Lucy is pretty much a new experience for me. She belongs, in fact, to a social category that I've barely come across: polite, interested, slightly disdainful. Whatever she says – and she uses upper-class little-girlisms like 'gosh' and 'frightful' (as in 'frightfully expensive' and 'frightfully sweet') – has, you feel, a permanent sub-text, something like: *I may have to work at the BBC, times being what they are, but I went to Oxford and I know my way round a gallery or two and whatever cultural topics we may stray into the probability is that I know more about them than you.*

'Will there be any money in this?' I asked at the end of the pitch.

'There'll be a bit,' she said briskly. 'Not very much, though. After all, this is the BBC, darling.'

I was a bit reassured by the 'darling', which clearly came in quotation marks, a conversational flounce she'd borrowed from somewhere and wasn't overly happy with. Looking at her as she ate her salad and drank sparingly from a glass of mineral water, I wondered if I hadn't got her slightly wrong, mistaken reserve for bitterness.

Lucy turned out to be unexpectedly knowledgeable about Upward & King.

'I ordered some of your tapes up from the library. The last TV series. One or two live performances someone had filmed.'

'What did you think?'

'I thought one or two of the studio things were a bit before their time. The one about Mrs Thatcher in the shop I mean . . . But some of the live material was, well, rather old-fashioned.'

'Old-fashioned?'

'A bit dated.'

She meant 'offensive to women', of course. The sexism thing hit comedy like a tidal wave in the early Eighties, alongside and sometimes in association with the alternatives – a whole new set of rules that most people in the business could barely grasp. They threw Benny Hill off the networks for sexism. I can remember in about 1982 doing a student charity gig with an old bloke called Eric Hopkins, whom we rather liked, who'd spent twenty years working the northern club circuit. Eric, who was a great one for flowered suits in the Max Miller style, bounced on stage, took a look at the audience and began 'People say you are what you eat . . . Well, I'm a cunt.' I think he lasted a minute before they booed him off.

'I'll be perfectly honest,' Lucy said, giving her lips a delicate little pat with a napkin. 'I was quite impressed. I mean, my *father* used to like you. He said you were like Morecambe & Wise. But when I looked I thought he was completely wrong, that the personalities were quite different. Kind of sad in a way.'

Kind of sad. Outside there were leaves bowling down Mortimer Street, and a policeman on a horse was trying to negotiate a row of bollards that someone had placed in the road. The horse came juddering to a halt on the far pavement. In profile, leaning across the table with one hand on the Perrier bottle, caught suddenly in the early-afternoon shadow, Lucy's face looked less intent, less of today. She had little tendrils of hair that fell away from her blonde, page-boy cut, down over her ears.

'Sorry. You must get terribly fed up with people talking about you like that.'

'You get used to it.'

Whether Lucy took this as a rebuke I don't know, but she became noticeably less brisk. Even so, whatever signals she was giving off I found difficult to decode. One thing was unmissable, though. Rather like Kev from the school gates, she was a great volunteerer of information: time in job (six years, before that something in publishing), domicile, career path.

'Where do you live?'

'South-east. Plumstead. Abbey Wood way.'

'Gracious. That's a long way out. We live in Putney, but my boyfriend says he needs to be nearer to work.'

'What does your boyfriend do?'

'He's a management consultant.'

I don't know if I was supposed to be impressed by this, or indeed whether Lucy is impressed herself. Afterwards we ended up walking back together towards Oxford Circus, her departure point for a trip to interview an ex-Home Secretary ('Honestly, I think he'll be hopeless, but Graham says he once appeared on the Morecambe & Wise Christmas Show'). Ten, perhaps eleven inches shorter than me, she bobbed along at my side like a cork. She agreed to get back to me with a preliminary treatment within a week.

'Should I send it to . . . Lennie, is it? Or straight to you?'

'I should keep Lennie out of this.'

'I saw the other tape, you know,' she said soberly. 'The one where he . . .'

The one where he . . . I let that pass, walked off along Oxford Street, past the rows of Queen Mum calendars, hot-dog vans and leaflet purveyors. Looking back I could see her poised on the lip of the stairs and delving into her bag, the wind whipping her hair up into a kind of helmet. She talks extraordinarily, by the way. The way I imagine Virginia Woolf talking. Or George Eliot.

As I suspected, DI Stevens turns out to be a policeman. I find him on the pavement one morning as I come back from a stroll by the river, one arm sprawled over the roof of a red Mondeo, the other scanning the upstairs windows. Fiftyish, I suppose, with grey-black hair made comic by a pair of much darker eyebrows. As I swing into the doorway – I can see he's waiting for me, but don't feel like making the first move – he flaps his ID card in the air a yard away from my face.

'Ron Stevens. Fraud squad. Mind if I come in?'

'*Fraud squad?*

‘’Sall right,’ he says matily. ‘Not about your tax return. Just a few questions, okay?’

Apparently policemen still have those working-class Londoner names: Ron, Dennis, Harold. Back in the Seventies Upward and I did a parody of one of the current cop serials, in which everyone was called Dennis and talked in what we imagined to be police argot: ‘Dennis, did you lean on Harris like I asked?’ ‘That’s right, Dennis, I fingered his collar good and proper.’ ‘But did he sing, Dennis, that’s what I want to know?’ ‘Sung like a bleeding canary, Dennis. Proper nark’ etc. etc. Once inside, Stevens slips up to the first floor with surprising eagerness and starts looking at the pictures, the Water Rat charity night and the Palladium ensembles.

‘You know,’ he says delightedly. ‘I used to watch you on the TV. Friday nights. You’d come on in a coat and he’d be sitting there by the lamp-post, and you’d say “Me and him, we’re here to entertain you.” ’

‘And did we?’

‘What? Entertain us? More often than not. You should have stayed in the business,’ he says, dropping his voice a tone. ‘I don’t like these young blokes. Too chippy.’

I make us tea and he trips round the room a bit more turning over Daniel’s schoolbooks, takes a squint at the pile of videos stacked above the television.

‘Still,’ he says. ‘It’s not easy on your own, is it? Like Ernie without Eric. Ah well. You ever come across a character called Martin Cartwright?’

‘The MP?’

‘Was.’ Stevens picks up one of Daniel’s ping pong balls, flicks it in the air and catches it in the palm of his hand. The effect is surprisingly disconcerting. ‘Lord Cartwright of East Mersey he calls himself now. Labour peer. Ever met him?’

‘Now and again.’

‘And when would that have been, sir?’ Given the previous affability, the ‘sir’ snaps in the air like a cap pistol.

‘I don’t know. 1975. 1976.’

‘It’s all a long time ago, isn’t it?’ Stevens says helpfully. ‘1976. Do you know I was a bobby on the beat back then? Twenty-five I would have been. Would that have been about the time you knew Gavin Newsome?’

'I suppose so. Yes.'

'It's all right sir. It's amazing what they have in the files these days. Even the showbiz gossip.' He improvises gamely: ' "TV comedians Upward & King were on hand to entertain guests at Gavin Newsome's lavish charity ball. Arthur Upward remarked, 'I told the ones down the front that if they didn't feel like clapping they could rattle their jewellery.' " Remember that?'

'A bit. It was a long time ago.'

'I'm with you there. Think about it. You were a TV comedian and I was a bobby on the beat. But some people have long memories. You'd be surprised. Did you see the stuff in the papers last week?' Without waiting for me to nod, he goes on: 'Newsome's an old man now. Must be seventy at least. Most of the money's gone, too. But somebody's blown the whistle.'

Outside there are low grey clouds hanging over the approach to the river, gleaming white light beyond. Perhaps one of Turner's ships is out there instead of the tourist boats and the PLA barges. Nothing would surprise me about London now.

'What about?'

'Newsome and Cartwright. Backhanders. *Money*. Where did it all come from? Where did it all go? That charity do in 1976. The 25th of June 1976 to be exact. Who was there?'

'You tell me.'

'Gladly. Half of London. If I looked out the *Who's Who* entries we'd be here till tea-time. It's all right sir. Nobody thinks you had anything to do with it. Nobody even thinks you knew what was going on. But, well, we'd like to know.'

'About what?'

'Who you saw. Who you talked to. Where you went. I know, it was twenty years ago and you were the cabaret. Or whatever. But let me tell you sir, there's old blokes in their sixties shitting themselves just now about what's coming out of the woodwork. Old women too.'

Stevens loves all this, of course. Who wouldn't? The Ngongi have a series of elemental rituals designed to enliven cold nights around the desert camp fire: The Bringer of Bad Tidings; The Teller of Tales: He Who Saves the Scattered Flocks. From the age of three, according to the ethnologists, Ngongi children have a reasonable understanding of mimesis.

'Anyway,' he says. 'I'll come back, if I may. Give you time to think. A period of quiet reflection. If anyone rings you up – anyone out of the ordinary, that is – you'll make a note of it, won't you?'

Back on the pavement, mist is slowly descending. Stevens peers at it, steadying himself. He has terrible skin, full of smashed veins and odd runways of flesh.

'Do you know the sketch of yours I most liked?' he says, by way of a farewell. 'The one where you talked about women. You know, he'd be bragging about what he'd done the other night and you'd just say something quiet like to bring him down, and the look he'd give you would be sheer poison.'

I watch him drive off. There is, of course, no such thing as a lost world.

Talking About Boys

KING (Greta), in blonde wig and tank-top, sits in café. UPWARD (Shirl), hair cascading round his shoulders, in polka-dot dress, joins him.

KING (*gives appraising look*): Purple suits you, you know.

UPWARD: Aye. You can either wear it or you can't, and I'm one of the ones that can.

They look at each other.

UPWARD: Give us a fag.

KING: Honest Shirl, I'm down to me last forty.

UPWARD: Y'tight cow . . . so who was it last night then? Him as works in the abattoir up McElligot Street?

KING: Him? No . . . him as works in the funeral parlour on Inkerman Terrace.

UPWARD (*impressed*): Oh yeah? Where'd he take you then?

KING: Oh, you know. The usual.

UPWARD: What? I thought the chip shop shut Thursdays? Or was it round the bus shelter in Slug Street?

KING: As if any self-respecting girl'd let herself be taken there! The idea! I read that Mrs Whitehouse as writes in the papers, you know. I know what they're after.

UPWARD: What's wrong with the bus shelter in Slug Street? I've had some very happy moments in the bus shelter in Slug Street.

KING: Actually he took us to the Frog and Toadstool.

UPWARD (*gives little squeak*): Ooh! *Posh.* I suppose you'll be telling me you were drinking Babycham next?

KING: And anyway Shirl, you'll never believe what he said . . . Thing is, Shirl . . . Well, we're *engaged.*

(*both rise from their seats, punch the air in triumph, then sit down again*)

UPWARD: How many times have you been engaged now, Gret?

KING: Six . . . seven. But the thing is I've got a kind of *feeling* about this lad.

UPWARD: What's his name?

KING: Trevor. Trevor Ramsbotham.

UPWARD: What kind of a feeling?

KING: You know, a land of dreams, the two of us . . . doing things . . . together. You know. Like unblocking that drain under me mam's sink. Or putting out the rat poison last thing.

UPWARD: I'm happy for you love, I really am . . . have you told your mam?

KING: Actually Shirl, we haven't seen mam for a couple of nights, and – (*her gaze strays out of the window*) – oh my God! Shirl!

UPWARD: What's the matter, pet?

KING: It's him. Trevor. With his arm round some floozie. Look.

They look

UPWARD (*dispassionately*): Aye, you're right. A real painted harlot. You're well out of that, love.

KING: I suppose I am.

UPWARD: And it's no way a classy job. I mean, fiddling around with a lot of, well, dead people.

KING: Convenient, though.

UPWARD: What?

KING: If anyone dies, that is.

UPWARD: I suppose so. So what are you doing tonight?

KING: We could go down the bus shelter in Slug Street.

The voices fade

1972

Light Goes Green

Did you hear about the disturbance at the butcher's? The butcher sat on the bacon slicer, and all the customers got a little behind with their orders.

Life, Upward used to say, was pretty much like the experience of telling jokes in front of a crowd of 300 people. I always thought there was something in this. The hasty arrival on stage, the pleased or at any rate tolerant faces of the audience, high expectations, the confidence with which you spoke the opening lines, leading to a period of uncertainty, the audience wondering if its money mightn't have been laid out better, the comedian worrying about his choice of material, wondering if there weren't time to change tack, finally either triumph or collapse, graceful withdrawal – showered with praise – or death.

'Think about it,' Upward used to say. 'The stand-up's a kind of metaphor for how most people live their lives, only more compressed. You're out there. Everybody's watching you. You want to stop, think a bit about what you're saying, work out if they like you or not, but there's no time, you just have to press on regardless, and in the end they'll either start clapping or chuck things at you.'

Like most of Upward's opinions about life, or Upward's opinions about comedy, it was hard to know how seriously he meant you to take this. Newspaper articles about 'the secret of laughter' always annoyed him: they struck at the uncertainty which I suppose was his own definition of its mystery.

'Just imagine,' he would say, gloomily, 'how bloody awful it would be if there really was a secret. Suppose Arthur Haynes' (a comedian Upward disliked) 'really did know the trick of telling a joke that made you laugh, every time, bang on the button. Think how tedious it would be. Like asking some absolutely unattainable girl for a shag and knowing all the time that she was going to say "yes".'

For some reason I've always connected these remarks to the atmosphere of Temple Chambers – part of a compound made up of red buses in the Strand, endless marble corridors and the scent of coffee beans. In fact they date from a slightly later period, and in the case of Upward's theories of comedy come from as much as two or three years farther on. Perhaps this is just an example of Upward's ability to impose himself on things, to dominate situations or stretches of time in which he was only fleetingly present. I don't know. At any rate, it was impossible to separate him from Truefitt & Hislop's duck-egg-green carpets, high ceilings and the clogged, blue-grey Embankment skies.

What was I doing in London? For a couple of months after Mary had walked out I hung around in Yarmouth wondering what to do with myself – I had this vague feeling that if I bided my time she'd miraculously turn up on the doorstep again – but in the end I could see it was no good. Even more than that, though, I was tired of Yarmouth and the life I'd been living there all those years. It wasn't dislike – after all, I'd been born there and most of the important things that had happened to me had done so in the couple of square miles between St Nicholas's church and Southtown – just boredom with the gulls and the sight of the pleasure beach ferris wheel looming over the horizon and the eternal smell of salt. God knows there are worse things to smell outside your front door first thing in the morning than salt hanging in the air, but at the time I didn't see it. Maybe if Mother had wanted me to stay I'd have done it, but the truth was that she didn't seem particularly interested. I can remember going over to Uncle Ralph's one night to break the news that I was off, and her staring vaguely at me – Mrs Moss was prowling around in the kitchen as we talked – not really seeming to take it in.

Looking back I'm a bit shocked at how easily this severance was effected. In a way it's proof of how little there was to keep me. For a while I worried what to do about Kenilworth Road, which was still full of stuff the Parmenters had given us. In the end, though, I just sold the furniture off to a secondhand dealer and sent the money to the farm. I can remember standing in the front room after they'd come to take it away with an odd sensation of something lost and irretrievable that I could never call back. A day or so later I went to London, took digs in Hammersmith – they were kept by a dusty old woman who said she'd once been ladies' maid to a duchess – and got the job at Truefitt & Hislop.

Even now I don't quite know why I was so set on the place, wanted to live there or thought it would give me what I wanted. The papers hadn't yet come up with the notion of the 'Swinging Sixties' but already there was an idea that this was the place where smartly dressed blokes were pulling in the big money. I'd absorbed plenty of this kind of propaganda in the back rows of cinemas throughout my teens. Apart from the obvious things, though, I hadn't the faintest idea of what I'd find when I got there. I can remember the first Sunday morning taking a bus into the centre with the aim of finding Chelsea, and getting hopelessly lost somewhere in Kensington, which seemed to be all dingy little squares mouldering in the rain and the shriek of kids playing in the fenced-off gardens.

Once in a blue moon Mother wrote. It was mostly stuff about people in Yarmouth and Uncle Ralph – all the old talk that I'd listened to for years, since before Father died. But at the same time I could tell that something had happened to Mother, that beneath the usual complaints about money and her relatives, she was excited about something in a way that I hadn't ever seen before. It turned out that Mrs Moss's husband had died and she'd proposed that the two of them should set up house together, and Mother, who was heartily sick of cooking Uncle Ralph's meals, was itching to accept. At the same time, Mrs Moss had some harebrained scheme for buying the lease of a cheap shop somewhere in Cromer or Sheringham and setting up as secondhand dealers. They'd even, I later found out, opened a joint bank account in anticipation. Naturally, all this was just nuts to Mother – I think she saw it as a chance to get back within sight of the old life she'd had – but it shocked me in a way. It wasn't just the surprise of Mother being galvanised out of her awful little world of slaving for Uncle Ralph, or the thought of its probable consequences – I had this dreadful vision of Mrs Moss, grinning her deathshead grin, guarding the till of an empty shop crammed with flyblown lumber – as the realisation that nothing was certain any more, that all the fixed points were gone.

Truefitt & Hislop were coffee brokers, with offices in one of those big, labyrinthine buildings between Fleet Street and the river. The *News of the World* was fifty yards away in Bouverie Street and people said that the file of expensively dressed but slightly unreal-looking women you could sometimes see disappearing through its revolving doors were call-girls come to sell their stories. I got the job by replying to a newspaper ad, using a reference that I'd taken the precaution of getting from old Penworthy before I left Yarmouth. Before I arrived I had the idea that the place would simply be an outsize warehouse, but in fact most of the real business got transacted in the London and Commercial salerooms in Mincing Lane where I sometimes got sent on errands. This was an enormous hall where you could buy and sell anything from coffee, cocoa, hemp and jute to exotic stuff like shellac or soya beans. Temple Chambers was where the administrative side went on, and the only clue as to what the firm dealt with was the tray of samples inside the front door.

Even by the standards of the Sixties, Truefitt & Hislop was an old-fashioned concern. The senior partner appeared in a morning suit, and I once saw the office manager – an extraordinary old character named Huckerby – telling off a secretary he'd spotted eating an ice-cream in the street. But I liked the atmosphere in the great silent chambers – and they always were silent, even when a dozen men and women were busily at work – and the people I met there. They were quiet, youngish blokes, mostly, with their sights set on jobs as commodity brokers, who thought this would be a good place to learn the trade. But what really struck me about Truefitt & Hislop was its complete detachment from anything resembling modern life. The Sun Alliance might have been a provincial insurance office with business practices that would have disgraced Mr Gradgrind, but at least the people who worked there knew which decade they lived in, knew, too, of the effort that would be needed to maintain themselves into the next. At Truefitt & Hislop, despite occasional panics over bad harvests in Brazil, the sense of detachment was absolute. I remember seeing one of the junior partners pick up a newspaper a day or so after the 1964 General Election. The City had been in a flap about a Labour victory for nearly a fortnight, there was talk of a run on the pound and money leaving the country, rumours of this agitation had even penetrated as far as Temple Chambers, but no, this young exquisite simply registered the picture of Harold Wilson standing on the steps of Number Ten, sniffed slightly and then flipped the paper over to the sports page. Wilson, you see, was just some dreary little man who'd bamboozled the public into electing him Prime Minister, not someone you could take seriously.

As for the clerical duties required of you at Truefitt & Hislop, these were slightly less arduous than the upkeep of old Penworthy's boxes of address cards. Essentially, as a clerk your job was to file orders as they came in and liaise with the warehouses – these were mostly down by the docks – to make sure that they got filled on time. There was the occasional flap about getting letters ready in time for the early-evening post, but by and large you were left to yourself and provided that you got on with your work nobody took the slightest interest in you. Oddly enough I didn't mind the sense of anonymity that working in a place like Truefitt & Hislop gave you. After what had happened in the last couple of years I was happy enough to be left alone. From a window in the big staff room at the back of the building, which doubled up as a kitchen, there was a view out over the Thames and I used to stand there sometimes in the autumn afternoons as the dusk stole up over Temple Gardens and the lights began to go on along the Embankment, watching the distant passage of the boats. Other times I used to sit on a bench outside the Howard hotel watching the taxis thunder up towards the Strand, interested in the throng of aquarium faces behind their glass. It seems to me that I was perfectly happy. And yet all the time I knew I was waiting for something – I had no idea what it was, simply that it was there – that would swoop down and alter my life for ever.

It was a dull, grey morning in November – not much of a day, I remember – with fine rain falling over the roof of Temple church and its dingy gardens. In the distance a church clock – not Temple, but another one, further away towards Fleet Street – was striking eleven. Time hung heavy at this hour. With the first post sorted and dealt with, there was usually nothing to do until after lunch, sometimes not even then. I used to go and stand in a kind of communal office, halfway between the partners' rooms and the main area where most of the clerks worked, where there was a notice-board and an old jellygraph machine for copying circulars that was always breaking down. I was hanging about here smoking a cigarette and reading an announcement about the firm's Christmas dinner – which sounded a melancholy affair – when another of the clerks, a bloke called Benson, wandered diffidently into view.

'There's a chap wanting you in reception.'

'Someone from London and Commercial?'

An occasional visitor from the saleroom was about the limit of my dealings with the outside world at Truefitt & Hislop.

'Don't think so. Never seen him before. Funny little bloke in a Trilby hat.'

This was unprecedented. I went off in pursuit. To the left of the reception area, always manned by the same grim receptionist, there was a small room where messengers from the warehouses and the other City firms that Truefitt & Hislop 'corresponded' with were sometimes put to wait. Here, behind panelled glass windows, head down over the *Daily Mirror*, a short, squat man with red hair sat smoking a cigarette. It was Upward. Seeing me, he dropped the cigarette into a cup of coffee that rested on the arm of his chair and folded the paper under his arm.

'You took some finding.'

'So did you.'

'I wrote to your mam,' Upward said, a touch accusingly. 'Took near on a year to get a reply.'

'Never mind.'

At twenty-five – which was the age I reckoned him to be – Upward seemed to be hurtling towards middle age. He was fatter than I remembered, and the set of his face was more pronounced than it had been in the Catterick days. He looked – and I'm conscious of thinking this at the time – like a number of things: a prosperous northern businessman in London on a daytrip, a 'likely lad', an extra from an Ealing comedy. All these images were somehow enhanced by the suit he'd got on: a weird, three-piece affair in a dazzling red check. Upward caught me looking at the suit.

'Nice cloth, isn't it? Apparently the Household Cavalry use it for making up hunting caps.'

'It looks like a carpet.'

'I'm thinking of wearing it on stage,' Upward said easily. 'Like Maxie. Look, this is a line of old women in a bus queue, see?'

He went into a kind of crouch and made a few movements that for some reason were extraordinarily like that of someone elderly holding a heavy bag and becoming steadily more irritated by the non-arrival of a bus. I laughed out loud.

'Got to see someone in Aldwych. What time d'you get off for lunch?'

'Half-past twelve. Quarter to one.'

'I'll come back then then. All right?'

'All right.'

We said goodbye at the lift, and I walked back to the room with the notice-board and the jellygraph machine, where a secretary was copying a circular that had something to do with sugar futures – an area in which Truefitt & Hislop took a subsidiary interest: '*beetroot first running 88 per cent analysis f.o.b. Continental parts . . . 96 per cent c.i.f. London/Liverpool*'. I stayed there for over an hour, aware of my surroundings, but mentally detached from everything except the spectacle of Upward standing by the lift shaft in his scarlet suit.

He was waiting in the street when I went downstairs at twelve-thirty. In the interval the wind had caught his hair, lifting it off his head to show the beginnings of a small bald patch beneath.

'You're going bald.'

'Am I?' Upward fingered the crown of his scalp without much interest. The intervening hour seemed to have depressed him a bit, somehow taken the bloom off our reunion. The scarlet suit, I noticed, badly needed brushing.

'See your bloke in Aldwych?'

'Wasn't a bloke.'

Being encouraged to admit that he'd spent the last hour with a woman, however innocuous the meeting might have been, had a galvanising effect on Upward's spirits. His eyes sparkled. He aimed a small, delicate punch at my shoulder.

'Anyway. 'Ow've you been?'

As we walked up the hill towards Fleet Street, past the *News of the World*, where print lorries jockeyed for position and fat men in raincoats clustered on the steps, I started to tell him something about why I'd left Yarmouth, Mary, London, the years that had passed. At intervals Upward nodded or made some barely relevant comment, but I could see that his mind was far off, wrapped up in its own affairs. This, it now seems to me, was completely typical of him. When he sought people out it was because he had something he wanted to say to them, needed an audience. Even now, striding up a London back street with someone he hadn't seen for four years, he was completely self-absorbed, listened out of politeness, waited for the moment when he could unload all the serious business collected in his own head.

There was a pub halfway along Fleet Street, round the corner from the *Daily Telegraph*, called the Cross Keys. It was one of those places – there were dozens of them in the Sixties – supposed to have an 'atmosphere', which in this case meant that bands of journalists hung around drinking brandy and treading their cigarette ends into the dun-coloured carpet. Upward claimed to have eaten an early lunch. I realised this was simply his way of making sure that the conversation proceeded on his lines. Sure enough, while I ate a sandwich, he started on one of the long, disconnected monologues that I remembered from army days, a kind of recapitulation of Upward's life to date in which fantasy, prejudice and fact came uncomfortably mingled together. Even now, over thirty years later, I can remember whole sentences of this harangue, so mesmerising was the way Upward delivered it.

'Had two years of it now, I mean doing it *professional*-like. Up north, mostly. You ever been up north, Ted? Well, y'should. Might teach you a thing or two. I mean, they're still livin' in the Dark Ages compared to, compared to . . .' He stopped and looked round for some point of comparison between northern doughtiness and southern softness, but found only journalists, brandy glasses and cigarette smoke. 'Was stopped on a train near Sheffield, and just to amuse myself I started counting the factory chimneys. Well, I got to thirty-seven before the train went on . . . Staying in the bed and breakfasts, too, boy. That'll show you a bit of life. Chamber pots under the bed, toast like bleeding paving stones . . . You know the one about the black man that walked into a pub in Hartlepool with a parrot on his shoulder? Talking parrot that ordered a pint and asked for a game of cribbage. And so the landlord says, interested-like, "Where did y'get that then?" And the parrot looks down at the black man and says, "There's bleeding hundreds of them in the jungle in Africa . . ."'

There was a lot more of this. Listening to it, I remembered another of Upward's characteristics, his trick of picking up conversations as if they had only just been interrupted, no matter how many hours, or in this case years, lay between them. In the end I lost interest and just stared out of the window, where leaves were blowing along the street and couples with umbrellas picked their way in and out of the traffic, back again at the now deserted bar.

'Sorry if I'm boring you,' Upward said, without irony. 'You know how y'mind runs on when you've not had anybody to talk to. What time is it?'

It was twenty past two.

'I must be getting back.'

'Must you? All right. Well, it's been nice seeing you,' Upward said vaguely.

We picked up our coats and stood for a moment around the bar – horribly bleak and cheerless, it now seemed to me – which contained only the barman polishing glasses, barely visible behind a blanket of smoke. Almost as an afterthought, Upward said:

'Doin' anything tonight?'

'No.' It was the truth, too.

'Well, come here then.' He fished in his pocket and produced a small rectangle of pasteboard. It read: *Minerva Club. London's finest niterie. Eight till late. Members only.*

'What happens at the Minerva Club?'

Upward smiled, a smile I remembered from the platoon details at Catterick – half pleasurable anticipation (things might get better), half gloomy foreboding (things will probably get worse).

'I do, you daft bugger. Arthur Upward entertains. Songs, sketches, jokes old and new. Come about nine.'

'All right.'

Outside in Fleet Street the afternoon was already turning grey. Upward swivelled on his heels, made a mock salute with two fingers against the side of his head, and then plunged off in the direction of the Strand. I waited until he was lost to view before turning back down Bouverie Street to Temple Chambers, where the afternoon post had come in and there was a pile of telephone messages over the desk together with a note from one of the partners asking me to go round to Weingott's in High Holborn to pick up a cigar humidor. For a time I tried to deal with these calls to duty, but it was no good. Something had wound down inside, ground to a halt, that could never be restarted. At the same time, something else had begun to march forward. Whether it was the memory of Upward haranguing me in the filthy pub in Fleet Street or the glimpse of something else beyond it that prompted this, I don't know, but I knew – knew beyond all shadow of a doubt – that my life would never be the same again.

Over the next few months, through a mixture of dropped hints and direct questioning, I managed to work out what Upward had been up to in the four years since we'd last met. Much of it, as he'd maintained, had been spent in the north of England, but not all of it – by no means all – as a professional comedian. So far as I could make out, there'd been one or two precarious periods ('dodgy times', Upward called them) when he'd been reduced to taking clerking jobs, at one point even selling things door-to-door. According to Upward, he had worked successively as a bookie's runner, a bakery assistant, an apprentice barman, a petrol pump attendant, a cinema usher and, finally, as a vacuum cleaner salesman.

For some reason Upward liked talking about his brief career selling vacuum cleaners.

'That was when I realised I had to do something – lugging the things round the back streets, trying to flog 'em to housewives on the never-never.'

'But I thought you said all you needed to sell things door-to-door was patter. Surely you could do that?'

'Aye, but it's *technical* patter ent it? How much dirt it could pick up and how you could poke it under chair covers. There was a bloke in our office who got fascinated by them. You know, so that if ever some woman wanted a demonstration he'd lay all the parts out on the carpet and show how they worked. Got dozens of orders, he did.'

There was a bitterness about Upward as he said this. Failure, even in the comparatively unexalted trade of vacuum cleaner selling, rankled with him.

'I thought being a door-to-door salesman was a good way of picking up women?'

'You thought wrong.'

In the end, however, chance had supervened. Somewhere up north in the course of his travels – Preston? Bolton? Skelmersdale? – Upward had fallen in with an old connection from the Eight Lancashire Lads, who now worked as a booking agent. This man had got him an engagement at a working men's club somewhere else in the north – Accrington? Leeds? Lancaster? – where someone from the northern branch of the BBC Light Programme had happened to hear him. This had led to two or three radio broadcasts, not too badly received, after which Upward had decided to chance his arm in London. By the time we met at Temple Chambers, he'd been there a couple of months.

Three years on the road in the north, whether selling vacuum cleaners or doing stand-up in working men's clubs, had made Upward even tougher, if that was possible, even more self-contained. In the army I'd had the feeling that though he kept himself away from people he was uncertain about them, and that the faintest overture of friendliness would have been returned with interest. All that had gone. In its place came a complete confidence in his abilities, mixed with an eerie single-mindedness over putting those abilities to work. Professionally, too, he'd moved off into different territory, talked about 'reveals' and 'snaps' (a routine where you use a small joke as a stepping stone to the crescendo), and 'holding' an audience. It was from Upward, for instance, that I first got hold of the idea that certain jokes couldn't be used because they were 'too funny'. I don't mind admitting that all this rather frightened me, that whereas in the past I'd been simply admiring of Upward's expertise, now I was rather awed by it, wondering whether it hadn't been achieved at too great a cost, whether the Upward I'd known in the army hadn't been pushed aside by this new, tough-minded intruder. All this, though, lay in the future.

The Minerva turned out to be in Frith Street, stuck between a strip club and a derelict Chinese restaurant. Armed with Upward's card, on which he had scribbled *Please Admit Bearer – A. Upward*, there was no trouble about getting in. Inside the path lay downward and ever downward, along sharply descending passages and flights of stairs, through doorways where burly men in dinner jackets lurked vigilantly, to a kind of cavern far underground containing a dancefloor, a raised stage and a small bar. Twenty feet above, around three sides of the room, a gallery stretched away into darkness. Here at the lower level about thirty people sat at rickety tables grouped round the edge of the dancefloor listening to a florid man in a tuxedo singing a medley of Beatles songs. I had been there less than a minute when Upward came shambling out of a side-door by the corner of the stage and veered over the dancefloor towards me, nearly colliding with a waitress dressed in fishnet stockings and a halter top who was approaching from the other side.

'I should leave the champagne,' Upward said, breathing heavily from the dash across the dancefloor. 'It costs two quid a glass. That's all right darlin'' (to the waitress), 'we'll have a couple of beers.'

We had a couple of beers. Upward drank his in tiny, fastidious sips. Dressed in an evening suit – something I'd never seen him in before – he looked pale, hugely ill at ease.

'Are you all right?'

'Course I'm all right,' Upward said belligerently. He looked around the room once or twice, getting nods from the bar staff and a stout man who stood by the stage. 'Not many here tonight.'

'How many do you usually get?'

'Depends. Fridays and Saturdays are the big nights. That's when you get people down for the weekend. And foreigners. Weekends, like I say, it depends. But it's quality that counts, not quantity. Y'see that bloke over there?' – he motioned up to the gallery, where a grave-looking man in spectacles was reading the *Evening Standard* – 'that's a Labour MP, that is. And them two there' (two crop-haired middle-aged men in raincoats by the bar), 'who d'y' think they are?'

'Peers of the realm?'

'Plain-clothes policemen, more like. Always coming in to see if we're breaking the by-laws.'

'Do you break the by-laws?'

Upward laughed nervously. It was difficult to know what to make of him in this new environment. Above our heads the gallery was filling up.

'Got to go,' he said, after a minute or so of silence. 'On in twenty minutes. You just stay here. Anything you want, ask the waitress.'

I watched him move off across the dancefloor, glance up for a moment at the man in the tuxedo, then disappear.

It was about half-past nine. The man in the tuxedo stopped singing abruptly, lit a cigarette and went over to talk to somebody in the small orchestra at the side of the stage. There was a faint ripple of applause. After a minute or two the orchestra struck up again and a line of chorus girls wearing sequinned skirts and elaborate headdresses – rather like the Variety performers I'd seen in Yarmouth ten years before – emerged stealthily from behind a curtain, and danced up and down while the man in the tuxedo shimmied unconvincingly in their midst. The buzz of conversation, which had lessened a bit while the girls came on, rose again. In the end the girls tramped away. One by one the stage lights were switched off until all that remained was a single spotlight trained on a microphone stand.

From the wings a voice said – slightly resentfully, as if this was a new arrangement, only just introduced to the club – 'Ladies and gentlemen, Arthur Upward!'

Nothing happened. The orchestra launched into a syncopated introduction, kept it up for half-a-dozen bars and then stopped. Somebody dropped a cymbal. Still nothing happened. Finally there was a kind of scuffle in the darkness to the right of the stage which ended with Upward flinging himself – rather than simply moving very fast – at the microphone. I looked at him carefully. Even paler than before, cigarette sticking out of his mouth, dishevelled despite the evening suit, he looked as if he were about to faint.

'She was only an Admiral's daughter,' Upward bellowed in a voice so loud that the microphone hummed with static, 'but she had discharged seamen in her naval base.'

There was silence, then a roar of laughter, which Upward quelled immediately by twisting the microphone off the stand and waving it in front of his face.

'Discharged . . . seamen . . . naval . . . base . . . It's not supposed to be funny you know.'

He was on for about half an hour. It was extraordinarily filthy, far worse than anything you heard then on the radio or the Variety hall stage, delivered with such relentless, machine-gun attack that the effect was simultaneously exhilarating and a bit exhausting. Watching Upward at the microphone stand, you wanted him to slow down, stand back, let other people in on the mystery of his private demons. The audience, I noticed, hardly knew what to make of him. They laughed at the obscenities, but you could see they found the wider spectacle – Upward's white face, jerky movements, hectoring voice – deeply unsettling.

Eventually, at the end of a complicated routine about a lodger and a vegetable marrow, Upward stopped, bowed perfunctorily and left the stage. At the time I wondered whether this was just another element in the air of mystique Upward wanted to drape over his performance. Questioned a day or two later, he put it down to simple boredom and fatigue.

'No, I just got fed up. Had to get off the stage. Happens to you sometimes.'

A bit later, when the man in the tuxedo had returned to the dais to sing 'That'll be the Day', he re-emerged from another door at right-angles to the stage and came slowly over to the table. Arrived there, he stood with his hands pressed together over the back of a chair, moving his feet up and down like an athlete limbering up.

'Why don't you sit down?'

'I can't. It's my nerves.'

Upward's face as he said this was deadly pale. He looked as if he was going to fall over. In the end he managed to lever himself downward on to the chair. A waitress brought more drinks. Upward drank half his off in a gulp.

'What did y'think then?'

'You didn't look as if you enjoyed it very much.'

'No? I suppose not. D'you think the people enjoyed it?'

'A bit. I think they were a bit scared as well.'

'You think so?'

The whole tone of Upward's questioning suddenly changed. Before he'd just been polite. Now, leaning across the table, cuffs of his white evening shirt dropping into the ashtrays, his face was creased with curiosity.

'Well, they're a rotten audience. Rotten. They don't come here to see me.'

'No?'

'Course not. The blokes come here to see if they can pick up the waitresses, or see if one of the chorus'll get her tits out. The women come cos they've been told to. Or to play cards in the back. I'm supposed to keep them *amused*.'

We sat there for a few minutes more as balloons – let slip from a restraining net beneath the rafters – cascaded through the air and collected in droves under the table. Looking back, I'm surprised to find how characteristic the evening was of Upward and the way he behaved. Annoyance, absorption in his audience, interest in technique – all of the things that later became obsessions with him were there in embryo. After a while he pushed his empty beer glass decisively towards the centre of the table.

'Come round the back,' he said. 'There's someone you ought to meet.'

At the outer doorway, where the passage wound on towards the street, there was a kind of cubby-hole, staffed by an immensely tall negro in a dinner jacket. Behind, harsh lighting showed another staircase rising steeply into darkness. Nodding to the negro, Upward took me up to a small landing, around which three or four tiny offices were grouped. In one of these, empty except for a couple of tables and chairs and some crates of beer, a youngish, red-faced man was making calculations in a pocket book. Hearing the noise of our footsteps, he looked up.

'Seen you before, haven't I?'

'Sir.'

Oddly enough, I wasn't in the least surprised to find Captain Groves sitting in a back room at the Minerva Club. It was all part of the net Upward had thrown over the evening, turning it into a sort of alternative world where nothing could take you unawares.

Out of uniform – he was wearing a smoking jacket and a bow tie – he looked younger, a bit fatter too.

'A lot different from when we last met?'

'That's right.'

'Enjoy the show?'

I gave a watered-down version of what I'd told Upward. Captain Groves looked interested.

'Always thinking that myself, you know. Try not to bludgeon your audience. Let them breathe. But Arthur's doing very well. I've the highest hopes for him.'

I took a look at Upward while these compliments were being pronounced. He was standing rigidly to attention, eyes staring blankly at the far wall, thumbs neatly positioned alongside the creases in his trousers. Even here, in the midst of a Soho November evening, it wasn't hard to remember the Catterick parade ground.

Without warning a buzzer on the desk exploded into life. Captain Groves stood up sharply.

'Trouble downstairs. You'll have to excuse me.'

Odd noises sounded in the near distance: a surge of footsteps, what sounded like breaking glass. Upward looked on unconcernedly as Captain Groves disappeared down the staircase.

'What kind of trouble?'

'There's always trouble. I got a bottle chucked at me last week. If you want to run a club in the West End you've got to pay for it.'

'Does Captain Groves own this place?'

'Up to a point. There's a bloke called Cooper hangs about too.'

By this stage we were back in the main body of the club. Here several things were going on simultaneously. Two or three men were scampering across the stage. Another man – the big negro I'd seen on the way up to Groves's office – was sitting next to one of the tables with his head in his hands. Smashed glass lay across the floor. Most of the people had disappeared.

'Let's get out of here,' said Upward matter-of-factly.

He led the way behind the bar to a kind of broom cupboard. Stepping through the door at its rear we found ourselves in the street.

'Does this sort of thing happen quite often?'

'First time in a fortnight,' Upward said.

He didn't seem particularly put out. This, too, I thought was a throwback to his army manner. Somebody would sort something out. The unit Upward had attached himself to would regroup, find a new position. Fresh orders would be issued. It was about ten o'clock, and Frith Street had turned bitterly cold. Beside us, taxis cruised silently past the heaps of piled refuse bags. From the club doorways an occasional tout edged forward, saw the look on Upward's face and edged back again. Twenty yards down the street, Upward stopped suddenly.

'I'm staying just round the corner. You want to come and have a drink?'

By this stage I was aware of feeling incredibly tired. There were a dozen questions that I wanted to ask. A few paces further down the pavement, Upward darted into a tiny alleyway full of entrances encrusted with doorbells. In one of these a steep flight of steps led up to a white-painted door.

'Been here a fortnight,' Upward said, jabbing a key into the lock. 'Best digs I've had in ages.'

Half into the hallway he stopped, overcome by the deluge of flaring light: strip-lights overhead, half-a-dozen table lamps and wall brackets.

'For God's sake, Brenda,' Upward said irritably. 'Turn some of these things off can't you?'

Upward's digs consisted of the largeish main room in which we stood, with a kitchenette in the corner, and a couple of other rooms beyond. In the doorway of one of these a tall girl with untidy blonde hair, wearing a short purple dressing gown, stood over an ironing board.

'Brenda,' Upward said, either introducing her or simply calling her to attention. 'This here's Ted King. That army chap I was telling you about.'

Brenda stared remorselessly back.

'The one you broke into the NAAFI with at Catterick?'

'No, not that one.'

'The one you said owed you two hundred quid?'

'Nor that one neither.'

Upward looked a bit embarrassed at this, probably because it represented a side of his life that I knew nothing about.

'Look,' he said firmly. 'I've got to talk to Ted here. This place looks like a knocking shop. Why don't you go out for a bit? I'll give you some money. Why don't you go to the Tin Tack or somewhere?'

'The Tin Tack doesn't open till eleven.'

'The Coal Hole then,' Upward said, losing his patience. 'Here's twenty quid. Go to the Coal Hole, there's a duck, and come back in an hour.'

Brenda put her head on one side.

'Will *he* still be here?'

'I shouldn't wonder.'

In the end she accepted the four blue five-pound notes that Upward produced from his wallet and went into the bedroom, where – oblivious to the open door – she started to put on some clothes that were lying over the bed. Upward fished out some beer bottles that lay cooling in the sink. A bit later the door slammed.

'Nice girl, Brenda,' Upward said, pouring the beer into tumblers. 'Nowt up top, though. Nowt at all.'

'Do you and she . . .?'

'Oh yes,' Upward said. 'Abso-bloody-lutely.'

I looked at him as he said this. There wasn't a flicker of irony. I realised that this, simply, was the world Upward had moved into, a place where blonde girls in dressing gowns stood over late-night ironings, while their boyfriends told jokes in night-clubs.

'Where did you meet?'

'She works in a club in Meard Street,' Upward said. Obviously Brenda, or at any rate the practical detail of Brenda's life, was of no interest to him. I tried one or two other conversational openings of this sort, but it wasn't any good. Upward wanted to talk about his performance. What did I think of the hurling himself on stage routine? Of the unexpected departure? What about the jokes? Were they too blue? Not blue enough? There was a peculiar intensity about the way he asked these questions. Finally he said:

'Look at these.'

There was a bundle of papers piled on the lip of the ramshackle sofa. Upward picked it up and dropped it into my lap. They were comedy sketches, quite funny ones. I browsed through them for a minute or two.

'Notice anything?'

'They're written for two people.'

'That's right. I need a feed.'

For a second I forgot what the word meant. 'A what?'

'A stooge. Someone to feed the lines. What about you?'

'I couldn't do it.'

'Yes you could.'

'No.'

We looked at each other for a bit.

Upward said: 'At least think about it. You could rehearse. No one'd let you on stage until you were sure of yourself. What have you got to lose?'

'I've got a job.'

'Give it up.'

By then I think each of us knew that though I'd eventually be worn down, it wasn't likely to happen on the spot. Upward looked at his watch.

'Sleep on it,' he said. 'Me, I'm going to bed.'

It was a quarter to midnight, too late to be sure of getting the last tube to Hammersmith. After some discussion Upward made up a bed for me on the sofa. Some time in the small hours Brenda came back and blundered about for a bit in the darkness. I listened to the sound of Upward and her scuffling for a while and then fell asleep.

What's a Greek urn? About seventy-five pounds a week.

Fifty-three years ago this summer, in a café on the front at Blackpool, George Hattersley stood Max Miller a plate of cheese sandwiches. I know this because George has told me. Several times.

'I'm just sitting there, the way you do, and this bloke standing by the till catches my eye and I see it's Maxie. Joke is, 'e's left 'is wallet at the hotel. So of course I say "Anything you like Mr Miller. Be my guest." And Maxie says, "I only came in for a snack. Not a bleeding banquet, you know." Must 'ave stayed talking for 'alf an hour.'

Over the years this tale has grown in the telling, starting off as a hastily borrowed half crown, returned to George that night at his own hotel in a manila envelope, blossoming into a kind of tableau – the famous comedian, publicly embarrassed, the willing acquaintance – ending up as a dramatically outlined double act, the two professionals putting on an impromptu show for the café's startled customers. Curiously, I don't mind these embellishments. The more George tries to evoke this far-off scene, the happier I am.

'But what did he look like? Describe him to me.'

'Maxie? Well, he looked like . . . You must have seen the pictures of him? Jewish, of course. Funny thing was, he only wore them clothes of his on stage. Time I met him he was just wearing a check suit and a Trilby hat. Though come to think of it, 'e had them trousers that roll up to the knee with long socks underneath, what d'you call 'em, plus-fours?'

We're sitting in the main room of George's flat in the sheltered housing complex George inhabits in Walthamstow. Outside the road winds through neatly scalloped grass verges and identikit low-rise bungalows, out of which occasional old folk emerge. On the mantelpiece are framed souvenirs of George's professional career: dinner-jacketed and fancy-tied, taking a bow at the Bristol Hippodrome in 1947, the fourth element in a close-harmony quartet swooping over a BBC microphone sometime in the Fifties. I've an idea that, forty years ago, probably at the Yarmouth Regal alongside Father and Mother, I even saw George perform myself. George is keen to abet this fancy.

'Every chance you did. Every chance. Used to do the eastern circuit. Yarmouth. Norwich. Cromer. Lynn. Three times a year. You *must* have seen me. Must have done.'

It was Lennie who shoved me in George's direction. (*This old bloke, amazing really. Used to know Max Miller and that. Before my time of course. But 'e remembers them all.*) I suppose George must be touching ninety. At any rate he remembers the day the First World War ended, seeing Queen Mary's coach once in Windsor, watching Winston Churchill turn up for the second house at the Holborn Empire in 1941. All this has impressed him in its way. You can tell that he feels it's been quite a romance, his career, that somehow these nine decades or so of English life wouldn't have been quite the same without him in it. He was *there*.

'Shall I get you a cup of tea, George?'

No reply. George has gone to sleep. He does this quite often, chin slumped down on the point of his breast bone, hands gripping the arm-rests of his chair. Knees sticking up towards his shoulders, he looks like an exceptionally frail grasshopper. I stand up to stretch my legs, smelling the room's distinctive smells: camphor, mint humbugs, old blankets, piss. George's wife died in 1978. His children packed him off here a good ten years ago. The idea of George standing in Windsor High Street watching Queen Mary's coach makes me think of Lucy from the BBC. George, undoubtedly, is a person in history. Accounts clerk in the dead 1930s. Turned pro in 1936 ('First night I was due on they closed the theatres on account of the old king dying'), ENSA concerts on Luneberg Heath. But I think Lucy wants something a little more up to date. The questions weren't bad. *Do you believe England is a better place now than when you were a child? What do you believe are the most significant changes to have taken place in English society in your lifetime? Who do you consider to be the politician who has most lived up to his or her promises in the past fifty years?* Plus a neat little note on rose-strewn writing paper conveying the writer's enjoyment of our lunch and looking forward to 'seeing you again'.

I was so amused by the questions – the idea that this kind of thing was even answerable – that I tried them out on Lennie. His answers, for what they're worth, were 'Don't make me laugh', 'The bleeding immigration' and, well, perhaps you can guess the last one. Lennie gave up on politics years ago. The last time he cried, he says, was watching the TV news report on Mrs Thatcher's resignation speech.

Lennie has been following the newspapers this last week. (*Would you believe it? All them blokes with their 'ands in the till?*) DI Stevens was right. Someone – nobody quite knows who – has been singing. The songsheet takes in all manner of familiar names, not heard of in twenty years. The Bank of Bristol. Mayflower. The pyramid selling scam. No one charged as yet, apparently, but then these are old men, ill men, famous men. There was a picture of Sir Gavin Newsome in the *Guardian* the other day: white-haired and stick-tethered at the end of his Surrey drive, shooing away reporters. Cartwright's gone to ground somewhere in Essex. The real interest, as far as I can make out, takes in the plans to buy up a chain of defunct theatres and relaunch them as casinos – fruitless in the end, but leaving mementoes in half-a-dozen south-coast council chambers. Backhanders for planning permission; committee chairmen on the payroll; councillors moonlighting as 'design consultants' – that kind of thing. There was another picture in the *Guardian*, too, next to the one of Sir Gavin (donations to the Conservative Party usefully listed alongside) of a balding man in thick spectacles, remnants of greasy black hair swept back over his head. Cooper, described as an 'entertainment magnate with property interests', didn't look to have changed much. There was some eye-catching stuff about his early-Seventies run-ins with the Obscene Publications Squad.

Lennie was particularly excited at the thought of Cooper's involvement.

'Dennis Cooper? Used to book acts for 'is clubs. Thirty years ago.'

'What kinds of acts, Lennie?'

'Singers. Dancers. What other kinds are there?' When I read him the bit in the paper about 'exotic floorshows' he sniffed a bit. 'You don't want to believe everything you read in the papers, Ted, mate.'

Oddly enough, for a theatrical agent Lennie maintains quite a high moral tone. (*Nah, I don't hold with it, all them girls showing off their tits.*) His idea of smut is Barbara Windsor in the *Carry On* films.

Outside the rain falls. A big Jaguar is nosing slowly through the tiny streets of this old persons' toytown, sending water spraying over the verges. George's eyes open and he blinks once or twice, startled by everything – gas fire glowing by his knees, family photos, silent visitor.

'I didn't think you were coming today,' he says.

'You were telling me about Maxie.'

'Maxie?'

'Max Miller.'

The Ngongi have a tradition of extending respect to their elders: the toothless jaws gibbering in the firelight; the line of dutiful faces. If this were equatorial Guinea George would be telling me about the lion hunts of his youth. As it is he is telling me about Max Miller. Twenty minutes later I leave him hunched over a cup of tea, face wreathed in steam, like an old wizard inspecting the latest draught from his protégé's cauldron.

'I like your house,' Lucy says.

Seated in the front room, workbag drawn up on her knees, Lucy has the inquisitive look women assume when they come to survey single men's houses. I can remember Paula putting it on a quarter of a century ago: the urge to throw open cupboards, alter the alignment of curtains.

'It hasn't been lived in a great deal recently.'

'You could do a lot with it,' she says.

Here on a visit, the space between us has lessened a bit. In particular, the fantastic unfamiliarity I'd diagnosed on our first meeting had cracked into more recognisable shapes. Among other things, it turns out that Lucy comes originally from Norfolk – Holt, on the other side of the county. Sitting on the sofa, turning over the copy of *Nintendo Warrior* bought as a present for Daniel, she looks less like a BBC ice-maiden and more elfin – the kind of girl who wouldn't have seemed out of place on the end of the TV dance troupes twenty years ago.

'Anyway,' she says. 'You can see from the running order which clips we're using. Still no sign of anything from Mrs Upward?'

'She was never the greatest correspondent. I'll try again if you like.'

'Only Graham' – Graham is the producer – 'is keen that we try all the angles, get as big a context as possible.'

Even now, the stuff about angles and contexts bothers me a bit. Lucy, I can see, has run through the tapes of the *Upward & King Show* and the radio programmes from thirty years ago and found something symbolic. Or if not symbolic then connected to time in a way that I can't see. Upward, for instance, always maintained that he hadn't any particular grudge against Harold Wilson, was even prepared to vote for him, simply found him funny.

'When do you want to do the interview?'

'Next week sometime?'

Lucy, on her own admission, is thirty-seven. There has been a lot less recently about the boyfriend and the house in Putney. Presumably even girls of thirty-seven feel their age, see the conveyor-belt of their future stretching out ahead. Once or twice, I notice, she gives me a look of what can only be shyness, a vulnerability drawn from an older world that she no longer inhabits.

'Where's Daniel? I must give him his magazine.'

'He's upstairs somewhere.'

Standing in the hall I shout up the stairs a couple of times. There is no response: Daniel takes fright at visitors.

'Never mind. You can give it to him for me.'

What sort of life does Lucy live? What does she do in the house in Putney? Always with women, even with professional helpmeets like Lucy, I've made phantoms I could later chase – images of things, known and unknown, tracked back across their lives. Lucy must have been to college. What did she do there? How have the intervening fifteen years in London passed? For some reason I badly want to know. Thinking about it, its secrets and mysteries, its dawns and departures, makes me unexpectedly miserable.

'I'd better go,' Lucy says. 'Stuff to do back at the office. I'll ring with a progress report in a day or so.'

Suddenly, not quite knowing where the impetus comes from, I find myself suggesting we have lunch again. Unexpectedly, Lucy assents. From the window I watch her moving away along the street, oddly purposeful and determined. On cue, Daniel appears in the doorway.

'Who was that?'

'Just someone to do with work. Look, she brought you a present.'

Daniel stares at the magazine. 'Why did she give me that when she's never met me?'

'I don't know. Perhaps she's just interested.'

The year Lucy was born was the year I met Mary. When she was at primary school I was doing cabaret in Soho. I think about these things as I cook Daniel's tea: sausages, chips and beans. Krieger, whom I have consulted, says that a growing ten-year-old needs all the carbohydrates you can throw into him.

. . . As for what makes Upward & King *funny*, the answer is as indefinable as in any other comic medium. Part of it is their grounding in the old atmosphere of the Variety halls, the way in which, as they advance to the front of the stage, at least half of their gaze seems to be concentrated on ghostly rows of faces above and beyond the studio audience. A great deal more lies in the rich vein of near-surrealist whimsy tapped in every third or fourth sketch: Upward fancying himself pursued by a giant bee; King filing outlandish expenses claims ('Six elephant's foot wastepaper baskets') matter-of-factly on his tax return; the two of them embarked on a kind of endless, absurdist dialogue between a shop proprietor and his customer, where the exceptionally alert viewer might just discern that the matter in hand had something to do with money for the Christmas Club. They did a marvellous sketch set at a doctor's surgery, another one featuring Harold Wilson as a seedy prep school master trying vainly to quell the irruptions of his class ('Now, just be quiet young Benn, d'y' hear?' etc.). Inevitably, physical and vocal dissimilarities give these exchanges their bite: Upward short, burly, pugnacious; King tall, saturnine, pacific; the one urgent and loquacious, the other restrained and reticent. If I had to find a single word capable of supplying the essence of their performance, that word would be *tension*, the tension that exists between two people who, broadly speaking, like each other, each of whom is sometimes exasperated beyond measure by the other's behaviour. King's interventions in Upward's by now trademarked monologues about girls are a pattern example of this: barely disguised resentment that altogether fails to conceal ruefulness at his own lack of success, while contriving, with lavish subtlety, to puncture each revelation as it looms up before him . . .

Kenneth Tynan, *Observer*, 1973

Frith Street

Waking at half-past five, even in the depths of winter, the first thing you became aware of was the shouts from the street, near at hand but strangely subdued – like drowning men summoning their last energies before disappearing beneath the waves. These came from the drunks stumbling home from the drinking clubs. Before this came the noise of the refuse carts, which I was never awake to hear. From six to half-past it was more or less quiet, apart from the whirr of an occasional milk float, but by seven the street would be alive with the sound of footsteps, tradesmen taking down shutters, lorries reversing into the narrow alleyways. Upward – not the only one – resented the twenty-four-hour quality the place seemed to possess. Up half the night, rarely in bed before three, he used to spend most of his afternoons asleep, sometimes in bed, more often than not simply collapsing on the sofa in the corner of the rehearsal room.

It's odd how you can turn nostalgic over somewhere as battered and tuppence-coloured as Soho. I can't have lived there for more than eighteen months, but for some reason the place is as vivid to me as the front room in Southtown, or Yarmouth harbour, and if you put me down blindfolded at the end of Old Compton Street I could probably find my way to the French Pub or the Colony Room or half-a-dozen other places where I used to spend my time. Dean Street! Berwick Street market! I don't suppose they mean much to you, but for about a year and a half they marked the boundaries of the world I lived in. There was a run-down café where I used to have breakfast – Café Continental, I think it was called – at the top end of Frith Street, and I can remember the inside even now: the squares of mirror stuck on odd places over the walls, the steaming urns and old Walenski, who owned the place, sitting at the back reading a copy of *Polska!*

It was a strange time to be around in Frith Street, Brewer Street and the square mile or so of back-alleys and tumbledown mews where I spent most of my time. In theory Soho was still 'respectable'. There were strange old shops which looked as if they'd been there for a hundred years; the streets were full of tiny family firms who made violins or bound books; but everyone knew that the rents were rising and the crooks were moving in. People used to talk about the old villains of the Fifties – Melvin and Muller, Jack Spot and Billy Hill – with a sort of nostalgia, merely because they weren't the sort to throw paraffin heaters through shopkeepers' windows, which was the favourite trick of the Maltese gangs (whom everyone called 'Maltesers') from Wardour Street. Not that this meant very much to me, of course. The closest I got to a gang fight was having Reggie Kray pointed out to me once in a club in Greek Street.

It took only a couple of days hanging around with Upward to establish that the Minerva was not exactly a brothel – there was hardly such a place in Soho – but a well-known resort of prostitutes. The 'girls' – there were about a dozen of them, ranging in age from seventeen to an extraordinary old crone who claimed to remember Armistice Night – all had rooms in the nearby streets, which meant that Captain Groves couldn't be charged with running a disorderly house. I think his percentage was seventy per cent, and he wasn't above sending stooges along to make sure he wasn't getting short-changed. Apparently, just before my arrival there'd been some police trouble, but Captain Groves had smoothed it over somehow – being called Captain Groves helped, of course – and before very long he started expanding. There were a couple of drinking clubs he owned in Meard Street (which informed judges maintained was the worst street in Soho) and a restaurant up near the Square. I suppose in retrospect I'm a bit shocked to have been wandering around on the fringes of all this, but at the time I don't think the morality of it bothered me very much. I'd found something I wanted to do, and the fact that it took place in a hole in the ground in Frith Street where people went to pick up women was the price you paid for being a beginner. There was also the fact that, outwardly at any rate, it was difficult to see what all the fuss was about. I'd been brought up in Great Yarmouth, where the watch committee would have a fit if anyone had tried to stage what was then known as 'indecent dancing'. Here I was in what Father and Mother would have marked down unhesitatingly as a den of vice, and yet apart from the fact that some of the girls weren't wearing very much it was all horribly ordinary: men in evening suits with those frilly collars, 'hostesses' sipping Coca-Cola at a guinea a glass (whatever they left of it was poured straight back into the bottle), Frank the barman's head bobbing up from behind the soda siphons to keep an eye on the drunks. Later, of course, I found out about some of the things that went on beneath the surface, but by that time I was getting ready to leave the place and it could all be washed away, rather like the glitter powder some of the hostesses dusted into their hair, which got everywhere in the club and stuck to your hands at all times.

I suppose if I'd been the carefree spirit Upward hoped I was I'd have chucked in my job on the spot. As it was I spent another three weeks at Truefitt & Hislop working out my notice. Upward, though he accepted this, was contemptuous of the attitudes he thought it reflected.

'The trouble with you,' he used to say, 'is that you're too bloody middle-class. Seeing out your time for a bunch of shit-stabbers who couldn't care less whether you stay or go. The idea!'

He was right, of course. God knows what Father and Mother would have thought if they knew I'd thrown over a job without abiding by the statutory conditions. Those last three weeks were the time I enjoyed most – watching the light fade across the Thames, or dodging the buses in Fleet Street. In the pub on the last afternoon I let on that I'd got another clerking job somewhere in the City. Three days later, with a suitcase in each hand and £200 in my wallet – my entire savings – I was walking up Frith Street towards Upward's flat.

Queerly enough, quite a lot survives from that period – I mean actual sketches that eventually resurfaced on radio or TV. The one about the two men on the life-raft was written maybe a week or two after I'd turned up. And there's a piece about a bloke taking his dog to the vet that later went through endless rewrites and restagings but probably has its origins back there. All this time, of course, Upward was still doing his one-man show at the Minerva, but in the afternoons we used to rehearse in an old, high-ceilinged room on the top floor of a house in Lexington Street. Some of my sharpest memories of Upward are from that time – seeing him in the doorway, red-faced and furious, rubbing his hands against the cold, or bent over one of the old packing cases with which the room was littered with a cigarette in his mouth striking out a line of dialogue in the script. At the outset I'd been worried that it would collapse around my ears, that having found me again Upward would throw me aside the instant he discovered I wasn't up to his own lightning pace. Gratifyingly, this didn't happen. All the same I don't think I ever quite worked Upward out, established what it was he wanted from me, how he thought I might provide it. He had fixed routines – lumbering round the room for an hour or more in silence until his mind got going, vanishing on odd errands I was never party to. 'Got to go out', 'Got to see a man', 'Something to pick up'. Sometimes Brenda would come and collect him – a subdued-looking Brenda in slacks and a pastel-coloured raincoat – and they'd disappear somewhere, leaving me in the empty room with its view out over the rooftops towards Regent Street, and the single-bar electric heater.

It was the same at the flat, where I spent a week kipping on the sofa before Captain Groves fixed me up with a room in Carlisle Street. In the army I'd had a fair sight of Upward's temperament, but it wasn't until I lived with him that I cottoned on to his utter gloominess, an awful depression of spirit that caught up everyone around him and eventually had them playing bit parts in a kind of tragic drama of which Upward was the undisputed star. In the mornings, while Brenda hustled round the flat in her dressing gown making vague efforts to 'tidy the place up' and I read the paper, he'd sprawl in one of the armchairs with his hands behind his back, not saying a word.

What puzzled me about these fits of gloom was their complete lack of connection to the patterns of Upward's life. I'd known melancholics before – Yarmouth had been full of grim little men fretting themselves behind shop counters or office desks – but in each case there'd been some explanation to hand, some basis on which this dissatisfaction with environment could be teased out. Upward's dejection, it seemed to me, was much more deep-set, in fact practically cosmic, never alleviated by conventional prods to the ego – money, comfort, a good audience – occasionally terrifying in its intensity. Even odder, perhaps, was Upward's habit of being cheered up by things going wrong. A heckler booing one of his jokes, a row with Brenda – these happened about once a week – a financial crisis: all these turned him unexpectedly gleeful. I was halfway up the stairs to the flat one afternoon when there was a loud crash, followed by the spectacle of Brenda, wild-haired and with a coat flung over her shoulder, in flight towards the street door. Inside I found Upward kneeling on the hearthrug sweeping glass – quite a lot of glass – into a dustpan.

'Christ!' he said savagely. 'D'y' know what that mad bitch has just done?'

'No.'

'Chucked a fucking table lamp at me, that's all.'

There was no mistaking the note of exaltation in his voice. It had been there at Catterick when the PE sergeant had broken his collar-bone. There was no doubt about it. Upward liked having table lamps thrown at him, liked noise, upset, passionate arguments, bitter reconciliations. The smashed glass lay in a heap on the carpet for a fortnight.

As for Brenda, there was no getting away from Upward's original judgement. She was quite the stupidest girl I'd met in my life. At first, confronted with Brenda's ignorance over who was Chancellor of the Exchequer or how to send a telegram, I'd marked her down as residing in the same category as the Parmenters, but this, I soon saw, was a mistake. The Parmenters, not counting Horace, were merely badly informed, and if a piece of information looked as if it might be useful to them they remembered it. Brenda, on the other hand, was simply stupendously, invincibly ignorant. It used to puzzle me how a woman could exist in the second half of the twentieth century on the mental resources Brenda had at her disposal, but she managed it somehow. She could just about read, but arithmetic, geography – any kind of calculation – was more or less beyond her. Upward, who had a sadistic streak where Brenda was concerned, wasn't above exploiting these weaknesses by way of ghastly, unsparing question and answer sessions.

'Now Brenda, lass, here's a question for y'. What's the capital of France?'

'Don't know.'

'If you wanted to go to America, how would you get there?'

'Ask you and you'd take me.'

I used to look at Brenda's face sometimes during these interrogations, but it was devoid of feeling. You could see that at periods in her life, various people – parents, schoolteachers perhaps – had tried to engage her in these strange rituals, and she'd decided that this was the only way of keeping her dignity.

'You oughtn't to talk to her like that,' I told Upward one time.

'Why not?'

'It's humiliating for her.'

'No it isn't. You'd be surprised how much she likes it. Likes me talking to her, that is.'

There was something in this. When not throwing table lamps at him, Brenda was devoted to Upward. She spent long hours in the shops in Carnaby Street buying him presents. Upward, I noticed, never knew how to respond to these gifts, usually ostentatious bits of clothing that showed no understanding of the things he liked to wear.

'Christ,' he would say later, staring at some magenta waistcoat or a pair of yellow wash-leather gloves. 'What am I supposed to do with this? Hang it on a bleeding flagpole?'

At the same time he was genuinely glad to receive them. I've an idea that in sketching Upward's relations with Brenda through dialogue, I'm in danger of misrepresenting them, conveying only the patronage at the expense of other currents running deep beneath the surface. Probably that was how Upward wanted it. For her part, Brenda was capable of the most fantastic projections of their life together. There was one extraordinary conversation along these lines that took place about a month after I arrived in Frith Street.

'Do you think Arthur's going to make a success of this comedy thing?'

'I shouldn't wonder.'

Brenda had a trick of shooting out more or less unanswerable questions at random: 'Do you think it will rain on Sunday?' 'Why do Chelsea play in blue?'

'You'd be surprised how serious he takes it. All day in that rehearsal room.'

It was about six o'clock on a January evening – mid-morning, Soho-time – and we were alone in the flat. Upward had disappeared on one of his errands. Outside snow was falling gently over the tops of the surrounding houses. Abruptly Brenda changed tack.

'Snow always makes me feel sad,' she volunteered.

'Does it?'

'That's right. It makes me remember when I was a little girl.'

Somehow there was no way of entering into this, of working out what Brenda might have been like as a little girl. She got up from her chair, picked up a pile of clothes that lay on the sofa, rearranged them to her satisfaction, and sat down again.

'Do you know what we're going to do when Arthur's made his money?'

'No idea.'

'Open a hotel.'

'A what?'

'Open a hotel. Up north. Manchester maybe, or Leeds. Not commercial travellers or anything. You know, a *posh* place.'

Of all the things Brenda had said to me in the month or so that I'd known her – and she was a confidential girl – this was by some way the most bizarre, so outlandish as to be practically unreal. I hadn't any idea what to say.

'A posh hotel?'

'That's right. We've often talked about it. Two dozen beds, say. Arthur'd work out front, I'd be in charge of the kitchen and that.'

For some reason I assumed this was one of Brenda's momentary whims. These were quite common – to be snuffed out by a word from Upward or a second thought. In this case, nothing could have been further from the truth. For the next ten minutes, while the snow fell over the rooftops and car-horns sounded in the street below, Brenda talked about the hotel. She did this with utter seriousness. There could be no doubt she believed it would happen:

'Not too grand to begin with, of course . . . a *French* restaurant, that's what people like these days isn't it? . . . Cotton sheets, not those nylon things . . . Dancing on Saturday nights . . . None of them unmarried couples coming in with fake wedding rings . . .'

Eventually Brenda stopped.

'When it's finished,' she said, 'when it's all done, Arthur and me'd take it kindly if you'd come and stay with us.'

'Thank you.'

'There wouldn't be a charge, of course.'

'No.'

Upward came back at eight, frowning, with the faintest suspicion of a bruise above his left temple. Later on Brenda and I went to see him at the Minerva. Nothing more was ever said about the hotel.

So you can see, it was an odd kind of life I was leading here in the mid-Sixties in Frith Street: mornings spent frowsting in my room in Carlisle Street (it was above a butcher's shop and in summer the stink from the bins filled the house); afternoons rehearsing with Upward; evenings at the flat with Brenda or at the club. Small things and big things came mixed together. Churchill died, and even the dirty bookshops closed down for a couple of hours and Captain Groves shut the Minerva for the day as a mark of respect. Apparently he and Churchill had been to the same school. The £200 I'd brought with me from Hammersmith was dwindling away now, but after a bit Captain Groves gave me a job helping out behind the bar, which basically meant making sure the hostesses were ordering enough drinks, and bringing up crates of brown ale from the cellar. A while later I was promoted to what was known as 'liaison man' (Captain Groves ran the place on military lines), which consisted of ferrying messages from the bouncers out on the door to the main office, keeping an eye on the people in the main body of the club and lending a hand when things got nasty. Once or twice I've tried to imagine the person I was in those days, tried to work out what I was like and what went on in my head, but I never got very far. A photo or two survives from that time – on the steps of the Minerva, with a ferocious crew-cut (long hair hadn't quite come in by then) and a Crombie coat, alongside Upward in a pavement café somewhere – but they don't amount to much. I turned twenty-five that year, which back in Yarmouth would have had people muttering about what you were 'doing with your life', but that didn't worry me in the least. I was gripped by the oddest feeling of exhilaration, of doing something I liked, and not worrying about what Father or Mother or anyone else thought, and not caring a damn about the future. It used to astonish me sometimes. Two years before I'd been glooming away at Kenilworth Road, and now here I was in a dinner jacket with my hair smarmed up in little wrinkles on the top of my head telling fruity-voiced old blokes and women with a thousand pounds' worth of jewellery round their necks where they could leave their coats. There were women, too, half-a-dozen of them at least: cashiers, receptionists, dancers – the kind of girls Soho was full of in those days. I can remember taking the first of them, a blonde girl whose name I can't even recall, back to the room in Carlisle Street, getting her clothes off and then falling on her in a kind of frenzy, I was so desperate. As for the others, all that remains is a jumble of fragments: a girl called Alice who worked in a club in Brewer Street standing stark naked over a chest of drawers searching for a packet of cigarettes; black sheets on a bed belonging to a woman called Selina who was probably a tart, though I didn't enquire at the time; rain falling on a window somewhere near Soho Square. I'm not proud of this, and I don't recall there being very much pleasure in it, but I remember having a kind of feeling that it was something I had to do, a way of getting rid of Mary and all the other ghosts from long ago.

In any case, all this was much less important to me than the real business of Upward and the rehearsal room. I don't think I could ever quite convey the excitement of those winter afternoons in 1965, with the electric fire gleaming through the murk and footsteps clanging on the wooden stairs outside. At first I'd just assumed that Upward wanted me for the role of straight man, the stooge who offers lines to the comic and gets annihilated in return. It turned out, though, that he had something more ambitious in mind. Comedy double acts in those days operated on a rigid formula: the 'lead', usually small and bumptious, and the stooge, usually taller, or at any rate physically differentiated in some way. The stooge's job was simply to volunteer lines of varying degrees of innocuousness, and give the lead a chance to score off him. At its most basic level – the kind of thing you saw at the Yarmouth Regal – this would find the stooge saying, in a faintly lugubrious way, 'Turned out nice again today', so that the lead could immediately turn it into a put-down: 'Pity you couldn't turn out nice again to match it.' This always got a laugh. At the same time it encouraged the audience to side with the lead, the 'smart man' who was running rings round his lead-booted adversary. Upward's idea was that the stooge, if not actually undermining the lead's jokes, should be nearer to his fighting weight, certainly capable of challenging his pretensions, sometimes overthrowing them altogether. There was a whole range of sketches, loosely titled 'Talking about girls', that followed this blueprint – Upward blustering, contemptuous and superior, gradually being brought down to earth.

UPWARD: Saw you with that Alice Hackthorpe the other night.
KING (*shyly*): She's my girlfriend.
UPWARD: Oh yes! Does she know?
KING (*slow on the uptake*): Does she know what?
UPWARD: That she's your girlfriend.
KING (*hurt*): Of course she knows . . . She knows more than you think . . . I bet she knows more than you know.
UPWARD (*outraged*): Knows more than I know? Let me tell you, there's not many people know as much as I know . . . For instance, did you know that the capital of Ecuador is Quito? There's professors of Geography at Oxford University don't know that.
KING (*obligingly*): There's people living in Ecuador don't know that.
UPWARD: What?
KING: Hundreds and thousands of them. Never done geography. Sad, isn't it?

The ending was typical of the way Upward worked. In his solo show at the Minerva, whenever the audience turned restive or a gag looked as if it was about to fail, he'd shout out something like, 'Look at that pink rat over by the fire escape', or pick some woman near the front and yell: 'It's all right love, there's just the two of us. Give me a moment to put my trousers on and I'll be with you.' This might not raise a laugh, but it always got people's attention. For all these attempts to subvert the usual patterns of cross-talk, I knew that once we got on stage it was Upward who would carry us. Permanently aggrieved, put-upon, bouncing with conceit, a bit like Hancock but angrier, tougher, he was the kind of comedian people laugh at on sight, who then makes himself funnier by seeming to hate himself for raising the initial laugh. An early sketch that we didn't perform much – it needed too many props and assistants – always seemed to symbolise this talent for comic exasperation. It took place in a police station where a detective (Upward) was preparing to interview a suspect (me). Leading the suspect into the interview room, Upward discovers that the electric light has failed. They find a second room. After ten seconds the second light fails and plunges the room into darkness. In a third, the table at which the suspect sits suddenly collapses. The sketch ends with Upward calling for a toolbox and making repairs while continuing to ask questions: 'So where were you on the night of the 13th?' (*bang*) 'Just look in that box and see if there's a nail, will you?' etc. No one watching it could doubt that Upward really was cross, or that the properties of a comedy sketch hadn't ignited some wider anger – a universal dissatisfaction, practically, deep inside him. There was a sense of relief when it was all over. You felt – something Captain Groves once said, watching from the wings – that it was all a bit much, faintly exhausting. Oddly I remember much more about Upward in the act of performing than off-stage – standing there pale-faced under the arc light with the sweat pouring off his forehead, tossing the microphone anxiously from one hand to the other. Given what happened later, perhaps that's not such a bad thing.

Mother died in the spring of 1965. I hadn't even known she'd been ill. There was a mix-up in forwarding letters from the old address – I'd moved out of Carlisle Street by this stage – and I didn't find out until a week later. By the time I got through to Uncle Ralph's on the phone they were already clearing up after the funeral. I wonder if you can imagine how I felt about that? Mother dead, and me not even there to stand over her grave? But it was all par for the course for our family. No one at Uncle Ralph's would have had the first idea of how to go about getting in touch with me in London, and I suppose it was my fault for not keeping better contact.

It turned out that she'd died of heart failure. I don't mind telling you that Mother's death cut me up. I hadn't seen her for a bit, but every so often there'd be a letter, usually about the shop and Mrs Moss and how the council wouldn't let them display the bigger stuff out on the pavement, and I'd kind of gathered, reading between the lines, that Mother was having the time of her life. Yarmouth, when I got there a day or so after the funeral, seemed a bit smaller than I remembered, and even more flyblown, and I recall walking around the streets in a new suit I rather fancied myself in – it had very slight bell-bottoms, which were all the rage just then – hoping to meet someone I knew but not finding anyone, and noticing the changes since I'd last been there. The square was much the same, except that Wedderbury's had sold out to one of the big outfitting chains, and Father's shop was a kind of ice-cream parlour. I remember standing there for a long time under one of the beech trees – they'd grown to an enormous size and badly needed pruning – smoking cigarettes, admiring the bell-bottoms of my trousers, but somehow seeing Father's face like a ghost in what had been the shop window as he bent over the till or weighed out sweets into a paper bag, and thinking, of all things, of the day – it would have been thirteen years before, now – that Betty disappeared.

After a bit I cheered up slightly and went round to Uncle Ralph's. He'd gone out somewhere, but one of his daughters, Aunt Hilda, whom I hadn't seen for six or seven years, was there hoovering the front-room carpet in a vague kind of way. She was a gaunt, stringy woman with her hair perpetually done up in curlers whom I don't suppose I'd ever really exchanged a word with, but she seemed happy enough to see me, launched into a detailed account of Mother's last days and eventually took me upstairs with the idea of going through Mother's things. There wasn't a great deal to see. All the clothes I told Aunt Hilda she could keep or chuck out as she wanted to. Mother's secret vice was revealed in the pile of paperback novels with titles like *Hawaiian Romance* hidden under the bed. The other things – odd bits of jewellery, an old diary or two and a photograph album – barely filled a carrier bag. I stuffed this under my arm and went off into the centre of Gorleston with a definite idea of having a talk with Mrs Moss, but somehow I couldn't face it. I got as far as the shop – it was a bit more superior than Mother had let on, and there was a sign advertising 'Teas and light refreshments' – and then stopped. I could see Mrs Moss by the till talking to someone and looking more than ever like a deathshead, and I've an idea that she even glimpsed me through the window, but in the end my courage simply failed me. Somehow the thought of standing there amid the dirt and the mothballs talking about Mother with old Moss while people came in and haggled over dirty mattresses was more than I could bear, and I slunk off to the cemetery, where it was raining and the entranceway was blocked by half-a-dozen black Daimlers carrying the mourning party of some Yarmouth councillor who'd died that week (I'd read about this in the *Mercury* at Uncle Ralph's). They'd buried Mother alongside Father, and someone had added 'Eunice Mary, loving wife of the above' and her dates further down his headstone. It was raining pretty hard by now, but I stood there for half an hour or so while Alderman Bumstead's interment went on ten yards away and some workmen came and started on another grave in the next row, listening to the noise of the sea booming in the distance and somehow seeing Mother's face there amidst the newly cut flowers, the bright grass and the dripping trees.

Later in the train I turned the contents of the carrier bag out on to the spare seat beside me piece by piece. There wasn't much, and what there was was the kind of stuff you wondered about. Why had Mother wanted to keep a brown envelope containing a packet of beads and a Union Jack button? The photo album I remembered from childhood, and it didn't seem to have been added to since then, although there was an odd, grainy picture of Father and Mother from quite late on in the murk of Uncle Ralph's front room, with Father looking kind of dreary and faded behind the *Mercury*. In the past they'd sometimes talked about letters that Father had sent home during the war. There was no sign of these. The diaries were standard Letts' 'commercials' from the early Fifties, stamped with the name of Smith Brothers, who were the big wholesale grocers in town, and whose boss Father might just have known at the Buffaloes. They weren't much more than three inches square, with four or five lines available for each day, but beneath the reminders of *Annunciation of BVM* and *Maundy Thursday*, and *Dividends due* Mother had scratched in a telegraphic account of her life in the back-parlour at Southtown. It took me a minute or two to penetrate the particular shorthand she used for this task – Father was 'F', for instance, I was 'T', while the shop was 'S' or simply 'it'. A typical entry might go: *Van came at 8. Boxes all over street: Mr H not pleased* ('Mr H' would have been Mr Hargraves, the sub-postmaster). *F worried about it. Fixing up to see bank again. T in new uniform. Back late from school.* Or: *Picnic on dunes. T upset about something. F up late doing books. Nice day.* Christ! I remembered that day – the trek to the beach with our lunch done up in paper bags, the endless search for a spot 'out of the wind', Father's pale face as he champed his sandwiches and the breeze flattening the coarse grass. God knows what I was upset about, but reading this brought it all back. The effect was unexpectedly shocking – not just to have bits of your life set out before you, but the fact that Mother had done it at all. In all the years I'd known her I'd never twigged she'd kept a diary, and it wouldn't have surprised me if Father hadn't either. The last volume dated from 1956. Inevitably it was all about the shop, the bank, the wholesalers stopping deliveries and 'F' being 'very worried'. *Letter this morning. Don't know what we shall do. T to school to do exam. Geography, he said.* I remembered that morning, too: half the shop's stock piled up in the middle of the floor, Mother in tears and an atmosphere you could have cut with a bread-knife.

The train rattled through Ipswich and the Suffolk market towns, over the Stour and the huge expanse of black marsh with curlews picking at the water's edge, on into Essex, but I kept on reading. It was like a drug: Father, Mother and the old days, with the rain falling over the square and the lights going on in Wedderbury's, and the boys coming round delivering the evening paper, and Mother's voice in the yard and the smell from the bakery. Heaven knows I wasn't sentimental about it, but it made me think about

Father and Mother in a way I hadn't done for years. I don't believe I reached any startling conclusions about them – except that Mother's urge to set things down on paper revealed a side to her that I'd never known about – I just felt a bit guilty about all that misery burning itself out in the parlour behind the shop while I went around chasing girls and nagging Father and Mother for extra pocket-money. It's what children do, of course, but it doesn't help to have it explained to you. But there it was, Mother was dead – her last few months hadn't been too bad from the sound of it – and Father too, there was nothing to be done, nobody could ever come into Lutterworth's again in search of a packet of Player's Navy Cut, and the whole thing was over. The carriage was starting to fill up by now – it was late afternoon on a Friday with people heading up to town – and in the end I put the things back in the bag and started thinking about the weekend, when Upward and I were actually going on stage together for the first time, and praying that it would be all right. I knew, you see, that these were old ghosts, and that though they'd come to haunt me from time to time the old world – Father, Mother, Yarmouth, even Mary and the Parmenters – was gone for ever.

Curiously enough, though I hadn't told anyone the time of the train, Upward and Brenda were there to meet me at the station. I remember it as a typical Upward moment, typical of the way he did things, the impression he wanted to create, the eventual sacrifice of everything to his own egotism: the handshake in the dusk of Liverpool Street, the pat on the back –

'You all right?'

'Yes.'

'It go okay?'

'More or less.'

It's all mixed up in my mind with the trip back across London in the Friday-night crowds, Brenda loitering behind us to look at the ads on the tube, Frith Street, and posters stuck to one side of the Minerva's battered door announcing the first public performance of 'Upward & King'.

My dreams are keeping me awake. Father and Mother back in the shop with the blinds drawn down and yellow light winking off the surfaces. Flat, even fields with distant sea. Waking up at these times – three or four a.m. – in silence except for the far-off traffic noise, the room seems too small, airless, fenced in. Members of the Ngongi, fetched up in cities or dragooned into the medical centres, will often be found at night straining at the walls that surround them. They think they're slowly moving forward to crush them, apparently.

Daniel sleeps uneasily too. Whatever he dreams rolls up to the surface and pulls him awake. Sometimes he drifts into my room and stands there by the bed, a quarter conscious. He has this curious, fresh, little boy smell – warm and somehow nourishing. Once, at one of these times, he said:

'Am I going back to live with Aunty Shena soon?'

'Soon.'

'After Christmas?'

'Probably.'

This is not a lie. Not necessarily. Who knows what will happen? Another letter came yesterday, on whose top left-hand corner someone had gone to the trouble of writing URGENT PLEASE OPEN THIS. I didn't open it. Urgency, as Upward often used to say, means different things to different people.

Kev and I are mates now. Big mates. We shout 'how do?' and 'all right?' madly to each other across the asphalt, have matey halves of lager in the pub down the road from the school before it's time to pick up Daniel and Neil. Unprompted, Kev has worked out where he first saw me: on television when he was fifteen or so. All this has a curious, two-way effect on Kev's attitude towards me. On the one hand, Kev is definitely admiring of the TV connection, with its attendant claims to expertise, power and money. On the other, Kev's a little bit puzzled – no, a lot puzzled – that I'm sitting with him in a pub in south-east London when I could be schmoozing with the chatshow hosts. Kev likes having me around, I deduce, but the fact of having me around is a kind of confirmation that I've failed. If I had power, money and expertise I wouldn't be talking to Kev.

What do I think about Kev? What interests me is his ability to switch between temperamental styles at the drop of a hat: apoplectic in the pub over some TV football match (*Kill the cunt! Go on, stamp on 'is 'ead!*) one minute, amiably nodding at his son the next. Professionally, I'd say Kev's life was governed by the roles he creates for himself: bloke, parent, jack-the-lad, consumer (like everyone else Kev is a mobile phone/cable TV/playstation obsessive). Demanding roles, too. Half the time when I see him Kev looks resentfully exhausted by the stresses of having to fix that stare, make that call (all Kev's mobile calls are, of course, completely unnecessary – calls to the football chat lines and the astrologers), yell amicably *Neil will you stop fucking about and get over 'ere* across the street. And yet I *like* Kev. I don't quite know how to put this into words. You could do worse than Kev, with his clueless observations about sport and the things he reads in the papers, and his bristled bald scalp, a whole lot worse.

Kev's outside the school gates now as I arrive to collect Daniel, Neil in tow, and smiling with edgy excitement. It doesn't take long to establish that something is up here in the asphalt playground and the polished corridor. There's a police car drawn up by the gate and a little cluster of anxious faces round the main door. Kev waves a hand up when he sees me, flicks a finger at the throng.

'What's up, Kev?'

'I dunno. Some bloke comes in and goes after one of the teachers or something.'

'Did they get him?'

'Nah,' Kev says. ''E's holed up in one of the offices or something, saying 'e's going to kill 'imself and that.'

Or something. And that. Kev's speech is peppered with these redundancies. He can't let a sentence out of his mouth without larding it with something that will nullify its meaning. Worried about Dan, I start off across the playground, stop as I see him loping towards me out of one of the side-doors. He looks wide-eyed rather than frightened, mildly amused. It turns out that Miss Cox's boyfriend, recently evicted from her flat, arrived on the premises half an hour ago to plead his case. He did this in front of a class of thirty ten-year-olds. Frostily received, he opted to cut his losses by chasing Miss Cox out into the corridor while trying to throw a chair at her.

'What happened then?'

'It was okay, Dad. Jamal had his mobile so he called the police. And Justin went off to get Mr Crisp.'

Mr Crisp is the PE teacher, a six-foot-three-inch hooligan popularly supposed to have been a commando in the SAS. Nothing will please him more, I suspect, than the chance of incapacitating Miss Cox's boyfriend. What kind of children are we bringing up here, I wonder? For a moment a part of me is enraged at the thought of a brushed-off moron picking up the pieces of his self-esteem by chasing a girl round a classroom while some ten-year-old kids cower behind their desks.

There's a minor commotion going on over by the main doorway. The crowd parts and a couple of policemen – one older and bald, the other young and self-important – appear, propelling a handcuffed figure between them. Miss Cox's boyfriend is impossibly weedy, with one of those ridiculous paintbrush goatee beards. He looks as if he writes poems, or whatever the modern equivalent of writing poems is. No wonder Miss Cox told him to go.

As they reach the gate and the waiting police car the silence is unexpectedly broken.

'All right my son,' Kev yells delightedly. 'Give her one for me, eh?'

One or two people laugh. The younger of the two policemen grins. Miss Cox's boyfriend looks, if anything, even more doom-laden and ground-down. Far off, in the grey, clouded distance, I can see the gulls massing over the river.

* * *

Several phone calls from Lucy. I have an idea, reading between the lines, that the boyfriend is, or will shortly become, an ex-boyfriend. No explanation is forthcoming. I don't ask for one. She seems particularly keen to know if I can glean any more Upward material. I tell her I'll write another letter to Audrey. 'How's Daniel?' she asks, several times. I get an odd sensation of something running beneath the surface, a kind of willed complicity I can't quite put my finger on moving across the wires between us.

The red Mondeo is parked outside the house when we get back and DI Stevens is leaning negligently against the door. How long has he been here? Twenty minutes? Half an hour? When he sees us he skips down the steps and waits for us to pass. A brown paper parcel containing something flat and oblong sticks out from under his arm.

'Thought this might be a good time to call,' Stevens says. 'Mind if I come in?'

'Be my guest.'

Inside there is post lying on the doormat – circulars, electricity bills, another buff rectangle with PLEASE OPEN! inked on the corner. The answer phone light pulses. Daniel moves off into the front room and switches on the TV, not in the least interested in Stevens, or me. Stevens picks up the envelope and looks at it knowingly.

'Someone here's pretty keen to get in touch with you by all accounts.'

'I shouldn't wonder.'

'Don't mind me pointing it out, do you? Only it's the kind of thing that tells you about people.'

'What does it tell you?'

Stevens pirouettes on his heels with surprising grace for a short man of fifty running to fat. 'Well, in your case it says that you don't like opening post, doesn't it?'

We go down into the kitchen where I make tea while Stevens prowls nervously round cupboards and sinks, pulls out a recipe book and looks at it, slots it back. Seen for a second time, he looks much more extraordinary than before: hair rising off his scalp like spun sugar, the dark eyebrows half comic, half sinister. In the end he says:

'You'll have seen the stuff in the papers?'

'Some of it.'

'Amazing isn't it, the memories people have? Twenty years, a quarter of a century ago, and it's just like yesterday isn't it? Secretaries. Commissionaires. All lining up to dish the dirt. I interviewed Lord Cartwright the other day. Interviewed! Pretends he's gaga half the time. But I know better. Ever come across him, sir?'

'Once or twice. He was at Sir Gavin Newsome's place once when I stayed there.'

'Was that when they talked about bringing in the army? Doesn't seem possible, does it, these days? But I can tell you, there were others used to talk about it. Coppers too. Now, your pal Upward. He knew Cartwright well, didn't he?'

I try to remember what Upward had said about Cartwright.

'He used to talk about him now and again.'

'Lots of hospitality, too,' Stevens says. He recites in a curious, high-pitched voice. 'I've a note of a luncheon at the Gay Hussar, March 1984, attended by among others Mr Arthur Upward and his wife Paula.'

'His wife was called Audrey. My wife – my ex-wife – was called Paula.'

'Sorry, sir. My mistake. And your friend never said anything about that occasion? These occasions?'

'Nothing. Besides, we weren't working together by then.'

'No, of course you weren't, were you? But you saw him, didn't you? You and your ex-wife? Remind me what Mrs King's name is again.'

'Was. Paula.'

'I'm sorry, sir.'

Upstairs I can hear the low rumble of the TV. Outside the window the light fades over low, cheerless rooftops. Three weeks to Christmas. Stevens blinks seriously up at the crockery shelves, hefts the brown paper parcel under his armpit, squints at his watch.

'Tell me sir, what did you think about that lot when you knew them? Newsome and Cartwright and the others. Cooper. When you used to see them. When you used to tell them jokes. What did you think of them?'

What did I think of them? I ponder this for a while as Stevens takes the packet out from under his arm and swaps it back from hand to hand.

'I don't know. It was part of the world I was caught up in, I suppose. You never knew who you were going to meet. What they were going to say.'

'And now you don't meet them and that's that?' Stevens says. 'Do you know what I think, sir? I don't think it'll come to court. All too long ago. Or rather not the kind of thing we want to remember. After all, it's a brave new world now isn't it, and we're all working for the same things?'

'Are we?'

'Oh yes, sir. Not the shadow of a doubt. Now, before I go would you do me a favour?'

Unravelled and laid out on the kitchen table, the parcel turns out to contain a copy of Upward's autobiography. I pick it up and leaf through it for a moment, marvelling at the cheek of some of the pictures, the one side by side with Sammy Davis the result simply of Upward's happening to leave a restaurant at the same time.

'What do you want me to write?'

'Oh, I don't know. Something like "from the other half". That should do it.'

I do this. Stevens pores over the inscription for a bit, smiling slightly.

'Thank you, sir,' he says. 'Much appreciated. I'll try not to bother you again. Leave you to yourself and your responsibilities, if you take my meaning.'

We wander upstairs to the hallway. I can see Daniel's silhouette framed by the light in front of the TV. Stevens stoops down and picks up the envelope marked PLEASE OPEN!

'Do you know what I'd do if I were you, sir?' he says. 'I'd open it.'

Twenty minutes later Daniel comes into the kitchen to raid the biscuit tin. He looks round once or twice as if expecting Stevens to rematerialise.

'That bloke. Was he a copper?'

'Yes. What do you know about coppers?'

'I know a bit.'

I look at him as he says this, striving to find something that will connect him to the ten-year-old I was, Father and Mother in the shop, Southtown and the rest. I suppose it shouldn't surprise me that there isn't anything. Does he wonder about it? Or does the past simply not exist to a ten-year-old boy? The children of the Ngongi have a kind of folk memory, apparently: drought, rains, emigration, the red ants in the dunes. Real events blend effortlessly into symbolic high points. A wedding is always 'the wedding', a death always 'the death'. I gather him up in a half-embrace, head bent against my shoulder, which he accepts for a while before twisting away. Searching for something that will keep him here, keep his face in front of me, I say:

'Do you like living here?'

He thinks about this. I can sense him meditating likely answers, weighing the relative advantages of truth and not giving offence.

'If you wanted we could live somewhere else.'

'Where?' He looks less interested now, as if he knows I began the conversation without any definite end in view.

'Dan,' I say. 'When that man came into the classroom after Miss Cox, were you scared?'

'A bit. Neil said he was a wuss though.'

He stacks the biscuits up in the palm of one hand, half-a-dozen of them at least, claps the other hand over the top and wanders out.

Later, when Daniel is eating his tea, I go out round the corner for a packet of fags. Early in December the place undergoes small but significant changes. The off-licences break out in a rash of artificial snow and special offers. Orange peel accumulates in the gutter. Even the Rashids' shop isn't immune to these ghostly twitches on the seasonal thread. Approaching the window through the early-evening shadow I can see what might just be an approximation of a yule log propped up on a bed of artificial grass and a stencilled sign that says 'A MERRY XMAS TO ALL OUR CUSTOMERS'. Inside vegetables rot under the sickly strip-lighting. Mrs Rashid sits stark and motionless at the till, as if in a trance. Her husband is at the back of the shop arranging the little bags of crisps marked 'Not to be sold separately from multi-pack' on a shelf. Something in the way he bends over the cardboard box at his feet stirs a memory of someone else, a long way off. I pay for the cigarettes in a silence broken only by the jangle of the till, the rustle of the crisp packets and Mrs Rashid's ponderous breathing, walk out into the road again. Invisible here, a quarter of a mile away beyond the housefronts and the backs of warehouses, the river declares itself by its smell, that odd reek of stagnant water and burnt oil. On the instant I realise that Mr Rashid, head down over the wholesaler's boxes, reminds me of Father: the same pious absorption in the task, a punctiliousness not at all excluding a sense of pride. One of my sharpest memories of Father, oddly enough, is of coming into the shop to find him standing by the door, arms folded across his chest, raptly surveying the rows of chocolate boxes and the jars of pipe tobacco, a little monarch all alone in the world he'd created.

Suddenly I feel an irrepressible urge to go back there, back to the square, to Father and Mother's ghosts and the old world, to see what's become of it, what shapes and colours it's taken on. It's thirty-four years since I went to Yarmouth but it can't all have changed, surely? Railway station, churches, familiar landmarks – surely they'd still be there? Or at least there'd be something remaining that you could fasten on to, keep for yourself? If it comes to that, Father's shop will still be a shop. Or even if it isn't, there'll still be enough to remind you of what had been: beech trees in the square, say, or Wedderbury's big high windows gleaming in the twilight. Walking back down the empty street, past the lines of cars, watching the helicopter lights moving through the violet sky, I start making plans. Even allowing for the change at Norwich, Yarmouth isn't more than three hours away by train. With someone to look after Daniel, I could manage half a day there and still get back in the evening. Half a day would be enough for the kind of thing I have in mind: Father and Mother, the beech trees and Wedderbury's windows.

Back at the house, Daniel is perched in front of the TV, hands cupped beneath his chin. Down in the kitchen I sit listening to the bump and judder of a train moving in the distance towards Plumstead, trying to remember what Yarmouth station looks like. Try as I may, I can't manage it. The incidentals – the approach, the wide hall beyond the ticket barrier, the curved street outside –

are all there. For some reason, though, the thing itself, the point of it all, utterly escapes me.

Later in the evening Lucy phones. She seems a bit subdued, but interested in the Yarmouth trip.

'Who's going to look after Daniel? Will he be okay on his own?'

'There's a kids' party he can go to that afternoon. And then I can collect him later in the evening. It's not a problem.'

The children's party, which I'd forgotten about until reminded by the strip of fluorescent cardboard on the mantelpiece, is Neil's eleventh, courtesy of Kev at the flat.

'So what will you do when you get there?'

'Walk around. Take a look at the sea. How's the programme?'

'All the things I told you about have been fixed. They should finish cutting it together in a week.'

'That's good then. Makes me feel like a radio celebrity again.'

There's a pause.

'How's the boyfriend?'

'Actually,' Lucy says, 'we've split up. At least he's not here at the moment.'

'I'm sorry.'

'There's no need to be,' Lucy says. 'I'm glad I found out about the things I found out about when I did. Look,' she goes on, 'there are one or two things I need to go through. Little details for the voiceover. Can I come over some time next week?'

Once again I get the sense of something stirring through the distance between us, something that Lucy knows about and I don't.

'Come next Thursday,' I tell her. 'The day after I get back. And then I can tell you all about it.'

'Yes,' Lucy says. 'That would be nice.'

TV Times

INTERVIEWER: How would you describe yourself as comedians?

UPWARD: Us? We're funny comedians. That kind. Seriously, we're the sort you could take your wife to see. Even leave her there, if you wanted to.

INTERVIEWER: What would you say your influences were?

KING: Gordon's. Teacher's. We're not fussy.

INTERVIEWER: Seriously. Is there anyone you've consciously modelled yourselves on?

UPWARD: Harold Wilson, now he's funny. But he needs management. And too much of it's unscripted.

INTERVIEWER: Do you differentiate yourselves? Would either of you say you were the straight man?

UPWARD: I do the talking. He's the quiet one.

KING: . . .

INTERVIEWER: I beg your pardon?

UPWARD: He says he's the quiet one.

INTERVIEWER: You've been together a long time?

UPWARD: Like my fiancée's knees.

KING: You shouldn't talk about his fiancée. It's a sore point.

UPWARD: I'll say it is.

INTERVIEWER: What do you hope to do in television comedy?

KING: Stay in it. Seriously folks, we've seen the competition. Morecambe & Wise. Mike and Bernie. *Songs of Praise.* We're just happy to be here.

UPWARD: *You* might be.

KING: But you haven't got my sunny disposition, have you?

UPWARD:	Never touched it.
INTERVIEWER:	Is there a life after comedy?
UPWARD:	Is there a life after what?
KING:	You're not taking us seriously.
UPWARD:	But we don't take ourselves seriously.
KING:	We're professional comedians. I don't think you could get much more serious than that.

1973

What It was Like

So what was it like being on stage? People were always asking you that. Women, sometimes, but mostly men. You'd be walking down Oxford Street, say, on your way to the BBC, coming out of a pub round the back of Langham Place, sauntering into some hotel foyer somewhere (Blackpool, Bournemouth, Morecambe) and there they'd be, edging surreptitiously across the road, the pavement or the carpet to nod – they always nodded – paw at your elbow – they always did that, too – and ask, shyly but as if they really wanted to know, '*What's it like being on stage then?*' Thinking about it, it was mostly blokes. Fat ones. Thin ones. Prosperous-looking ones. Down-at-heel ones. And always the nod – as if in some long-ago schoolyard you'd swapped cigarette cards together – always the tug at your elbow – as if they wanted to reassure themselves that you weren't made of ectoplasm – and the urgency. '*What's it like being on stage then?*' As if the answer would get you a better life, a better wife, a better job, a better car. And you'd say 'Sorry' or 'Pardon' or 'In a hurry', or stop and scratch your signature on a piece of paper, or a fag packet or a calling card, which was usually enough for all but the most persistent ones (who were capable of following you down the street, to the door of your car, to the door of your house, at which point you said 'Bugger off' or 'Calling the police', which finally sent them away). But you didn't stop thinking about the question, which was an interesting one and had exercised your mind ever since you first did it.

So what was it like being on stage then? Funnily enough, being on stage was a lot like *not* being on stage. Apart from the lights, that is. And the smoke. And the faces. Which is to say that there were two of you talking to each other, to all intents and purposes having a normal conversation, except for the pauses, the gaps in this world you were creating, where the laughter flowed in. Laughter, you found out pretty soon, had a life of its own. You could say something, wait for the laugh, feel it start to fade, open your mouth again, and suddenly another wave would roll in from somewhere, somewhere you couldn't see, and nearly drown you in its intensity. Laughter also had – and you found this out even sooner – a death of its own as well. You could build the waves up, have them crashing round your head as you clung on to the microphone stand for support, stretch out for that last paroxysm of delight, and suddenly, without warning, there'd be utter silence. And you'd smile – you always did that – stare back at the faces – you always did that, too – while you worked out just what trick you'd failed to master, just exactly where you'd gone wrong.

The worst thing was the faces. It's not true that comedians don't see the people they're performing to. What else are you supposed to look at? You saw them all: animated, impassive, grim, eager, loving it, hating it, missing it. Sometimes they were tiny rows of pin-heads back in the far distance. Other times they were great balloons with the features sketched on in charcoal. You could never tell, just as you could never tell how you wanted them to react. You didn't want them to turn away, because that meant they'd lost interest, but you didn't want them staring at you full-on, because that meant you couldn't get away from them. All the time you looked at them you were in danger of coming apart from the person you were working with. It was a double act, so you wanted the faces on your side against him, but you knew you could never take the faces for granted, because if you gave them an inch they'd be back on the other side. You loved them, but you hated them, you wanted them to go away, but you also knew that if they did that you'd want them to come back again.

The next worse thing about being on stage was Upward. Upward was like the faces only not quite so bad. You wanted Upward to like the way things were going – you always wanted that – but you knew that the worse things went, the greater the chance of Upward making some face-saving intervention – and you wanted that, too.

You wanted to come in on cue, and you wanted not to as well. You wanted to be certain what was going on in Upward's head – and you never could be certain – and you wanted, mentally, to be all over the place because you knew that made for better comedy. You wanted what you were doing to coast zestfully through gag after gag, which meant, of course, that there was a danger of you being predictably unexpected, or unexpectedly predictable, depending on what the audience wanted from you. When you were on the stage you wanted to be off it, but when you *were* off it, back in the dressing room, say, under the bright lights with Captain Groves fisting you a champagne flute, emerging lightheadedly into the stone-cold, small-hour air, you wanted to be back on it. You were always planning some of the act, and you were always stopping yourself planning it because you knew that, if you did, what you said would probably be funnier. And then, at the end, when you stood side by side on the shiny, slippery stage with the sweat sizzling off your wrists, wide-eyed in the smoke, while the audience clapped or whistled, or did whatever they did – and somehow you were always too tired to notice – you were always vaguely disappointed, annoyed that you'd spent a second too long coming back at the line Upward had dropped without warning into the middle of the last-but-one routine, or ridden the laugh instead of driving it off elsewhere.

And what was it like being on stage with Upward? People were always asking you that, too. Men sometimes, but mostly women. You'd be cruising down the front at some blighted holiday resort, pondering your prawn cocktail in a restaurant window, tripping up the steps of some suburban theatre somewhere (Croydon, Wimbledon, Romford) and there they'd be, edging nervously across the esplanade, the doorway, the coconut matting, to blink – they always blinked – come to rest a foot from your shoulder – they always did that, too – and ask, anxiously, but as if they really wanted to know, '*What's it like being on stage with Upward?*' Thinking about it, it was mostly women. Young ones. Old ones. Unassuming ones. Brazen ones. And always the blink – as if in some long-ago dancehall you'd held hands together in the corner – always the coming to rest a foot from your shoulder – as if you had a force-field around you that couldn't be breached – and the urgency

– '*What's it like being on stage with Upward?*' As if knowing the answer would get you a better life, a better husband, better sex, a better figure. And you'd say 'Fine' or 'Cheers' or 'Meeting someone', or stop and scrawl your signature on a table napkin or a menu card or an envelope, which was usually enough for all but the most persistent ones (who were capable of turning up in your hotel corridor, in your room, in the back of your car, at which point you said 'I'm married', whether you were or not, or 'Calling the police', which finally shooed them away). But you didn't stop thinking about the question, which was an interesting one, and had exercised your mind ever since you first did it.

So what was it like being on stage with Upward then? Funnily enough, being on stage with Upward was a lot like *not* being on stage with Upward. Upward, you found out pretty soon, had a life of his own. You could say something, something scripted, something you'd gone through a dozen times that week in the rehearsal room, and suddenly Upward would be off somewhere, somewhere you couldn't follow, leaving you stranded on the beach while the real action was half a mile off in the billowing surf. Upward also had – and you found this out even sooner – a death of his own as well. You could build the routine up, have the gags snap into place like a row of suspender clips, almost unable to believe your luck, stretch out to offer Upward that final line – proudly yet humbly, because it would bring your final humiliation – and suddenly, without warning, there'd be utter silence. And you'd smile – you always did that – stare back at Upward's red, perspiring face – you always did that, too – while you wondered just what trick you'd failed to master, just exactly where you'd gone wrong.

Upward always liked to say that we'd never done the same show twice. Strictly speaking, this was only half-true. Upward had certainly never done the same show twice in his life. On the other hand, I had. About two or three hundred times, in fact.

Upward had original views on why an audience came to see us, even more original views on what an audience was. He used to say:

'Let's say a hundred people turn up. Twenty might be there because they genuinely want to see you. You know, what you do strikes them as funny. Another ten might be there because they've got it into their heads that they might like to see you. Another thirty don't care either way – they're just the kind of people who turn up to things. Another twenty will be people who've come along with other people. Another five will be there by mistake. *Seriously.* That's your first problem, right? That everybody's come to see you for different reasons.'

'Or for no reason.'

'Exactly. There might be people there who're actively hostile. I once did a show up north where the place had been in trouble with the watch committee over smutty jokes, and the front row was full of Salvation Army lasses. But you've got another problem, and that's the range of your audience. Let's say sixty of them are men and forty of them are women. Ten of them might be fairly intelligent. Eighty of them will be varying degrees of average. Another ten of them might be imbecilic. What do you do? How do you get the bottom ninety to laugh at something the top ten are interested in?'

'Aren't there supposed to be universal absolutes? You know, a man who slips on a banana skin is just funny, whether you're an Oxford don or a dustman?'

'It doesn't work like that.'

'Laughter the unifying force?'

'No.'

Upward's theory of comedy – why people came to see us, why they laughed – was frankly elitist. He believed that the members of an average audience, at any rate the sort of audience you got at the Minerva, didn't really know how to respond to what they saw. They might want to laugh, but there wasn't any guarantee that they would laugh. Nothing could be taken for granted. Worse, Upward thought, the audience was in the grip of a collective neurosis, wanting to laugh but worrying that other people would despise them if they laughed at the wrong things.

'So what do you do?'

'What do you do? You go for the top man, of course.'

According to Upward, every audience had two, or at most three, controlling intelligences – people who knew what was funny, were prepared to respond to what was going on on stage and, most important of all, could influence the other spectators. The problem, according to Upward, was that such people weren't easily swayed. If they weren't impressed, their silence could damp down the enthusiasm of other people by a kind of telepathy. This meant they needed careful handling: reassurance, discreet asides, catchphrases. As Upward described it, there were actually two performances going on – one in which you fished for, and flattered, a handful of sophisticates, another in which you encouraged them to take their discovery of how funny you were to the masses.

Watching Upward as he rocketed around stage at the start of a show, quickly throwing out feelers into the audience, working out where the laughter lay, I used to understand something of the difference between us. Whereas I was part of a picture made up of the faces, the smoke, the stage light and Upward himself, Upward lived in a world of his own. But there was more to it than this, I realised. I repeated my lines; Upward wove patterns. Sometimes at the start of a routine he'd pick up a phrase and play with it, throw it out to the audience and catch it back, and then store it for later use – bringing it out again, say, halfway through the next sketch. At these times whatever we were doing teetered like a juggernaut in mid-lane. There was no knowing which way it would turn. There was nothing you could do. You merely had to wait until Upward had finished, hoping that the stopping-off point bore some resemblance to the original running order.

So what was it like being on stage with Upward? Being on stage with Upward was a lot like *not* being on stage with Upward. Except that everything had moved up a gear, got brighter, louder, more extreme. Sometimes in mid-sketch, especially when Upward had gone off into one of his closed, private whirls, you'd shoot him a mute, imploring look – an access-requested look, an exclusion-zone look – and watch it break on the shoreline of his stare. Or you'd miss something – some catchphrase you didn't know about, some gesture that hadn't been rehearsed – and spend the rest of the half-hour wondering what would happen afterwards. We used to have fights in those days. Most double acts end up fighting, of course. But these were proper punch-ups. Back in the dressing room, grim and furious after ten seconds or so of weak applause, Upward would suddenly put down the cigarette, the bottle or the towel he was holding and wing a fat hand into my face. I might respond by picking up the chair that lay between us and throwing it at him. In reply, Upward might launch his head meatily but unhurriedly in the region of my shoulder. Eventually, after a minute or so, as if at some pre-arranged signal, we'd stop, light cigarettes, negligently rearrange the furniture, give each other playful little cuffs and slaps, sink down into chairs. A bit later Captain Groves, whose office lay along the corridor, might put his head round the door and say unconcernedly, 'Everything all right boys?' And you'd say 'Fine', or in Upward's case 'Champion', or 'With you in a minute'. Once, by some fluke of anticipation, Captain Groves arrived in mid-scuffle. He stood in the doorway for a minute or two, with the ash collecting on the end of his cigar, and a slightly puzzled look on his face, watching the sailing chairs and the savage head-butts. Then we heard him marching back along the corridor.

There are patterns now, figures visible in the mist. For some reason this time has a kind of clarity that's absent from earlier parts of my life. Later parts, too. Where did it come from, that heightened sense of awareness? What produced it? It's difficult to tell. But the late Sixties are very vivid to me in a way that other times are not. Not simply in the things that happened around me, but in the contours of my own life. Brighton sea front in 1968, a girl whose name I can't remember sitting in a hotel bedroom a year or so later, Upward's face in the rehearsal room – all this is much more real to me than vast tracts of recent life. Loafing with Upward once in a seaside café in the rain one Sunday morning at some resort where we were doing summer season, a train-ride north one November through the South Yorkshire slag-heaps where you waited for a daylight that never came, horses seen in a field somewhere in the West Country – grey horses, they were, with long steelwire manes – lolloping away through the mist. There was a feeling of well-being, too, that I can't quite put into words, the sensation of having left certain things behind – Father and Mother, Mary and the gulls – and not being worried about what might take their place. It's not true to say that I forgot Yarmouth at this time – how could I? It was there every time I smoked a cigarette, or went past a corner shop, or saw one of those maps of southern England that makes it look like an angel taking wing, and the east coast is the angel's head. But there was a way in which it was all somehow filed and docketed, ready for me to take up again when I wanted it, not when it wanted me.

We left Soho early in 1966: 'not before time' according to Upward. The official line was that the BBC wouldn't give airtime to a double act that played three nights a week at places like the Minerva, but at bottom I think it was simple restlessness on Upward's part, that he was tired of the flat, the grey Soho dawns and performing to fat men in tuxedos. Brenda disappeared somewhere. Counting up what we'd put away in the past six months we found it came to £500. The plan was to go on the road, log up experience, get our names known outside Soho and then come back to London for a proper go at the BBC, which in those days was the Holy Grail of anyone who took themselves at all seriously. Sometimes we'd be in a pub in the West End and some fat little middle-aged man would march in with the *Daily Mail* under his arm and a couple of sidekicks trailing in his wake, and Upward would go rigid with suppressed emotion. There was never any need to ask him who it was.

We had an agent by this time – an old white-haired bloke who claimed to have represented Tommy Handley – and there was talk of a 'sound test', which was the name they gave to radio auditions, but in the end it all fell through and we went off on the road.

So what was it like going out on the road? Funnily enough, nobody ever asked you this. All that's left now is a jumble of impressions – the colour of the fried egg yolk at breakfast in the boarding houses, which wasn't so much pale yellow as a kind of light green, spending the night once in a bed and breakfast somewhere up north where they didn't even have beds, just a couple of mattresses spread out on the floor waking up one morning in some Godforsaken room in Liverpool and seeing a rat perched on the chest of drawers feeding off a packet of sandwiches that Upward had left there the night before. Out of interest I totted up the number of different beds I slept in that first year, and it came to 129.

In those days there were recognised routes around the country for comedy acts. The south coast was one: Ramsgate, Brighton, Bournemouth. Another was what was known as the 'east run', from Skegness up through Grimsby and Hull to Harrogate. Variety was long gone by this time, but in its wake lay a chain of concert halls and theatres that managers were still trying desperately to fill. This meant that you ended up in some weird line-ups – fifth on the bill, say, behind a beat group, a male-voice choir, an impressionist and a gang of plate-spinners. A bit later we moved up to the northern club circuit, when the money was better but you had to keep an eye on your material. Upward had warned me about the working men's clubs:

'Two hundred piss-heads out of the pit or the foundry on a Friday night with their wives dressed up like parrots, and if it isn't about mothers-in-law or niggers you might as well go home.'

He was right, too. When we went on stage the first time – it might have been in Worksop or Chesterfield – doing the set we'd used on the south coast, not a soul clapped. I remember looking out into the crowd – they used to sit five or six to a table with a forest of beer bottles piled up in the middle – and no one was even looking at us. They weren't hostile, they'd just marked us down for what we were: 'smart', know-all southern comedians. Even then there were huge differences in what the audiences wanted out of comedy. Southern audiences liked you to score off your opposite number; northern crowds preferred you to tell jokes against yourself. We played a few dates in Scotland around this time, and it was even worse – if you told jokes about religion people would walk out. On the other hand they'd scream with laughter if you mentioned death, which was something you couldn't touch south of the border. In the end Upward wrote some stuff which was nearer to the old northern variety routines – sketches where we played Lancashire housewives at the bus-stop or mill-girls out courting, and implied, without stating it in so many words, that we both came from somewhere west of the Pennines.

As for the life you were living off stage, it was scarcely worth the name. On average each engagement lasted three nights, which meant that you'd barely settled yourself in before it was time to pack your bags and head off to the next place, which might take as little as an hour or as much as a day. Upward was in charge of the bookings. One of my chief memories of him in those days is on the phone, in coin boxes near railway stations, in hotel foyers, in lodging house back rooms with the landlady grimly reckoning up the cost behind the door. Usually he managed to stick to some kind of pattern, but there were dreadful days when we ended up trekking halfway across the north of England on buses and rattletrap trains. Once, I remember, owing to some mistake in the arrangements, we played a night in Leeds, upped sticks for a couple of days in Carlisle and then rushed back to Leeds again to perform in front of a dozen elderly domino players in what looked like somebody's front room.

Worse than this, perhaps, was the sheer unreality of the places we fetched up in. I'd never been in the North before, and it took me at least a month to get used to it: huge sprawling cities where every surface was black with dirt, and the bricks looked as if they'd been dipped in creosote; the endless rows of back-to-back houses with front doors opening into the street, which people like Father and Mother would have died rather than inhabit; and beyond the towns the rolling countryside, with hills rather than flat fields, the stone walls running across them like piping over a dress, and in the distance, drawn up beneath smoke clouds, the next clump of houses and billowing factories. Upward, I noticed, was completely matter-of-fact about all this. I watched him once on a train-journey from Leeds to Sheffield – the filthiest landscape you ever saw in your life, with pools of stagnant water gleaming at the edges with chemicals, where even the grass had a brownish sheen – and his face was quite impassive. I couldn't look at it without thinking of the line in 'Jerusalem', which we'd sung at school, about 'dark, Satanic mills', but to him it was simply the train-ride from Leeds to Sheffield. Curiously, this feeling of being in another time followed me everywhere we went. Even in the lodging houses – these tended to be run by people with some connection to 'the business' as they put it – you were suddenly back in a world that was thirty years out of date, with pictures of old Variety stars on the wall and 'Father' proudly admitting to have appeared on stage with Will Hay in 1933. It was just the same out in the streets. The Sixties – long hair, mini-skirts and the rest – really only happened in London. North of the Trent the towns were still full of women in granny coats, bee-hives and drain-piped Teddy boys.

What Upward made of all this – grey streets, the working men's clubs, even the Sixties themselves – was anyone's guess. It wouldn't be true, for example, to say that he was 'at home' in the north of England. Set down in some northern city – Leeds, Sheffield, Newcastle – he had a trick of emphasising sides of his personality that were slightly at odds with local tastes in speech, dress and diet. These transformations were all the more unexpected in that they represented a complete reversal of his London get-up. Seeing him in Frith Street – hearing him order a drink, or clapping a friend on the back – it was impossible to believe that he had been born anywhere south of Lancashire. Fetched up west of the Pennines, on the other hand, he could suddenly turn back into a Londoner. Perhaps this is too sharp a distinction to explain the series of carefully engineered cultural collisions that Upward enjoyed provoking. Watching him in a restaurant in the north east, carefully asking a waiter to explain the meaning of 'hot pot' or 'barm cake', it was difficult to know what game he was playing, or if a game was being played at all.

In the end I decided that there were bits of his professional life that he simply couldn't bear to give up, the fake Upward walking off stage into the real world, but even this somehow begged more questions than it answered. Irritable, nervy, selfconscious, Upward was capable of lightning shifts of gear, guaranteed to wrongfoot anyone not familiar with the way he operated. Once, a bit after this period, I watched him being interviewed by a journalist for a Manchester evening paper. The interview began with the two greeting each other virtually as long-lost brothers. Upward may even have called the interviewer 'wack'. Within the first few minutes he used half-a-dozen dialect expressions unknown to me. There were references to 'up here' and 'us Northern folk'. Then, without warning, the atmosphere started to change. After a bit I realised that Upward was having to have explained to him the existence of the Manchester Ship Canal. Shortly after that he claimed not to know that there were two local football teams. It was all much too flagrant to be ignored. Afterwards I asked him:

'What did you think you were doing?'

'What d'y' mean?'

'Pretending not to know about the Roses Match. Or Len Hutton?'

'There's too many of them bloody northern mascots,' Upward said with surprising bitterness. 'Ken Dodd. Cilla bloody Black.' He broke into mimicry. ' "My dad worked in t'pit, and we allus went to Morecambe for us holidays." They're not getting me on that lark.'

It was impossible to work out what he meant by this. Nobody, outwardly, could have been more 'Northern' than Upward. At the same time, nobody could have hated more the kind of things northernness was supposed to consist of. In the end I decided that it was simply Upward using one highly significant part of himself – where he came from – as a weapon, an infinitely adaptable weapon, too, as it could be turned on friend and foe alike. And yet knowing this didn't at all solve the problem of Upward, what he wanted, what he was after, where he was going to stop. I remember once asking him, not in any deliberate sense but simply to keep the ball rolling, what he 'wanted'. Upward put down the newspaper he was reading and gave me his full attention.

'What do I want? I'd like to shag every girl in Lancashire, eat off gold plates and have Bobby Charlton ask me for my autograph. And then I'd like to sit down and think about it.'

Some of this I noticed and thought about at the time. A bit more I simply absorbed and filed away for future reference. I was twenty-seven then, twenty-eight, and for all the claustrophobia of the lodging house bedrooms and the cheap rehearsal gaffs, I had things to think about apart from Upward. I was seeing places, too, in a way I'd never done before, not since the old army days. The names ran on in my head in clusters – Bristol, Exeter and Penzance; Broadstairs, Deal and Ramsgate; Clacton, Southend and Felixstowe. Dead English towns, for the most part, sleeping in the summer sun or the winter fogs, but I'd never seen them before. I don't remember much about them – a recreation ground near Margate, once, where I sat and smoked cigarettes for a whole summer afternoon, watching the children swarm over the slides, a boating lake somewhere on the Essex coast which had iced up in the frost, with bird tracks pittering over its surface – just the pleasure of being there, taking things in. I was growing up. It was five years since I'd last seen Mary or worked at the Sun Alliance. Somehow it seemed a lot longer – all tied up with Father and Mother and my teens rather than the immediate past. From time to time on my travels I'd send postcards back to the people I remembered from those days – Uncle Ralph, Uncle George and

Aunt Sheila. I don't know if they ever received them, much less what they thought if they did.

Meanwhile, in a small way, I'd begun to enjoy myself. For a start we were seeing glimpses of a life beyond the boarding houses and the seedy theatres. Late in 1967, just as Upward had promised, we started getting radio work. Nothing very much, usually just guest spots on other people's shows, but it meant that the bookers and the club managers treated you with respect. A bit later we did warm-ups for Frankie Howerd at Blackpool. We even – God knows how Upward fixed this – had bit-parts in *Magical Mystery Tour*. If you look very carefully in the coach tour scenes, where Ringo's aunt is telling him not to be so 'historical', you can see a couple of characters sprawled over the back seat. The one in the straw hat and the carmine and blue boating blazer is Upward. The other one is me. We started doing private dates as well: a hundred businessmen in a country hotel, say, wanting jokes about Harold Wilson and devaluing the pound. There was a weird afternoon once in the very early days, when we were fixed up to play at a private party in the East End, and no one would tell us whom we were performing to. We went there by cab, down the Mile End Road, then off into a warren of side streets. All the time I could see Upward getting more and more nervy.

'Who do you reckon it is?' he kept asking. 'Bloody Krays or someone?'

Eventually we pulled into a square where forty or fifty people – middle-aged men in overcoats, mostly, wearing war medals – were standing in rows outside a pub. Suddenly a Daimler swung into the square from the far side and there was a forest of salutes. Nazi salutes. Dumped on the pavement by the pub door, I looked on while the men – there were a few teenagers with short hair and Crombie coats – filed past and Upward skulked inside to make enquiries. He came back looking white and furious.

'Mosley,' he said bitterly.

'What?'

'Like I said. Sir Oswald bloody Mosley.'

Without even stopping to discuss it we headed back across the square, past the empty Daimler, towards the nearest side street. Reaching the car, something struck Upward.

'Hang on a sec,' he said.

Simultaneously a volley of cheering erupted inside the pub. Shouting voices, feet drumming on floorboards, the boom of the smashed glass as Upward hurled the half-brick through the Daimler's windscreen, the stillness that mysteriously returned to the square twenty seconds later – all this has stuck in my head.

In the Sixties people began to tie up their own experiences with history. Where were you when Kennedy died? When England won the World Cup? When the slag-heap tipped over on to Aberfan? When the other Kennedy died? When Armstrong and Aldrin walked on the moon? It says something for the kind of life Upward and I were living all this time that I scarcely noticed. I remember watching the World Cup final in a hotel bedroom somewhere in the Midlands, while Upward (who hated sport of any description) worked on a script. The Aberfan disaster made a bit more of an impression, if only because we were in Wales at the time and there were collecting boxes outside every shop. Bobby Kennedy I remember reading about in the *Daily Mirror* one morning while Upward sacked our agent over the phone. As for the moon landing, who knows where we were, what we were doing back in July 1969 a fortnight or so before my twenty-ninth birthday. Needless to say I can't recall that either. Like Mosley's face, the joke John Lennon told me in 1967 and the colour of the south coast buses, the whole thing has simply disappeared. Upward, who had the better memory, would have remembered.

From the street the bare wooden steps went up sharply and apparently indefinitely – the effect was a bit like the Minerva in reverse – through the building. Just at the point where you thought you could go no further, where the view downwards became a dizzying prospect of jutting banisters, they reached a summit: a wide landing with a single door set in the farthermost wall. Inside, two long, high-ceilinged rooms – there was a kitchen and bathroom on the floor below – looked out over the sea front: rows of shops on the further side giving way to a rickety esplanade, nondescript boats drawn up on the shale, beyond that the sea itself. Of all the places we stayed in, it was by far the most memorable: detached, deserted, eerie. Climbing the stairs at night – there was a push-button light switch that gave out on the second flight – you were lost in absolute darkness. Whether the other flats were inhabited or not – and in a fortnight's residence I never set eyes on another lodger – no light ever burned behind their doors. Upward used to say that it was the kind of place where you could expect to find a corpse lying on the stairs, its throat neatly cut, as you went down for the post. This may have had something to do with the principal event of our stay there; perhaps not. However sinister, its influence always seemed to be out of all proportion to the time we spent there. It was here, for instance, that I first heard Gavin Newsome's name, found out some things about Upward that had previously been hidden, other bits of information.

'Of course,' Upward used to say, 'it's not as if we do a proper job or anything.'

This was true. All the same what we did do – both on the stage and off – could be uncomfortably hard work. It was hardest of all when Upward was in one of his moods. These – they descended without warning and often went on for three or four days – were completely disabling. Struck down by one of them, Upward was quite capable of not speaking for several hours, occasionally not even moving. Marooned in a chair – and the effect was oddly like someone left on a tiny desert island – he simply stared in front of him until for some unknown reason, something Upward claimed to have no control over, the spell broke. It was always hard to know what to do when this happened. Talking could be worse than useless (Upward always said that at these periods the sound of a human voice was reduced to a kind of droning). On the other hand there were things that had to be said – stuff about that night's performance, travel arrangements and so on. In the end I usually adopted a policy of carrying on as usual – something which Upward always said irritated him beyond measure, but sometimes produced dramatic improvements in his condition.

Reaching the top of the stairs that Sunday morning, pint of milk in one hand, a couple of newspapers wedged under the other arm, I knew by a kind of sixth sense that in the twenty minutes I'd been gone Upward had been gathered up by another of his moods. It was the last week of September, and bright sunshine was streaming through the skylight directly above the stairhead. The door of the flat was half-open, but the radio left playing pop music had been turned off. Upward sat, still in his dressing gown, at the far end of the battered sofa. Unshaven, strands of red hair plastered low over his forehead, he looked utterly woebegone, even tragic. From the end of the room steam was rising dramatically from an electric kettle: I switched it off. Everything else – the uncleared table, Upward's current stage costume (purple three-piece suit with a bright yellow check) hung over a chair, a jumble of odds and ends over the floor – seemed much as I'd left it.

'Do you want a cup of tea?'

Upward was silent. I sat down on a chair by the window and, allowing for the incongruity of the figure in front of me, tried to read the *News of the World*, wondering at the same time what had brought this particular crisis on. Upward's moods weren't entirely arbitrary. A hostile audience or a professional snub – the 'star' two rungs up the bill who pretended not to notice him – was usually enough to plunge him into gloom. However, nothing like this had happened for weeks. In fact the day before had brought a letter from the BBC offering us two or three slots in a series of comedy half-hours. Professionally, things were looking up. On the other hand, Upward's subconscious had an uncanny ability to sniff out trouble in advance. The cancelled date, the TV comedian not wanting to shake hands – frequently Upward's moods ran in advance of these slights rather than reacting to them. It could be that something unpleasant was going to happen that only Upward, or rather some secret part of Upward, knew about.

'Do you want to know what's in the papers?'

Again, Upward said nothing. At these times I usually found myself talking to him as if he were a deaf, elderly hospital patient whose mental state couldn't be relied on. Many years later Upward told me how much he hated this. Somehow, though, no other tone seemed suitable. I rolled out the *News of the World* on my knees, looking for something that might interest him.

'It says here that Val Doonican's just bought a new Bentley.' Nothing stirred. I went on: 'Seated at the wheel of his impressive new purchase, the popular singing star said: "*I haven't shown it to my mother yet, but she'll be glad the old pushbike's going into retirement.*" '

This kind of thing always annoyed Upward. As a general rule he hated any kind of showbiz success story, however deserving the personality involved. I read on for several minutes: starlets holidaying in the Barbadian surf, gnarled veterans of the wide screen and their teenage companions.

'Oh, and Mike and Bernie Winters have just landed a six-part series with ITV.'

'Give me that.'

Upward's face as he said this was almost deathly white. I handed the paper over and he stared balefully at it for a bit. Outside the wind whipped against the high windows. Not more than ten yards away there were gulls hovering on the current, wings raised awkwardly above their bodies.

'Not a good idea?'

'You said it.'

'It could be worse.'

'I suppose so.'

Having spoken, and thereby broken the spell, Upward cheered up a bit. At any rate he consented to be made a cup of tea and look over the picture of Mike and Bernie, while restating one of his most deeply held theories about comedy: that talent existed in inverse proportion to the exposure granted to the comedian.

'I mean, why don't they put an ad in the paper. "Are you talentless? Are all your jokes thirty years out of date? Well, ring a TV producer and he'll give you something really special. Oh, and lots of girls will be waiting backstage for a quick knee-trembler after the show."'

Eventually the animus burned itself out. Upward drank two cups of tea in quick succession. Then he said in a curiously humble way:

'D'y' think it went okay last evening?'

'Absolutely.'

'You think they got the end of "Talking about girls"?'

'Seemed to.'

Upward paused, lost in some remote world of laughter and acclamation.

'What about me?' he demanded sharply. 'Was I funny?'

Oddly, there wasn't any vanity about Upward as he said this. He simply wanted to know.

'You were funny.'

There was no guarantee that Upward would be pleased by this. In fact he was quite likely to start criticising you for your own shortcomings ('We can't just rely on one of us getting a laugh' etc.). But now the compliment seemed to satisfy him. He rolled off the sofa, clutched the flapping folds of the dressing gown to his chest (this was a deliberate gag – we had a routine about a woman surprised by a Peeping Tom) and lit a cigarette.

'You open any of that post?'

'Not yet.'

There was a pile of letters lying on a table inside the door, sent on by the London agent. Upward picked them up and took them into the bedroom. From within I could hear him pulling his clothes on, interspersed with the sound of tearing paper, occasional gusts of laughter.

'What's so funny?'

'There's some grand stuff here.' Upward's head appeared for a moment, half in and half out of the door. 'Listen to this. "*Dear Arthur Upward. My husband and I enjoyed your show at the Lewes Civic Theatre last week, especially the sketch about Harold Wilson, who my husband cannot stand, and I agree. My husband is often away on business, and it gets very lonely in the evenings. I was wondering if . . .*" D'you think it's genuine?'

'Bound to be.'

There were about a dozen letters: cheques, an unpaid bill or two, the agent's account, some fan-mail. The fan-letters were always for Upward. Once or twice Upward came out into the room, half dressed, to confer on particular points.

'There's an invite here to the Kent Federation of Master Builders' Christmas ball. Think we should do it?'

'Can't do any harm.'

'Bloody bore, though, jacking down to Whitstable two days before Christmas. What about this one? Private dinner at the house of Gavin Newsome. Morrie's dead keen.'

'Who's Gavin Newsome?'

'Bloke that has his picture in the paper advertising commission selling. The Bank of Bristol. *You* know. Tried to stand as a Labour MP last time around, but they wouldn't have him.'

At this stage in my life I knew nothing about Gavin Newsome short of his name. The commission selling scheme; the Bank of Bristol; his ambition to become a Labour MP – all this lay in the future. At the same time I wasn't at all surprised to find that Upward knew all about them. Uninterested in newspapers, bored to distraction by TV news programmes, he had a trick of picking up information about the personalities of the day by a kind of osmosis. A footballer sacked by his club, a bankrupt pop star, a disgraced politician: somehow Upward dredged them up from the choppy, late-Sixties sea into which they'd tumbled.

'How did Gavin Newsome find out about us?'

'Morrie says he heard us on the radio. Deeply impressed. Just the ticket for his mates at dinner.'

By now Upward had finished dressing. He came out of the bedroom for the final time, hooking the door to behind him with the toe of his shoe.

'What d'you think? Every popsy's dream?'

The question had to do with the suit – a slighly quieter version of his stage get-up, topped with a pink shirt and a bright red tie – but it was difficult not to take a wider view. At thirty, Upward looked older than most forty-year-olds: hair definitely going now, skin oddly red and abraded, as if the hair colour was working its way downward by way of compensation. Outwardly nobody could have looked more ordinary than Upward, more of a face in the crowd. At the same time there was a way in which everything about him was faintly exaggerated, larger than life. Looked at for a minute or two he suddenly seemed monstrous, extraordinary. In the beginning the fan-letters Upward got – at first no more than a trickle, now five or six a week, always from women – used to puzzle me. Now I accepted them as an inevitable part of the person Upward was. It seemed perfectly logical that women who saw Upward on stage should want to write to him. The wonder was that more of them didn't do so.

'I'm off out,' Upward said. 'Down the pub. You coming?'

'Not now. Later, perhaps.'

'Suit yourself.'

There were good reasons for not going into pubs with Upward. The version of himself that he carried into this kind of social life was basically a projection of the character he touted around on stage: loud, cocky, assertive, occasionally tragic. Put down in a bar with Upward, there was no guarantee that he wouldn't start eyeing up women who were quite obviously with someone else, argue with the landlord, or challenge someone to a bout of arm-wrestling.

I heard rather than saw him go out: a colossal slam of the door followed by the noise of feet moving regularly down the endless stairs, another slam – muffled but still fairly loud – of the street door as he stepped outside. It was about half-past twelve. Beyond the window, traffic moved sluggishly along the sea front. In the far distance, almost at the point where the sea met the sky, there were yachts tracking back and forth. Nearer to hand I could see Upward's squat, powerful figure moving purposefully through the knots of people, the pale girls still in summer dresses, arms clasped elbow to elbow against the breeze, boys in parka jackets wheeling mopeds along the pavement. If I had a plan for Upward's absence – and the odds were that he'd be gone for at least an hour or two – it was to phone a girl I'd met the week before in Folkestone, maybe even arrange some kind of meeting. Life on the road was full of these hasty assignations: phone numbers scrawled on the back of cigarette packets, afternoon trips to towns a dozen miles away heavy with the knowledge that you were never going to see the girl again, the whole thing dominated by Upward's shadow. Curiously, nearly all the girls, even the biddable ones, wanted to talk about Upward. I was once actually in bed with a girl who asked me whether he was married. As it was, the phone call was never made.

Three-quarters of an hour went by. Then, quite distinctly, I heard the sound of the street door – not usually kept locked during the day – slam shut. Somebody was coming up the stairs. My first thought was that it was Upward, unexpectedly depressed by the atmosphere of the pub, or even, as had happened in the past, thrown out. But the footsteps didn't sound like Upward's heavy tread. Interested, I went and stood on the landing. Twenty or thirty feet below a figure – a woman's figure judging from the glimpses of pink skin beneath a skirt – was moving slowly nearer. After what seemed like several minutes, several pauses for breath and at least one fruitless knocking on a door two floors below, the figure turned laboriously into the last stair-flight. Standing to one side of the stairhead, view obscured by the sun streaming in from the skylight, it took me a second or two to make out the shock of blonde hair and the scissor legs. It was Brenda. Seeing me, she stopped a step or two up the final incline and plumped the heavy canvas bag she was carrying down on the step.

'Didn't expect to see me, did you?'

'Not really.'

'Well, I've come anyway,' Brenda said ambiguously.

I came down the steps to pick up the bag. Brenda seemed to approve of this gesture, as she gave me a tiny pat on the arm.

'Nice manners you had,' she said. 'I always said.'

'Are you all right?'

Brenda looked very far from being all right. Never at all fresh complexioned, her face was horribly pale. For someone whom I remembered – it was one of Father and Mother's phrases – as 'a strapping girl', she seemed a whole lot thinner. For some reason the clothes she was wearing – a shortish skirt with a kind of smock over her upper half – exaggerated both her pallor and her skimpiness. This was the great age of skinny models, of course – Twiggy and Jean Shrimpton. Brenda looked worse than that, ill rather than fashionably slim. Without answering, she went through the open door of the flat and started looking despondently around her.

'Is *he* here?'

'Gone out to the pub, I think.'

'Figures,' Brenda said. She sat down heavily in the armchair, so heavily that little flurries of dust rose up on either side of her forearms. 'It's nice to see you again, Ted.'

'And you.'

In fact I didn't know whether I was glad to see Brenda at all. Not just because she fell into the category of business concluded, even though that business was someone else's, but because she belonged to a part of my life that I'd assumed to be over. It was as if – to choose someone else whose appearance would have made me deeply uneasy – Mr Parmenter had suddenly turned up on the doorstep, or Horace been discovered parking his motorbike out in the street.

'I don't suppose you expected to see me?' Brenda said again. 'Did you?'

'Not really. No.'

Brenda wagged her head at this. Settled in the armchair, lighting a cigarette from a packet Upward had left on the table on the butt of one she had in her mouth, she looked even more unhappy. There was a restlessness about her, too, that I didn't remember from the Frith Street days. Once or twice a noise from the street caught her ear and she jerked round to the door.

'Do you suppose that's him coming back?'

'It doesn't sound like it.'

I don't mind admitting that I had no idea how to deal with Brenda. The old Brenda, who talked placidly of her future in the hotel trade, I could handle: the trick was simply to listen and make encouraging comments. The new Brenda – a shrunken, faintly hopeless version who chain-smoked and chewed her fingers – was beyond me. By rights, I suppose, I should have asked what she was doing here, a good sixty miles from London – what was the matter with her, why she wanted to see Upward. Somehow this wasn't something I could bring myself to do. Neither, oddly enough, did Brenda seem to expect it. However pleased she might be to see me, I was a factotum, the welcoming party that would eventually make way for the master of the house, when whatever business lay between them could be transacted.

Brenda smoked another cigarette. 'Make us a cup of tea will you, Ted?' she asked.

I was standing over the boiling kettle when the noise of the street door slamming resounded beneath. It was Upward this time: no question. Distracted by something she had taken out of her bag, Brenda seemed not to hear it. Muttering something, I ran out of the door. Upward, halfway up the second flight, stopped when he saw me.

'It's Brenda.'

'Here?'

'In the flesh.'

'Christ!' Upward's face sank dramatically. 'Christ! That's all I bloody needed.' He was genuinely shocked. 'Look, hang about a minute will you?'

'Hang about where?'

'Anywhere. Christ!' Upward said again.

I watched him disappear above me, taking the last few steps at a run. The door slammed behind him. There was a sound of raised voices, then silence.

It was nearly two o'clock. There was no telling how long this would go on. In the end I left the building and walked along the front to a makeshift pier where teenagers stood jamming sixpences into slot machines and there was a kind of pram park of sunburned mothers and their children. There were long grey clouds coming in from the west – 'rainheads' Yarmouth people used to call them – and the sky threatened thunder. Sure enough, after twenty minutes or so, a storm blew up, sending the teenagers scuttling into coffee bars further along the front. The promenading mothers gathered up their belongings and disappeared. I took shelter under the pier's metal stanchions, wondering how long I could decently give it before going back, what I'd find when I got there, why Brenda had come, other things.

Coming back at four, I found the street door half open and the wind blowing leaves into the hallway. There was no one about. Upward sat on his own in one of the armchairs reading the *News of the World*. He looked sober, cautious, not especially put out.

'Brenda gone then?'

'As far as I know.'

'She seemed a bit upset.'

'Suppose she did.'

Somehow with Upward the questions you wanted to ask never got asked. What was Brenda doing here? What trouble was she in? Why should this involve Upward? There was silence for a minute or two. The scent Brenda had been wearing – it was cheap and overwhelmingly pungent – still hung in the air. I walked through into the bedroom. There, for some reason, the smell was even worse. Upward, still sitting in the armchair, was gearing himself up to say something.

'I gave her fifty quid, y'know.'

'Fifty quid?'

'Said she was having a bad patch,' Upward said, a bit defensively. 'It was all I had.'

'That was good of you.'

Upward looked as if he might be going to say something else. Then he stopped. His eye fell on the letters.

'Let's have a cup of tea,' he said. 'Something I want to talk to you about.'

I made the tea. Outside fine rain was streaking the surface of the window. Settling himself back in his chair, Upward talked for nearly half an hour with huge, unselfconscious seriousness about changes he wanted to make to several of the sketches. '. . . Reckon we might take out that line in the Wilson sketch . . . Never gets much of a laugh . . . Important that you look at the audience while you say that stuff about his mother . . . Tell the joke *with* them, not *at* them.'

The room began to go dark. Upward had forgotten all about Brenda, I realised. It was as if she had never been there.

For some reason the month or so after that afternoon is very clear in my mind. A week later we went back to London to start work on the BBC shows and perform at Gavin Newsome's private dinner. Upward had his picture printed in the *Radio Times.* Not quite knowing why I did it, I put twenty five-pound notes in an envelope and sent them by registered post to Brenda's last address. There was no acknowledgement. Not so very long after that I met Paula.

What I Remember Most

What I remember most is the journey back from York. With the boy on the other side of the table reading a comic, but looking up every so often – shyly? Hopefully? Who can tell? And the train taking a while to get going, struggling a bit to leave the city and the wooded country beyond the outskirts. Eating biscuits out of a Tupperware box Shena had packed for us, and thinking Shena disapproved. The boy not wanting the biscuits or the Coke I fetched him from the buffet. Saying: 'Aunty Shena doesn't like me drinking Coke.' And me answering, 'I'm not Aunty Shena', and then regretting it. Speeding south, finally, over the plain and the sun rising suddenly from nowhere – the day overcast till then – pulsing over the grass. And me and the boy having to shade our faces from the glare. Trying to talk to him and not getting anywhere. About school, and the house, and football, that kind of thing. The boy nodding. The odd question. Computer games? Staying up late? And me agreeing to it all, all these things I haven't thought about, all these things I don't know. What does a ten-year-old boy eat? What time should he get up in the morning? How much pocket-money should he have? And the boy sensing this, the uncertainty, and quietening down again, back in his seat, watching the sun speed across the fields, the other people in the carriage, me.

Not a long journey, two hours perhaps, King's Cross, the tube to Charing Cross. The boy tired but looking interestedly at the escalator ads, wanting to put the pound coins in the ticket machine. And then the taxi, the afternoon sun less intense now, burning over the water and the blackened wharves down by the river. Bermondsey, Rotherhithe and Greenwich. London names. The boy nearly asleep now, waking up near the station, sloughing through the hot streets. The house, silent as the grave, gaping with disuse. Me opening windows, switching on electricity, while the boy explores, padding wide-eyed from room to room, looking at the photographs on the wall, the framed posters. The telephone ringing, and Shena's voice charged with tension, the boy talking to her while I hover in the background, half not caring, half wanting Shena's approval. Ransacking the cupboard for old tins – sausages, beans, tomatoes. The boy saying: 'This is two years past its sell-by.' 'It doesn't matter. Tinned stuff always keeps.' 'How long? For ever?' 'Well, nearly for ever.' Eating tinned custard, cold, with dessert spoons, as the cars go past in the street.

And before that, a month before, being in the room with Paula, with more sunshine pouring in through the open window. And Paula hunched up in her bed-jacket, hands pressed together on the coverlet, looking thinner than you could believe a person could ever look, not talking but just looking at each other. The boy away somewhere, at school, out with his friends, I don't know. And me – a terrible admission – trying to remember how old she is. Forty-five maybe? Forty-six? But no age to look like a bundle of sticks tied up in a sheet. Shena in the next room showing her dislike with sharp, heavy clumps. And me thinking of Father before he died, face the colour of oatmeal, hair all gone. And going out into the kitchen, closing the door, and Shena saying 'Three weeks', like that, no tone or feeling in the words. Hearing a noise from Paula's room, going back to find she'd dropped a library book, reached down and not been able to raise herself, propping her up again and seeing the bone of her arm, a dreadful thing, no flesh on it, the jars of pills on the shelf beside the headboard, and saying 'Can I get you anything?' and her shaking her head.

Then later, talking about Daniel, how old he is, things she sees in him, attitudes. 'Like you.' 'How?' 'I don't know. Just like you.' About Shena, the house, the doctor. 'He's a strange one, that Dr Mackay.' 'Why?' 'I don't know. Nothing you could pin down. Nothing I could pin down.' And me thinking how long I'd known her, and coming up with a quarter of a century near enough. And forty-five, forty-six no age to die at, no age at all. Younger than me, younger than Father and Mother, younger than all of us. And all the things that should have been said not said, just lying there between us, because there was plenty of time, always plenty of time, until the last time of all, when suddenly there was no time, her arms on the coverlet like spindles, nothing there at all, except the things not said, Shena moving in the corridor, the sun cascading in over the empty bed.

White Stag Hunting

Did you hear about the Irishman who applied for a job at ICI? They asked him what nitrate was, and he said 'Time and a half'.

What Upward used to call 'it' – he meant success, fame and money – lasted about seven years, perhaps a bit longer. From 1972, say, to around 1980. After that, after the final TV series and the last Variety Performance, we could see things were winding down, that we were back where we'd been before, a rung or three from the top of the ladder, with younger people – 'kids' Upward used to call them dismissively – hurtling past and nothing in the world you could do to stop them. The odd thing about this ascent was how quickly it happened. One moment we'd been going backwards and forwards to dates in the train, the next we were being driven to them in a limo. Sandwiches in pubs suddenly became four-course meals in places that a year before we wouldn't have dared to set foot in. That's how it seemed at the time, though I suppose there was actually a period of about a year when you could see things moving into gear, taxi-ing forward and taking flight. I can remember a bank statement arriving some time in 1972 or 1973 telling me that I had £2,000 in my current account, and feeling hugely elated and at the same time faintly guilt-ridden on account of Father and what the money would have meant to him. I don't suppose there was a time in the whole of Father's life when his total assets amounted to more than £500.

The first TV series went out in 1972: eight half-hour episodes on Wednesday nights, just after *Coronation Street.* There was another one a year later, then a film – one of the last of the *Carry On*s, as it happened – with Upward as a randy, wench-fancying highwayman and me as his dim assistant. It was a disaster, of course, but by the time it came out this didn't matter for we'd moved up another notch. We were in panto that year in Croydon with Rod Hull and Emu, then out on the theatre circuit. By 1975 we were filling the Manchester Palace, the biggest theatre in the north in those days, for a week at a time. Oddly enough, I don't remember a great deal of it. The early years with Upward are full of sharp, vivid little memories, even down to the look on Upward's face when a line went across, but what came later isn't much more than a blur, a kind of whirl of expensive restaurants, the faces in the big theatres going back what seemed like hundreds of yards, the TV gantry lights burning down on your face. What remains, predictably enough, are one or two incidentals – cruising back in the small hours from some date up north, with Upward asleep with his head on the leather arm-rest and the Midlands towns going by in a sprawl of lights gleaming out of the darkness; ghastly dawns somewhere at the southern end of the M1, with the early lorries zipping past on the north-bound carriageway, sky the colour of a fish's underbelly, and the bulk of London gathered up in the mist below.

As you'll have gathered by now, perhaps, none of this appealed to me in the way that five or six years before I'd assumed it would. I used to drift through rooms – the high, cream-coloured rooms where Upward sat surrounded by the people who appealed to him – wondering what I was doing there, when I could decently get away. The faces came and went – I shook hands with the Queen once, backstage after a Royal Variety Performance, met Harold Wilson and talked football with Bobby Charlton – but they were never real, somehow, in the way that the old world had been. The Queen was simply a smile, Wilson a tetchy little man smoking a foul pipe, Bobby Charlton a bald thirty-five-year-old wondering what to do with the rest of his life. I wonder if you'll believe me when I say that I used to keep a list of the famous people I met? Lulu, Sir Gerald Nabarro, Rodney Marsh, Alvin Stardust, Little Jimmy Osmond, John Stonehouse, Len Murray, Malcom McDowell. Not many of them cut much ice these days, I dare say, but that was the kind of world I wandered through, made up of charity lunches and receptions, celebrity parties and trading back-chat with the showbiz columnists. What was worse, perhaps, was that I'd gone into it thinking I could preserve a sense of detachment, keep a bit of me at one remove from it all. And yet somehow the life you were living sucked you into it. However much you tried, you could never get away. I used to disappear sometimes for the odd weekend in between tours or recordings, decamp to a hotel somewhere off the beaten track or even take a furnished room in a town miles away from anywhere, and it was always the same – stacks of phone messages, telegrams, Upward appearing out of nowhere to spirit me away. Somebody – Upward, some under-strapper from the agency, even the local police force once – could always find you. Other people, too. Occasionally the old life that I hadn't given a thought to for a decade jumped up again to scare me. Once Uncle George and Aunt Sheila turned up backstage after a show we'd done at the Ipswich Gaumont and I took them out for a meal, but we just sat and stared at each other. The past, which I'd thought I could summon back on my own terms, walk into at will, turned out to have a wall round it. Worse, all through the meal, I could see that Uncle George was intent on touching me for fifty quid. He got it, too.

Upward, on the other hand, enjoyed himself tremendously.

I remember once, right at the beginning of the tornado years, perhaps even when we were signing some contract or other, asking him what he wanted from all this. Upward hardly paused to consider.

'The White Stag,' he said. He then quoted a piece of poetry he'd picked up somewhere which contained the line 'It's the white stag, fame, we're hunting'.

This admission, which Upward made quite matter-of-factly, seemed to me to reveal a huge amount about Upward. I could even visualise it physically: the stag, elusive, practically mythical, constantly disappearing among the highest rocks and pathways; Upward, grim-faced, determined to bring it down, convinced – and this was the most important thing – that he knew exactly what he'd find when, finally, the beast lay dead on the mountain path in front of him. In a sense I suppose this was what I envied most about him. Upward – and there was no getting away from this – knew exactly what he wanted success to consist of: the smiling hostess, the welcoming maitre d', the vacant table. For some reason these demands were nearly always met. All the same, Upward had to be treated on his own terms. This valuation could sometimes be rather high. Not everybody shared it. Once, I remember, the *Observer* sent quite a well-known novelist – Kingsley Amis, it might have been, or Anthony Burgess – along to interview him. Even now bits of what got printed still float around in my head: 'an undeniable panache and intelligence, compromised by innate and somehow gratuitous vulgarity', 'brash, over-confident, assertive . . . an apocalyptic door-to-door salesman metamorphosed into a comic titan'. Upward claimed he'd simply taken the man out to lunch and talked unrevealingly to him for an hour or so. Clearly, though, it had gone deeper than that. Somehow, without meaning to, Upward had given huge and lasting offence.

All this, though, was typical of the post-Sixties Upward, a character I found just as mystifying as the grim clown of the Catterick fatigue parties. The fixation with newspaper interviews, in particular, showed a side to him that I never got to the bottom of. Though he hated giving away details of his personal life, Upward was simultaneously ravished by the idea of journalists bringing accounts of him back to the paying public. Upward's favourite football team (Manchester City), Upward's political preferences (Labour, but with occasional dizzying lurches rightwards), what Upward smoked, thought about female beauty, the Archbishop of Canterbury and the European Economic Community – these were all subjects which a certain kind of newspaper reader in the mid-Seventies would have known all about. All this gave Upward a kind of notoriety, liable to break out in TV impersonations of him by other comedians, jokes in *Private Eye*, which I don't think he much minded. It was all part of the package. The truth was – and this is something I don't think I grasped until much later on – that Upward felt at home in this new world (shaking hands with the Duke of Kent, pictured with Mike Yarwood, boozing with Sid James) in a way that I didn't, could adapt himself to the people he came across (Lord Longford, Danny La Rue, Geoff Boycott) in a way I couldn't, showed effortless brilliance in matching what he had to offer (cheek, 'Northern commonsense') to whatever was needed.

Our trail stretched all over the Seventies. Look for our tracks anywhere in that odd, dead landscape of unrest and false dawns and pious hopes, decaying pasts and shiny futures, and you'll find them – on TV carol services with Angela Rippon and the cast of *Dad's Army*, umpiring the annual cricket match between the Lords and Commons, doing warm-ups for the Miss World Contest (Upward in a scarlet wig and sequins as 'Miss Galapagos Islands' claiming that his hobbies were looking after tortoises and world peace), guesting on the *Generation Game* as a couple of fantastically inept plate-spinners. Such an odd, unlikely, alarming world, but with its own walkways and purlieus, its neighbourhoods and backyards: the Thames studios at Teddington Lock early in the morning with the cigarette smoke already gathering under the ceiling; Leicester Square; the Ivy, where Upward would often eat lunch *and* dinner, sometimes not even bothering to leave the restaurant between the two; the cover of the *TV Times*. I've kept some of these pictures, which used to puzzle me. Upward, you see, looked like Upward, whereas I looked like someone paid to impersonate me, to keep the show rolling in my absence.

All the same, I wouldn't want you to think I was unhappy. There was money coming in. Even then, ten years in the trade, I still got a terrific kick out of the patterns that Upward and I wove on stage. And despite the dawns and departures, the expensive cars nosing out of the Midlands dusk, I liked the feeling that I was in control of my life in a way that I've not been before or since. It's difficult to explain this, hard to pin it down, but back in the days with Father and Mother, in the army, even under Upward's wing in Frith Street, I never had a sense of being able to act on my own. Now all that had changed. In hotels sometimes I used to dial room service late at night simply for the kick of having someone run around on my behalf. Quite often I'd take holidays abroad – sometimes with Paula, more often on my own – just for the pleasure of seeing new places at my own speed. All this is very clear in my mind: Bordeaux, once, in a week in June, with the villages asleep behind hedgerows of loosestrife; Venice, another time, on a day in November, with the water lashing over the flagstones. All pretty small beer, I suppose, but I liked it, liked the unhurriedness, the foreign voices, the slow pace of unknown lives.

Ask me what's left of those days and there it is: Upward swallowing oysters at Wheeler's; Cartwright and Newsome round the big table; Tracy Jacks peering out into the December twilight; Paula's face caught in the frame of door and jamb. All gone, of course, and long dead, but vivid for a while, and part of me.

At this height – two or three hundred feet – the view was disconcerting. Gathered up in the jumble of brick and concrete, buildings and landmarks that you knew turned unfamiliar. Only unmistakeable objects – the Post Office tower to the east, Green Park unfolding in the distance to the south – persuaded you of the reality of what you saw. The wind, thudding in against heavy plate-glass windows, made this feeling worse. Looking out at various points in the proceedings I used to lose my bearings completely, get confused by the lowering sky and the alien rooftops, until a voice or a slammed door dragged me back.

Outside it was already getting dark. The green recording light, which had been turned off ten minutes before, flickered unexpectedly into life again and then went dead.

'I should really like to wrap this up in the next half an hour,' Tracy Jacks said brightly. 'Say three-quarters of an hour. How does that sound?'

There was a silence. The two technicians who had come into the main studio from the smaller ante-room fenced off with glass nodded meekly. A third man – the assistant producer, who might have been called Jacobson – scribbled something in the margin of his clip-top pad. In the distance, beyond the glass, girls' heads could be seen bobbing up and down under the light.

'What's the hurry?' Upward said.

Shirt-sleeved, with an unlit cigarette in his mouth, seated alone at the circular table, he looked pretty irritated, but still more or less friendly. Upward liked Tracy Jacks, hesitated before complaining about or to him, but he was still capable of losing his temper.

'The power's going off again at four apparently,' Tracy Jacks said. 'Not in here, of course, but it makes things difficult.'

'I can see that.'

'There's another couple of pages to get through. We can deal with the other stuff later.'

'We could deal with the other couple of pages later,' Upward said. 'I don't care about bloody power cuts.'

Tracy Jacks and I swapped glances. He was a tallish, blond, heavy-featured character of about twenty-five, whose deference to Upward occasionally reached fantastic heights. On one occasion he'd been seen to stop whatever he was doing at the desk, descend through several levels in the lift and trek through half a mile of corridor to fetch Upward a bottle of stout from the staff canteen. Another time, waiting unseen in the doorway, I'd watched him scoop up some crumbs from the chair where he knew Upward would sit into a paper handkerchief.

'Arthur . . .' Tracy Jacks began.

For him to use Upward's Christian name meant that a kind of pleading had begun. Upward knew this, and appreciated it. Bored by this routine, which had been enacted countless times both here and at Teddington, I walked out into the ante-room where there was a coffee machine and a stack of newspapers and somebody had left the radio on.

> '*Dance on moonbeams, slide down rainbows*
> *In furs or bluejeans, you know what I mean*
> *Do the Strand* . . .'

It was the week before Christmas, a fortnight into the power workers' go-slow. There would be an election soon: everybody knew. The Prime Minister's face stared out of that morning's *Daily Mail*, lying on the newspaper rack: wooden, unresponsive. Upward had tried and failed to produce an imitation of Mr Heath, succeeded only in taking off the odd, champagne-bottle set of his shoulders. He was on much firmer ground with Wilson (all to do with the availability of props, Upward claimed, instancing the pipe). I looked back through the window where Upward, the unlit cigarette still clamped in his mouth, was listening to Tracy Jacks in much the same way that Father had listened to reps from the sweet companies that he didn't want to deal with: civil but unimpressed. Fatter now than he had been a year or two ago, Upward looked tired, but still extraordinarily energetic. He was only waiting for the right cue, you thought, to get up and whirl round the room, take

Tracy Jacks in his arms, start doing high kicks. I decided to go back into the studio.

'Plenty of time for a drink,' Upward was saying. 'Then nip back here and bugger the power workers.'

For all his air of barely suppressed energy, Upward liked to work at a leisurely pace. We had been here for a couple of hours. Upward's plan was that we ought to go to the BBC Club round the corner from Langham Place, and then wind the recording up later in the afternoon.

'Arthur . . .' Tracy Jacks said again. 'Arthur. In another hour or so there won't be any lights down there. I rang up to check.'

Arguments between Upward and Tracy Jacks weren't unusual. There was no telling how long this one might go on. The technicians had disappeared, I noticed. In a bit, unless he could be got to see reason, Upward would turn petulant.

'Well, let's see what Ted says about it,' Tracy Jacks went on, not very hopefully. 'What do you think, Ted?'

'If there's only another couple of pages to get through, we ought to do them now. Then you can go off down the club.'

Upward looked suspicious. He hated the idea that Tracy Jacks and I were, as he sometimes put it, 'ganging up on him'.

'*I want a drink*,' he said suddenly. 'It's not much to bloody ask for, is it? *I want a drink*.'

'Have a drink then,' Tracy Jacks said encouragingly. 'Have it here. I'll send someone to go and fetch it.'

'I don't want it here. I want it downstairs.'

It was a quarter to three. Paula would be expecting me soon. A slow fuse, which had been burning for the last ten minutes or so, finally reached the powder store.

'Why don't you get off your arse you fat cunt and do what Tracy says for a change? Go on, just do it for once.'

'Ted!' Tracy Jacks looked genuinely horrified, as if he scarcely believed anyone would be capable of talking to Upward like this. Upward, on the other hand, shifted uneasily in his chair, sat bolt upright, pulled out a box of matches and lit the cigarette.

'All right,' he said, not sounding very put out. 'Have it your own way.'

Arguments with Upward often ended like this. In fact Upward sometimes admitted that he only started them as a means of staving off boredom. While he smoked the cigarette, Tracy Jacks recalled the technician and spoke to the girls in the ante-room before finally settling himself at the sound board.

'Anyway,' Upward said, waiting until he was out of the room. 'It's a bloody awful script.'

'We should have done it ourselves.'

'It's only radio.'

Upward's annoyance about the missed drink now had a context. He was bored by the BBC, Tracy Jacks, dog-eared scripts with the producer's comments written on them in green biro, had moved on into a world of TV studios, restaurants and showbiz columnists. A world, too, in which Upward's word, if not exactly law, counted for more than it had done three years before. Upward liked imposing himself on situations: changing his mind about food; sending a waiter off into the night for a packet of cigarettes; telling drivers to make unexpected detours. Sometimes this ended up as outright bullying, usually with people whose position in life left them with no obvious means of defence. Humiliated doormen, floor managers vaguely aware they were being 'got at' – Upward's path through this period of his life was littered with casualties. To do him justice, I don't think he ever realised what a nuisance he made of himself, or why such violent offence was sometimes taken. I once saw a barman whom Upward had not exactly insulted but verbally sparred with for a minute or two pick up a soda siphon and squirt it over his head. Upward was genuinely shocked.

'Why would he want to do that for?' he asked, as they sponged him down afterwards. 'Why on earth should he want to do that for?'

It was as if one of Marie-Antoinette's gardeners had suddenly jabbed her in the eye with a pruning fork.

'All right then,' Tracy Jacks said keenly. 'Page seventeen. Let's take it from the top, shall we? Green light coming up in five seconds and *away* we go.'

It was the last instalment of an old series, begun way before the TV contracts and the newspaper profiles, in which Upward played the owner of a lacklustre travel-agency, with me as his faithful but none too intelligent sidekick. Two years ago it had been quite funny. As Tracy Jacks had promised, the rest of the session took about three-quarters of an hour. Upward read his lines without emphasis. By twenty to four we were finished. Outside the sky was turning blue-black.

'Are you coming down the club?' Upward asked, tossing his copy of the script pointedly into a wastepaper basket near the door.

'Not today.'

'Tarts,' said Upward theatrically, to no one in particular. 'Can't keep away from them. Well, give her my love.'

Safely behind the studio door, looking back through the square of glass, I watched Tracy Jacks heave into sight with an ashtray, already keen to catch the inch or so of ash that hung from Upward's cigarette. Then I went out into the corridor, past the photographs of Arthur Askey and Michael Bentine, Roy Castle and Eric Sykes, to the lift, thinking, as I so often did those days, restlessly and a bit uneasily, about Paula.

I met Paula in 1973, at a hotel somewhere in Croydon which the cast of a revue we'd been headlining at the Fairfield Hall had colonised after the show. At that point she'd have been about twenty-one – a thin, dark-haired girl who undulated about in the front row of something called the Marsha Flett Dance Troupe. Don't laugh. That's the kind of thing the second- and third-tier acts were called in those days – the Mike Sands Singers, the Butterfly Chorus, the Harry Grayson Quartet. The Marsha Flett Dance Troupe – Marsha Flett was a tough old witch in her fifties who looked on keenly from the side of the stage – consisted of a dozen girls in their teens and early twenties with names like Samantha and Patch – again, that's the kind of thing chorus girls were called in those days – whose job was to open and close the show and possibly transact a bit of business with the comedians midway through the second half. Upward, in particular, wasn't above routines which involved him walking up and down a line of female dancers inspecting the generously framed *décolletage*. Presumably I'd seen Paula before – had to have done, if it came to that, as there was a sketch in which the dancers doubled up as night-club hostesses – but it wasn't until afterwards that I properly became aware of her. I have a particular memory of her, head in profile, with a cluster of other girls, laughing at a joke that someone –

probably Upward – was telling, having supper a bit later with her and another girl called Antonella who Upward claimed had allowed herself to be 'done' earlier that evening on one of the hotel's snooker tables.

Paula! My God, what can I tell you about Paula? What could you tell me about someone you were married to for twenty years? What I remember about her now is coloured by what came afterwards, of course, but I know the things I felt about her at the time were more or less genuine. I can remember a Sunday afternoon two or three weeks after we'd met, wandering around one of the London parks for hours on end, trying to work it all out, and then going to a phone box to call her number and being furious when she wasn't there. A couple of days later I even went to a theatrical agency in Wardour Street and got them to look up the Marsha Flett Dance Troupe in the files on the off-chance there'd be a picture – that was how I felt about Paula back in the days of the oil crisis and the three-day week.

Paula (her surname was Marriot)! The Marsha Flett Dance Troupe! The Fairfield Hall, Croydon! It's another part of time, of course, a big old amphitheatre with space for two thousand, packed with people who'd brought their kids to gawp at faces they knew from the television, no smut, incidental entertainment provided by Ali Bongo and his Mysteries of the Orient and a couple of all-in wrestlers. Oddly enough, when I think of Paula – which is something I've never stoppped doing – it's always that world she seems to inhabit: girls in leotards glimpsed through half-open dressing-room doorways taping their breasts up with sticking plaster, microphones whining feedback at you whenever you approached, Upward's face through the smoke, Marsha Flett working out her percentages on the back of an envelope in the cubby-hole beyond the safety-curtain. The later days, in Surrey or at the big house looking out over the Stour, might just as well not be there.

What did Paula look like ten years later? I can barely remember. But I can tell you what she looked like in 1973. I don't think it's patronising her to say that she had a Seventies face. People grow out of the landscapes you place them in. Marjorie Lovelace looked like a Fifties schoolgirl, which is what she was. Mary looked like the daughter of a Norfolk farmer who'd led an exceptionally sheltered life – an exclusive category, maybe, but one that would have meant something to the people she knocked up against, and certainly meant something to me. I'm not saying that Paula looked like Susan Hampshire or Felicity Kendal, but her face belonged to that kind of world: trusting, friendly, a bit uncertain, willing to make the best of a bad job. At the same time this hint of vulnerability was deceptive, as it came combined with a huge amount of professional *nous*. The Marriots, it turned out, were a real showbiz family. Paula's father had been some kind of agent back in the Fifties, and old Mrs Marriot was an ex-Variety girl who looked as if she could have shown Marsha Flett a thing or two. I went round their house once or twice – they lived in Penge or Sydenham – and it was a kind of museum, full of signed photographs of Variety stars and Mrs Marriot executing the Can-Can in 1948. Naturally enough, what I did cut no ice with them at all. I can remember Paula once starting to talk about some TV show we were doing and old Marriot not even bothering to listen. To him TV was just an abomination that had killed off proper entertainment.

But the Marriots were friendly enough in their way, if a bit worried about Paula and the kind of situations she might be getting herself into. I used to go down there sometimes on a Sunday night for supper, and doze in front of the TV while Mr Marriot criticised sitcom actors and his wife nagged Paula about not eating enough. Shena, Paula's older sister, worked in a bank but I don't suppose I met her more than two or three times at this point. And though it wasn't in the least like the old days at Southtown I'm sure that the kind of routine with which the Marriots invested their lives deeply appealed to me. There's a lot to be said for knowing that your dinner's going to be on the table at seven p.m. sharp and that it'll either be shepherd's pie or baked cod.

Mother would have looked Paula appraisingly over in a vague sort of way and pronounced that she was a 'nice girl'. This wasn't necessarily a compliment. It simply meant that from the limited materials available for scrutiny Mother couldn't find anything openly antagonistic to her own interests. As for the Marriots and the terraced house in Penge, I can't imagine what she would have said – it was all so beyond her experience as to render all previous social judgements useless. None of this, perhaps, has much of a bearing on Paula, the kind of life we lived together, what was said. On the other hand, you couldn't get away from these connections. At least I couldn't. Entering Paula (something I accomplished on the fourth or fifth time we met, with every encouragement) I knew I was entering a world, that however much the Marriots, Penge, family ancestry, kept to the back of the stage they were still there, so to speak, liable to be brought up to the spotlight or otherwise involved at the drop of a hat. What I liked about Paula, I suppose, was her eagerness to please, and to be pleased. I don't mean in relation to myself, but in a whole mass of tiny details and sensations. An hour of sunshine when the forecast said rain, a lost five-pound note run to earth in the bottom of her handbag – these brought out an enthusiasm that was faintly childish.

'Gosh, that was fun,' she said when we'd been to bed that first time – I can remember her sitting up against the pillow with her fine hair falling down over her face – and it was quite genuine.

Later I used to wonder what she really thought of me at this time, but I never found anything to change the original estimate, or alter the conviction that it was all my fault.

Standing in the doorway of Broadcasting House after an hour or so in Tracy Jacks's lofted studio, you got an odd feeling of having returned to a different world. Waved on by the smiling commissionaire, the door held open by a Radio One DJ on his way into the building, it took a moment to recover. Outside it was nearly dusk. In the distance a line of buses had come to a halt in Regent Street. Not far away, on the steps of All Souls' church, a Salvation Army choir was singing Christmas carols. I started to thread my way north east through the warren of streets that separated Langham Place and the Euston Road.

Paula lived in a basement flat in Nottingham Place, next door to a launderette and a students' hostel. Oddly enough, Upward had had a flat around this way a year or two back. Just now he was living in Fulham, with whom nobody quite knew. What Upward got up to remained completely his own business, ever since the day Brenda had turned up at the south-coast lodging house. Quite often he'd produce girls at social events, usually bottle-blondes of incredible gormlessness, but there was no way of knowing how they fitted into the scheme of things. More than once, recently, Upward had talked about getting married.

There was a light on in the basement: the rest of the house was dark. In the area rotting leaves and old newspapers crackled underfoot. As I rang the bell the door opened and Paula's face appeared behind it.

'Hurry up. The power goes off in a minute.'

'Have you just got up?'

She was wearing a dressing gown, with a towel wound round her head like a turban.

'I was having a bath, silly.'

Paula kept odd hours. It was quite likely that she had only woken up half an hour or so ago. I followed her into the flat's main room, where there was a children's programme flickering on the TV and a kettle boiling in the corner.

'What do we do when the lights go?'

'Candles,' Paula said. 'Look.' She pointed to a row of jam-jars ranged along the windowsill. 'And a couple of torches. We can hang them from the curtain rail or something.'

'Wouldn't it be simpler to go to bed?'

'Don't be naughty. Anyway, there are some blankets.'

I watched her as she skipped round the room making tiny rearrangements and adjustments to the scheme, completely absorbed and delighted. Without Paula, it had to be said, the flat would have been hugely uninviting. It was basically a single, not very large, room with bedroom, kitchen and bathroom running off at the sides. Most of Paula's clothes lay between paper tissue on the sofa, owing to the damp, whose reek was at this point overlaid rather than disguised by the smell of burnt toast. Every available wall surface was covered by pictures of Paula: Paula aged seven in a line of infant tap-dancers; Paula at ten in a pierrot's outfit; teenage Paula in ballet gear; in an amateur version of *Oklahoma!*. For some reason the effect wasn't at all self-advertising. You simply got a sense of effort, hard work, awareness of the distance yet to climb.

A church clock somewhere nearby began to strike the hour. On cue the electric light, the TV and the kettle went off simultaneously. I fished a box of matches out of my pocket and started lighting the candles. Paula dropped down on the sofa amid the piles of evening dresses and spangled stage costumes. Now that darkness had fallen, the bounce seemed to have gone out of her.

'I hate this,' she said. 'They ought not to let it happen.'

'I don't suppose the government wants it to happen any more than you do.'

Paula quite often said things like this. It was her one connection with Mother: the idea that 'they' – a mysterious organisation, never exactly defined but probably taking in all forms of civil administration – spent their time conspiring to ruin the lives of ordinary people.

'That reminds me,' Paula said. 'Upward rang with a message, just before you came. Something he'd forgotten to tell you.'

'I didn't know he had your number.'

'Well, he rang anyway. Said not to forget the Mayflower meeting in the morning.'

'Thanks. I hadn't.'

I was struck by the fact that Upward knew – had managed to get hold of, as I certainly hadn't told him – Paula's phone number. Normally Upward showed no interest in the girls I knew.

'No offence or anything pal,' he'd once said. 'But they're all just *women*, aren't they?'

At the same time he liked keeping tabs on people. Abroad once or twice on solitary holidays, I'd been slightly startled to come back to the hotel and find telegrams from him lying on the reception desk. This habit of Upward's had produced a TV sketch, in which a husband desperate to get away from his wife relocates to ever more far-flung destinations – the Faroe Islands, Greenland, Krakatoa – only for the silence to be broken by the tap on the door, the phone call, the whirr of the carrier pigeon and so on.

'Is that another of those advertising agency things?'

'Sort of. The meeting's in the City. London Wall somewhere.'

Paula cheered up a bit. 'I thought we were going off somewhere tomorrow.'

'We can go away at the weekend if you like.'

'Can't. We're doing the Winter Dance Spectacular at Kensington Town Hall. Marsha would go up the wall if I wasn't there. What's Mayflower, anyway?'

What was Mayflower? It's true to say that at this point in my life I barely knew. There were ads for it in all the newspapers – I'd seen one only that lunch-time, waiting in Tracy Jacks's ante-room. Essentially Mayflower was the latest scheme dreamed up by Gavin Newsome – Sir Gavin Newsome as he now was – with the aim of encouraging the 'small entrepreneur'. The goods involved were mostly cosmetics. The idea was that interested parties put up a small sum – I think it was a thousand pounds – to start a small business to sell the stuff on commission. There were inducements for persuading other people – 'go-ahead friends and neighbours' as the ads put it – to join in. As the scheme was aimed at the less well-off, there were intermediaries at hand to fix up capital loans. I had an idea that the Bank of Bristol – this was a cooperative bank in which Newsome had an interest – was involved somewhere. So far Upward and I had done two quite funny TV ads in which I featured as a doubtful housewife and Upward as a glib neighbour who contrives to sell her a bottle of toilet water. I explained some of this to Paula. Outside, Nottingham Place looked even eerier than usual, the darkness of the buildings relieved only by occasional glows and pinpricks of light. Paula discovered that the water in the kettle was still reasonably hot and made two cups of lukewarm tea.

'He's a bit *grand*, isn't he, Sir Gavin Newsome? I've seen him on TV.'

I thought about this. It depended what Paula meant by 'grand'. Smartly dressed? Upper-class? Well spoken? Gavin Newsome was all of these things, but I'd have hesitated to call him grand. Dukes and duchesses, members of the House of Lords were grand. What Paula meant was a faintly distinguished-looking character in a three-piece suit who talked with what Mother would have called a 'half-crown voice'. Paula having heard of Gavin Newsome – she was bored by news programmes – was a tribute to his impact on popular life. He wrote articles in Sunday newspapers about the 'commercial spirit'. There'd even been talk at one point about co-opting him into the cabinet.

'Anyway, he's Upward's friend, not mine.'

It was Upward's old trick of knowing people. Pop singers. Cabinet ministers. Tycoons. Whoever they were, Upward somehow managed to get talking to them, draw them out, draw them in.

Now I remembered, he'd even managed to spend a weekend at Newsome's country estate in Sussex.

'It was all right,' Upward had reported back. 'Good grub. Drinks trays when you wanted them. Isla – Lady Newsome – she's all right. Doesn't give herself airs like some of them. You ought to come next time.'

This being Upward, quite a lot of cake had been had and eaten too. I later found out that, amid much grand company, he'd made a point of sitting down to Sunday lunch in his shirt sleeves, loudly demanded a bottle of stout instead of whatever vintage was offered, and called the Tory MP placed next to him 'old cock'.

The room was getting cold. Paula's cat – a ginger tom called Tigger – stalked through the kitchen doorway, looked at us unconcernedly and went away again.

'When does the power go on again?'

'Not for ages. Seven or eight.'

'Where are those blankets you were talking about?'

Using the blankets and a couple of sleeping bags Paula pulled out of a cupboard, we made up a kind of nest on the floor beyond the sofa and climbed into it. Lit only by the row of candles, wavering in the draughts of air that blew through the front door, the photographs of Paula in her ballet gear, as the lead in *Oklahoma!*, looked a bit grotesque.

'It's cold,' Paula said. 'You'll have to warm me up.'

The usual things happened. Afterwards, while Paula slept – she did this rather like a baby, both hands gripping an imaginary parallel bar just above her head – I smoked a cigarette, watched the reflections that the lights of the passing cars made on the walls of the buildings opposite, and thought about it all: Paula, Upward, the Mayflower meeting. Nothing particularly out of the ordinary had happened that afternoon, unless you counted the power cut. Tracy Jacks. Upward in the studio. Paula's flat. I'd been there before. I'd be there again. Somehow, though, I could feel myself reaching decisions about things that I could barely put into words.

A bit later Paula woke up. Shortly after that the lights came on again.

We got married – eventually, and with various delays and rows – in the summer of 1975 at a church not far from the Marriots' place in Penge. Paula's face beneath the veil. Upward standing ostentatiously to one side with the ring case. A patch of grass outside the church where three or four bridesmaids – they were distant cousins of Paula's, I think – played ring-a-ring-a-roses after the service. It's all utterly distinct and real in my mind, an endless procession of smiling faces and expensive suits. Terry Wogan was there, Benny Hill and Michael Crawford. Morecambe & Wise sent a telegram. On the wedding photos Paula and I look a bit swamped, pressed into the dead centre of the throng of faces, familiar and unfamiliar, and a bit diminished by them. After the service old Marriot, who'd now decided I was a good thing, confided in me that he thought his daughter had more talent than anyone had ever suspected and the important thing was to get her into films. Upward got drunker than I'd ever seen him and the wedding cake was carried into the room on the shoulders of the Marsha Flett Dance Troupe. It was a proper showbiz wedding.

And afterwards, what happened then? I'd like to say that we went back to the big house in Weybridge I'd bought with the proceeds of the first three TV series and lived happily ever after, but of course it wasn't like that. I was thirty-five then, and if I try to remember the person I was in those days for some reason it's much more difficult to get to grips with than the boy in the square in Southtown. The odd thing – something I'd never had to deal with before – was that I had time on my hands. Upward & King had been three years in the limelight now, and the pattern of what we did was pretty much established. A TV series a year, usually in the spring or autumn. Six or eight weeks in summer season at Blackpool, Bournemouth or Margate. A Christmas pantomime maybe, if the money was good. Odd club dates around the country and bits of advertising work. Beyond that, though, time hung heavy. Occasionally I saw Upward and we'd sift through ideas for sketches, but that was a morning's work. Newspapers used to make out sometimes that we lived in each other's pockets – the TV series, of course, was based on the idea that we lived in the same house – but that was all rubbish. When we weren't working I never saw him more than once a week. It was odd when you thought about it. For five or six years we'd barely been apart for more than a few hours, and now he was simply someone I made time for in my diary now and again, like a business partner or an accountant. He used to come for Sunday lunch sometimes, or we'd play golf – that was the trendy celebrity sport in those days, you were always having your picture taken playing golf – but it never really worked. He nearly always came on his own, which meant Paula and I had to sit there staring at him, or else he brought some more or less unsuitable girl whom you were glad to see the back of. As ever, Upward's private life – his whole life outside comedy – remained a complete mystery. He had a big house down in Kent somewhere, where we went a couple of times, but I don't think he lived there often. In any case I had other things to think about. A year after we got married, Paula miscarried. I can remember her standing in the bathroom with the blood running down her legs and a look of absolute horror on her face such as I'd never seen before in anyone. There was another a year after that, then another six months later. Sometimes we used to talk about what we wanted to do with the rest of our lives – Paula's ideas were always abstract suggestions like 'go to America' or, even vaguer, 'see the world'. Nothing ever came of them. There wasn't anything wrong between us, I don't think, simply that she was faintly dissatisfied with the situation she'd ended up in: stuck in the big house at Weybridge – the neighbours, of course, barely acknowledged our existence – childless, with a husband who sat upstairs reading. I'd discovered books, you see, by then. I used to order them up in great parcels from Foyles and Hatchards and go through them like a child in a sweetshop. In fact that's how I remember the whole of the late Seventies – sitting upstairs in the study at Weybridge, with the view out over the lawn to the fields and the Surrey hills in the distance, Paula in the kitchen, only the occasional ring of the phone to bring us back to the world beyond, above all the feeling that you were happy, reasonably happy, with what you had but knew – feared – suspected – that it couldn't last. Like so much of life, I suppose.

The Wednesday-morning arrangements worked out fine. By eight-fifteen I had Daniel packed off to school and was waiting for one of the commuter trains to Charing Cross. A quarter-circuit of the Circle Line got me to Liverpool Street with ten minutes to spare before the nine-thirty to Norwich. I slept for half an hour, woke to find the train already running through Chelmsford, with its strew of soccer pitches and genteel factories, on over the Essex flats. All the time as we went east I found myself searching for familiar things. They weren't hard to find. The view out over the Stour beyond Manningtree looked exactly as I'd left it seven years ago. Ipswich was a jumble of sidings and smoke-blackened bridges. The Suffolk market towns didn't seem to have changed since I was a kid: the lines of faces drawn back beyond the safety line; the dopey porters staring out of the door of the waiting room; the rows of cars in the station forecourt. Almost before I knew it I was in Norwich, where the buildings around the football ground had been torn away to create a wasteland of car-parks and road-schemes, but the station was pretty much the same. I bought a cup of coffee in a Styrofoam cup and a copy of the *Eastern Daily Press* and took them along to one of the outer platforms where a three-coach sprinter was waiting to take me the last twenty miles to Yarmouth. There was no one much about: a few old women with shopping bags and a couple of chaps in suits who talked about insurance. Needless to say, I didn't drink the coffee or read the paper. I spent the time staring out of the window, watching the landscape change and then settle down, from the spongy green meadows that marked the edge of the Broads to the flat, level plain of the Acle Strait.

And then suddenly there we were. Inevitably it was all a bit inconsequential and out of focus: a couple of slate-grey platforms, ticket office with crowing advertisements, taxis in the street beyond. It was one of those sharp, clear days that you only get on the east coast in winter – bitterly cold, with every gull in the North Sea coming inland for food – and I pottered about for a while on the forecourt getting my bearings before I headed off into the town. Before I did this I took a look at myself in a shop window, and I didn't look too bad – decent coat, most of my hair still there, not that far removed from young Ted King who'd come here a dozen times a year back in the Sixties. All the same I didn't kid myself that anyone was going to know who I was. I wasn't sure I even wanted them to. I just wanted to stalk around the place for an hour or two, see how things had changed or hadn't changed and then come back, not intrude on anything. And so I set off, stopping every so often to look in windows or stare at the skyline, along the approach roads that led into the centre. Do you know, it was the oddest sensation? Like looking for the body of a human being or an animal and finding only the bones. Most of the things I remembered were still there, but they'd been changed in such a way that you had to stop to think twice or even three times about the original. The churches were still the same, and the market square, but the Sun Alliance building where I'd stared out of the window all those afternoons had been swallowed up into a huge wall of marble and glass, and fantastic things had been done to some of the shops. There was a bloke standing on the edge of the market stalls selling copies of the *Big Issue* and I went over and bought one. Lo and behold if he didn't turn round and say 'Thanks, pal,' in an accent straight out of *Brigadoon*. Surely there didn't used to be Scottish people in Yarmouth? Of course there did, but they used to come to work on the herring catch sixty years ago.

It was lunch-time now, and the town centre was a bit crowded: young blokes in suits stepping out of the big offices, crowds of girls in coats. Most of the big businesses I remembered from forty years ago were still there, but they'd been joined by a whole roster of newcomers. I headed on towards the sea, intending to take a look at the bowling greens (presumably they were still there) and the pleasure beach, whose ferris wheel I'd been able to see out of the corner of my eye for the past five minutes, and there it all was, Yarmouth front in all its glory. It was out of season, of course, and most of the fish and chip restaurants and the amusement arcades were boarded up, but the whole thing cheered me up beyond measure – it was all so horribly vulgar and basic, the kind of thing you had to be practically half-witted to enjoy, run by canny Norfolk businessmen who'd swindle you out of your last fifty pence if you'd let them. I had half a mind to go into one of the arcades and blue five pounds on the machines, but I knew it would be a waste of time, and besides there were more important things to do. It was even colder down here in sight of the sea, and I crossed the road to the wider pavement on the far side, next to some raked-over flowerbeds and a display board advertising the marina. Eastwards the sea was grey-white, and there were a couple of tankers sliding by along the horizon, on their way from Harwich to the Hook I supposed. I went on a bit further and then pulled up sharp. Where the road bent round towards the pleasure beach and a municipal car-park there was a barrier across the pavement made up of a metal bar stretched lengthways across some packing cases. Ten yards away a police car was idling at the verge with a bored-looking constable leaning against the bonnet eating a Mars bar. Seeing me staring at the barrier he stumped across and gave me a look.

'Sorry sir, road's closed.'

'What's the trouble?'

He was a huge, beefy lad with a corrugated face and an accent that could almost have been Fram. A bit puzzled that I needed any kind of explanation, he gestured in the direction of the car-park.

'It's the travellers, sir. Parked up by the pleasure beach. We've closed the road off.' He poked at the *Eastern Daily Press* under my arm. 'There's been enough about it in the papers.'

A furious little old man with iron-grey hair and spectacles balanced on the bridge of his nose – the kind of little old man who'd stood in the shop talking to Father half a century ago – came cruising across the road just in time to hear the last half sentence or so.

'That's right. Bloody gyppos parked up on council property and too idle to use the toilets. There's human excrement piled up on that beach, and what are your lot bloody doing about it, eh? You ought to run them and their fancy cars off the site and back to Ireland.'

'It's a point of view,' the policeman said.

He looked embarrassed by the intervention, but not unsympathetic. Possibly he had ideas of his own on the subject. I walked back the way I'd come, not altogether surprised but wondering what Father and Mother would have thought if they'd lived to be told that you couldn't use a municipal car-park in their town because a gang of travellers had taken up residence in it. Even Father – mild-mannered Father, wincing as he broke the rabbit's neck – would have had something to say about that. Thinking about Father and Mother, which oddly enough I hadn't been doing while I was drifting past the shopfronts and along the esplanade, made me remember what I was doing here. It was just after one o'clock. I set off towards the quayside in the direction of Southtown.

For a while – down by the quays and across the bridge – I knew exactly where I was. Even the river was the same – a greeny-grey, like washing-up water with odd shapes and protrusions visible way below the surface. But then, going down one of the approach roads to what I thought was the square, I got into trouble. Doubling back towards the river I tried again, only to resurface in a sort of cobbled courtyard packed with expensive-looking cars. There was no one about or I would have asked somebody. As it was I kept on through the yard – the buildings on either side were all smartish business premises – until at the end it opened out into a tarmac plaza with tropical plants growing in tubs and lumps of artistically arranged concrete roped off with chains. I was just about to turn back again when something in the set of the windows made me stop. On the instant I realised – and it hit me with an actual pain – that I was standing on the west side of what had been the square. I looked around once or twice wondering if I'd mistaken things, but there was no getting away from it. After I'd stood there for a bit and taken another look at the buildings on the far side I managed to work it out. All the shops had gone, except for what had been Wedderbury's – it was the long, gleaming windows that had given me the clue – which was now an up-market marine suppliers. In their place was a row of what looked like municipal offices – three-storey affairs with green-and-white signs plastered over the frontage. The main part of the square, where the fenced-off garden and the row of beech trees had been, had disappeared altogether.

On the east side were more offices and a property developer's showroom. Dodging a few people in suits moving in the direction of the courtyard, I went over to take a look. That was it all right, where Father's shop had been, and the sub-post office and the bakery, or rather it wasn't, because you couldn't tell where the original buildings were. I dare say if I'd have had a map of the place from the Fifties I could have worked it out. As it was, all I could do was the vaguest kind of superimposing. In the end I walked up to the spot I thought most narrowly approximated to the site of Father's shop, which turned out to be some sort of employment clinic, and hung about for a while. Curiously, I wasn't as shocked as I'd thought I'd be. The past is never there when you want it, or how you want it. All the same, it shook me to see the place where I'd watched Father going bankrupt, smashed up the kitchen with Betty and chased after Marjorie Lovelace, turned into an office-block. For a second or two I wondered about going inside, inventing some excuse that would let me sit down in a chair for a moment, but in the end I thought better of it. All I could think of was Father and Mother and how the fact that the place they'd lived in had disappeared had somehow diminished them and taken them further out of my grasp.

There was a taxi creeping along the far corner of the asphalt, and I flagged it down. Pretty soon we were bowling along a B-road south of the town in the direction of the farming country. The cabbie was about my age, with an accent that wouldn't have been out of place in the square forty years ago, but he shook his head over the various names I tried him with. He remembered the shops in the square, though, and volunteered the information that most of them had kept going in one form or another until the early Eighties when the council had redeveloped the site. All the time I was staring out of the window for landmarks, thinking that there used to be cows in a particular field or that surely beyond that hedge was where the houses began. The cabbie looked on with interest.

'Where exactly are we going, guv?'

It was a good question. 'It used to be called Parmenter's Farm. Ever heard of it?'

He hadn't, of course, so I sent him through the village and up the hill on the farther side. As far as I recalled in the old days the track – it wasn't much more than that – had wound off the road about half a mile out. We cruised along, past fresh-painted new houses set in the clearings (surely they hadn't been there before?) and spruce little meadows – all the raggedness I remembered from forty years back had gone – without seeing anything except a sign or two advertising what looked a fairly plush hotel. Another half-mile and I knew we were past the turn where the track had been, so I made the cabbie retrace our steps. Sure enough, there was the sign again, set back from the road to the right of a broad concrete drive.

WAVENEY HOTEL MICHELIN LISTED

Afternoon teas Full dinner menu

Again, just as it had done when I stood in the square, something clicked. The Parmenters had gone, died or sold up, and this was the result.

'Just drive up here a bit, will you?'

In the old days it had been a rutted track, where the cow parsley grew eight feet high and you could see the banks of rhododendrons leading away to the house. Now it was a kind of small highway going through neatly kept hedges with passing places and little chained-off arbours with gravel floors. The cow parsley had gone, along with the rhododendrons. In the distance, up the hill, I could see the outlines of the house. There were several cars parked about, and what looked like the first hole of a golf course. For a second or two again I hesitated, even wondered about seeing whether they did lunches for non-residents. Then in the middle distance I saw a couple of figures coming down the hill towards me. They were men, a bit older than me, in their sixties perhaps, done up in the standard retired persons' golf gear – Pringle sweaters, checked caps and trousers and huge golfing brogues – each of them trundling a little golf trolley behind them like an outsize shopping bag. The cab slowed to let them by and I caught a glimpse of the lined, expensive faces – not particularly smug or pleased with themselves but relaxed and confident, as if there was no better destiny than to be strolling down a hill in Norfolk in your sixties with a golf club under your arm. After that I knew it was no good, that I simply couldn't face the sight of whatever they'd done to the Parmenters' farm, and the people who'd be hanging round it. It wasn't that I disliked it, or them, merely that I knew what it would be like – the menu done up in French and little brass table lamps stuck in the alcoves where Mrs Parmenter – my mother-in-law if it came to that – had left her knitting patterns, all this come to disturb the ghosts of people I'd known and lived with. In the end I made the cabbie reverse back down the drive – there wasn't enough room to turn round – past the golfers, who were smoking cigars under a tree, and back on to the road.

'Anywhere else, guv?' the cabbie wondered, sounding a bit puzzled. You could see his point.

'The church. Another mile down the road.'

It was impossible for anyone to muck that about, surely? We went on following the bend in the road – there were more new houses dotted about – passed another tiny hamlet with a pub done up in mock-Tudor, which I just about remembered, and there it was, set back on the hill behind the trees, the church where I'd got married back in 1961, with Mother scowling in the back row, old Parmenter resplendent in his best suit and Mrs Parmenter sniffing into a cotton handkerchief. I left the cab at the foot of the hill and walked slowly up, past the trees, through the lych-gate, on towards the porch. For some reason everything looked very small. There were a couple of benches and a notice or two about flower-arrangements. They didn't even have their own vicar, just a rota with half-a-dozen other parishes. I wondered how many people came here now on a Sunday? Twenty? Thirty? There'd have been a couple of hundred crammed in for Harvest Festival in the Fifties. Inside the church itself there was flaking plaster all over the floor and a huge hole in the roof of the belfry, where the bells had been taken down. I prowled about for a bit, took a look at the Bible lying on the big eagle's head lectern – it was a massive King James with the 's's all 'f's, open at the Book of Ecclesiastes – and then walked out into the churchyard. Most of the gravestones were green with moss, but there were a handful of new ones over by the far side, and I wandered up and down the line for a while, certain that if I looked long enough I'd find what I wanted. And sure enough, there it was, an outsize marble slab commemorating the passing of George Ernest Parmenter, born 1901, and his wife May Elizabeth, born 1903.

Oddly enough, the Parmenters hadn't died that long ago. The old man, it turned out, had gone on well into his seventies and Mrs Parmenter hadn't followed him until as late as 1985. It seemed queer to think of Mrs Parmenter alive in the world of Mrs Thatcher, Princess Diana and *glasnost.* I was so intrigued by this that I nearly missed the last line of the inscription, which read simply: 'And Mary Margaret, daughter of the above, born 16 May 1942, died 22 June 1988'. I stood looking at this for a moment or two, quite unable to take it in. June 1988. About the time Upward and I did the comeback show. There was nothing else to see and I walked back down the hill, not really knowing what to think, wondering of all things what had happened to Horace, the last of the Parmenters. Still alive, presumably, frowsting in some defectives' home or being 'looked after' somewhere. But what about Mary? What kind of life had she had in the quarter-century after we'd split up? Stayed at the farm watching her parents grow old? Got married again? It seemed unlikely. For a moment or two I tried to plot the life she might have led alongside the one I'd had, but it was no good, there was no connection, no juxtaposition worth the name.

'Turning colder,' the cabbie said as I got back into the car.

It was, too. High above us flocks of birds were wheeling low over the ploughed fields. We drove back to Yarmouth with the sky turning blue-grey, wind coming in off the sea.

'My dad was a fisherman,' the cabbie volunteered. 'Wouldn't fancy being out there now.'

'No.'

'Sure you've seen all you want?'

'Quite sure.'

Well, that was true. In fact, I'd seen rather more than I wanted, a whole lot more. I got the cabbie to drop me in the town centre

('Nice talking to you guv. See you again') where the clocks said two-thirty. There was a train back just after three, but in the meantime there was something else I wanted to do. When I was a kid, half a century ago, there was one duty that every holidaymaker in Yarmouth was expected to perform: send a kipper home. There were even shops that existed simply to sell the things to trippers, smoked and in special packages so they didn't perish *en route.* Did they still have kipper shops in Yarmouth? Striding back towards the station with a sausage roll in one hand – I hadn't eaten since breakfast-time – I came across an up-market fish shop. Inside two teenage boys with red, well-scrubbed faces, dressed in pinstripe blue overalls and gumboots, were swabbing the floor with mops and buckets. I pretended to inspect the display trays for a bit – they were full of lobsters and shellfish which I suspected didn't come from anywhere near Yarmouth – and then swung round on them.

'I wonder if you can help me. I want to send a kipper.'

They just gawped at me, of course. A middle-aged man walking into a fish shop and asking if he could send a kipper home. You could just see them telling their mates about it in the pub that night. I tried explaining about the West Midlands holidaymakers sending fish back to their next-door neighbours in Digbeth and Dudley, but it was no good. I tried one or two other places and got exactly the same response. Oddly enough, it was this that upset me more than anything – more than the square, more than the Parmenters' farm, more than Mary – the discovery that you couldn't send a kipper home any more. It felt – I don't know – like some eighteenth-century aristocrat coming home from the Grand Tour to his country estate, stepping out into his walled garden, moving daintily towards the peacock lawn, only to find that some hooligan had pinched the sundial. In the end I simply bought a kipper from a stall on the market, took it into a stationery shop, up-ended it into a padded bag, stuck some stamps on it and wrote Lucy's name and address on the front and shoved it in the postbox on the corner by the station.

So there it was. That was what had happened to the old life, to the Parmenters, to Father's shop, to the room at the farm where I'd woken up to find Mary asleep beside me and the pigeons clacking in the eaves – all blown to smithereens, only this time by sane, sensible Norfolk people rather than the German bomb-aimers who'd done for the town my parents knew. And the truly awful thing was that I'd known it would be like this, known somehow about the square and Mary dying, known everything. I hadn't wanted it back, but at the same time I hadn't wanted it to change.

Apparently the Ngongi recognise the nondescript watering holes where they fetch up through smell. Put them down next to a dried-up pond and a few scrubby trees, and even if they haven't passed that way for years and the sand dunes have shifted to form an entirely new horizon, they'll know where they are. Well, I'd been back to the place where I'd been born for four hours or so and I couldn't smell a thing. Only the salt hanging in the clear, dead air.

On Parkinson

PARKINSON: J. B. Priestley – another northern sage, like ourselves – says somewhere . . .

KING: I'm not a northern sage. I come from Norfolk.

UPWARD: Ee! You've offended him there. He's very sensitive about his roots.

PARKINSON: His roots?

UPWARD: That's right. Didn't you see the bottle of lotion he keeps in the dressing room? (*turns to audience*) Carries it everywhere, you know.

PARKINSON: Sorry about that. J. B. Priestley says somewhere that comedy is society protecting itself with a smile. Do you have any comment on that?

KING: Is he a comedian?

UPWARD: Come on Ted, he's from Bradford. No, no comment there.

PARKINSON: I suspect that what I'm trying to ask you is, do you ever think about the nature of what you do?

KING: Absolutely.

UPWARD: Oh aye. But it's more fun thinking about the things you don't do.

PARKINSON: Let me try again – that sounds like the beginning of a song, doesn't it? Somebody else once said that the best kind of comedy encourages people to laugh *with* themselves rather than at other people. Communal, not discriminatory. Now, a lot of your jokes have victims, don't they?

KING: We never try to hurt people. It's just that certain things – certain situations – are simply funny.

UPWARD: It depends on what you mean by victims. Now, a government minister, some celebrity that's shot his mouth off in the press, they're fair game. That's what comedy's about – getting back at people like that. I mean, how else are you supposed to get back at them, eh? But then if you laugh at someone tripping on a banana skin does that make that person a victim? It depends who they are. It depends what's happened in the minute before they slip.

PARKINSON: So you're saying that humour has a moral dimension? That the comedian – excuse me if I get all highbrow here – is an ethical policeman?

KING: Everything's got a moral dimension.

UPWARD: We're not interested in people's morals. The Archbishop of Canterbury can look out for them. We just want to have a laugh.

PARKINSON: You've said many times that your background lies in the old Variety halls, and several critics have noted the enthusiasm with which you've reinvented some of the old routines. What do you think about, let's call it the new style of humour of the last few years?

UPWARD: Harold Wilson? He's a little better.

KING: Monty Python? That kind of thing?

UPWARD: College kids, isn't it?

PARKINSON: College kids?

UPWARD: That's right. Read a few books and want to show off about it. No mass appeal is there, jokes about Sartre? I mean, it's telling the people who've not heard of him to piss off. (*pause*) Am I allowed to say that? The animations aren't bad, though.

KING: Not original either. People talk about surrealism. Well, you should have heard Tommy Handley.

UPWARD: And what about us? We do surrealism, we do. *Avant garde* we are, up there with the best of them. René Magritte. Margaret Thatcher. Seriously, though, Mike – is it all right if I call you Mike? – we're a cross-talk act. A music hall act. I'm short and fat. He's tall and gloomy. I take the piss out of him, he takes the piss out of me, and sometimes it doesn't work, sometimes it does. And then – I'm not saying it happens all the time, mind – people laugh.

KING (*seriously*): And I'm from *Norfolk*.

1976

1979

'Christ,' Upward said peevishly.

'What is it?'

'Left my fags back at the house.'

'Go and get them then. It'll only take you five minutes.'

'I've only just bloody got here,' Upward said. He looked a bit put out, much more upset than a packet of mislaid cigarettes would normally have warranted.

'In any case,' Audrey said, with surprising firmness, 'it'll do you good not to have another one. Stay where you are, that's what I say.'

For some reason Upward looked even more upset. He stared first at me, then at Audrey, finally back towards the small beechwood from which we'd just emerged.

'It's no good,' he said. 'Better get back. Anyway, Peter might have phoned and left a message.'

'I suppose so.'

Hands plunged deep into the pockets of his sheepskin coat, breath steaming above his head in enormous, vaporous clouds, Upward marched off through the beech trees, disappeared into thickets of foliage, re-emerged, growing smaller by the minute, on the far side.

'I don't know why he came out in the first place,' Audrey said mildly. 'He hates the wet anyway. I told him he'd be better off in bed.'

'Safety in numbers. Everyone else seems to have come out of doors.'

In the distance, beyond the beech copse and the stretch of ground across which Upward's figure could just about be seen walking, perhaps a dozen other people were out taking the Saturday-morning air. Some of them were standing on the peacock lawn, on which – as it was early February – no peacocks could be seen. Several were clustered round the back of the house, like Upward probably waiting for an excuse to get back indoors. One or two more were inspecting the edge of a large artificial lake. At this distance I couldn't recognise a soul. Higher up, the roofs and turrets of the house gleamed and sparkled with frost.

'It's a big place, isn't it?' Audrey said. 'Quite scared me, the thought of staying here, I can tell you.'

'I know. But still.'

Audrey, Upward's wife of six months, had taken some coming to terms with. This wasn't because Upward's getting married was unexpected – for the last few years he'd talked of nothing else – but simply because Audrey was so utterly unlike any woman that Upward had previously produced in the two decades that I'd known him. Supposed to be exactly Upward's age, she looked, if anything, a good bit older: forty-five, even. Seeing her for the first time – a fortnight ago when Upward had brought her to lunch – I'd been irresistibly reminded of the women Mother knew in Yarmouth: hair going grey under headscarves, preoccupied expressions. In fact Audrey was fairly cheerful, but she seemed to accept that her youth was behind her.

'It was all very different when I was a girl,' she said more than once.

Upward's explanation of why he was getting married had been relayed in a few sentences: 'Audrey's an old friend of mine. We've known each other for years. We're probably even distantly related. I've been thinking of getting married for a good long time now. I talked it over with Audrey. We agreed it was the right thing to do.'

There were other ways in which Audrey differed from the tribes of showgirls and TV hostesses 'done' on snooker tables and in other places. For a start Upward was prepared, in fact eager, to be ordered about by her: not to have extra drinks when she said so, to behave when she told him to. Also, he told me, he 'didn't want her name in the paper'. All this was so unlike Upward as to make you wonder about it. But then Upward, too, was unlike Upward these days. It was difficult to put this into words: not exactly quieter, but a bit warier, cross about something. As I later found out, there were reasons for this.

I watched Upward trailing back through the outcrops of trees. He'd found the cigarettes and was smoking one in short, furious puffs. There was another man with him whom I recognised as a journalist on one of the dailies. He was doing most of the talking. Upward stopped once or twice, took the cigarette out of his mouth and said something in reply.

At the edge of the wood there was a kind of rubbish dump, heaped up with dozens of black refuse sacks. They looked, and smelled, as if they'd been there a long time, probably since the start of the current round of industrial disputes. Audrey and I retreated back the way we had come, as Upward and the other man beat a path towards us.

'He's not been well you know,' Audrey said, smoothing her thick tweed skirt further over her knees.

'What's the matter with him?'

'Says he's got pains in his arms. The doctor can't find anything wrong with him though.'

'He looks all right.'

Close up, Upward didn't look so much ill – though his face was certainly a bit drawn – as preoccupied. He would be about forty now, but it was hard to work out how he'd altered in the time that I'd known him. A bit less squat, perhaps. But the essentials – wispy red hair, redder face – were exactly the same.

'Peter hadn't rung,' Upward said, as he came closer. 'Leastways there wasn't any message. I told the girl if he did ring she was to come out here and tell me.'

'She won't like doing that.'

'She watches the shows,' Upward said. 'Gave her my bloody autograph didn't I? Told her she could have yours, too.'

Peter was our agent. Negotiations for the upcoming series, which everyone had previously thought to be going all right, had suddenly stalled. Nobody quite knew why. I suppose, looking back, I should have seen this as a symbol, a pointer to the way ahead. At the time, though, it didn't seem like this. It was just something that Peter, Upward and the TV executives would sort out.

Upward went off to talk to Audrey. I could hear her lecturing him about the cigarettes. It was wet underfoot and there was rain coming through the soles of my shoes. The journalist, whose name was Sexton, came up and shook hands.

'Your wife here?'

'She's in bed with flu.'

'Well, there's nothing much to get up for is there? Do you know they're not even burying the corpses up in Liverpool?'

We stood looking back at the house, while Upward and Audrey started on another conversation, conducted in furious whispers. Most of the people had gone back inside. A few still hung about by the lake, moving this way.

'Always surprises me,' Sexton said, 'that Newsome can afford to keep this place up.'

'I thought he'd made a fortune out of property in the boom. That's what everybody said.'

'Well, everybody said wrong.' Sexton looked as if he got quite a lot of pleasure from saying things like this. 'Look at that pyramid selling scheme of his – Mayflower was it? Stunk to the high heavens, that did. Streets full of people in Birmingham, or wherever it was, paying forty per cent on loans that the agents had actually fixed up with Newsome's own bank. There weren't many takers next time he went into the City wanting a float. Lost a couple of directorships too, by all accounts.'

'What's he up to now?' I wanted to know this simply as a means of impressing Upward.

'Something to do with the entertainment industry, if I hear rightly. Buying up old theatres or something and leasing them out. Something to do with a bloke called Cooper. That name mean anything to you? I expect you've come across him, doing what you do?'

Sexton went on like this for a minute or two longer, not interested in whatever replies I lobbed back. Upward and Audrey had stopped whispering and were slapping their arms against their sides. It was definitely getting colder. Probably it would snow.

'I'm going back to the house,' Upward said. He seemed a bit happier now. 'Someone must have put a bloody fire on by now.'

Together we walked quickly towards the beech copse, nearly colliding with two men, until then concealed by the trees, who were coming out of it. There was a flurry of nods and apologies.

'Hello, Sir Gavin,' Sexton said eagerly.

It was the only time I really set eyes on Sir Gavin Newsome at close hand. I'd sat at the same table as him the night before, but been reduced to a fleeting glimpse or two. He was a tall, white-haired bloke of about fifty, apart from that difficult to describe. On the one hand he looked exactly like the pictures of City gents you see in newspapers proceeding in and out of the Guildhall. On the other there was something fantastically alien about him, hard to pin down. This effect was reinforced by the tall Russian hat he wore. The man introduced as Cooper I recognised immediately: a bit older than me, with greasy black hair. If Sir Gavin looked more or less at home here in the middle of a wood on a freezing Saturday morning, Cooper – wearing a white mac and suede shoes that were taking in water – looked completely incongruous. He was breathing heavily.

'Don't think we've met properly,' Sir Gavin said easily. 'Seen Arthur here dozens of times. Looking forward to your thing tonight, of course. Anything new for us, or just stuff we've seen on the box?'

'I dare say there'll be a surprise or two.'

'Well, that whets my appetite I must say.'

There was a faint trace of accent: nothing I could place. Upward had once or twice declared that Sir Gavin was 'a regular northern gent', but then Upward had claimed the same thing about Enoch Powell and a man who turned out to be the captain of the Welsh Rugby XV. What struck you was command of environment. You got the feeling that if a would-be assassin had jumped out from behind one of the beech trees Sir Gavin would have somehow dealt with him, disarmed him, drawn him into the conversation, asked after his wife. I looked at the rest of the group. Upward seemed bored: nothing he wanted to say would have been any use here. Sexton looked desperate for Sir Gavin to say something to him. Cooper, muttering faintly, was examining the waterlogged sole of his shoe. Audrey, who had her hands drawn up under her chin, simply looked worried and respectful.

Nobody said anything. Sir Gavin looked carefully around him. 'Excellent,' he said. 'Very good. See you all later then.'

He and Cooper set off in the opposite direction, where a path led through waist-high bracken towards more trees. Sexton looked as if he badly wanted to tag after them, then thought better of it. As we went back to the house a few flakes of snow came fluttering down from the darkening sky. In the entrance hall, making sure that Sexton was out of earshot, I grabbed hold of Upward's arm.

'Isn't that . . .?'

'The very same.'

'The one that Captain Groves . . .'

'Conked on the napper with a soda siphon. I was there. It just goes to show.'

I remembered it too. The argument spilling out of Captain Groves's office into the main body of the Minerva, Groves languid at first, then finally losing his temper and picking up the first weapon that came to hand, Cooper – he wasn't badly hurt in the end – being taken away.

'Still in Soho then?'

'Owns most of Frith Street from what I've heard. And some other things, too.'

That night we were booked to perform a couple of sketches for Sir Gavin Newsome's dinner guests. This kind of celebrity showcase happened quite often. In the past we'd appeared in front of a roomful of cabinet ministers, the England football team and the Queen Mother and her entourage. I never enjoyed these occasions: not enough people, forced intimacy, the reminder that you'd have to talk to your audience twenty minutes later. This one wasn't any better except that for the first time – I'd seen it in rehearsals but never taken much notice – Upward unveiled his imitation of Mrs Thatcher. It was unbelievably funny, a kind of humour impossible to convey in words, so funny that I forgot all the professional protocols that had been dinned into me for the last fifteen years and burst out laughing myself. You might not think that a balding, red-faced man waving a finger the size of a saveloy in front of his face could imitate Mrs Thatcher, but somehow Upward managed it. Cigar smoke rising to the ceiling, starched white shirtfronts, fat hands curled round brandy glasses, greying heads thrown back, black air beyond the window – that was the rest of it.

Afterwards I went to bed. Upward stayed downstairs. Next morning when I came down to breakfast I found him hanging about in the hall. He was horribly excited, so excited that he might still have been entertaining Sir Gavin's guests.

'Well, I had a weird evening last night,' he said instantly. 'You want to hear about it?'

'All right. Now?'

'Come in here,' Upward said.

To the right of the front door, a dozen feet or so from the stairs, there was a large cloakroom with a row of coat-pegs and a jumble of expensive-looking boots and shoes leading to a lavatory. The room had a sliding door, which Upward now pulled shut.

'If anyone comes I'll pretend I'm having a crap.'

'What shall I pretend I'm doing then?'

'You'll think of something,' Upward said.

Assuming this was a joke, I started to laugh. Upward glared back. Paler than usual, he didn't look as if he had slept much.

'Are you all right?'

'Champion.' He paused for a second and then started off on what was clearly a different tack from the one he'd first intended. 'This is an extraordinary place. D'y' know what I saw last night before we went in to dinner? I was wandering around outside the drawing room where Isla – Lady Newsome – was putting on her gloves. You know them long evening gloves she wears, the ones that come up to your elbow?'

'Yes.'

'Well, get this, Ted. When she'd pulled them on she got out a bottle of cow gum or white spirit from a drawer under the writing table and do you know what she did?'

'Drank some? Started inhaling it?'

'Don't be bloody silly. No, she dabbed a couple of blobs on the inside of each of her arms. So the gloves wouldn't slip down. Can you beat it?' Upward seemed completely entranced. '*Sticking your gloves to your arms so they don't slip down!* Do you suppose the Queen knows that trick?'

'Is that what you wanted to tell me?'

'Of course it bloody isn't.' Upward looked suddenly furious. 'It was just something I noticed. 'Ow the other half lives, that kind of thing. The really important stuff was later.'

'What was that?'

A soft tapping noise had begun on the other side of the sliding door.

'I say,' a well-bred voice said diffidently, 'is there anyone in there?'

'Hold on a minute,' Upward shouted loudly. 'I'm just having a crap.'

There was a noise of footsteps receding.

'Well, after dinner, after you'd gone and that little bloke Sexton had pushed off – said he had to get back to London – there was about ten of us round the fire. Audrey had gone to bed too. Can't stand late nights. Lady Isla as well. Me. Sir Gavin. That chap Cartwright, the MP. The bloke about seven feet tall who looked like an army officer. You know the one I mean?'

'Sort of.'

'Him then. One or two others. What do you think they were talking about?'

'The state of the country I should think. That's all most people talk about these days. Was it the bins not being emptied or "Crisis what crisis?"?'

'Good guess. It *was* that, up to a point.' Upward paused again, winked and bent forward impressively. '*Treason.*'

'Treason?'

'Not in so many words. Nobody said "I've got a file of tanks and I'm going to drive them up Whitehall", or "that Bill Sirs ought to be shot and I'm the man to do it", but take it from me there was some pretty odd stuff flying about. Army committees. Sympathetic newspapers. *Money.*'

For some reason – probably because of the strangeness of the setting – I always remember this as the most unreal moment of my life: the rows of Wellington boots lying on their sides, a ventilator fan whirring in the background, Upward's face nearly purple with emotion, fireside chatter about army committees.

'But Cartwright's an MP isn't he? A Labour MP at that.'

'A solid parliamentarian if the chips were down,' Upward nodded. 'Which I don't suppose they ever will be. Don't you worry, Ted. No one was talking about stringing Jim Callaghan up on a lamp-post. I'm just telling you that there was half-a-dozen blokes – *important* blokes – saying things that, well, you wouldn't want to hear.'

'What did you say?'

'Not a lot. Kept quiet mostly.'

'What are you going to do?'

'Nowt,' Upward said, reverting to stage northerner for an instant. 'But I'm going to ring up Frank' – I knew from hearing the name dropped before that 'Frank' was the Chairman of the Parliamentary Labour Party – 'and tell him about it.'

Someone was tapping at the door again, a bit louder.

'All right,' Upward shouted again. 'Just wiping my arse.'

A moment later we filed out, past a startled-looking elderly gentleman in a tweed suit, into the breakfast room. During the meal I found myself looking at Lady Isla's forearms. On each of them, just beneath the elbow where the bone ran into flesh, there was a small red blotch.

Whether or not Upward spoke to the Chairman of the Parliamentary Labour Party I never found out. At any rate he never mentioned it again. There were several reasons why all this might have been driven out of his head. A few days later we heard from Peter that there was to be another TV series, for transmission in the autumn. Then, a fortnight after that, Upward had a minor heart-attack and spent some weeks in hospital recovering. Though his face frequently stared out of newspapers or appeared on television, I never spoke to Sir Gavin Newsome again.

Outside Ipswich it began to snow. By Chelmsford the fields were turning white and the flakes were silhouetted against the blue-black sky. From time to time commuter trains whipped by heading east. Here the carriage was nearly empty. No one much travels into London at five-thirty on a Wednesday afternoon. Oddly enough, the train smelled of fish. Perhaps I'd unwittingly brought some of Yarmouth back with me? The only other souvenir was the copy of the *Eastern Daily Press*, with its reports of day care centre openings in Fakenham and sea defence repairs on the North Norfolk coast.

Watching the snow cheers me up, to the extent of making plans about Daniel. Come the weekend, if it's still there, maybe we could make a sledge, head down into Kent somewhere and find a hill. I can see the expression on Daniel's face – that desperate intentness children have – as the sledge comes over the lip of the incline. Tonight, I think, I'll read him *The Hobbit*, which has been lying around in his room for a week unregarded among the video games and the Michael Owen souvenir magazines. The train comes out between a gap in the low hills, and I can see the motorway lights winding away across Essex, down into the deadlands of the east, down into my country.

Back at the estate in Plumstead – four monstrous towerblocks rearing into the night sky – the remnants of Neil's party are still on their way home. As I head towards the lift shaft the doors open and a crowd of kids stream out waving balloons and soccer scarves.

Up on the fourth floor Kev stands in the hallway, can in one hand, unlit Marlboro Light in the other. He looks a bit puzzled, almost worried, as if seeing me is a contingency he hasn't planned for, wonders how to deal with.

'Yes, mate?'

'I got back sooner than I thought. I hope Dan's been behaving himself.'

''E went off 'alf an hour ago with 'is aunt. Thought you knew.'

'His *aunt*?'

'That's right. Tall woman in a raincoat. Turned up on the dot with some other parents. With some bloke she said was driving them.'

Behind Kev, at the end of a pink-carpeted corridor, I can see Mrs Kev, a friendly-looking woman in goggle glasses, hearing the noise and coming to investigate.

'Let's get this straight. A woman came to collect Daniel from the party who said she was his aunt?'

Kev looks a bit unhappy at this, like someone whose professional judgement has been called into question.

'Wasn't saying nothing,' he says. 'As soon as your Daniel sees her he goes "Hello Aunty Shena". What am I supposed to do? Ask for ID? Anyway, she says she's come to take him home.'

'Kev,' I say weakly. 'She's my ex-wife's sister. She lives in Yorkshire.'

Even now, with my pulse booming away, I can see the excitement on Mr and Mrs Kev's faces as the implications sink in. They know about this kind of thing from the soaps and the tabloids. *Custody dispute* I can see them thinking. *Who'd have thought it eh?* In the kitchen, while Mrs Kev makes tea, Kev replays the events of half an hour before.

'That's right. Bang on the dot of half-past seven. You was in the kitchen, wasn't you, Jen? And there's this bird in a trenchcoat looking as if she's from the Social Security or something, says "I wonder if this is the address where Daniel King is attending a party?" *Anyway*, we let her in – knew who I was, knew who you were – she sees Dan, he comes running in, that's it.'

'What did he say? What did he look like?'

Kev thinks about this, staring hard at the table top in front of him. 'He looked like a kid whose aunt's come to collect him from a party.'

'We're dreadfully sorry,' Mrs Kev says, now assuming collective responsibility. 'But what were we supposed to do? Do you want to phone the police or anything?'

'No.' Daniel will be in a car by now, halfway round the M25, off towards the idiot north. 'Seriously,' I say again. 'Thank you. No.'

Something of the gravity of the situation has now communicated itself to Kev.

'Awful thing to happen,' he says suddenly. 'With a kiddie and that. Fucking awful thing to happen. What can I say?'

'Kev!' Mrs Kev says indulgently.

I leave them in the kitchen – the rest of the children are still romping around in the front room bursting the balloons and swearing – and go out of the flat, back along the corridor and into the urinous lift. Outside the snow lies crisp and even on the car bumpers and the tarmac surround. Caught in the sodium glare of the streetlamps it looks faintly unreal, like the fake snow we used to use in the carol singers' routine for the Christmas show. I walk up the hill, shoulders hunched against the cold, thinking of Daniel in the car, Shena, the sledge coming up across the lip of the hill that I will never see.

Untouched, exactly as it was twelve hours ago, the house seems unexpectedly changed by my absence. There are messages on the answer phone: Lennie telling me that the booker for a chain of south coast pubs will be ringing me; the booker himself telling me that he's just spoken to Lennie; somebody offering voiceover work; finally Shena calling from a mobile – you can hear traffic noise in the background – sounding quaintly formal. '*You ought to know that Daniel is quite safe and I am doing this in what I consider to be his best interests. You can expect an official communication in the next twenty-four hours.*' Somewhere in the crackle and whine of static I am sure I can hear Daniel's voice. I replay the tape seven or eight times but can't catch it. The dialback facility gives me the mobile number. It has been switched off.

Daniel's room has lost its charm, its invitation. It is just a place where someone has left a wallful of football posters and a few pre-teenage paperbacks, old Mars bar wrappers and crisp packets. Even the Daniel-smell is fading away, heading up north in the speeding car. I imagine him again, half asleep, with his head pillowed on the arm-rest, looking out of the window at the drifting snow.

The phone rings.

'Isn't the snow wonderful?' Lucy says. 'You wouldn't believe how I've been enjoying it. How was your trip?'

'Dan's gone.'

'What do you mean "gone"?'

I explain into a silence broken by the intake of breath and tiny sussurations: Shena's raid on the party, the car, the flight to the motorway, details real and imagined. They might not be on the motorway at all, but holed up in some hotel. Halfway through I realise that Lucy's silence is one of immense, sorrowful respect, that, mysteriously, having Daniel removed from my life has somehow confirmed something she likes about me.

'Oh God,' she says. 'That's dreadful. Truly dreadful. Have you called the police?'

'I don't even know where they are. I need to talk to Shena.'

'You ought not to be on your own. Do you want me to come over?'

'It'll take for ever. Come tomorrow. Like you were going to.'

'Fuck the script changes,' Lucy says. It is the first time I've heard her swear. 'You must take care of yourself.'

'I'll try to.'

Shena, reached by phone at nine-thirty a.m., is predictably businesslike.

'I'm sorry to have to do this, Ted, but you didn't leave me any choice.'

'Where is he?'

'Daniel? He's just had his breakfast. Gary's taken him down the park.'

'Gary being the minder you brought along yesterday, I take it?'

'I don't think that's got anything to do with you Ted, really.'

'Seeing he's looking after my son at the moment I think it's got everything to do with me, don't you? When do I get to see him again? I mean, do I have to come up and do a repeat performance?'

'Look, Ted.' Shena sounds unexpectedly worn down by the complex manoeuvring required of her. 'There's a lawyer's letter coming this morning. By registered post. That'll tell you exactly where you stand.'

'I'm impressed by the homework,' I tell her. 'I mean, picking him up from the party. That was a stroke of genius.'

'I could just have met him out of school,' Shena says matter-of-factly. 'It wouldn't have made any difference. I don't know how to say this, Ted, *but he wanted to come.* I wouldn't have taken him if he hadn't.'

'When's he get back from the park? With his escort, I mean. When can I talk to him?'

'Actually,' Shena says, 'I don't think that would be a good idea. In a bit, perhaps. Not now. He's a bit upset.'

'Of course he is.'

'I don't mean that. I mean about the life he's been leading in the past three months. He's told me about it. You leaving him alone in the evenings when you went out. I'm not one to criticise, Ted, but that school . . .'

'It's just a school.'

'That's as maybe. I'm sorry, Ted, I should never have agreed to let you have him for the three weeks. I knew it would be difficult, that all this would happen. Did you know Daniel used to phone me in the evenings?'

'No.'

'Well, he did. Two or three times a week. Asking when he could come home. How do you think I felt about that?'

'How do you think I feel about this?'

'I shouldn't think you feel very happy. But then – don't mind me saying this, will you Ted? – Paula didn't feel very happy. Not for a long time. You can't just wander back into people's lives when you feel like it.'

'If I find you're keeping him against his will it'll take more than Gary to stop me bringing him back.'

'But I'm not,' Shena says exasperatedly. 'I'm not keeping him against his will. It's not about *owning* him. It's about Daniel. Look,

I'll ring you in a couple of days and tell you how he is, all right? But if I look out of the window tomorrow morning and see you there I'll call the police. And from what the lawyers say they'll listen to me, not to you.'

Lucy arrives an hour later, her head done up in a kind of Afghan bonnet like the mini-cab drivers. Meeting in the hallway, we peer uncertainly at each other for a second or so.

'I'm so sorry,' Lucy says fiercely. 'So sorry about Dan. I just wanted you to know that.'

So much of my life has hinged on a failure to accept invitations. This time I don't need any prompting. She falls into my arms in a kind of slow-motion jog, jacketed shoulder coming to rest against my chin. She smells of what? New-mown hay? Expensive toilet water?

'I thought and thought about it after you told me,' she says. I can feel her fingers digging into my shoulders.

There is no explanation for these things. They happen. They are there. Moving through the hall I see her face caught suddenly in the mirror above the phone: white, sharp-featured, like the other Lucy, the girl in the Narnia books that Mary had by her bedside all those years ago.

The Last Sketch

UPWARD: It's good to see you again.

KING: It's good to see you again.

UPWARD: I thought you'd have changed, but you haven't. Not taken a bath either, by the smell of you.

KING: You haven't changed either. (*reaches over to feel the lapels of Upward's suit*) Still making your own clothes I see.

UPWARD: Huh! My mother was a champion dressmaker y'know . . . Her and me father in the shop, they knew all about *haute couture*.

KING: I've never heard it called that before.

UPWARD: Listen! Do you want to know what happened when Mrs Thatcher and half the cabinet had dinner with the European Council of Ministers in Brussels last week?

KING: No, but go on.

UPWARD: They asked her what she wanted to eat, and she said 'I'll have the roast beef of Old England.' And then they said, 'What about the vegetables?' And she said, 'Oh, they'll have the roast beef as well.'

KING (*admiringly*): You're a one, you are.

UPWARD (*proudly*): I am. I am a one. That is exactly what I am. So what have you been doing with yourself?

KING: Oh, the usual things. Sorting my stamp collection. Taking the dog out.

UPWARD: I'm surprised at you. With your money you could afford a woman.

KING: I borrowed yours, remember, but it had a puncture.

UPWARD: . . .

KING: What's that?

UPWARD: . . .

Witham Sports Arena, June 1988

The Comedy Man

Do you know the difference between a cavalry charger and a brewer's nag? Well, one darts into the fray . . .

Where did it all go wrong? In all the time that followed I regularly used to ask myself that question. Sometimes I used to believe that it was simply a series of pieces of bad luck, that if we'd somehow managed to push things like Upward's heart-attack to one side we'd have been able to jink round the obstacles we found in our way, come bouncing back into the spotlight. What if Upward hadn't been ill? If we'd got the next series, and the one after that? Done the film that Peter wanted us to, but Upward refused? I used to agonise over these mistakes – if they were mistakes – for hours at a time. In the end, though, I realised that there was a perfectly simple explanation. Upward being ill didn't help – he took a long time to recover, and even when he was fit again you could see that it had frightened him, that something had stuck in his mind that hadn't been there before, changed him and chastened him. At the same time – it's something you do when you can feel the ground slipping beneath you – we made some stupid mistakes. Not going back to radio was one, and the two or three films we did around that time were simply diabolical – just girls taking their clothes off and Upward smirking, with me looking hang-dog in the background.

But the thing we were involved in, that we'd spent our lives doing, was changing and we hadn't even noticed. Or rather, we had noticed and there wasn't anything we could do about it. I remember once out of curiosity climbing a set of back stairs in

Brewer Street of all places around the time of the Falklands to see an outfit called Dogface and Haddock, and thinking that once you took away the shock tactics they were probably quite funny, but that anyone who laughed at them would think twice about laughing at us. Upward, in particular, hated anything that described itself as 'alternative comedy' or anyone who described himself – worse, herself – as an 'alternative comedian'.

'Stupid hair and silly voices and the Tories and no fucking punchlines and bad language and the Tories and jumping up and down,' he once complained. 'Well, it doesn't make *me* laugh.'

Which was accurate, if beside the point.

Naturally enough, none of this happened overnight. As late as 1981, I remember, we were still coming fourth in the polls of 'Comedy Favourites'. But it was all quietening down, fading away. You put out your hand to touch something that you'd assured yourself would always be there and it was suddenly gone. Six million people watched the last TV series we did. Three years before it had been ten or eleven. A TV executive we'd known for years took us out to lunch and explained, politely but firmly, why there wouldn't be another. Upward cried after that lunch – Upward! Who when I first knew him genuinely couldn't care less about anything. I remember sitting there looking at him as he tried to light a cigarette with his hands shaking so much that he could barely hold the lighter, and then issuing a mock-defiant challenge that got printed in the tabloids, towards the back of the tabloids now: WE'LL BE BACK SAYS OUSTED UPWARD! TV BOSSES ARE OUT OF TOUCH – SACKED COMIC'S SHOCK CLAIM! That kind of thing. We did a summer show that year somewhere down in the West Country, and I remember looking out into the stalls a couple of times (the place was still half full – you never lose your audience completely) and thinking that the game was up. Worse, that I didn't care, certainly not as much as I ought to, or Upward seemed to think I should.

After that we started to drift apart. There was no big flare-up or anything. We just saw less of each other, didn't telephone so often. Paula and I had moved to Suffolk by this time, to the big house looking out over the Stour Estuary, and I suppose that wasn't an incentive. He used to come over at odd times though. I'd get home from a trip to London, back from Manningtree station in a cab late on a dull autumn afternoon and find his car in the drive, Paula and him looking out of the window as the cab swerved into the gravel. You got the feeling – nothing was ever said – that Audrey kept him on a pretty tight rein. Even when he was with us he was always phoning her, worrying about whether it was time to leave. There was always vague talk about plans, reunions, a live video some director was going to shoot in a pub in the East End. Of the pair of us, I'm sure it was Upward who was the harder hit. He was still a bit of a figure in his way – you saw him now and again on the TV gameshows that go out in the afternoon when nobody's watching – and it must have hurt him, the thought that he'd never get back where he'd been before, however much he tried. I remember when Eric Morecambe died he was bitterly upset, not because he'd known Morecambe especially well but because of the symbolism: the good man gone, the toppling over of something you'd thought fixed and irrevocable, the conveyor-belt rushing on empty.

And all the while time was moving on. It was 1984, 1985, and we hadn't been on a stage together for four years. It used to puzzle me sometimes, coming back from a walk over the marshes, watching the teal take flight into the winter sky, how you could lose something that had been a part of you and not seem to mind. Once or twice I had offers from other people – younger blokes looking for 'guidance', deadbeats of fifty wanting to head back to the theatre circuit. I always turned them down. I wasn't far off fifty myself if it came to that. And what about me? What did I do? The answer is, I suppose, that I sat tight, read more books, tried to look after Paula. There'd been another miscarriage in the early Eighties, after which we'd stopped trying. I used to walk for hours over the flats near the house, all the way down to Shotley sometimes on the furthermost tip of south-eastern Suffolk, watching the birds and thinking about it all, all the way back to Father and Mother and the square, Mary and the old days at the farm, so far away now that it might have been another world, and someone else living in it, not me at all.

As to the life that Paula and I led, I can't begin to describe it. We'd spend whole days together in the house, walking over the wet fields, driving up to Pin Mill on the north side to look at the boats. Everything around the place was to do with water, from the yacht masts passing down the estuary a quarter of a mile away to the smell of the brine which slapped you in the face like a dishcloth whenever you stepped out of the door. In winter huge flocks of geese, two or three hundred at a time, came and camped on the meadows. I used to watch them from the study window upstairs, taking flight momentarily when a ship's horn sounded out in mid-stream, hanging in the air for a second or two then slowly descending to the emerald turf. Sometimes at night you'd be woken by the sound of them flying overhead, a curious rub-a-dub noise like an old-fashioned laundry. What Paula and I talked about over our solitary meals, the summer days we spent out in the water meadows, exploring tiny, forgotten churchyards where the newest gravestone dated from the 1890s, I don't remember. I can recall the substance, but not the words spoken. Was she happy? I don't know. Perhaps I should have asked her.

Backstage, you suspected that the dressing room had recently done service as a furniture store. Bits of jumble lay all over the floor. An elderly wind-up gramophone with a rearing loudspeaker. Three or four cane-backed chairs. A case of books. A colour photograph of the Queen Mother dating from the Fifties. Stepping past these obstacles, bending to avoid a low-swinging light bulb, I was reminded of other, similar clutter. It took a second or two to connect it with the shop that Mother and Mrs Moss had kept in Gorleston a quarter of a century before. That was where the memory came from, though: a compound of chalk-dust, mothballs, old dresses hung in rows, Mrs Moss's deathshead face leering from the till.

'Not the bloody Winter Gardens, is it?' somebody said.

In the ten years since I'd last seen him, Tracy Jacks had clearly made some stark decisions about his sexuality. He had lost weight, a great deal of it, and his once curly hair, which in the early Seventies had nearly reached his shoulders, was reduced to a savage crew-cut. As a final touch there was a metal stud drilled into his right ear. None of this, it had to be said, was especially convincing. There was a weird sense of someone got up in fancy dress. Upward, who had been reintroduced to him the day before, had taken this transformation about as badly as could have been expected.

'Christ,' he had said. 'It's going to be bad enough already without that little pansy mincing round the changing rooms.'

'You used to like him.'

'Who'd have thought it?' Upward had sighed mournfully. 'Tracy Jacks turned into a bum-bandit.'

Upward sat on a chair at the far end of the room. He didn't look well. Like Tracy Jacks with his short hair, lean face and thigh-hugging chinos, it was hard to say exactly what was wrong. Dressed in a brightly coloured suit, much more outrageous than anything he'd worn in the past, he seemed unable to work out what kind of mood he was in. Two or three jokes, snapped out on arrival twenty minutes since, had given way to a gloomy silence.

'Bloody hell,' Tracy Jacks said, not quite as respectfully as he'd done fifteen years ago in the studios at Broadcasting House. 'You're not going on stage in that, Arthur?'

'And what if I am?'

'For a start that jacket'll strobe every camera in the hall.'

'I'll wait for the director to tell me that, ta.'

This exchange definitely did Upward some good. He laughed loudly and started to talk to another man who had something to do with the video company. Tracy Jacks watched him for a moment, as if he couldn't quite work out whether or not he'd caused offence, and then moved back in my direction. This too made you feel that what he was dressed in, hairstyle and general appearance, was a kind of disguise. Ten years older and two or three stone lighter, he still gave an impression of lumbering, of being ready to crash into anything left in his path.

'Glad to hear about your missis,' he said, sending a stool skidding across the floor. 'Been a long time, eh?'

'A hell of a long time.'

'When's it due then?'

'Another three months. Two and a half, maybe.'

I was still completely unable to come to terms with Paula being pregnant. Expecting the worst, then finding that the worst didn't happen, was deeply unsettling. Away from her, I used to break into a sweat whenever a telephone rang or someone I knew came purposefully towards me. With her, I'd stare at her stomach, fists clenched, willing the baby to grow. Paula was a bit unnerved by this.

'So no jokes about expectant mothers?' Tracy Jacks said.

'None at all.'

'Fair enough.' Flicking up a finger, he began to massage the earlobe where the silver stud hung. 'Jesus, I'm sure this is infected. I mean, it shouldn't hurt like this, should it?'

'Probably not.'

The reunion concert had been Tracy Jacks's idea. Sacked from, or bored with, the BBC – no one quite knew – he was something to do with an independent production outfit. Tonight's performance would be going straight to video, unless, as had been vaguely rumoured, Channel Four were interested.

'What do they use this place for anyway?' Upward asked. He was taking pairs of spectacles out of his pocket – three or four of them lay on the table top before him – and balancing them one after another on the bridge of his nose.

'Sports hall, I reckon,' Tracy Jacks said. 'There's a couple of basketball nets either side, but I've got the sound boys taking them down.'

One or two other people started to drift into the room, making it a bit crowded: the director, sound men, a security guard. A make-up woman came in and, without speaking, began to scoop up the ends of what remained of Upward's hair into place with the end of a comb. Upward ignored her. He seemed to be floating somewhere, far away from the dressing-room throng. With the view obscured by several bodies, I heard Tracy Jacks trying to restart their conversation.

'I read your book,' Tracy Jacks was saying. 'D'you know, I even went out and bought it.'

'Oh, aye?'

Most people would have stopped at this point. Tracy Jacks went on gamely: 'I thought it was a bit, well, *personal*.'

'Of course it was personal,' Upward said with extraordinary savagery. 'What's the point of writing a book like that if it's not bloody personal?'

Whatever Tracy Jacks said in reply was cut off by the director clapping his hands for silence. He was a small, seedy-looking man of about forty with chronically inflamed eyelids. For a moment I tried to concentrate on what he was saying, but it was difficult to take in more than fragments.

'All feeling our way a bit here . . . Important *not* to play to the camera . . . Just do your normal act, and leave the technical stuff to us . . . Language. It'd be a good idea if nobody said "fuck" or "cunt". Anything else we can probably get away with . . . Same goes for jokes about ethnic minorities . . . Take a break after thirty minutes, just to make sure we've got the levels right . . . All professionals here I know . . .'

At the mention of the word 'professionals' I stopped listening. Faintly in the distance, as warm-up act gave way to warm-up act, music was playing.

> '*They're playing our tune, by the pale moon*
> *We're incognito, down the Lido*
> *And we like the Strand.*'

It was the same music that had played in Tracy Jacks's studio fifteen years before. I moved forward with the idea of pointing this out to him, but the room was losing its population. Someone said: 'Ten minutes then,' quite loudly. In the distance there was a noise of scattered applause. Tracy Jacks, glimpsed for a second in the doorway, made a thumbs-up sign. I waved back. Then the door shut and I was alone with Upward.

Very slowly, as if they were immensely fragile and expensive pieces of china, Upward was stowing the pairs of spectacles back in the inner pocket of his jacket. This took him several minutes. Doing it he looked a bit decrepit, deflected once or twice by pieces of cloth or his own fingers. When he'd finished he straightened up and said, comparatively normally:

'How's Paula?'

'Very well. She said to say hello.'

'Too late for owt to go wrong now, I suppose?'

'It's never too late. Especially for things to go wrong.'

'That's true enough.'

There was a silence. 'You know,' Upward said, 'I always wanted to have a kid. Too late now, of course. But there's no denying it would have been difficult.'

God knows what Upward meant by this. That it would have been difficult for Audrey to have a baby? That something in Upward's temperament would have stopped him being a good parent? I realised that Upward was in a state that I'd only witnessed three or four times in the thirty years I'd known him: the confidential. While I was working this out there was a knock on the door, which then opened a foot or so, and a voice – owner unseen – muttered, 'Five minutes' and withdrew. Upward seemed not to notice.

'Always fancied it,' he said. 'You know. Taking him out places.'

'It would have to be a boy?'

'Oh I always think you'd want a boy, don't you?' Upward said.

There was another muted burst of clapping in the distance: the second warm-up act had finished. Upward looked vaguely around him.

'We're not on yet, are we?' he asked.

'Three or four minutes, I suppose.'

People always talk about a light going on in someone's head. That was how it seemed with Upward at that moment. He sat bolt upright, drummed his fingers on the table, squinted at himself in the mirror: tired, maybe, but ready to make a go of it.

'If this goes okay it won't be the last time.'

'You think so?'

'Positive. Shouldn't have left it so long in the first place.'

Coming from anyone else, this would have been taken as an apology. As it was, Upward somehow made the long delay sound as if it was my fault. Then, quite unexpectedly, his mood changed. He looked worried, ground-down, much worse than when I'd first seen him earlier that evening.

'Are you okay?'

'I'll do. Look, afterwards . . . There's something I want to tell you.'

'Tell me it now if you like.'

'No.' Upward looked appallingly nervous. 'Can't tell you now. Do you understand?'

'I suppose so.'

There was another scuffling noise beyond the door. Upward started indulging himself in another pre-performance ritual I remembered from the old days – tying and retying his shoelaces. Already we seemed to have got through an eternity of waiting. Upward looked up, nodded, smiled, bent down to reapply himself to his shoelaces. Thirty seconds later we were on stage.

There was a kind of roar of appreciation, scattered applause. Upward, stage-centre, was bowing low, making elaborate gestures with his hands. Still dazzled by the light, I stood on the lip of the stage and stared out into the darkness. The sports hall's immense height – much bigger than an ordinary theatre – made it seem like a huge, dark cavern. There were about three hundred people there, some empty seats to the rear, hut not too many. It was a fair turn-out. The applause, which was showing signs of falling away, renewed itself as Upward went into another of his old routines: sliding forward on his knees with arms outstretched on either side. Somebody threw a bunch of daffodils on to the stage. Upward picked them up and pressed them to his heart. Breathing heavily, scarlet-faced, he stayed like this for a moment or two, clambered up and picked one of the microphones out of its stand.

'Ladies and gentlemen,' he bellowed. 'We're not here today and gone tomorrow.' There was a pause. 'We pissed off last night.'

There was another roar of laughter. Upward swung the microphone up in the air, caught it expertly as it fell.

'This is my friend Ted,' he shouted. 'Did you know he had a Chinese cousin? That's right. Keeps an oriental restaurant in Walthamstow. It's true. I rang up to order some chow mein and a voice said "Good evening, I am Fu King the manager," so I said "That's okay, I'll call back in a minute."'

I was still looking at the faces: rows of them. Middle-aged, mostly, but with a scattering of younger people. By now Upward was prowling restlessly near the back of the stage.

'He doesn't say much,' he announced, veering towards me. 'He keeps himself to himself.'

'You should see some of the things *he* keeps to himself,' I lobbed back.

The laughter was coming in tiny ripples now, important to play it out.

'I went up to his room the other day and there was this teenage girl coming out. She said: "I'm a foreign languages student. Mr

Upward's kindly been helping me to brush up my Greek." ' More laughter. 'I said, "Well, I've never heard it called that before." '

The laughter reached crescendo. Just as it fell away, Upward whipped round and tried to do the splits, stuck halfway and remained there like some grotesque children's toy that had stopped working, needed a prod to set it functioning again.

Up until now we'd simply been mucking about. All the time, though, I'd been waiting for Upward to launch into the first sketch. The cue for this was that Upward would turn to me and say 'It's good to see you again.' Upward was quite capable of spending five minutes marching round the stage saying anything that came into his head. By this time, I noticed, he'd worked out where the cameras were. There were two, one immediately between the stagefront and the first row of the audience, another on the far right-hand side.

Crouching down now, with the microphone almost vanished between tightly clasped hands, he murmured: 'They're taping this, you know. That's right . . . Playing it to the buggers at ITV.'

Three or four people laughed: not many. Upward swivelled round, winked at me lavishly.

'It's good to see you again.'

'It's good to see you.'

The sketch unfolded. An innuendo about *haute couture.* Mrs Thatcher at the Brussels summit. All the time Upward was glancing around him, at the cameras, at the front row of the audience, back at me. Drenched in the bright light, the eyes of the electrical equipment blinking out of the darkness, it was difficult to get a proper sight of his face, but he looked drained, panic-stricken. He'd got the microphone stand in one hand now and was using it as a prop, waving it in front of him, leaning on it as if it was a walking stick. Halfway through the routine, after the Mrs Thatcher joke, he coughed a couple of times, lost the line, grabbed at it and retrieved it before the audience knew it had gone. I grinned at him but he didn't respond. When it happened, halfway through the joke about the inflatable woman, I thought for a second it was part of the act, some unrehearsed piece of slapstick he'd invented just to spice things up: me feeding him the line, Upward goggling, me feeding him the line again, Upward sinking slowly on to his knees, the microphone stand wedged under his arm like an outsize swagger stick, then rolling over on to his back with his eyes wide open and his teeth bared making little waving motions in the air while the audience laughed and I stood there, looking for a sign that it was all a joke, all make-believe, but not finding it and rushing forward, Tracy Jacks suddenly bobbing up on to the stage from his vantage point at the side, the laughter suddenly falling away, Upward lying motionless under the harsh, white light.

And that's nearly all there is to say about Upward. As it happened he didn't die until the early hours of the next morning, in a hospital out in the wilds of Essex with Tracy Jacks and me prowling up and down the corridors and waiting for the police car that was bringing Audrey up from Kent. I think she got there with half an hour to spare. I was wandering round the grounds anyway, by then, smoking cigarettes and not knowing what to do with myself. Various people lobbied for a proper showbiz funeral, but in the end Audrey put her foot down and there were just a couple of dozen of us at a tiny church in a field near Canterbury, not far from where they lived: Paula and me, some cousins from up north, family of Audrey's. I remember odd things: the wind suddenly sweeping in across the churchyard and dragging Paula's coat tight across her stomach; a couple of youngish women that nobody could identify who sat at the back of the church and left early; Tracy Jacks standing mournfully by the grave after the coffin was lowered into the wet earth.

If I'd expected any great revelation about Upward at that moment – some blinding flash of light about where we stood in relation to each other – then it didn't come. Life stopped for a second or two while I thought about him at Catterick with the PT instructor breaking his collar-bone, marching down Bouverie Street, then began again. Going back to the car, Paula and I started a little bickering argument that flared up and absorbed most of the journey home. And that's really what I remember about Upward's funeral: Paula's voice, the endless crawl back round the M25, reaching the big house in the marshes at dusk, switching on lights, wondering what to do with the rest of my life.

I haven't heard from Audrey for six or seven years, but a day or two ago she replied to my letter in search of Upward memorabilia. Even for Audrey, with whom there'd been a fair amount of correspondence in the months after Upward's death, the tone was grimly matter of fact. The fact that I'd known Upward, on and off, for thirty years; that someone wanted to make a radio programme about him; that the whole question of Upward's reputation might be up for grabs: none of this apparently was of much account. In fact the letter – there weren't more than a few lines, but looking as if they'd been much laboured over – and the things that accompanied it seemed to confirm what I'd suspected about Audrey since the evening twenty years ago when the four of us had sat down to dinner in Surrey, that in some respects she was the oddest person I'd ever met, far odder, if their respective characters were ever compared, than Upward.

The package that Audrey enclosed – a largeish brown envelope bound round with Sellotape – had my name written on the front. However, the handwriting was faded in places to the point of illegibility, as if years ago it had been left out in the sun, was Upward's. Had Audrey ever opened it? The tape wound round the seal looked just as ancient as the address. It was possible that Audrey had simply found it at the bottom of a drawer, in a remote attic, under piles of newspapers in a garage, decided to send it on. Perhaps, if it came to that, its discovery explained the chill of Audrey's covering note – Audrey suspecting a secret between the two of us that good manners prevented her from exploring.

Perhaps, on the other hand, Audrey had looked at the envelope's contents and then resealed it. It was impossible to tell.

For some reason seeing Upward's writing on the corner of the envelope – even an Upward who'd been dead ten years – produced the most tremendous feeling of excitement. It was as if some piece of music, half-remembered from childhood, its cadences hanging tantalisingly out of reach for years, had suddenly poured out of the radio, complete and unblemished. As if, too, it had been magically possible to re-create the sensations you'd experienced on first hearing it. Picking it up, holding it in the palm of my hand, I could hear Upward's voice, wouldn't have been surprised to look up and find him walking into the room. Predictably the contents, turned out and spilled across the table, looked unexciting. There was a bundle of photographs, most of which I'd seen at one time or another, showing the two of us on stage – summer season shots, I guessed, probably dating from the early Seventies – a small handful of theatre programmes and several sheets of paper, mostly in Upward's handwriting, occasional additions in my own, containing unfinished sketches. Some of these looked as if they were thirty years old. A crumpled white envelope turned out to harbour half-a-dozen postcards I'd sent back from foreign holidays in the Seventies: France, Venice, Crete. Try as I might, I couldn't remember writing them. Despite all this, despite the poverty of Upward's showbiz leavings – a few photographs, creative tryouts, other odds and ends – the sense of him that these fragments threw up was very strong. Looking at the lines of cross-cut dialogue, unpunctuated, bare stage dialogue printed in capitals (HE PICKS UP HIS HAT/GIVES LOOK OF DISGUST) you got an instant feeling of what Upward was like, how he went about things, the effect he had on people.

There were one or two other things: some fan-letters, mostly commiserating with Upward about the end of the TV series; some stuff about Upward's autobiography; finally – the very last thing that fell out of the envelope – a little bundle of foolscap letters tied up with embroidery thread. Something about this parcel drew my eye towards it: the neat bow that held the collection in place; the regular slant of the handwriting. I untied the bow and let them spill out over the table, pushed them apart with my finger. There was no doubt about it. The handwriting was Paula's.

All of a sudden, without warning, a huge amount tumbled into place: Upward's unexpected appearances in Suffolk; Stevens's mistake over Audrey's name; the last conversation in the dressing room. To have what you'd not exactly suspected but worried about, feared, was – what? A relief? Something else? I picked up the first letter – it was dated early 1988 – read the first paragraph – innocuous-enough-sounding stuff about the weather as it happened – and then put it down again. Now that the evidence had so dramatically come to light, why read on? I remembered reading Mother's diaries on the train back from Yarmouth thirty years ago. They'd had the power to startle merely because I had no idea what they might contain. Whatever I guessed about Paula writing to Upward would be preferable to what was there to be read. As to how long it had gone on, there was no way of telling. Shuffling the letters back together and carefully ignoring their contents, I glanced at the top right corners of the pages where Paula had scribbled the date. They were all from the early part of 1988, just before Daniel was born. That needed thinking about as well.

I left the letters on the table for a while, came back and stared at them again. The fact that even in death Upward exercised the same influence as he'd done in life wasn't lost on me. For a bit I wondered what Upward would have said had he ever got round to telling me about it. Though he hardly ever talked about his love affairs, Upward had always liked to present them as unavoidable, providential nudges, something he was quite unable to escape from, predetermined by the stars. What had he thought about Paula? What had Paula thought about him? Suddenly it struck me that there was absolutely no point in posing these questions, that they would never be answered, that they were probably best left unsolved. There was nothing left to be done. Separating the letters out from the rest of Upward's leavings, I put them back in the larger bag. Even then it was hard to stop my mind racing, wondering when, and how, and in what spirit Paula had written them, in what spirit they'd been received. Finally, though, I put them in the sink, lit a match and watched them burn. It was a triumph of a sort.

'So there's a chance that Daniel isn't your son?' Lucy asks.

'It's a possibility that has to be faced.'

'But what do you think?'

'I don't know. Sometimes I think he is. Sometimes I think he may not be. But it doesn't make any difference.'

'No?'

'Not to anything that matters. I've spent ten years assuming he's my son. He's spent ten years assuming that I'm his father. Pulling that apart isn't going to do either of us any good.'

'Surely you must want to know the truth?' Lucy wonders.

'I don't think there is one, not one I could find out. I could try asking Audrey if she knows anything about it. Can you imagine how she'd react to that? I don't think she even knew about the letters.'

'I think you're being very brave,' Lucy says, a bit uncertainly, the way people say things unthinkingly. *It's tragic. You must be very upset.*

Am I being brave? I don't think bravery comes into it. What do I know about Upward that is 'true' if it comes to that? That I worked with him for a quarter of a century on and off? That he was an edgy, secretive man whom I never really got to the bottom of? That I liked him, admired him, found him funny, whatever that means? That he could be as unscrupulous towards me as to anyone else? It is hard to feel that this amounts to much.

'But what about the practical stuff?' Lucy asks. 'Daniel not being here?'

'I'll sort it out.'

'You must let me help.'

'You are helping.'

This is true. Lennie has reported several flurries in advance of the radio doc. *Phone 'asn't stopped ringing* was how he put it. Professionally, things are looking up.

A week or so later Daniel telephones. It's three-thirty on a grey December afternoon. Outside there are children's voices in the street.

'It's me, Dad, Dan.'

'Does Aunty Shena know you're phoning me?'

'No. She's out somewhere. I just got back from school.'

For a week I've been relishing the prospect of this conversation. Now it's upon me I have no idea what to say, no idea how I want Daniel to respond.

'Are things okay? Are you all right? What's it like?'

Daniel thinks about this for a moment, working out what he can reasonably tell me and what he ought to leave out.

'It's smooth,' he says after a bit. 'Uncle Gary took me to the football last week at Leeds. And there's cable.'

'That's good.'

Silence for a bit. Then: 'Dad . . . Am I going to be staying here?'

'Probably. Is that all right?'

'I missed Aunty Shena.'

'I miss you.'

'Aunty Shena says . . .' Another silence. In the distance the sound of a door opening. 'Listen Dad, I've got to go.'

Daniel seems to have settled back into his life here without too much difficulty, Shena wrote in a letter that arrived yesterday. *Gary and I think, however, that the important thing is to disturb him as little as possible while he reacclimatises himself.*

In English: keep your distance.

People in History: The Comedy Men went out a fortnight after Christmas. Coming at the dead season of the early new year, it got some goodish reviews. Half-a-dozen radio critics wrote knowledgeably about influences given and received and what one of them called our 'place in the English comic tradition, halfway between Miller and Morecambe & Wise'. Afterwards somebody looked out the tapes of *The Upward & King Show* and put out a thirty-minute assemblage on Channel Four. Listening to it, while Lucy curled up nervously on the sofa ('After all,' she explained, 'you might not like it'), I took some time to come to terms with the cross-section of professional voices, the lilt and crackle of the ancient tapes. There was a definite sense of past time, even of past time regained, simultaneously a feeling that past time had been knocked out of kilter, reassembled into shapes that bore no resemblance to the landscapes I remembered. As the programme went on, this feeling of slight bewilderment hardened into deep unease. Eventually, just before the end, there was a minute or two of one of Upward's monologues – the one where he impersonated a politician who wanted to give away free beer on the NHS. Listening to Upward's voice gradually rising to crescendo, the dutiful laughter of the studio audience, I realised that I'd become cut adrift from it, left behind. It was simply a voice screaming on into the silence.

Lucy phones most evenings. We talk about ourselves in the way I suppose most people beyond their twenties tend to do: family, heritage, expectations. Sometimes I catch myself in the middle of one of these conversations and marvel at it. Once, a week ago, she said suddenly:

'Why did you send me the fish?'

'What do you mean, the fish?'

'I'd forgotten about it until now. Just before Christmas, I got back from work one day, and there was a dirty great padded bag with a Yarmouth postmark on the doorstep stinking of ammonia. When I opened it out came this rotting fish. It could only have been you.'

'It was what people staying in Yarmouth used to send back to their friends.'

'Well I had to throw this one straight away, I can tell you. But it was a nice thought.'

Several times lately I've had a peculiarly vivid and arresting dream. Daniel and I are climbing a hill somewhere. It's a slow and fairly laborious process: through small outcrops of woodland, across a stream, along steadily rising rutted paths, up to a distant prospect of meadows, head-high bracken. Eventually we start running, off through the rising grasslands towards the summit, so high that the flat country stretching out on either side looks like stage decoration rolled into place by scene-shifters who, after we'd gone, would merely roll it away again. Whatever I say to Daniel is blown back by the wind, lost in the endless climb towards the horizon and the shiny sun.

In dreams begin responsibilities.

The Comedy Man

Looking out of the window suddenly
in the midst of the usual chatter, with some arse
or other holding forth about nothing that matters,
I saw, for some reason, the two of them
stuck on some stage, maybe Brighton, or up north,
at any rate somewhere I'd found myself silent and
solitary in an ocean of fools, amused in spite of it all
– idiots with ice-cream, the w-oman that coughed. Well-schooled
in these routines, I note how the tall one, always spurned, carries on
regardless, the lessons not learnt in a year,
or a decade, try as he might, and the fat one, toothy and slab-faced,
reeling him in like a fish on a hook made of spite.
With the audience pissing themselves, and me wanting to shout
'*What in God's name was funny, what on earth were you laughing about?*

1974